Mark Morris was born in
and began writing short s
government's enterprise s
writer. *Toady* is his first ful.... .g... novel to be published.

TOADY

Mark Morris

CORGI BOOKS

TOADY
A CORGI BOOK 0 552 13632 8

Originally published in Great Britain by
Judy Piatkus (Publishers) Ltd

PRINTING HISTORY
Piatkus edition published 1989
Corgi edition published 1990

'Death and Night and Blood (Yukio)' by The Stranglers
Lyrics reproduced by permission of Complete Music Ltd

'Hybrid' (Severin/Steven/Sioux) © Chappell Music Ltd
Words reproduced by kind permission of Chappell Music

This book is set in 10/11pt Plantin by
County Typesetters, Margate, Kent

Corgi Books are published by Transworld Publishers Ltd,
61–63 Uxbridge Road, Ealing, London W5 5SA, in Australia
by Transworld Publishers (Australia) Pty Ltd, 15–23 Helles
Avenue, Moorebank, NSW 2170, and in New Zealand by
Transworld Publishers (N.Z.) Ltd, Cnr. Moselle and
Waipareira Avenues, Henderson, Auckland.

Made and printed in Great Britain by
BPCC Hazell Books
Aylesbury, Bucks, England
Member of BPCC Ltd.

Dedication

This book is dedicated:

To Nel, my best friend, whose love, support, faith and patience has never wavered, who has helped me through the bad times and shared in the good;

To my mum, Eileen, for her sacrifices and love, and to whom I hope I can help bring back happiness;

To the memory of my dad, Jack, for teaching me independence and how to be positive, and for showing me the humour that others often miss.

Acknowledgements

My heartfelt thanks go out to so many people.

To Ramsey Campbell, Charlie Grant, Jo Fletcher, Anita Mason, Di and Mike Wathen, and Dave and Jeff at *Dark Dreams* for professional advice and encouragement.

To Sue, Danny, Lisa, Bob, Frank and Rebecca for services rendered in the writing of this book.

To Paul S, Paul B, Nick and Chris, Jo and Gerry, Jo and Brendan, Arek and Jean, Trevor and Margaret, Dave and Jonesie for friendship, favours and loadsa laughs.

To Nellie, for all of the above and much, much more.

To Judy, for taking the risk.

If I've missed anyone out, my humblest apologies. Slap me around the head and I'll put you in next time around (promise).

PART ONE

Playground Twist

'Hell has no limits, nor is circumscribed in one self-place: for where we are is Hell, and where Hell is, there must we ever be.'

Mephistopheles: Doctor Faustus

CHAPTER ONE
The Horror Club

1

Thursday

The bell rang, and the school vomited screaming, laughing children into the playground.

When all his classmates turned right, Richard Gardener turned left, towards the lockers. He was a small boy made smaller by his blazer, which was one size too big. His hair was short and neat, a wad of tape held the arm of his spectacles in place, and his green and black school tie hung slack as a noose around his neck. He kept to the side of the corridor, fighting against the tide of bodies, flattening himself into the wall when they threatened to drag him back.

'Playing football, Rich?' he heard someone say, and turned to see Philip Kershaw tossing a football from hand to hand.

'No,' Richard replied. 'I might play later. I'm a bit busy just now.'

Kershaw rolled his eyes. 'Not that stupid Horror Club again?'

'It's not stupid!' Richard protested.

'OK,' Kershaw said, 'please yourself.'

Richard quickly shrugged off his resentment and hurried on. It was easier now; most people were in the playground, only a few stragglers trailing behind. He rounded a corner to see the lockers, a dull-grey metal wall punctuated by keyholes, on his right, the science labs on his left.

Quickly he crossed to his locker, fumbled the key into the lock, pulled open the door, and took out a heavy book. He slipped the book into his bag, slammed the locker shut, and hurried towards the nearest door that led into the playground.

As he stepped outside he shivered at the cold January wind, the promise of snow. Even with ice in the air he could smell the sea, though it lay two miles away, beyond buildings stacked like boxes. The playground was a mass of shrieking, running bodies across which balls hurtled like ammunition. Richard wove his way through, skirting a group of girls who were jumping over skipping ropes in time to their own chanting.

The shrieking died behind him as he crossed the main carpark and headed towards the kitchens. Already he could see the other three members of the Horror Club waiting for him on the ledge by the enormous school dustbins. Toady once claimed he'd seen a rat slinking between the castors, but Richard didn't believe him. He thought it a shame that Toady felt he had to lie in order to impress people.

'You're late,' Toady snapped when Richard was close enough to hear.

'Aw, don't start,' Richard said. 'I had to get something from my locker.' He unzipped his bag and took out the book. Bela Lugosi and Boris Karloff shared the limelight with a George Romero zombie. Yellow slime dribbled from the title above their heads: *Horror Movies 1910–85.* Toady sneered.

'Kid's stuff!' he said. 'That's all you're interested in. Why don't we ever do anything worthwhile in this club?'

'Like what?' asked Nige. He was slim and dainty looking with straight black hair and olive skin.

Toady shot him a glance. 'The real thing. A seance.'

There was a moment of silence, then Richard pulled a face. 'Aw, I dunno, Ade,' he said doubtfully.

'Why not?' Toady snapped. 'You scared?'

'No, course not,' said Richard, and held Toady's gaze,

12

aware that the others were watching the exchange with interest.

Since Toady had joined the Club a few weeks ago, his manner had become increasingly hostile. He attempted to monopolize meetings, pressing forward his own suggestions, deriding the views of others. It was rare for him to get his own way for the boys usually stood firm, but then he went into a sulk and made the meetings uncomfortable. He was not a popular figure in the school, and the Club members were beginning to see why.

Richard held Toady's gaze until the fat boy looked away. Though they had not said so out loud, he sensed that Robin and Nige considered Toady his responsibility as he had been the one who had invited Toady to join the Club in the first place. Richard had done it out of kindness and pity for Toady's loneliness, but already he was regretting his charity.

'Well, why not?' Toady said sulkily, frowning. 'We never do anything in this club except talk and swop books and watch stupid videos.'

'But a seance?' Richard said. 'I don't see the point. None of us knows how to carry out something like that.'

'I do,' Toady said eagerly. 'I've read up on it. I'll arrange everything. All you have to do is show up.'

Richard sighed, looking out over the carpark. The weak sun gleamed white on windscreens; the smell from the kitchens confirmed that beefburgers and cabbage were on the menu again. 'What do you think?' he asked, turning to Robin and Nige.

Nige shrugged. 'We could give it a try. It might be a laugh.'

'Rob?'

Robin squinted beneath his long fringe of blond hair and self-consciously fingered his acne. 'I'm not bothered. Yeah, if you want to, I suppose.'

'All right,' Richard said to Toady, 'we'll give it a try.'

Toady grinned, his wide mouth curling up at the edges. Richard thought that Toady was the only person he knew whose smile made him look more grotesque than he did already. 'Great,' he said. 'At last we're doing something.'

If that remark was directed at Richard, he chose to ignore it. Instead he asked, 'When shall we hold this seance?'

'Tonight,' replied Toady, 'at my house. My parents will be out, so we'll have the place to ourselves.'

Richard nodded. 'OK. What time?'

'Midnight.' Toady grinned with relish.

'Midnight? I can't stay out that late,' protested Nige. He saw the others looking at him. 'Well, not on a weekday anyway,' he amended.

Toady tutted and flicked his greasy hair out of his eyes. 'This has to be done properly,' he said. 'It's not a game. We want to do it right.'

'Yeah, but midnight is a bit *too* late,' Richard said diplomatically. Toady shrugged, looking sulky again.

'What time, then?' Nige asked.

Richard looked at Robin, raised his eyebrows questioningly. 'Seven o'clock?' he suggested.

'Seven o'clock!' spluttered Toady, and shook his head scornfully. 'If it's gonna be that early, we might as well not bother.'

'All right then,' Nige said, 'why don't *you* suggest something? All *you* do is slag everyone else off all the time.'

Toady looked at the sky, half-smiling as though amused by Nige's anger. 'Ten o'clock,' he said after a moment.

Richard started to agree, then noticed that Nige still looked dubious. He guessed his friend was thinking about his mother. 'How about nine?' he suggested.

Nige nodded gratefully. Toady shrugged. Robin said, 'Yeah, yeah, any time,' and picked up his sports bag, eager to be off.

'Is there anything—' Richard began, but another voice broke in.

'Well, well, look who's here. Toady Tibbett and the frog chorus.'

14

The four of them looked up, startled. Three boys and a girl, all fifth-formers, were standing a few feet away. Immediately Richard realized he and his friends were in trouble. His mouth went dry.

The leader of the fifth-formers was an ape-like sixteen year old with straggly red hair and hard, brutal features. His cheekbones were sharp as knuckles; he had three studs punched into his left ear; a cigarette jutted from the corner of his mouth. He grinned, and it was not a nice grin.

'Hello, Rusty,' Robin said uncertainly, and immediately wished he hadn't. Eyes blazing, the red-haired boy swung round on him.

'How dare you fucking call me that!' he snarled. 'Only me mates call me Rusty. I'm Mr Oates to you.'

Robin paled. He nodded and hung his head, looking down at his shoes.

'Say sorry to Mr Oates,' one of the boys standing behind Rusty ordered.

Robin said nothing. The boy stepped forward and slapped him hard across the head. 'I said say sorry!' Robin flinched, instinctively putting up his hands to defend himself.

'Look, he's fighting back!' squealed the girl excitedly. She was a well-developed fifteen year old who, despite school rules, wore her make-up like a mask.

'So he is,' Rusty leered, and grabbing a handful of Robin's hair in one nicotine-stained fist, wrenched his head back. In a voice so reasonable he might have been asking the time, he said, 'You wanna fuckin' scrap, zit-face?'

Robin opened his mouth, lips trembling. 'No,' he whispered.

'Oh, I think you do,' Rusty said. His hand tightened, made Robin cry out. He turned, smiling, to his cronies. 'What shall we do with him?'

'Burn his eyes out!' the girl cried. The two boys sniggered.

'Yeah, go on,' one of them encouraged, 'burn the twat.'

Rusty plucked the cigarette from his mouth and regarded it, grinning. Replacing it between his lips, he drew long and hard, then blew the smoke into Robin's face. Robin began to splutter and gag, eyes streaming. Rusty laughed.

'Burn his eyes out,' he murmured. 'Yeah, I like it.' He took the cigarette from his mouth again, pinched it between the thumb and forefinger of his right hand, and directed it slowly towards Robin's eyeball. Frenziedly Robin began to struggle. Rusty yanked hard on his hair, making him yelp. Robin struck out, knocking the cigarette from the bully's hand. Rusty saw red.

'You fuckin' little turd,' he snarled, and yanked even harder on Robin's hair, trying to bring him to his knees. Desperately Robin began to flail out, aiming blows and kicks at Rusty's ribs and groin. The fifth-former winced as a fist caught him in the solar plexus, and drawing back his right hand he struck Robin hard on the cheekbone and wrestled him to the ground.

Up to this point the others had been standing in a kind of frozen tableau, too frightened to intervene, but now Richard rushed forward to try to help his friend. Immediately Ratz, the thick-set Polish boy who had hit Robin, grabbed Richard and yanked him back. Almost casually he banged him against the wall, then shoved him in the direction of the third boy. Bruno, pale and sleepy-eyed, with black spiky hair, caught Richard and twisted his arms behind his back.

Rusty was now sitting on Robin's chest, knees pinioning his arms to the ground. His right hand still gripped Robin's hair and with the left he was lighting another cigarette.

'Now then,' he murmured when he had done so, 'where were we?' He glanced up at the sky, face creased in concentration as though in an effort to recall the gist of the earlier discussion. At length he said, 'Ah, yes. I was just about to burn your eyes out, wasn't I?'

He pinched the cigarette between thumb and forefinger once more and held it above Robin's eyeball. Robin squeezed his eyes tight shut and made a renewed effort to struggle free. It was no use; this time Rusty's dominance was indisputable. With sadistic deliberation, Rusty began to lower the cigarette towards Robin's rapidly blinking eye.

When the glowing tip was an inch away Rusty froze, looked up, and quipped, 'Medium or rare?'

Ratz sniggered stupidly. Everyone else was silent. Rusty sighed, as though lamenting the fact that his joke had not been better appreciated, and slightly shifted position. He looked for all the world like a surgeon about to perform a very delicate operation.

In a small, broken voice, Nige suddenly sobbed, 'Stop it! Leave him alone!'

'Shut it, wimp,' Ratz ordered, stepping forward and smacking him hard across the face. A crimson handprint sprang up on Nige's cheek.

Richard, his arm still twisted behind his back, said calmly, 'Why *don't* you leave us alone? We've done nothing to you.'

'You're friends of the Toad,' Rusty said without looking up. 'That means you're shit.'

Toady had pushed himself into the space between two dustbins and was cowering there, looking not unlike the amphibian he was supposed to resemble. Glancing at him Richard said, 'We can be friends with whoever we like.'

Rusty turned now and his eyes were daggers. 'Shut it, Gardener, or you'll be next.'

The hate in the fifth-former's voice made Richard wince, as did the increasing pressure in his already numb arms as Bruno gave them another twist. He knew that Rusty was more than capable of carrying out his threat. Two years ago he had spent nine months at a remand centre for putting a lit firework into a kid's duffel coat hood and then pulling the hood tight over his head. The kid still showed the scars from that little jape and would

17

have to wear a wig for the rest of his life.

Images of violence swelled in Richard's mind, muffling his thinking. How could they get out of this one? Could they surprise Rusty by running at him, knocking him off-balance, and making a dash for freedom? Looking around, he realized they could not. Even if he could break free of Bruno's hold, it was unlikely he would have the support of his friends. Toady was still cringing between the dustbins and Nige was nursing his red, tear-stained face, Ratz looming behind him, still clutching his blazer collar.

The sight of Rusty, still waving the cigarette butt in Robin's face, reminded Richard of a cat tormenting a mouse before the kill. He watched, horrified, as lingeringly, almost lovingly, Rusty touched the cigarette to Robin's cheek. The smaller boy squealed in pain, tried to flinch away, but the fifth-former's grip was unbreakable. After seconds which seemed like minutes, Rusty took his hand away, leaving a weal of red skin stained by ashes.

Richard felt sick. He was about to kick back at Bruno's leg in a last attempt to break free when the bell for the end of break shrilled out. Next moment Mr Carter, the English tutor, strolled round the corner humming to himself. Immediately Rusty let Robin go, stood up, dropped his cigarette and stamped on it. Then, releasing their prisoners and pushing their hands harmlessly into their pockets, the fifth-formers slunk away.

Robin was dabbing at his burn with a handkerchief when Mr Carter approached them. 'Were those boys bullying you?' the teacher asked, peering after Rusty, Ratz, Bruno and the girl who were sauntering across the carpark.

'No, sir,' Richard said; he knew that tale-telling would only lead to more trouble.

Mr Carter looked sceptical. 'Hmm, well, if you *should* have any problems, you know where to find me.'

'Yes, sir,' Richard said. He liked Mr Carter. The English tutor was young and friendly, and unlike most teachers seemed to know exactly what interested his pupils. He knew the bands they liked, what clothes were in fashion, who their heroes were. He was even receptive to gossip from the pupils' grapevine; he knew who was dating whom, and – more importantly – who was bullying whom. Richard watched him out of earshot, then said, 'You OK, Rob?'

'Just about, I think.'

'Nige?'

'Yeah, I suppose so. That Ratz is a fucking gorilla.' Nige touched a hand to his burning cheek and tightened the knot of his tie. 'I'm going to keep away from that lot this lunchtime. It's Chess Club for me.'

'Yeah, I'll join you,' said Richard. 'I don't fancy running into Rusty on my own.'

Toady emerged from between the dustbins like the rat he once claimed to have seen. 'What about me?' he whimpered.

'What *about* you?' said Nige.

'Well, I don't want to be left on my own either. They hate me, Rusty and that lot.'

'If it hadn't been for you, none of this would have happened,' Robin said unsympathetically.

'It wasn't my fault,' wailed Toady. 'I don't *ask* Rusty to pick on me, you know.'

'It's all right, Ade,' said Richard. 'If you like you can come to Chess Club with me and Nige.'

Nige looked ready to protest, but Richard, catching his eye, gave the tiniest shake of his head. It was unfair to blame Toady for what had happened. He was a lost, sad, rather pathetic figure, an ugly duckling embittered by a lifetime of being bullied.

As though picking up Richard's thoughts, Nige smiled and said, 'Yeah, why don't you come with us?'

Instead of feeling grateful, Toady was immediately wary. Painful experience had taught him that friendliness was often a mask for deceit. Past ordeals had included being lured into the subway and debagged, given sweets that were really soap tablets, invited to join in games only to find he was the scapegoat for violence. Inevitably he had learned to trust no-one, and his deepest scars came from those incidents which had begun innocently, with a smile and an invitation.

'Well?' Nige said, taking Toady's silence as a refusal. 'Don't you want to?'

Toady hesitated a moment longer, then nodded 'Yes . . . Yes, all right.'

'OK, see you in the dinner queue at half twelve.'

Toady nodded again.

'See you tonight, Rob,' Richard called after Robin, who was heading towards his woodwork class. 'Nine o'clock at Ade's.'

Robin raised a hand. 'I'll be there.'

2

Whistle-crack . . . Whistle-crack . . .

Toady heard the sound even before he turned the corner, and immediately his mouth went dry. Why? he thought. Why did it have to happen now, just when he thought he was safe? Fearfully he peered round the edge of the wall, already knowing what he would see.

Rusty was standing by the school gate, scanning faces in the crowd. Behind him slouched six other boys, hazy ropes of blue smoke drifting from the cigarettes in their mouths. One of the boys was Ratz; Toady saw him take something flat and metallic from his pocket, and brandish it. The fact that it was a comb gave Toady little comfort. But the belt which Rusty carried was worse even than a knife.

He flicked his wrist and the belt cracked again. Its black leather gleamed almost as bright as its metal studs. Toady shuddered, then turned his attention to three girls who wandered across and began to talk to the boys in shrill voices. To cement their bond with the group they were given cigarettes. Ratz performed his trick with the comb again, prompting squeals of admiring laughter. One of the boys, a skinhead with tautly muscled arms, rolled up the legs of his jeans, displaying his Doc Marten boots as though showing off an armoury.

Toady ducked back out of sight and wondered what to do. He could bypass the gate by using the subway, but Rusty probably had guards posted there. He considered going back into school and waiting until Rusty and his friends got bored – but he knew that Mr Pike, the caretaker, would be along in a few minutes to shoo everyone out.

That left only one alternative: to go the long way home, across the fields, which meant it would be dark by the time he reached his street. He sighed, swung his satchel up on to his shoulder and pushed himself away from the wall.

Before he could turn, however, a hand slammed into the centre of his back and sent him sprawling. Toady's satchel swung in an arc above his head, thudding into his knee as he fell. The hand he instinctively put out to cushion himself skidded along gravel and became embedded with shards of stone. He closed his eyes as his elbow smashed on to the cold ground and a zigzagging wall of concrete came up to meet him.

When he opened his eyes again, seconds later, all seemed quiet. His satchel lay a few feet away, books spilling from its open mouth. His arm hurt terribly, stemming from his hand which was raw and bleeding. He struggled on to one knee, levering himself up with his good arm.

Philip Kershaw and Peter Strider, both from his own year, were standing over him. 'Sorry, Toady, only a joke,' Kershaw grinned, and stretched out a hand which Toady glared at and refused to take. Rage burned in his throat, but he could not convert it into words. He had been the whipping-boy for so long that his body had become conditioned to accepting punishment mutely.

Kershaw shrugged, withdrawing his hand. Toady began to pick up his school books, brushing the gravel from

21

their covers, scooping them into the battered satchel.

'Piss off, Kershaw, this runt belongs to us.'

Toady's head snapped up at the voice. Rusty was walking towards him, his stooges a couple of steps behind. A block of ice settled in Toady's stomach as he saw again the loop of studded belt that Rusty was banging casually against his leg.

'Sure, Rusty,' Kershaw said, 'no problem.' He began to back away. The skinhead with the muscly arms stepped forward and indicated to Strider that he wanted the football the boy was holding. After a nervous glance at Kershaw, Strider handed it over. The skinhead tossed the ball into the air and punted it towards the carpark.

'Now run along and play, little boys,' he said. Relieved, Kershaw and Strider turned and fled, leaving Toady alone with the group.

Rusty grinned, tapping the loop of belt into his open palm. 'Right then, down to bus—' he began, but before he could complete his sentence, Toady was up and running.

'After him!' Rusty yelled.

3

Toady's lungs were burning. Behind him he heard pounding feet, whoops of delight, the belt singing in the air as Rusty whirled it round his head. Every second Toady expected that belt to take off the top of his skull, or to wrap round his legs and bring him crashing to the ground. He raced across the carpark and headed for the playground and the playing fields, though he had no real plan. Just staying ahead of the pack was good enough for now.

He had never been a sportsman (among his peers that was another black mark against him), and how he kept ahead he would never know. But keep ahead he did, his spare tyre slopping and jouncing about his middle, the blood pounding in his head. How close his pursuers were, Toady had no idea, but by the time he reached the playing fields and had still not been caught he began to think that maybe, just maybe, he would get away. As a result he slowed down just a touch, and that proved his undoing.

Something – a stick, a boot, a stone – hit his legs, and he stumbled and fell on his stomach. As they surrounded him he curled into himself, drawing up his knees, tucking in his head. He felt a kick in the back, another on his arm, a fist in the base of his spine. A moment later the belt sang, and Toady felt the heavy leather bite him, the studs sharp and cold even through his jumper.

He squeezed his eyes tight shut and tried to blot everything out. It was a technique he had almost perfected over the years. He would curl up, his mind elsewhere, until the beating was over. And then, when the sounds had died away, he would come back into himself, take stock of his injuries, and be thankful he was still alive.

This time, however, it didn't work out that way. His mind was just beginning to drift when he realized the pain had stopped. For a moment he was uncertain: surely Rusty and his friends hadn't chased him half-way across the school grounds just to kick him and then run off? Raising his head cautiously, he peered out from behind the screen of his arms.

Something was going on. Some conflict that didn't involve him. The figures around him seemed to have multiplied, and Toady noticed that this new group were cleaner, smarter, dressed in school ties and blazers. He heard a name he recognized and suddenly everything clicked into place.

'Just fuck off, Gardener, this has got nothing to do with you.'

Neil Gardener, Richard's elder brother, captain of the sixth-form rugby team, faced Rusty without flinching. His eyes were cold and hard. Even when Rusty half-raised the belt they did not stray from the bully's face.

'It's got everything to do with me,' he said quietly. 'Now you just take your scumbag mates and piss off.'

Rusty sneered. 'You gonna make me?'

'If I have to, yes.' Neil's stance seemed casual – left hand tucked in his trouser pocket, right hand holding the handle of his Puma sportsbag – but Toady saw the knuckles tighten into sharp white points as he spoke.

'I'd like to see you try,' Rusty spat, and suddenly struck out with the belt. The studded leather flashed through the air, but Neil leaped nimbly out of the way, at the same time throwing up his bag as a shield. The belt rattled harmlessly against the plastic.

'What brave little boys you are,' he said mockingly. 'Only seven of you on to one third year. You must have real guts.'

'I'll have *your* fuckin' guts, you cunt!' Rusty screamed, and raised the belt again.

Before he could bring it down, Neil dropped his bag, stepped forward, and drove his fist into the middle of Rusty's face. Rusty fell backwards, blood gushing from his nose. Immediately Mo, the skinhead, aimed a kick at Neil, which was quickly countered by one of Neil's friends. Within seconds the situation had degenerated into a free-for-all.

Toady scrambled to his feet and began to run. He heard someone call his name. Looking round, he saw Richard a short distance away. Toady kept on running, his one thought to put as much distance as possible between himself and Rusty before the fight was over. It didn't occur to him to thank Richard and Neil for their intervention; in a way he even resented it. He found being bullied humiliating, and having to rely on others only added to that humiliation. When Richard called his name again, Toady didn't even look back.

4

'Thanks, Neil,' Richard said at the garden gate.

Neil looked at him. 'Well, at least someone's grateful,' he replied.

Richard winced. He had guessed from his brother's silence that he was annoyed about the way Toady had fled. 'Sorry, Neil, I don't know why he ran off like that. He must have been scared.'

'Yeah. Well, that's the last time I do one of your mates a favour. I don't enjoy getting smacked in the face, you know.'

'No, I know. Sorry, Neil,' Richard said again.

He hated having to make apologies for Toady. It was not fair that he should take the blame, especially since it was he who had seen Toady being chased across the carpark and had managed to waylay his brother as he was walking out of the school gates.

'I don't know why you go around with that little runt anyway,' Neil was saying. 'You never used to. He's nothing but trouble.'

'He's a member of the Horror Club,' Richard replied defensively.

'The Horror Club!' Neil repeated with scorn. 'And it's time you grew out of that too.'

'God, you sound just like Mum.'

Neil looked at his brother for a long moment, and then smiled. 'Talking of which' – he indicated his black eye – 'she'll do her nut when she sees this.'

'It wasn't your fault.'

'Huh, try telling her that.'

'I will. You never started anything, you were only sticking up for me.'

Neil pulled a face. 'Let's hope she sees it that way.' He pushed open the gate and they went up the path.

Inside the house, Richard yelled, 'Mum, we're home!'

The kitchen door opened and Sam, their boxer dog, came to greet them. Neil took Sam's huge head in his hands. 'Hello, boy, how are you?' When their mother emerged from the kitchen, he bent and began to pick at his shoelaces.

'Oh, both together I see.' Eileen Gardener's hands were

ghostly white, crusted with bits of pastry. 'This *is* unusual.'

'We, er . . . we had a bit of trouble after school, Mum,' Richard said nervously.

'Trouble?' Eileen repeated, her face hardening. 'What sort of trouble?'

Neil raised his head and Eileen's hand flew to her mouth. 'My God, what have you done? Have you been fighting?'

'It wasn't Neil's fault, Mum,' Richard said quickly. 'Some fifth-years were beating up a friend of mine. Neil came to help . . . er, to help my friend, that is, not the fifth-years.'

Eileen tutted and wiped her hands savagely on the apron she wore. 'I don't know why you can't keep out of these things. Especially you, Neil; you're old enough to know better.'

'Aw, come off it, Mum. You don't expect me to just stand by and watch a little kid get mashed to pulp do you?'

Eileen grimaced, both at his tone and terminology. 'I'm sure it wasn't like that. Schoolboys fight all the time.'

'It wasn't just a fight, Mum,' Richard said. 'That lot would've killed him. It was Rusty Oates and his mates. Rusty was the one who put the firework in that little kid's hood a couple of years ago. They were hitting Adrian with this massive studded belt.'

Eileen turned to Neil. 'Is this true?'

'Every word. Honest Mum, if Richard hadn't come and got me, that kid would be a hospital case by now.'

'Then this is obviously a matter for the headmaster, or even the police. I'll ring the school first thing in the morning.'

'No, don't,' Richard said, 'it'll only make things worse.'

'But you can't just pretend it never happened!' Eileen exclaimed.

'Look,' Neil said wearily, 'if we got Rusty into more trouble he'd only be out for revenge.'

'But what if he *keeps* picking on your friend? What if he

26

does put someone in hospital? Will you still keep quiet then?'

'No, of course not,' Richard said. 'If it got that bad then we'd have to tell someone. But just at the moment it's better to leave things alone. I mean, there was no harm done . . . well, apart from Neil's eye, of course.'

'Well, I don't think it's right,' Eileen replied. 'People shouldn't be allowed to get away with these things.'

'Oh, he didn't get away with it,' Richard said. 'Neil hit him a real beauty in the nose. You should have seen the blood.'

Eileen Gardener withered her son with a look. 'There's no need to gloat, Richard. Violence doesn't solve anything. I know it was a noble cause, but I don't want to hear of you – either of you – fighting again. Is that clear?' Both boys nodded. 'Good. Now, Neil, let's put something on that eye of yours. Come into the kitchen and I'll make you up an ice pack.'

Neil followed his mother into the kitchen, grimacing at Richard as he did so. Richard grinned and slapped his brother on the back. 'Go on, Rocky, the boss knows best.'

The kitchen door closed on the smell of stew, and Richard went upstairs, intending to do at least some of his homework before dinner. He set his books out on the desk by his bed and sat down. Above him, on the shelf, black-spined horror novels were guarded by a Wolfman model that he'd got for Christmas. Behind him a blood-drenched Carrie White glared out at the world through hate-bulged eyes. Richard picked up his pen, but after all the excitement at school he found he couldn't concentrate on revision. He put his pen down and looked out of the window. There was still half an hour or so before it began to get dark; seemed a pity to waste it. He grabbed his jacket and went downstairs. He would do his homework later, after he'd taken Sam for a walk on the beach.

5

Starmouth was in deepest hibernation, so still and silent you might almost have thought it was dead. On the seafront empty tram-lines waited patiently for migrant trams; the shops and stalls, now shuttered, were winter havens for beachballs, postcards and 'kiss-me-quick' hats; lonely hotels stared out to sea, pink or yellow or white, like giant ice cream blocks masquerading as buildings.

Richard strolled down the promenade, Sam at his heels. To his right a wall topped with a hand-rail dropped twenty feet to the beach; ahead of him marched cast-iron lamp standards festooned with strings of dead fairy-lights. Further along, the pier was a long probing finger testing the water. Though it was closed, Richard could see reclining deck-chairs, striped like candy.

He stared beyond the pier to the fairground, a graveyard of mechanical dinosaurs waiting for summer's resurrection. Yet despite its desolation, Richard preferred the town this way. He hated summer, when the dinosaurs came to life and Starmouth danced to the tourists' tune. He hated the way they crawled over the beach – dropping litter; playing radios loud to prove how clever they were; showing off peeling lobster bodies that sizzled with coconut oil. Apart from the weather and the long school holiday, Summer's only consolation was that Olive Pierce could make enough money to pay her bills and buy Christmas presents for her friends when winter came round again.

Richard looked over towards Olive's booth, which was on the corner by the closed souvenir shops. Behind glass were photos of Olive dressed as a gypsy and chatting with celebrities. Here was Ken Dodd, here Frankie Vaughan, here Terry Wogan. Above the booth was a black sign bedecked with gold stars and the legend: Madama Zaria – Fortune Teller.

Richard smiled. Olive was a friend of his grandmother's. She had lived in Starmouth all her life and was no more a gypsy than he was. She did have some psychic ability – Richard had seen evidence of that for himself – but her knowledge of palmistry came not from any mystical source, but from books borrowed from the local library. The same was true of her knowledge of Tarot, and the cards themselves she had bought in Woolworths. Twenty years ago, bored with being a shoe-fitter, she had decided to set up stall down at the market, charging a shilling a reading. She had been so successful that when a place came free on the seafront she had drawn her savings from the bank and snapped it up immediately. The rates were high, and the flat above the booth small and cramped, but Olive was happy. Richard looked up at her window, at the ghost of a vase behind the net curtains that covered the bottom half. When he had been down the beach, he would call in to see how she was.

'Come on, Sam,' he said, and ran along the promenade, past the pier entrance to where a set of stone steps led down to the sand. Sam galloped at Richard's heels, and then, when the steps came into sight, streaked ahead and began to scramble down them.

'You should have been a mountain goat,' Richard said a minute later when he reached the bottom to find Sam waiting for him. The dog wagged his tail and streaked back up the beach, towards the pier.

At this time of the afternoon the tide was going out, leaving the sand patterned with ridges and ripples from the departing waves. Richard walked along the sea's edge, stepping on bladderwrack and popping its plastic blisters, crushing tiny sand sculptures that were worm casts. Ahead of him, below the promenade twisting right and merging with the interlaced streets leading away from the sea, gaped caves in the cliff, black as throats. One of them belonged to the Horror Club. It was where they met at weekends, when weather and the tide allowed. Richard decided to walk along to the cave, make sure everything was in order, clear away any rubbish that might have been washed up or left by kids.

29

Near the pier the beach became a little rocky. Sam was jumping from rock to rock with nonchalant ease, unwittingly disturbing crabs and anemones stranded by the outgoing tide. Richard took more care, his feet sliding on sea-moss. At last he came to the pier.

It was an impressive structure. Built originally of wood in the 1860s it had been destroyed by fire during the Second World War. In the 1950s a local businessman had put up the money for its reconstruction, and a new iron framework had been erected, the buildings on it closely resembling their original Victorian counterparts.

Sadly, however, the pier was now falling into decline. The theatre and restaurant had been replaced by a bingo hall, an amusement arcade, a fish and chip stand, and a shop that sold cheap souvenirs. But despite its commercialism Richard still loved it. To him the pier was a majestic place. He enjoyed walking its length, catching dizzying glimpses of sea through the boards, leaning over the railings at the end and watching the water crashing against the girders. And at low tide, such as now, he loved walking underneath, between iron supports like the petrified trees of some primeval forest, the pier's underbelly bearing down like a bank of storm clouds.

He passed underneath, breathing in the smell of seaweed, and trudged towards the cliffs. The caves here were deep and dark; the finding of an iguanodon skeleton in 1975 had spawned schoolboy rumours of dinosaurs living deep underground and coming out at night to feed. Five years ago, as an impressionable nine-year-old, Richard had accepted those rumours as gospel. Even now he was reticent about venturing too far along the tunnels. In some of the caves the darkness was so absolute you could walk less than ten feet, hold up your hand in front of your face, and see nothing but blackness.

The cave which belonged to the Horror Club was at the foot of the cliff which the boys had dubbed 'Grandad Rock'. It was Nige who had first noticed the face in the cliff; two skew-wiff depressions that were eyes, a jagged outcrop of rock that was a nose, the cave itself the mouth. The impression of age had been given by two curtains of rock which formed the cave entrance, thought to resemble the two ends of a drooping moustache.

Richard clambered over the rocks, passed beneath the moustache and went into the mouth. The boys had chosen this cave because it was relatively dry, and because a hole in the low ceiling went right up to the surface, forming a natural chimney and letting in plenty of daylight. Richard wished the boys were meeting here tonight instead of having this stupid seance at Toady's house. Apart from the likelihood of it being a complete waste of time, he was not relishing the walk through the Piling Hill estate in the dark.

He sighed and looked around. Everything seemed fine here. The candles and matches were still on the ridge inside the flue where the tide couldn't get at them, and the initials 'HC' scratched on the wall had not been tampered with.

Richard whistled Sam and the two strode back along the beach, under the pier and along the sands. Overhead gulls wheeled like kites, calling mournfully.

On the promenade, Richard took off his trainers and emptied out some grains of sand that were irritating him. That done, he stood up, stamped his foot, and crossed the road. A few moments later he was ringing Olive's doorbell.

Above the star-decked sign the net curtains stirred. The window opened and a grey head popped out. 'Hello? Who's there?'

Richard stepped back from the door so that Olive could see him. 'It's only me. I was walking along the beach so I thought I'd say hello.'

'Oh, how nice,' the old lady said. 'Wait a moment, I'll be right down.'

'I've got Sam with me. Is that all right?'

'Oh yes, of course. He's a well-behaved dog. Very partial to digestive biscuits, if I remember rightly.'

She drew her head back in and closed the window.

Moments later Richard heard a lock being turned and the booth door opened.

'Hello, Richard, come in,' Olive said. She was a plump woman, wearing a dress patterned with small blue flowers, and a brown cardigan. Her eyes were bright green, enlarged by her spectacles, and her hair grey and tightly curled. Sam wagged his rump enthusiastically when he saw her, and Olive obliged by patting his shoulders.

Richard followed her into the booth, the interior of which, in summer, was mysterious, almost surreal. Wall hangings, a canopied ceiling, a curtained-off alcove and dim, concealed lighting gave an impression of indeterminate shape and size, in complete contrast to the gaudy realism outside. Now, however, the room was bare: the walls were empty of wall hangings, which had been taken down for their winter wash; props were packed into cardboard boxes marked 'Persil' or 'Winalot'. Small items of furnitue – an antique card table, two bamboo chairs – were suspended in limbo beneath dust covers.

Olive opened a further door which in summer was invisible, and ushered Richard into a small hallway and up a short flight of stairs. Her flat was simply a corridor that branched off into four rooms: kitchen, bathroom, bedroom, lounge. Handled wrongly it could have been claustrophobic, but Olive had managed to make it cosy.

'Now, Richard,' she said as she carried a tea tray into the lounge, 'how are you?'

Richard took the tray and set it down on the low table before the sofa. 'Fine, thanks,' he said, spooning sugar.

'And your gran?' Olive asked as she sat down. 'How's she?'

'Oh, she's fine too, apart from her varicose veins. It's her birthday next week. She'll be seventy.'

Olive looked shocked. 'Richard Gardener! Don't you know it's impertinent to reveal a lady's age.'

Richard opened his mouth to apologize, then realized Olive was joking. 'I think it's silly not telling people how old you are,' he replied. 'I'd be proud to be seventy.'

'Oh, it's not such an achievement,' Olive said, giving Sam a digestive biscuit. 'It's more the luck of the draw. Some are taken early, others are allowed to stay around awhile.' Her eyes twinkled. 'Anyhow, you know what they say – only the good die young.'

'Well, I still think it's something to be proud of . . . Are *you* seventy yet, Olive?'

'Impertinence again,' Olive said, smiling. 'Let's just say I'm getting there.'

Richard nodded and dunked his biscuit. 'What does it feel like?' he asked.

'It feels . . . slower. As though gravity's pulling you down. You can't run and jump and swim like you used to. Just going to the shops makes you tired some days, and at nights you get sleepy early.'

'Sounds awful.'

Olive laughed. 'Oh, it's not as bad as that. Frustrating sometimes, but not awful. It happens slowly, you see, not all at once. You get plenty of time to get used to it.'

Richard nodded. 'Still, I wouldn't like it.'

'Oh, I don't suppose anyone *likes* it. You just learn to accept it, that's all.'

Richard sighed. Olive punched his arm. 'Hey, come on, I'm not dead yet. Let's change the subject; tell me about the Horror Club.'

Richard grimaced.

'What's the matter? Are things not going well?'

'Oh no, it's all right really. It's just that this new member, Adrian Tibbett – the one I told you about, the one everyone calls Toady – he just doesn't fit in. He keeps trying to run things all the time. Nobody really likes him, especially Robin. Since Toady joined, Robin's gone dead quiet and moody. It wouldn't surprise me if he left pretty soon.'

'Well, if it's as bad as that, why don't you ask this . . . Toady to leave?'

Richard shrugged. 'I suppose we should really, but it's not as simple as that. Toady's never really had any friends,

33

you see; he's always been bullied at school. If we dumped him now, we'd look just as bad as everyone else.'

'Then why not have a quiet talk with him, let him know where he stands.'

'He's not really the kind of person you can talk to,' Richard said. 'He'd only take things the wrong way. He's very touchy.'

'Then I don't know who I feel more sorry for, you or him.' Olive paused to sip her camomile tea. At length she said, 'Maybe he just needs more time. You say he's always been bullied at school; that can make a person very bitter and mistrustful. Perhaps he's afraid to make friends. Perhaps his "touchiness", as you call it, is simply a defence mechanism.'

Richard wrinkled his nose. 'I don't know if he's that complicated.'

'Oh, everyone's complicated,' Olive said, laughing, 'even small boys.'

'We're not *that* small,' Richard said indignantly. 'I'm fourteen, you know.'

'And I'm nearly seventy,' Olive said firmly, 'so I should know.'

'Yeah, I suppose you're right. Still, I don't like the idea of having it out with him. I wouldn't know what to say.'

'Well, why not speak to the others first, see how they feel? You say that Robin doesn't like this boy – has he told you that?'

'Well no, not exactly, but I can tell. Like I say, he's been dead moody just recently; he always gets like that when he's fed up about something.'

'Perhaps he's having trouble at home again,' Olive suggested. 'Maybe that's what worrying him. Or maybe he's just growing up.'

'Well, *I'm* growing up too.'

'Yes, but Robin's sixteen – two years older than you. Believe me, two years makes a big difference at your age. He's got his career to think about; he'll be leaving school in July. And just at the moment he's probably more interested in girls than horror films.'

For some reason this reference to girls embarrassed Richard and he looked away, picking at a thread on his knee. Olive noticed his embarrassment, but pretended not to. Stroking Sam, she said, 'Just talk to them, Richard, find out what their feelings are. Talking's important, you know; sharing your thoughts with people your own age.'

Richard shrugged. 'Yeah, I suppose.'

'Never mind "suppose". Just do it. Talk to them.'

'Yeah, yeah, OK . . . I'll talk to them tonight.'

'Promise?'

'Scouts' honour.'

'You're not a scout.'

'All right, Horror Club's honour, will that do?'

Olive nodded. 'Yes, that'll do. You've having a meeting tonight, then?'

'Yes, at Toady's house. We're having a seance.'

Olive sat up so suddenly that Richard jumped. 'You're what?' she snapped.

'Having a seance,' Richard repeated, startled by the anger in her voice.

'Richard, you mustn't,' Olive said, concern blending with the anger. 'Tell me you won't.'

'Why?'

'Because it's dangerous.'

'It's only a bit of fun.'

'*Fun?*' Olive cried. 'You call it fun? I've been to seances, Richard – real ones – and I've seen the results. Believe me they aren't fun. They have to be carried out by professionals. There are – for want of a better word – *forces* which must be controlled. Having a seance unsupervised is like giving toddlers matches to play with.'

'It was Toady who suggested it,' Richard said defensively. 'Anyway, nothing'll happen. He's not a medium or anything.'

'How do you know?'

'What?'

35

'How do you know he's not a medium? Not all mediums are strange old ladies like me, you know. They can be quite ordinary people.'

Richard squirmed in his seat, at a loss for words. He wished he hadn't come to see Olive, after all. At last he said, 'Well, I can't do anything now. It's all been planned.'

'Then unplan it,' Olive said simply. 'Call it off.'

'I *can't*,' Richard insisted. 'It would make me look soft. They'd think I was scared.'

'You should be scared. Better to jump from a window than to stay in a burning house.' She leaned forward. 'Call it off, Richard.'

He said nothing. Olive reached out, took his hands in her larger, more wrinkled ones – and suddenly leapt back, snatching her hands away as though she'd received an electric shock.

'What's the matter?' Richard said, alarmed. Sam looked up from his place on the hearth rug, disturbed by the commotion.

Olive massaged her fingers as though they were cold. Her face was haggard. 'Call it off,' she said hoarsely.

'Olive, what happened? Why did you jump back like that?'

'I . . . felt something,' she said.

'Felt something? What do you mean?'

'I felt . . .' Olive's mouth moved, but no words came out. She shuddered violently. 'Just call it off, Richard,' she whispered.

Richard stood up, his throat clogged, close to tears. 'You're just trying to scare me.' He thrust his hands into his jacket pockets as though concealing evidence. 'I've got to go now. Come on, Sam.' He stumbled from the room. Puzzled, the dog leapt up from the hearth rug and followed him.

Olive sat still, hearing him thump downstairs, draw the catch, slam the door. She made no move to follow him; she felt too weak, too drained. Her legs were solid and heavy as tree trunks. Her hands ached. She formed a fist and the fingers seemed to creak.

'Call it off,' she whispered. *'Please.'*

6

Robin sat on his bed and drummed his knee with a pencil. Beside him a Ramsey Campbell novel lay untouched. He had thought that losing himself in a book might help drown his anxieties, but he had not been allowed to escape.

He sighed. Outside black clouds rolled across the sky like a spreading ink stain. Mr Treeborn, who owned the house that backed on to theirs, was sticking newspaper to his windscreen to stop it from freezing up. In the back garden the washing line supported a row of flapping silhouettes, and Robin looked away, embarrassed, when he recognized a line of his mother's panties. They were beckoning to Treeborn like an invitation. Why did she have to flaunt herself like that?

Savagely he yanked his curtains closed and switched on his bedside lamp. Maybe shutting out the night would help him to think. Just lately he'd felt so down that each day was an ordeal. 'It's adolescence,' his mother had said with apparent unconcern, 'everyone your age goes through it.' But if that were the case, why did everyone at school except him seem always to be having a good time?

He touched his face. His skin was a moonscape, pitted with acne: he must be the spottiest boy in school. He knew that everyone stared at him, even though when he confronted them with a stare of his own they had always just looked away.

Perhaps he ought to list his problems; maybe that would help him to solve them. He reached into his bag for his English exercise book, and on the inside back cover wrote: 'Problems. 1) Spots – can't get girlfriends 2) Mum and Dad – always arguing, getting worse 3) Horror Club – getting too old? Don't fit in. Toady an arsehole, Rich and Nige best friends 4) Job or "A" levels? Don't know what to do.'

He paused and looked at the list. Already his problems seemed insurmountable. Almost grudgingly he put 'Solutions' on the opposite side of the page. He thought for a moment and then wrote: '1) Go to doctor's for better spot cream. Wash face thoroughly. No crap food 2) – 3) Tell Toady to get lost? Just go to weekend meetings not to school ones? Spend schooltime with class mates? 4) Decide after GCSE results. See careers teacher.'

He paused again, chewing the end of his pencil. The solutions seemed sensible, but already Robin could see difficulties. Why would any other spot cream be better than the one he had now? What if his careers teacher couldn't suggest anything? What if Richard and Nige objected to him not coming to all the meetings? What if his mum and dad's arguing just carried on getting worse?

Angrily, he threw his book on the floor. Fuck it, it was so unfair. Here he was, trying to be constructive, and all his solutions seemed to do were breed more problems. He flicked through his record rack, found *The Rocky Horror Show* and put it on, turning up the volume. His walls shook to the Timewarp. The music made him feel a little better, and Robin bopped to it while he got changed. The cigarette burn on his face still smarted a little, reminding him that perhaps he ought to add Rusty to his list of problems. He glared at his exercise book and deliberately kicked it under the bed. When he had applied his spot cream and brushed his hair he was ready. Despite his doubts about the Horror Club, he was quite looking forward to this seance.

7

The pale blue house looked like one of a set, packed tightly between its neighbours as though the architects had been playing sardines. In the window a sign read: 'Vacancies'. Richard rang the bell and watched as a large silhouette wavered closer behind the frosted glass of the front door.

'Hello, Mrs Figg. Is Nigel in?' he asked.

The woman standing before him was pink and doughy as a marshmallow. When she began to speak, Richard's gaze was drawn, as ever, to the severity of her crimson lipstick.

'He's up in his room, doing his homework. I don't think you ought to disturb him just now.'

'Oh, but he's expecting me,' Richard said hastily. 'He said to be here by eight-thirty.'

He didn't know whether Mrs Figg's grimace was intended for him or her son, but holding the door wide she said, 'I suppose you'd better go up and see if he's finished then.'

Richard stepped into the house which, as always, was intolerably hot. He wiped his spectacles, which had steamed up, then took off his parka, unwound his scarf, and went upstairs. When he knocked on Nige's door an angry voice snapped, 'Yes, what?' and immediately Richard knew that Nige was having problems with his maths revision. He pushed the door open a crack and poked his head through.

'It's only me, Nige. Can I come in?'

At the sight of him, Nige's scowl disappeared. 'Oh, Rich, hi. I thought you were my mum.'

'How's it going?' Richard asked, picking his way through a jungle of books, papers, pens, and the scattered contents of a geometry set. Nige sat back against the bed, massaging his aching neck.

'Crap. I don't understand these bloody logarithms.'

'Join the club,' said Richard.

Gloomily Nige began to gather his papers into a pile. 'I'm bound to get detention again. I hate maths. It's my worst subject.'

Richard nodded sympathetically and sat on the edge of the bed. He was dying to tell Nige about his visit to Olive's, but was not sure how to do so without making the

39

episode seem over-sensational. Thinking back, he found it difficult to rationalize the events of that afternoon even to himself. And yet he knew he had to tell someone.

He watched as Nige rummaged beneath his bed for a mislaid ruler. If he was going to tell him, then now was the best time, when he didn't have to look him in the eye. Circumspectly he asked, 'Are you looking forward to this seance?'

Nige's voice was muffled beneath the bed. 'Yeah, it'll be a laugh. Better than bloody maths revision any day.'

Richard nodded, though Nige couldn't see him. 'I went to see Olive today,' he said.

'Oh yeah?' The indifference in Nige's voice only fuelled Richard's resolve.

'Yeah. I told her about tonight's seance.'

'Did you?' Nige squirmed from beneath the bed and placed the recovered ruler in his geometry set, then closed the lid with a snap.

'Yes. Do you know what she thinks?'

'No, what?'

'She thinks we should call it off.'

'Does she? Why?'

'She says seances are dangerous. She thinks that having a seance unsupervised is like giving little kids matches to play with.'

Nige shrugged. 'Oh well, you know how batty Olive can be.'

'Yeah, but she really was serious, Nige. In fact, she frightened me, she was so angry.'

'Oh, come on, Rich,' Nige said, grinning, 'don't tell me you let Olive get to you. All that supernatural crap she comes out with. She makes most of it up, you know.'

'Yeah, I know, but this was different. This time she really meant it. I told her about the seance and she tried to persuade me to call it off. Then she touched my hand, and suddenly . . . well, she sort of jumped back . . . as though she'd seen something really terrible.'

Nige rolled his eyes and tapped the side of his head, the

action so smug that it made Richard angry. 'Aw, she's an old lady, Rich, probably going a bit senile. You don't want to take much notice of what she says.'

'Don't be stupid,' Richard snapped. 'Olive's as sane as you are. If you'd been there you wouldn't be taking the piss. I'm only trying to warn you, Nige, that's all.'

'Warn me? About what?'

'About this seance. I agree with Olive. I think we should call it off.'

'Oh, come on!'

'I mean it,' said Richard. 'I've got bad feelings about this. Olive doesn't say these things just for the sake of it. I reckon if we stick together we can pressure Toady into cancelling it.'

'But I don't want it cancelled,' Nige replied. 'I'm looking forward to it. You're just acting stupid, Rich, getting your knickers in a twist just because of what some loony old woman says.'

'Olive is not a loony!' Richard retorted, unable to stop his voice from rising in anger. 'She's psychic; you know that as well as I do. Remember that time when Tommy Lepton came with us to see her, and suddenly she went all funny and told him to go home straight away, and when he got home he found out his little sister had been knocked down by a motorbike? Well, she does that sort of thing all the time; I've seen her do it. I mean, she puts it on for the tourists, yeah, but she wouldn't have told me to call off this seance if she didn't know something was going to happen.'

Nige looked unsure, but said, 'Aw, she was probably just trying to scare you, pretending to have one of her turns just to give you the willies.'

'No, she wasn't!' Richard insisted. 'That's what I thought at first, but I just know she wouldn't do a thing like that. She doesn't scare people into doing things; she just tells them, plain and simple. This seance is a bad idea, Nige, a *really* bad idea.'

Nige was generally a rather timid boy, the result of years

41

of molly-coddling by his mother. He looked unsettled by Richard's conviction, and yet reason dictated that he couldn't bring himself to take Olive's warning so seriously. He had met Olive two or three times, and that occasion with Tommy Lepton had been the only one in which he had seen her do anything remotely psychic. Yet so matter-of-fact had she been about the situation that it had not seemed particularly unusual or spectacular. Persuasively he said, 'Aw, c'mon Rich. You know as well as I do there's no such things as ghosts and ghoulies. I mean, what the hell can happen, eh? Four kids pissing about, holding hands round a table. I mean, be serious, Rich, think about it.'

A sudden banging made Richard think for an insane second that the door had joined in the discussion. Then a female voice, harsher than either of the boys', shouted, 'Nigel! Nigel!'

Nige rolled his eyes, but was secretly pleased by the interruption. 'Come in, Mum.'

Mrs Figg entered like a giant advertisement for confectionery. 'I heard raised voices,' she said, glaring at Richard. 'What the devil's going on?'

'Nothing, Mum,' Nige said. 'Me and Rich were just having a minor disagreement.'

'A minor disagreement?' The crimson lips writhed like red worms. 'It sounded more like war.'

Richard smiled stiffly. 'Oh, no, nothing like that, Mrs Figg.'

Rosemary Figg gave him a 'who asked you' look. 'Have you finished your homework?' she said to Nige.

'Yes,' Nige lied. He knew that if he said 'nearly' or 'more or less', she wouldn't let him out.

'Are you sure?' Her doughy face creased suspiciously. Obviously she thought that Richard had been persuading Nige against his better judgement.

'Yes, Mum. We didn't have any homework as such. We just had to learn for a maths test tomorrow.'

'And you know it all, do you?'

Nige hesitated, looked quickly at Richard. 'Yes, I think so.'

'You *think* so?' Mrs Figg's voice was triumphant at having rooted out the uncertainty. 'I don't think you should go out until you're sure.'

'I know it as well as I can do,' Nige replied quickly. 'Honestly, Mum, I've been working solid since tea-time. I'm starting to get a headache.'

Mrs Figg looked sullen, frowning at Richard as if it was his influence that was making her son argumentative. 'Well, all right, you can go out,' she conceded reluctantly. 'But don't be late home, and wrap up warmly. It said on the weather that it was going to snow tonight.'

Nige nodded. 'OK.' He began to root in a drawer, searching for a clean pair of jeans. His mother watched him for a moment, then turned and waddled downstairs.

'I don't think your mum likes me,' Richard said when she was out of earshot.

Nige found his jeans and yanked them out, scattering socks. 'Nah, it's just her way. She doesn't really trust anyone who isn't family. It's with being a seaside landlady. Half the guests nick anything that isn't nailed down.'

Richard watched as Nige changed from school trousers to jeans. When Nige began to lace up his trainers, Richard said, 'About this seance—'

'Oh, God, let's not start arguing about that again. Look, Rich, just give it a try, OK? Nothing's going to happen.'

Richard looked unhappy, but reluctantly nodded. 'OK,' he said. 'I suppose I'll have to go along with it. But if anything *does* happen, we've got to stop straight away.'

'Fair enough,' said Nige, 'but nothing will. As with most of Toady's ideas, it'll probably be a complete waste of time.'

Before going out, Nige had to show his mother that the clothes he was wearing were warm enough. He emerged from the sitting room muttering, 'Mothers.' Richard grinned and the two boys went out into the night.

8

The soughing of the sea was like a mournful old man complaining about the weather. As the two boys walked through the myriad sidestreets, Richard felt like a mouse in a maze.

During the winter, boarding-houses were depressing places. They huddled together as though for warmth, the 'Vacancies' signs in their windows like hopeless pleas for companionship. As the boys progressed inland, away from the seafront, their surroundings gradually changed. Streets began to widen out, houses became larger and less congested, regiments of graceful trees appeared on grass verges. This was Beachside, or, as it was often referred to by the locals, the stockbroker belt. This was where those comfortably well-off families lived who had always had a desire to be near the seaside without having to be too close to the vulgarities of the tourist trade. Richard and his family lived here, in a house almost exactly two miles from the beach. Though Toady lived beyond Beachside, closer to Richard than to Nige, Richard always went to call on Nige rather than the other way round.

There were two reasons for this. One was that Nige's mother would be unlikely to allow him out if nobody went to call for him (she would probably claim that all his friends were at home doing their homework), and the other was simply that Richard liked being near to the sea. Though he moaned about having to call for Nige all the time, it was really only token resistance; in truth he rather enjoyed the extra walk, hearing the rush of the waves grow louder and closer with each step.

Now, though, the boys were trudging through the wide, well-lit streets of Beachside, with names like Acacia Avenue and Shakespeare Drive. Though the houses here were larger, they looked gloomy as the shops on the promenade.

As they progressed yet further inland, the houses became even newer, though they were so shabby it was difficult to tell. They were nearing the Piling Hill estate now which lay three miles from the seafront, beyond Beachside and the school. Toady lived here, on the estate's outskirts. In Starmouth, Piling Hill was notorious, a place where, it was joked, even the pensioners carried flick-knives. Tonight that comment didn't seem so funny.

As the boys passed a row of disused factories, Richard told Nige about the fight with Rusty after school. When he had finished, Nige pulled his coat tighter about him and shivered.

'Oh, that's great,' he moaned. 'He'll really be after us now.'

'Or maybe it'll work the other way,' Richard said. 'I mean, now that Neil's cracked him one, he might leave us alone.'

'Nah, no chance. He'll be out for revenge. He'll go away to lick his wounds and then he'll be back, and if he can't win with fists he'll use knives, bricks, bottles, anything he can lay his hands on.'

Richard thought that Nige might very well be right, but he refused to let the fear of Rusty hang over him like a cloud. Slapping Nige on the shoulder, he said, 'Oh, come on, let's forget about him. All we have to do is keep out of his way for a few days. He'll soon get bored and start bullying someone else.'

'How can we forget him?' Nige said gloomily. 'He lives in Piling Hill, remember. For all you know, he might be lying in wait for us at this moment.'

'Don't be stupid,' Richard said, though all the same he felt uneasy. Around them loomed the factories, silent and threatening, towering into the night sky. They seemed diseased, their brickwork black and crumbling, broken windows gaping like jagged wounds. On walls beneath street lamps graffiti glistened; Richard made out the name RATZ in yellow paint amid a jumble of football slogans and obscenities. Forcing a smile he said to Nige, 'If you're worried we can walk in the middle of the road. That way we'll have plenty of time to run if someone jumps out at us.'

Nige nodded, and the two boys stepped off the pavement and on to the road, and began to walk along the white lines up its middle. They passed black archways that led into cobbled yards where old machinery rusted and decayed. As they neared the end of the road, something stirred in one of the archways, and Nige jumped, but it was only a fish and chip wrapper, unfurling greasily. Within a few minutes they had left the factories behind and were entering the estate proper.

Immediately Richard's stomach began to tighten. Whereas before he had felt enclosed, prey for ambush, here he felt the opposite – out in the open, conspicuous and vulnerable. The estate was quiet, though it seemed a hostile, heavy quiet, charged with tension. They passed squat shoebox houses, the windows flickering luminous blue, jerky with television images. Reggae music drifted from one house like a ghost, then faded away as they walked by.

As they hurried up Buckingham Road, the sign to which graffitists had made the obvious amendment, Nige said, 'I don't like this place. It's too quiet.'

'There's no pleasing you, is there?' Richard joked, but he understood Nige's unease.

Both boys leaped back, startled, as an old man suddenly staggered around the corner, clutching a half-empty wine bottle. Muttering to himself, the man unzipped his flies and urinated up a lamp post. The boys rushed past.

Toady lived on Latimer Street. As the boys passed a sign which read: 'King Street leading to Latimer Street', Nige stopped and peered ahead.

'What's the matter now?' asked Richard.

'I saw something moving up there.' Nige pointed towards an abandoned house on the corner. Its roof had caved in. Boards were nailed across the house's downstairs windows, giving it a blind, somehow sinister look.

'Oh, for God's sake,' said Richard, 'it was probably only a bloody dog or something. I wish you'd shut up, you're making me nervous.'

'But I *did* see something. I'm sure it was someone ducking down behind the garden fence.'

Richard gave him a withering look. 'Come on,' he said, and started forward.

'All right, clever dick,' Nige said, catching up with him, 'if you're so brave why don't you go into the garden and have a look?'

'Why should I?' Richard replied. 'It was you who saw something.'

'You daren't,' Nige said.

Richard rounded on his friend. 'Christ, Nige, it's only an empty bloody house. I'm not getting my feet wet traipsing around in that garden. Have you seen the grass? It's at least three feet high.'

'Well, I dare you to go up the garden path then and knock on the front door.'

Richard shook his head. 'You're a pillock sometimes,' he said, trying to sound superior.

'And you're shit-scared!' Nige exclaimed triumphantly.

'No, I'm not,' Richard retorted. 'I'm just not as much of a dickhead as you. People will think I'm a right prat if I knock on the door of an empty house.'

'What people? There's no-one about.'

Richard groped for another excuse. The fact was, he didn't really fancy the idea of getting too close to that old house, and he particularly didn't fancy the idea of standing among all that long grass. His imagination was conjuring up creatures with large, jagged-toothed mouths, just itching to make a meal of his legs and feet. He moved his hand, and the glinting of his watch under the street lamp gave him the excuse he had been looking for.

'Shit, look at the time. It's nearly ten past, and we're supposed to be there by nine.' He strode ahead, hoping Nige would forget his childishness.

Unfortunately he didn't. As the boys came in line with the broken, graffiti-scrawled gate, Nige sidled up, looking smug. 'Scaredy,' he taunted.

Richard glanced at him, intending to ignore the jibe,

but Nige's complacent grin coaxed a retaliation. 'I'm not scared, I'm just not a stupid little prat like you. OK, if it'll make you happy I'll knock on the bloody door. But don't blame me if Toady starts moaning about how late we are.'

Viciously he shoved the gate open and marched up the garden path. His face was defiant as he walked, but inside Richard felt uneasy. The tall grass on either side of him appeared to stir restlessly. As he came up to the peeling front door, the house seemed to cast out silence and gloom like a net. Out of the corner of his eye Richard thought he saw a light flare in an upstairs room, but decided it must have been a reflection of the street lamp or the moon.

The front door was grey, the paint hanging in strips to reveal red beneath. The house smelt rotten – of wet toadstools and diseased wood and something animal that might have been cat's piss. Richard turned and saw Nige looking at him with wide shadow-smudged eyes. From here the distance between himself and the gate seemed immense, the path snaking through a vast desert of restless quills. It was surely only imagination that made the grass appear to have encroached a little further over the path. Richard waved, though his hand felt like lead, and turned back to the door.

His hand formed a fist and he rapped on the blistered wood. Before the echoes of his knock had died away, he was back on the path, striding swiftly but with dignity towards the gate. The grass was not really slashing impotently at his ankles; it just felt that way because he was walking so fast.

He was halfway to the gate when a clump of undergrowth to his right seethed. Richard leaped to his feet, his hand automatically flying to his mouth. He was vaguely aware of Nige stepping back sharply from the gate at the same moment, and realized he must have seen the movement too.

'What was that?' Nige whispered.

'Nothing, just a dog,' Richard replied quickly. After a moment he began walking again. The grass had settled now at any rate; whatever had been there must have gone.

He was less than eight feet from safety – he could even make out the name 'Rusty' carved on the wooden gate – when the grass before him erupted outwards, and a black figure leaped up and slowly raised its arms.

9

The electric clock above the cooker whirred remorselessly. Toady looked out of the window again, grimacing at the depressingly familiar view: the feeble street lamps, the flat sodium carpet that was the road, the shabby excuses for houses imprinted with darkness and dirty orange light. Where the hell were the others? They were already fifteen minutes late. Why was he surrounded by incompetence?

His mother came into the kitchen and Toady winced. Did she really have to dress like that? What sort of bar was it she worked in anyway? She was much too old for leopard skin tops and satin trousers. Trousers? The way they clung to her legs they were more like tights.

She snapped open her shoulder bag, extracted a brush, and dragged it through her permed, peroxide-blonde hair. 'Doesn't look as though your friends are coming, does it?' she said.

'Yes they are,' Toady snapped.

His mother's eyes widened, the false eyelashes reminding Toady of Venus fly traps. 'All right, love, don't bite my head off. I was only making conversation.'

Toady grunted and continued to stare out of the window. His mother struggled into an imitation fur coat.

'Well, I'm off to work,' she said. 'Tell your dad there's a steak'n'kidney pie in the oven if he wants it when he gets home; and beans and stuff in the pantry if he wants anything else . . . oh, and cake and biscuits in the tin.'

'Yes, all right,' Toady said irritably, 'I'll tell him.'

'Right, well, I'll be off then. You make sure you look after Simon.'

'Yeah.'

'See you later then, love.'

'Yeah, bye.' Though Toady sensed his mother hovering, he kept his gaze steadily on the street outside. He knew that eye-contact would only encourage her to come across and give him a good night kiss, and he couldn't bear the thought of having those red lips and that sticky mask of a face slobbering over him. He was relieved when her high heels finally clicked away over the lino and the door slammed shut behind her.

Now he turned, wrinkling his nose at the reek of perfume his mother had left. He sat, listening for the sound of the front door closing, and only when it had done so did he slip off his stool and go upstairs.

He enjoyed having the house to himself. Indeed, his mother and father were so seldom here that he regarded them more as lodgers, even intruders. He was sure that, given the opportunity, his father would rather take up residence in the pub he inhabited for five hours every evening. There were some weeks when Toady didn't see his father from one Saturday to the next, though lying in bed he often heard him – falling through the front door, staggering into the kitchen, swearing incomprehensibly to himself. Toady was ashamed of his father, so much so that the mere sight of him made his skin crawl with embarrassment. On the occasions when their paths did cross, his father would often grin companionably, his breath sour with the previous night's alcohol. He would ask something banal like: 'And what have you been up to this week, son?' And Toady would mutter, 'Nothing much.' And his father would nod and turn away, satisfied that he had done his duty as a parent.

Toady now stood on the landing with his ear to the door of his brother's room. Hearing nothing he pushed the door open and peered in. A shaft of light from the landing squeezed in with him, mingling with the glow from the Snoopy night-light.

Simon's cherubic face, crowned with a halo of blond

hair, was half-turned into the pillow. His small fist was curled up by his head, his eyelids flickering in some infant dream.

'You'll be all right if I go out for an hour won't you, Simon?' Toady whispered. He took the toddler's silence for affirmation. 'Course you will, you won't let Adrian down. You'll sleep till morning like a good boy.' The exploratory shaft of light, as though afraid of being trapped inside, sprang back into the corridor as he pulled the door shut.

In his own bedroom he grimaced at the unmade bed. What had his mother been doing all day that she couldn't even perform this simple task? Smoking and drinking coffee and yakking to the neighbours most likely. With the house in the state it was, there was no wonder his father stayed away.

He opened the door of his wardrobe, with its picture of Freddy Krueger, and dragged out a rucksack, dislodging a stack of *Fangoria* magazines. The shape of the rucksack, the outline of the articles inside, gave Toady a thrill of excitement, made him eager for the night's events to begin. 'Come on, come on,' he urged, looking at his watch, 'what the hell are you doing?'

Suddenly it occurred to him that maybe he had been deceived again, that maybe they had chickened out, or, worse still, had not intended to show up in the first place. It wouldn't be the first time it had happened. He had once been invited to a party four miles out of town, and after having caught three buses and spending a small fortune on fares, had discovered the address on the card to be an old folks' home. 'Oh, please, not this time,' he begged silently. 'Please, please, please.'

He sank on to the unmade bed, eyes closed, hugging the rucksack to him like a baby. Silence, in turn, hugged him. Silence, that is, except for his watch, wickedly ticking away the seconds.

Richard's heart rose to the back of his throat. His legs felt hollow and fragile as matchsticks. The black figure before him was trembling, apparently with malign energy. It raised its hands to its black dome of a head, dug its fingers into its own neck, and dragged slowly upwards. Its skin came away – a balaclava that revealed Robin's grinning face beneath.

There was a moment of stunned silence, then Nige roared, *'Rob, you bastard!'* and crashed through the gate to pummel their tormentor. Robin fended him off as best he could.

'Your faces,' he wheezed through great gouts of laughter. 'You should have seen your faces.'

Richard was shaking: fury, relief and amusement spun in his head, chasing one another round and round. Nige, still punching Robin, cried, 'You big, crazy bastard! If you hadn't taken off your balaclava just then, you wouldn't have seen me for dust.'

Richard leaned back against the gate. Shakily he asked, 'How did you know I'd be coming into the garden?'

'I didn't,' Robin replied. 'In fact when I saw you come through the gate, I thought you'd seen me. What were you doing? Why did you knock on that door?'

'This pillock dared me to,' Richard said, relief making him grin too.

'But why were *you* in the garden?' Nige asked of Robin.

'I saw you at the top of King Street. I saw Nige point, but then when you didn't wave or anything I decided to hide in here and give you a fright as you walked by.'

'You did that all right,' Nige said, and then added again with feeling: 'You bastard.'

'Come on,' Richard said, glancing at his watch, 'we'd better get to Toady's. It's late enough as it is.'

The three boys walked towards Latimer Street. Nige was still chatting to purge his nervousness. Robin folded up the balaclava and stuffed it into his pocket. Glancing at him, Richard said, 'What do you reckon to this seance, Rob?'

Robin seemed surprised by the question. 'How do you mean?'

'Do you think it should go ahead?'

'Yeah, course. Why not?'

Nige rolled his eyes and said in a mock-hushed voice, 'A strange old gypsy woman has given Rich a warning.'

'A gypsy woman? Who?'

'Olive said we should call this seance off,' Richard said angrily. He had agreed with Nige that they should talk this matter over with Robin. Now Nige's messing about would undermine anything that he had to say. Indeed, it seemed it already had, for Robin tossed his head dismissively and said: 'Oh, Olive.'

'Yes,' said Richard firmly. 'Why does no-one take what she says seriously?'

'Because she's a loony,' Nige replied.

'She is not!' Richard snapped. Turning to Robin, he said, 'I went to see her today and she told me how dangerous having a seance can be.'

As they walked down Latimer Street, Richard told Robin what had happened at Olive's that afternoon. When he had finished he felt disappointed at how empty his words sounded. In the tiny flat the events had seemed significant and terrifying, but now those same events seemed over-dramatic and – yes, he had to admit it – even a bit loony. And from the condescending look on Robin's face it was obvious he thought so too. Richard braced himself against a barrage of patronizing words and casual dismissals of Olive's sanity. When they had come and gone he felt drained and defeated, but tried desperately once more.

'But what if something *does* happen tonight?' he said. They were standing outside Toady's gate now.

Robin scowled. 'Such as?'

'I don't know: anything. What if something happens that we can't control?'

'It won't.'

'But what if it does? What would we do?'

Despite his teasing, Nige looked uncomfortable. 'I dunno. I hadn't really thought about it.'

'Exactly! You're all just treating this as a laugh, but Toady was serious. He said he'd read up on seances and he knew what to do. And remember what I told you about Olive? I've never seen anyone look so scared. You can make fun of me all you like, but that doesn't alter the fact that I've got bad feelings about this. If it was up to me, I'd call this seance off now.'

'Look,' Robin growled, 'no-one's forcing you to come. You can go home now if you like.'

'No, I can't,' Richard said. 'If you're determined to go through with it, I've got to be there. I've got to see what happens.'

'Nothing's going to happen,' Nige said, his voice almost a plea. 'Nothing's going to happen.'

Richard mustered a smile. 'I hope you're right.'

Robin shoved open the gate and they trudged up the path to the front door.

11

Despite the cold, Toady was sweating. Suspense was a terrible thing. For some minutes now he had been staring at Freddy Krueger and urging the doorbell to ring downstairs; and with each silent second that passed, his grip on the rucksack had become tighter and tighter.

When the doorbell did finally ring it made him jump. Subconsciously he realized he had all but given his friends up, had put their non-appearance down as another mark of deceit in his register of experience. He got up from his bed, limbs trembling, and still clutching the rucksack, thumped downstairs, almost falling in his eagerness. When he opened the door and saw them looking so casual, his relief turned to anger.

'Where the hell have you lot been?' he said. 'You were supposed to be here at nine.'

Nige and Robin seemed taken aback, but Richard stepped forward, eyes blazing. 'And where did you go this afternoon?' he returned. 'My brother's got a black eye because of you, and not a word of thanks.'

Toady turned away, stung by Richard's verbal assault. 'I never asked you to help,' he muttered. 'I could've managed on my own.'

'*You could've managed?*' repeated Richard incredulously. 'You'd be in hospital now if we hadn't come along.'

'I'd've been all right. I always have before.'

Richard gripped Toady's arms, forcing him to meet his gaze. 'You mean you've been kicked in before, and so far you've managed to avoid getting badly hurt. But that doesn't mean you'll be as lucky next time around.' Toady shrugged, tried to look away but Richard shook him to regain his attention. 'Why won't you accept our help, Adrian? We want to be your friends. Why do you make it so difficult?'

Toady stared back, but said nothing. Richard released his arms and shrugged. 'Well, don't say I didn't try.'

Toady bent and picked up the rucksack he had dropped when Richard had grabbed him. Indicating it, Nige asked, 'Going camping, Ade?'

Toady looked at Nige as though he were retarded. 'It's for tonight,' he said abruptly.

Richard watched him, his stomach shifting slowly like oil. As the seance approached he was becoming increasingly nervous, which was one of the reasons he had flown off the handle so easily. He had already decided to say nothing to Toady about his visit to Olive's. If he couldn't discourage Nige and Robin, what chance would he have with the instigator?

'Aren't you going to invite us in?' Robin asked.

Toady shook his head. 'No, we're not having it here. There's been a change of plan.'

'Where, then?' The flicker of hope Richard felt was cruelly dispelled with Toady's next words.

'At the abandoned house in King Street. We can get in through a window round the back. I checked this afternoon.'

Richard was horrified. 'No, not there! Anywhere but there, Ade. I don't like that place.'

'Me neither,' said Nige. The thought of the abandoned house, with its blind window and its sense of decay, filled him with misgiving. Toady however, was scornful.

'Why not? There's nothing to be afraid of. It's only a house.'

Ironically, Richard recognized echoes of his own words to Nige in that statement. However, now that Toady's intentions had been revealed, Olive's warning seemed especially significant. 'It might be dangerous,' he said desperately. 'The roof's already caved in. If we go in there, we might bring the whole lot down on us.'

Toady shook his head. 'No, the ground floor's quite safe. A bit damp, but we can put up with that.'

'I still don't like it,' said Richard.

'Well, if you don't like it you know what to do,' Toady replied angrily. 'You've been against this idea from the start, haven't you? Just because it wasn't you who suggested it.'

Richard shook his head. 'No, that's not true. It was only since Olive said—'

'Olive, Olive, Olive, that's all we've been hearing tonight,' Robin interrupted. 'Change the record, Rich, will you. I'm sick of hearing about that stupid old woman.'

'Well, I agree with Rich,' Nige said timidly. 'I don't mind having a seance, but I don't want to go into that house.'

Toady shot him a look of pure disgust. 'You're just a big baby, Figg; Mummy's little boy. Reading Stephen King and watching *Dawn Of The Dead* is just about your limit. Anything like this comes along and it's a different story.'

'Piss off,' Nige said uncomfortably. 'I'm not scared. I . . . I just meant I agree with Rich that the place might not be safe.'

'It's safe,' Toady said wearily. 'I was there this afternoon. The ground floor is perfectly OK. As long as you follow me, you'll be fine.'

Nige, unsure, glanced at Richard. Robin said, 'Oh, come on, Nige, don't spoil everything now. Just 'cos Richard's soft doesn't mean you have to be as well. You don't have to do everything he says, you know.'

Nige was silent for a moment longer, then he reluctantly nodded. 'Well . . . OK. As long as Ade promises it's safe.'

Toady smirked. 'I promise.'

They started down Latimer Street, their shadows thrown out bold beside them. As the house came into sight, Nige said weakly, 'How will we be able to see? It'll be dark in there.'

Toady jerked a thumb at the rucksack. 'What do you think I've brought this for? There's a couple of torches in here.'

When they came to the gate, Toady turned and grinned, his wide lips appearing to curl back into shadow, the teeth springing forward like claws unsheathed. Behind him the house crouched in darkness, a blind, dead face with a bashed-in head. Toady led the way up the overgrown path and round the side of the house to where the street lamp's influence was minimal. When they rounded a corner into the back yard, the darkness hemmed them in completely.

The boys stood for a moment, trying to defy the darkness with their eyes. Here moonlight was screened by the house, though traces of it filtered through, picking out details in ice-blue luminescence. In one corner of the yard, Richard made out a mangled piece of metal grille, an ancient parka with a fur-lined hood, a smattering of cans like the debris from a shooting gallery. The ground ahead seemed littered with small, lumpy objects that he could only guess at. Rotting food? Waiting rats? Animal excrement? None of the possibilities were pleasant.

Toady was standing by the back door, rooting about in his rucksack. He pulled something out and handed it to Robin who was standing by his side. Richard's guess that it was a torch proved correct. In the next moment the beam was exploring the yard, discrediting threatening shadows for the harmless objects they really were.

'Hurry up,' Robin said, 'this place stinks.'

A second torchbeam joined the first, then played over Toady's features, stretching his mouth wide, blurring his nose and eyes. Flashing the torchbeam around, he said, 'People use this yard as a rubbish dump. Whenever their bins get too full they just chuck the crap in here.'

He handed Robin the rucksack and moved to a window by the back door. It hadn't been boarded up; either that or the boards had been removed. A crate advertising oranges was set conveniently beneath the sill. Climbing on to it, Toady said, 'Here, hold this,' and held his torch out for Richard.

Richard took it and directed the beam on to the back of the house. Grunting with effort, Toady took hold of the window frame and levered it up. The window came open bit by bit, shedding dry slivers of paint and rotten wood with small crackling sounds. When the gap was wide enough, Toady heaved himself through head-first. For a moment his stubby legs kicked wildly, trying to gain a foothold, then they slid forward as though the house had sucked him in.

For what seemed a long time the boys waited in silence. Richard's torch still illuminated the back of the house, but its beam revealed nothing. The glass in the upper portion of the window threw the torch's reflection back as a dazzling sheet of white light, and the room beyond was black as the deepest pit. Suddenly two hands appeared on the window sill and Toady's face poked through.

'Hand me the torch,' he said. Richard did so. 'Now the rucksack.' That was passed through also. 'OK, now you can come in. Just let yourself slide head-first. There's an old sink on your right which you can grab hold of for balance.'

He moved back from the window and Robin stepped forward, silently handing his torch to Nige. Nige took it, and as the beam travelled briefly over Robin's face, Richard saw the trepidation there. However Robin took hold of the crumbling window frame without hesitation, and, using the crate for leverage, pushed himself through. In his determination to prove himself he went through faster than was necessary, and Richard heard a muffled thump and a curse as he hit the floor on the other side.

'You all right, Rob?' he called nervously, afraid of raising his voice. Almost immediately Robin appeared at the window, dusting himself down.

'Course I am.' He glanced at Richard, and then suddenly grinned. 'Come on, Rich, don't look so worried.' Richard smiled back, though he found it difficult.

Nige stepped forward, passed the torch to Robin, and said, 'Me next.' He tried to make his willingness sound like bravado, but Richard guessed he had volunteered so as not to be the last one left in the yard. It took only a moment for Nige to climb in. He was small and agile, and with Robin and Toady's help slipped through the window like a rabbit down a hole.

Now it was Richard's turn. As his head disappeared into the maw of the house, his immediate thought was that it was even colder in here than outside. Robin and Toady were trying to aid him with torchlight, but succeeded only in creating confusing shadows and throwing up brief, dazzling shapes. Taking a deep breath, Richard plunged forward, his right hand scrabbling for the sink which Toady had mentioned. He found it and his hand closed around grimy porcelain. The next moment he was lying on the debris-strewn floor and fingers were curling around his arms to drag him up. A musty, dank smell stifled him, like a welcoming embrace.

12

'This is the kitchen,' Toady said, shining his torch around.

In the harsh light the kitchen looked colourless, its floor littered with dust and rubble, wallpaper lolling like strips of flesh from walls that were sweaty with damp. Snug against the left-hand wall were skeletons of cupboards which looked as though only cobwebs held them together. Against the right was the sink, grimy and furred with dust, and the cooker, a rusted-out shell of itself. From somewhere nearby Richard could hear sounds of scratching: mice, he thought, or maybe even rats.

'What a dump,' he said, and the empty walls took up his cry and clogged the echoes with dust.

'Come on,' Toady said, 'I'll show you the rest of the place.'

Eagerly he led the way to a gaping door frame, the lack of a door like an invitation to explore further. Beyond the frame was a narrow hallway, panelled in wood so rotten it seeped and bulged like fungus. It smelt too, bringing to Richard's mind images of putrefying slugs, cabbages slimy with age, rivers slick with pollution. When he slipped and his hand brushed the wall, the wood gave like a sponge, releasing a gooey brown leakage on to his fingers. He took a tissue from his pocket and wiped his hand obsessively, continuing to do so even when all trace of the slime had been cleaned away.

They crept to the end of the hallway. To the left was what Richard guessed must be the front door and a flight of stairs leading upwards. Robin flashed his torch briefly in that direction, and Richard saw that the top of the stairs was choked with lengths of timber and large chunks of masonry from the collapsed roof. To the right was a door that had once been glass-panelled: now only fragments were left, protruding from the frame like knives.

Toady pushed at the door and it grated inwards over a carpet of dust. Beyond was a sitting room with wooden boards nailed across the windows, allowing only a faint glimmer from the street lamps outside. Opposite the door a fireplace wore a mask of soot, its grate a yawning mouth with beercans for teeth. Across the walls, graffiti was king

– names, slogans and crude diagrams of copulation overlapping to form a grotesque and ugly tapestry. In the corner by the window a stained, piss-stench mattress sprawled, breathing squalor.

'Don't,' Toady warned as Robin made to lower himself on to a settee that was one of only two items of furniture in the room. Robin paused, his bottom inches from the upholstery.

'Why not?' he asked.

By way of reply, Toady shone his torch along the length of the settee. It was wet and rotten, colonies of teeming woodlice having a party in the puddles.

'What a shithole,' Nige said in digust.

Toady shot him a look. 'It's not. It's all right.'

'It stinks,' said Nige. 'This whole place stinks.'

Toady shrugged. He unslung the rucksack and rooted through its contents. After a moment he pulled out a white bedsheet, rolled up small and bound with string. As he untied the string, Richard asked, 'What's that for?'

Toady passed over his torch so he could use both hands to shake out the sheet. In the dark room it billowed like a ghost, sending dust scuttling and swirling. 'We need something to sit on,' he explained, and allowed the sheet to settle over the floor. The boys watched him as he crossed the room and took hold of a rickety bamboo side table, the second item of furniture. This he placed in the centre of the sheet.

'Now what?' said Robin.

From the rucksack Toady produced two packets of cellophane-wrapped candles, a large box of matches, some plasticine, and two dozen eggcups. 'Light the candles,' he said, handing a packet to Robin and one to Nige. 'Fill the eggcups with plasticine and stick the candles in and then place them all round the room, but not too close to the walls or to that mattress.'

Robin nodded. Nige plucked unenthusiastically at the cellophane on his candle wrapper. 'Why do we need so many candles?' he asked.

'For light, of course,' Toady said, 'and energy. Heat'll provide us with energy.'

Richard stood by the wall, saying nothing. The room and the preparations were unsettling him, making acrobats of his innards. In his mind's eye he kept seeing Olive, her nice old lady's face twisted in panic, her mouth moving desperately. 'I tried to get them to stop, Olive,' he thought, 'I tried, but they're still going ahead. Even now I can see them lighting the candles, Toady grinning as they flare up one by one. I can see graffiti glistening on the walls, things crawling in the ruin of the settee. I can feel the house closing around us like something alive, can smell its stench and feel its chill. I know there's no such things as ghosts or devils or monsters, I know that, but I also know that you're never wrong, Olive, that you saw or felt something this afternoon, something so awful you wouldn't or couldn't even talk about it. I know we shouldn't be doing this, but it's not up to me, Olive; I can't make them stop. I've tried, but I can't!'

Despite the cold Richard felt sweat slithering down his body, whilst behind him his hands lay palm-down against plaster that had the consistency of clammy skin. He screwed his eyes shut in the hope that darkness would assuage the fear that was building and building inside him, but instead the blackness behind his eyelids only brought into sharper relief the image of Olive, leaping back in her chair, snatching her hands away. With a new clarity he saw the look of horror on her face, heard her panicked voice begging, 'Call it off, call it off . . .' And he knew that he had to try just one more time, that it was his duty to make his friends see that what they were doing was bad and wrong and dangerous.

He opened his eyes and saw Toady grinning like a Halloween pumpkin. He tried to speak, but his lips were so dry that they seemed to tear apart like paper. For a few seconds he couldn't even generate enough saliva to breathe. Then, with a supreme effort, he managed to force out three tiny, whispered words: 'Don't do it.'

Toady, kneeling on the floor by the rucksack, looked up. 'What?'

'Don't do it,' Richard repeated, unable to raise his voice above a croak.

Nige frowned. 'Are you all right, Rich?'

'Aw, he's just got the shits again,' Robin said, both amusement and annoyance in his voice.

Richard pushed himself away from the wall. 'There's something in this house,' he said, and all three looked at him, surprised by his sudden certainty.

At last Nige said quietly, 'What do you mean?'

'There's something here,' Richard repeated. *'In this house.'*

A pause like a heartbeat – then Toady said, 'Don't be stupid.'

Richard felt like shaking him, battering some sense into his ugly, cunning frog-face. Trembling he said, 'I'm telling you, there's something here . . . We shouldn't be doing this. It's wrong.'

Robin tapped his head. 'You're going loony, Rich. Either that or you're just trying to scare us 'cos of what that stupid old woman said.'

'No,' Richard said, 'no, I'm not trying to scare you. I'm trying to warn you, can't you see that? We've got to leave this house now. There's . . .' he searched for the word, '. . . there's evil here.'

'Evil?' scoffed Toady. The look on his face was almost triumphant. 'Come on, you don't expect us to believe that?'

'I don't care what you believe. All I'm saying is, we should get out now.'

'Aw, give it a rest, Rich,' said Robin, yet it was obvious from his voice that the intensity of Richard's plea was unsettling him. 'Look, you get out if you want, but we're staying here. Just because you're scared doesn't mean you have to spoil it for everyone else.'

'You don't understand.'

'I'm warning you Rich, just *shut it!*'

Toady took stock of the situation at a glance and added his own weight to the argument. 'Yes, just sit down or go home. We're going ahead with this seance whether you like it or not.'

Richard was about to argue further, then, looking at his friends' faces and realizing it was hopeless, he slumped silently to the floor. For a moment Toady watched him, smiling.

'Are we going to get started now?' Robin said. 'This place is making me seasick.'

Nige sniggered nervously. The room did indeed seem to be rolling and flickering with light, splashes of flame dancing up the walls. Toady nodded and reaching into the rucksack for the last time, extracted two objects. One was a whisky tumbler and the other a block of dark varnished wood. Nige looked at them and noticed that there were carvings in the wood: words or symbols.

'What's that?' he asked.

'A ouija board,' Toady said, and placed it on the table where it could be seen clearly. It was simply a flat wooden board with the letters of the alphabet carved in a rough semi-circle across the top, and the word 'Yes' carved in the bottom left hand corner and 'No' in the right. As soon as he saw the board, Richard leaped to his feet again.

'No,' he said, shaking his head. 'No, I can't let you do this. Ouija boards are the worst things of all. You've got to stop now.' He advanced determinedly across the room. Immediately Robin rose to meet him.

'Leave it, Rich,' he said warningly. Richard ignored him, tried to push past, but Robin was the bigger and stronger of the two. He caught hold of Richard's arm and dragged him back towards the wall. 'Come on, Rich, just sit here and don't cause any more trouble.'

Richard began to struggle. 'You don't understand,' he said, and just for a moment the tone of his voice almost persuaded Robin to let go. Then panic caused him to aim a rabbit-punch at his friend, who ducked easily. Roughly,

Robin flung him back against the wall which boomed with the impact.

'Just sit!' he snarled, and bunched his fists until Richard had done so. Nige came across and put his hands on Robin's wrists.

'Hey, Rob, calm down,' he said.

Robin turned, breathing heavily, his fists tightening rather than slackening, 'He fucking started it,' he muttered. 'It was him who threw the first punch, not me.'

'Yeah, I know,' Nige said, smiling nervously, 'but . . . look, this was supposed to be a bit of fun . . . I mean, bloody hell, why's everyone getting so uptight?'

'Because something's going to happen,' Richard said bleakly.

'No, it isn't!' Nige replied. 'What the fuck *can* happen, eh? We're not bloody mediums, we're only fucking kids . . . I mean four kids with a lump of wood! Come on, Rich, just ignore what Olive said; she doesn't know everything.'

Richard sighed. In a strained voice he said, 'You didn't see her, Nige. You weren't there. I know something's going to happen. I just know it.'

'Oh, you're a fucking psychic now as well, are you?' Robin grunted. He had now rejoined Toady on the sheet and was sitting probing at a spot on his chin.

Richard glanced at Robin, but ignored the jibe. Nige said, 'Look, Rich, if anything does happen we'll probably all run like hell anyway . . . I mean, there's no way we'd sit around if some fucking demon or something started appearing in the middle of the room, is there?' Richard shrugged. Nige continued, 'Course there isn't. So come on, promise you won't mess this up for us? We don't all want to fall out over something stupid like this, do we?'

Richard shrugged again and palmed sweat from his forehead. His eyes were wide behind his spectacles as he said, 'I can't promise anything Nige . . . And don't treat me like a kid.'

'Well, stop behaving like one, then,' Nige retorted. He

stood up, a look of frustration on his face. People were always saying he was soft, but Richard was walking away with the prize for biggest wimp tonight. He opened his mouth, half to renew the argument, half to offer consoling words, but nothing of either emerged. In the end he muttered, 'Aw, fuck it,' and joined Toady and Robin.

As he sat down, Robin said petulantly, 'I don't know why he bothered coming in the first place if he's so scared.'

Toady sneered. 'Yeah, he's a real baby.'

'Just leave it, Ade,' Nige warned. Toady pulled a face.

Robin said, 'Look, can we start now?'

Toady nodded. Carefully he placed the whisky tumbler upside-down in the exact centre of the ouija board and knelt before it. He motioned to Robin and Nige to join him, one on either side.

'Now what?' said Robin.

'Each place the index finger of your right hand on the glass,' Toady instructed. When that was done, he said, 'Now, concentrate.'

'What on?' whispered Robin. Toady frowned.

'On the glass, of course. Empty your mind of all other thoughts. Think only of the glass.'

Robin grinned surreptitiously at Nige and raised his eyebrows. Nige grinned back, relieved. Richard's attitude had frightened him, but if Robin was not really taking this seriously, maybe everything would be OK. He relaxed slightly and focussed his eyes on the glass. It seemed that minutes elapsed before anyone spoke again.

'Concentrate,' Toady said quietly. 'Concentrate.'

The order was unnecessary. Nige was staring at the glass in fascination, watching its multi-faceted surface wink and sparkle with a million tiny flames. The more he stared, the more sensually soothing the flames became, until it seemed that only the glass existed, its heart glowing and dancing, its veins pulsing with pure fire. From somewhere came a voice, syrupy-thick with heat, in rhythm with the flames. 'Concentrate.'

Nige felt his eyes growing heavy as though he was being hypnotized; his finger on the glass looked miles away, not part of him at all. He closed his eyes and flame continued to flicker behind his lids, red as blood.

Slumped against the wall, Richard was growing colder and colder. Outside a car rumbled past, the sound of its engine a voice from another world. Richard shivered, drawing in his legs, pulling his parka tight around him. His lips felt numb, his spectacles pebbles of ice pressed against his eyes. He watched the ceremony before him with a kind of detached horror, like witnessing atrocities on the news that the small screen made unreal. The three figures looked to be in a trance, their eyes wide, their breathing shallow. Toady, sitting in the middle, opened his mouth to speak, and immediately shadows swarmed into the contours of his face, making it look as though it was created from fire and darkness. Richard's teeth began to chatter softly as Toady's low voice probed the air with a question.

'Is anybody there?'

Richard's hair quilled in anticipation of a reply, but none came. He longed to say something, to cleave the oppressive atmosphere, but the sweating cold had pasted his tongue to the roof of his mouth. He hugged himself tightly with hands like blocks of frozen meat, and watched Toady's face. After a moment shadows blossomed from Toady's mouth and the question came again.

'Is anybody there?'

The minute shifting of glass on wood was loud as granite on granite. Richard expelled air from the puncture wound of his mouth. He put his arms down rigid on either side of him and dug his fingers into the floor. The wall at his back held him like flypaper as the glass shifted again.

Nige watched as the glass came towards him, its surface now literally dancing with flame, sending off sizzling white sparks like a catherine wheel. He felt vague surprise that the sparks weren't burning his finger, but his overwhelming feeling was one of elation and achievement.

He urged the glass on, beckoned it like a father encouraging a baby with its first steps. When the glass stopped on the word 'Yes' his triumph was complete. His head swelled with pride.

And then the pain began.

13

Despite Richard's belief that something was going to happen, his immediate thought on seeing the glass move was a desperate urge to rationalize.

'They're pushing it!' his mind yelled at him, 'one of them's pushing it, Robin probably. It's subconscious, auto-suggestion, self-hypnosis, something, it must be something like that. It's not real. It's not! One of them's pushing it.'

His reasoning was frantic. He felt as though he was performing a highwire act where the rope was reality and the abyss beneath was a land of crazy thoughts – *The Twilight Zone*, as Rod Serling might so glibly have said twenty-odd years ago. Yes, Richard was perched on a rope overlooking The Twilight Zone. Ha, Ha! Only it wasn't funny, because Nige's scream pushed him right over the edge.

Richard shook his head, trying to shake off the muggy haze which had invaded the room like a dream's after-image. Had Nige really screamed or had it just been sound conjured from the dream-state? He looked at his hand as though it was a specimen under a microscope. Then, thoughfully, he bunched it into a fist and hit himself as hard as he could in the face.

Pain threw him a lifeline. Richard grabbed it and, gasping through his stinging nose, dragged himself back to reality. Yes, Nige *was* screaming, screaming fit to burst. His back was arched, his right arm rigid before him, index finger still poised delicately on the glass as though he couldn't let go. The screams that were coming from his mouth were bouncing around the room like rubber balls full of echo. The candles were roaring, changing colour – blue to red to white to green. There was a stench in the air; urine and unwashed animal, and something heavy and deep and rich like the blood-red beating of a heart. Richard saw shapes swarming before his eyes as though ropes of graffiti were playing lassoes in the shadows. His mouth struggled for speech – and found it.

'Nige!' he screamed. The name mingled with Nige's pain, zig-zagged round the walls. 'Nige!'

Nige turned, his mouth still open, sweat pouring down his face. Toady and Robin were watching him, crouched over the ouija board, their expressions rapt. Nige's left hand waved feebly, a drowning man begging for aid.

'Hold on, Nige, I'm coming!' Richard pushed himself up, climbing the wall with his hands, tottering as though his legs had been clamped in splints. Gritting his teeth, he waded towards Nige, through a wave of freezing heat and stench that was thick as treacle.

Nige was sinking to his knees, his eyes closing in a dead faint, his screams becoming weak and ragged. Richard reached him at last, took hold of him beneath the armpits and pulled. Nige flopped like a rag doll, and Richard lost his grip, his hands slipping on sweat like iced water. He swore in desperation and grabbed him again.

Releasing Nige from the glass was like trying to drag a toy back through a mangle: it couldn't be done. Changing tack, he let Nige drop to the floor and took hold of the glass itself. Almost immediately, however, he released it, yelping in pain. The bloody thing was red hot! Pulling his sweater sleeve over his hand, he tried again.

This time the glass came away easily; Toady's, Robin's and Nige's fingers flopped to the table. Nige slid to the floor and lay there, unconscious, whilst Toady and Robin stared at him stupidly like doped monkeys. Immediately the glass began to burn Richard's jumper, and drawing back his arm, he threw it with all his failing strength at the wall.

It left his hand gravityless, floating like a weird satellite. Then, as though it was metal and the wall a magnet, it speeded up, faster and faster, so fast that impact with the wall ground it immediately to powder which billowed over the boys like a flour bomb.

The glass destroyed, the room began to settle again. The graffiti stopped swaying, the smell died down, the candles dimmed, many of them guttering out completely.

And Richard, his head spinning, slid to the floor and slept.

14

'He's waking up,' Nige said.

Richard opened his eyes to see faces looming at him. He stretched out a hand and touched one of them. It was Toady's. He flinched away.

'Hey, what're you doing?' he cried, as disgusted as if Richard had spat at him. Richard sat up, and the room and the smell came back, hitting him with hard, unpleasant memories.

'Nige! Nige, you're all right . . . I thought . . .'

Nige looked confused. 'You thought what?'

'What happened? What happened when you touched the glass?'

'Nothing happened. I said nothing was going to happen, didn't I? You slept through it all.'

'Slept?' Richard put a hand to his forehead. The cuff of his jumper was black and burned. 'No, I didn't sleep. I was awake. I was awake when you screamed.'

Nige laughed uneasily. 'Screamed? What are you on about? Why should I scream?'

'You screamed,' insisted Richard, and gripped Nige's shoulder. 'You were all in some sort of trance, and the glass moved, and you screamed. I managed to pull the glass away, and smash it against the wall.' He became aware that all three were staring at him as though he were a

70

lunatic. 'You don't believe me, do you? You think I'm making it up?'

'Aw, you've just woken up,' Robin said. 'You're getting dreams mixed up with reality that's all. Nothing happened, Rich. We just sat here and got cold and nothing happened. A real waste of time.'

'No. No, something did happen. What about this?' Richard held up his arm where the black and tattered remains of his cuff flapped from his parka sleeve. Nige's eyes widened.

'Shit, Rich, you must've done that on a candle. Christ, you could've burned the place down.'

'I didn't do it on a candle,' Richard replied, frustrated. 'I did it on the glass. It was red hot. It burned a hole in my jumper.'

'Look, do we have to listen to this shit much longer?' Toady snapped. He was leaning against a wall, arms folded like a grumpy old gnome. Richard looked at him, then beyond him to the table.

'OK,' Richard said, 'OK, if I was dreaming, do you mind telling me where the glass is?'

Nige turned to point it out. 'It's on th—' He stopped, puzzled. 'At least, it *was* on the table a minute ago. One of you two must've got it.'

'Not me,' said Robin, shrugging.

'Ade?'

'Course not,' scowled Toady. 'I'm not interested in playing stupid games.'

For the first time Nige showed real unease. 'But it was there a few minutes ago. We left it there when we finished. Someone must've moved it.'

'I smashed it,' Richard said. Nige frowned fiercely, as though on the verge of believing or remembering.

Then Robin said, 'Where are the pieces?'

Richard looked up, 'What?'

'The pieces,' Robin repeated. 'If you smashed it against the wall, there would be bits of glass all over the place.'

'Ah,' said Richard. How could he explain what had

71

happened and make it sound believable? 'The glass didn't shatter when I threw it. It just went faster and faster, and then when it hit the wall it just . . . well . . . sort of vaporized.'

'Vaporized?' Robin laughed. 'Vaporized?'

'Well, maybe vaporized isn't the right word. What I meant was, it just sort of . . . turned to powder.'

There was a moment of silence. Nige stared, Robin shook his head in amusement. The silence was broken by Toady, who pushed himself away from the wall. 'Look, I'm not going to stand around here any more listening to stupid fucking fairy tales. I must've put the glass away or something; whatever, it'll turn up. All I want to do now is pack up and go home. It's nearly twenty-five to eleven. We've been gone over an hour.'

This, more than anything, got a reaction from Nige. Horrified, he said, 'I'm supposed to be back by eleven. Mum'll kill me.'

Toady smirked, whether at Nige's discomfort or because he had diverted attention away from Richard was difficult to tell. He said, 'Come on then, give me a hand blowing out these candles and packing them away.'

The torches were switched on and the boys began to move about the room, taking down candles as though dismantling a holy shrine. Richard helped, moving mechanically, his thoughts elsewhere. He knew he hadn't been dreaming, he knew something had happened, but even now he couldn't convince anyone. Nige appeared to have suffered no ill-effects from his experience, the powdered glass had blended with the dust on the floor, and his scorched jumper had been explained away as a result of getting too close to a candle. Richard felt it was almost as though there was some sort of conspiracy against him, that he was the butt of some sick practical joke. Ah well, he thought, at least nothing more serious had happened; his quick thinking with the glass had prevented that.

He gathered up the last of the candles and gave them to Toady, who stuffed them into the rucksack. Then, with a final torch-sweep around the room to ensure nothing had been left behind, the boys left.

15

When they got outside it was snowing. Richard pulled up the hood of his parka; Robin shivered and patted his pockets for gloves; Nige looked at his dirty hands as though they were a part of him he had never seen before.

'Can we come back to your place for a wash, Ade?' he asked. 'Mum'll murder me if I go home in this state.'

Toady scowled and reluctantly said, 'I suppose so. But hurry it up, my dad'll be back soon.' He stomped away. Robin pulled a face behind his back.

The snow was just beginning to dust the rooftops when they reached Latimer Street. The sky was grainy with flakes, glowing orange around street lamps where they fluttered and spiralled like moths. Toady wafted the snow away – perhaps angry that his seance hadn't worked, Nige thought – and pushed his key into the lock. The hall he led them into was cold as an ice-box and smelt of too many chips. Robin held out hands grimy with house-dust and asked, 'Where's the bog?'

Toady pointed upstairs. 'Third door along. But be quiet, my brother's asleep.'

Robin nodded and went upstairs. Richard and Nige stood blinking in the bright light of the hallway whilst Toady heaved the rucksack from his shoulders.

'Shit, Rich,' Nige said, 'you're really filthy.'

'You're not exactly Miss Persil Automatic 1989 yourself,' Richard replied. The two boys looked at themselves in the half-length mirror and laughed. For Richard it was a release from tension, gratitude that he had prevented anything more serious from happening back at the house. Nige giggled and prodded Toady's fat belly, but he simply glowered, swiping the hand away.

'Oh, come on Ade, cheer up a bit,' Richard said. 'Look at yourself.'

Toady looked, but the frown remained.

'What's up?' said Nige. 'Are you pissed off because the seance was a waste of time?'

'It wasn't a—' Toady retorted, then stopped. 'No, of course not,' he mumbled. 'I'm tired, that's all.'

'You didn't really expect anything to happen, did you?' said Nige.

Toady shrugged non-committally.

'Right, next one,' Robin said, coming downstairs. He was cleaner now, though the hot water had made his acne stand out in red blotches. Nige grinned and reached for him with filthy hands, and Robin backed up the stairs, laughing.

'Stop that!' Toady hissed. The boys turned to look at him. 'I've told you to hurry up and be quiet. Now will you please get washed and go?'

Robin tutted and came down, passing Nige on the stairs. 'You're a real bundle of laughs, you know, Ade. We were only having a bit of fun.'

'I've told you, my brother's asleep. I don't want him woken up.'

'We weren't going to wake him up. We were being quiet enough.'

Toady turned to Nige, who was still hovering on the stairs, interested in the argument. 'Will you hurry up?' he snapped. 'I thought Mummy was waiting for you.' Nige shrugged, embarrassed, and trotted upstairs.

'Fucking Toady,' Robin muttered.

'What did you say?'

'Look,' Richard said, 'just calm down, OK? We don't all want to go home in a bad mood, do we?'

Toady shrugged and sat on the stairs; he looked at his hands, sulking again. The boys lounged in the silence of the hall, listening to the splash of water from upstairs, the muffled grumbling of the taps. Nige reappeared a few moments later, looking clean, though his clothes were still grubby. Richard went upstairs, had a quick wash, and came down again.

'Right, we'd better be off,' he said. 'See you at school tomorrow, Ade.'

Toady nodded without looking up. 'Yeah, I suppose so.' He sat on the stairs, looking down at his hands, until the boys had left. When he heard the front door slam he raised his head and smiled.

'Thank you for coming,' he said quietly.

CHAPTER TWO
See No Evil

1

Olive was thinking about curlers – the silliest-looking things ever invented, and damn painful too if you forgot you had them in and leaned back in the armchair – when the telephone rang. She snatched up the receiver, knocking her library book, *The Thorn Birds*, to the floor.

'Hello?' she said, breathlessly.

'Olive Pierce, is that you?' The voice wasn't Richard's, but his grandmother's, Constance Gardener, which might be worse.

'Yes, of course it's me, Constance. Who else would it be?'

'Well, it's obvious there's nothing wrong with you,' Constance said.

'Wrong? Why should there be anything wrong?' answered Olive.

'Oh, I just wondered, with you not showing up at the club tonight, whether you might be sickening for something?'

'No, I'm fine thank you, Connie. I just didn't feel up to it tonight. The cold's starting to get to my old bones a bit.'

'Pschaw,' said Constance. 'Major Bowers was most disappointed.'

'Oh, go on with you,' Olive said, blushing in spite of herself. 'Major Bowers isn't interested in me. Too much Mills and Boon, that's your trouble.'

'Of *course* he's interested,' Connie said. 'I reckon if you play your cards right, it could be wedding bells in the not too distant future.'

'Wedding bells? At my age? Come on, Connie, I'm much too old for all that.'

'Nonsense,' Constance said firmly. 'You're never too old for love. My Albert still brings me a bunch of flowers every Sunday morning. Been doing it for nearly forty years now.'

'Yes, but that's different,' Olive said. 'That's long-standing love. I'm talking about new love, courtship. I'm not going through all that palaver again at my time of life.'

'Still,' said Constance wistfully, 'the major is a very nice man.'

Olive chuckled. 'You old matchmaker. You started looking after me when I was ten, and you've been doing it ever since.'

'I just don't like the thought of you in that flat on your own, Olive, especially not now. You need someone around in your old age, someone you can depend on.'

'Connie, I'm fine, I'm happy. I don't want some man around, cluttering up the place. I like it here on my own. I've got my friends and plenty of visitors; I don't need anybody else.'

Constance sighed. 'You're a stubborn old battleaxe, Olive Pierce.'

'Thank you,' Olive replied. 'I'll take that as a compliment.'

Constance made an exasperated noise, though Olive recognized the humour there. 'I trust you'll be coming to the club next Tuesday?'

'I may do. Why do you ask?'

'May do? May do?' Constance was outraged. 'I insist upon it. It's my birthday party. Or had you forgotten?'

Olive laughed out loud. 'Simmer down, you daft old trout. Of course I hadn't forgotten. I wouldn't miss it for the world.' Before Constance could say anything else Olive abruptly changed the subject, but tried to make it sound casual. 'Umm . . . Richard isn't with you by any chance, is he?'

'No,' Constance said. 'Why do you ask?'

'Oh, nothing. Is he at home, do you know?'

'I've no idea, Olive. Is something the matter? Is he in trouble?'

'Oh no, no, nothing like that. He . . . er . . . he just came to see me this afternoon and left something behind, that's all. Not to worry. I'll give him a ring in the morning.'

'Mm,' said Constance vacantly. 'Look, Olive, I'll have to go. Albert's just come back from taking the dog out; he'll be clamouring for his cocoa in a minute.'

'Yes, all right. I may pop round tomorrow. Will you be in?'

'In the morning. I'm having my hair done at two.'

'The morning it is then. Bye until then.'

'Cheerio. See you tomorrow.' There was a click as she put down the phone.

Olive held the receiver in her hand, debating whether to call Richard's house. She got as far as lifting the phone book on to her lap, but then shook her head and replaced the receiver. She looked at the phone for a moment, let her hand hover over it, then tutted and reached for her book. As she found her page, she glanced at her watch. It was ten-twenty.

At ten twenty-one the room became abruptly and unbearably hot.

Olive gasped and put a hand to her forehead, which was pouring with sweat. How could she be as hot as this? Snow was forecast for tonight. Did she have a fever?

She propped her book on the arm of the chair and made to push herself up to open a window – and it was at that moment that the room around her exploded with shattering glass.

2

The illusion lasted only a second, but in that time Olive

78

threw herself to the floor and covered her head with her hands. A moment later, when she looked up, everything was normal; the furniture in place, the ornaments untouched, the window unbroken. With the aid of the armchair, she scrambled painfully to her feet, trembling like an alcoholic desperate for a drink. Something *had* happened to Richard. She knew that now as surely as if Constance Gardener had told her over the phone.

Her hands were shaking so much that she knocked the telephone receiver off its cradle and on to the floor. 'Damn and blast,' she cursed, and groped beneath the table where the receiver lay buzzing like a trapped insect. 'Come here, you ridiculous contraption,' she panted, and snatched it up.

She rifled through the telephone directory so frantically that she tore some of the pages. 'Come on, come on,' she muttered to herself, her finger passing down the endless list of Gardeners, a soft roar in her ears that was either the hum of telephone wires or the rushing of her blood. She came to the end of the list and went back to the beginning again, forcing herself to look at each entry more carefully. At last she found it: Gardener, D. 28 Cedar Grove, Beachside. She dialled the number, snapping, 'Is that Mrs Gardener?' when a woman's voice said hello.

'Erm . . . yes it is,' the woman said, surprised. 'Who is this, please?'

'It's Olive, Mrs Gardener, Olive Pierce. I . . . is Richard there?'

'No, he's out with his friends, I'm afraid, Olive. He should be back around eleven. Can I give him a message?'

'Er, no. Could you ask him to ring me as soon as he gets in?'

'Yes, of course, if that's what you want. Olive, is something the matter?'

'No, no, nothing to worry about,' she said bluffly. 'Richard left something here when he came to see me this afternoon. I thought he might need it for school in the morning.'

79

'Oh, I see. Well, I'll get him to ring you just as soon as he gets in.'

'Thank you very much. Sorry to have bothered you at this hour.'

Olive sat staring worriedly at the receiver for a full minute after Eileen Gardener had rung off, then replaced it gently in its cradle and stared at it some more. Heat and breaking glass, what did that mean? And that afternoon, when she had touched Richard's hands, what had really happened then? One moment she had been sitting in her armchair, and the next she was in a black empty space, a dream-pit, where bristling nightmare shapes heaved at the edge of her vision. She remembered turning her head, feeling giddy with the hot stench of offal, seeing lamps, red lamps, rushing at her out of the darkness. A moment later a great swinging thing had come at her, like a hand with rotting elephant's tusks for fingers. She had closed her eyes and something had smashed into her body, slamming her back against the wall . . . Then her eyes had opened to find that the wall was the back of her armchair, and the only thing hovering over her was Richard's worried face, almost luminous in the sudden glare of daylight.

Remembering, Olive felt her gorge rise, and rushed to the window for air. She tussled with the curtain for a moment, then flung it aside and pushed the window open. A cold sea breeze met her, and snow fresh as rose petals. Olive leaned out as far as she dared, drinking the air, watching black waves carry slivers of moon on to a black beach.

When the nausea had passed, she pulled the window closed again and went back to her armchair, picking up the telephone on the way. She sat down, the telephone perched in her lap like a cat, and waited for Richard to ring.

80

'Some of these pieces must be missing,' Mr Figg said. 'I can't find the traffic warden's hat anywhere.' Perplexed, he sifted through the cardboard box whilst staring glumly at the picture of Oxford Street on the lid. Mrs Figg, languishing in the armchair, turned round.

'Well, if you will play with such childish things,' she replied. 'Honestly, I gave up jigsaws when I was ten.' She turned back to the television, where a raucous comedy was trying to be funny, pausing only to pop another chocolate liqueur into her mouth.

Richard finished his coffee and stood up. 'I'd better go,' he said. Nige nodded and stood up too. They went through into the hall, which was as cloyingly hot as the fuchsia pink sitting room, though not as inundated with Mrs Figg's powdery scent. 'Can we talk now?' Richard asked when the sitting room door had closed behind them. Nige seemed taken aback.

'What about?'

'About tonight. That's why I came here. You don't think I've come a mile and a half out of my way just for the fun of it, do you?'

'I don't know. Didn't you?'

'Of course not. God, sometimes you're so dim. It's blowing a blizzard out there. I came because I wanted to talk. I wanted to convince you that what I saw happen tonight really happened.'

Nige groaned. 'Oh, don't start all that again.'

'Look,' said Richard through gritted teeth, '*can* we talk now or not?'

'I don't know,' Nige said doubtfully. 'It's pretty late and I've still got to go over those logarithms before I go to bed. My Mum doesn't like me staying up past half eleven on a school day.'

Richard sighed and yanked his parka from its hook on the wall. 'All right, forget it,' he said. 'Well, thanks very much for the coffee – it was worth coming an extra mile and a half through a snowstorm for – three miles actually because I've got to walk back now, but who cares eh? That's what life's all about. Enjoy your revision, and when you're switching off your bedside lamp think of me stuck in a snowdrift somewhere.' He felt better, though breathless, after his outburst. He wound his scarf angrily round his neck, almost strangling himself. Nige watched, bewildered, not really sure why his friend was getting so het up. He hadn't asked Richard to run all the way home with him, had he?

Richard pulled open the front door, admitting a squall of snow on to the doormat. He felt oddly satisfied to see the temperature in the hall barometer drop like a stone. 'Good night,' he muttered, and stomped off down the path without closing the front door.

'Night, Rich, see you tomorrow,' Nige called. He sounded conciliatory, but Richard had made his grand exit now and refused even to wave. As he reached the end of the path, he heard the door close after him.

He reached the gate, opened it, and began to walk along the road. The snow was coming thick and fast now, descending from a sky that looked heavy as a lead shutter. Drifts of snow had transformed the road into a moonscape where cars and houses were shapeless mounds of rock. Street lamps puffed out orange fog that was grainy with snow flakes. Somewhere behind him the sea whispered, though its words were hidden by the moaning of the wind.

Richard bent and scooped snow into his hands. He packed it into a ball and lobbed it towards the nearest lamp post. It missed and plopped into the snow beyond. He sighed and continued walking.

It was not easy to get into a rhythm. His feet felt dragged down, footsteps crunching and creaking in the powdery snow. He was sweating inside his parka, could feel it pouring off him, though his extremities were numb with cold. He felt the night's events crowding in on him again, so strong he could almost taste the empty house's darkness. He shivered and huddled yet deeper inside his parka, thrusting his hands into the pockets.

After another mile he stopped, his breath coming in short, ragged bursts of steam. He was reaching Beachside now, the road broadening out, the houses growing in size. The snow was relentless but somehow remote, its intricate patterns always just ahead of him, seeming to lure him onwards. After a few moments' rest, he began walking again.

He was halfway up Churchill Grove when he heard the sound: a low, shivering growl that blended briefly with the wind and then faded away. Richard stopped and looked around him, expecting to see some bad-tempered dog trembling with cold in a driveway. Seeing nothing, he pulled down the hood of his parka. The sound had been so transient that he couldn't even be sure he hadn't imagined it. He listened for a moment, but hearing nothing further, continued walking.

He looked at his watch: almost twelve o'clock. His mother would be getting worried now. He would probably get a right bollocking when he got in – Where the hell have you been? Do you know what time it is? School in the morning, blah, blah, blah – and he still hadn't done his maths revision for tomorrow. He groaned, though the prospect of sitting in a warm classroom working out equations seemed almost comforting after tonight. He would just have to trust to luck in the test tomorrow and blunder his way through – he was much too tired to do any work for it now. All he longed for was a warm bed and a deep, dreamless sleep.

The swirling patterns in the snow seemed to swallow Richard's thoughts, and almost before he realized it, his legs had carried him to the end of Cedar Grove. He had all but forgotten about the noise, when suddenly he heard it again. This time it was closer, louder, and even over the wind, unmistakable: it was the low, threatening snarl of an animal.

Richard whirled round, his heart pounding, cursing the

snow which blurred his spectacles. There was nothing behind him, but had he caught a glimpse of something ahead just before he turned? He spun back to see, and was met with a harsh swirl of snow that blew into his face like stone-chips. He held up a protective hand, cringing against snow that stung his cheeks. Through the swimming lenses of his spectacles he saw a dark shape creeping through the blizzard towards him.

Panic gripped him and he swept off his spectacles and cleaned them frantically. When they were clear he put them on again. Whatever had been there was gone.

He was trembling now, his hair drenched, his skin stretched like freezing rubber over his face. Ahead of him Cedar Grove should have been bright with snow, but most of the houses were in darkness. Along the edges of the pavement mournful black shapes cast shadows – gesticulating men frozen into trees.

Richard began to stride briskly forward. The wind kept pace with him, moaning softly in his ear. Trees loomed as he walked, each one a potential hiding place, shadows smeared about their bases like crouching shapes. As he neared his house, number twenty-eight, he slowed down. Was there something there, by the gate, waiting for him? He peered closer, but the snow and the blackness of the hedge made it difficult to tell. Gingerly he walked forward.

As he approached, the shadows seemed to clot, to crawl about the hedge as though searching for substance. He edged closer, and suddenly something dropped from the hedge and on to the ground, making a sound like a small animal. Richard peered at it as it writhed, but could make no sense of its structure. It was almost as though the thing were enclosed within its own pocket of darkness, a creature that was hatching from shadow.

All at once Richard heard a cracking sound, like a bursting egg, and the shape by the hedge began to grow. Blackness bloomed upwards, and among the blackness Richard saw a flash of white that might have been teeth or eyes. Panic-stricken, he scooped snow from the ground and packed it into a ball, the nearest he could get to a weapon. Already he felt his mind becoming sluggish, his thoughts dragging like boulders. Before he could enter the dream-state he had experienced at the house, he threw the snowball with all his strength.

The patch of oily darkness split and separated, scattering like pieces of a mirror hit by a stone. The snowball followed through as if nothing had been there, and broke up on impact with the hedge. Richard ran across the road and through the garden gate, oblivious to the snow that stung his face. He didn't stop running until he was at the top of the path, and only when he had fumbled his front door key into the lock did he turn round.

Something *was* there, outside the gate, watching him. Shadow and snow made its form unclear, but Richard was almost certain he saw a shaggy lupine shape, crouching as though to spring, with slanting red eyes that seemed to glow. And, carried to him on the wind, he heard that low animal snarling once again.

He shuddered and turned away, twisting his front door key so hard he thought it might snap in the lock. Behind him the garden gate creaked open, and the snarling grew louder, accompanied by soft padding footsteps. Heart pounding in his chest, Richard pushed open the door and leapt inside.

4

'Where the bloody hell have you been?' Eileen Gardener said. She was in her dressing gown and slippers: a bad sign. It meant she'd been waiting up for him.

'Sorry, Mum, I lost all track of time,' he panted. His head ached with cold; melting snow dribbled down his neck.

'Olive Pierce rang,' Eileen said tartly.

'Did she? Why?'

85

'She says you left something at her house this afternoon. She wanted you to ring her back.'

Richard nodded and reached for the phone. 'Not now,' Eileen said. 'Get those wet things off first and dry your hair. Look at you, you're shivering like mad.'

Richard sighed and pulled off his parka. He sat on the stairs and picked at his wet shoelaces with fingers that felt like ice lollies. Eileen went upstairs to get a towel, which she dropped over the banister on to his head.

'You dry yourself off properly and then get to bed,' she said. 'You can phone Olive in the morning.'

'But, Mum,' Richard protested, 'it might be important.'

'In the morning,' Eileen said firmly. 'Anyway, I told Olive you'd be back by eleven. She's probably in bed herself by now.' She moved off down the corridor and Richard heard her enter the bathroom. Cautiously, rubbing his hair with the towel, he crept to the front door, lifted the flap of the letterbox and peered out.

He saw the front path covered in snow, the garden gate squeaking softly on its hinges, the tree-lined pavement beyond. Apart from that, nothing. It was snowing so hard now that even his footsteps, and any that might have been following, had been obliterated. Somewhat reassured he let the flap drop and went through to the kitchen.

Sam was curled in his box, an old blanket covering him. When he saw Richard he looked up, wagging his tail.

'Hello,' Richard said, and stroked the dog's head for a minute. He helped himself to a biscuit from the tin, but after one bite didn't feel like any more and gave the remainder to Sam. He switched off the light, pulling the door closed on the chomping sounds.

Despite his mother, Richard phoned Olive. He listened to her phone ring once, twice, and then a sleepy voice said, 'Yes, hello.'

'Olive, it's me,' Richard hissed, glancing upstairs to make sure his mother wasn't around. 'My Mum said you rang me earlier.'

Immediately Olive's voice became sharper, more alert. 'Richard, what happened tonight?'

Richard hesitated for a moment. 'I'm not sure. I'm a bit muddled. Can I come and see you tomorrow?'

'Please, yes, straight after school if you can. If not, in the evening. But tell me, are you all right?'

'Yes, I'm fine. Scared but . . . OK.'

'And the others? How are they?'

'Oh, they're fine. As far as they're concerned the evening was a complete waste of time. They say that nothing happened. But it did, Olive, I know it did. I wasn't dreaming. And I think . . .' He broke off, suddenly afraid to say what was in his mind.

'What?' Olive prompted. 'What do you think?'

Richard cupped the mouthpiece, glancing at the front door as though it were an eavesdropper. In a thin whisper, he said, 'I think something followed me home tonight.'

He heard a sound that could have been a sigh or an intake of breath, then Olive said, 'We need to talk, Richard, but together, face to face, not over the telephone. Something happened here tonight, too.' When Richard began to speak she said, 'No, not now. I'll tell you tomorrow. Be careful until then. God bless.'

The solemnity in her voice frightened Richard. 'Good night,' was all he could whisper, and gently he replaced the receiver. He stood for a moment, listening, feeling the oppressive weight of snow, like a cold shroud chilling the house. He shivered. Even here he felt that eyes were watching him. As quietly as he could, he ran upstairs. Quickly he washed and brushed his teeth, then went into his bedroom. Vague shadows were moving on the walls; snow was building a screen of white across the window. Averting his gaze from the garden for fear of seeing a dark lupine shape standing on the lawn, Richard closed his curtains. He stripped quickly, touched his hair to make sure it was dry enough, then climbed into bed. The sheets were clammy and unwelcoming at first, and Richard brought up his legs, bending his knees and elbows into the foetal position. He closed his eyes, his body humming with exhaustion. But it was a long time before he slept.

5

Friday

Robin started awake, scrappy disturbing images fluttering through his mind like ash from a bonfire. His sleep had been deep, but not restful, plagued with murky repellent dreams which he could not now recall. He sat up quickly, shaking himself like a dog. His bedsheets were crumpled and twisted around him. He pushed them away, feeling hemmed in, and plucked open his curtain. Immediately he screwed up his eyes against the glare of snow.

His room smelled; the pungent sweat of nightmare. Robin stood on his bed and opened his window. The air that breezed in was so crisp he felt he could snap it between his fingers. Below his window, birds bickered by the bird table; Mr Treeborn swore as he dug his car out with a shovel. A couple of streets away a gritter rumbled by, spraying sand like buckshot.

Robin yawned and stretched. Already his dreams were receding, swamped by normality. He stepped down off his bed, wincing at the cold, cursing his broken radiator. He pulled on his dressing gown, stepped into his slippers, and went along the corridor to the bathroom.

As always he groaned at his reflection. Every morning was the same. He would get up, half-hoping that his acne had magically disappeared overnight, but one glance in the mirror always confirmed the worst. Rather than disappearing, his spots actually seemed to be spreading. They peppered his forehead, his cheeks, his chin, his throat. His face was a battlefield; he looked like a case of terminal measles. Gloomily he urinated, washed his hands, then applied his hated spot cream. The smell of the stuff was a constant reminder of his horrendous condition.

Back in his room he switched off his alarm. It wasn't due to go off for another ten minutes, but Robin didn't feel like getting back into bed. Instead he pottered around – collecting his schoolbooks together and packing them into his bag; sticking up a poster of a Porsche Spyder that had been drooping off the wall for a week; putting records, which had been accumulating dust, back into their sleeves. When he had exhausted all the options, he went downstairs for his breakfast.

The kitchen was large and bright, the view from the window cheerful as a Christmas card. As Robin poured muesli into a bowl he heard bumps and groans and footsteps above him, followed by his mother's voice, sharp with anger. Automatically he switched on the radio to drown out the argument he knew would follow.

Five minutes later his father stomped into the kitchen, scowling with annoyance. 'Paper's not come,' he grunted, and clattered about in the fridge, taking it out on the milk bottles. Robin wolfed his muesli, hoping to get out of the kitchen before his mother made an appearance. From his father's mood he knew that a quarrel was imminent.

'Can you fix my radiator this weekend, Dad?' Robin asked. 'It's freezing in my room.'

His father nodded. 'I expect so. I'll do it tomorrow when you're at work.'

'Thanks,' Robin said and put his breakfast dishes by the sink to be washed. 'At work': it sounded important, though it was only a twelve-hour-a-week job in a super-market, packing shelves. Still, it was worth an extra twenty-odd quid, money that Robin didn't know what to do with. And, as he had only got the job two weeks ago, the novelty of putting on his blue nylon overall had not quite worn off yet.

On the way upstairs he passed his mother. She was a slim, attractive, dark-haired woman in her late thirties. Robin suspected that one of the reasons why she and his father argued so much was because his father resented her attractiveness. He was overweight with prematurely grey hair, and always seemed to be tired. She, on the other hand, was vivacious and energetic with more men friends than his father approved of. True, most of them were hairdressers like herself and tended to be pretty weird, but for some reason that only irritated his father all the more.

'How's your face this morning, Robbie?' she asked.

He put a self-conscious hand to his cheek and half-turned away. 'It's OK,' he mumbled, embarrassed.

'Well, it doesn't look it,' Sylvia said, 'it looks awful. Have you put your cream on yet?'

'Yes, Mum,' Robin said, feeling even worse.

'And did you wash your face first like the doctor said?'

'Um, no Mum, not yet. I was just about to now.'

'Oh, Robbie,' Sylvia sighed, 'what's the use of putting your cream on and then washing your face? Do it the other way round in future.'

'But Mum, this cream's brown,' he protested. 'It makes me look like I've got make-up on.'

'Who cares what it looks like so long as it does the trick? Now, get along to the bathroom and do as I say.'

'All right,' said Robin grudgingly, and plodded upstairs. Why the hell did they have to make the stuff brown? They probably just went for the most embarrassing colour they could think of.

In the bathroom he ran hot water into the basin and peeled off his dressing gown and pyjama top. He shivered at the chill, goose pimples springing up on his back and shoulders. Bending low over the basin he scooped hot water into his face. He worked his special soap into a lather and washed his face, neck and arms thoroughly. Dripping, eyes screwed up against the soap, he groped to his right for a towel.

When he was dry he raised his head and looked into the bathroom mirror. It was steamed up now, water droplets clinging to the glass through a cloud of vapour. Peering at himself, Robin frowned. He could see his face only as a vague pink blob with dark, smudged features, but it was not this that made him frown. In the blurred glass something white and shadowy seemed to be perched on his left shoulder.

Robin brushed at his shoulder, simultaneously twisting his head to see what was there. Of course, there was nothing; he looked around the bathroom, and then into the mirror again. The white blur was still there, hovering above his head like a bird or a halo. Frightened, he rubbed the layers of steam from the mirror, fingers squeaking on the glass. This time the reflection showed only his wide-eyed face and pimply shoulders, with pale green wall tiles and a glimpse of the darker green lampshade behind.

Robin stared at the mirror for a moment, then suddenly shivered. More goose pimples sprang up, this time from fear, not cold. Robin snatched up his pyjama top, his dressing gown and his spot cream and hurried to his bedroom. He tried to convince himself that what he had seen was an optical illusion, a glare of snow reflected in the mirror, something like that. But what shook him was the fact that the thing had looked as solid as he was.

Quickly, he re-applied his cream, got dressed and combed his hair. It was only ten past eight, but suddenly he wanted to be out of the house. Its confines felt oppressive, disturbing. From downstairs he could hear Radio One and his mother's laughter. It wasn't often his mother and father laughed together, but today even that couldn't shake off his unease.

He went downstairs, still thinking about the ghostly white thing above his head. Perhaps it had been the Finger of God singling him out. Maybe he would hear a booming voice, 'Splatto!' just before a gritter ran him down on the way to school. No, don't think of such things, even in fun. It was tempting fate to think that way.

He said goodbye to his parents and then started off to school. He was going to be ridiculously early, but it was better than sitting around the house. Already he could feel himself calming down, the air clearing his head. The snow was so dazzling he had to screw up his eyes. He should have brought his Polaroids with him; hadn't he heard that the glare from the snow could be just as dangerous as staring at the sun?

All at once Robin stopped. Across the road an oak tree in a long, snow-blanketed garden cradled a tree-house among its branches. Staring at the planks that made up the tree-house had suddenly brought Robin's dreams back to him with startling clarity. Of course, now he remembered their location. It had been the room in the house in which they'd held the seance.

6

'Red eyes,' Richard thought. 'Had that thing in the snow really had red eyes?'

He sighed and looked across the classroom to where Nige was scribbling away. In fact everyone seemed to be writing except him. He picked up his pen and turned his attention to the questions on the paper in front of him. After a moment he jotted down a hesitant answer, then crossed it out and wrote something else. He began to flick through his book of logarithm tables, but the numbers were a meaningless blur. His mind began wandering again.

Red eyes.

'Ten more minutes,' Mrs Charlesworth said.

Over by the window Nige was just finishing question nineteen. The test had been a struggle, and some of his answers were so ludicrous that he knew they couldn't possibly be right, but he felt he had done enough to pass. He put down his pen and allowed himself the luxury of flexing his fingers. He still had ten minutes to go; just time for a short rest before he began the final question. He sneaked a glance over his shoulder. Richard appeared to be working now at any rate; every other time Nige had looked he had been staring into space. Idly, he wondered where Toady had got to this morning. Probably skiving. He hadn't shown any signs of being ill last night. He might have picked up some bug from that old house, though; it had certainly been cold and dirty enough.

Still flexing his fingers, Nige glanced out of the window. The school playground was covered with snow dirtied by footprints; over on the playing fields a snowman drooped, overcome by a snowball barrage; the beginnings of ice-slides glimmered like slug-trails on concrete paths. Nige enjoyed the view from the maths classroom window. By leaning slightly to the left he could see as far as the school gates and the path beyond. During particularly boring lessons he liked to watch the people come and go. At the moment he could see a young mother in furry snow-boots, pushing a pram, a blind man with black spectacles and a black suit probing the air with a white sick, a bearded youth with long hair and a loping stride.

'Five more minutes.'

Nige picked up his pen again. He found the last question surprisingly easy. When he had finished he glanced around, caught Richard's eye, and pointed at the door. Richard nodded.

'How did you do?' Nige asked a few minutes later as they walked down the corridor.

'Crap,' answered Richard. 'I only got up to question fifteen. How about you?'

'OK, I think. Enough to pass anyway.' Richard nodded, though he seemed preoccupied. Nige said, 'Are you OK?'

'I'm worried. Let's go and talk somewhere, away from the snowball fights.'

'OK.'

The boys skirted the playground, managing to avoid flying snowballs. They headed for the dustbins, but smokers had claimed the area, so they went over to the gymnasium instead. The changing rooms were always quiet and empty during break, and they knew they could talk there in peace. On the way they looked for Robin, but he was nowhere to be seen. Secretly Richard was pleased; it would be easier to convince Nige on his own.

'OK,' Nige said when they had sat down, 'what do you want to talk about?'

'Last night,' Richard replied firmly.

'Oh no, not that again. What is there to say? Nothing happened.'

'No, Nige, something *did* happen, and not just at the seance. Afterwards. When I was walking home.' He told Nige about the sounds he had heard, and the thing by the hedge, and the creature with the red eyes that had watched him from the gate.

'You're sure you're not imagining all this?' Nige asked. Richard shook his head vehemently.

'No chance. Besides, it wasn't just me. Something happened to Olive as well.'

'To Olive? What?'

'I don't know yet. I rang her, but she wouldn't tell me over the phone. I'm going to see her tonight. I want you to come too.'

Nige wrinkled his nose. 'I don't know, Rich. I'm not sure my Mum would approve of two nights in a row. You know how she is.'

'All right, then, we'll go this aft, straight after school.'

'We can't. You've got to take Toady's satchel back, remember.'

'Damn,' said Richard. He had forgotten about that. At registration that morning their form teacher, Miss O'Brien, had held up a battered satchel covered with size eight boot prints and had asked if anyone knew why Adrian Tibbett had left it in the playground after school the previous day. Richard hadn't told her that, but he had volunteered to take Toady's satchel back to him. He was curious and a little worried by Toady's non-appearance at school that day. 'Well, we'll go to his place first and then to Olive's,' he said. 'If we're quick we can do both before tea. Tell your Mum you were held up at choir practice or something.'

'I'm not in the choir.'

'Well, tell her you joined. Come on, Nige. If nothing else, just do it to humour me.'

Nige sighed. 'OK. But if I'm not convinced by the time

I've seen Olive, I don't want to hear another word about it. Deal?'

'OK,' Richard nodded. 'Deal.'

7

Walter Treeborn was an obsessive man. His life was a perfectly balanced routine of order and efficiency. Each morning at eight o'clock he got up, and each evening at eleven o'clock he went to bed. He showered twice a day, he brushed his teeth after every meal, he combed his hair (which was trimmed once a fortnight) whenever he saw a mirror, and he never wore the same pair of underpants two days running.

His house was a reflection of his character. It was meticulously furnished and spotlessly clean. Anything in it that had the temerity to look the tiniest bit shoddy or worn or threadbare was immediately thrown away. Treeborn loved machines, loved them for their cleanliness, and as a result technology gleamed in every room. A computer and a word processor graced the study; a video tape recorder, colour television and compact disc player the lounge. The bedroom displayed a digital clock radio and a teasmaid, the bathroom an electric toothbrush, sun-ray lamp and electric razor. A fridge freezer, washing machine, spin dryer, blender, electric can opener and various other culinary marvels enhanced the kitchen. However, despite all this, the house never looked cluttered. Full, yes, but never cluttered. Treeborn had a place for everything.

But it wasn't just the inside of the house; the outside, too, was immaculate. The garden was a tribute to symmetry, the lawn like a billiard table; the garage was cobweb-free and hung with gardening tools you could see your face in. The car, a blood-red Cavalier, was showroom clean. Each evening Treeborn could be seen carefully wiping dirt from the bumpers, the hubcaps and the licence plates.

The cause of Treeborn's obsession was simple; he had

never married. And the reason he had never married was that no wife could possibly have lived with his obsession. It was a vicious circle, a clean, sterile, beautifully ordered Catch 22. He was a balding, bespectacled, very successful, very lonely sales rep. And today he was in a bad mood.

Treeborn's car was the most precious commodity of his occupation: without it he could not do his job. And so when, that morning, he had dug it out of the snow to find it wouldn't start, he was naturally very annoyed. Already it meant that his routine had been disturbed and that he was going to have to re-arrange his schedules. He phoned for a mechanic, who promised to be out within the hour, and settled down with his plan of action.

However, three hours had now passed since that phone call and still the mechanic hadn't shown. 'I'm afraid we've got a bit of a job on, guv,' he had said on the four occasions that Treeborn had called him, 'I'll get to you as soon as I can.'

Treeborn was furious. His day was in tatters. Even if he had the whole afternoon to work, which now seemed unlikely, he couldn't possibly get through his calls. He sat on the sofa, his papers on his lap, and looked anxiously out of the lounge window. With each minute that passed, his stomach tied itself further into knots.

At precisely twelve-thirty Treeborn went into the kitchen to make himself a cottage-cheese sandwich. He didn't really feel like eating, but he made it a rule never to skip a meal. He carried his sandwich into the lounge and watched the lunchtime news whilst he took small, precise bites.

There was more fighting in Angola, the newscaster informed him. A plane had crashed, killing forty-seven people. A teenage girl had been missing from home for four days and police now feared for her safety. The royal couple had officially opened a youth centre in Bristol.

It was to the background of Angolan gunfire that Treeborn first heard the noises coming from his cellar. He paused like a bird, his sandwich suspended two inches from his mouth, and listened.

Yes, there they were again. An unmistakable series of scratches and bumps coming from the floorboards beneath him. Treeborn pushed his plate aside and looked down at the carpet, half-expecting it to burst apart and the cause of the sound to erupt into the room. What could possibly be down there? Surely not mice! The thought chased away the last of his appetite. He took his plate into the kitchen, deposited the half-eaten sandwich in the pedal bin (after first wrapping it in cellophane, of course), then thoughtfully washed the plate and put it away in the cupboard.

Perhaps it was someone's pet down there, he thought as he brushed his teeth, a cat or a dog that had somehow got in through the coal bunker. He combed his hair and shuddered. Treeborn was not a great animal lover; in his opinion they were dirty, smelly things that shed hairs and fleas wherever they went. If it *was* an animal down there, and he didn't see what else it could be, he would have to scrub the place after he'd got it out.

Gloomily he pulled on rubber gloves and a pair of waterproof over-trousers on top of his grey pin-stripes. He considered taking a weapon, a walking stick or a spade in case the animal was savage, but in the end decided against it. Much as he disliked animals, he didn't think he could bring himself to hit one with a spade. The thought of getting blood on his clothes made him feel quite sick.

The cellar door was tucked away in a corner of the kitchen. Treeborn didn't use the cellar (it was a long time since the house had relied on coal for fuel, and Treeborn didn't believe in storing things), but nevertheless he cleaned and de-bugged the place once a month. As he pulled open the door a rush of cold air swept over him like a breath of winter. He shivered and peered into the darkness below. Nothing seemed to be moving. Perhaps the animal had found its own way out.

Treeborn sniffed. The cellar always smelt of disinfectant and, however much he cleaned it, of coal-dust. Now, however, another smell could be detected. It was so faint it was unrecognizable, but nevertheless it caused him to wrinkle his nose in disgust. Tentatively he sniffed again, trying to pinpoint the source of the odour, but like the colours of an oil-slick, it seemed to change constantly. One second it was like ammonia, the next he could have sworn it was fish. Then petrol. Then wet animal fur. Then stagnant water. Whatever was down there certainly had an impressive olfactory repertoire. His spirits sinking fast, Treeborn braced himself to deal with the filthiest-looking mongrel he would probably ever see.

Reluctantly he started down. His hands felt clammy in the rubber gloves, but the rest of his body was numb with cold. In fact the cellar was much colder than it ought to be, which seemed to support his theory that the coal bunker doors had come open.

Three steps down he reached out his left hand to the light switch and flicked it. Nothing happened. The bulb must have gone. Damn, he thought. His whole world seemed to be collapsing around him today. He considered going to his garage to get the big torch he kept there, but then remembered he had lent it to Mr Treadwell, whose house backed on to his, a couple of days before. Treadwell should have returned it by now; he'd only needed it to change a lightbulb in his garage. Treeborn's resentment boiled into anger and he glared into the darkness below.

'Come out of there you . . . you . . . you bloody animal!' he hissed. The only response was a fresh waft of stink, this time reeking of bad eggs.

Treeborn went down another couple of steps. The cellar was pitch black. Already the door behind him looked a long way away. The blackness seemed to be moving and rolling like water, trying to form itself into shapes. Treeborn stumbled another few steps. He was halfway down now, and to him it felt like limbo. Below was an abyss, a black unknown pit, and way, way above, so far it looked unreachable, the welcoming rectangle of light that was the cellar door.

All at once Treeborn felt sleepy. How ridiculous, he thought, to feel sleepy at a time like this. It was almost as though the cellar was a dream into which he was being lured. He was weightless, his mind drifting like a balloon. Below him, in the darkness, two red eyes suddenly blinked on like lamps. Treeborn watched, bemused, as they bobbed towards him, bringing with them a stench so vile it made his eyes water. As the red lamps came closer, Treeborn saw the blackness beneath them part like paper and white, glistening teeth flash through.

'Good doggy,' he murmured. 'Good boy, good doggy.'

Then the stench overwhelmed him and he fainted dead away.

8

If it were possible, the Piling Hill estate was even more threatening by day than it was by night. On street corners gangs of kids, some no more than nine or ten years old, stared in hostile silence, daring Richard and Nige to establish eye-contact. Teenage mothers, their faces as jaded as their clothes, trudged resentfully through the snow, pushing prams which contained grubby, squalling infants. Tattooed men with hard, unrelenting features glared as though the boys' uniforms were a challenge.

Richard's senses were working overtime, weighing every sight, every smell, every sound for its potential menace. Shattered windows, boarded-up shops, piles of rubble and gutted furniture, bludgeoning music from a seedy cafe: all intensified his discomfort.

He and Nige spoke little on the way to Toady's house. They crunched through snow whose contours had been marred by boots and passing traffic; they cowered beneath a bleak sky, against a wind like pincers of ice. As they turned on to King Street, Richard gestured and said, 'There's the house.' Nige looked at Richard, then at the house, but said nothing.

Passing the house, Richard shivered. In the daylight it looked even more grotesque. The collapsed roof meant no softening mantle of snow, which gave an impression of the house as a huge maw open to the sky, squatting in a fenced-in nest.

'I feel like it's watching us,' Richard said quietly.

'It's just a house,' Nige replied – but Richard noted that he was careful to avert his gaze as they passed by.

Latimer Street was quiet, the grey houses like a dormitory of tramps sleeping under dirty blankets. A dog, shivering as it inspected a lamp post, seemed to be the only sign of life. Richard noticed that Toady's curtains were closed and pointed it out to Nige.

'Maybe he *is* ill then,' Nige said.

'I hope so,' Richard replied before he realized how bad that sounded.

Nige laughed. 'You're charming, you are.'

'You know what I mean.'

They went up the path and banged on the front door. Richard thought he saw Toady's curtain flicker, but the movement was too quick for him to be sure. They waited a few minutes then tried again. Still no-one came.

'Maybe he's too sick to answer,' suggested Nige.

'If he's that bad, someone should be looking after him,' replied Richard.

They tried knocking a third time. Richard stayed by the door while Nige went around the side of the house to peer in at the windows. He came back, shrugging.

'I can't see anyone. Maybe they've all gone away.'

'If they have, it's pretty short notice. And why would they leave in the middle of a snowstorm?'

'Family business? Perhaps someone died or something.'

Richard nodded. 'Yeah, you're probably right,' but still he stared up at the house for a few moments. Finally he said, 'Come on, we might as well go. It looks like we've had a wasted journey.'

Nige nodded and the two boys trudged down the path. At the gate Nige turned back briefly. Richard pushed the gate open, but Nige stopped him.

'Hey, wait a minute.'

'What's up?'

Nige pointed. 'Toady's curtain moved. I'm sure of it.'

The boys went back up the path and stood beneath the window.

'Ade? It's me – Richard.' There was no response. He held up the satchel like a peace offering. 'We've brought your bag back.'

A few seconds passed, then the curtains twitched open and a fat, unsmiling face peeked through.

'There he is,' Nige said, and waved. Toady didn't wave back. His head at the window was motionless, his face impassive: the eyes were so glazed they looked painted. Then the head mouthed something and the face disappeared. Nige turned and said, 'He must be coming down.'

The boys waited, stamping their feet against the cold, until a lock rattled and the door inched open.

'What do you want?' Toady asked, peering at them suspiciously.

'We've brought your satchel back, Ade,' Richard said.

'Oh, yeah. Thanks.' Toady reached out a pyjama-clad arm and snatched the bag away. He seemed reluctant to open the door more than a few inches.

'Are you all right?' Nige asked.

'Yes, of course I am. Why?'

'Oh, nothing. Just that you didn't come to school today, that's all.'

Toady nodded. 'Oh, yeah, that. Well, I've not been too well.'

'Sorry if we got you out of bed,' Richard said.

'Bed?' Toady looked down at his pyjamas. 'Oh, yeah, bed. Well, that's all right, I was getting up anyway.'

Richard frowned. 'Are you sure you're all right?'

'I've said so, haven't I? I'll be fine by Monday. Well, I'd better go. Thanks for the satchel.' He eased the door shut.

Richard made a move to stop him, then changed his mind. Something was wrong, he was sure of it, but what

101

could he do? He voiced his suspicions to Nige, who said, 'I thought so too. What is it, do you think?'

'I don't know, but he didn't really look ill to me. Tired, yes, but not ill. His eyes were red, his hair was messy. He looked as though he'd been up all night.'

'Perhaps he was too ill to sleep?'

'Perhaps, but I don't think so.' Richard looked up at the house, searching for inspiration, but ideas failed him. Nige hugged himself. He was getting cold.

'Well, there's nothing we can do now,' he said. 'If he doesn't show up at the meeting on Sunday we'll just have to wait till Monday. Come on, Rich, I want to get to Olive's and home before tea.'

Richard nodded reluctantly. 'I suppose you're right.' He walked back down the path, aware that he was turning his back on a mystery. He may have been one satchel lighter, but his mind was heavy with questions.

9

Toady watched them go through the gap in his curtains. When Richard turned for a last look at the house he pulled back into the shadows, anxious not to draw attention to himself a second time. If Richard saw him watching it might further arouse his suspicions.

His room smelt stale, but Toady didn't notice. Neither did he notice his own fatigue. He was too close to worry about minor discomforts; he needed just a little more time.

When he was certain that the two boys had gone, he returned to his task.

10

Snow didn't belong on a beach. Though Olive had lived in Starmouth all her life, she had never got used to that strange sight. Snow and sea. They came from the same source, yet it was like a meeting of opposites, a confrontation between two of nature's enemies. Of course, the outcome was always inevitable. The sea was stronger, permanent, it was on home ground and it had motion on its side. The incoming tide ate away the snow like corrosion until all that was left was a blending that was not even discernible.

Olive was drawn to the sea, always had been. She watched it for hours, fancied she saw faces, scenarios, whole episodes from her past, acted out before her eyes. She saw life and death in the waves, heard voices disguised as wind. The sea was alive, as much of a living being as she was; more so, perhaps, for it was always moving. It had its moods and its tempers, its friends and its enemies. Olive liked to think of herself as one of its friends, and an intimate one at that. She had spent hours engrossed in its company, and even when the sea had been at its most furious and lives had been lost, she had never felt threatened or afraid.

But every coin has its flip-side. Olive detested flame, was terrified by it. It had been fire which had killed her father in his bed, and which, eleven years earlier, in the form of lightning, had killed her fiancé, Harold. Harold had been twenty-four when he'd died, Olive two years younger. Though she had not been with him at the time – he had escorted her home from a dance and was walking back over the golf course to the house he shared with his parents – Olive had seen his death many times. She had seen it in the waves: the lightning streaking down, Harold raising his head slightly, his mouth widening in astonishment. And then the impact: his body jerking as his head was engulfed, a sizzling sound, a funnel of smoke as though from an overheated plug. Harold had fallen, stunned, his hair aflame. And there, as he had slept, the fire had slowly and meticulously done its work: spreading over his face, down his back, along his limbs, cooking and devouring at its leisure.

Olive shuddered, not because she had seen the body but

because she hadn't. There had been no chapel of rest for Harold, no weeping relatives coming to pay their last respects. No cosmetic job, however elaborate, could have concealed the fact that there was little left but charcoal.

Now, whenever Olive wanted to remember him, she had to look at photographs to bring back his features. Her own thoughts betrayed her, conjured up an image from a nightmare. This distressed her not just because the image was upsetting, but because fire had corrupted her memory of Harold. Was this all he was to her now? A blackened husk for which she could feel only terror and disgust? She had loved him once, had come close to marrying him. It pained her to think that in April he would have been celebrating his seventieth birthday.

The doorbell was a welcome intrusion into Olive's thoughts. It was talking over old times with Constance Gardener that morning that had stirred these memories. Now Constance's grandson, Richard, was bringing her back to the present.

'Olive, are you up there? It's only me.'

Olive went to the window, pulled back the net curtain and waved. Her walk that morning had stiffened her joints, and she winced as she descended the stairs. Coldness seemed to linger in her body much longer these days; sometimes she found it almost impossible to get warm at all.

Richard had brought a friend with him, a dark-skinned boy with black hair and delicate features. 'You remember Nige,' he said. Olive nodded.

'Of course. I never forget a face. How are you, Nigel?'

'Fine, thank you, Mrs Pierce.'

'Good, good. Well, come on in, you must be freezing cold. I know I am.'

They followed Olive into her booth and up the stairs to her flat, Richard looking around anxiously. Olive had said something had happened here last night, and she had sounded distressed on the phone, but as far as he could tell nothing was out of place.

She ushered them into the sitting room and went to make tea. Nige perched on the edge of the settee, looking uncomfortable, stealing glances at the clock.

'I can't stay long,' he said, 'We have tea at six.'

Richard leaned back in an armchair as though showing Nige how to relax. 'Don't worry,' he said, 'we've got plenty of time.' Yet he too wished Olive would hurry. All day long he had been wondering what she was going to tell him.

'It's cold in here,' Nige complained, hugging himself.

'Yes, Olive hardly ever puts the fire on. I don't suppose she can afford it.'

Nige rubbed his arms and craned his neck to look out of the window. Beyond the railings of the promenade, the sea was nibbling the snow. The wind off the sea was making banshees of the clothes that the few passers-by were wearing: a figure with a rucksack encased in a blue cagoul, a schoolgirl battling with the wind for her satchel, a man with a black suit and black spectacles who was tapping the way ahead with a stick. The scene made Nige feel even colder, and he looked around with a shudder as Olive came in.

'Here we are,' she said. She set the tray down and lowered herself into her favourite armchair. Richard played mum without being asked. He passed the cups round, and then before anyone had had a chance to drink, blurted: 'What happened to you last night?'

Olive sipped, then set her cup down. 'Patience, Richard,' she said. 'I want to hear your side of the story first.'

Richard looked disappointed. 'Aw, why?'

'Because I think it will help me to understand better what happened to me. It's a matter of cause and effect. It's no use giving the answer even before the question has been posed.'

Richard shrugged, conceding defeat. 'All right, my version first,' he said. He began the story haltingly, starting with the boys climbing into the old house. He found it difficult to describe his feelings, to relate the sheer terror he had experienced to what had actually taken place. 'Something was there,' was the only way he could think to describe it, 'something was in that house, but it was only me that felt it. Nobody else seemed to feel anything.'

'It was just a house,' Nige said from his perch on the settee. 'It was spooky because it was dark, and it stank to high heaven, but that's all it was, just a house.'

Olive listened to both those explanations, nodding gravely, her green eyes thoughtful, fingers steepled to her lips. When Richard came to the part about the glass and the candles flaring up, and the oddities in temperature, she leaned back and very quietly said, 'Ah, that's it.'

'What?' Richard asked.

Olive waved the enquiry away. 'Never mind, I'll explain later. Go on. Oh, just one question. What time did you smash the glass?'

Richard shrugged. 'I'm not sure. Ten? Half ten?'

'Yes,' Olive said, 'that would fit. Go on with your story.'

Richard told her the rest of it, about the creature in the snow, the red eyes that had watched him from the gate. Throughout, Olive said nothing, though her expression grew a little more intense, and, Richard fancied, a little more fearful.

'That's it,' he said when he had finished. He spread his arms and laughed shakily. 'Pretty unbelievable huh?'

'Very unbelievable,' Nige muttered.

Olive turned to him. 'You don't believe Richard's story?'

Nige looked embarrassed. 'It's not that,' he said, 'I don't think he's lying deliberately. It's just that . . . well, I was there last night, and as far as I'm concerned, nothing happened.'

'What do you remember?' Olive asked.

Nige blushed slightly. 'We lit candles and sat around the table with our finger on the glass. Richard was in the corner. I remember staring at the glass for ages and feeling a bit sleepy. That's all, nothing else. After a bit we packed up and went home.'

'And you remember no pain? You don't remember calling out?'

'No, of course not.'

'So what would your honest opinion of all this be?'

Nige flashed Richard a hesitant smile to show he meant no harm, and said, 'Well, it was obvious that the house was getting to Rich. I mean it was getting to me a bit too, but Rich was really scared, you know? I think he had a nightmare and dreamt it all, and then later, because of the nightmare, he imagined that something was following him. I mean, it was snowing quite badly. I've done it myself at times, seen shapes in the snow that aren't really there.' He shrugged. 'I think this thing's got a bit out of proportion, that's all.'

'I take it you haven't experienced anything out of the ordinary, then?' Olive said.

Nige shook his head. 'No.'

'Well I have,' Olive said firmly. 'Perhaps when I've told you my story you'll be a little more convinced.' She finished the last of her tea and told the boys what had happened to her last night – the sudden, unbearable heat, the way the room seemed to shatter around her. 'It was just as though, for a moment, the room and everything in it was made of glass. You've never heard such a noise. I threw myself on the floor and covered my ears. When I looked up I expected to see glass everywhere, but there was nothing, not even a broken window.' She paused a moment to allow this to sink in before delivering the *coup de grâce*. 'It must have happened at the same time that you threw the glass at the wall.'

There was silence in the room for a moment. Richard's mouth felt dry. It was not that Olive's story confirmed his fears – he trusted his own feelings enough to know that something awful had happened – but it did seem to indicate that the repercussions of what they'd done were much more far-reaching than he had imagined.

He glanced at Nige to see how he had taken it. His friend was staring at Olive, his eyes wide, his mouth slightly open. Richard swallowed, and finally managed to croak, 'Well? Do you believe us now?'

Nige's eyes flickered away from Olive and focussed on Richard. Very quietly he said, 'I don't know what to believe.'

Gently, as though all three of them were treading through a verbal minefield, Olive said, 'I know how we can make Nigel believe, but he would have to be agreeable.'

'How?' Richard asked.

'I have a friend,' Olive said, 'a man called Nathan Buttrick. He's a hypnotist. If anyone can unlock Nigel's subconscious, he can.'

Richard nodded slowly. 'Yeah, good idea.' He turned to Nige. 'What do you think?'

Nige looked unenthusiastic. 'I don't know. I've heard hypnotism's dangerous. Sometimes people don't come out of the trances properly.'

'Pshaw,' said Olive, 'there's no need to worry about Nathan on that score. He's an expert, not some shabby sideshow hack. I give you my word that no harm will come to you.'

Nige was still doubtful. 'But how will I know what I've said,' he argued. 'I mean, if I'm going to be in a trance, I can hardly convince myself, can I?'

'We tape it, of course,' said Olive. 'This boudoir of mine is not entirely without its technology you know.' She gestured over to a wooden cabinet. 'Richard, would you be so kind as to bring me my cassette recorder? It's in the left hand side of the cabinet.'

Richard grinned and did as Olive asked. The recorder, despite Olive's protestations, was at least fifteen years old and somewhat archaic. As she plugged it in, Olive explained, 'I like to listen to my own choice of music – Wagner, Strauss, Brahms – without having to rely on the whims of these so-called disc jockeys. I would have bought

108

a gramophone, but it would have been too large for my flat.' She selected a blank tape and put it in the recorder. 'Are we agreed, then?' she said.

Nige squirmed on the settee, looking distastefully at the tape recorder. 'I don't know,' he said. 'I have to be home by six.'

'Then we have plenty of time,' Olive said brightly. 'Nathan only lives five minutes drive away. I can ring him immediately.' She picked up the receiver, but paused before dialling and looked at Nige. 'That is, if you want me to.'

'Go on, Nige,' Richard prompted, 'you'll be all right.'

Nige still looked unhappy, but at last he nodded. 'OK, but I do have to be back by six; no later.'

Olive was already dialling. 'You will be. Nathan will have that information out of you and on to tape quicker than you can say Jack Robinson.' She paused. The telephone was ringing at the other end. 'Hello? Nathan? . . . Hello, lovey, it's Olive. Look, I wonder if you could do me a favour?' Ten minutes later she stood as a car pulled up outside. 'Here's Nathan,' she said. 'I'd best go let him in.'

When she had gone, Richard said, 'Are you sure you want to go through with this, Nige? Just say no if you don't.'

Nige shrugged. 'I'll do it if it'll help. I can't back out now anyway, not now the man's here.'

The boys fell silent as they heard voices on the stairs. Next moment Olive and Nathan entered.

'Boys, I'd like you to meet my good friend, Nathan Buttrick.'

Buttrick sprang forward, his small pink face wreathed in smiles, and took Richard's hand. Richard was surprised by his appearance. He had expected someone tall and imposing, but here was a mouse of a man – small, white-haired, with dainty hands and a smile like a leprechaun. Richard didn't find him the slightest bit impressive until he spoke.

'And you are?' Buttrick asked. Richard stammered his reply, not least because Buttrick's voice was deep, rich, melodious; it seemed totally at odds with the man who owned it.

'Ah, then *you* must be Nigel!' Buttrick said.

Nige nodded, disconcerted by Buttrick's close gaze. The hypnotist unbuttoned his overcoat and draped it over a chair. Beneath he wore a dark serge suit that had seen better days. 'We'll begin immediately, shall we?' he said.

Olive primed the tape recorder. Nige, taken aback by the abruptness of events, looked alarmed. Richard settled himself in his armchair to watch.

'Now,' Buttrick said, 'Olive here informs me that last night an incident occurred which you have seen fit to lock away in your mind. Is that correct?'

Nige, realizing he was being spoken to, shrugged, 'I . . . I don't know. I can't remember anything happening.'

'Of course you can't,' Buttrick said soothingly. 'That's why I'm here, to help you remember. You do want to remember, don't you?'

Nige couldn't take his eyes off the old man. 'Well, y-yes . . . I suppose so.'

'Of course you do,' Buttrick replied, nodding. 'Now all I want you to do is relax. Can you do that for me? Just sit back and relax?'

Nige nodded and leaned back on the settee, his hands limp by his sides. Buttrick smiled.

'That's right, just relax. Close your eyes and let your mind drift. Imagine that all the tension is seeping away, leaving your bones and your joints. You feel warm and sleepy and contented. Your mind is drifting . . . drifting.' He was silent for a moment, though the echoes of his honeyed voice seemed to swirl lazily about the room. When he resumed, his voice was a drawl that seemed to slow time. 'Can you hear me, Nigel?' he said.

'Yes.' The affirmative was barely audible.

'Good. Now, could you raise your right arm for me?'

Nige did so. 'Good, now lower it again.' Nige did that too. 'Good, good, very good . . . Now, Nigel, I'm going to ask you some questions and I want you to answer me truthfully. Do you understand?'

Nige's eyelids gave the barest flicker. 'Yes.'

'I want you to imagine that you have gone back in time. But you haven't gone far. It is ten o'clock yesterday evening. Thursday evening. Now, Nigel, can you tell me what time it is?'

'S'ten o'clock.'

'Good, that's right, ten o'clock. Now, can you tell me where you are?'

There was a slight pause. Richard held his breath. Beside him the tape whispered. At last Nige managed to get his mouth around the word he was struggling to say.

'House.'

'You're in a house? Is that right, Nigel?'

'Yes, house.'

'And where is this house, Nigel? Can you tell me that?'

A frown appeared on Nige's face, then just as quickly vanished. 'King Street,' he drawled.

'And can you tell me what the house is like? Can you describe it to me?'

Nige appeared to consider again. When he next spoke, his voice was much clearer. 'S'big . . . No roof . . . Black . . . boarded . . . boarded windows.' A sound like a snigger escaped him. 'Smells. Round th'back. Smells.'

'And is that how you got in, Nigel? Round the back?'

'Yes . . . round the back . . . window. Toady first . . . then me . . .' He frowned. 'No, then Rob . . . then me . . . then Rich.' He fell silent.

'And where are you now, Nigel?'

Nige raised his eyebrows. 'Kitchen, of course.'

'Good, that's good. Now I want you to go out of the kitchen and tell me where you are. Can you do that?' Nige nodded. 'Good. Now where are you?'

'Hall.'

'Good, now go along the hall and what do you come to next?'

'Room.'

'Can you describe the room, Nigel? Can you tell me what it looks like?'

'Smells,' Nige said immediately. 'Pooh, stinks! Fireplace . . . table . . . mattress . . . windows.' His finger jabbed at each item as though checking them off.

Buttrick glanced at Richard to confirm that this was the room in which the seance had taken place. Richard nodded.

'All right,' Buttrick continued, 'now I want you to tell me exactly what happened in that room, Nigel. Think carefully now. Can you do that for me?'

For a moment Nige's face was blank, his lips moving slightly. Then abruptly he moaned. 'No,' he said, shaking his head, 'no, I can't.'

'You must, Nigel,' Buttrick said gently. 'You must remember. Just take your time. Tell me slowly and carefully what you saw.'

Nige swallowed, then let out a long, shuddering breath. 'Lit candles,' he muttered, 'sat down. Table had . . . things on it . . . It . . .' He trailed off.

'What sort of things, Nigel?' Buttrick prompted.

Nige lifted both arms slightly and made a soothing gesture with his hands. 'Cloth,' he said, 'eeja board.' He turned his head aside, like a baby distastefully refusing a mouthful of food.

'A ouija board, is that what you mean, Nigel?' Buttrick asked, and Richard felt Olive stiffen beside him.

Nige nodded slowly. 'Yes . . . eeja board.'

'Anything else?'

Nige's eyes flickered. 'Glass,' he whispered. Buttrick leaned forward.

'And what did you do with the glass?'

'Put our fingers on it,' Nige replied, his voice suddenly very distinct. His head nodded and his speech became drowsy again. '. . . fingers on it . . .'

'And then what happened?' Buttrick asked.

This was the key question. For a moment Nige didn't answer. Richard held his breath as his friend's brow furrowed and his lips moved soundlessly. Outside the wind seemed suddenly to die, the gulls to stop squalling. All Richard could hear was the tape, whose whirring seemed to accentuate the tension that they all felt.

'Is anybody there?' Nige said suddenly, and Richard felt gooseflesh crawl down his back. The cadence of Nige's voice imitated Toady's perfectly. Again he said it, though quieter this time: 'Is anybody there?'

There was a pause, apparently to represent the wait that followed. Then Nige moaned.

'Glass moved,' he said. Another pause. 'Moved again . . . coming towards me . . . the lights . . . lights in the glass . . . pretty lights . . . in my head . . . came into my head . . . but they're sharp. Ow! Claws, not lights, teeth . . . tricked me . . . owww! Tricked me. Owwww!' Nige began to thrash his head from side to side. Sweat sprang up on his brow. His hands jerked frantically, clawing the air. 'Owwwww! No! Let me go! Leave me alone! Nooo, you're hurting me! Let me go!' He began to scream, high and endlessly, like a trapped animal. Richard clapped his hands to his ears.

'Stop him, can't you!' he shouted at Buttrick. 'For God's sake, stop him!'

Buttrick was trying, but his low, soothing words were being ignored, lost in the ululations. Nige's back began to arch as Richard had seen it do last night. His keening was now so high it felt like it was tearing the room apart. Richard could hardly bear to watch. He felt sure that any moment Nige's spine would snap in two.

Then suddenly it was over. Nige's screaming stopped abruptly, his body became limp. He flopped on to the settee, panting, his face drenched in sweat. Gradually, as before, the tension left his body. Richard glanced at Buttrick.

'Is he all right?'

The old man was trying hard not to appear flustered,

113

but his face was red, his hair awry. Sweat dotted his upper lip. He nodded shakily.

'I . . . I think so. At least physically.' He gestured at Nige's limp body.

'Please wake him up.'

Buttrick looked smaller now than when he had come in. He cleared his throat, struggling to reproduce his earlier tone of authority. 'When I count to three,' he said, 'you will awaken, and you will remember nothing of what has just occurred. Do you understand?'

There was no reply. Nige slept on. Buttrick glanced fearfully at Olive. 'Do you understand?' he repeated, and the desperation was evident in his voice. Still Nige failed to respond.

'What's wrong?' Olive whispered.

Buttrick had no answer. For a moment they all sat there, too frightened to do or say anything. Then Richard ordered: 'Count to three.'

Buttrick looked at him, then nodded and turned back to Nige. Keeping his voice steady, he said, 'One.' Nige's face was still and peaceful, his breathing heavy. 'Two.' Nige's finger twitched; he murmured once, then fell silent again. 'Three.' A second hovered infinitely; then Nige yawned and sleepily opened his eyes.

'Nige!' Richard yelled delightedly. 'Nige, you're back!'

Nige smiled bemusedly. 'What do you mean, back? I haven't been anywhere. I've been asleep, that's all.' He struggled to sit up and looked round at the relieved faces. 'Well?' he said. 'Did it work?'

11

'Where's the bloody pickled onions?' a red-faced man with a bald head demanded. Robin thought for a moment, then flapped his hand to the right.

'Er, um, just down that aisle. You see where the jars of beetroot are?' But the man had already gone. What was it

114

about supermarkets that always made people so bad-tempered? Robin wondered.

He moved on to the tinned fruit. He was pushing a skip on squeaking castors, collecting cardboard trays which had been rifled for their tins and jars and bottles. Above him music, bland as the pristine walls, dribbled from loudspeakers. Robin hated the music, hated it even more when he found himself humming along. In fact he was rapidly coming to the conclusion that he hated the whole place. The music, the shoppers, the rows of Tony the Tiger and Jolly Green Giant, the smells of cardboard and disinfectant and spilled tomato sauce and coffee and vinegar and sweaty people and potato dust; it was like drowning in consumerism, being brainwashed by packets and tins and banal forgotten songs.

'Will Robin Treadwell go to the warehouse, please? Robin Treadwell to the warehouse.'

Robin groaned at the voice over the tannoy. What did McCourtey have in store for him now? McCourtey was the warehouse manager, one of life's bullies. He'd taken an instant dislike to Robin and had had it in for him ever since. Robin went through the strips of thick plastic that served as the warehouse door, and stood blinking for a moment, trying to adjust his eyes to the gloom.

'Ah, Robin, you got my message. Good.' It wasn't McCourtey who stepped forward from the shadows, but Mr Wilson, manager of the entire grocery section. He was friendly enough, though a little daunting. Robin found himself touching the knot of his tie nervously to ensure it wasn't askew.

'Yes, sir, you wanted to see me?'

'Yes, I have a new boy here,' Wilson said. 'I'm hoping you'll show him the ropes.'

Robin looked at the new boy and gasped. He immediately recognized the shaven head, the arrogant leer, the scarred knuckles. This was Mo, one of Rusty's trusty entourage. Mo grinned savagely, recognizing Robin too.

'Well, I'll leave you to it then,' Mr Wilson said. 'Put

115

Maurice on floor service for a while, Robin. Then later, when you start filling the shelves, get him to give you a hand.'

He strode away. Robin felt an urge to run after him, to catch hold of his sleeve and tell him there must be some mistake, but he did neither of these things. The threat of Mo's presence was enough to keep him stationary.

'Well, well,' Mo said when Wilson had gone, 'so this is where Spotty gets to on a Friday night, is it?' He stepped forward and Robin flinched, though the skinhead merely prodded him in the chest. 'My mate Rusty wants a word with you.'

Robin looked round as though expecting Rusty to step from the shadows. 'Why does he want to talk to me?' he asked nervously.

'You and him have got some unfinished business. Oh, and your mate Gardener too. Him and his brother are gonna die. You tell 'em that from me.'

The remark was so casual that it chilled Robin to the bone. Swallowing, he said, 'L-look, we never started anything.'

'Fuck you!' Mo sneered, and bunching his fists took a step forward.

'You'll get the sack if you start on me,' Robin said quickly.

Mo lowered his fists. 'I'm not stupid. I know better than to start somethin' in here. But you just wait till after work.'

Robin knew his father would be there to pick him up, but still the threat made his mouth go dry. 'Look,' he said, 'while we're both working here, can't we at least try to get on? You know, sort of see the supermarket as neutral ground? I mean—'

'Get fucked!' Mo interrupted. 'You're a wanker, Spotty, and I don't like wankers. You just fuckin' show me what to do and then piss off.'

Robin had no alternative but to obey. If he didn't, he would be going against Mr Wilson's orders. He dragged an empty skip out on to the shop floor, his stomach feeling as though it had been scraped out and tossed back in again. His mind was in a turmoil.

How could he be expected to work with Mo the psychopath breathing down his neck? It wasn't exactly the ideal environment, was it? But then again, how could he afford not to work? He couldn't pack in the job and scrounge off his father again: there was pride at stake here. Besides, his father would be furious. He had always taught Robin to stand up for himself, not to give in to bullies; but turning theory into practice was not as straightforward as it sounded.

'Come on, cuntface,' Mo said, 'hurry up. Looking at your zits makes me wanna puke.'

Despite Robin's misgivings, this latest insult was the final straw. His body revolted, fear became fury. His hands, anticipating the revolution, balled into fists.

'You just shut your mouth,' he heard himself saying. 'One more insult and you can find out for yourself what you've got to do.'

'Oh, yeah?' Mo said, sounding amused. 'Look, shithead, the quicker you tell me, the quicker you'll get away from me, right? Oi, where you going?'

Robin was walking away from Mo, striding determinedly towards the lift that would take him up to the manager's office. 'I'm going to see Wilson to report you,' he said. 'I can't be expected to work in these conditions.'

Mo ran after him and caught hold of his arm. 'You lose me this job and you're dead,' he said quietly.

Fear was overtaking anger now, but Robin tried hard not to let it show. 'I'll get the police on to you,' he warned.

'Oh, yeah, and tell 'em what? That a bloke at work is calling you names?'

'I'll tell them that you've been threatening me with violence. I don't have to stand here and take this, you know.'

'That's up to you,' Mo snarled. 'But like I say, you lose me this job and I'll hit you so fuckin' hard you'll have eyes in your arse.'

117

'It seems to me that you're out to get us anyway, so what have I got to lose?'

Robin glared at Mo, but knew he could not keep it up. The skinhead annoyed was not a pretty sight. Veins in his temples were standing out like worms under the skin; his jaw was clenching and unclenching.

'I'm warning you,' Mo hissed, and would have said more, but the tannoy intruded.

'Will Robin Treadwell go to the warehouse, please? Robin Treadwell to the warehouse.'

'I'll have to go,' Robin said. 'Let go of my arm.'

'You tell me what I'm supposed to be doing first.'

'Floor service. It's easy enough. You just take that skip round, collect all the loose cardboard and face up the cans to make them look neat. If something's running low, you replace it with stock from the warehouse.'

Telling Mo this felt like admitting defeat, but it couldn't be helped; Robin didn't want to get in McCourtey's bad books tonight if he could avoid it. Mo let go of his arm and gave him a shove.

'Right, now piss off, zitface. I'll see you later, after work.'

'Where the fucking hell have you been?' was the first thing Robin heard when he entered the warehouse. He groaned inwardly. *Why* was everyone so hostile?

'N-Nowhere, Mr McCourtey,' he stammered, looking around for the source of the voice, 'I was just showing the new boy what to do.' He finally located McCourtey over by the racks of biscuits and hurried across. McCourtey was a fat, sour-faced man in his early thirties with wiry black hair and bushy sideburns. His hands were large and hairy, the fingers brown with nicotine stains.

'Fucking about instead of working more like,' McCourtey said. 'Well, it's time you made up for it. I'm going to give you some real work to do.'

Robin didn't like the sound of that, though he tried to look interested. He had discovered over the last few weeks that it was impossible to communicate with McCourtey on

118

a human level. The best one could hope for was to keep on the right side of his temper and his snide remarks.

McCourtey prodded a fat brown finger straight into the air. 'I want you to climb up there and get me some bourbon creams,' he said. 'They're on the top shelf.'

Robin looked up. The warehouse was a gloomy dirty place, vast and echoing, fifty or sixty feet in height. A metal framework was laid across with wooden boards to form shelves; this was where all the stock was kept. The framework reached up to the ceiling, which seemed so high that Robin felt dizzy and sick just thinking of the climb. Clinging to the vain hope that McCourtey's instructions were a joke, he said, 'Why can't you use the forklift?'

'Because it's knackered,' McCourtey snapped.

'But I saw you using it earlier,' Robin argued. McCourtey glared at him.

'It was all right earlier, now it's knackered. So stop fucking arguing and get climbing or I'll dock your wages.'

Robin stood for a moment, unable to speak, the back of his throat hot with tears of injustice and anger. Finally, in a strained voice, he said, 'I don't have to go up there. Mr Wilson says it's against safety regulations to climb more than five shelves, and those biscuits must be at least fifteen shelves up.'

McCourtey leaned forward and laid an unfriendly hand on Robin's shoulder. Robin tried to hold his breath. McCourtey's smell was one of stale cologne and rank sweat, and when he opened his mouth there was a waft of something sweet and sickly.

'Look, sonny,' McCourtey said, 'you're nothing but a snotty little part-timer, a fucking schoolboy out to make a bit of extra money to go with Daddy's allowance. Well, I'm going to make you work for that money. When I say jump, you jump. And when I say climb, you climb. Got it?'

Robin felt confused and tearful. What could he do? He daren't report McCourtey. Even if he did get the

119

warehouse manager into trouble, it would be nothing to the trouble that McCourtey would then make for him. Swallowing his frustration, he said, 'What was it you wanted?'

McCourtey grinned, enjoying his victory, and thrust a grubby piece of paper into Robin's hand. 'Bourbon creams. The details are on here. And don't take all fucking night about it.' He stalked away, sniggering to himself.

Robin watched him go, then shoved the piece of paper into his overall pocket and began to climb. It wasn't difficult, though he had never been beyond shelf five before. The topmost shelf looked unbelievably high, almost lost in gloom and shadows. He gritted his teeth. It was better not to think of the height. Just keep climbing, that was the thing to do, just keep climbing and look neither up nor down.

On level six he stopped for a rest. Taking hold of a metal strut, which was so cold it made his hand numb, Robin heaved himself on to the shelf on his stomach. When he felt secure he knelt back on his haunches and brushed the dirt from his clothes. Sitting amongst the grimy cardboard boxes, he looked down.

Already it was high enough to make him feel giddy. The warehouse was spread out below like a dingy parody of the supermarket it served. The only sound was the clatter of men at work, the scrape of boxes and crates, the throb of voices whose words were lost amid grime and echoes.

Despite his fear of heights, Robin felt peaceful sitting among the boxes; so peaceful in fact that he felt like curling up and going to sleep. Somewhere below him he heard McCourtey's hoarse laughter and then some of the other men joining in, and felt certain it was him they were laughing at. Well, let them laugh, he thought. He didn't care. He was better than the lot of them put together.

After a few minutes he reluctantly began climbing again. His arms were beginning to ache now, and dust was catching at the back of his throat. Two-thirds of the way up he clung to a strut and let a coughing fit overtake him, refusing to move until it was over. Though he knew it was only his imagination, the shelves seemed to be set wider apart the higher he climbed, making him stretch further for each handhold.

He was on level twelve when his left hand, stiff with cold, groped mechanically for the metal strut he knew would be there. As his fist closed around it, something writhed under his thumb and the next moment, a very large spider was scuttling up his arm. Without thinking, Robin let go, and his body swung out over empty space.

Desperately he clung on, with his right hand taking the weight of his body. For a few seconds the warehouse swayed sickeningly around him. He looked down to see the spider slide from his arm and tumble towards the ground, and a shudder convulsed him. Closing his eyes, his right hand still clinging desperately, he clawed for a handhold.

Finally he located the wooden shelf and snatched at it, trying not to wince as a splinter slid neatly into his thumb. When he was stable, and his heart had stopped pounding, he hauled himself on to the shelf.

Extracting the splinter was more painful than acquiring it had been. He picked at the protruding sliver of wood with bitten-down fingernails, but succeeded only in forcing it deeper. His teeth did a more efficient job, though he hissed in pain as the splinter came free.

As he sat sucking the blood from his thumb, he looked down again. A real and violent nausea came over him as he realized how close he had come to falling. He closed his eyes and breathed deeply, certain he was about to throw up. If he did, he wanted McCourtey to be standing directly underneath. His temples were thumping, and something seemed to be fluttering, probably his heart. By the time the thumping had died down, Robin realized that the fluttering was outside his body.

Nervously he looked round. The shelf was a gloomy three-foot high corridor, piled with boxes and with a sheer drop on both sides. The fluttering was coming from the far end. Despite his curiosity, Robin decided to ignore it, to climb on, get the biscuits and get back down to ground level as quickly as possible. Then the fluttering came again, accompanied by a flash of white, and Robin's gaze was drawn to the end of the shelf.

What was along there? Was it a piece of paper caught in an air-conditioning duct? It was possible, for the far end of the shelf was flush with the warehouse wall, which made it very dark. Robin strained his eyes, but the shelf was a jumble of struts and boxes and shadows. The fluttering came again, reminding him of something, and giving in to his curiosity he began to edge his way towards it.

He had to go slowly for the boxes were a hazard and the 'ceiling' – in reality the shelf above – was low. He kept his head hunched tight into his shoulders, yet even so he banged it twice on the shelf above.

He glanced up as the fluttering came again, more frantic this time, and saw something white rise briefly from behind the boxes, then disappear. Suddenly he realized what the sound reminded him of: when he was nine or ten a crow had flown down his grandad's chimney and got stuck in the flue. The fluttering he heard now was very similar to the frenzied beating of the crow's wings against the brickwork. Was this what had happened here then? Had a bird somehow got into the warehouse and become trapped between the boxes? Robin crawled forward on all fours, manoeuvring around boxes with difficulty, sneezing from the dust that billowed up around him. At last he reached the end of the shelf.

There was nothing there: no bird, not even a fluttering piece of paper. Robin frowned, puzzled. What had happened? Had the bird seen him coming and worked itself free in panic? Surely not, for he would have seen it, would have heard the beating of wings. What then? It couldn't have disappeared.

Bewildered, he peered over the edge of the shelf, checked behind the boxes, even lifted a couple of them and had a look underneath. There was nothing; or rather, not quite nothing. He shrugged and was about to turn back when he caught a glimpse of something white out of the corner of his eye. Crawling towards it, he realized it was a feather, a white feather about the length of his hand. Robin picked it up and turned it over, recognizing it as a seagull feather. So there *had* been a bird; the proof was sitting here in his hand. But where had it gone now? Perplexed, he pocketed the feather and shuffled back along the shelf.

Later, on the way home in the car, Robin told his dad about the bird. He reached into his pocket to show him the feather, but was surprised to find it empty.

'I must've dropped it,' he said.

'Never mind,' his father replied, 'it doesn't matter.'

Robin shrugged and looked out of the window. The mystery nagged him, but he tried to put it from his mind. It was difficult, for the snow against the car roof was like the fluttering of wings, and out of the corner of his eye a shape seemed to be forever forming from the snowflakes, like a large white bird following the car.

12

The worst thing for Sylvia Treadwell was that she had no idea in which direction she wanted her life to go. Her present situation, her family ties, she found stifling and depressing, yet breaking away would be more depressing still. Her marriage, she had to admit, had lost its sparkle, yet divorce would only leave her empty and frightened. Besides, divorce was too final, too messy, and the mere thought of telling her parents that she and Mike were separating after eighteen years of marriage caused her to break out in a cold sweat.

So if not divorce, what? Perhaps the answer lay not in her but in her husband? If only Mike were more alive, if only he was still the happy-go-lucky, unconventional man who had attracted her all those years ago. She sighed. What was the point of hankering after the past? Like herself, Mike was older now, tireder. Age had brought different outlooks, worries and responsibilities. Maybe their mistakes lay in their lack of sharing. Maybe if they had been less selfish with their troubles, things would be different.

But what use were maybes? They had trodden their paths and made their choices. If mistakes had been made, they should be rectified, not mourned over. But where to begin? Did the answer lie in reviving their marriage or in outside interests? Should she talk to Mike or simply let things run their course? They had tried talking before, or at least she had, but their discussions always degenerated into arguments. Maybe there were no solutions to their problems. Maybe there were no answers.

Sylvia went over to the drinks cabinet and poured herself a whisky. She took her drink back to the armchair, and sipped as she stared out of the back window. She felt trapped in the house, suppressed within its confines. Here there were so many rules to observe, rules which she herself had set. Usually the curtains of the window she was looking out of were closed by now, pulled to when the dark began encroaching. It was almost a ritual, a superstition, as though shutting out the dark could keep all of life's troubles at bay. Tonight, however, the curtains were open and the blackness was staring in. Sylvia shivered, yet she was damned if she was going to move from this spot. The thought came, depressing her even more; was this what her rebellion amounted to? A refusal to shut the curtains? God, how pathetic.

Angrily she drained her glass, lit a cigarette, and stalked to the window. Smoking like a vamp – a habit she had picked up from watching Bette Davis as a teenager – she glared into the night.

The dark was swirling, shedding snow that gently prodded the glass. The back garden beyond seemed almost luminous under its covering, and the trees at the end of the garden were like ghosts of themselves, their branches picked out in white.

Sylvia's gaze drifted further, to the house opposite. Suddenly she started, almost dropping her cigarette. She rubbed her eyes, which felt tacky with mascara, and looked again. They were gone now, but she felt certain they had been there: twin points of red light bobbing in an upstairs room of Walter Treeborn's darkened house.

For three minutes she stared, but the lights did not come again. The fact that the house was dark was strange in itself. Treeborn was a creature of habit; Sylvia couldn't remember the last time she had seen the house completely black. Even when he went out, which was rare, he usually left a downstairs light burning, invariably asked them to keep an eye on the place for him and stipulated precisely what time he would be home. Chewing her lip, Sylvia glanced at the telephone. Ought she to call him and make sure everything was all right? Of course there were many explanations for a dark house, especially in this weather with some of the roads impassable, but still . . . Annoyed with her indecision, she snatched up the telephone and dialled.

She listened to the ringing at the other end go on and on. She was about to replace the receiver when there was a click and a voice said, 'Hello?'

Sylvia almost cried out in relief. 'Mr Treeborn?'

'Yes.'

'I'm sorry to bother you, Mr Treeborn. This is Sylvia Treadwell from over the back. I noticed your house was dark and I saw some . . . some red lights upstairs. I just wondered whether you were all right?'

There was a sound at the other end which puzzled Sylvia for a moment; then she realized that Walter Treeborn was chuckling. Strange, she had never heard him laugh before. Indeed, she had once remarked to her husband that Treeborn was the most humourless man she had ever met. The chuckling stopped and Treeborn said, 'Thank you for your concern, Mrs Treadwell, but really

I'm perfectly all right. The reason my house is dark is because the fuse box couldn't stand up to the cold. I've just been down in the cellar fixing it.'

'Oh, I see,' Sylvia said. 'I felt sure there would be some rational explanation, but I thought I'd better check.'

'It was very kind of you,' Treeborn said silkily. 'In fact, to show my appreciation, perhaps you'd care to come over for a drink? I'll have the lights working again in a jiffy.'

Coming from Walter Treeborn, the offer of hospitality was almost an indecent suggestion. Sylvia found herself blushing and stammering like a schoolgirl.

'I . . . um, well, actually, I . . . I'm waiting for my husband to come home. He shouldn't be very long. He's only popped out to pick up Robin – that is our son – from work.'

'Of course, I understand,' Treeborn said. 'Ah well, some other time maybe?'

'Y-yes,' said Sylvia, 'some other time.'

'I shall look forward to it. Goodbye, Mrs Treadwell, and thank you once again for your concern.'

'Yes, goodbye,' Sylvia said. She replaced the receiver and realized she was sweating. Immediately she felt annoyed with herself. Why had she balked at Treeborn's offer like that? She was supposed to be a mature woman, not some silly simpering schoolgirl. She suddenly realized that in her confusion she had forgotten to ask what the red lights were, and glanced at the receiver again. However, she couldn't bring herself to ring Treeborn a second time: he was bound to think she was being pushy.

A moment later she blinked. A downstairs light had come on in Treeborn's house. Sylvia peered across, and then, embarrassed, ducked away out of sight. A dark figure had stepped into the light and stood there as though watching her. For a few moments Sylvia crouched beneath the window, cheeks burning, then cautiously raised her head. She peered across at the house once more, and was relieved to see that the window was now empty, that the figure that had been standing there was gone.

126

Rusty was pissed as a fart. Slouched across a table in The Glamour he hugged his pint close, oblivious to the spilt beer soaking into the elbows of his denim jacket. On the dance floor Ratz was gyrating obscenely with Michelle Short. Bruno, over in the corner, was swearing at the fruit machine as it gulped his money. Raising his glass, Rusty took a huge swallow and felt the alcohol rush to his head like a swarm of bees.

The music ended. Couples drifted back to their tables. Ratz and Michelle came across and sat down. 'Fancy a pint?' Ratz said, nodding at Rusty's nearly empty glass.

'Couse I fuckin' do,' Rusty slurred, draining his glass and banging it down. Ratz grinned and pushed his way to the bar.

Rusty stared at Michelle, trying to focus on her face. It was a pretty face, though you could see where she'd blitzed the zits with make-up. Getting his mouth around the words was difficult, but finally he muttered, 'Y'all right?'

Michelle nodded, and, looking uncomfortable, rummaged through her handbag. Rusty snorted with laughter. The knack he had of unsettling people delighted him.

'He's hung like a fuckin' donkey, you know,' he said, nodding at Ratz. A look of alarm or interest, Rusty was too drunk to tell which, flickered across Michelle's face. She shut her handbag with a snap.

'Really?' she said in a terse voice.

'Oh, yeah. You won't be able to walk for a week when he's finished with you.'

Michelle reddened, and Rusty sniggered to himself. 'What's the joke?' Ratz asked as he returned, doing a balancing act with the glasses. Michelle shook her head.

'Nothing.'

'I was just telling sweaty-tits here what a massive dong you've got,' Rusty said, and slung back half his pint in one go. Ratz looked embarrassed.

'Oh, just ignore him, 'chelle,' he said, 'he's only pissin' around.'

Michelle nodded timidly. Rusty stared at her, but she refused to meet his gaze. Up on stage the deejay had cleared away his equipment and a middle-aged man in a cheap suit had taken his place. The crowd turned expectantly as a spotlight fell on him and he began to speak.

'Ladies and gentlemen,' he said, 'could I have your attention please?'

'No, you fuckin' can't!' Rusty yelled. Laughter rippled through the crowd. The man smiled uncertainly and shielded his eyes from the spotlight to see who had shouted. Unable to identify the culprit he continued: 'And now the moment I'm sure you've all been waiting for. Will you please put your hands together and welcome . . . Brenda!' He thrust his arm to the right and backed out of the spotlight. Into it walked a buxom, heavily made-up blonde in a black leather jacket, high-heels and tight leopard skin trousers. The crowd cheered and clapped and wolf-whistled. Rusty turned away.

'Pathetic,' he said. 'Grown men going after a tart like that.' He looked at Michelle. 'You'd never do nothin' like that, would you?'

Michelle bridled. 'Course not.'

'Pity,' said Rusty, and grinned crookedly.

Accompanied by a tortured version of 'The Stripper', the blonde began doing her stuff. She unzipped the leather jacket and swung it round and round her head to a chorus of male-throated encouragement. Bruno wandered across, having lost his all on the fruit machine.

'Oi, lads, here's Mo,' said Ratz. Rusty turned and stuck up two fingers in greeting.

'Oi, Mo, you old bastard, over here!' he shouted.

The skinhead squinted into the gloom, then raised a hand as he located the group. He made a drinking gesture and turned to the bar.

'Piss artist,' said Rusty.

Brenda tossed the leather jacket into the audience, and immediately the announcer in the cheap suit bustled forward to retrieve it. Bruno was standing, mouth agape, eyes like organ stops. 'I'm in love,' he gasped.

'Sit down, pervert, before you cream your jeans,' said Rusty, dragging on Bruno's arm. Bruno sat, but his eyes remained fixed on the gyrations on the stage.

Mo sauntered across, drinking beer as though the glass was stuck to his mouth. In the dingy nightclub his head was like an upside-down face, the crown like stubble. He pulled up a chair and put down his glass. 'Oi, Rusty, listen to this,' he said.

'*Mr* Rusty if you don't mind,' Rusty said imperiously.

Mo tutted. 'Fuck off, Rus, just listen to me a minute, willya?'

Rusty shot out a hand, almost knocking over his pint, and grabbed Mo by the throat. 'How dare you tell me to fuck off,' he snarled.

Michelle, being a newcomer to the group, huddled up to Ratz, alarmed by the violence. He put a meaty hand around her shoulders and sniggered. 'Don't worry,' he said, 'they're only messin'. They do it all the time.'

As though to confirm this, Mo disengaged Rusty's hand from his throat and said, 'Stop arsin' around a minute, Rus. I've got somethin' to tell you.'

Rusty stood up, banging his glass down like a gavel. 'Right, you lot,' he said, 'listen.' When Bruno didn't respond, Rusty cuffed him across the head. 'I said listen.'

'Aw, Rusty, I wanna watch,' Bruno said, nodding at the stage.

'Shut up, pervert. Mo here has got somethin' to say. And when Mo speaks, you listen. All right?' He sat down, indicating that Mo should stand up.

Ignoring him, Mo said, 'It's about that twat Gardener.'

Immediately Rusty's face hardened. He seemed to go from drunk to sober in one second flat. Fingering his bruised nose, he muttered, 'What about him?'

Mo smiled, satisfied that at last he had got Rusty's

attention. 'Well, actually,' he said, 'It's about one of his mates. You know that spotty git, Treadwell?'

'Yeah.'

'Well, he works at the supermarket, Friday night and all day Saturday. I thought you might be interested.'

A nasty smile crept across Rusty's face. He patted Mo on the back. 'You've done well, my son,' he said, 'very well indeed.'

Ratz leaned forward. 'Let's go and arsehole him tomorrow, Rus,' he said eagerly, 'give him a right good kicking after work.'

Rusty laughed and patted Ratz on the head. 'Whoa, down boy,' he said. He slapped Bruno, whose attention was straying to the stage again. 'Listen, dickface, this is important.' Bruno, with a reluctant sigh, turned his back on bountiful Brenda.

'Now,' Rusty said, looking around, fixing them one by one with a drunken stare, 'this is a situation that calls for planning and efficiency. I mean to get those fuckers, and they're gonna get more than just a kick in the bollocks. Nobody busts my fuckin' nose and gets away with it.' He rooted clumsily in his jacket pocket. 'This is what I'm fuckin' talkin' about,' he said quietly, and held up his hand.

The flick-knife blade sprang eagerly from its sheath. The boys looked at it: Ratz smiling, Mo nodding his head grimly, Bruno trying to conceal his nervousness.

'Hey, put it away, Rus,' Bruno said after a moment, 'someone'll see.'

Rusty grinned, retracted the blade and pocketed it. To Mo he said, 'Here's what I want you to do, Maurice, old son.'

Nobody but Mo heard Rusty's next words. The crowd was erupting as, up on stage, Brenda finally revealed her true colours. Bruno's gaze wandered back to his heart's desire but Ratz kept his eyes on the plotters. And, as Rusty outlined his plan, he saw a slow, poisonous grin filter across Mo's face.

14

Starmouth belonged to Alfie Bessle. He was known by everybody and a friend to all. Children gathered at his feet to hear stories; police came to him for advice on local matters; seafront landlords provided him with a free Guinness and a seat by the fire every night. He ate well courtesy of the fishermen and the market stallholders, he dressed well courtesy of Oxfam, and he slept well courtesy of the Salvation Army. Yes, Alfie wanted for nothing in life. The town was his, the sea was his, and sometimes, when he was especially contented, he felt the whole damn world was his.

Tonight, however, he was cold. He huddled into his overcoat, ingrained with someone else's pipe tobacco, and grumbled into his beard. The leftovers he had been given at the chippy were sitting in his stomach like a lump of cold lard, though Alfie's view had always been that it was better to have something in there than nothing at all. He stamped his feet, encased in hob-nail boots, and flapped his arms about him. Leaning over the railings of the promenade, he stared out to sea.

It was in a vicious mood tonight. The surface was dark and fitful. Beneath, Alfie knew, the water would be sharp as sliced glass. Some nights, late on, Alfie liked to bathe; but not tonight. Tonight all the gold in all the teeth in China would not have drawn him to the water.

The beach was a mush of ice and sand, too wet for the snow to settle properly. However, despite the conditions, Alfie wandered to the end of the promenade, where the steps led down to the beach. He was damned if he was going to let a bit of snow stop him from taking his nightly stroll along the sands before he retired.

Heard close up the sea was roaring, reminding Alfie of a sluggish animal caught in a net. He looked up at the moon, its fat cold face illuminating the land, and began to make his way along the beach. Ice disguised as wind grappled with his clothes, seemed to cleave right through his skin and squeeze his bones with glacial hands. Alfie shuddered and drew his overcoat tightly around him, thinking longingly of his warm bed in the Sally Army shelter, of the hacking coughs of the vagrants – sounds which he paradoxically associated with night time and sleep. Sister Ethel might even give him some of her cocoa tonight if he was lucky. When the weather was particularly fierce, and he looked especially forlorn, she had been known to do so.

But first, Alfie thought, his walk. Something like pride drew him on. To forsake his walk just because of a bit of wind and snow was like an admission of old age. As the years passed the wind grew colder, sharper, stronger, but that was because of these atom bomb tests, all this radiation in the air, not because his body was ailing.

A dead crab swirled at Alfie's feet, its tiny claws drawn up in the vain hope of protecting itself from the ice. Ahead of him, the pier stood on tip-toe in the water. When Alfie breathed, the wind seemed to grasp at his throat as though trying to snatch his breath. Resolutely pulling his hat down over his ears, he shuffled on.

The pier stepped towards him as he approached, its girders like props supporting the sky. Alfie passed beneath it, listening to the drip-drip of melting snow, adjusting his eyes to the barnacled dark. On the other side the moon sprang out of hiding, and suddenly the beach was much clearer. Alfie could now detect the angry ripples of the sea, the patterns in the sand. The caves, which before had been simply black scars in the cliffs, now had a cold, flat definition.

Suddenly a girl, barefoot and clad only in shorts and a shirt, ran from one of the caves then, giggling, back in again. Alfie blinked. Surely he had been mistaken! Nobody would be dressed like that in this weather.

'Mermaids' was the word that rose suddenly to his lips and, despite himself, licked his heart with fear. Mermaids: those mythical beauties whose singing lured boats on to rocks. But this had been no mermaid. It had been a young, attractive, teenage girl. He had seen the muscles in her legs move as she ran, picked out in cold blue moonlight; had seen the way the shirt, tied in a knot at her navel, clung to her breasts.

For the first time in years, Alfie felt a stirring in his abdomen, a glimmer of sexual re-awakening. The sensation alarmed him: sexuality was about attraction, and Alfie had lived quite happily with his own non-attraction for the last five decades. He looked down at himself and sighed. His clothes were cast-offs, his beard unkempt, his skin slack and wrinkled on his bones. He had B.O., halitosis, and, much to his own amazement, had picked the occasional louse from his thinning hair.

But, despite his inadequacies, he felt his old penis hardening like some ancient gnarled plant determined to bloom one final time. Nervous as a schoolboy, he trudged towards the cave where he had seen the nymphet emerge, half-hoping that he had been mistaken.

But no. As he approached the cave he smelt burning, heard the crackling of flames, saw the glow of a fire touching the rocks. 'Hello?' he called, and his voice was an old man's voice; thin, frail, withered as dry leaves. 'Hello?' he called again, and this time detected movement, a stirring among the shadows. And then, suddenly, there she was: his vision, his fantasy, standing at the mouth of the cave, bare legs gold in the firelight. And she was smiling at him.

'Hello,' said the girl, 'who are you?'

Alfie stumbled forward, feeling wretched but at the same time entranced, ravenous with desire. 'I-I'm Alfie,' he stammered. 'I-I live here in Starmouth. I'm a local celebrity.'

The girl's smile widened. 'Of course you are,' she said. 'I recognize you.'

Encouraged by the smile, Alfie clambered up beside her, the girl putting out a hand to steady him. Up close she was even more beautiful than ever. Her skin was perfect, her hair, reaching down to her bottom, shone like a halo.

Her lips were full, her eyes large with long luxurious lashes. Alfie had to thrust his hands into his overcoat pockets to stop himself reaching out and grabbing her.

'Would you like to warm yourself by my fire?' she asked, gesturing at the cave. Alfie nodded and the girl led the way inside.

The fire was small (Alfie wondered where the girl had managed to find dry wood), but the cave felt suffused with heat. Alfie touched the glowing wall and warmth lapped at his hand. The girl sat down, cross-legged, produced an apple from somewhere and held it out to him.

'Are you hungry?'

Swallowing his pride, Alfie nodded and sat beside her. He took the apple, his fingers briefly touching hers, and bit into it. It was sweet and warm; juice ran into his beard. His mouth full, he asked, 'Aren't you eating?'

The girl shook her head. 'I'm not hungry.'

'Who are you?' Alfie asked.

'Who would you like me to be?'

The reply threw Alfie and he didn't answer straight away. Changing track, he asked, 'Where do you live?'

'Here,' said the girl, 'in this cave. At least for the time being.'

'But your parents,' Alfie insisted, 'don't they mind?'

The girl smiled, and her eyes, a glittering blue, regarded him openly. 'I have no parents,' she said.

She was an orphan, Alfie realized, an orphan like him. So there *was* an affinity between them! Excited by this revelation, he said, 'Me too. I mean . . . I never knew my parents.'

The girl nodded. Uncrossing her legs, she drew up her knees and rested her chin on them. Idly she began tossing handfuls of sand into the fire, watching them sizzle and flare. Almost as though she were talking to herself, she said, 'You can touch me if you like.'

Alfie dropped the apple. 'What?' he exclaimed, morsels of fruit spraying from his mouth. The girl turned to face him.

134

'That's what you want, isn't it?' she said calmly. 'To touch me? Isn't that what you want more than anything else in the world?'

Alfie's mouth worked, but no sound came. 'Say something, you old fool,' he urged himself, 'say something before the moment passes.'

But there was no need. With long, delicate fingers the girl untied the knot at her waist. Her shirt came open to reveal round, dark-nippled breasts. 'Here,' she said, and taking his right hand placed it gently on her left breast as though it were a baby's mouth.

Alfie's body felt like an echo of the girl's heart, a huge thick pulse of sensation. Inside his trousers his penis throbbed with desire. Clumsily, almost tumbling into the fire, he scrambled towards her, right hand still clamped to left breast. She made no objection as his other hand found her right breast and began to knead. He stared, transfixed, at the mounds in his hands, as though they were giant pearls that he had found washed up on the beach.

The girl made no sound as Alfie squeezed and stroked. Gently she placed her hands on his shoulders and then, a moment later, behind his neck. So engrossed was Alfie that he didn't feel the heat running down his back until it began to itch between his shoulder blades. He contracted his back muscles to rid himself of the sensation, but the itch persisted.

'I'm wet,' he thought vaguely, 'sweat is pouring off me.' Then he yelped as he felt the first stab of pain.

Something was digging into the back of his neck, something that felt like worms burrowing, searching for his vertebrae. As the realization came so the pain increased, intensifying until it felt as though his whole neck was a hot throbbing mass of agony.

Alfie's hands left the girl's breasts and groped behind his neck for the hurt, climbing her wrists to find the source. What he discovered there caused him to scream out in terror through vocal cords that felt stretched like elastic.

135

The girl's fingers were embedded in his neck, sunk in skin and muscle up to the first knuckle. Blood was flowing freely down his back, shooting out in little spurts. Alfie thrashed and screamed, though it hurt him to make any sound. He clawed at the girl's wrists and hands, pummelled at the breasts that had so tantalized him seconds before. But it was no use; pain had given him the strength of a kitten.

All at once something cracked, a sound like splintering wood. Alfie's head suddenly became an intense, unbearable weight on his shoulders. He felt it slipping and knew his vertebrae had snapped. His tongue ballooned in his mouth; his brain throbbed. As his vision clouded over he looked up at the girl's face and saw she was smiling distractedly, her eyes glowing red. Then he died.

The girl laid the corpse down, the head lolling on the shoulders like a rock in a sack. Humming, she wiped blood on her shirt and looked around for the apple core. This she tossed into the fire, watching as it fizzed and popped. When it had been consumed she turned her attention back to Alfie.

Then slowly, methodically, she began to do unspeakable things to his body.

15

Saturday

Toady was beginning to think he should have gone back to the house. Maybe the 'poltergeist' was not as strong as he had anticipated. Maybe it couldn't even hear him, let alone respond – yet last night he had been so sure. He had seen its display of power, been awed at the influence it had exerted over Robin and Nige. Like Richard he had resisted its pull, had engaged in a grim game of tug of war with his mind as the rope. The 'poltergeist's' strength had been both frightening and impressive, but on his own territory, away from the house, Toady had been certain he could control it.

He cast his mind back to last Saturday, to the chance find that had spawned the idea for the seance. He had been in the local library, doing work for his school project. In the reference section he had come across the headline in a copy of *The Starmouth Gazette*.

The newspaper was dated 17 November 1979, and the headline read: COUPLE FORCED TO FLEE HOUSE BY POLTERGEIST. It was only a small article, tucked away in the bottom left hand corner of page five, but Toady noticed it immediately, and as he read his excitement mounted:

John and Hilary Crutcheon yesterday fled their house in panic because, they claimed, a poltergeist was wreaking havoc in their home. Mrs Crutcheon, 33, was close to tears as she said: 'It was terrible. I was in the kitchen when I heard a crash. I turned round and there was a cup lying on the floor smashed to pieces. I bent to pick it up, and the next thing I knew there were pots, pans, cutlery flying all over the place. I had to crawl out on my hands and knees to avoid getting hit.'

John Crutcheon, 37, claims this is only one of a number of strange happenings that have occurred at the house. 'First it was little things,' he said. 'We'd come down in the morning to find a tap turned full on or an ashtray upended on the carpet. After a bit, though, things started getting worse. We'd hear banging from the living room at night, and once we heard a crash and came downstairs to find a picture smashed in the fireplace.' Asked whether he and his wife would be going back to live in the house, Crutcheon said, 'No way. You wouldn't catch us spending another night in that place.'

Not everyone was impressed by the Crutcheon's story, however. Mr Steven Trellini, whose company were responsible for building the row of houses in King Street, Piling Hill, said: 'All this talk of ghosts and spooks is stupid. Those people are either off their heads or it's a hoax to make a bit of money out of the papers. It's more than likely they're exaggerating what they've seen. Some of these new houses take a while to settle, or maybe they've got a bit of subsidence, though we checked the land thoroughly before we built on it. It's something we'll have to look into.'

We asked an expert, Dr Rudyard McKenzie, professor of parapsychology at nearby Sailsford University, what he thought of the Crutcheon's claim. He commented: 'Poltergeist phenomena in new houses is rare, but not unknown.' Asked whether he thought the King Street poltergeist was genuine, Dr McKenzie replied: 'Having not investigated the premises, I am not really in a position to comment.'

The house in King Street will be going up for sale later this week.

Toady sat back, enthralled. King Street! Why, that was only a couple of streets away from his own house! School project forgotten, he eagerly set to work rooting through more microfiche copies of *The Starmouth Gazette*, trying to find further details of the poltergeist. For a while his search was fruitless. Page after page of local trivia flashed before his eyes. He searched restlessly, wishing silently that what he was looking for would be on the next page; the next page; the next page. It was almost an hour before he found it.

The paper was dated 30 March 1980, and the headline read: GHOST HOUSE HIT BY STORM. Toady leaned forward excitedly, devouring the story with his eyes.

The 'ghost house' in King Street, Piling Hill, from which a young couple recently fled, was badly damaged in a storm yesterday. Police believe that the house, which has stood empty since the couple vacated it four months ago, was struck by lightning, though a spokes-man commented: 'It's very strange. The roof of the house appears to have fallen in completely. Whether that's because the house was struck by lightning or whether it's due to some inherent structural weakness is difficult to say. The place is uninhabitable now at any rate. We'll just have to hope that the other houses in the row aren't affected.'

Toady read the rest of the article without really taking it in, for he now knew which house it was they were talking about. He pictured the caved-in roof, the boarded up windows, the overgrown garden. Of course. He should have realized! There was no other house it could realistically have been.

That Saturday afternoon, less than two hours after reading the story, Toady climbed into the house for the first time. He stayed there until early evening, wandering around the rooms, walking the downstairs corridor back and forth, peering up the stairs to see if anything was moving. He spent a lot of time in the kitchen and the living room, where the main disturbances had taken place, just standing, waiting for something to happen. But nothing did.

By Sunday evening Toady was intimate with the house. He felt, or fancied he felt, a presence there: something lonely and trapped that wanted company. For much of that second day, he sat cross-legged in the sitting room, watching the daylight gradually darken through the boards of the window. And as he sat, he came to a conclusion: something had to be done; some sort of contact had to be made.

That Monday, after school, he went to the library again and took out three books on seances: *The Spirit World* by Jemimah Micklewhite, *Talking to the Dead* by Valerie Leaworthy, and *Voices from Beyond* by Stephen Gunn. He spent all his spare time over the next two days reading the books, and then on Wednesday he locked himself away in his father's toolshed and made the ouija board. He was gong to make a planchette too, but in the end decided that a glass would probably work just as well.

Thinking back, Toady found it hard to believe that a week ago he had never even heard of the King Street poltergeist. Within that short time, the 'ghost house' had become an obsession with him. He had been delighted last night with the partial success of the seance, but it had frightened him too: he hadn't expected quite so much power. Although he'd felt resentful at the time, perhaps Richard had been right to smash the glass.

Wearily he yawned and rubbed his eyes. He hadn't slept last night, had sat up with the ouija board trying to re-establish contact. Now, after an unsuccessful twenty-eight hours, his throat was hoarse, his eyes like chunks of grit in his face, his limbs like weights attached to his body. He was hungry too (all he'd eaten today was a bowl of cornflakes, a hunk of cheese and four slices of bread), but too tired to make himself anything now. Soon, he knew, he would have to sleep, despite his fear that such an interlude might break the fragile link with the 'poltergeist' forever. Some sign was all he required, some sign that the 'poltergeist' had heard him.

He got up from the bed and went to the window. Outside the world looked stark, the snow reflecting moonlight that hurt his eyes. Toady looked at his watch and saw it was almost three a.m. Sleep: he would have to get some sleep. Empty and irritable, he turned to his bed. It had never before looked so inviting. He lay down, sighing as he let himself relax, feeling as though his body were sinking into the mattress. His mind released its hold gradually, so that his thoughts, his fears, his hopes seemed to dissolve, to blend and merge into sleep. Just one sign, he thought as he drifted away, just one small sign that you're there. Exhaustion picked the words apart and sleep came rushing in like the sea.

He felt warm and snug, his sleep black but comforting, a soft-sculpture landscape stitched from the velvet night. Suddenly something clawed into the blackness, ripping a jagged white hole. Toady murmured, blocking his ears as it burst in through the hole like a shriek of wind. It came again, then again, ripping the hole wider, shredding his sleep, filling his dreams with harsh white noise.

He struggled awake. The clock by his bed read 3:05. The sound was still here, though louder, more ragged. It took Toady a few moments to realize it was coming from a human mouth, and another moment to realize it was Simon.

'Shit,' he whispered, sitting up in bed, rubbing his eyes. 'It's you, isn't it? This is the sign I asked for? It's really you?'

The screams continued, a long ragged ululation similar to the sounds Nige had made at the house. On the surface Toady felt cold and numb, yet beneath, deep down, he felt a kind of horrified elation. He heard the creaks and bumps from his parents' bedroom, then his mother's voice raised in panic, and his father's bad-tempered but frightened reply. He heard the door open, footsteps on the landing, then another door open and Simon's screams momentarily increase in volume, decreasing again as the door was closed. Toady hugged the blankets to his chin, shaking his head at the dark. 'All right, leave him alone now. Leave him alone.'

The screams stopped abruptly. Toady listened to his father's voice, which sounded awkward and embarrassed, trying to comfort his son, and he hated him for his inadequacy. His mother's voice, querulous and shrill, asked what the matter was, and his father muttered something about a nightmare. Toady settled back in his bed. For a few moments he lay, wide awake, staring at the javelin of light that had crept in through the curtains and was now hovering on the ceiling. Then, layer by layer, sleep claimed him again. Toady closed his eyes. As he drifted away his last idle thought was to wonder why the dark, hunched figure across the room was sitting in the chair and watching him sleep.

16

The day was frozen, too cold for snow. Richard rubbed his gloved hands together and shivered inside his parka. Above him the sky looked drained, littered with gulls that screeched mournfully. Along the kerbs of every street, cars covered in frost sparkled like Christmas decorations. As Richard walked, he wondered vaguely whether it was cold enough to freeze the sea. However, nearing Nige's house he heard it, roaring as usual, and the sound made him feel even colder.

The gate creaked as he pushed it open. The spangled path was deceptively slippy, and, as his foot shot from under him, he put out a hand to the fence. Heart thumping from reaction, he shuffled forward and rang the doorbell.

Mrs Figg came to the door with a smile on her face, but it froze when she saw Richard. 'Yes?' she said, her blood-red lips pressing into a terse line.

'Is Nigel in?' Richard asked.

Mrs Figg frowned and sighed, though she must have been anticipating the question. 'I'll have a look,' she said. 'I think he's doing his homework.'

Her tone implied that Richard ought to be doing the same. She went into the house and shouted up the stairs. Richard heard thump-thump-thump-thump and then Mrs Figg saying severely, 'Don't run, Nigel, you'll break your neck.'

Richard was interested to see how Nige looked this morning. Yesterday, after a pale and flustered Nathan Buttrick had left Olive's flat, Olive had presented Nige with the tape of the afternoon's events and had told him to listen to it. 'If that doesn't convince you,' she had said, 'nothing will.' The boys had parted at Nige's gate and had not seen each other since.

Now Nige appeared at the door, fighting off his mother who was trying to re-arrange the scarf at his neck. 'Mum, stop it,' Nige said, pulling free, 'you'll strangle me.'

'But it's cold out,' Mrs Figg twittered, bosom heaving, fat face creasing anxiously. 'You have to take care of yourself in this weather.'

'I'm fine,' Nige said, and walked briskly up the path, pulling Richard clear of his mother's range. 'I'll see you later,' he called over his shoulder.

He opened the gate and the boys half-ran up the road and around the corner. When he was out of his mother's sight, Nige stopped and scooped snow from a low wall. 'What shall we do?' he asked, idly packing the snow into a ball, poking holes in it to make a face.

'I'm not bothered,' Richard said, watching him closely, 'what do you want to do?'

Nige shrugged. 'Dunno. Nothing really. Let's just walk for a bit.'

'OK,' Richard said as Nige lobbed the snowball into the air and kicked it. They turned left at the end of the next road and walked past a small line of shops. 'Shall we go to the beach?' Richard suggested, but Nige pulled a face.

'Nah, too cold and windy. Let's go this way.'

Richard was disappointed, but he said nothing. He could see Nige was troubled, and he suspected it was because of the tape. He wished Nige would talk about it before he had to ask.

They passed a snow-covered primary school whose black windows made the building look like a negative, and a bus shelter with only one pane of glass remaining where people were moaning about the lateness of the bus. Nige led the way past a pub called The Plough and, crossing the road, through a gate into some playing fields.

The wind was strong here, as though relishing the wide open spaces, and Richard thought irritably that they might just as well have gone on the beach. In a set of goal posts a group of kids were attempting to play football but their ball kept getting bogged down in the snow. Nige sat on a bench and stared blankly at a line of scrappy trees, each of whose trunks were painted with a white cross as though marking them as lepers.

143

He stayed that way for a long time, saying nothing, just staring. At last Richard impatiently said, 'Well?'

Nige looked at him, 'Well, what?'

'Did you listen to the tape?'

Nige turned away, focussing his attention on a man walking a Pekinese. 'Uh-huh.'

'And?'

'It was . . . weird.'

'How do you mean – weird?'

Nige frowned. 'Well, y'know . . . hearing my own voice, talking that way, all slow and slurred like I was drugged.' He shrugged. 'Just weird.'

'But do you believe us now?'

Nige said nothing for a moment as though considering the question. Then he said dully, 'I have no choice really, do I? I mean I've heard it straight from the horse's mouth, so to speak.' He laughed humourlessly. 'I still don't know what it is we're believing *in* though.'

'No, me neither,' Richard said.

The boys sat in silence for a while, Richard hunched forward, rubbing his gloved hands together nervously. At last he said, 'Perhaps we're making too much of this. I mean, nothing's happened since Thursday night, has it? Maybe we did over-react a bit at the house. Maybe there's some perfectly logical explanation.' He tailed off, acutely aware that he was grasping at straws. Now that he'd got Nige to believe, he wasn't sure he wanted to believe himself.

'Yeah, but what about that thing that followed you home?' Nige said.

Richard shrugged. 'I dunno. All that seems a bit of a blur now.'

Nige sighed. 'So what do we do about all this?'

'I've no idea. There's nothing much we *can* do, is there?' Richard stood up, troubled by the conversation, and began walking again. After a moment Nige followed him.

The kids had given up their game of football now and

were trudging away, throwing snowballs at one another. The man with the Pekinese was standing self-consciously, pretending not to notice the squatting dog on the end of the lead. Nige looked at the dog, and then at Richard – and suddenly he laughed. Richard joined in gratefully, the laughter reducing the knot of tension inside him.

'Why don't we get our sledges and go up on to the ridge?' he suggested. 'It'll take our minds off all this seance stuff.'

Nige looked at his watch. 'It's a bit late now. That'll have to wait till this afternoon. We could build a snowman, though, in our front garden. There's a massive pile of snow there that I cleared off the path yesterday.'

'OK. But what about your Mum? Won't she mind?'

Nige rolled his eyes. 'Nah, as far as she's concerned it'll be keeping us out of mischief.'

On the way back, Nige bought a Crunchie Bar and shared it with Richard. The chocolate was cold, splintering like ice between their teeth. Munching, Nige said, 'It was really strange being hypnotized, you know? I thought it'd be just like being asleep, but it wasn't really. There was no sensation of time passing, nothing like that. It was almost as though that ten or fifteen minutes hadn't existed for me at all. One second I was feeling sleepy, and the next I blinked and woke up, and it was over.'

'Don't you remember anything?' Richard asked.

'No, nothing. Certainly no dreams about the house.' All at once he shuddered. 'Did I really scream like that?'

Richard nodded slowly. 'Yeah. And back at the house too.'

'God,' Nige said quietly.

As they walked in through the Figgs's garden gate, Nige pointed at the snow piled in the front garden. 'Start building that up to make a body and I'll go and get some stuff from the house,' he said.

Richard nodded and set to work. Some of the snow which had been shovelled from the path had frozen into heavy blocks, and he was soon sweating with the exertion of heaving one on top of the other. When Nige reappeared, Richard's arms were beginning to ache.

'Carry on, you're doing a fine job,' Nige grinned. Richard stood up, placing one hand in the small of his back.

'What have you got?' he asked.

Nige showed him. He had a grubby pink beret that had belonged to his mother, one of his father's old pipes, a plastic joke-mask comprising spectacles (complete with painted bloodshot eyes), bulbous red nose and black moustache, and a checked scarf and four black buttons.

'Great,' said Richard. 'He's going to look really good when we've finished. C'mon, give us a hand shifting this snow.'

The boys spent the next half-hour building up the blocks of snow to form a basic trunk shape, padding it out half-way up to give the impression of arms. They made a head-sized ball which they heaved on to the snowman's shoulders, then Richard packed snow around the 'neck' area to keep the head in place whilst Nige collected the things from the windowsill where he had put them.

When the snowman had been 'dressed', the boys stood back to admire their handiwork. Richard laughed.

'He looks brilliant. That beret and moustache makes him look French.'

'A continental snowman,' Nige said, smiling.

So taken were they with their creation that they didn't see the man in the black suit until he had reached the fence.

'Excuse me,' he said, his voice deep and rich as though he might once have been an actor.

The boys turned. The man was gaunt with a heavily-stubbled chin and hair that was stringy and style-less. It was difficult to tell his age because of the black pebble-glasses he wore, but Richard reckoned him to be about seventy. The man's head was tilted slightly upwards as though he were looking not at the boys but at an upstairs window of the boarding house. Richard thought it curious, then noticed the white stick that the man held in his right hand and realized he was blind.

'Excuse me,' the man said again.

Nige glanced quickly at Richard then, frowning, said, 'Yes?'

'Ah, young man, I wonder if you can help me? I'm looking for Parson's Terrace, number forty-one. I understand it's somewhere round here?'

Nige gaped. Richard felt a tingle of something he couldn't identify squirm briefly in his stomach. Clearing his throat, Nige said, 'This . . . this is forty-one Parson's Terrace.'

'Ah, splendid,' the man said. 'Then I am at my destination.' He twirled his white stick foppishly in the air and pushed open the gate with the carpet bag he held in his left hand. Nige hurried forward, and just for a moment Richard was unsure whether he intended to aid the blind man or refuse him entry.

Then Nige took the man's arm and said, 'I'd better help you. The path's not been sanded yet.'

'Thank you, young man. Most kind. You are a credit to your generation.'

Leaning heavily on Nige's arm, the man allowed himself to be led up the path.

'Have you reserved a room?' Nige asked.

'Indeed I have. I spoke to a Mrs Rosemary Figg on the telephone.'

'That's my Mum,' Nige said.

'Ah, then you must be Nigel. Your mother has told me all about you.'

'Has she?' Nige grimaced.

'Yes, indeed. She thinks very highly of you, you know.'

'Mm,' Nige said, 'here we are.'

He leaned forward and opened the front door. The blind man probed the area ahead with his stick, then stepped inside. Nige followed, hovering in a way that reminded Richard of his mother. When Nige was satisfied that the blind man was not going to bump into anything, he squeezed past him and shouted, 'Mum, there's someone here for a room, a Mr . . . ?' He turned questioningly.

'Robespierre,' the blind man enunciated. 'Donald Robespierre.'

CHAPTER THREE

I Am The Shadow

1

Robin was amazed. He couldn't believe what had just happened. Since getting up at six forty-five that morning, he had been dreading this day, praying that it wasn't going to be too bad; and now, incredibly, it seemed his prayers had been answered.

He had been standing in the locker room of the supermarket when the miracle had happened. The clock on the wall read 8.24, and Robin was due to start work at 8.30. The supermarket was empty of customers at this time, but still the insufferable music droned from the speakers, like a brainwashing technique to deaden thoughts of rebellion. Robin could smell the bakery and hear people chatting; the occasional 'ching' as they clocked in for work. They were quiet, busy sounds, the first stirrings in what was soon to become a hive of activity. Normally he found these sounds restful, almost comforting, but today he had found them troubling. Not just the sounds, but everything about the supermarket had distressed him almost to the point of nausea.

The reason for this could be pinpointed in one small word: Mo. Robin had not been relishing a full day of Mo's company. The night before he had gone out of his way to avoid the skinhead, had turned in the other direction whenever he saw Mo approaching, had even ensured that Mo was occupied before sneaking off to the toilet. The fear that the skinhead had induced in him annoyed Robin, made him feel ashamed and angry, but there'd been nothing he could do about it, fear was fear. He had tried to rationalize it, had thought to himself, 'What's the worst that can happen?' But it had been no use. Despite thinking up reassuring answers, his fear had remained, hot and ugly, something that churned in his gut.

So there he was, at 8.24 in the morning, dreading the day, his stomach curling slowly as though something was alive in there. He had been buttoning up his overall when Mo had walked into the locker room.

Immediately Robin had begun to sweat. His fingers had felt clumsy as they'd fumbled with his buttons. He'd gazed steadily at his locker door, pretending that he hadn't seen Mo come in. He'd wanted to clear his throat, but hadn't dared in case Mo had interpreted the gesture as provocative. Behind him he had heard the grinding of a locker key, a clatter as the metal door was pushed back. He'd been about to make a break for it when Mo's voice had stopped him in his tracks by saying, 'All right, Treadwell?'

Had Robin heard that correctly? The skinhead's words had sounded like a greeting, not a threat or an insult. He had turned slowly, trying on different expressions to face Mo, none of which seemed to fit. He'd cleared his throat at last, but still his voice had betrayed him. 'Sorry?' he had finally managed to croak.

Mo had been knotting his tie in a mirror, long neck stretched, jaw jutting out aggressively. Without turning he had said, 'I said, all right? You know, hello. It's something people say to one another when they meet.'

Robin had stared, trying to work out the catch. In a way Mo's friendliness had been even more unsettling than the expected hostility. At last he had managed to stammer, 'Oh . . . oh, yeah. Hi.'

Mo had finished knotting his tie, had adjusted it slightly, and then had nodded in satisfaction. To Robin he said, 'You'd better get a move on. We're due on the floor in two minutes and that bastard McCourtey will give you a right bollocking if you're late.' And with that he had left.

150

Robin had stood there, stunned. He could not have been more amazed if a vision of the Virgin Mary had appeared before him. And what's more, as the day wore on, Mo's friendliness persisted.

He helped Robin shift some heavy boxes from one warehouse shelf to another, he told him jokes, he began calling him Rob, he offered him a stick of chewing gum. By mid-morning Robin's mind was in a turmoil. Why was Mo behaving like this? At eleven-fifteen, during the busiest hour of the morning, the skinhead sidled over to where Robin was pricing jars of gherkins and asked, 'Y'all right, Rob?'

Robin nodded, warily eyeing the Stanley knife that Mo held in his hand. 'Yes,' he said. 'I hate the supermarket at this time, though, it's so bloody hectic.'

Mo looked around as though he hadn't noticed the shoppers before and distractedly ran his thumb along the blade of the knife. Robin winced as the knife cut into Mo's flesh and drew blood. Mo merely tutted and put his lips to the wound.

'What I came across for,' he said, his words muffled through the mouthful of thumb, 'was to see whether you fancied going for a pint this lunchtime? This shelf-stacking's pretty thirsty work.'

Robin shrugged, trying to hide his nervousness. It crossed his mind that maybe this was what Mo's friendliness had been leading up to. Perhaps it was simply a ploy to lure him out of the supermarket where he would be easy prey for ambush.

'I . . . I'm not sure,' he said. 'We're not supposed to go drinking at lunchtime, you know. If McCourtey smells it on our breaths we'll get the sack straight away.'

'Aw, we'll be all right,' Mo replied. 'McCourtey's got the afternoon off. Janet told me.'

Janet was the floor supervisor, a pretty red-haired woman in her late twenties. Robin could see her now, armed with a clipboard, patiently explaining something to one of the checkout girls. In his mind, Robin weighed up the pros and cons of Mo's suggestion. He would rather have Mo as a friend than a foe, but was he prepared to risk trusting him? On the other hand, if Mo and Rusty intended to get him, they would manage it one way or another. Feeling as though he were taking his life into his hands, he sighed and said, 'All right, but we'd better not go to The Wasp. Some of the managers go in there on a lunchtime.'

Mo winked. 'That's all right,' he said, grinning. 'I know just the place.'

The Glamour by day looked even more shabby than it did by night. At first, when he saw Robin, it seemed the bouncer wasn't going to let the boys in. Then Mo said, 'All right, Terry?' and the man, recognizing him, nodded and stood aside.

They entered what Robin at first thought was a cave of smoke. The walls were drab, discoloured by beer stains and patches of damp. To the ceiling clung an iron framework which supported a pitiful selection of disco lights. The tables and chairs looked as though they might fall apart at any minute. The Glamour at this hour was filled mostly by men – hunched over tables, drinking and smoking, exchanging sporadic fragments of rumbling conversation or watching the horse racing on the television above the bar.

'What do you want?' Mo said, pushing his way through. Robin looked at him uneasily.

'Er . . . it's all right, I'll get my own. I've only got enough money for one anyway.'

'Aw, forget it,' Mo replied, 'I'll get you one. Just tell us what you want.'

'Um, I'll have a shandy then, please.'

Mo nodded, flapped his fiver in the air and whistled. The petite, dark-haired barmaid in the red satin skirt looked up, surprised. Seeing Mo, she smiled. When she had given an oily-faced man in blue overalls his change, she came across.

'Yes, Maurice?' she said, wiping her hands on a bar towel. 'What can I get you?'

'I'll have a pint o' bitter and a pint o' shandy please, Irene,' he said. A few people, who had been waiting for a drink longer than Mo, turned and glared at him. Mo glanced up, fixed his gaze on a blond-haired man with buck teeth and asked mildly, 'What you fuckin' starin' at, Goofy?' The man looked away, feigning a sudden interest in the fruit machine.

'Here, you, don't go causing no trouble,' Irene said, hurrying back with the drinks.

'Who, me?' Mo said, adopting an expression of wounded innocence. 'As if I would.' He passed Robin his shandy and collected his change, laughing at Irene's pursed lips.

'Shall we sit down?' Robin said, indicating a table whose last occupants had been drowning cigarette butts in flat beer.

Mo shook his head. 'Nah, not yet. I wanna go on the fruit machine first.' He stalked across, rooting in his pocket for change.

Robin followed, and watched as Mo pumped money into the machine. After a while he got bored of the spinning reel and the flashing lights. Sipping his shandy, he asked the question he'd been aching to voice all day. 'Why are you being so friendly today, Mo?'

At first he thought Mo wasn't going to answer. The skinhead scooped up his meagre winnings and began to feed the coins back into the machine. At last he said, 'I just got to thinking about what you were saying yesterday – you know, about us working together and that? – and I decided that you were right. As we do have to work together, we might as well try and be mates, eh? I mean, Rusty doesn't like you, but that doesn't mean that I have to be the same. So this morning I thought: "I'll give him a chance, see what he's really like." And you're all right really, aren't you? You're not the wanker I thought you were.'

'Thanks,' said Robin, not sure how to take this back-handed compliment. He was beginning to feel more relaxed now in Mo's company. The visit to The Glamour didn't seem to be a trap at any rate, and Mo's explanation for his change of personality certainly sounded feasible enough.

Mo held up a ten pence piece. 'Last one,' he said, and fed it into the machine. The reels spun. Mo muttered, 'Come on, come on,' clenching his fist in triumph as the middle reel stopped on the jackpot symbol. The other two reels stopped a couple of seconds later, a lemon and a cherry. Mo muttered, 'Bastard,' and kicked the machine, which burbled smugly.

'C'mon,' he said grumpily, 'let's sit down.' He made his way to a spare table, Robin trailing in his wake. Robin wondered what his parents would say if they could see him now. He supposed that Mo was the 'bad company' they had always warned him against keeping.

'Fancy another?' Mo asked, draining his glass. Robin looked down at his half-finished shandy and wondered how Mo had managed to drink so quickly and play the fruit machine at the same time.

'Um, n-no thanks,' he said. 'I'm fine with this.'

Shrugging, Mo said, 'All right, please yourself,' and made his way to the bar.

Alone, Robin looked round. He imagined this as the kind of place in which drug pushers plied their trade, prostitutes touted for business, criminals planned their next job. Some of the men looked so mean they seemed barely human: Neanderthals in camel-skin coats with camel-shit cigars; gorillas with tattoos that championed tribalism; weasels with quick fingers and darting eyes.

'Do you come here much?' Robin asked Mo when he returned.

'Yeah, quite a lot. It's the best place in Piling Hill. They have a disco on Fridays and Saturdays, and most nights there's a stripper on. They've also got a club licence or something, which means the bar stays open until two in the morning.'

Robin nodded as though familiar with such things as

strippers and nightclubs. He turned nervously as a cheer erupted behind him, but it was only due to a favoured horse romping home in first place.

'What do *you* do on a weekend?' Mo asked.

Robin shrugged, embarrassed. How could he say he watched videos at Richard's, went to Horror Club meetings every Sunday, did his homework on Fridays before work? He wracked his brain, trying to think of some activity that Mo would find acceptable. Finally, lamely, he said, 'I used to go down the football on a Saturday afternoon, but I can't any more, not now I'm working.'

'Yeah, me too,' said Mo. 'I got banned for hittin' a copper with a corner flag.'

Robin smiled as though the act was worthy of admiration, though he felt nervous when Mo talked of violence.

'Got anythin' lined up this weekend?' Mo asked.

'Going to a party tonight,' said Robin.

'Oh, yeah? Where's that?'

Robin hesitated, worried that Mo might be hankering for an invitation. 'It's at the Sports Centre in Beachside . . . it's somebody's eighteenth,' he added as though that was an excuse for not having to invite Mo.

To Robin's relief, however, Mo didn't seem too eager for an invitation. The skinhead took a long swig from his glass and then asked casually, 'Who you going with?'

'Oh . . . just some mates,' Robin replied.

'Gardener, you mean?' Mo said. He grinned, slow and cunning. Robin felt his ears burn. He nodded, trying to seem indifferent.

'Yeah, Richard's going . . . and his brother, Neil.'

'That little fucker, Toady, isn't going, is he?'

Robin shrugged. 'I don't think so.'

'Why the fuck do you go around with that little shit?' Mo asked. 'It's only because of him that Rusty started on you the other day, you know.'

Robin shrugged again, feeling uncomfortable. He couldn't really explain about the Horror Club to Mo. He

155

sipped his shandy, hoping his silence would act as an incentive to drop the subject. Thankfully it did, for now Mo was looking at his watch.

'Come on, we'd better get back,' he said. 'We're due on the floor again in ten minutes.'

Robin finished his shandy and the boys left. It wasn't until they got outside that Robin realized how hot and dark The Glamour had been. The cold was piercing, and the snow made him screw up his eyes. 'Come on,' Mo said, speaking as he might to an erring pet dog, and stalked off.

The walk back to the supermarket was undertaken in silence. Robin struggled for conversation, but could think of nothing to say. A small part of him resented the way Mo made him feel, like a little kid trying to impress his elder brother, but the larger part yearned for acceptance. Maybe he had insulted Mo by not inviting him to the party or by disclosing that he was going with Richard and Neil Gardener. He glanced across to try and judge the expression on the skinhead's face, and was surprised and a little uneasy when he saw that Mo was smiling.

2

Another uneasy soul in Starmouth that day was Olive Pierce. She had woken up with the feeling. When she opened her eyes, she felt a weight settle inside her as though her anxiety had found solid form. She got up, scowling, searching for her slippers as the cold froze around her feet. She shuffled to the kitchen, plugged in the kettle, and then, shivering, went into the sitting room and drew back the curtains.

The sky was a harsh white, causing her to shield her eyes. She felt at odds with the sea today, seeing the grey foamy mass as a blemish, like having a rubbish tip on the horizon. The shapes she could see from her window depressed her: the empty pier, the silent ferris-wheel, the rows of lamp standards. They all seemed heavy and industrial, their colours muted, their magic gone. 'It's just the weather,' she thought, 'just this damn cold and the crotchetiness of old age.' But as she sat sipping fennel tea, trying to warm her hands on the cup, she knew it was something more.

Starmouth had been invaded. No, not invaded . . . infiltrated. Yes, that was the word. Suddenly the town felt sick, listless, a laboratory rat injected with some slow-acting virus. As yet the disease was all but dormant, the symptoms barely noticeable, but they were there, no doubt about that.

She finished her tea and poured herself another as she debated what to do. How does one combat a disease? By striking at its source? But what was the point of that if you didn't know what it was you were trying to cure? She sat, deep in thought, and decided the thing to do was to gather information, to find out as much as possible and then to equip herself accordingly. She smiled wryly. But how does one go about gathering information? Where does one start? . . . Well . . . she supposed the best place would be the house. Its history might throw up some clues. And then after that . . .

Her smile faded into a grimace. Despite her sensitivity, despite knowing that Starmouth was under threat, she couldn't help feeling like a medical charlatan about to remove a malignant tumour with a hacksaw.

She finished her tea and went to the bathroom. Her body felt sluggish, an old machine that was slowly running down. She washed and dressed methodically and was out walking by eight-thirty.

The cold wind blew the cobwebs from her mind, but it seemed to slough off a layer from her body too, leaving her feeling exposed and vulnerable. She shuddered, and dragging her coat around her, hurried the length of the promenade. To her left the sea hurled itself at the foot of the cliffs, scattering surf like confetti. Above, gulls sailed into the wind, hovering on the thermals like gliders.

157

Olive left the sea behind and walked into Starmouth proper. Here, away from the seafront, the wind was not so fierce and the cold not so biting. She loosened her headscarf, and acting on intuition entered the first estate agent's she saw.

'Hello, can I help you?' the girl behind the counter asked.

Olive sat down. 'I've come to enquire about a house,' she said. 'I don't want to buy it, mind, I just want some information.'

'Oh yes?' the girl said warily.

'Yes. The property is on King Street in Piling Hill.'

The girl flicked through her files. 'What number?' she asked.

'I'm not sure. It's at the end of the row, so I assume it's either one or two.'

The girl sighed. After a moment she said, 'I'm afraid neither of those is listed. The house you want can't be for sale at this agency.'

'Oh no, no, it isn't for sale,' Olive explained. 'It's uninhabitable, you see. The roof has fallen in. It's an abandoned house.'

The girl stared at her. 'Is this some kind of joke? We're estate agents, we don't deal in demolished property.'

'No, you don't understand. The house isn't demolished either. It's just that . . . oh, never mind. The thing is, I just want some information about the place. I thought you might be able to help.'

The girl shook her head. 'I'm sorry, madam, but I don't think we can.'

'Oh dear,' said Olive. 'You've no idea which agency dealt with the property, I suppose?'

'No, I'm afraid not. We don't keep such records here. You might try the housing department.'

'The housing department, yes. Erm . . . have you any idea where that might be?'

'Town Hall, I suppose,' said the girl, shrugging.

Olive stood up. 'Right, well, I'll try there then. Thank

you very much, you've been most help—' She didn't finish her sentence, for at the moment a door to an inner office opened and a tall thin man with a pencil moustache and wearing a blue suit emerged.

'Has Mr Cork rung back about Bronson Terrace yet, Janet?' he asked. Then he noticed Olive and smiled obsequiously. 'Ah, good morning, madam. Everything all right?'

'Yes, thank you, Mr . . . ?'

'Pilling.'

'Mr Pilling. Yes, everything's fine. The young lady here has been most helpful.'

'Ah, splendid,' Pilling said, rubbing his hands together. 'Then I trust we've been able to accommodate you?'

'No, I'm afraid not,' said Olive. 'I'm on my way to the housing department.'

Pilling's smile faded. 'Indeed? Did our selection of properties not meet with your requirements?'

'She wasn't interested in buying anything, Mr Pilling,' the girl piped up defensively. 'She just wanted some information about a condemned property.'

Pilling's smile returned, though he was obviously puzzled. 'Ah, I see. Yes, I think the housing department is probably your best bet in that case. You'll find it . . .' He tailed off, for Olive was staring at him intently. 'Is, er, is everything all right, madam?'

'I know you,' Olive said suddenly, wagging a finger in the air. 'Aren't you Dorothy Pilling's boy? What was his name now? Ah, yes, Michael.'

Pilling nodded uncertainly, as though nervous of what this might lead to. 'As a matter of fact, madam, I am, but I don't see what—'

'I haven't seen your mother for years,' Olive said. 'Did she move away from the area?'

Pilling looked down at his fingernails. 'I, er, I'm afraid she died, madam. She had a bad heart, you see.'

'Oh, I'm sorry,' Olive said, 'I didn't mean to upset you.'

'No, no, that's perfectly all right, madam. It was quite a

159

number of years ago now.' The estate agent mustered a smile and cleared his throat nervously. Olive stood back to look him up and down.

'My, my,' she said, 'Michael Pilling. Who would've thought such a snot-nosed little boy would grow up to be such a well turned-out young man?'

Behind the counter Janet stifled a snigger. Pilling glanced at his watch and blushed red. 'Yes, well, Mrs . . . er, I'm sorry we haven't been able to help you.' He took Olive's arm and coaxed her gently towards the door.

'I don't suppose *you* can tell me anything about this house, can you?' Olive said.

Pilling smiled stiffly. 'I rather think the housing department will be better—'

'Number one or two King Street? I don't suppose you ever handled the property?'

Pilling let go of Olive's arm and stepped back. 'The "ghost-house" you mean? Now why would you be interested in that?'

Olive was delighted, though she felt a spark of fear at the words 'ghost-house'. 'You know it!' she exclaimed. 'I knew you would. I have a feel for these things.'

'Yes,' Pilling said distractedly, 'I'm sure you do. But . . . why does the property interest you so much? It's been empty for a number of years now.'

'I'm writing a book,' Olive lied smoothly, 'about local ghosts, strange phenomena and suchlike. I take it this house has a certain . . . reputation?'

'Indeed it has,' said Pilling, rubbing his hands together again as though relishing the chance of a gossip.

'I wonder,' Olive said, smiling sweetly, 'whether you would be so kind as to tell me about it?'

'Certainly, madam, if you'll just come through to the office.' He held the door open and Olive stepped inside.

Half an hour later she emerged, pensive and thoughtful. At the prospect of getting his name mentioned in Olive's book, Pilling had been positively effusive on the subject of the house. He had shown her the files on the King Street property, which included the yellowing newspaper clippings from *The Starmouth Gazette*, and had even given her an in-depth report on the ramblings of the couple who had wanted to sell it. He seemed a little disconcerted that she wasn't taking down his story word for word, especially since he so generously informed her that she should feel free to quote him on the matter. Olive, however, assured him that everything he had told her was engraved on her mind.

At the door of the shop, Pilling called, 'Be sure to send me a copy of the book, when it's finished, won't you?' Olive merely waved and lost herself in the bundled-up crowd of Saturday shoppers.

She trudged, unseeing, back towards her flat. 'Poltergeist', she thought scornfully. 'Is that the best they could come up with?' She knew that whatever the boys had awakened in the house, it was no mere poltergeist. Poltergeists were undirected forces; mindless, destructive, amoebas on the spirit scale. No, she was certain the resident of King Street was much more complex than that.

When she came to the promenade she leaned on the railings and looked out to sea. On the whole the morning had been a waste of time; next to nothing had been achieved. All Olive had really done was to confirm something she already knew. 'So what now?' she thought. 'What is the next step that must be taken?' She remembered how she had pictured herself earlier, a medical charlatan with a hacksaw. 'Well then, we shall go into battle blind,' she murmured, feeling as though she were quoting, but not quite sure from what. Her attention was suddenly caught by something cartwheeling over the sands, something greeny-brown that scampered with frightening speed. She tensed; then, recognizing the object, relaxed. It was nothing but a battered old trilby being bowled along by the wind.

Grandstand was just starting when Toady woke up, so he knew it was around lunchtime. He lay in bed for a while, unwilling to move even though his bladder was heavy and his stomach rumbled for food. Slats of lights, poking through gaps in the curtains, lay across the far wall, one reaching as far as the wardrobe where it cut Freddy Krueger in half. Toady traced the shape of the light with his finger, and thought idly that if he didn't get up soon he would wet the bed.

He looked across the room at the chair which he was sure had been occupied the night before. The figure in the chair had been large, shadowy, powerful-looking, but somehow basic, like a human shape cut from black paper by a child. The figure hadn't frightened Toady: in fact, quite the opposite, it had soothed him. Had it spoken to him? He didn't think so, yet somehow he remembered being reassured that his brother was unharmed.

He closed his eyes, but the ache in his bladder intensified, angry at being ignored. Groaning, he crawled from his bed, shivering as he searched for his dressing gown. He found it at last, stuffed behind the wardrobe, and pulled it on. After he had opened his curtains and been to the toilet he went downstairs.

As was usual for a Saturday, his father was lying on the settee, watching telly. The racing pages were open on the floor beside him and the names of various horses were ringed. He looked up as Toady entered, the index finger of his right hand rooting in one nostril.

'Hallo, son,' he said as though he had forgotten Toady lived here, 'you're up late.'

'I've been ill this week,' Toady replied curtly.

His father withdrew his finger from his nose and regarded it with satisfaction. 'Have you?' he said. 'What was it? Flu or something?'

'Just a bug,' Toady said, tight-lipped.

His father nodded, though now his eyes were fixed on

the television where the next race was getting underway. 'Go on, Mister Custard,' he yelled, 'go on, my son!'

'Where's Mum?' Toady asked, raising his voice.

'Gone shopping, I think. Come on, you stupid horse! What's wrong with you today?'

'Did she take Simon with her?' Toady said, determined to make himself heard.

'Oh, I don't know. She must've if he's not here. Bloody hell, would you look at that! He's fallen!'

'Is he all right this morning?'

'Huh? What? Is who all right?'

'Simon. Is he all right? I heard him screaming last night.'

His father picked up the racing pages and began to study them. 'Oh, yeah. It was just a nightmare, that's all.' He tapped the page. 'Jolly Gee. I'll have a couple of quid on that.'

'What do I do about lunch?' said Toady.

'Oh, I don't know. You'll have to go down the chippy or something.'

'Can I have some money then?'

'What?'

'Some money. For the chips. Or do I have to buy my own meals now, too?'

'Oh, bloody hell,' his father said and rummaged in his pocket. 'Look, here's a quid. Now stop pestering me. I've got to get this bet on before the next race starts.' He heaved himself upright, groaning as he did so. He was not a big man, though he looked heavy, his skin puffy and colourless as lard. He dug his fingers into his armpit and began to scratch. Toady grimaced and left the room.

Sometimes he loathed his father so much it made him sick. How he wished it was his father who had been made to scream last night, and not Simon. If that had been the case Toady would not have asked for the screaming to stop. He would have urged it to go on and on, until the men in the white coats came and took his father away.

He swayed on the stairs and grabbed at the banister to steady himself. For a moment his hatred had been so

163

overwhelming it had almost caused him to black out. His head felt stuffed with animosity; it was almost as though something had latched on to the emotion and intensified it. A small part of him felt alarmed at the feeling, but the larger part rose to it, his face cracking into a huge smile. His father was a nothing, a nobody, a crawling thing on the earth. Toady was strong, powerful, special; he had something that set him apart. He glanced up the stairs and for a moment he almost grasped what that something was. Then it was snatched tantalizingly away again, out of reach.

He moved slowly up the stairs, feeling exhilarated, high on his own loathing. Above him the landing was still and expectant, cold thin light whitewashing the walls. 'I hate my father,' he heard himself say, and laughed aloud at the words. Elation zipped and popped in his joints. 'I hate my father,' he said again.

He came to the top of the stairs. The landing was silent, the racing commentator's voice a million miles away. His bedroom door stood ajar; Toady walked across to it, his footsteps muffled by the carpet. He stretched out a hand to push the door open. But before he could do so it swung slowly inwards with a faint whoosh of air.

For a few seconds Toady stood motionless, his heart beating steadily. His mind felt alert, his body lithe as a panther's; it was as though his whole being had been transformed. He swallowed and the sound was rich and pure, an evocation of his new perfection. Calmly he stepped into his bedroom.

His eyes quickly scanned the room, taking in the unmade bed, the clothes and shoes that littered the floor, the desk piled with schoolbooks, the daylight gleaming on sellotape that affixed horror posters to the walls. For a moment Toady saw the room through someone else's eyes. It was not an unfamiliar room, but it did not belong to him. Then, slowly, his perception shifted. He recognized the bed as his bed, the desk as his desk, the chair as his . . . He looked again. It was hard to tell, but there appeared to be a faint man-shaped shadow sitting in the chair.

Toady felt nothing; no fear, no unease, no horror at the apparition. He walked slowly across the room, and as he did so, it grew dimmer, objects becoming insubstantial, daylight turning flat and insipid. It was only the chair, and the shadow sitting in it, which became sharper, more clearly defined.

The shadow curdled and writhed, drawing darkness to itself. Slowly it thickened, became solid, until at last a black, faceless figure was sitting in the chair. Toady reached out a hand and the shadow responded, extending a grey-black sinuous limb.

Fingers touched, and Toady felt a hot-cold tingling sensation, a feeling as of hundreds of insects scuttling up his arm. The blackness began to engulf him: it was orgasmic, a hungry sexual ecstasy, like being coupled with a storm cloud. Toady looked for his lover's eyes, and saw two tiny red points glowing somewhere in the distance. Sibilant, seductive, a woman's voice murmured: 'My love, my darling, succumb.'

Toady's lips parted to say yes.

'Chippy'll be closed if you don't hurry up, you know.'

The voice was a sledgehammer, shattering his world. Toady's eyes opened, eyelids ripping apart as though they had been sewn together. His mouth was all tongue, his stomach queasy and feeble. When he moved, his limbs felt like chunks of wood tied to his torso.

'What?' he squealed, making the noise through instinct. His father frowned in at him, roving index finger now exploring an ear for wax.

'I said if you don't get a move on, chippy'll be closed. Look at you, half-past one and you're not even dressed.'

Toady pushed himself up out of the chair in which he was sitting. Despite the cold, his body squelched with sweat. He wrinkled his nose, smelling something animal on him. When his father had left the room, he sniffed his sleeve and recoiled.

His dressing gown reeked. It smelt hot and vile, like a mangy dog in high summer. Toady peeled it off distastefully, carried it to the Ali Baba basket on the landing and dropped it inside. His pyjama top was clinging to him, the bottoms too, and Toady was alarmed and embarrassed to discover he had ejaculated.

Trying to fight down his nausea, he locked himself in the bathroom and began to run a bath. He peeled off his soiled pyjamas, and after rinsing away the tell-tale stains as best he could, dumped them in a corner. When the bath was deep enough he climbed in. He immersed himself in the water, reached for the soap and began to wash his body thoroughly.

As he did so he thought about what had happened. There was no doubt now that the seance had been a success, that whatever they'd evoked at King Street was here in the house with him. This fact filled Toady with a fearful excitement, yet he also felt distaste and unease at the incident that had just occurred. Somehow things had got a little out of his control, somehow the shadow had almost managed to gain the upper hand. 'I brought you here,' Toady muttered. '*I* brought *you*. You have to do as *I* say.' He heard a scratching outside the window and looked up.

Something was there, something dark that fluttered like a bat. 'No,' Toady murmured as the scrabbling sounds the thing was making became a host of whispering voices. They seemed to be trying to burrow into his mind – enticing, evocative, promising paradise and more. 'No!' he said again, more forcefully this time. 'No, this isn't how it should be!'

The voices paid him no heed. Their words dug deep, barbs that tore at his thoughts. Toady tried to block them out, jammed his hands over his ears, but it was no use. Relentlessly, insidiously, the seduction was beginning again.

4

Nige sat in the armchair by the fire, feeling baked. Outside the window the sky was already dark. He was eating his sandwiches as fast as he dared and eyeing the clock on the wall. It was 6.25; Richard and Neil were due to pick him up at 7.30.

'Robespierre,' Mr Figg mused, reaching for a sandwich. 'It's a strange name. Isn't it something historical?'

'It's French, dear,' Mrs Figg said, smiling an apology at the blind man which he couldn't possibly see.

'I know it's French,' Mr Figg replied, 'but it's also something else. I'm certain I've heard the name before. Something to do with the French Revolution, isn't it?'

Robespierre smiled and nodded, stretching out his legs, reminding Nige of a black, spindly insect unfurling slowly. 'Yes, you're thinking of Robespierre's Reign of Terror in Paris in the 1790s,' he murmured.

'That's it!' Mr Figg exclaimed, turning to his wife. 'There, you see. I knew I was right.'

'There's no need to gloat, Colin,' Mrs Figg snapped. Her voice softening, she asked Robespierre, 'Are you related to this . . . this Frenchman?'

Robespierre smiled. 'I hope not, madam. He was a ruthless, evil man, forever chopping off people's heads.'

Mrs Figg's podgy hand flew to her even podgier neck. 'Oh dear!' she exclaimed. 'How perfectly dreadful.'

'Yes. It was rather a distasteful episode in this long, bloody history of ours.' Robespierre smirked, and Nige shifted uneasily in his seat.

The blind man was an unsettling character. His black suit was clean and neatly pressed, but frayed like an undertaker's cast-off. Despite the heat of the sitting room he was not sweating as most new guests were apt to do; indeed, he didn't even look flushed. His face was rigid, strangely immobile, though Nige guessed that effect was due to his spectacles, black lifeless coins that shut off the mirrors of his soul. He stirred on the settee as though sensing the boy's unease, his fingertips softly caressing the white stick.

'Who did you say recommended this place to you?' Mr Figg asked. He took his pipe from his pocket, but Mrs Figg frowned fiercely and nodded at the piled plates to show that they hadn't finished eating yet. Sighing, Mr Figg put his pipe away.

'It was Captain Patchett. I understand he stays here every summer?'

'Oh, yes, indeed he does,' Mrs Figg trilled. 'Always stays in the same room. In fact, I've put you in his room – number three.'

Robespierre smiled his appreciation. Mrs Figg reached for a plate heaped with cakes that were bright as poster paints. 'Care for a French fancy, Mr . . . er?' she said.

'No thank you, Mrs Figg. It's very kind, but I really am quite full.'

'Have you known Captain Patchett long?' Mrs Figg asked.

'Oh, yes,' the blind man replied. 'We served in the army together. It was there, in fact, that I was blinded. A stupid accident really. A bomb blew up in my face.'

Mrs Figg gasped, red lips forming an O of shock. 'How awful! And are you completely blind?' She spoke the word like a taboo.

'I'm afraid so. Twenty-four years now. It's strange, though, how one gets used to it. I've taught myself braille and I can get about without too much trouble.'

Nige, sitting in the chair, stared at Robespierre. If what the blind man had said about the bomb was true, his face certainly bore no signs of disfigurement. There were no burn marks, no healed-over scar tissue. Perhaps he had had extensive plastic surgery. Yes, that must be it: that would account for the smooth, unyielding waxiness of his features.

'Did it hurt when the bomb went off?' he asked before he could stop himself. His mother stared at him, aghast.

'Nigel, how can you ask such a question?' But Robespierre held up a hand.

'Please,' he said, 'I'm sure the boy meant no offence.' He raised his hands to his eyes as though re-living the experience. 'I'm afraid I remember nothing of the incident. The only thing I can recall is coming round in hospital six days later and not being able to see. I panicked at first, of course, but as I said, one gets used to it.'

There was a pregnant silence. Then Mrs Figg asked, 'More tea, Mr . . . er, Robespierre?'

Robespierre stood up, using the white stick to steady himself. 'No thank you, Mrs Figg. Actually I'm rather tired. If you'll excuse me, I think I'll take a nap.'

Mrs Figg nodded. 'Oh, of course. And remember, if you need anything don't hesitate to ask. Perhaps we'll see you later this evening? Feel free to come down to join Colin and I whenever you like.'

Robespierre thanked her and tapped his way around the furniture to the door. Nige shivered as the blind man passed him. The odour from Robespierre's clothes was musty, stale, like the smell of old books in a damp room.

'How could you ask such a question?' his mother hissed when the door was closed.

Nige shrugged uncomfortably. 'I'm sorry, Mum, I didn't mean anything. It just sort of slipped out.'

'Can't you see you've upset the poor man?' Mrs Figg said, and Nige shrank further into his seat. His mother furious was an awesome sight: fat cheeks quivered, stiffened strands of lacquered hair bobbed out of place.

'I'm sorry,' Nige said again, 'I never really thought.'

'No, that's your trouble! You never *do* think, do you? I've got a good mind to make you stay in tonight. Perhaps that'll teach you some manners.'

Nige stared in disbelief. 'You can't do that!' he said shrilly.

'Oh, can't I? Just you watch me!'

Nige's stomach was churning. He gripped the arm of the chair until his knuckles showed white. 'But, Mum,' he pleaded, 'everyone else is going. You can't make me stay in, I'll be a laughing stock. I didn't mean to be rude.'

'You should have thought of that before. I will not have my guests upset. Heaven knows, we get few enough in winter as it is.' Mrs Figg went to the window and yanked the pink curtains across as though to emphasize her anger.

Nige said bitterly, 'You're just using this as an excuse. You never wanted me to go to this party in the first place, did you?'

Mrs Figg refused to comment. She moved agitatedly about the room, shifting ornaments, re-arranging the antimacassars, piling up plates which scraped harshly. Nige raised his voice, refusing to allow her busyness to act as a ploy to curtail the argument.

'You didn't, did you?' he said.

'I don't know what you mean!' Mrs Figg snapped, savagely folding a tablecloth.

'Oh yes you do!' Nige snapped back, and glared at his father who was perched on the settee, trying to light his pipe. His father looked up and sighed, recognizing Nige's stare as a demand for moral support.

Abandoning his pipe-lighting, he said, 'I do think you're being a little hard on the boy, Rosie.'

Mrs Figg whirled, more strands of hair loosening, and banged down a clock which she had been unnecessarily winding. 'Oh, do you?' she snarled. 'And whose side are you on?'

'I'm not on anybody's side,' Mr Figg said, 'I'm neutral. And speaking as a neutral, I think you're being too hard on the boy.'

Mrs Figg stumped forward and pointed at Nige. 'He was rude to our guest!' she accused.

'Yes, but not intentionally. The question was just a little ill-considered, that's all.'

'Oh, is that what you call it? Ill-considered?'

'Yes, as a matter of fact I do.'

'And that makes it all right, I suppose?'

Mr Figg kept his temper, which made his wife all the more angry. He said, 'No, I'm not saying it was all right. Certainly Nigel spoke out of order. But I don't think his

170

offence really warrants the sentence you advocate.'

'There's no need to get pompous,' she raged.

Nige, recognizing that his mother was getting flustered, pressed home his advantage. 'I really am sorry, Mum. I'll go and apologize to Mr Robespierre if you like.'

Mrs Figg turned away to pick up the plates and refused to say anything. Mr Figg nodded diplomatically.

'Yes, perhaps that would be the best thing to do, Nigel. If I were you, I'd go now.' He gestured with his eyes, making it obvious that things would be better if Nige were out of the room. Gratefully, he stood up and sidled towards the door.

When the door had closed, he heard his mother's voice start up again, shrill as chalk. Trying to block out the argument, he hurried upstairs.

Winter stilled the house, making it feel hollow as a shell. Nige hurried along the landing to his room, on the door of which was a small plaque, 'Nigel's Room', and a sign beneath that read, 'Silence. Genius at work.' Nige turned the handle and went inside.

A shred of night whirled from the window to face him. Nige stepped back, banging his head on the closing door. The gangly black figure held out its white cane and rapped, 'Who's there?'

'It's . . . it's me,' Nige said in a small voice. 'This is my room.'

Robespierre smiled slowly and lowered the cane. The night at his back swallowed his dark suit, giving emphasis to his white, hollow-cheeked face. He raised his head and ice-blue light slid across the black lenses of his spectacles like fleeting vision.

'Do forgive me,' he purred. 'I must have entered the wrong door by mistake. It's the unfamiliarity, you see. I'm sure I'll get used to it soon enough.'

'That's all right,' said Nige, though he thought it an unlikely mistake. Robespierre's room was three doors down on the other side of the landing. As the blind man strode towards him, white cane swinging, he flinched back. Too late: the cane caught him across the side of his leg, forcing a muttered, 'Ouch!'

Robespierre spread his hands to profess his clumsiness and cocked his head in apology. 'I am so sorry,' he said. 'I just can't seem to do a thing right today.'

'That's OK,' Nige said, rubbing his leg. 'Anyway, it's me who should be apologizing to you.'

'Really? What for?'

'For asking you the question about the bomb. It was pretty thoughtless. I'm sorry.'

Robespierre gripped Nige's shoulder. 'My dear boy, think nothing of it. We all make mistakes, do we not?' He laughed, a sharp hoarse sound, and his grip tightened as though to goad an answer. Nige winced and nodded.

'Yes. I suppose we do.'

After a final squeeze, Robespierre released his grip and groped for the door handle. Finding it, he pulled the door open. 'Would you be so kind as to escort me to my room?' he asked. 'I seem to have lost my bearings somewhat.'

'Yes, course,' Nige said, and took the old man's arm. He led him along the corridor, Robespierre's white cane bumping the carpet and chattering against the skirting board. At the door of room three, Nige said, 'Here it is. You can tell it's your room because there's a number on the door.'

Robespierre reached out, traced the '3' with the tip of a finger. 'Ah, so there is,' he said. 'How stupid of me.' He unlocked the door and pushed it open. 'Well then, I'll bid you good night.'

Nige nodded. 'Good night, Mr Robespierre, see you in the morning.'

'Oh, indubitably,' Robespierre said, and was gone.

5

The men had departed in a cloud of shampoo and aftershave, leaving Sylvia behind to mourn for her social life. She remembered a time, not so very long ago, when Mike would not have dreamt of going out without her. Nowadays he didn't even bother to ask.

Feeling close to tears, she went across to the drinks cabinet. It was a place where she sought comfort more and more these days, and it worried and angered her. Worried her because she didn't want to go the same way as her grandmother (a bottle of gin a day for the last seven years of her life, and a drunken fall downstairs deciding her fate before her liver could), and angered her because it was her goddamn bastard husband's fault that she should feel the need to drink at all.

She pulled a glass from the cabinet and banged it down on the sideboard, half-hoping it would shatter. Perhaps if she hurt herself, cut herself badly, slashed her wrists even, Michael would care. But if she had to resort to self-abuse to attract his attention, then it wasn't bloody worth it, was it? She removed the cap of the Scotch bottle with small, savage twists.

She poured a large whisky and gulped it down, feeling in a strange way as though the action was spiting Mike's selfishness. Snatching up the bottle she poured herself another, filling the glass almost to the brim. She carried the glass to an armchair and sat down, folding her legs beneath her.

The house was cold, like a dead thing, but Sylvia sat and shivered, refusing to switch on the heating. Mike would expect it of her, would take it for granted that she would do so. But she was so resentful that she was prepared to sit and freeze just to see his disgruntled expression when he came back; back from his night of leering and vulgarity and pouring beer down his throat to prove his machismo.

Oh, how she hated men! She seared her throat with whisky to add fuel to her fury, and her eyes brimmed with tears. Seeing Robin going out tonight, self-conscious in his best clothes, smiling through his spots, she had felt an urge to hug him and plead with him not to go. It was as though she was seeing Mike again, an unsure sixteen-year old Mike, setting out on his first steps of manhood. Tonight Robin would be doing the same as his father – swigging pints, swapping dirty jokes, ogling girls – and that was something that infuriated and depressed her deeply. She wanted Robin to be different, she wanted to teach him about love and caring and sensitivity, wanted to sit down and talk to him about how not to be like his father. But she knew she never would. Already Robin was being drawn into the pathetic, brutish world of masculinity, and her promptings would be discarded as silly female misconceptions.

She sipped whisky again, licking lips which tingled with alcohol. Already she felt her mind shutting down, her thoughts drifting to a lower level because the emotions they spawned were too much to bear. The rest of the night she would spend aimlessly. She would have a couple more drinks, just enough to help her sleep, stare unseeingly at the television for a few hours, read a romance, go to bed. In the morning she would wake, look at her overweight husband snoring beside her, and feel depressed all over again.

As she raised her half-empty glass to her lips, the doorbell rang. Sylvia looked up, startled. She glanced at her watch, frowned, and balanced her glass on the arm of her chair. Who could this be? she wondered. Perhaps Mike had forgotten his keys. She unstretched her legs and stood up, thinking that if it was her husband she would insist he take her out.

The doorbell rang again. 'All right, all right, I'm coming,' she muttered, and went through to the hall, surprised at how light-headed the whisky had made her feel. She put the chain on the door, twisted the Yale, and pulled the door open, looking through the gap to see who was there.

A man stood outside holding a club. That was Sylvia's first impression a split-second before she recognized the smiling face of Walter Treeborn. He held up the wine bottle he was carrying.

'I haven't forgotten about that drink I promised you,' he said, 'only I thought I'd bring it over here. That is, if you don't mind?'

For a moment Sylvia was too startled to say anything; then, recovering her wits, she slid the chain from its snip and held the door wide. 'Of course I don't mind, it's a lovely idea,' she said. 'Please come in.'

Treeborn stepped over the threshold, smiling broadly. 'I hope you like red wine,' he said. 'Perhaps I should have brought white?'

'Red is perfect,' said Sylvia, taking the bottle, though she wondered what the consequences of combining the wine and whisky would be. Still, time to worry about that in the morning. 'Just go through, Mr Treeborn,' she said, and gestured towards the sitting room.

'Please, call me Walter,' Treeborn said. 'Mr Treeborn is so official, don't you think?'

Sylvia nodded. 'Walter it is then. And I'm Sylvia.'

'Sylvia.' He repeated the name as though tasting it. 'A pretty name, very feminine.'

'Why thank you, kind sir,' Sylvia said, blushing. She hovered until Treeborn had settled himself on the settee, then sat in the armchair to his right. 'Did you manage to fix the lights?' she asked.

'The lights?' Treeborn looked puzzled, then realization dawned. 'Oh yes, thank you.'

'Good, good.' Sylvia smiled, rubbing her knees with the palms of her hands. 'Well, shall we have a drink?' she said desperately.

'If you like.' Treeborn picked up the bottle from where Sylvia had put it on the coffee table. 'Do you have a corkscrew?' he asked.

'Yes, it's . . . um, it should be over there,' Sylvia said, wincing with embarrassment to see the drinks cabinet yawning open, the whisky bottle capless. She watched as Treeborn rooted in the cupboard, took out two wine glasses and found the corkscrew.

'Here we are,' he said, coming across to Sylvia. 'A

charming little plonk. Marks and Spencers '88.'

Sylvia smiled. 'Nothing but the best.' She sipped and tried not to grimace. The wine was rough; after the whisky it was like swallowing sour fruit. However, she bravely took another swig. 'It's not bad, is it?'

'I've tasted better,' said Treeborn. He sat down, put his glass on the coffee table and leaned forward. 'I . . . I'm glad I came round tonight,' he said. He seemed about to go on, then thought better of it and cleared his throat self-consciously.

Sylvia smiled. 'So am I.'

Treeborn looked round as though searching for eaves-droppers. 'Are you, er, are you on your own this eve-ning?'

Sylvia nodded warily, unsure where this was leading. 'I'm afraid so, yes.'

'Your husband not around then?'

'He's out with the boys,' she said, unable to hide the bitterness in her voice.

Treeborn raised his eyebrows. 'Oh? You don't approve?'

She sighed, running her fingers gently round the rim of the glass. 'Oh, it's not that,' she said, 'I don't begrudge him a drink with his friends. It's just that . . . well, I always seem to be the one stuck at home nowadays. I can't remember the last time he took me out.'

Treeborn nodded sympathetically. 'Some men just don't know how to treat women.' When Sylvia didn't respond, he went on, 'I didn't mean that as an insult to your husband. I hope you won't take it the wrong way.'

'Oh, no, that's not why I didn't say anything,' Sylvia said. 'No, you can insult him all you like. He's a pig in my opinion. No, the reason I didn't say anything is because I wasn't entirely sure what you meant. I mean, how do you think men *should* treat women?'

Treeborn curled his fingers around the wine glass as though trying to conceal it in his hand. 'W-well,' he stammered, 'with respect, of course.'

Sylvia smiled. 'You're a true gentleman, Walter. There's not many like you left.' She reached out and touched the sleeve of Treeborn's jacket. He seemed uncertain about the physical contact for a moment, then he smiled.

'Michael doesn't know how lucky he is,' he said quietly.

Sylvia looked away, as though interested in something outside the window. She said, 'It's cold again tonight.'

'Yes, it is,' Treeborn agreed.

'I'll put the fire on, shall I?'

'If you like.'

Sylvia put down her glass and knelt in front of the fire. She lit a match, turned on the gas. The fire gave a dull 'whoomph' and exploded into blue flame. She flinched back, snatching her hand away, and laughed nervously. 'I hate doing that. I always think the thing's going to blow up.'

'You should have let me,' said Treeborn.

'Never mind, it's done now.' She sat back in the armchair and sipped her wine, shivering. It really was cold in the house tonight. Treeborn must be thinking that they couldn't afford to have the heating on all the time. She stole a glance at her visitor. He was leaning forward, elbows on knees, cupping the wine glass in both hands. As always he looked well-groomed, though he seemed more relaxed than Sylvia had ever known him before. He was staring into the fire, blue flames reflected in bluer eyes. For the first time, Sylvia became aware that Walter Treeborn was a very attractive man.

'There's something different about you tonight,' she said, numb lips and tongue making it difficult to form the words without slurring. Treeborn looked up sharply.

'Oh?'

'Yes, don't you usually wear . . . whatsits . . . specs?' Sylvia circled her eyes with her index finger to emphasize the question. Treeborn relaxed.

'Oh, yes I do,' he said, 'but I don't need to wear them constantly. Only for reading, driving, stuff like that.'

'I have glasses for reading too,' said Sylvia.

'Do you?'

'Yeah, little gold-rimmed ones with half-moon lenses. They make me look like a school marm.'

'A very attractive school marm, I'm sure.'

Sylvia snorted with laughter. She was beginning to feel quite drunk. 'Oh, you're terrible, Walter,' she said, 'a born flatterer.'

'Well,' said Treeborn, 'it's not often I'm in the presence of a pretty lady.'

'A pretty drunk lady,' Sylvia giggled.

'Aw, who cares about that? We're having a good time, aren't we?'

Sylvia nodded. 'We certainly are.'

Treeborn held up the wine bottle, jiggling it so its contents sloshed. 'Come on, drink up,' he said. 'I want to propose a toast.'

Sylvia did as she was asked, draining the remainder of her glass in one gulp. The wine slid harshly down her throat, sat hot and burning in her chest for a moment, and then slipped lower. She touched her stomach, imagining the alcohol fermenting in there, and held down an acidic burp.

'All finished?' said Treeborn. 'Good.' He refilled her glass, then his own. Holding up his wine like an offering, he said, 'I propose a toast.'

Sylvia sniggered and held up her glass too.

'To us,' Treeborn said quietly.

Sylvia looked at him, momentarily surprised, then nodded. 'To us,' she agreed.

They chinked glasses.

6

Madonna was urging people to get into the groove when Richard, Nige and Neil entered the Beachside Sports Centre. It was a large building of brick and glass that had been completed only last summer. A large 'Sport for All' emblem flanked the wall behind the entrance desk like a family crest. The boys showed the moustached man on duty their invitations, then headed towards a door marked 'Private Party' beyond which the music was coming.

Neil led the way into a long low room with a bar on the right. Tables and chairs were set in front of the bar and up both sides of the room. At the far end, on the stage, sat the deejay, a young man with spiky blond hair and a Hawaiian shirt. He was staring glumly at the empty dance-floor which changed colour constantly under a panoply of disco lights.

'There's not many people here,' Richard said, looking around.

'No, we're early yet,' replied Neil. 'Don't worry, it'll soon fill up.'

'Where's Dennis?' Nige wanted to know.

The boys peered into the gloom, trying to fit identities to shadowy figures. At last Neil pointed. 'There he is, sitting by his grandfather at the family table. His mother's seen us, she's coming across.'

Dennis's mother was a jolly, rotund woman. She was wearing a blue dress with a lilac flower pattern on it. Squeezing between the tables, she made her way over to the boys.

'Hello, Neil, how are you?' she said. She proffered her cheek and Neil pecked it self-consciously.

'Fine, thank you, Mrs Leeman. This is my brother, Richard, and his friend, Nige.'

Mrs Leeman said she was pleased to meet the boys; Richard was relieved that he didn't have to kiss her too.

'I've got Dennis a present,' Neil said, taking a small package from his jacket pocket. 'I'll pop across and give it to him, shall I?'

Mrs Leeman's cheeks were flushed with sherry and excitement. 'Yes, but you'll have to pry him away from his grandad. The old man's been moaning about the music all night, says it's bad for his ears. He's giving Dennis a lecture now on how he'll be deaf by the time he's forty. Heaven knows what he'd say if he knew Dennis had got a Sony Walkman for his birthday.' She took Neil's hand and began to drag him across the dance-floor. Richard and Nige made to follow, but stopped when Neil turned back and mouthed, 'Get some drinks.'

'Charming,' said Richard as Neil and Mrs Leeman waded into the sea of lights. 'Leaves me to get the first round and I'm not even old enough to buy alcohol.'

'Do you think they'll serve you?' Nige asked, eyeing the barman.

Richard nodded confidently. 'They ought to. I mean, it's a private party, isn't it? It's not like in a pub.' He took a crumpled five pound note from his pocket and straightened it out. 'What do you want?' he asked.

Nige looked at the glowing signs above the beer pumps and wondered how his mother would react if he came home drunk. Quashing the thought, he said, 'Er . . . a pint of lager, thanks.'

Richard went to the bar, standing on tiptoe to make himself look taller. The barman eyed him suspiciously as he ordered, but said nothing. When they had the drinks, they trooped across the dance-floor, their skin pulsing green to red to yellow under the disco lights. 'Aha, sustenance!' Neil cried, standing up to take his pint. Chairs scraped as people made way for the boys. They shuffled through, avoiding toes, and sat down next to Neil.

Introductions were made. Richard and Nige smiled and nodded at uncles and aunts, who smiled and nodded back with multi-coloured faces. When Richard leaned forward and said, 'How do you do?' to Dennis's grandfather, the old man glowered at him, mouth so puckered it seemed in danger of caving in.

'I can't hear you, young man,' he complained, 'this music's too loud.'

Richard smiled sympathetically and the old man sat back, muttering into his beer glass.

The boys felt uncomfortable at the family table, as

though they'd infiltrated a clique. Only Neil seemed relaxed, chatting animatedly to Dennis about rugby. Some of Dennis's relatives made an attempt to ask the boys about themselves, but the questions had to be shouted above the music and sounded more like interrogation than smalltalk. After a while the conversation ebbed away from them, and they sat, sipping their drinks and feeling awkward, trying to think of an excuse to get away.

'Look, there's Rob!' Nige exclaimed after the boys had sat in silence for some minutes. Richard looked up, relieved. Robin was at the door, peering into the gloom, trying not to look lost. Seizing the opportunity, they jumped up, squeezed through the maze of chairs and hurried across the dance-floor.

'Rob, hi!' Nige called.

Robin turned and grinned, his acne much less prominent under the shifting paint of the lights. 'So there you are,' he said, and nodded at the glasses that both boys held. 'At it already, I see. How long have you been here?'

'Oh, ages,' Richard said airily. 'This must be at least our sixth or seventh pint.'

'Liar,' Robin said good-humouredly. 'Nige would be unconscious by now if it was. He was out of his head after three on Christmas Eve.'

Nige squirmed, embarrassed, but managed to grin. 'Ah yes, but that was a month ago,' he said. 'I've become a hardened drinker since then.'

'I'd better catch up then,' Robin said, and turned to the bar.

More people began to drift in. Most of them were Neil's age or older, and Richard sighed, feeling like a kid. Mrs Leeman seemed to be everywhere, greeting people, making smalltalk, accepting presents as if it were her party. When Robin had got his pint, the boys sat at an unoccupied table by the bar and looked around. They felt slightly isolated, but were enjoying the atmosphere nonetheless.

'Do you know many people here?' Richard asked Robin.

181

Robin shook his head. 'I recognize some from school, but I don't really know that many. There seem to be some nice girls here, though.'

Richard nodded cautiously, looking at his friend. Robin's expression was eager, but also a little desperate. Though he had never said so, Richard knew how much Robin wanted a girlfriend: because of his acne he had never had one. As though Robin already needed an excuse, Richard said, 'The only trouble is, most of the good-looking girls seem to be with someone.'

Robin smiled wryly. 'It's always the way,' he said.

All at once a group of girls stood up and made their way to the dance-floor. The deejay, who had been slouched, bored, over his equipment, perked up immediately. 'That's the spirit,' he enthused, his voice booming over the music. He turned to the tables that were now slowly filling up. 'Come on, fellers, where are you? These lovely ladies need dancing partners.'

'Shall we go and have a dance?' Nige said, eyeing the girls as though they might bite. Richard wrinkled his nose. Robin looked undecided for a moment, then his hand curled protectively around his glass.

'Nah,' he said, 'let the dance-floor fill up a bit first.'

Nige shrugged and swigged his pint. Richard asked, 'How's the blind man settling in?'

'All right, I suppose,' Nige said, looking uncomfortable. He fell silent for a moment, then added, 'He's a strange one, though.'

'Strange? In what way?'

Nige paused again, looking down into his pint. 'I dunno. He's just . . . weird. Nothing I can really put my finger on.'

'Who *is* the blind man?' Robin said. 'I don't know what you're on about.'

Briefly Nige told him about Robespierre's arrival that morning.

'Talking of weird,' Richard said, 'has anything . . . out of the ordinary happened to you, Rob, since the seance?'

Immediately Robin thought about the fluttering thing in the warehouse last night and the lost feather, and then the blurred image in the mirror yesterday morning. But he shook his head, 'No, why?'

Richard looked uncomfortable, glanced at Nige. 'Well, it's just that there seem to have been a few strange things happening, that's all.'

'Like what?' Robin said guardedly.

Richard told him about the lupine shape with the glowing eyes he'd seen on his way home, and about Nige being hypnotized at Olive's. Also about her vision of shattering glass at the time of the seance, and the phone call he'd received from her this afternoon. 'Apparently that house is supposed to be haunted. The couple who lived there moved out because plates and stuff used to fly around, and a picture flew off the wall and smashed into the fireplace. The house was empty for about four months and then one night the roof just fell in. They reckon a bolt of lightning struck it, but Olive doesn't agree.'

Richard looked round at his audience for their reaction. Nige, who hadn't heard about the phone call, was wide-eyed, but Robin simply scowled.

'Aw, I dunno, Rich. I think you're reading too much into it all.'

'But what about the wolf?' Richard insisted. 'What about Nige being hypnotized?'

Robin refused to meet his eyes. 'That wolf must have been an illusion; you said yourself there was a blizzard. As for being hypnotized – well, I'm sure a good hypnotist can make you do anything when you're in his power.'

'It wasn't like that,' Richard said. 'He didn't tell Nige to scream. You ought to listen to the tape, Rob. You'd believe us then.'

Robin simply shrugged and took a long swig of his beer. There were a few moments of awkward silence, then the older boy suddenly grinned. 'Hang on,' he said. 'As a matter of fact something weird *did* happen to me today.'

'What?' Nige asked, alarmed.

'Well, you know Mo? That skinhead who goes around with Rusty? He bought me a drink at lunchtime.'

There was another silence. Though Robin's experience had not been quite what they were anticipating, both Richard and Nige were stunned.

At last Richard said, 'Are you joking?'

Robin grinned and shook his head.

'It must have been poisoned then,' said Nige.

'Ha! Ha! Funny,' replied Robin. 'No, as a matter of fact he's started working at the supermarket. He was pretty mean last night, but he was really friendly today. He's not as bad as you think, once you get to know him.'

'Did he say anything about Neil?' Richard asked quickly.

'No, not really. He just smiled when I mentioned he would be here tonight.'

'You told him Neil was coming here?'

'Yeah, why not? I've told you, Rich, he's all right.'

Richard said nothing. He looked around for his brother and spotted him on the dance-floor with a fifth-form girl. Despite Robin's assurances, he felt uneasy. He couldn't quite believe that outside Rusty's jurisdiction Mo was just a normal, friendly guy. He had seen Mo on his own, and in his opinion the skinhead didn't need Rusty's influence to make him mean and dangerous.

'Party's really getting going now,' Nige said, tapping the table in time to the music.

Richard nodded. He tried to put Rusty and Mo out of his mind, but glanced round nervously every time someone came through the door. He reassured himself with the thought that even if Rusty and his cronies did make a surprise appearance, there were plenty of people here to deal with them. Most of the squad of the sixth-form rugby team, for instance, who were sitting around a table sagging with beer glasses; or even some of the dads who were clomping awkwardly with their wives on the dance-floor. And then of course there were the barstaff, especially the head barman, who was so large his white shirt looked in danger of bursting apart at the seams. Yes, thought Richard, relaxing, with such a display of brawn Rusty and Mo wouldn't dare show their faces tonight.

'I'm getting another drink,' said Robin. 'Do you want one?'

Richard gave up his empty glass. 'Yes please. Bitter.'

'Nige?'

Nige was struggling with the last quarter of his pint. He drained it at last, wiped his mouth and burped. 'Lager, please,' he said. Robin took the glass and joined the crush in front of the bar.

The boys looked round as a cheer erupted from the rugby table. A boy with permed hair jumped up, beer dripping from his white shirt. A girl who was collecting empty glasses tutted disgustedly and went to the bar for a towel.

'Come along, boys, we're going to do the Chicken Dance,' Mrs Leeman said, appearing from nowhere. Richard groaned inwardly, but managed to smile.

'We'll be right there, Mrs Leeman,' he said, hoping it would get rid of her. He hated the Chicken Dance. It was a novelty record where the general idea was to cluck and flap imaginary wings. 'We're just waiting for a friend of ours to come back from the bar,' he explained.

'Well, don't be too long now,' she said, 'we want as many people as we can get.' She bustled away to requisition another group.

Nige smiled at Richard. Both boys felt superior, too adult to be organized. Smoke was rising in the room like swirls of pure colour under the disco lights. Bodies gyrated languidly on the dance-floor to a slow song. Robin returned with the drinks.

'Here we are,' he said, setting the glasses down. He passed Nige the one which contained the lightest liquid. 'There, that's yours.'

The Chicken Dance began. People flapped wings and strutted around imaginary farmyards. The deejay stilled the music half-way through to see how loud everyone could cluck. The rugby table clapped and wolf-whistled every time a girl in a leather mini-skirt squatted to lay an egg.

'Christ,' Robin muttered, and cowered behind his pint to avoid conscription. Richard and Nige did the same.

The dance was soon over. People drifted back to their tables or to the bar for refreshment. The deejay announced, 'We'll be having a break for food in about five minutes, but first here's a song especially for our birthday boy, Dennis. It's Stevie Wonder and *Happy Birthday To You*.'

The song began; people danced. When it was over the lights came up, the doors to the buffet room were opened and a queue began to form. Inside, Richard met Neil.

'What's her name, then?' he said as they waited with paper plates.

'Lisa,' replied Neil. The food came into reach and he selected two sausage rolls. 'She's all right, isn't she?'

'Not bad,' Richard said with a grin. 'Where is she now? Not hungry?'

'Nah, she's gone to the bog. I'm keeping a place for her.'

The boys piled their plates with sandwiches, sausage rolls, crisps, chicken legs, vol-au-vents, pizza. When the plates couldn't hold any more they went back to their table and began to eat.

After the food they were full, though Richard went to the bar and bought more drinks. By the time the plates had been cleared away and the music started again, he was feeling quite woozy.

'Are we gonna dance or what?' Nige said, swaying like a marionette. His alcohol threshold was even lower than Richard's; twice he had almost knocked his drink over.

'You'd have trouble walking, never mind dancing,' Richard said.

Nige waved his hand vaguely. 'Rubbish,' he argued, and belched, jerking upwards in his seat. Richard began to snigger uncontrollably.

'Shaddup,' Nige said, though he was sniggering too. He reached over and grabbed Robin's arm. 'Come on, Rob, let's go and chat up some birds. Let's go and have a good old boogie.'

186

Robin disengaged Nige's fingers. As the evening had progressed he'd become more and more introverted. 'Nah, there aren't any decent birds here,' he growled. 'I'd rather just get pissed.'

'Rubbish,' Nige said, and almost overbalanced as he leaned forward. He put out a hand and patted Robin's shoulder. 'C'mon, Rob, cheer up.' He tried to stand, but bumped his thighs on the table as he did so and sat down again, giggling. Abruptly Robin jumped up, pushing his chair back with a screech.

'I'm off for a piss,' he snarled, and stalked out of the room.

'Wass wrong with him?' Nige said muzzily.

'Aw, you know how he gets when he's had a few pints. He wants a girlfriend, but he won't talk to any 'cos he thinks they'll laugh at his spots or be disgusted by him or something.'

'He doesn't wanna worry about that. Lotsa people have spots.'

'Yeah, I know,' said Richard, 'but you try telling Rob that.'

7

The foyer was cool and quiet after the party. Robin stood for a moment, the faint smell of chlorine and sweat in his nostrils. Frustration had almost choked him in there, had almost pushed him into taking his anger out on Nige. When he felt calmer he made his way to the toilet.

As he urinated, thoughts of his own inadequacy tormented him. Why didn't he talk to girls? Why didn't he just go right up and talk to them? Because he was ugly, that was why. He was a freak, a junk-food leper. Why, oh why, did it have to be him who was so hideously disfigured? Why couldn't it have been some other poor sod?

He looked in the mirror and felt sick. His spots seemed redder than ever, as though they'd been feeding on the beer and converting it into pus. Below his battlefield of a face, his smart clothes looked grotesque. What was that old saying: You can't dress mutton up as lamb? In Robin's case it seemed depressingly appropriate.

He sighed as he washed his hands. Just give it time, his mother had said, it's only a phase, lots of people go through it. But here he was, his youth ebbing away, and with each day that passed his torment only increased.

When he came out of the toilet he heard voices raised in anger and looked round. Outside the entrance doors a group of boys were arguing with the moustached man from the desk. Thinking they were just kids, Robin was about to turn away, but before he could do so one of the boys struck a match. Robin looked again, his attention drawn by the spark of flame, and his stomach tightened. In the sudden flare of yellow light he saw a greasy mop of ginger hair, and beneath it the hard, brutal features of Rusty.

Instantly he remembered Richard's words, 'You told him Neil was coming here?' and he went cold all over. 'Oh, shit,' he murmured, glancing at the functions' room door. 'Oh bloody hell.' He stood, undecided, wondering what to do. Should he try and handle things himself, or go back to the party and fetch reinforcements? Part of his mind desperately wanted to believe that the boys meant no harm, that they had simply come to join in the fun; but the frightened, unhappy face of the man standing defensively in front of the doors told him otherwise. Rusty and his cronies looked mean and nasty; they had come here to fight. And Robin saw that Mo was with them, his head like a suede egg in the moonlight.

He was still hovering, uncertain, when Mo looked up and saw him. Immediately the skinhead came forward and banged on the glass.

'Oi, Rob,' he yelled, the words jetting out as vapour, 'come out here a minute.'

Unwillingly Robin walked towards the glass doors, limbs stiff with nervousness. 'I should be getting help,' he was thinking, 'I shouldn't be walking towards them like this, I should be getting help.' His mind jittered, nervous as a trapped moth. 'Lamb to the slaughter,' he thought crazily. 'Mutton dressed as lamb to the slaughter.'

His hand closed around the thick steel handle and tugged. The heavy door groaned open and he stepped out into the night.

It was the cold that hit him first, squeezing his face, clawing at his ears. It was as though the six figures standing before him were icemen, breathing out winter. Robin glanced at the moustached man and saw fear and gratitude on his face.

'What's up, Mo?' he asked as casually as he could, then coughed as cigarette smoke, blue and harsh in the cold air, caught at his throat.

Mo plucked the cigarette stub from his mouth and dropped it on the floor. He brought his heel down, killing it. 'It's this pillock here,' he said, jabbing at the moustached man's face, forcing him to flinch back, 'he won't let us join the party.'

Robin tried a sympathetic smile, but felt as though tics were hatching out under his face, transforming it into a twitching mask. 'Yeah, I'm sorry, Mo,' he said, shrugging, 'but it's invitations only, I'm afraid. It's not my party you see. If it was there'd be no problem, but . . . well . . . I don't really have any say in who comes in and who doesn't.'

He glanced round at the other boys, looking at them properly for the first time. As well as Rusty and Mo, Ratz was there, creaking in a leather jacket, and three others in their late teens whom Robin had never seen before. One of them was enormously fat with a scrappy beard and piggy eyes set in rolls of flesh. Robin looked away from the eyes with a shudder, but still felt them boring into him like knives dissecting his nerves.

Mo spat on the floor and leaned forward conspiratorially. 'Come on, Rob,' he wheedled, 'who's gonna know if you just let us in? I mean there must be – what? – a hundred and fifty people in there? A few more won't make much difference.' He put a hand on Robin's shoulder and leaned closer still. 'Come on, whaddya say?'

Robin tried not to flinch at Mo's touch. The threat from the group was almost tangible, and Robin felt his nerves tingling, his stomach tying itself into knots. Clearing his throat, he said, 'Look, Mo, it isn't up to me. And besides, most of the people in there are from school. They'd recognize you straight away; they'd know you hadn't been invited.' He paused, glanced at Rusty who was squinting through cigarette smoke. 'Neil Gardener's in there,' he continued, 'and most of his rugby mates, and . . . well . . . I mean, you lot don't exactly get on with them do you?'

Rusty's voice suddenly cut in, harsh and mean as a blade. 'Aw, come on, I'm sick of this, let's go in.' And before anyone could react, he grabbed the moustached man by the throat and shoved him roughly aside.

Taken by surprise, the man staggered, almost regained his balance, then sprawled to the ground. Before he could get up the fat, bearded thug lumbered over and began to kick him.

Robin was appalled, not so much by the violence, but by the suddenness of it. He had time to do nothing, not even to think, before a fist like a mallet blocked his vision and slammed him back against the glass doors. Curiously he felt no immediate pain – his adrenalin was pumping too hard to allow it – but he did feel fear as the glass doors shuddered under the impact of his body. He scrabbled for the door handle as Mo swung for him again. This time he saw the blow coming and partly parried it with his free hand. Then the door opened inwards behind him and he fell into the lobby.

8

'I don't feel too good,' Nige groaned, and slumped over the table, arms out before him.

'You're not going to be sick again, are you?' Richard said. He remembered Christmas Eve all too well. Mrs Figg

190

had almost hit the roof when her son had come home with vomit down his shirt.

Nige's head moved slightly on the table. 'No,' he groaned, and turned away to show that the exchange was at an end.

Light spilled suddenly into the room as the door leading to the foyer was flung open. Richard stood up as Robin staggered through, blood pouring from his nose. 'Rob, what's—?' he began, but the words dried in his throat when he saw Rusty coming through the doorway behind Robin.

Heads turned to look at the new arrivals. People stopped dancing and peered nervously round to see what was going on. Richard saw Neil across the room speak urgently to Lisa, then put a hand on her shoulder and rise from his seat.

'Gardener!' Rusty screamed, and his voice cut into the music like a discordant note. 'Where the fuck are you, Gardener?'

Richard cowered behind the table, his stomach turning over. Robin was being seen to by two girls, who had dragged him away from the dance-floor and were now using handkerchiefs to wipe the blood from his face. The music stopped abruptly, executed in mid-sentence, 'Baby, I Love—', though the disco lights still fluttered, soaking the scene in gaudy, nervous colour.

'Come on Gardener!' Rusty yelled, veins bulging in his temples. 'Come and fight!'

People had now begun to take in the scene, to make sense of the confusion. The head barman threw down the cloth with which he'd been wiping glasses and bore down threateningly on the group.

'Right you lot, out!' he ordered, pointing at the door. Almost in unison six hands reached into back pockets. There were half a dozen dry clicks, and suddenly six flick-knives were glinting and flashing under the lights.

'You gonna make us?' Rusty said quietly.

The barman halted, the anger on his face now diluted with a wary fear. 'Come on, lads,' he said, his tone changing, 'put those things away and get out before the coppers get here.'

'Go fuck yourself,' Rusty snarled. 'We're not leaving till we've seen Neil Gardener.'

Richard was still crouching behind the table. Across the room he saw the rugby team eyeing the knives and debating quietly. Neil was still standing up, but for now he was just one of a hundred shadowy figures.

'Come on, Gardener,' Rusty said, addressing the room at large, 'either you come out now or we're gonna come lookin' for you.' He flicked the knife from side to side as though to indicate they would literally cut through the crowd to find their quarry.

'No,' Richard breathed as he saw Neil begin to move. He watched, sickened, as his brother made his way between the tables and out on to the dance-floor.

Rusty grinned slowly, eyes bright. He took a step towards Neil, waving the knife in front of him as though cutting slices from the damp air. 'Come on, Gardener,' he purred, and jabbed forward, the blade gleaming as the lights splashed it with colour.

Neil swallowed, looking from the knife to Rusty's face. There was a tremor in his voice as he spoke, but the words were mocking.

'You're so brave aren't you, Rusty?' he said. 'Six of you with knives versus me. That's what I call really fair. What's the matter? Are you too scared to fight me on your own?'

Rusty's face twisted. 'Fuck all that!' he spat. He indicated his nose which was still swollen and bruised. 'You're gonna pay for this,' he said, 'and you'll have more than just a fuckin' broken nose by the time I've finished with you.' Without warning he lunged forward, slashing out with the knife. There were a few gasps and screams as Neil jumped back, almost falling over his own feet. The knife made a slit in his shirt across the stomach and nicked the skin beneath. A tiny spot of blood appeared on the material and began to blossom slowly.

'You fucking moron!' Neil screamed, but now there was real panic in his voice.

Rusty laughed and moved forward, his gang following like obedient dogs.

People now began to stand up and rush out on to the dance-floor, shocked into action. The gang slashed out on all sides with their knives, effectively keeping a distance between themselves and the incensed crowd. One man who ventured too close was gashed badly across the arm and leaped back with a cry of pain. He staggered to a seat and sat down, his blood black under the disco lights.

Neil was backing up against the stage. Behind him the deejay watched the scene in horror.

'Got you now, you cunt,' Rusty snarled and leaped forward. At the same instant one of the rugby players jumped up on to a table and hurled a glass, which came sailing through the air and shattered against the stage. Although it missed Rusty, it distracted him just long enough for Neil to act.

Throwing himself forward, Neil took Rusty round the legs in a perfect rugby tackle. Rusty fell back, banging his head on the floor. Before he could recover, Neil leaped on top of him, snatching at the hand that held the knife. Rusty bucked and struggled frenziedly, spitting like a wild animal. Neil punched him in the face to quell him, then succeeded in grabbing his arm and pinning it to the floor.

'Watch out!' he heard someone scream suddenly. Instinctively he ducked and half-turned. Out of the corner of his eye he saw a flash of steel and then something cold and hard struck him on the back. He didn't realize he'd been stabbed until he saw Mo pull away, the knife in his hand trailing blood.

All at once his arms and legs felt weak and sickly; his head spun. Rusty struggled easily out from beneath him and Neil fell sideways, thinking he was going to faint. Somewhere nearby a distorted, roaring voice formed the words, 'Come on, let's get out,' then drums or pounding feet jarred him, performing a sick tattoo on his dwindling consciousness.

Muzzily he looked up, saw a sea of faces and hands washing over him. Then reality bled away and dissolved into black.

9

Toady was sitting in the armchair in the lounge, knees hunched up to his chin like a goblin on a toadstool. The only light came from *The Curse Of The Werewolf* which was being shown on television for the umpteenth time. Everyone was in bed except for his mother, who was at work; yet even as he wondered what time she would be home, he heard the front door open and she entered, shivering. 'Why aren't you in bed?' she asked him as she stepped into the darkened room.

'I'm just watching the end of this.' Toady's voice was flat, weary.

'What time does it finish?' Pauline asked, squinting at the clock on the mantelpiece.

He followed her gaze to the clock. 'Ten more minutes,' he said.

'All right, I'll go and get dry. Do you want a coffee?'

'Mm, please,' said Toady, turning his gaze back to the screen.

His mother exited, leaving Oliver Reed to rampage about the rooftops.

In fact, Toady was not really watching the film; he was simply postponing the moment of going to bed. He had overcome the seduction that morning by plunging his head underwater and holding it there for as long as possible. When he'd finally come up, gasping for air, the voices had gone, as had the dark bat-like thing at the window. Since then he had kept his mind alert, feeling that if once he lapsed they would start all over again.

'Here we are,' his mother said. She entered the room with two steaming mugs and handed one to Toady. She was dressed in a cream-coloured dressing gown which showed off her long legs. Her hair had been scrubbed semi-dry with a towel. Toady took the mug and sipped gratefully.

His concept of time had been affected too, but as he had been experiencing these chronological shifts all day, they didn't really alarm him any more. Take just now, for instance: it had seemed only a moment since his mother had left the room, but here she was, back already, dried and changed. He glanced at the television. Oliver Reed had been despatched, the credits had rolled, BBC2 had turned to a whining grey – and all, it seemed, in the twinkling of an eye.

'Turn this telly off, it's getting on my nerves,' Pauline said, but she got up to do the job herself. She clicked on a lamp, them came and sat next to her son, picking up her mug from the floor as she did so. 'You look tired, petal,' she said gently, stroking his fringe and feeling his forehead at the same time.

'I'm all right,' Toady said. 'I've been feeling much better today.'

'That's good. You feel cool at any rate, but you're still pale. Have you eaten anything?'

'Yes,' Toady lied.

His mother put her arm around his shoulders and gave him a brief hug. 'Do you think you'll be fit for school on Monday?' she said.

'Oh, yeah,' Toady replied. 'I should be all right by tomorrow. We've got a Horror Club meeting in the afternoon.'

Pauline frowned. 'Yes, well, we'll have to see about that, won't we?'

Toady said nothing. He knew he would get his way; he always did. He drank his coffee, warming his hands on the cup, and then pushed himself up out of the armchair. 'I'm going to bed,' he announced.

Pauline smiled. 'Yes, you go and get a good night's sleep.' She caught him and kissed him on the cheek before he could get away. 'Good night, Adrian.'

'Night, Mum.'

On the stairs he wiped his cheek, still smelling his mother's perfume. Above him the darkness seemed soft and stealthy as a thief. He reached the landing, stepped on to it, then jumped as from behind him there came a whoosh and a soft clattering sound. He smiled at his own nervousness. It was only sleet blowing against the window. The darkness hovered before him, a barrier that threatened to collapse at any moment. Taking a deep breath and drawing his thoughts into himself, Toady stepped into it.

He found himself in a glittering, incandescent cloud, surrounded by sparks of light that were magical, hypnotic, frantic with energy. He squeezed his eyes tight, imagining his mind as a series of heavy doors that were swinging shut against the invader. Around him the cloud fizzed angrily like sherbet mixed with water. The exposed parts of Toady's flesh twitched and crawled as if stung with pinpricks of energy. He clung on to his thoughts, refusing to acknowledge the attempted violation of his shell. If his mind slipped for one moment, the energy would form into recognizable shapes, would come together as the voice of his seductress. Toady was clamped within himself, his only outward probe the hand that groped for the door handle.

He found it, reassuring metal, cold and hard. Putting the whole of himself into the action, he pushed down. The door came open and Toady slipped inside.

His room was a sanctuary – for now. The air was cool and clear as spring water. Toady breathed it in, feeling refreshed, and wondered how powerful his seductress was. Could she take him any time she wished? It was a question he tried not to reflect on too deeply. All he knew was that up to now he had survived; he tried to keep from his mind the thought that maybe his resistance was all just part of some greater plan.

He undressed slowly, put on his pyjamas and climbed into bed. The sheets were cold, clammy, but comforting because they were real. The house today had been a peculiar domain. Only by concentrating had he been able to hold its reality together. It had been like sampling a strong drug and then fighting tooth and nail to keep the hallucinations away. Toady's head ached with the exertion. Within minutes of getting into bed he fell into an exhausted sleep.

He sat up in bed, feeling that things were different. He looked around. His walls were moving.

Toady closed his eyes. 'No,' he murmured, '*I* control *you*. I brought you here. I can send you back.'

He opened his eyes again. His walls were writhing yellow flesh that pulsed with stringy blue veins. Toady could smell their sweat, hot and rancid.

'No,' he said, 'no.' He looked down. The floor was white, uneven, the carpet had disappeared. As he watched, cracks appeared through which poured hundreds of candy-striped spiders. Though they continued to pour through the cracks, they dissolved as they appeared, like vampires thrust into daylight, with little squeals of pain.

The door to his room clicked open. Toady watched as a figure entered, sinister in cape and cowl. The figure limped slowly across the floor until it stood at the foot of his bed.

'Just who *are* you?' Toady whispered, dragging the sheets up to his neck in feeble defence. 'Why are you doing this to me?'

The figure stirred slightly and began to speak. Its voice was hollow, as though it came from inside a cave.

'Don't you know me?' it asked.

Toady shook his head. 'No. No, I don't know you. Please go away.'

The figure ignored the plea. 'You must know me,' it insisted. Limping, it came around the side of the bed. Toady smelt earth and sourness. 'You must know me and I must know you.' The figure raised its arms and, fingers clicking hideously, pulled back its cowl.

Seeing what was before him, Toady's mouth opened, but he was too terrified to scream . . .

. . . and suddenly he awoke, amid sheets that clung like a web.

10

It was several minutes before he could stop shaking.

He lay staring at the ceiling, listening to his own panicked breathing. Around him his bedsheets lay tangled like a skein; his pyjamas were damp and crumpled with sweat. When he moved, his head began to throb thickly as though the dream was still trapped inside.

He struggled to sit up, feeling suddenly claustrophobic. His room was normal, and silent as loneliness. Toady listened for the sound of sleet or his father's snoring, but there was neither. Pushing the sheets away he swung his feet over the side of the bed.

At once the coldness settled on him, turning his sweat to ice. Toady's teeth began to chatter as he took off his pyjamas, peeling the top from his back like flypaper. Despite his nakedness he immediately felt warmer. He padded across the room, switched on the light and pulled open his chest of drawers. Selecting a T-shirt and a pair of clean underpants, he put them on.

Now he felt calmer, more able to think. Sitting in the armchair which faced his bed he looked around the room. All was as it should be. The dream had been terrifying and realistic, but not strong enough to encroach on the reality of his own world. Toady felt pleased, for didn't that mean by waking he had defeated it?

Not for the first time, he wondered how all of this would end. His hope was that by resisting and resisting and resisting he would force the shadow to realize he could not be controlled, would try to make it communicate with him in some other way. Despite his suffering Toady still did not regret the seance at the house. He had wanted communication – still did – but he wanted it on his own (or at least equal) terms. In moments like this, quiet moments, he felt sure he could resist and thus force the shadow to comply. It was only when he was fighting the shadow's insidious attempts at subjugation that he began to have his doubts.

He swallowed and winced. His throat was sore and

inflamed, his mouth dry. His head throbbed, as did his sinuses. Now he felt he really did have flu. He crossed the room to his bedroom door and pulled it open.

The landing beyond was quiet and still. Light struggled behind the curtains. Toady stepped out, feeling the carpet soft beneath his feet, enjoying the sensation of gooseflesh springing up on his arms and legs.

All day he had sensed the shadow in the house – somewhere, lurking – but now the feeling had gone. The house was just a house again – cold, shell-like, empty of influence. Did that mean that by defying the dream he had finally proved his strength? No, he didn't believe that; it seemed too easy. And yet his mind felt freer now than it had done for a long time.

He went down to the kitchen, the lino sending little shocks of cold into his feet. Balancing on his heels he searched through the Rowntrees tin that his mother used as a first aid box. He found two Anadin, put them on his tongue and washed them down with water, gasping as it sent needles of ice into his head. He rinsed out the glass he had drunk from and upended it on the draining board. Then, walking as gingerly as if the floor were littered with razor blades, he left the kitchen.

Still nothing stirred in the house. Toady took the stairs two at a time, feeling new confidence flowing through him. He was beginning to believe that maybe he *had* won after all, that maybe by waking up he *had* finally proved that he could not be manipulated. 'I'll talk to you,' Toady said. 'I'll talk to you as an equal.' The house remained silent, which made him feel as though the shadow was prepared to listen. Increasingly reassured he said, 'We can be friends if you like. We can help each other.'

He continued up the stairs. When he got to the top he pulled back the curtains and looked out. The sleet had mellowed to snow again, which was drifting lazily as though it knew it had all night to complete its task. Already it was painting over the previous layer with a new brightness. Toady watched it for a while, enjoying the soothing effect it was having on his eyes. His headache was beginning to ease; further proof that the shadow was withdrawing, considering his proposal.

After a while he began to get sleepy and cold. Turning reluctantly away from the window, he walked back to his room, thinking with distaste of the damp tangled sheets that awaited him. He decided that the best thing would be to strip them off and get his sleeping bag out of the wardrobe. He would snuggle so far down that not even nightmares would reach him.

As he entered his room, he immediately felt the shadow's presence again. He looked around, his heart thumping with anticipation. Everything seemed normal . . . and yet Toady knew he was not alone.

Suddenly he staggered as the floor tipped beneath his feet. Yes, there was no question now; the shadow was here all right. It had probably been here all along, storing up its energy, waiting for him to return. He tried to keep calm as the room came alive around him.

His walls rippled, unstable as water. Toady put a hand out to one of them and felt his fingers tingle as though electricity was running beneath the plaster. A slight movement drew his attention to the bed. He shivered. It reminded him of a mortuary slab, a single white sheet spread over a still, human form. Suddenly the thing on the bed shifted, and Toady knew that whatever was beneath the sheet was real and alive.

'Well?' he said, his voice trembling with nerves. 'Come on, show yourself.'

The sheet was pulled slowly back and a figure sat up. Its hair was tousled. It wore an inane grin. As Toady saw it he gasped and fell to his knees.

He was looking at himself.

200

PART TWO

Jigsaw Feeling

'Hey, little baby, don't you lean down low
Your brain's exposed, and it's starting to show
Your rotten thoughts, Yuk!'

The Stranglers: *Death and Night and Blood*

CHAPTER ONE

Fragments

1

Starmouth was divided into tones of black and white –
snow and shadow; blank walls and dark side-streets; earth
and sky across which sleet scurried. From the ambulance
Richard saw the moon leering like a giant malevolent
hailstone that threatened to drop and crack open the
planet. He looked away, wincing, as the ambulance jolted
and his brother moaned again.

'All right, son, soon be there now,' the ambulance man
said gently. He reached out and touched Neil's pulse.

Richard saw him frown. 'How is he?' he asked for the
hundredth time. The ambulance man smiled, but there
seemed little conviction in it.

'He's stable, son, try not to worry. I've seen worse than
him survive.'

'But why is he so white?' Richard asked, touching his
brother's face.

'He's in shock,' the ambulance man said. He tried to
sound reassuring. 'It's quite common in cases like this. He
doesn't seem to have lost much blood.'

'What will they do at the hospital?' Richard asked.

'Examine the wound, make sure there's no internal
haemorrhaging. Give him an intravenous infusion.'

'That sounds serious.'

'No, no, it's fairly routine procedure. It's done mainly
to keep the vein open in case of deterioration. Nothing to
worry about.'

The ambulance jolted again as it took a corner, rattling
its interior like loose bones. Richard gripped the metal

struts of the bed he was perched on, clenching his teeth in sympathy as Neil let out a gasp of pain. Landmarks of Starmouth flashed past like an expeditious sightseeing tour: The Town Hall with its columns and its intricate stone-work; the lions which guarded the library; the statue of a soldier who tried to look dignified beneath his coat of bird droppings. The ambulance, wailing, reduced them all to blurs, but still it was too slow for Richard.

Finally, they reached their destination, the ambulance swinging in through the gates of the building, past a large neon sign which said: 'Hospital. Quiet Please'. They came to a halt outside Casualty, the driver pulling up as close as he could to the glass-doored entranceway. He cut the engine, jumped out of his cab, and ran round to the back. The ambulance man with Richard stood up as the doors were opened and night-cold and sleet rushed in like ghoulish voyeurs.

The metal four-wheeled stretcher was lifted quickly out and set down on the snowy ground. Richard jumped from the ambulance just as a white-coated doctor and two nurses came hurrying out of the hospital to help.

'How is he now?' the doctor asked, looking down at Neil's still form. He was a tall imposing figure, gaunt-faced with wiry grey hair swept back from his forehead.

The ambulance man, a shorter, stockier figure, shrugged. 'He's in shock, of course, but he seems fairly stable. He hasn't lost that much blood – less than a pint, I'd say.'

The doctor nodded, his face grim. 'Right, well, we'll get him seen to straight away. Who are you, his friend?' Before Richard could reply, the doctor turned abruptly and led the way inside.

Though Casualty was cosily warm, it made Richard's skin crawl. He had always hated hospitals – the chemical smell, the pristine functional corridors, the aura of human sickness. As a toddler he had swallowed some pills and had had to be rushed in to have his stomach pumped. Though he had no clear memory of the incident, the sight of a hospital's interior always brought a vague nightmarish impression of being held down whilst tubes were pushed down his throat.

He started to follow the stretcher as it was wheeled away, but a nurse took his arm and steered him into Reception, towards a row of back-to-back chairs with skeletal frames and square brown leather seats.

'If you wouldn't mind waiting here,' she said. She gestured at the receptionist, a dark-haired woman in her mid-thirties. 'And could you just give Lynn some of the patient's particulars – name, age, next of kin, that sort of thing?'

'Will Neil be all right?' Richard asked, glancing back at the stretcher as it squeaked out of sight.

The nurse smiled. 'Let's hope so. He's in the best possible hands.' She indicated the machine across the room. 'Would you like a coffee?'

Richard nodded, though he didn't know if he could drink anything, and wandered in a daze to the Reception desk. He mumbled answers to Lynn's questions, then went to sit down. The events of twenty minutes ago were still fresh in his mind; even now the disco lights seemed more real than the antiseptic brightness of the hospital. From somewhere down the corridor he head a clanking sound, footsteps, a phone ringing. 'Here we are,' the nurse said, returning with a plastic cup and handing it to him.

Richard took it, holding it gingerly because the coffee had made the plastic hot and pliable. He sipped, burning his lip. No sugar. The taste was awful.

He put the cup on the floor beside him. 'When will there be any news?' he asked.

The nurse shook her head. 'Not for a while yet. These things take time. Has Lynn phoned Neil's parents?'

'I think so,' Richard said.

'And how about the police? Have they been informed?'

'Erm . . . yeah. Someone at the Sports Centre phoned them.'

The nurse glanced at her watch. 'Have you spoken to them yet?' When Richard shook his head, she said, 'Well, no doubt they'll send someone round, and they'll want to speak to you when they arrive. Do you think you're up to it?'

Richard nodded, though the prospect alarmed him.

'Right, well, I have to go away for a while. You'll be all right here, won't you?'

Left alone, Richard leaned back in his chair and tried not to think about his queasy stomach. The alcohol he'd drunk seemed to sour as he recalled the sound of catches being released, the appearance of blades like gleaming splinters in the gloom. He shuddered, closed his eyes, wishing he could just sleep and find that everything was all right when he woke up. He sighed, opened his eyes, looked about relentlessly. The clock on the wall said six minutes to twelve.

He heard a murmured conversation somewhere down the corridor and turned expectantly. The murmur became a whisper, then faded away altogether. False alarm. Probably the first of many tonight. He sighed, and for want of anything better to do, took off his spectacles and began to clean them with a handkerchief.

A car suddenly pulled up outside, its headlights sweeping the front of the building, and Richard half-rose, thinking it must be his parents or the police. He sat down again, however, when two young men entered, one bleeding badly from a head wound, the other supporting his semi-conscious friend as best he could. A nurse appeared, and, hurrying forward, supported the injured man from the other side.

'That looks nasty,' she said as she ushered him away. 'What happened?'

'Some bugger hit him with a brick,' the friend replied. Their voices and footsteps faded as they moved off down the corridor.

Richard settled into his seat again, feeling numb, staring at the blood that streaked the floor. One of the boys had walked through it and trailed a broken line of red footprints down the corridor. Gulping, Richard closed his eyes; looking at the blood made him feel a little nauseous.

In point of fact, it reminded him of Neil's blood, black and glutinous under the disco lights.

Suddenly he heard a clanking sound and opened his eyes again to seen an orderly approaching with mop and metal bucket. He was in his fifties, small and dumpy, with a crabbed, worn face and hands rough as sandpaper. He began to hum 'Anything You Can Do I Can Do Better' as he wiped up the blood, and Richard smiled to himself despite his anxiety. A few moments later the orderly ambled away and Richard looked up as another car came to a halt outside.

This time he instinctively knew it was his parents. He stood up as he heard the engine die, doors slam, hurrying footsteps. A moment later his mother entered, wearing a headscarf and an old sheepskin coat with a ripped pocket. She looked pinched and drawn and grey, and as soon as she saw Richard her eyes filled with tears.

'Oh, Dickie, Dickie,' she said, hurrying forward, 'are you all right?'

Richard nodded, crushed in a hug. His mother hardly ever called him Dickie any more; it had been his pre-teen name. Hearing it now filled him with love and sadness.

'Yes, Mum, I'm fine,' he croaked, trying to swallow the lump in his throat. He broke away in time to see his father enter, 'brring' from the cold, brushing sleety snow from his overcoat. His father came across, a well-built, straight-backed man with a clipped moustache and prematurely grey hair that made him look steely and dignified rather than old. Unconsciously imitating his wife, he asked: 'You all right, son?'

'Yes, Dad, fine,' Richard said.

Derek Gardener nodded in approval, and rubbing his hands together, perused his surroundings. 'Where've they taken Neil?' he asked.

'I don't know,' replied Richard. 'The bloke in the ambulance said he'd need an invenus infusion.'

'Intravenous,' his father corrected automatically. 'A blood transfusion, you mean.'

207

'A blood transfusion!' Eileen gasped. 'Did he . . . did he lose a lot of . . . blood then?'

'No, not all that much,' Richard said cautiously. 'The ambulance man told me that having a blood transfusion was fairly routine in things like this. He said it was to keep the vein open or something.'

'Yes, well, he would say that,' Eileen said. She reached out and clutched her husband's sleeve. 'Oh, God, Derek, can't you talk to someone? Ask how he is?'

Derek nodded and strode over to the reception desk where Lynn was now embroiled in a crossword. Richard and Eileen sat down, he slipping an arm around his mother's shoulders.

'He'll be all right, Mum, don't worry,' he said.

Eileen responded with a tearful smile. 'How . . . how did it happen?' she asked.

'It was that Rusty and his mates – you know, the ones we had a fight with the other day? They gatecrashed the party and they all had knives. Rusty was after Neil 'cos of Neil busting his nose.'

'Well, the police'll have to be told now,' Eileen said. 'We can't let this happen again.'

'They've been told. They should be here pretty soon.'

Eileen sighed and sniffed. 'Was anyone else hurt?'

'Someone got his arm cut, but I don't think it was serious.'

Derek returned and sat down on the other side of his wife.

'Any news?' she asked.

'He's in radiology at the moment, having X-rays on one of his vertebrae. It'll be a while before there's any news. If he has to have an operation we may be here most of the night.'

'But how is he? Is he going to be all right?' Richard detected a hint of panic in his mother's voice.

'They don't know, love. We'll just have to wait and see.' Derek gave his wife a squeeze and turned to Richard. 'Is there somewhere I can get a coffee in this place? I'm parched.'

Richard indicated the machine on the wall and his father moved away. A few minutes later he returned, his teeth gritted against the hot plastic that burned his fingers. He gave a cup of insipid looking tea to his wife and placed his own cup, which seemed to contain milky sludge, on the floor beside him. Settling back in his seat, he asked, 'How did all this happen then, son?'

Richard groaned. 'Do you mind if we just leave it for now, Dad?' he said. 'The police'll be here soon. You can hear all about it when I tell them.'

Derek nodded. 'All right, if that's what you want.'

Richard looked at his father as he sipped his coffee, unbuttoned his coat, and suddenly he found himself admiring him in a way he had not admired him since childhood. His father had aways been calm and practical, never prone to extreme emotions, but this was the first time Richard had ever seen him in a real family crisis. He admired now his patience, his understanding, his sensitivity. Without his father's influence, low-key though it was, he was certain he and his mother would be wearing one another down with worry. In that instant he wanted to give his father a hug, but he didn't really know how. He knew his father loved him, but he had never been a man who expressed his love physically and Richard wondered how he would react to such a show of affection. He was still wondering moments later when the police arrived.

Richard saw the reflection of the headlights first, fluttering across the walls. Once again, he heard doors slam, footsteps padding across the snow-covered carpark, crunching on the gravel beneath. A moment later two policemen entered, large and dark in their uniforms.

'Evening, Sergeant Glennon,' Lynn said as they removed their hats and stamped the snow from their boots. The larger and older of the policemen, a solid figure with curly red hair and a chin like Desperate Dan's, came forward.

'Good evening, Lynn,' he replied. 'How's it been tonight? Quiet?'

'Yes, very. A few broken bones because of the weather, but most people seem to have had the good sense to stay indoors.'

Glennon nodded and turned to his younger blond companion. 'Pop and get us a cuppa would you, Kev? One sugar, not much milk.'

The young policeman called Kev rolled his eyes. 'Bloody tea-boy, that's all I am to him,' he said, addressing the Gardeners. Richard smiled and the young constable smiled back.

Sergeant Glennon looked at Richard. 'You're not Richard Gardener by any chance, are you?'

Richard nodded, nervous in spite of himself.

'Ah!' said Glennon, and placed his cap on the reception desk. 'Just the feller we wanted to see.' He lifted a moulded plastic chair from a stack against the wall and set it down so he could speak to Richard face to face. 'And I assume you're the boys' parents?' he said, turning to Derek and Eileen.

'That's right, yes,' Derek said.

Glennon turned to take his tea from Bailey. 'Have you had any news of Neil yet?'

When Derek shook his head, Glennon pulled a sympathetic face and said, 'Perhaps you'd like to tell me in your own words exactly what happened, Richard?'

Richard smiled nervously and began, recounting the evening's events in a low, halting voice. He felt tired and rather intimidated by his close, intent audience. He was aware that Glennon was watching him thoughtfully, sipping his tea, occasionally putting the cup down to jot something in his notebook. When Richard had finished his account, Glennon glanced quickly at his notes and asked, 'This "Rusty"? Am I right in assuming his real name is Steven Oates?'

Richard nodded.

'Is this boy known to you, sergeant?' Derek asked.

'Oh yes, sir, I'm afraid he is. He's a regular trouble-maker – a real bad lad.'

'Do you know where to find him?' Eileen asked.

'Yes, madam, we have all his particulars. We shouldn't have too much trouble picking him up.' He paused to consult his notebook again, at the same time draining the last dregs from his cup. 'Are you sure,' he said, 'that it was Maurice Landen – Mo – who actually stabbed your brother? Nobody at the Sports Centre seemed too certain.'

'Yes, I . . . I'm fairly sure it was,' Richard said. 'Neil was sitting on Rusty's chest, trying to grab his knife, when it happened, so it couldn't have been him. Yes, I'm fairly positive it was Mo who came up behind him.'

'OK,' said Glennon, 'not to worry. We'll find out for certain later on. Now, do you know the names of any of the others who were there?'

'Ratz. He's Polish. His name's Krystof something. He's in the fifth-form at school.'

'Yes, we have his name – Krystof Wlodarczyk – but it's the names of the three others I'm really after. Any idea who they were?'

'No,' said Richard. 'I didn't know any of them.'

'Descriptions?'

Richard shrugged. 'They were older than Rusty – eighteen, nineteen, I'd say. One of them was big and fat and had a beard. I didn't really notice the other two.'

Glennon nodded and closed his notebook. 'Right, well, I think that should be enough. We'll find out who the others are when we pick up Oates and Landen and the Polish boy. Thanks very much, Richard. We'll let you know how we get on.'

Richard smiled, relieved that it was over. Perhaps now he could get some rest, maybe even sleep – he certainly felt tired enough. Despite Neil's injury, the knowledge that Glennon and his partner were on their way to pick up Rusty's mob cheered him considerably. He began to think that maybe his wish would be granted after all; maybe he *would* wake up in the morning to find that everything was all right again.

The next two hours passed in a dreamy blur. Richard dozed fitfully in his seat, constantly drifting between sleep and wakefulness. He remembered episodes only as vague and hazy snatches of memory: the nurse who told him that Neil was undergoing surgery and that it might be best if they went home and waited for a phone call; the boy in the dressing gown who entered in a wheelchair with an inflatable splint around his leg; a doctor who ran into casualty, coat flying, and hared down the corridor. When Richard was finally shaken awake by his mother at twenty past three, he wondered how many of these events had actually taken place.

'What's up?' he said, coming out of his doze, the words thick as old leather in his mouth.

'Neil's out of surgery,' Eileen said. 'A nurse has just told us that the doctor should be along in a minute to let us know how he is.'

Richard came awake, squinting his eyes against the glare. His back and neck were throbbing, his legs a tingling ants' nest of pins and needles. He stood up, stretching and groaning and stamping his feet, then went across to the drinks machine for something that would make his mouth feel real again. He selected hot chocolate with sugar, which in the time it took him to reach his seat had formed a thin membranous skin. Scooping it out with his finger, Richard drank. The chocolate was sickly and gritty, but he was grateful for the sensation of hot liquid in his mouth.

He looked up as he heard footsteps approaching, and his heart began to thud as he recognized the grey-haired doctor who had been attending Neil. The doctor looked haggard and weary; the lines in his face seemed to be grooved a little deeper than before. Richard began to feel sick as he strode towards them.

'Mr and Mrs Gardener?' he said when he was close enough.

212

'Yes,' said Derek warily.

'I'm Doctor Padwell. I'm pleased to tell you that your son is going to be all right. We've given him a blood transfusion and a thorough examination, and stitched him up. He's sleeping now and will probably do so for another twelve hours. The wound was not as bad as we first thought. No major organs were punctured, although the knife did grind against one of his vertebrae and he'll probably be very sore for a while. We'll keep him in hospital for four or five days, perhaps a week, until he's healed. In the meantime I suggest you all go home and get some sleep. You look as though you need it.'

Derek closed his eyes and exhaled, then stood up and gripped the doctor's hand. 'Thank you, doctor,' he said. 'Thank you very much indeed.'

Eileen began to weep again and Richard put a hand on her shoulder. He felt elated, almost giddy with joy. He wanted desperately to express his gratitude to the tall grey-haired man standing before him, but could think of no superlative strong enough. Instead he contented himself by simply nodding in agreement with his father's thanks.

'Can we see Neil before we go?' Eileen asked, dabbing away tears.

Padwell shook his head. 'Not now if you don't mind. As I say, he's had a traumatic evening and is thoroughly exhausted. I suggest you come back tomorrow afternoon. He should be awake by then.'

Richard could see that his mother was dissatisfied with that, but before she could say anything his father interceded. 'That's all right, doctor, we quite understand. Well, thank you once again for all you've done. We really do appreciate it.'

They got up to leave, and after a further round of goodbyes, trooped out into the carpark. Richard felt so exhausted that not even the sleet and the cold could revive him. As he climbed into the car he thought that, like Neil, he too could sleep for twelve hours, and *he* wouldn't need an anaesthetic to help him. As his father started the engine, Richard closed his eyes. He was asleep before they'd even pulled out of the carpark.

2

Sunday

As Nige had expected, his mother was waiting up for him when he got home. He could see a lamp glowing behind the sitting room curtain like a luminous stain on the material. Leaning over the front seat of the car, he pointed.

'That's my house, Mr Treadwell; the one there with the light on.'

Robin's father nodded and pulled into the kerb with a whoosh of snow.

Nige got out, thanked Robin's father for the lift and said his goodbyes. Robin, sitting subdued in the passenger seat, murmured something in reply. Nige watched as the car pulled away and drove off down the road. Then he stood for a few moments, face upturned to the sleet in the hope that its freshness would clear his mind.

At the party the drink had made him largely unaware of what was going on. He recalled chaotic images – shouts, screams, the sound of breaking glass. Only when the fracas was over – when the lights had come on and the ambulance was on its way – had he really come to his senses. And then the sight of Neil's blood pooled and smeared across the dance-floor had sent him scuttling to the toilet to be sick.

For a time the shock had sobered him, but now the alcohol was beginning to buzz again. Nige shook his head to clear it, rubbed snow into his face, cupped his hands over his mouth to see if he could smell beer on his breath. If his mother found out he'd been drinking she'd go mad. Both she and his father were virtual teetotallers, and, especially since Christmas Eve when he'd come home from Robin's drunk and covered with his own vomit, she'd put an unconditional ban on his intake of alcohol. Feeling a little unsteady Nige walked up the garden path, and let himself quietly into the house with the keys he'd sneaked from his father's coat pocket.

'Nigel,' his mother called as soon as he stepped through the door. He groaned. She must have radar for ears; either that or she'd had an alarm installed underneath the doormat.

With a heavy heart he approached the sitting room and pushed the door open. His mother was curled up in an armchair with a Barbara Cartland paperback in one hand and a half-eaten chocolate biscuit in the other.

Forcing a smile, Nige said, 'Hello, Mum. You still up?'

'I waited up for you,' Mrs Figg said. 'How did you get in?'

'Dad lent me his keys,' Nige lied smoothly. 'Everyone else in bed?'

'Yes, your father went an hour ago. I haven't seen Mr Robespierre all evening. Did you have a nice time?'

'Mmm,' said Nige, and made a big show of yawning and stretching. 'I'm really whacked though. I think I'll go up to bed myself.'

Mrs Figg frowned. 'I'd prefer it if you didn't use words like that, Nigel. It's vulgar.'

'Words like what, Mum?'

'Like . . . like what you just said.'

'Whacked, you mean?'

'Nigel!' Mrs Figg snapped. 'You don't have to repeat it.'

'But it's not swearing. It just means tired, exhausted. It's not like saying knackered.'

'Nigel!' Mrs Figg exclaimed, shocked. Nige closed his mouth. His mother said primly, 'If you feel tired then please say so, but I don't want to hear any of this . . . this uncouth street-talk from you. I expect you pick it up from Richard Gardener and those other boys you go around with. Your father and I certainly never use such terms.'

Nige sighed, but said nothing. He didn't want to get into another argument with his mother this evening.

'Come and help me up,' Mrs Figg said, stretching out a hand. She waggled her fingers at him as though in grotesque enticement.

Nige left his place by the door and moved into the room. As always the fire was blazing, the room like a hothouse. Perhaps his parents were really reptiles, he thought, perhaps they needed the heat to survive. He grasped his mother's podgy pink hand and pulled her up. It was a difficult manoeuvre: she had to rock backwards and forwards to gain momentum before heaving herself to her feet.

'Have you been drinking?' she said as her face came level with his.

Nige shook his head guiltily. 'No.'

'Well, what's that I can smell on your breath, then?' she said.

'Coke, I suppose?' replied Nige, turning away.

'Are you sure?' his mother asked suspiciously.

'Of course I'm sure. I've had Coke, that's all. That must be what you can smell.'

Mrs Figg plucked at her son's sleeve. 'Just come here and breathe on me. I want to know if you're telling the truth.'

'No,' Nige said, and stepped back from her sausage-thick pincers. 'I've been drinking Coke, Mum, that's all. If you don't believe me, that's too bad. I'm going up to bed now, I'm very tired. Good night.'

He turned and began to walk across the room. Behind him his mother said, 'All right Nigel, there's no need to take offence. I wasn't accusing you.'

He sighed and turned to face her. She was smiling obsequiously.

'I just worry about you, that's all,' she said.

Nige smiled back, though it was a strain. 'You don't have to. I'm old enough to look after myself now. I'm not a little kid any more.'

His mother wobbled over and began to pick strands of fluff from the shoulder of his jacket. 'I know that, Nigel, but you're still my son, and I've still got to do what I think is best. This is an important time of life for you. You've got your GCSE's in two years. I don't want you getting in with the wrong crowd and throwing away the chance of making something of yourself.' She touched his cheek. Nige felt smothered by her perfume.

'I'm not in with the wrong crowd,' he said a little tetchily. 'Richard and Rob are hardly juvenile delinquents. They come from good homes, they work hard at school, they've never been in any sort of trouble. I mean, what more do you want?'

Mrs Figg pouted. 'I just think you can do better for yourself, that's all,' she said. 'Since you started being friendly with those boys you've become more impertinent, you've started using slang, you go out a lot more than you used to. I'm just a little worried, that's all. Lord knows, jobs are hard enough to come by these days as it is. If you don't get your exams you'll have no chance of finding work. You'll end up on the slagheap like the rest of the layabouts.'

Nige gritted his teeth. 'I'm sorry if you think I'm impertinent, Mum,' he said. 'I don't mean to be, and it's got nothing to do with my friends. I'm just growing up, that's all. I need more freedom, more independence. I've tried to explain to you a hundred times, but you don't seem to understand.' He broke off. He could see he was not really getting through. During his little speech, his mother's pout had grown more and more pronounced so that she now resembled a spoiled schoolgirl. 'Oh, I'm off to bed,' he sighed. 'I'm really tired. Good night.'

'Good night,' Mrs Figg said sulkily. As Nige opened the sitting room door she added, 'Now you be quiet when you go upstairs. Mr Robespierre's asleep.'

Nige slipped out of the room and hurried upstairs. He knew that his mother would be busy for the next few minutes – pulling out all the plugs, meticulously checking that the doors and windows were locked – and he wanted to be in bed before she came up. On the top landing he could hear his father snoring and the murmur of a television from next door. In the bathroom, whilst brushing his teeth, he wondered how Neil was, and felt a pang of guilt at the thought that Richard was probably still at the hospital, worrying himself sick. Nige hadn't told his mother about the stabbing because he knew it would add fuel to her argument that he went around with a bunch of delinquents.

He heard the sitting room door close and his mother puffing and panting as she began to climb the stairs. Hastily washing his mouth out, Nige switched off the bathroom light and sprinted across the landing to his bedroom.

A wall of heat hit him as he entered. His mother had turned the radiator full on. Nige turned it down, taking care not to touch the hot metal, and crossed the room to open his window. However, when he got there he decided against it; in this weather the room would cool soon enough. Outside, the snow and the streetlamps produced a deadening luminosity that made the landscape seem soundless, somehow lunar. From his window Nige could just see the sea, a tiny triangle of it trapped between the sloping rooftops of two buildings. It looked black and oily, discernible only by the shards of moonlight reflected in the moving water. He shivered. Despite the warmth of his room the sight made him feel cold; the thought of its depthlessness chilled him. He stretched out a hand to the curtains, and then suddenly went rigid.

From the corner of his eye he could see a figure standing in the garden below, looking up at him. It seemed bloated, its unfinished features like slabs of lard. Nige looked down, apprehension causing him to screw up the curtain in his clenched fist.

His heart skipped, then quietened. Relief made him smile. It was only the snowman that he and Richard had made that morning, and it wasn't looking up at his window at all. In fact, it must have been his imagination that had conjured the impression of a face, for all Nige could see was the top of the pink beret that was perched on the snowman's head.

Still smiling, he pulled his curtains across. They were patterned with large blue roses, the same as his wallpaper. He grimaced. He didn't like his room; it reflected his mother's personality, not his. He much preferred Richard's room – cluttered, untidy, the walls covered in posters. Nige's mother didn't allow him to have posters, only a couple of framed pictures and a cork board above his desk where he could stick photographs and stuff. She didn't allow clutter either; at least twice a day she came in to tidy up and threw out anything she considered superfluous to his needs. Conkers, comics, horror novels, weirdly shaped bottles and shells from the beach – all went out with the trash if not carefully hidden. As a result, Nige felt constantly under siege. Feeling resentful, he undressed, put on his pyjamas and climbed into bed. He lay for a moment, staring at the ceiling before switching off the bedside lamp his mother always left on for him. Immediately he felt sleepy, as though the disappearing light had taken his alertness with it. He was wondering how Neil was when he fell asleep.

The landing was dark and chilly. Nige blinked. How had he got here? He looked around for the door of his room, but the dark seemed to swallow everything up. He realized he couldn't even remember where his room was supposed to be, and shook his head, deciding he must still be disoriented by sleep. He put out his hand to the wall and groped along it, looking for the door handle.

All at once his hand bumped against a solid object. Nige clutched at it eagerly. It had felt almost as though the handle had grown from the wall, but of course the darkness and his sleep-muffled mind must be responsible for that illusion.

The silence was cloying, heavy; Nige felt wrapped in a thick, invisible blanket. Suddenly, permeating the silence, came a sound: a high mewling cry like a lost cat or a baby. Nige stood still, listening hard. Though the sound had been close, it had reached his ears only faintly, fighting its way through a wall of silence.

'Who . . . who's there?' Nige called. His own voice seemed lost, reduced to a feeble buzz in the dense quiet. However, whether in answer to his query or not, the mewling cry suddenly came again.

'Help! Help me!' were the words Nige heard, and the voice was unbearable, heart-rending. He gasped and put a hand to his throat; he couldn't help but respond to it.

'Where are you? I can't see you. Please tell me where you are.'

This time the reply was immediate. 'Here. Behind the door.'

Suddenly, Nige knew that the voice belonged to Robespierre. 'The poor man,' he thought, 'what's happening to him in there?' Without a moment's hesitation, he turned the handle and pushed inwards.

He gasped. There was nothing beyond the door except an absolute blackness; a void of purest night. Cautiously Nige stretched out a hand, and although there was no sensation, the blackness swallowed it like mud. He felt his heart thudding. Robespierre was somewhere in here and he was in trouble. There was no alternative but to look for him.

Nige stepped into the room and began to walk forward. He could see nothing, hear nothing, feel nothing except the carpet beneath his feet. He held up his hand in front of his face, but saw only blackness. He looked back the way he had come and was chilled to see that the doorway and the corridor had gone. It was as though the darkness had sucked him in, closing ranks behind his intrusion.

He kept expecting to bump into furniture, and after five or six steps put out his hand to prevent himself from walking into the opposite wall. However, there was no need; nothing obstructed him. The wall must be a few steps further then, Nige thought; he must have misjudged the distance in this darkness. He took three more cautious steps, then four, five, eight, thirteen, twenty. After twenty-five he stopped, gripped by a hideous, overwhelming panic. There was no opposite wall, no furniture, no nothing. What the fuck was this place? Limbo? Purgatory? He fought down his panic with difficulty, told himself he was being stupid, irrational. He was obviously overlooking something here, and tomorrow morning, when he was fully aware, he would laugh about what it was.

He stood for a moment, undecided. What should he do? Go on or go back? If he went on, he might get lost forever, but if he went back he would be deserting Robespierre, and the thought of leaving someone to fester in this nothingness made him feel wretched. Nige decided to try calling to see if the old man would respond. If he did he would go on, if not he would go back and get help, or at least a torch. At the top of his voice he yelled, 'Mr Robespierre, where are you? Can you hear me?'

Unlike before his voice now seemed to echo inside a vast cavern, to boom hollowly away over a distant invisible horizon. He strained, listening for a reply, but none came. He was about to turn back when suddenly he heard a tiny, almost imperceptible cry: '*Help meee!*'

Nige tensed, experiencing a strange blend of elation and despair. The voice certainly belonged to Robespierre, but what horrified him was the realization that the dimensions of the place must be colossal, judging by the faintness of the cry. He wondered how far he would have to walk before he reached the old man.

He tried to put the thought from his mind and proceeded cautiously into the blackness. If he stayed calm and clear-headed, he should be all right. He had read about experiments where subjects were deprived of all senses, even hearing and touch. After a while the subjects began to 'invent' senses, to live in a world of hallucination. It struck Nige that maybe he hadn't heard Robespierre's voice at all, maybe it had been an hallucination created by his mind to compensate for the quiet. He shook his head angrily. No, he had heard Robespierre's voice out in the corridor, hadn't he, when all his senses had been intact? And besides, he hadn't been in this room long enough to hallucinate, or at least he didn't think he had. It was difficult to tell, for like everything else even time seemed suspended here.

He had been walking for what felt like a few minutes when he decided to call again. 'Mr Robespierre!' he shouted, and was alarmed to hear a ragged tinge of panic in his voice. No, he mustn't let this place get to him. He must remain calm. *Calm.* Clearing his throat he tried again, and this time his voice was stronger.

'Mr Robespierre, where are you?'

The answer came surprisingly quickly, and Nige was overjoyed to discover that the old man sounded closer than he had expected. 'Here, boy. Over here. Here I am.'

Nige turned in the darkness. It seemed as though Robespierre was somewhere to his left. He began to stumble in that direction, putting up his arms as though to ward off unseen obstacles. 'Shout again,' he called. 'Say something so I can follow your voice.'

'Here, boy. Over here.' Robespierre was much closer now.

Nige blundered on, his eyes straining into the blackness. 'Not much further,' he kept repeating silently to himself, 'not much further now.'

Then, suddenly, he saw it: a glimmer of white-blue light flashing in the darkness. He let out a cry of triumph and ran towards it, panting. 'Don't move, don't move,' he gasped, 'I can see you.'

The light grew sharper as he approached, and Nige slowed, then stopped, when he saw what it illuminated.

Robespierre was lying naked on his bed. His sheets were ripped and crumpled and soiled with faeces. Nige was appalled at how thin the old man was, all skin and bone, though with a hideously distended stomach. He appeared to have been beaten, his body blackened by bruises, his mouth and nose covered in blood. Grotesquely he still wore his black pebble-glasses which, from a distance, made his face look like a skull. He was illuminated in ice-blue light, displayed like an exhibit in some macabre museum.

'Oh my God,' Nige said, stumbling forward, 'Oh my God, what's happened to you?'

He reached the bed, almost gagging on the stench of human waste. A shiver trickled through his body when he saw that Robespierre was grinning manically; obviously the old man's ordeal had caused his mind to snap. Robespierre lifted a trembling stick-like arm, twig-fingers reaching up to his spectacles. And then, with a movement that was swift as a striking viper, he whipped them away.

Nige gasped, stumbling back from the bed. Robespierre had no eyes – just flat red discs that were slanted, almost lupine in shape. Suddenly he seemed transformed from a pitiful old man into a lean, hungry beast, muscles rippling beneath the pale frame. As Nige watched, the blind man's mouth opened and he hissed like a snake, a forked tongue flickering between his lips. He raised his hands and hooked talons sprang from the ends of his blunt fingers with a sound that reminded Nige of the flick-knife blades springing from their sheaths. Snarling and spitting, Robespierre drew the talons across his white chest, tearing himself. Until then Nige had been riveted, unable to take his eyes from the scene, but as soon as he saw the blood he ran.

This time the darkness seemed to contain shapes, buildings, like the debris of a ruined city glimpsed through black fog. Nige, however, had not time for exploration. He concentrated all his energies on running; running and running, back the way he had come, hoping that the abomination from the bed was not following him.

A grey concrete pole surrounded by buzzing orange suddenly loomed out of the night. Nige was running so fast that he had time only to register it was there before he crashed into it, knocking himself to the ground.

He lay for a moment, stunned, trying to regain his senses. He had the confused impression that a drink was being pressed to his lips and he turned his head aside in refusal. The water was hard and bitter, crunchy as dirt in his mouth. His hands, his face, the entire front of his body was cold and wet. His head throbbed like an egg about to hatch. His eyes opened, drifted slowly into focus, and he found himself staring at the base of a lamp post.

Groggily he sat up, and was astonished to find himself sitting on the pavement outside his house. His pyjamas and dressing gown were soaked; his slippers felt like lumps of squelching newspaper wrapped round his feet. The wind was howling, probing at the wound in his head like an exploratory scalpel. Feeling dizzy and sick, and shivering with the cold, Nige stood up.

He wondered what had happened. Had he sleepwalked out of the house, down the path, and then gone smack into the lamp post? He supposed he must have; he felt confused and disoriented, though relieved. The dream about Robespierre must have seemed so real because he had been stumbling about the house, looking for an exit.

Pushing open the garden gate he began to walk up the path. As he did so he heard a sound: a loud slurping plop. It was the kind of sound a limpet might make as it disengages itself from a rock, though amplified a hundred-fold. Nervously, his head throbbing, Nige looked around.

The garden was still and deserted, glittering beneath a layer of snow. In the centre of the lawn stood the snowman, pink beret at a jaunty angle, pipe jutting from beneath the plastic novelty mask that comprised spectacles, nose and moustache. Nige's gaze skittered further, to the house, but that too was dark and silent. As he looked up at his bedroom window he glimpsed movement to his left and spun round. Had he been mistaken or had he really seen the pipe in the snowman's mouth move from right to left as though the snowman had lips to move it with?

Curiously he stepped from the path on to the lawn. Snow flurried around him, catching in his hair, dusting his shoulders. The snowman, of course, was immobile. It was only a snowman after all: the movement he'd seen must have been the movement of flakes in the air, tugging at the edge of his vision. He looked at the snowman one last time and then made to turn away. As he did so his eyes widened and he swung back. The bowl of the pipe in the snowman's mouth was glowing as though tobacco was being inhaled from it, and, bizarrely, smoke was drifting from the nostrils of the plastic novelty mask.

Nige watched with horror as the snowman's round head turned slowly towards him. He heard a sucking plop, the same as before, and the snowman lifted its stumpy left leg clear of the ground. Desperately, his own legs like water, Nige began to back away. The snowman took a few cautious experimental steps and then came shambling over the lawn.

Nige reached the gate and groped at the catch with numb fingers. Behind him the snowman was getting closer, its huge body making a ponderous crunching swish as it moved. Panic-stricken, Nige tore blindly at the catch and at last the gate swung open. Without stopping to think, he rushed out into the road.

He began to stumble away, his heart pummelling. He couldn't move fast because he kept slipping and sliding in the snow. His feet felt so numb that his legs felt chopped off at the ankles. He blundered and cried, too exhausted to scream, as behind him the snowman gained momentum. It was striding now in pursuit – remorseless, machine-like, smoke billowing behind it.

Nige turned left at the bottom of the road, heading – though not consciously – towards the sea. Around him, Starmouth looked grainy, unreal, clouded by his terror and the swirling screen of snow. At the end of the road he turned right, and suddenly he was on the promenade, exposed to the dull bellow of the ocean. The water was restless, the waves rhythmic as breathing. Nige began to stagger down the promenade, the wind roaring like a crowd urging him on. He was at the pier entrance before he risked a look back.

The white, bloated figure was less than ten yards behind him. Despite the wind, its pink beret was still perched on its head and its plastic mask still in place. It puffed out smoke in clouds as though it ran on steam. At the sight of the apparition Nige stumbled and almost fell. He exhaled, breath raw and sobbing, through lungs that felt shredded with fear. He forced himself to turn his back on the snowman, and without giving thought to the fact that he was running into a trap, staggered on to the pier.

The snowman followed, slower now, as though it knew it had its prey. Nige's feet pounded on the snow-covered boards as he ran, though not half as loudly as those of the presence behind him. He reached the pier's end and leaned over the railings, gazing out to sea. The wind roared like an ogre, buffeting him, drenching him with spray. Behind him he heard the thundering footsteps slow, then stop, and the smell of pipe-smoke pinch his nostrils. From the corner of his eye he saw a great white paw, a slab of snow that broke into fingers, reaching out for him. He climbed up on to the topmost railing, teetered for a moment, then dropped.

Before he hit the water, he woke up, floundering in bedsheets. He whimpered and clutched at the headboard to stop himself from falling. Eventually his senses levelled, the room ceased its sickening tilt, and Nige lay in the dark and the quiet, sweating and panting with relief.

A dream, a dream. The thought was driftwood to which he clung desperately. He repeated the word over and over, whispering it like an incantation. However, despite his relief, fear remained. Twice already he had woken up only to find the nightmare had persisted. But surely this time he was right? Surely waking up in his own bed was proof that his ordeal was over?

Unwilling, as though drawn, he pushed back his covers and climbed out of bed. Much as he would have liked to have stayed there, he had to find out. He padded to the window, reached out a trembling hand and yanked back the curtain. Then, taking a deep breath, he looked down.

226

'No,' he murmured. 'Oh God, no.'

It was as he had feared. The front lawn was snow-covered, all except for the centre, where there was now only a circle of grass.

3

It was after one in the morning when Glennon and Bailey were able to get to Rusty's house. However, despite the lateness of the hour, lights were still burning in the downstairs rooms of the shabby two-up, two-down.

'Looks like we might be in luck,' Glennon said as he unfastened his seatbelt.

'I hope so,' his partner replied. 'I'm not in the mood for traipsing round after a bunch of stupid kids all night.'

The policemen got out of the car and pushed open the garden gate. The garden's covering of snow was deep, but not deep enough to conceal the rubbish strewn beneath – tin cans, broken bottles, an old boot, the rusted frame of a toy pram. Glennon turned to the younger man and shook his head. 'What a dump,' he muttered.

Bailey nodded in agreement, though he wasn't sure whether Glennon was referring to the garden or the whole area. Certainly this part of Piling Hill was the dirtiest, most run-down district of town. The houses here were small and squat with exteriors as seedy as their occupants; graffiti was sprawled across every available wall like an urban fungus. Bald patches of wasteground, piled with rubbish and crawling with vermin, blotched the landscape like outbreaks of scabies. And everywhere telephone boxes had fallen victim to vandals – battered, their innards ripped out, cowering amongst fragments of their own glass.

Glennon strode forward and rapped on the door. The policeman waited for a few moments, steam wreathing their faces, before Glennon tried again. Eventually they heard footsteps approaching and stopping on the other side of the door. 'Who is it?' a disgruntled voice demanded. 'What do you want?'

The policemen exchanged a look. 'Mr Oates?' Glennon said.

There was a pause, and then tentatively the voice asked, 'What's it to you?'

'It's the police, Mr Oates. Will you open up, please? We want a word with you.'

There was an even lengthier pause this time before the voice warily enquired, 'What about?'

'It's about your son, Steven,' Glennon said. 'Look, sir, if you'll open the door we'll give you all the details. Do you usually keep callers standing on the doorstep?'

'At this time of night I do. For all I know you might not even *be* police.'

'Oh, for God's sake, man!' snapped Glennon. 'Have a look through the bloody letter-box if you don't believe us!' He snorted in exasperation and stamped his feet, then his and Bailey's gaze flickered to the letterbox as it clattered open. They saw two mistrustful eyes peering up at them from waist level. Glennon squatted on his haunches and said with forced patience, 'Now, sir, would you be so kind as to open this door?'

The eyes frowned, the letterbox snapped shut. A moment later the policemen heard the sound of a catch being released and the door was opened. A fat, unshaven man with dandruff-flecked hair, wearing a grubby shirt and trousers, stood glaring at them.

'What is it *you* want?' he demanded, scratching his crotch.

'Just a few words, Mr Oates,' Glennon said, mustering a smile. 'Is your son in?'

'No, he isn't,' Oates replied. 'He's out with his mates.' He continued to stand there, his bulk blocking the doorway.

'Well, aren't you going to invite us in?' Glennon said pleasantly.

Oate's gaze skittered, half-aggressively, half-fearfully,

from one policeman to the other, then he sighed and stepped back from the door.

'I suppose so,' he grumbled. 'If you must.'

'Thank you,' Glennon said, and the policemen stepped into a dingy hall, taking off their hats as they did so. Oates skirted round them, closed the door and dropped the catch. Bailey wrinkled his nose at the sour smell of sweat and stale beer that emanated from the man's body, and also at the smell of the house itself – dirty nappies and greasy food.

'This way,' Oates said, and led them down the hall and into a pokey sitting room. The furniture and carpets were threadbare, the wallpaper grimy. Cheap knick-knacks in need of a dust littered the mantelpiece and sideboard. In one corner stood a television and video recorder, both of which looked startlingly new against the drab background. On the TV screen a grainy video image held on 'pause' depicted a bare-breasted black woman sucking a penis-shaped lollipop.

'I . . . er, was just watching a video when you called,' Oates said, grimacing at the screen.

Glennon glanced at the TV, but said nothing. 'May we sit down?' he asked, indicating a weary-looking armchair.

Oates nodded reluctantly and Glennon sat, holding out his hands to the two orange bars of an electric fire. Bailey strode across the room and sat in the other armchair. Nervous as an aged pedestrian, Oates glanced right and left and then lowered himself gingerly on to the settee between them.

'Now then, Mr Oates,' Glennon said, his tone cordial, 'have you seen your son this evening?'

Oates's eyes continued to shift from one policeman to the other. Speaking carefully he said, 'No, I haven't, not since he went out with his mates.'

'And what time would that have been?' Glennon asked.

Oates shrugged. 'Seven? Eight? I'm not sure.'

'And you're certain your son's not been back home since then?'

'No. Look, what's this all about? What's he done?'

'Have you any idea where your son might be, Mr Oates?'

Oates shook his head. 'No, how should I? He doesn't tell me where he's going.'

'Might he be at one of his friend's houses? Maurice/ Landen's for instance?'

Oates looked briefly uncomfortable, but shrugged again. 'I don't know. He might be.'

Glennon sighed and let his eyes stray to the image on the TV screen. 'You're not being very helpful, Mr Oates,' he said. 'New, is it?'

Oates looked up, startled. 'You what?'

'The video recorder. Is it new?'

'Oh . . . oh, aye . . . fairly new, I suppose.' The tremor in his voice was obvious; his gaze was straying around the room, alighting on everything but the topic of conversation. The two policemen remained silent and Oates felt obliged to go on. 'I . . . er . . . I got it from a friend,' he said.

'A friend? Really?' Glennon raised his eyebrows.

'Aye,' Oates said and began to fidget nervously. 'Just a mate, that's all. Someone I know who sells 'em cheap.' He cleared his throat and palmed a trickle of sweat from his face.

Glennon smiled. 'Say no more, Mr Oates. We understand perfectly – don't we, Constable Bailey?' He glanced at his partner who nodded.

Oates's head swivelled back and forth, giving him the look of a turkey cornered by two butchers. Smiling ingratiatingly he said, 'Look, didn't you come here to talk about my son? I mean, what's all this about videos? I bought it from a mate, that's all. Wasn't it my son you wanted to see?'

He flinched back, putting up his hands as Glennon suddenly lunged forward; however the big policeman merely brought his face up close to the fat man's and murmured in a silky-steel voice: 'Look, Oates, you're not very good at lying so I'd advise you to stop doing it. Now, either you tell us where your son is or we're taking you down the station and charging you with handling stolen property and possessing obscene materials.' He sat back again and smilingly spread his hands. 'The choice is yours.'

Oates stared at him. Sweat was breaking out on his face like pimples, but he looked too frightened to wipe it away. He licked his lips and his Adam's Apple bobbed as he swallowed. Finally he said, 'All right, I'll tell you where Landen lives. Our Steve often goes back there on a Saturday night after the pubs have shut.'

Glennon beamed. 'Now that's more like it. Only there's one small problem. You see we already know where Landen lives. What we want you to do is to ring up Landen's house, ask if your son's there, and if he is, tell him to come home. Say it's important, but don't say we're here – we want that to be a surprise.'

Oates was horrified by the suggestion. 'Are you asking me to con my own son? My own flesh and blood?'

Glennon nodded encouragingly. 'Got it in one! Well done!'

Something like pride asserted itself on Oates's face. 'I . . . I won't do it!' he declared.

Glennon shrugged as though unconcerned. 'That's up to you. Got those cuffs, Kev?'

Bailey produced a pair of handcuffs and jangled them in the air. 'Yep, here they are, sarge.'

'Ah, good lad. Slap them on our friend here, would you? He's got a few charges to answer at the station.'

Bailey moved in on Oates. The fat man shrank back against the settee, raising his hands in a conciliatory gesture.

'Now, hang on,' he whined. 'Wait just a minute.'

Bailey halted his advance. Glennon, who was almost out of the room, turned back in apparent surprise. 'Yes, Mr Oates?'

'I'll make your fucking phone-call for you,' Oates muttered.

Glennon smiled. 'Good man. I knew you'd see reason. Now, where's the phone? Out in the hall?'

Oates nodded sullenly and Glennon led the way out of the room. In the hall he picked up a telephone directory and began to leaf through it. Oates watched in hostile silence.

'Ah, here we are!' Glennon said, and turned the book round so that Oates could see. 'There's the number. Now get dialling.'

Oates took the book from him and picked up the receiver. He dialled the number slowly to show he was performing the task under duress, but Glennon was unmoved. When the dialling had been completed, the sergeant leaned forward to hear both sides of the conversation.

The phone rang for a long time before it was picked up. Finally, however, there was a click and a woman's sleepy voice said, 'Hello?'

'H-Hello, Mrs Landen?' Oates said.

'Yes, who's this?' said the woman.

'It's Mr Oates, Mrs Landen – Steven's dad. I'm sorry to bother you at this time, but – is our Steve there?'

Mrs Landen sounded bemused. 'No, he isn't. Neither's our Maurice as it happens. Why, is something wrong?'

'Oh, no,' Oates said, glancing at Glennon, 'nothing to worry about. But if our Steve should turn up can you tell him to come straight home?'

'Yes, I'll tell him. Or rather, I'll leave him a note. I'm going back to bed now. It's half-past one in the morning you know.'

'Yes, I know. I'm sorry about that, but it was pretty important. Well, thanks for your help anyway. Good night.'

'Good night,' Mrs Landen said.

Oates put the phone down and turned to the two policemen. Unable to hide the satisfaction in his voice, he said, 'He's not there.'

Glennon was irritated by the man's smugness, but

232

refused to show it. 'Oh, well, I suppose we'll just have to come back in the morning. If your son should happen to show up in the meantime, tell him to stay put. We'll want to speak to him as soon as possible.'

He put on his cap and made his way down the hall, Bailey following. At the front door he paused and turned back. 'Oh, and another thing, Mr Oates. I'll send someone round in the morning to take a statement about the video recorder. Sleep well.'

Then he and Bailey left, leaving Oates glowering after them.

4

The rocks were slippery with sea-slime and slush. When Robin awoke he found he was sitting on one of them.

He blinked his gummy eyes and confusedly looked out on the expanse of beach before him. It was dark and uninviting, a murky blend of half-melted snow and muddy sand. Groggily he stood up, realizing he was wearing only pyjamas, slippers and dressing-gown. His body ached with the cold; his hair was a freezing cap on his head. After the initial dream-shock, the moments of disorientation, real fear began lancing through him. What was he doing here? Why wasn't he at home in bed? Surely he hadn't sleepwalked over two miles through the snow in his pyjamas?

He stood up and began walking, his feet sinking into the mushy sand with each step. The wind from the sea was a bully, jeering and howling and trying to knock him down, but determinedly he kept on, heading towards the steps that led to the promenade. He was about half-way there when he stopped, a frown grooving his forehead. He turned and looked at the caves, struggling with the idea that had just planted itself in his mind. He could find shelter in the caves, could rest there until he felt strong enough, could *then* set off for home. Though he longed for his bed more than anything else in the world, Robin suddenly found himself turning away from the steps, walking back along the muddy beach.

The caves and rocks were beautiful in the moonlight, licked by a shimmering phosphorescence that seemed to rise and undulate as though in imitation of the waves. Robin stepped on to the rocks, thinking dreamily that this sculpture was more beautiful than the real thing. The sea to his left was hissing and clawing at the land; a huge hand of pitch that strained and withdrew, strained and withdrew, as though chained to the horizon.

Through the darkness, Robin could just make out something sitting on one of the rocks. It was waiting for him, he thought without hesitation; a small, hunched figure dressed in rags that ruffled and stirred round its body. He drew closer, his head clearing, feeling a warmth permeate his bones. He saw that the thing on the rock was in fact a bird, a large white gull that watched him impassively. The corners of its yellow beak were turned up in what appeared to be a smile.

He drew closer, but six feet from the gull he stopped and looked at it expectantly, as though waiting for it to speak. The gull stared at him, its eyes small and baleful, the wind hackling its feathers. At last it opened its beak wide, revealing a gullet in which a delicate pink tongue flickered like a worm. It screeched once, raucously, shuffled from foot to foot, and then, spreading its wings, took off into the wind.

Robin scrambled over the rocks in pursuit, keeping his eye on the bird as it soared gracefully over the cliff-face and finally came to rest outside the black wound of a cave. It twisted its head as though to ensure he was following, then hopped forward into the darkness.

Robin stopped, uncertain. Should he follow? It seemed his feet had already made the decision, for a moment later he found himself approaching the cave cautiously.

Before the cave mouth was a huge boulder, a sight which caused Robin to stop, to experience a peculiar sense of *déjà vu*. Something here was acutely, distressingly familiar, yet he couldn't quite put his finger on what it was. His mind felt webbed, veiled, as though it were being manipulated. Frowning, he stepped back, his eyes roving over the cliff – and that was when he saw the face, and with it came sudden realization.

This was Grandad Rock which 'belonged' to the Horror Club. Without quite knowing why, Robin felt affronted that the gull had led him here. From inside the cave, the 'mouth', he detected a flicker of orange; just a touch, like a barely moving tongue. Carried to him on the wind was a smell, not strong but enough to make him wrinkle his nose distastefully.

He stood for a long moment, wondering what to do. Suddenly he heard a muffled roar like a furnace, and a moment later flame gouted from the cave entrance. Feeling the intense heat, Robin stepped back, but almost immediately the flame disappeared, retreating into the cave, and the furnace-roar died to a campfire-crackle. Warmth lapped over the rocks towards him, and Robin moved forward, eager for its touch.

A silhouette appeared in the cave mouth. Though its outline was blurred with heat, Robin could see it was a girl. She was perhaps a year or two older than himself. When she stepped forward, he gasped.

She was the most beautiful thing he had ever seen. All those stupid, clichéd love-images – lips like cherries, eyes like limpid pools, hair like spun gold – came to mind, except suddenly they didn't seem stupid any more. He thought that if there could be an embodiment of perfection, then this girl was it. He continued to gawp, his mouth hanging open, as she came towards him. And when her luscious red lips curled into a smile he felt, quite literally, love-sick.

She held something in her hands, but Robin was too entranced by her face to register what it was. She extended the something to him and he heard a word, '*Come,*' echoing through his mind. Had the girl spoken the word?

He wasn't sure. Certainly it had seemed as though the smile on her lips had remained closed and intact.

Robin put a hand on the boulder as though to pull himself up, but all at once, despite the enchantment, he felt uneasy. His senses seemed to drift together as though coming into focus, and he sniffed, then almost gagged at the stench in the air. His eyes flickered downwards, past the girl's blonde hair, the breasts that strained through the thin material of her shirt, to her hands. His stomach flipped at the sight of what she held, though it was more impression than recognition. He saw only that it was red and ragged and juicy, and that it was drooling on to the rocks and splashing on to her legs. The image of her golden thighs stained with blood seemed hideously obscene. Yet more obscene still was when she held up her hands and brought the thing to her mouth.

Robin saw her lips part, perfect white teeth bared as though she were playing at wild animals – and then suddenly, voraciously, she dipped her head. He watched, horrified, as her mouth snarled open and she chomped down on the bloody mass in her hands. A moment later her blonde hair was tossed back as she dragged her head up, a stringy morsel of flesh clamped between her teeth.

She chewed and swallowed, the symmetry of her face marred now by the blood that dribbled from her lips. Robin recoiled, chilled and repulsed by her rapacity. He felt the warmth draining from him, his strength ebbing like the tide, and just for a second saw something hideous and corrupt crawling beneath the girl's perfection. There was nothing he could pinpoint, but the impression was enough to make him turn and run.

He slithered and stumbled away, his feet raw and tender inside his slippers. Bladderwrack, straggling everywhere, popped beneath him. Things crunched and creaked as though the rocks were giving way; ice and sea-moss joined forces, bringing him down once when his left foot skidded out from his body. Despite the bruises he got up and stumbled on, his fear greater than his pain.

At last he reached the edge of the rocks and jumped down on to the beach. Immediately the sand swallowed him, slurping him in up to the ankles. Robin pulled his feet free with difficulty, leaving his slippers stuck in the mud. Barefoot, he began to wade across the beach, heading towards the black skeletal shape of the pier and the steps beyond that led to the promenade.

When he felt far enough from the cave, he looked behind him. The girl was still on the rocks, thankfully making no attempt to follow. Robin tried not to look at the thing she held, the thing that had once been human, but was now a ragged, torn mass of bloody flesh and gristle. As though to taunt him, she tossed the thing in the air, caught it and swung it by its hair. Robin turned away, feeling sick.

His panic lessened as he got further from the girl. Despite the icy cold of the water he began to jog along the sea's edge. The incoming tide fizzed and swirled about his feet. Behind him the rocks and the caves gradually receded, blending with black. Only the occasional peak or shimmer of ice was picked out by the white-blue moon-light.

Ahead of him the pier loomed, its underside a forest of struts and curdled shadow. As Robin approached he heard drums, two contrasting rhythms that overlapped like a crazy heartbeat. The first was fast and light – boom-boom-boom-boom – and the other louder, more ponderous – BOOM . . . BOOM . . . BOOM . . . Robin looked around for a moment, then craned his neck as he realized the sound was coming from the pier itself. At first he saw nothing; then, suddenly, he glimpsed a flash of move-ment. He saw a running figure – small, panic-stricken, dressed as he was in pyjamas and dressing-gown. The figure was staggering, clearly near to exhaustion. Behind it came another, dressed in dazzling white, bloated like a spaceman.

Robin watched, fascinated, as the first figure reached the end of the pier and leaned over the railings. Then the

237

figure half-turned towards him, and with a jolt that was almost physical, Robin recognized the olive-skinned face and the black hair that flapped in the wind.

'Niiiiigellllll!' he yelled, rushing forward and waving his arms. He saw the fat white figure stop a few yards behind his friend and extend a stubby, powerful limb.

'Niiiiiigelllllllll!' he screamed again, but it was no use; the wind whipped away his voice for a plaything. Robin could only watch, horrified, as the creature's fat white limb broke into fingers which stretched wide as though to crush Nige's skull.

For a moment Robin thought Nige was unaware of his pursuer, but then he saw him give a quick backward glance and climb on to the railings. The creature made a sudden lunge forward, but too late. Robin saw his friend waver for a moment, then plunge towards the sea.

He never saw Nige hit the water, for a second later he was sprawling in the sand, something hard and sharp having gouged him in the back of the head. Instinctively he rolled over, his arms coming up to protect himself. The gull that had been sitting on the rock was hovering a few feet above him, treading air, wings spread wide to embrace the wind currents. Robin had time only to see that it had blood on its beak before it swooped at him again.

This time he got his fingers badly cut, his index finger right through to the bone, for the gull's beak was like garden shears closing on his hand. He screamed and scrambled away, his heels digging into the soft ground. Behind him the sea was bellowing as though invigorated by the contest. Robin felt its spray on him like beads of cold sweat breaking on his face.

The gull came again, a flying living weapon, swooping and darting, gouging where it could. Robin kicked at it as it went for his groin, and was satisfied to feel his foot making contact with the soft feathered body. However, rather than incapacitating the bird, the kick only seemed to enrage it further. Its next attack was frenzied, its razor-beak slashing, prodding, stabbing, until it was a blur of white above him. Robin was slippery with his own blood, but his adrenalin was pumping too fast to allow him to feel pain. He flapped and kicked and punched and screamed; once his grasping hands closed around the bird's leg. However before he could gain a proper grip, it slashed out with its beak, opening his hand from knuckle to wrist.

At last Robin felt his defences beginning to weaken, his reactions slowing. 'Please,' he whispered, the words sighing out through lips that felt viscid with blood, 'please, leave me alone.'

The bird paid no heed. It broke through his flailing arms time and again, snipping off flesh as a barber might snip hair. Robin felt consciousness ebbing with his blood; he could no longer manipulate his arms quickly enough to protect himself. He continued to flap and lunge, but now his resistance was only token. A moment later the gull found his face.

Robin used the last of his strength to scream as the hateful eyes and blood-drenched beak filled his vision. The bird struck, and Robin heard a pop, felt indescribable pain, was half-aware of an eruption of warm jelly down his cheek. He lay, twitching and whimpering, as the soft body of the gull burrowed into his face. The sound of the sea retreated . . . retreated . . . became a clattering . . . a muffled wet sound against glass . . .

And Robin opened the eye he had just felt punctured and found himself crying into his pillow.

5

For a brief second, when he heard the key in the lock, Oates panicked, thinking that the police had come back early. He threw himself off the settee, landing on all fours in front of the video, and jabbed at a button. On the screen fellatio was replaced by fuzz. Oates ejected the cassette from the recorder and was trying to stuff it down the back of the settee when his son and Mo walked in.

Rusty stared at his father's antics with an expression of bewildered disgust. 'What the fuck are you doin'?' he said.

Oates looked up and almost collapsed with relief. 'God, I thought you were coppers,' he replied, and wiped his mouth with the back of a trembling hand.

Rusty and Mo exchanged glances. 'Oh, yeah, we'd make a fuckin' great Crockett and Tubbs, we would,' said Rusty.

'It's no joke,' panted Oates, trying to extricate the cassette from the furniture, 'they've already been round once tonight. They wanted to speak to you. They even made me ring up Mo's house to see if you were there.'

'Fuck,' Rusty muttered, but didn't sound surprised. He crossed the room, pulled back a curtain and peered out. 'What time did they come?'

'I dunno,' Oates said. 'About an hour ago, I suppose.'

'Shit, we'll have to get out then,' said Rusty, and crossed to the door. 'Wait here Mo. I'll just go get some stuff together.'

'Hold on,' Oates said before his son could leave the room. 'Just what's this all about? What have you done?'

'Aw, it's a long story, Dad. I haven't got time to explain now.'

'It must be something pretty serious. The police don't come round for nothing. What is it, Steve? Drugs? Burglary? You been mugging old ladies or something?'

Rusty snorted a laugh. 'Nah, course not. They're just making a big deal out of nothing as usual.'

'Oh, yeah? Then why are they so keen to see you? I mean, I used to get in bother when I was your age, but never as much as you. I reckon if you don't watch it, you'll be in nick before you're much older.'

Rusty snorted again and stepped into the hall. Oates followed him, farting loudly.

'Just where do you think you're gonna go?' he said. 'The coppers'll want to talk to you. They told me you were to stay here.'

Rusty sneered. 'I dunno, we'll find somewhere. Don't worry about it.'

Oates opened his mouth to protest further, but Rusty put a finger to his lips. 'No more questions, Dad, eh? You'll wake the baby.' And with that he turned and started up the stairs.

Oates felt impotent as he watched his son. He knew he ought to put a stop to all this before it got out of hand, but he couldn't for the simple reason that Steven scared him. A ridiculous and demoralizing feeling, he knew, but one that he could do nothing about. Sometimes he even found it hard to believe Steven really was his son. The boy had something about him, a look in his eyes, that evoked fear. He was like a human time-bomb, the mechanism finely balanced, one jolt enough to induce an explosion.

Oates sighed. In his waking hours he felt he was merely marking time, patches of grey between the sleep that allowed him to forget his troubles. And what troubles! No money, no job, a delinquent son, and now, to cap it all, another bloody mouth to feed on account of his stupid cow of a wife forgetting to take her pill one morning last year. Oates rubbed a hand vigorously over his face as though trying to wipe his features away. After five months of screaming babies and the smell of dirty nappies he was just about sick to death. A few times his wife had pleaded for help in the bringing up of their new daughter, but Oates refused to have anything to do with the child. After all, it had been her mistake, not his; why should he be dragged into it? There was the drawback, of course, of his wife refusing to sleep with him now, claiming she was too tired for sex after spending all day caring for the baby, but that was a sacrifice Oates was prepared to accept. After all, he had his videos, and often they were a damn sight better than the real thing. He thought savagely that if the police *did* nick him for watching them he would make his wife pay the bloody fine.

His impotent rage was making him feel sick and hollow, so he stomped back into the sitting room where Mo had succeeded in fishing the cassette from the back of the settee. The skinhead was now sitting in front of the screen, peering at the writhing bodies as though searching for birthmarks.

'Mo,' Oates said guardedly.

The skinhead stirred. 'Yeah?'

'Just what the hell *is* going on?'

Mo looked up. Oates searched for some clue in his expression, but the bony face was blank. Mo's response was equally as neutral. 'What do you mean?' he said.

'I mean all this.' Oates gestured vaguely towards the open door. 'What have you and Steve been up to?'

Mo shrugged, 'Nothing,' and turned back to the video.

The skinhead made him nervous, but Oates persisted. 'Come on, it must have been something. The police don't come after you for nowt.'

'Don't they?' Mo responded, and smiled bitterly. 'Aw, there was a bit of a scrap at a disco, that's all. I think someone was stabbed.'

'*Stabbed?*' Oates half-rose from his seat as though the word had been thrust into his gullet.

Quickly Mo said, 'Yeah, but it wasn't us. Someone said it was, but it wasn't.' He glanced round, saw Oates's doubtful expression and spread his arms wide. 'Hey, come on, Mr O! Search me if you want. I'm not even carrying a blade.'

Oates didn't move and after a moment Mo lowered his arms. Heavily Oates asked, 'What will you do?'

Again Mo shrugged, as if his problems were that easy to remove. 'Lie low for a couple of days, I suppose, till it all blows over.'

'And meanwhile you'll leave me to carry the can!'

Mo's face tautened in reaction to the anger that had crept into Oates's voice. 'Just tell the cops you haven't seen us,' he muttered. 'Tell 'em we never came back.'

Thumping feet sounded on the stairs and Rusty reappeared, a rucksack slung over his shoulder. 'I'm just gonna get some food from the kitchen,' he said, and stared at his father as though daring him to protest.

A moment later he was back with a handful of tins and half a loaf of bread. The loss of the bread meant there would be no breakfast in the morning, but all Oates could think of to say was, 'You got any money?'

Rusty nodded and patted his pockets. 'Yeah.' He shoved the tins into the rucksack and heaved it on to his back. 'Right. You ready?'

Mo nodded and stood up. Rusty said, 'See you, Dad.'

'Yeah, see you, Mr O,' Mo echoed.

Oates's lips twitched into a smile. 'Take care, lads,' he said, and watched as the boys slouched down the hall and out of the front door into the cold. He waited until the door had slammed shut, then ran back to the sitting room and looked out of the window. Mo and his son were tall dark figures, their shadows preceding then following them as they walked beneath the streetlamps. Watching them, Oates felt restless, worried, and in a strange way, though he would never have admitted it, envious as hell.

6

The window reflected the room back as a ghost-image. Olive's gaze passed through it, concentrating on the black boiling sea, the cream-tipped waves of which were the only indicators of movement. The wind whipped and howled as though the house was its focal point, and despite being snug and warm beneath her numerous layers of clothing, Olive shivered at its ferocity.

She had been unable to sink back into sleep since waking a couple of hours ago. Each time she closed her eyes, feral images were there waiting to pounce. An ordinary setting with a nightmare implication: two boys, identical, staring at each other across a stifling bedroom. Even now Olive could not recall what had been so frightening about the scene, but it had something to do with the boy in the bed pushing back the sheet and smiling at his twin. Sighing, she closed her eyes.

243

Pushing back the sheet and smiling at his twin.

Her eyes opened and she shuddered. No, the significance once again eluded her. All she was left with was a lingering sense of defilement.

Her hands clasped more tightly around the mug she was holding and she sipped. The fennel tea smelled strongly of aniseed, but its taste was surprisingly delicate. Olive's feet were beginning to ache, the result of supporting her increasingly aged frame for nearly an hour; yet, despite her discomfort, she was reluctant to move. Even in its dark and sinister moods the sea provided her with an illusion of friendship, a semblance of stability.

Since she had returned from the estate agent's yesterday morning, Olive had passed the time in a flurry of indecision. She now knew a little more about the house in King Street's history, but how did that really help her? She still had no clear idea what they were up against, though theories, notions, questions played in her mind, tumbling over one another, each more bizarre than the last. Was their enemy animal, vegetable, mineral, spiritual? Was it some kind of force, creature, something that used dreams, fear, hallucination as its arsenal? Yes, maybe that was it. Maybe it was some kind of parasite, something that attacked the mind like a virus. But if that was the case, was it sentient or merely random? Were its actions planned or perhaps the result of some type of psychic contagion? Olive paled at this thought, recalling all the people she and the boys had come into contact with in the last couple of days. She pictured Starmouth going slowly crazy, each individual becoming gradually ensconced within their own delusions. The idea seemed ludicrous and far-fetched, too idiotic to contemplate. But was it any more ludicrous than the possibility that some huge invisible chameleon was stalking the town?

Olive pushed a hand through her wispy hair and realized she was trembling. She put down her tea and crossed her arms fiercely against her chest. All day she had been sifting through the evidence and coming up with nothing but riddles. She felt trapped in some insoluble conundrum, unearthing clue after clue only for each to blossom into even more questions.

The facts, then; the cold, hard facts.

In November, 1979, a young couple flee from their home in King Street, claiming to have been driven out by a poltergeist. Four months later the roof of the house caves in, presumably struck by lightning, which makes the house uninhabitable. Nine years on, four boys hold a seance in the house, awakening some apparently mindless force, though only one of the four remembers the incident. The contact in the seance is broken by Richard smashing a glass, an event which she herself had 'experienced'. That same night Richard is followed home by something which he says resembles a wolf. His friend, Nigel, recalls the seance under hypnosis. 'And I,' Olive thought, 'am suffering from someone else's bad dreams.'

She sighed. As before the possibilities and questions began to crowd in. 'Solutions,' she thought desperately. 'Solutions, solutions, solutions.'

Only one came to mind; the one which she had been putting aside all day in the hope of finding another. She had to go to the house; she had to go armed with whatever defences she could muster, and she had to confront whatever she found there. Comfort came in the thought that, as far as she knew, nobody had actually been physically harmed by this thing.

Yet.

She scowled at that little word and blinked, her gaze shifting to take in the room behind her which was reflected on the glass. Items of phantom furniture hovered in the darkness, distorting slightly now and again whenever the wind rattled the frame. Olive's attention was drawn to the armchair, the large one with the frayed arms and the sagging seat. She leaned forward slightly as though the room did indeed exist outside the window, and gasped at what she saw reflected there.

Harold, her dead fiancé, was sitting cross-legged in the

chair, watching her. Olive gawped, too stunned to turn round. Yes, it was Harold all right, his short dark hair gleaming with oil, his smile easy under his thin nose and heavy-browed eyes. He was wearing his best grey suit, the one he had . . . Olive gulped. The one he had died in.

Now she took a deep breath and turned slowly, her senses, her thoughts, her whole being concentrated into that one pivotal movement. The name was on her lips, 'Harold,' but it slipped away and became lost in the wailing of the wind.

For as silently and unexpectedly as he had appeared, Harold had gone.

Olive stumbled forward and gripped the arms of the chair as though by clutching at something solid she could fetch Harold back. She put out a hand, watched its violent trembling almost with detachment, as though it did not belong to her, and placed it on the seat. She felt her heart jolt. She was not going crazy; the seat was still warm.

'Harold,' she whispered then, tears filling her eyes. 'Oh, Harold, where are you?'

7

'Good evening, Mr Wlodarczyk. Is your son, Krystof, at home?'

The heavy-set man in the maroon dressing-gown looked confused and more than a little alarmed. 'Krystof?' he murmured. 'He's . . . yes . . . yes, he is.'

'Splendid,' said Glennon. 'Would you mind if we came in, sir? We'd like to talk to him.'

Wlodarczyk stood his ground a moment, confused, then stepped back, pulling the door wide as he did so. 'Yes . . . yes, please do. I'm sorry to keep you standing in the cold.'

The policemen stepped into a hallway which, though identical to the Oates's, was brighter and more cheerful. Wlodarczyk gestured to a door on the left. 'Come this way. We'll talk in the living room.'

246

He opened the door and motioned for the two police-men to take a seat. 'Can I get you anything?' he asked. 'Coffee perhaps? Or something stronger?'

'Not for me, thank you, sir,' Glennon said, holding up a hand. Bailey would dearly have liked something hot, but he reluctantly complied with his superior.

Wlodarczyk nodded, closed the door and crossed the room. His movements were quick and nervous. He perched on the edge of a rocking-chair which looked more ornamental than useful.

'Well, officers,' he said, shrugging, 'what has my boy been up to this time?'

'This time, sir?' Glennon said. 'You mean he's been in trouble before?'

Wlodarczyk looked as though he'd been caught out, then gave an uncertain smile. 'Well, at school, yes, but never with the police.' He shrugged again, clapped his hands against his knees and leaned forward. 'He's a good boy at heart, you know, but he keeps bad company.'

'Really, sir?' said Glennon. 'Such as who?'

'Oh, I'm afraid I don't know their names,' Wlodarczyk said, spreading his hands. 'But take it from me, they are not the sort of companions either his mother or I would have chosen for him.'

'Would it jog your memory if I mentioned a couple of names, do you think?' Glennon asked.

Wlodarczyk looked doubtful. 'I don't know. You can try.'

'How about Maurice Landen?' Glennon ventured, leaning forward.

Wlodarczyk mulled over the name as though tasting wine, but at last said, 'No, I'm sorry . . . that doesn't sound familiar.'

'Then what about Steven Oates?'

This time the response was more positive. Wlodarczyk sat back and wagged a finger in the air. 'Ah yes, the Oates boy. Both his mother and I have forbidden Krystof to have anything to do with that . . . that monster!' His face creased in sudden anger. 'Do you know what he did, sergeant? Do you know what he did to a little boy?'

Glennon nodded seriously. 'Yes, sir, we do. Have you any idea where Krystof has been tonight?'

Wlodarczyk shook his head. 'No, he never tells me anything. But he had been drinking, I could smell it on his breath. Is that what this is all about, sergeant? Has my boy been found guilty of drinking under age?'

'No-one's been found guilty of anything yet, sir. At the moment we're simply making enquiries. But in answer to your question, no, this has nothing to do with under age drinking. I'm afraid the matter is rather more serious than that.'

'More serious?' Wlodarczyk's eyes were wide, his voice alarmed. 'May I ask . . . how serious?'

'At a private party this evening a boy was stabbed by one of a gang of six gate-crashers. We have reason to believe your son, Krystof, was among the gang; also Steven Oates and Maurice Landen. The whereabouts of Oates and Landen are presently unknown, as are the identities of the other gang members. With your permission, Mr Wlodarczyk, we'd very much like to speak to your son about this matter.'

Wlodarczyk looked almost pathetic in his disbelief. He was shaking his head, mouth agape, one hand raking distractedly through sleep-tousled hair. 'No,' he murmured, 'no, my son could never have done such a thing. It's impossible, I tell you. He's a good boy. He would never . . . *never* . . .' His eyes held an appeal, a yearning to be told that this was all a terrible misunderstanding.

'If we could just speak to Krystof, Mr Wlodarczyk?' Glennon said politely.

Wlodarczyk looked from Glennon to Bailey, his mouth working, struggling for speech. At last he said, 'Of . . . of course. I'll go and get him. He's in bed, you understand . . . asleep.'

Glennon gave a smile of encouragement and Wlodarczyk left the room, shaking his head. A couple of minutes later he re-entered the room with Ratz, who, despite his bulk, looked young and frightened in his Paisley pyjamas.

'Hello, Krystof,' Glennon said in a neutral voice.

Ratz came in and sat down, his eyes darting everywhere. 'Hullo,' he mumbled.

'I think you know why we're here,' Glennon said. 'We want you to tell us exactly what happened tonight at the party. Just take your time and start from the beginning. It'll be better for all of us if we get this sorted out quickly.' He sat back, meshing his fingers together over his stomach, and looked at Ratz. The boy stared back at him, too frightened to speak.

'Well, Krystof?' his father said finally.

Ratz closed his eyes; his lip began to tremble. At last, in a halting voice, he said, 'I . . . I didn't stab the bloke, you know. It was Rusty's idea. He wanted to do it, to get Gardener back for . . . for smashing his face in the other day. There was only Mo who encouraged Rusty . . . I didn't want to, but I had to go along with them . . . I had to . . . but . . . but honest, I never did . . . anything.' His voice trailed off. He cleared his throat and wiped a hand across his eyes.

Glennon asked, 'Who stabbed Neil Gardener?'

Ratz blinked, sniffed. 'Is . . . is he dead?'

'No, but he's in a serious condition. He was still in surgery when we left the hospital. Come on, Krystof, tell us who did it. We're pretty sure we know anyway, so you won't be doing yourself any favours by keeping quiet.'

Ratz bowed his head and covered his eyes with his hand. 'Mo,' he whispered.

'Mo. You mean Maurice Landen?'

'Yes . . . yes, Mo.' He paused for a moment, then looked up, his words coming in a rush. 'I never did anything. I had a knife, but I never used it.' He looked at his father. 'Honest, Dad, I never used it . . . God, I wish I'd never got into this.'

Wlodarczyk shook his head, his face assuming a number of different emotions. At last he went over to his son and embraced him awkwardly. 'All right, son, all right. I believe you. You've been a stupid, bad boy, but it's all over now.'

'I . . . er . . . I'm afraid it's not, sir. Not quite,' Glennon said.

'Not? How do you mean?'

'Well, sir, I'm afraid Krystof will still have a number of charges to answer . . . causing an affray, possession of a dangerous weapon. And there are other enquiries to be made, not least finding out the whereabouts of Oates and Landen.'

Wlodarczyk hugged his son fiercely, seemed about to argue, then thought better of it and nodded. 'Yes . . . yes, I understand.' He frowned slightly. 'Will . . . will you be arresting Krystof, officer?'

Glennon glanced at Bailey. 'Um, no, sir, I don't think that will be necessary just at the moment. But I would ask you to keep an eye on the boy for the rest of the weekend. We'll give you a call when we want to speak to him again.'

Wlodarczyk nodded. 'Of course . . . So will that be all for tonight?'

'Just one or two more questions, sir, if you don't mind. It won't take a minute.'

Wlodarczyk took his arm from around his son's shoulder slowly and carefully, like a nervous sculptor unveiling a new work. Ratz looked up, bleary-eyed, swallowing and sniffing.

'Now, Krystof,' Glennon said, 'can you tell us what happened after the incident this evening? And more importantly, do you know where Oates and Landen are?'

Ratz nodded. In a voice devoid of emotion he said, 'We went back to the club, The Glamour, because one of our mates didn't show up – Bruno – and Rusty was furious with him. Luckily for Bruno he wasn't there when we arrived. I was glad really 'cos Rusty was really mad and he had a knife on him and . . . well . . . you never know what he's gonna do when he gets like that, even to his mates.' He paused a moment, rubbed his eyes, then continued. 'Anyway, we stopped for a drink, but we only had one 'cos Mo said one of the kids at the party – Robin Treadwell – knew we hung around there, and that he might tell the pigs – um, the police – so we all just came home. I came back and went to bed. Rusty and Mo went off together, and the other lads just drifted off somewhere.' He stumbled to a halt and shrugged. 'That's all I know.'

'And you've no idea where Oates and Landen went to?' asked Glennon.

'No, they didn't say. They sometimes go back to Mo's to watch videos.'

'Yes, we've tried there,' Glennon said. He thought for a moment, then shrugged. 'What about these older boys? Can you tell me their names?'

'Not really,' Ratz said. 'I'd never met 'em before. One of them was Rusty's cousin or something . . . they called him Haystacks . . . you know, after the wrestler. Another was called Stubbs, and the other one . . . no, I'm sorry, I can't remember.'

'Any idea where they live?'

'Erm . . . Piling Hill somewhere. Apart from that, I don't know.'

Glennon stood up. 'OK, well, I think that should do it for tonight. As I say, we'll be in touch. Now you stay home, Krystof, and don't do anything stupid. If Oates or Landen try to contact you, I want you to call us straight away. Is that clear?'

Ratz managed a watery smile. 'Yeah, OK.'

'Good. Well, sorry to disturb you at this hour, Mr Wlodarczyk, but I'm sure you'll appreciate how important the matter was.'

'Of course, officer.'

'Right then, we'll be off. You ready, Kev?'

Bailey nodded and stood up. At the front door Glennon said, 'Good night, Mr Wlodarczyk.'

Wlodarczyk opened the door. 'Yes,' he said, though he

251

seemed preoccupied with his own thoughts. 'Yes. Good night.'

8

'Get back! Pigs!'

Rusty dragged Mo into an alleyway, behind a mouldering wall that had once been part of an outside toilet. Where the toilet had been there was now only a hole emitting a foul smell like an open sewer. The boys watched from the shadows as a police car swept past, its wheels sounding like skis slicing through the snow. When it had gone, Mo came out of hiding and looked at the two lines of tyre-tracks which were even now beginning to fill up again.

'Reckon they were lookin' for us?' he said.

Rusty shrugged, hefting the rucksack into a more comfortable angle on his back. 'Dunno. Probably. It's great this, isn't it. Just like Bonnie and Clyde.'

'Bonnie and Clyde?' Mo said scornfully. 'Don't be a cunt, Rus. One of them was a bird.'

Rusty looked blank, said, 'Oh,' then began walking again. Mo followed him, scooping up snow to lob at a 'For Sale' sign. Rusty began picking his nose thoughtfully, hunched over from the burden on his back. After a couple of minutes he asked, 'Which one?'

'What?' Mo said, pausing in the act of packing snow around a chunk of house-brick.

'That Bonnie and Clyde? Which one was a bird?'

'Which do you think?' Mo snorted.

Rusty considered, then shook his head. 'Dunno.'

Raising his eyebrows incredulously, Mo threw his snowball which landed among a sea of bin liners with a crackle like a scurrying rat. 'Bonnie was a bird and Clyde was a bloke.'

'Oh,' said Rusty, and shrugged. A moment later he asked, 'Well, what about the Kray twins then? You're not gonna tell me one of *them* was a bird?'

'No,' Mo said wearily, 'they were both blokes.'

'Good. Well, we'll be them then. I'll be Ronnie, you be Reggie.'

Mo sighed. Rusty sometimes got into these childish moods, and from long experience the skinhead knew that nothing could shake him out of them. Ordinarily it didn't bother Mo, but now he could have done without it. In this state, Rusty was apt to be reckless, sometimes crazily so. Mo said, 'Look, this isn't a game, Rus. If Gardener snuffs it, I could get done for murder.'

Rusty looked at him, squinting through straggly hair. 'Aw, stop worryin'. The pigs'll never find us in King Street. They'll think we've fucked off out of town.'

Mo had his doubts about that, but said nothing. The deserted house that was to be their refuge was not unknown to the coppers due to the junkies and glue-sniffers who went there. However, being discovered was not the only problem on Mo's mind. There was also the question of how long they would have to lie low for. 'Until all the fuss has died down,' Rusty had said, but Mo was now beginning to realize just how vague that statement was. The pigs weren't going to forget about a murder (or even attempted murder) in a hurry – which meant big trouble ahead. For the first time in his life, Mo had to admit that he was shit-scared. One thrust of a knife in a fuckin' disco had pushed him over the thin line from delinquency into the big league.

The boys hurried on, their feet sighing through the snow. Progress had been slow because they were keeping to the back-streets, avoiding the main roads where headlights could pin them down. They had seen no-one on their route, though once an Alsatian had plunged from an alleyway, its teeth bared and its fur standing up in spikes. Rusty, however, had run at the dog, screaming obscenities, and it had turned tail and fled.

'Nearly there now,' Rusty said a few minutes later. They crept down an alleyway, backyards of houses on either side, dustbins huddled in alcoves like waiting muggers. Somewhere a gate was banging furiously; to their left, icicles formed a frozen drool from an overflow pipe. Mo massaged his scalp, which felt slimed with snow, and picked his way over cobblestones slippery as polished marble. He was grateful for his Doc Marten's, more so because of the obstacles which met his feet: old newspapers, tin cans, ripped dustbin bags which spilled their trash like guts.

Eventually they came to the last house in the row. Here darkness seemed to have made its home, settling on the eroding brickwork in layers like bats on a cave wall. In the backyard, rubbish congregated in mounds; from the upstairs window-frames shards of glass glinted as they caught the moonlight, silver-winking jaggedly.

'Christ, what a dump!' Mo said, picking his way through the litter of the yard. He reached the back window, which was half-open, and peered through. 'Hurry up with that torch, Rus. I can't see a fuckin' thing in here.'

Rusty was picking at the straps which held the rucksack together, his fingers reduced to insensate twigs by the cold. At last the strap came free and he rummaged among the tins and blankets for his torch. He found it and passed it to Mo, who turned it on.

'Shit! Would you look at that!' Mo exclaimed, directing his beam into the house.

Rusty joined him by the window. 'What?'

'A rat, a fuckin' massive one, about the size of a rabbit. It ran across the room and out that door.'

'Well, at least we won't be short of somethin' to eat,' Rusty said, and sniggered.

Mo passed him the torch. 'Hold this.' He climbed on to a crate which had been placed conveniently beneath the window and pushed at the window frame which juddered obstinately for a moment, then slid all the way up. Sticking his head through, he thrust his hand out again for the torch, which Rusty silently handed over. Mo shone it around, picking out details which sprang up harsh and bloated for a moment before slipping back into torpor. His appraisal over, he turned back to Rusty.

'It's like a bloody ice-box, but it seems sound enough.'

'Course it is,' Rusty said. 'Only the best for you, my lad.' He watched as Mo clambered into the house, the skinhead's long legs and tight jeans making his body look unnaturally elongated. When Mo was through, Rusty handed him the rucksack, then climbed through himself. He coughed at the dust that billowed around him, then grinned at his friend with delight.

'It's all right, isn't it?' he said.

'It'll do,' Mo replied.

The boys left the kitchen via the gaping door-frame and emerged into the hall. Mo shone his torch around, grimacing at the seeping walls and the mouldy-fungus smell. He started down the corridor, then suddenly stopped, putting a hand out to halt his friend's progress.

'What's the matter?' Rusty said.

'Look there,' said Mo, and pointed the torch at the floor. Though blurred, the boys could clearly perceive a jumble of footprints in the dust. Leading both to and away from the door at the end of the corridor.

Rusty shrugged. 'Aw, it's nothing. Just smack-heads and glue-boys, that's all.'

'Yeah, but what if they come back?' Mo said. 'What if they find us here?'

'No problem. Most of em'll be too far gone to notice us anyway.'

Mo frowned, but said nothing. At the end of the corridor he shone the torch up the rubble-strewn steps, unconsciously imitating the actions of the Horror Club just a couple of days before.

'No chance of going up there,' Rusty said. 'What a fuckin' mess.'

The debris was now coated with a layer of snow which had come in through the hole in the roof. An icy wind wafted down the stairs as though something huge and hungry was breathing on them. Rusty said, 'We'll stay in here,' and pushed at the door which led into what once had been the sitting room.

Here footsteps and indentations in the dust indicated more recent activity. There was a faint smell that was omnipresent, but hard to pin down. Rusty walked into the middle of the room and spread his arms. 'Fuckin' great, innit?' he said. 'Absolutely fuckin' brilliant.'

Mo found it hard to drum up any enthusiasm. 'Yeah, it's all right,' he replied and shivered involuntarily. 'Cold, though.'

Rusty opened the rucksack and dragged out a couple of blankets. 'Here, wrap this round you and sit against the wall. I would've brought sleepin' bags, but I couldn't fit 'em in.'

He passed a blanket to Mo, who did as his friend suggested, slumping down against the wall that was opposite the boarded-up windows. Rusty swept his blanket around his shoulders, whipping up a mini dust-storm, and dragged the rucksack over to where Mo was sitting.

'There you go,' he said, pulling out a fourpack of Pils and breaking off a bottle for Mo. The skinhead nodded gratefully and took out the bottle opener he always kept in his inside pocket.

'You hungry?' Rusty said.

Mo took a swig from the bottle, sighed, and wiped a hand across his mouth. 'Dunno. What you got?' he replied.

'Beans, spaghetti, corned beef, peaches, bread.'

'Yeah, give us some beans and a few slices of bread.'

Rusty took the items from the rucksack. 'Bread's a bit squashed, but it'll be all right. It'll still taste the fuckin' same,' he said.

Later, when the boys were eating cold beans from the tin using bread and their fingers, Mo smiled. 'You know, Rus,' he said, 'we're gonna do all right here, me and you. We're gonna do all fuckin' right.'

Rusty took a swig of Pils, smearing the bottle with bean juice from his fingers, and belched. 'Course we fuckin' are,' he agreed.

Richard sat up in bed, sleep falling away from him like a warm cloak. Outside the window winter raged, but Richard's room was dark and still. On a chair his digital clock radio transmitted the message 6.20 a.m. in sickly green numerals. He groaned and rubbed his face. He had been in bed less than three hours.

He shivered from the cold and pulled the bedclothes up to his chin, wondering what had woken him. His stomach felt tense and queasy; maybe it was the delayed effects of trauma, or perhaps it was simply the beer he had drunk earlier. He got out of bed, stepping into his slippers automatically and reaching for his dressing-gown. He needed a drink, Andrews or an Alka Seltzer, something to settle his stomach. Yawning and stretching, he pushed open his bedroom door and stepped on to the landing.

He heard the whining almost at once. It came floating up the stairs, lonely and mournful, like a lost scrap of wind that had somehow become trapped in the house. For a few moments Richard stood rooted to the spot; the whining seemed to drift through him, a thin skein of sound that made him shudder violently. Then it degenerated into a series of whimpers, and immediately Richard realized what the noise was.

It was Sam, their dog. He must be frightened of the storm, or, more likely, the storm had woken him and he now wanted to be let out for a piss. Hands in dressing gown pockets, Richard padded downstairs, drawing up his shoulders against the cold. The evening's intermittent drizzle had become sleet which had now thickened to a blizzard again. Although the snow had only been falling for two or three days, it already felt as though they had been plunged into deepest, darkest winter. At the bottom of the stairs, Richard turned sharp right into the corridor that led to the kitchen.

Before entering the kitchen, he clicked the light switch outside the door. He looked up at the crack between door and frame, watching the thin band of light flickering erratically. When he was sure the strip lighting had stabilized, he pushed open the door and went inside.

Three things struck him almost at once: the intense biting cold; the stench of filthy-wet animal, much more pungent than Sam's faintly doggy smell; and Sam himself, curled up and shivering in his box, whimpering quietly.

'Sam,' Richard said, stretching out a hand, 'Sam, what's the matter?' He was alarmed to see Sam cringe back from him, curling his lip, showing his teeth. He was about to withdraw his hand, back quietly out of the kitchen and go fetch his dad, when Sam's attitude changed. The dog relaxed, his jowls stopped their teeth-revealing curl and he began to wag his tail weakly. Richard breathed a sigh of relief and reached out to scratch Sam's head. Sam wagged his tail harder and licked Richard's hand. His tongue was rough and cold.

'That's a good boy,' Richard said soothingly. He squatted on his haunches, shuffled forward and took Sam's head in his hands. He inspected the dog closely, but could find no sign of injury. He stroked Sam for a minute or more until the dog's shivering had subsided, looking round the room as he did so.

The reason for the cold was immediately obvious. The back window, which led into the garden, had either blown or been forced open. A broken mug lay on the floor, evidently knocked off the sill when the window had swung inwards. Apart from that, the kitchen seemed OK.

Richard went to shut the window, inspecting the catch as he did so. No, it hadn't been forced, so obviously the wind *had* blown it open. He wondered why Sam had been shivering and tried to convince himself it was because of the cold. But he couldn't help recalling the way the dog's jowls had curled back from his fangs when he had first entered the room. There was no doubt that Sam had been scared: but of what? The window blowing open? The cup breaking? Both alternatives seemed unlikely.

Richard fixed himself an Alka Seltzer and took a couple of Ryvitas from the packet by the bread bin. He munched them dry, and as he ate he wondered about the dirty animal smell that had assailed him on first entering the kitchen. He sniffed tentatively, but the smell was almost gone now. Maybe it would be better just to go back up to bed and forget about it. Then in the morning he could pretend it had never happened at all.

He finished the last of the Alka Seltzer, wincing as the bubbles popped up his nose. 'You all right boy?' he said to Sam. 'You don't want to go out?'

Sam wagged his tail, but stayed put. Richard was relieved. He patted Sam's hindquarters, then stole a quick glance back at the window, suddenly and inexplicably afraid of what he might see. He saw only a deep blue-blackness meshed with snow. Smiling nervously he turned back, said, 'Good night,' to Sam, and exited the kitchen, switching the light off behind him.

Despite his absence, his blankets were still warm when he returned to bed. Outside the wind screamed and clawed at the window with icy fingernails, but in a strange way that only made Richard feel all the more sleepy. He snuggled deeper into his covers, drawing up his knees, unharnessing his mind and letting it drift. An effortless moment later he was standing outside a cave from within which came the sweet scent of straw and the homely smell of baking. Richard went inside and was surprised to find the place dark and cold. In the centre of the floor he could just make out a black lumpy shape atop an assortment of metal rods that reflected light in steely flashes. He moved closer. The shape resolved itself into a wheeled stretcher, like the ones they had had in the ambulance. His brother, Neil, was lying on the stretcher, flat on his stomach, face turned to the side, arms above his head as though sunbathing. Richard saw that Neil had a knife jutting from his back and there was a small trickle of blood – luridly, blazingly red against the bluish-white skin – emanating from the wound.

Moving forward, Richard said, 'Neil.' The figure failed to respond. Richard clasped the knife handle and tried to draw it from his brother's back, but the knife wouldn't budge. He though crazily: 'Whomsoever removes this knife shall become the next king of England.'

His attention was suddenly drawn to the back of the cave where something stirred. He peered into the shadows, but there was interference there, fuzzy and half-formed, like trying to focus through the onset of blindness. The only definite impression he received was that whatever lurked in those shadows was of an awesome size. He waited expectantly, one hand still resting on the knife handle projecting from his brother's back, the other rubbing obsessively against his trouser leg.

All at once the shadows broke open and the creature inside extended something – a limb? – towards him. It twined and twisted like a vine, it was grey, and it had a slightly deformed human hand on the end of it.

Richard's own hands flew to his face and he dragged his lips into a screaming position but could produce no sound. The spastic hand on the end of the grey vine scuttled blindly through the air like a spider. It alighted on the knife handle, flexed, and drew the knife slickly from his brother's back.

'The new King of England,' Richard thought with horror, and awoke.

His blankets were still warm, but now uncomfortably so. Richard pushed them away and sat up, enjoying the sudden rush of cold air that dried his clammy fear. For a moment the dark seemed to be a mess of limbs that groped towards him; then it settled into stillness. He breathed deeply, looking at the sickly green numerals across the room hovering on 7.15 a.m. Below the numerals something dark was crouched.

Richard started. 'W-who's there?' he said, hoping he was making a fool of himself by challenging a bag or a pile of school books or . . .

Breathing.

Richard froze into immobility, trying desperately to believe that the breathing he heard was an undertone of the wind, the soft pad of snow whispering to the ground. He imagined the snow, the sound it would make . . . it was no use.

Something was here, with him, in his room. Breathing softly.

'Who's there?' Richard said again. A stammer suddenly flowed through him like a cold wind. 'W-w-w-w-who i-i-i-is i-i-it?'

With an almost audible thrum of power, two lights blinked on in the darkness. Red. Slanted. Like eyes.

Richard cringed back, crushing himself against the headboard and the wall behind. He dragged out his pillow and held it up as a flimsy shield. The contents of his bladder screamed for release and all he could think of was what his mother would say in the morning if she found out he'd wet the bed.

The red eyes bobbed closer, bringing with them an animal stench. Richard whimpered as they reached the end of his bed, then screamed in a gobbling falsetto as they jerked towards him. Something heavy landed on his legs. Claws dug in and began to climb. Richard found himself pressed down into his bed whilst something shaggy and stinking slid up his body like an unwelcome lover.

In the darkness, below the eyes, he saw a long black snout, fangs that gleamed with saliva. The wolf-face, only half-seen, pressed towards him as though for a kiss. He felt the thing's paws on his shoulders.

Almost suffocating in the stench, Richard whispered, 'What are you?'

And incredibly he received an answer, though whether the creature actually spoke or whether the words simply formed in his mind he was not sure.

'I am all,' came the reply, 'I am the Shoggoth, the Manitou, the Vampire, the Demon.' There was a harsh rasping sound – a breath or a chuckle. 'I am the hungry wolf of your dreams . . .'

Then the eyes took him, and Richard screamed at what they held.

10

'What the hell was that?'

Derek Gardener came awake with a jolt and shook his wife by the shoulder. 'Eileen,' he urged, 'Eileen, wake up.'

Eileen groaned, rolling over on to her back. As her eyes squinted open, she raised a hand against the glare from the lamp her husband had switched on.

'What is it?' she asked thickly.

'I heard a noise. I'm sure it was Richard.'

'Richard? . . . What . . . what about him?'

Derek motioned her to silence and listened. Alarm bells were still clanging in his mind, but just why he couldn't say. 'I . . . I heard something. Something woke me up,' he told her lamely.

Eileen struggled into a sitting position and gave her husband a look which suggested she required a more concrete reason for being shaken out of her slumber. However, a moment later, her dubious expression changed to shock when a high ratcheting scream, a scream of mortal terror, tore the stillness apart.

'Richard!' she shrieked, throwing back the bed-clothes. Derek was already out and tearing open the bedroom door.

'Stay here,' he ordered, and before Eileen could protest he slammed the door shut. He hared down the landing to Richard's room and threw his son's door open.

He was met by heat, stink, and an array of yellow-black shapes that bloomed and withered like a speeded-up film

262

of flower growth. For a moment he staggered, his senses battered into confusion. He tried to focus on something, anything, but the room was psychedelia run riot. Then, through the oily sickness of imagery, he caught a glimpse of Richard tossing and turning in his bed. His son's hands were clawing at his throat; a shadowy shape was lying astride his body.

'Richard!' he yelled and threw himself into the turmoil. Sweat sprang up on his forehead, shapes bubbled and pulsed as though his brain were melting. He reached his son's bed and, noting that the shadowy shape was gone, shook Richard by the shoulder.

'Richard, wake up! Come on!'

Richard's hands fluttered at his throat like wings. His mouth was open and his tongue protruded slightly. Derek saw a bead of saliva glisten on his son's lip, then trace a silver chain of moisture down his chin. Digging his fingers in, he shook Richard again.

'Come on, Richard, wake up!' His voice was raw with panic.

Richard reacted. His tongue flipped back inside his mouth and he made a peculiar 'glubbing' sound. His eyes opened.

He looked straight into his father's face for a moment, terror lying across his sight like a thin film. Then he blinked, his nostrils dilated and he began to breathe normally.

'Dad?' he said in a weak voice. 'Dad, is that you?'

Uncharacteristically, Derek reached out and hugged his son hard. 'Yes, Rich, it's me. Are . . . are you all right?'

'Yes,' Richard said, frowning. He opened his mouth, closed it, opened it again. Suddenly he blurted, 'Did you see it, Dad?'

'See? See what?'

'The . . . the thing . . . the wolf.'

Derek frowned. 'I saw something . . . I don't know . . . it was all very confused.'

Richard sat up and clutched his father's arm. 'It was in

263

here, Dad. It spoke to me. It tried to take me. Can't you smell it?'

Derek sniffed. He *could* smell something. A dirty animal stench, and something else. Something greasy, ozoney, as though a massive and somehow corrupt charge of energy had been released. He nodded. 'Yes, I can smell something. It smells like an accident in a chemical plant.'

'It was the wolf, Dad,' Richard said earnestly. 'The wolf was here.'

'Wolf,' Derek repeated and gave an awkward smile. 'I . . . I don't understand, Rich. What wolf?'

'*The* wolf, Dad, the one that followed me home the other night. It was here in my room. It was on my bed. It spoke to me. You saw it!'

Derek smiled again, though now logic and order were asserting themselves in his mind. A little warily he said, 'Well, I'm not really sure *what* I saw, Rich. I mean, it was dark . . . I was half-asleep . . . you know how it is when you're suddenly woken up. And besides, I mean . . . well, a wolf!! There haven't been wolves in Britain for years.' He shrugged apologetically and looked away from his son's disappointed gaze.

'But, Dad—' Richard began, then broke off and sank back on to his pillow. Derek ruffled his son's hair.

'You've just had a bad dream, that's all,' he said. 'All the excitement and the panic, I suppose. You try and get your head down for a couple more hours. You'll feel much better when you wake up.'

Richard looked at his father, sighed and nodded. 'OK,' he said bleakly.

Derek smiled. 'Good lad.' He hurriedly left the room, closing the door behind him.

As soon as his father had gone, Richard got up, padded across the carpet and switched on the light. The time was now 7.35 and the sky was beginning to lighten, but at the moment it was still too dark for Richard to feel properly safe. He was cold out of bed and realized how much he had been sweating. Shivering, he pulled off his pyjama top and replaced it with a t-shirt. He opened his bedroom door, slipped out to the bathroom, urinated, then went back into his room and dived into bed.

The sheets were messy, but the wolf-smell had gone and it still seemed the safest place to Richard. He sat up, the sheet pulled to his chin, intending to remain there until full daylight painted his curtains with brightness.

A breeze swept across him and he shivered. It was cold in here, he thought, colder than it ought to be.

He looked to the window and saw a curtain billow slightly. He froze. Was the wolf still there, waiting for a second chance? The curtain billowed again, more strongly this time, and with the spit congealing in his mouth Richard got slowly out of bed.

He went to the window and took hold of the curtain. The thought of pulling it aside terrified him, but anything was better than the waiting. Standing as far back from the window as he could get, he yanked the curtain open.

His own wild-eyed reflection swung towards him, encased in glass, and Richard sprang back with shock. Because his hand was still clutching the curtain, he almost ripped the material from the rail, but let go just in time. The window swung again, revealing a different aspect of the room, and Richard sat shakily on the bed, breathing a sigh of relief. An open window, that's all it was, he thought, just an open window.

Feeling suddenly vulnerable with his light on and the darkness staring in, he went across to pull the window shut. Before doing so he looked outside.

Snow lay thick and fresh on the ground. A line of footprints, pawprints – *wolf prints* – crossed the carpet of glittering white in a slightly wavering line. They started beneath his window, where they were deepest, indicating that the creature had jumped from a great height. They were frighteningly big prints, each one comprised of a central vaguely heart-shaped pad and three flat-clawed toes. Crisp blue shadows collected in them, emphasizing their clarity, but even as Richard watched the falling snow began to blur them a little.

He sat at the window for a long time, elbows on the cold sill, chin in hands, and watched the prints disappear. This was evidence, he kept thinking, evidence that the wolf had been here; but at no time did he feel inclined to fetch his father.

When he finally went back to bed half an hour later it was almost light. Apart from a series of very slight indentations, the wolf-tracks had been completely obliterated. The snow was white and smooth again. Virginal. Richard wondered where the wolf was now and whether it would come back. He lay in bed, and, feeling strangely calm, listened to the singing of the birds.

11

A hand touched Toady's shoulder and he came awake at once. The figure who had woken him padded to the window and pulled the curtains open, allowing light to spill into the room. The covering of snow was dazzling, the sky a neutral grey. Toady's mind felt scrubbed, as clean as the house-roofs looked. Propping himself up on one elbow he asked, 'What time is it?'

The figure walked back across the room and sat in the large armchair. It crossed its legs, smiling slightly, and looked at its watch. *My* watch, Toady thought, but when he glanced at the dressing table his watch was still there, where he had put it last night.

'Nine o'clock,' the figure said. 'Time to talk before your parents get up.'

The figure smiled and Toady gave a little start. Was his own smile really that cruel, that mocking? 'Who exactly are you?' he asked, and immediately felt as though the conversation was becoming unreal. The figure's smile widened, making the face grotesquely frog-like.

'You know who I am,' it said.

266

Toady looked at himself, *at himself*, sitting across the room talking to him. The figure had his build, his face, his hair, even duplicates of his clothes – exact duplicates, right down to the grease-stain on the front pocket of his jeans and the slightly out-of-shape sweater collar that had been caused by his mother washing the garment at too high a temperature. Toady stared at this image of himself for a long time, a million possible explanations buzzing through his head. Finally he asked, 'Why do you look like me?'

The figure laughed (Toady thought: 'I don't laugh like that!') and said, 'I didn't think you'd be frightened of your-self. All the other things I tried just provoked resistance.'

Toady struggled to understand. 'So . . . so it *was* all down to you? All those dreams and . . . and that other stuff?' He blushed deeply, remembering the sexual nature of some of yesterday's experiences.

The figure that looked like him – *that was him* – inclined its head modestly. 'That was all me, yes. I wanted to communicate, but wasn't sure how. I was searching for an emotion that would make you receptive.'

'You exhausted me,' Toady said. 'You . . . you fright-ened me.'

'Yes, I know. I'm sorry about that.'

Toady struggled to express his thoughts and emotions. He felt clogged with them, but so complex and acute were they that paradoxically he seemed to feel nothing. A dreary numbness, that was all; a need to unravel things slowly. He certainly didn't feel the exultation, the wonder, the awe that he had anticipated. Probing cautiously he asked, 'How do you do all that . . . all that shape-changing? I mean, can you be anything you want? Can you go anywhere?'

The figure stretched and groaned, as though, like Toady, it had just woken up. 'Of course,' it said airily. 'Anything and anywhere at all.'

'But how do you do it? I mean . . . how do you do it?'

'It's easy. I don't know *how* I do it. I just do it, that's all.'

267

'But . . . but can you be in several places at once? I mean . . . how big are you?'

'Big?' said the creature. 'What's big?'

'You know. Size. Dimensions.' Toady spread his arms. 'This is me. This is all I am. This is my shape.' He lowered his arms slowly. 'What shape are you?'

The figure frowned, then raised its arms in a parody of Toady's own actions. 'This is my shape,' it said.

Toady began to feel frustrated. 'Yes, but not all the time,' he insisted.

'No, not all the time,' the figure agreed.

'Then what,' Toady said, 'is your proper shape?'

The figure considered the question carefully. At length it said, 'I don't know.' It held out a closed fist, palm up. Toady looked at it, eyebrows raised. The fist opened and a small creature sat there, a terrapin with a red and black spotted shell like a ladybird. 'This is me,' the figure said, indicating itself. 'And this is me.' It prodded the terrapin. The terrapin raised his head sleepily and began to plod across the figure's hand. The figure put the terrapin on the floor and stamped on it. Toady heard the crunch, saw the mashed remains of the terrapin clinging to the bottom of the rubber-soled Adidas trainer – *his* rubber-soled Adidas trainers – that the figure wore. He winced. The figure smiled.

'Does . . . doesn't that hurt?' Toady asked uneasily.

The figure's smile turned to a frown of puzzlement. 'Hurt? What is hurt?'

'You know – pain? Don't you feel pain?'

The figure looked at him as though expecting him to elaborate, then shrugged. 'No,' it said.

'Then what *are* you? What name do you call yourself?'

Again the figure considered, a frown on its face. 'Adrian.'

Toady sighed. 'No, no, what *are* you?' He broke off, frustrated. 'Are you . . . the Devil?'

'The Devil?' The figure looked bemused by the word.

Toady gesticulated with his hands. 'Are you . . . good or bad?'

'Good or bad? I don't know. I don't understand the question.' The figure poked Toady in the chest and a shrewd look came over its face. 'Are *you* good or bad?' it asked him.

Toady flinched as though struck. His eyes widened; his mouth opened and closed. 'I . . . I don't know,' he stammered. 'G-good, I suppose.'

'Then,' the figure said, satisfied, 'I must be good too.'

Toady sighed and closed his eyes. When he felt composed he opened them again. 'Why are you here?' he asked.

'You called me,' the figure said, smiling.

'No, no I didn't mean that. I meant – what's *your* reason for being here? *Why* did you come? Why are you here now? Like this? With me?'

'I've come to help you,' the figure said, and its smile widened.

'Help me? How can you help me?'

The figure pushed itself up from the armchair and walked across the room to the window, on the way picking up a tatty paperback that had been lying on the floor. The paperback's cover depicted a screaming man with maggots burrowing out of his face. The Toady-figure snorted and tossed the book on to the bed. 'You have enemies,' it said, looking out of the window.

Toady made no reply; he felt none was called for. However the silence stretched out, became uncomfortable – and angrily, with a distinct feeling that he was being manipulated, he snapped, 'So?'

The figure swung round and immediately Toady's mood changed from resentment to terror. The face that looked at him was no longer his own – it was the face of the man from the cover of the paperback. Maggots were squirming and wriggling from enlarged pores in the man's face. The mouth opened and perhaps two dozen more maggots spilled from between the distorted lips. Toady screamed and began to pedal his feet on the bed to put as much distance as possible between himself and the apparition. The tormented face laughed and abruptly changed again, becoming Toady's face once more. Even as Toady watched, the maggots withered like scabs and disappeared, and the pores from which they had come closed up. The Toady-thing said, 'With my help you can be anything you wish. You can crush your enemies as if they were flies . . . or maggots.'

Toady still felt sick, but already the implications of what he was being told were beginning to excite him. He imagined Rusty Oates squirming, pleading for mercy, and a warm thrill of pleasure spread though his body. Eagerly he asked, 'You mean you'll teach me how to change like you?'

His twin nodded. 'Of course. If that's what you want.'

'But . . . but how?' Toady said. 'How do I do it?'

The figure put its finger on the window and began to doodle on the condensation that covered the lower half of the glass. Abstractedly it said, 'It's quite easy. You'll soon learn.'

'Can you teach me something now?' Toady said.

The figure ceased its doodling and turned with a smile. 'If you like.' It came across the room and sat on the edge of the bed. Up close, Toady scrutinized the face it wore and marvelled at the creature's ability. Its resemblance to himself was astonishing, even down to the rash of spots on his forehead and the mole beneath his left ear.

'Right,' the figure said, 'what shall we do first? We'd better start with something simple.'

Toady thought for a moment, then held up his left hand, curling all but the index finger into his fist. 'Turn my finger into a twig,' he said.

His facsimile laughed, amused by the request. 'Very well. Concentrate. Concentrate on your finger. It is no longer flesh and blood. It can be moulded. It can become whatever you wish it to be.'

Toady stared at his finger, fascinated, looking closely at the bitten-down nail, the knuckles, the intricate swirls of his fingerprint. Suddenly he gasped, feeling a rush of heat, then cold, then pins-and-needles pervade the digit. The finger trembled, hooked over of its own accord.

And before his very eyes Toady saw it begin to change.

12

'Rob, I *know* something weird's going on,' Richard said. 'That wasn't a dream I had this morning. It was real. That wolf really was in my room.'

Robin scooped snow off a low wall to make a snowball, but it stuck to his gloves and broke up like powder. 'I dunno, Rich,' he said doubtfully. 'Dreams are funny things. That one I had last night about the bird seemed real at the time, but . . . well, I know now that it *was* only a dream.'

'But how do you know?' Richard demanded.

'Well, for one thing I got soaked in that dream, but when I woke up afterwards I was clean and dry. And that bird . . . it . . . ,' he faltered for a moment, '. . . it hurt me pretty bad. I mean, really cut me up, you know?'

Richard frowned. 'Yeah, well, I still say something's going on. We should never had had that seance. It . . . well, things aren't right, that's all.'

Robin shrugged. He had always been a sceptic, a strong believer that there was a rational explanation for everything, and all morning he had been trying to convince himself that last night's experience had been simply a nightmare. He thought he'd just about succeeded too, except that now and again he found his hands straying unconsciously to his eyes as though to ensure they were still there.

The boys turned the corner on to Nige's street, their footsteps thick and snow-muffled. Here, among the boarding-houses and holiday homes, Starmouth seemed like a ghost of happier days. The boxy houses painted in summer colours slept stoically beneath layers of snow; the only sounds were the ever-present sighing of the sea and the harsh scrape of metal on concrete as a sweating man further up the road cleared snow from his path.

Richard halted at Nige's gate, eyes widening. 'Bloody hell,' he said.

Robin followed his gaze to the front lawn. 'What's the matter?' He could see nothing amiss.

'The snowman,' Richard spluttered. 'It's gone!'

Robin frowned. In the centre of the lawn was a slight circular depression. 'What snowman?' he said.

'Y-yesterday me and Nige built a snowman. Right here on the lawn where that sort of circle is. It can't have just vanished overnight.'

'Perhaps it melted,' Robin suggested with a shrug.

'Don't be stupid, Rob! Snowmen don't just melt like that. No, someone must've nicked him. They must've come in the night and . . . and dug him up and . . . carried him off on a sledge.'

Robin shoved the gate open. 'Oh, well, you'll just have to build another,' he said. 'There's plenty of snow around.'

Richard followed his friend up the path, but he continued to shake his head and look at the place where the snowman had been. At the door Robin rang the bell and they waited. After a few moments they saw Mrs Figg's bulk wavering towards them through the frosted glass. Resentfully Richard thought: 'Why does it always have to be her who answers the door?'

Robin smiled when the door opened, but Mrs Figg didn't respond. Instead she looked at his spotty face as though he had some disgusting and incurable disease. 'Yes?' she said coldly.

'God, here we go,' Richard thought. At the same instant he switched on a smile and said, 'Hello, Mrs Figg. Is Nigel in?'

Mrs Figg glared at him and Richard could almost hear the cogs in her head whirring as she searched for some discouraging reply. However, this was Sunday – home-work had been completed and there were no shops open to which Nige could run errands. Her frown deepened but she said, 'Yes, I'll call him. You'd better come in.'

She stomped into the hall and Richard and Robin followed. In deference to Sunday, she was not wearing her usual flounces and frills. Instead she had opted for a simple blue dress with a white belt. Richard noted with some amusement that even her lipstick seemed a shade less severe today.

Her voice, however, was stentorian as ever. 'Niiiigelll!' she yelled up the stairs. 'Your friends are here.' She turned back to the boys, scorching them with a look. 'He'll be down in a moment.' Then she waddled into the sitting room, closing the door firmly behind her.

Richard and Robin exchanged a glance, half-amused, half-despairing. A moment later there was a sound on the stairs and Nige appeared. He looked tired and his smile seemed a little forced. 'Hi,' he said.

Richard and Robin returned the greeting, watching as Nige pulled on coat and scarf. Cleaning the steam from his spectacles, Richard asked, 'What happened to the snowman?'

He felt uncomfortable at the look Nige gave him. It was strange. Almost fey. In a halting voice, Nige said, 'I don't know.'

'Well, was it stolen?' Richard asked, trying to make his voice casual. There was a beat of silence during which some secret unspoken message seemed to zip between the three of them.

Then Nige said, 'I dunno . . . Yeah, it must've been.'

Robin opened the front door. The tension which had seemed to build between the boys was dissipated a little by the cold air. Robin and Richard stepped outside. Nige went to the sitting room door, opened it a crack and peeked in.

'I'm going out, Mum,' he said. 'I'll be back in time for tea.'

'You make sure you are,' came Mrs Figg's disapproving reply. There was an exaggerated shivering noise and she snapped, 'Quickly, Nigel, shut the door. It's freezing cold in here.'

Nige sighed and pulled the door shut, then followed his friends outside. Richard was on the path, again staring at the place where the snowman had been. Nige brushed past him, purposely avoiding his questioning gaze, and caught up with Robin. Both boys went out of the gate and began plodding down the road. After a moment Richard followed them.

They trudged in silence for a while, each occupied with his own thoughts. With each step they took, the softly hypnotic whoosh of the sea drew closer and closer. Eventually Nige asked, 'Is Toady coming today?'

Richard nodded. 'Yeah, he rang up to say he'd meet us at the cave.'

Nige raised his eyebrows. It was rare for Toady to ring any of them up.

'I dreamt about you last night,' Robin said abruptly. He looked at Nige in a way that Richard could not fathom; as though he was either affronted by Nige's participation in his dream or was seeking reassurance.

'Oh, yeah?' Nige said warily.

'Mmm. I dreamt I was on the beach, near the pier. I heard this sort of pounding. I looked up and you were there, running along the pier in your dressing gown. There was someone after you, a big fat man dressed in white. He'd almost caught you when you climbed on to the pier railings and threw yourself into the sea. I . . . I don't remember much after that.' He stumbled to a stop. The dream had been related at breakneck speed, as though Robin had felt an urge to get it out of his system. Now that he had done so he looked waxy, but somehow relieved.

The effect on Nige, however, was startling.

He began to shake, and suddenly staggered backwards as though about to faint, causing Richard and Robin to leap forward to stop him from falling. Nige, however, didn't fall. He stumbled back against a low garden wall, put a hand out behind him to ensure it was solid and sat down with a thump. He closed his eyes and let out a long steamy breath. Bit by bit his shaking subsided.

'Y-you all right?' Richard asked at last. His voice was so unexpectedly clear that it seemed to crack like a whip in the sharp air.

Nige nodded. 'Yeah, just give me a minute or two. I'll be all right.' He exhaled again, more strongly this time.

'I'm sorry, Nige,' Robin said, looking guilty, 'I didn't mean to frighten you.'

'It's . . . it's all right. It wasn't you. That dream just gave me a bit of a shock, that's all.'

'Shall we take you home?' Richard said. 'Do you need a doctor or anything?'

Nige gave a tight laugh. 'No, I've told you. I'll be fine. Just give me a minute or two.'

Richard crouched down by his friend. 'What was it about Rob's dream that got you so scared, Nige?'

The olive-skinned boy paused, looking down at his fingernails. 'Well, you know you asked about the snowman?' Richard nodded. 'Yeah, well, that was the fat man in white who was chasing me across the pier. I had this horrible nightmare where I was walking through all this blackness, and suddenly I came across the blind man, Robespierre, and he was all thin and white. He took his specs off and he had red eyes. And then he started to rip himself across the chest with his fingernails and . . . and I ran and suddenly I was outside and the snowman came alive and chased me on to the pier. I got away by jumping off, and I woke up in bed before I hit the water.' He stopped there, rubbed a trembling hand across his face. 'Pretty fuckin' weird, huh?' He turned to Robin. 'Well?' he said quietly. 'Do you still think there's nothing going on?'

Like Robin before him, Nige had related the dream in little more than a babble, but still Richard felt its potency. He shuddered. 'Yeah. Pretty fucking weird.'

Robin shrugged. He looked at Nige with an expression of almost fearful animosity. 'Dreams, that's all,' he said stubbornly. 'It was a coincidence that they were both similar.'

'A *coincidence*?' Richard exclaimed. 'Oh, come on, Rob, you can't mean that! I mean, you both *saw* the snowman, you both shared the same experience, and this morning the snowman's gone. It may have been a dream you both had, but in a strange way it also happened, just like me and the wolf. Surely you can't deny that?'

Robin shrugged again. He was glowering at the road and refusing to meet his friend's gaze. He muttered, 'I didn't say it *was* a snowman in my dream; just a fat man in white. And in fact, now I come to think of it, I don't think it was a snowman. No, I'm pretty sure it wasn't. So you see, Nige and I didn't share the same dream at all.'

He stumped towards the sound of the sea, making it clear the matter was at a close. Richard sighed, opened his mouth to argue further, then decided against it. If Robin was determined to believe that nothing was happening, then there was no way Richard would be able to change his mind. Maybe later, when he had had time to think things over, he would be prepared to admit what they all secretly knew.

Nige stood up and they trudged after Robin. Minutes later they reached the promenade, gasping at the thundering traffic of freezing air which bowled over and around them. Richard glanced towards Olive's booth and decided he would go and see her again as soon as he could. Maybe together they could work out some way to combat what was happening. As they descended the steps to the beach, Richard wondered whether anything strange had been happening to Toady since they'd seen him last. Certainly his friendliness on the phone that morning had made him sound peculiar.

'Hey! You lot!' came the cry from behind them, and the boys turned slowly. Toady was standing at the top of the steps in a shabby parka, the hood pulled tight around his head and tied in a bow under his chin. His jeans were tucked into black Wellingtons that flapped against his legs just below the knees. He was wearing no gloves and his hands looked red-raw and cold. 'Wait a minute!' he shouted.

Even as he came down the steps, Richard noticed a new and strange exuberance in his manner. Despite the cold weather his eyes were shining, his mouth twitched up into a smile. Again Richard felt disturbed by Toady's apparent cordiality. Normally he didn't call a greeting; he just slunk up to the boys and waited moodily for someone to greet him.

'Hello, Ade,' Richard said as Toady joined them.

Toady's smile widened. 'Hi,' he said, 'how are you?'

'All right, I suppose,' Richard replied, still bewildered and a little mistrustful. 'We, er, we've got a few things to discuss this afternoon . . . serious things,' he added.

'Serious?' Toady looked momentarily sullen, then glanced at Nige and Robin and shrugged. 'OK. Do you want to fill me in?'

As they trudged across the slushy sand-snow beach, under the pier and along the rockier flats that led to the cave, each of them told Toady of their experiences of the previous night. Nige again related his in a halting voice, though this time he filled in more detail. Robin related his only after some goading from Richard, and made a point of playing down any connection between Nige's dream and his own. Richard told Toady about the wolf, about Olive's sensation of shattering glass on the night of the seance, about Nige being hypnotized. And then, as an afterthought, he told him about the stabbing at the party.

'Shit,' Nige said, his eyes widening, 'with the snowman and everything I'd forgotten all about Neil. How is he, Rich? Is he going to be all right? How long were you at the hospital for last night?'

Richard held up his hand to stem the flow of questions. 'Yeah, he's OK,' he said. 'He's had surgery and the doctor says he should be up and about in a week or two. We were at the hospital till about three this morning. I'm going to see Neil later on this afternoon if any of you want to come.'

The boys nodded vaguely, though Richard looked at Toady, more concerned with his reaction to all he'd been told than anything else. He had looked interested in the boys' stories, though not once had he seemed horrified, shocked or surprised, not even when he heard about the trouble with Rusty, a fact which again caused Richard to feel uneasy.

'Has anything weird been happening to *you*, Ade?' Richard said, the question sounding like a challenge despite his attempt to keep it casual.

Toady regarded him a moment, licked his lips as though on the verge of a confession, then abruptly shook his head. 'No,' he said firmly, and turned away before Richard could say more.

As they clambered over the rocks that led to the cave, Robin, despite himself, felt his mouth going dry. He half-expected to see a girl standing at the cave-mouth, something bloody and torn in her hands. The noise of the gulls was raucous and hostile and his shoulders bunched as though anticipating attack.

'Someone's been here,' Richard said immediately they had entered the cave, and pointed at the remains of a fire in the middle of the sandy floor. Nige looked at Robin, saw him fighting down fear that was trying to hatch on his face, and saw that Richard had noticed the expression too. Toady untied the knot at his chin and pulled down his hood then moved forward, knelt, and put his hand in the ashes.

'Still warm,' he said. 'Must've been an old tramp or someone looking for shelter.'

'Yeah,' Robin croaked eagerly, and the others looked at him. As though embarrassed by the attention, he laughed sharply. 'That's all it was,' he said, 'just a tramp, nothing else.' He stirred his foot around in the ashes as if to assure himself they were real.

Nige, who was standing beneath the natural flue in the roof, suddenly slapped the back of his neck. '*Urghh*!' he said. 'What the hell was that?'

278

'Bird shit,' Richard said, and they all sniggered, releasing the tension inside them. However when Nige brought his hand round they all saw his fingers were smeared not with bird shit, but with blood.

They stared stupidly at the glistening redness for a moment before Richard asked, 'W-where did *that* come from?'

Nige looked bewildered and a little frightened. He stepped away from where he had been standing and cautiously looked up the flue. 'I . . . I don't know,' he said, looked at his fingers again, then suddenly grimaced and began to wipe them on the rock wall.

Robin suddenly gasped, 'L-look there,' and pointed at the floor.

Richard followed his gaze, and saw that where Nige had been standing there was a sticky pool of blood that looked dark, almost black, round the edges. A messy set of footprints – Nige's footprints – led out from the pool and trailed across the floor.

Immediately Richard was reminded of the hospital corridor last night, the broken line of red footprints that had glistened on the tiled floor. Nige moaned and plunged his blood-smeared Wellingtons into the centre of the dead fire. A cindery smoke billowed up and bits of ash clung to the blood. Richard and Robin watched this grisly cleansing with a kind of repulsed fascination, but Toady wandered over to the flue and stared up at it again.

'I still can't see anything,' he said. 'I think it must – oh, look here.'

Richard glanced up and saw Toady peering, fascinated, into the fissure. Toady beckoned him over and Richard came. 'That's where it's coming from,' Toady said. 'Just there.' He pointed into the flue.

Richard followed the line of his finger and saw Toady was pointing at the shelf on which the boys stored matches and candles and sometimes magazines. The shelf was just a couple of feet up the flue and led off from the fissure at a right angle. The only way that the boys could reach it was if one sat on another's shoulders, and even then they could only just get their fingers inside. It was a useful cubby-hole, but they had never explored it fully; they didn't, for instance, know how far back it went.

As Richard watched, he saw a bead of blood, black and shimmering, form on the lip of the shelf. It hung for a moment like an oily chrysalis, then dripped silently to the floor.

'Come on,' Toady said, 'give me a leg up. I'm going to see what it is.'

Robin's eyes widened. Nige took a step forward, half-raised his hand, then thought better of it and stayed where he was. Richard felt his stomach begin to churn, but made no move to oppose Toady's suggestion. Indeed, he crouched down so that Toady could climb on to his shoulders; he was as horribly curious as the rest of them.

Toady, although short for his age, was a weight, and Richard at first was unable to stand up. However, with Robin's help he got to his feet, his head bowed forward to accommodate the fat boy's gut. Toady peered into the flue. Though the gap way above afforded some light, it was still dark in there. He reached up and gripped the edge of the shelf.

'Found anything?' Richard said.

'No, not yet,' replied Toady. 'The shelf's all slippery with blood. Grab my feet and push me up a bit more.'

Richard did so, his biceps crying out as he took almost the whole of Toady's weight in his hands. He tottered slightly and Robin moved forward to support him. 'Found anything now?' Richard gasped as the top of Toady's head came level with the bottom of the shelf. Toady tried to peer into the crevice, but saw only blackness. Rashly he plunged his hand in and came up almost immediately against a slippery, but fairly solid object.

'I've got something,' he said. 'Hang on, I'll try and get a grip.' His hand explored the object, trying to find something he could grab hold of. He had the uncomfort-able impression that he was handling some sort of dead animal. He smelt something unpleasant and fought down the bile that was rising in his throat.

'Hurry up,' Richard gasped. 'My shoulders are slipping to my elbows.'

'Won't be long now,' Toady said as his exploring fingers found an orifice. He got a good grip and pulled. The object jammed for a moment, then popped from the opening like a cork from a bottle.

As soon as he got it into the light, Toady screamed shrilly and dropped it. The object landed at Richard's feet with a dull squashy thud. There was a moment of stunned silence then the boys began to yell like banshees.

The object lying at their feet was a human head. But it was not *just* a human head – it was a head that was battered, torn and eyeless. With a sick recognition Robin realized it was the object the girl had been feeding from last night in his dream. This message zipped from his brain to his stomach like an electric shock and he whirled and vomited into the fire.

From the shelf above Toady's head there now came a sort of shifting. He scrambled down from Richard's shoulders, almost rupturing himself in the process. Richard was still standing with the mutilated head at his feet, his face a mask of shock.

'*Come on,*' Toady said urgently, '*there's something else up there.*' One hand was clamped to his throbbing balls; the other reached out and grabbed Richard's arm.

Richard looked up, dazed, a strange whining sound coming from the 'O' of his mouth. He stood for a moment, ignoring Toady's attempts to try and drag him away; then all at once, his eyes widened and he looked into the flue. Toady's urgings suddenly made perfect and horrible sense, but by then it was too late to get clear.

A moment later Alfie Bessle's piecemeal anatomy was raining down all around them.

CHAPTER TWO

Fire, Fire, Burning Bright

1

The fire was only a small electric, but it made Olive nervous just the same. She daren't turn her back on it for fear an electrical fault would cause sparks to shoot out and set her lounge ablaze. Normally she refrained from putting it on at all, preferring to sit in her armchair, clad in so many layers she looked like the Michelin Man, warming herself with pot after pot of herbal tea. However, this morning, for only the third time this winter, it had been so cold that she had *had* to put it on. As always she had first gone into the kitchen to fetch a pan of water in case of emergency. Then, her fingers trembling, she had clicked the dreaded switch.

Now, several hours later, she was sitting, warm but wary, watching the orange bars as a babysitter might watch a mischievous child. She had been thinking deeply today, about Harold and wondering why he had appeared to her last night. Was he trying to warn her? Comfort her? She found some comfort from merely sitting in the chair which he had occupied. But truthfully his appearance had provoked in her an overwhelming feeling of sadness and . . . and *distance*. It was as though Harold were in some far, far unreachable place, and yet at the same time, agonizingly, near enough to touch.

On the wall in front of her, above the mantelpiece, was a mirror – an art deco mirror shaped like a cloud with a flat base. Normally, from this position, it gave a view of the opposite wall and the bottom left-hand corner of a framed print – Van Gogh's 'Sunflowers'. Today, however, the mirror seemed to have been tilted slightly downwards and when Olive looked in it she saw herself, an old lady – grey-haired, wrinkled, bespectacled – huddled in front of a fire trying to keep warm. Immediately a wave of despair washed over her. 'I can't do with all this,' she thought, 'not at my age.' She glanced at her hands on the chair arm – blotchy, feeble, the fingers like knobbly twigs. 'Not at my age,' she thought again. 'Not at my age.'

Suddenly she felt very tired. Despite the fire she felt her eyes closing. Less than a finger-snap later she was dream-thinking about Harold and how death had kept him young; and then, as though the subject were a natural progression, she began to think about hypothermia and how it could provide her with an easy, almost painless release.

She pictured herself, actually saw herself, leaning forward and switching off the fire. Then she was stripping off her layers of clothing, folding them neatly and putting them on the floor by her chair. As she did it she thought: 'Naked I came into the world and naked I will go out.' When that was done she simply sat back and waited.

A voice was speaking in her ear. A dreamy hypnotic voice that made her think of Nathan Buttrick. But this was not Nathan; he was still alive, and living people were not allowed to go where this voice was coming from. No, this was Harold; he was speaking to her, comforting her, telling her not to worry. He was saying: 'It's all right, Olive, my darling, soon we shall be together. Passing from your state to mine is so easy, so very much easier than people realize. In your case there may be a little shivering at first, but you can handle that, of course you can. After the shivering you will feel numb and sleepy, sooo, sooo sleeeepy . . . and then you will start to float. Float and drift, float and drift. Until at last you will wake . . . in my arms.'

Just then Olive did wake up, and was shocked to discover that someone was unbuttoning her cardigan. She was even more shocked a moment later when she realized that someone was herself. She shot out her arm as though it had betrayed her, and the empty teacup by her side went tinkling to the floor where it broke against its own saucer. Olive blinked wildly, her heart thudding, the taste of fear bitter on her lips. What had happened to her just then? What had happened? Had she become so frightened by this seance business that her mind had conjured up an image of Harold as an excuse for suicide? No, she couldn't believe that. She had always been a scrapper, a fighter. She would never – never – entertain such notions. Where there's life, there's hope, she had always said. And suddenly she felt a fury so hot, so terrible, that it obliterated her fear altogether. She thought with utter coldness: 'I am going to go to that house in King Street and I am going to destroy whatever it is I find there.'

She pushed herself defiantly to her feet, the sudden action causing her knees to crack like pistol shots. Ignoring the fire, the metal crackling as it cooled, she righted the mirror and picked up the pieces of broken cup, which she carried into the kitchen and deposited in the flip-top bin.

She was convinced now that the Harold she had seen last night had not been her Harold; it had been some part of that . . . thing, some ghostly offshoot intended as a lure. Well, Olive was not standing for that. From now on she would be on her guard. That thing was not going to trick her again.

She stomped back into the lounge, throwing a cursory glance over at the dying fire. She had switched it off in her sleep. That thing had made her switch it off. She crossed to the window to look at the sea, but what she saw out there on the beach chased all other thoughts from her mind.

There were four . . . creatures racing across the sand, screaming and wailing, their bodies splotched with red. It took a moment for the creatures to become boys, and then for the boys to become boys she knew.

Olive touched her throat in an almost religious gesture, though there was no crucifix or medallion there, and hurried into the hall. She took her coat from the peg and put it on. She glanced down at her feet, realized she was only wearing her house-shoes, and decided they would have to do. She ran, panting, down the stairs that led to her booth, and less than a minute later was crossing the wide road of the promenade and leaning over the railings twenty feet above the beach. Richard and his friends were still sprinting, heading towards the steps that would bring them back up on to the promenade.

Olive had a gift, a 'sixth sense', that (she had once told Richard) was like a huge and ancient radio that could now and again pick up snatches of obscure wavebands. If emotions were very strong somewhere nearby, Olive often got traces of them, red-hot flashes that were like physical blows to the system. The emotions she was receiving now, the waves of searing terror that were pulsing off the boys, was the most intense and frightening she had ever known. She could feel panic welling inside her, closing her throat, causing blood to gush round her body so violently she was sure she would pass out.

Then, as suddenly as it had come, the waveband shifted, slid over and around her, and left Olive shaking with relief and reaction.

Richard was very close now. Olive could no longer feel the terror but she could see it, stark and shocking, on his face. She felt an almost superstitious dread at the amount of blood that covered the boys, Richard in particular. It matted his hair, stained his clothes so completely it looked as though he'd been sprayed. The spotty boy who was just behind Richard was holding out his dripping hands as though to plead his innocence. A little way behind the spotty boy came the lissom, dark-haired, olive-skinned boy called Nigel whom Nathan had hypnotized; and bringing up the rear, panting with exertion, was a chubby boy whom Olive was certain she had never met, but who nevertheless looked vaguely and unsettlingly familiar.

285

She ran to the top of the steps and placed one hand on the railing for balance. 'Richard!' she yelled into the wind.

He looked up, saw her and tried to speak. He couldn't. After a moment he gave up and stumbled on.

Olive went down the steps, taking care not to slip, and reached the bottom at precisely the same moment Richard did. She grabbed his arm, but could not stop him from falling on to his knees in the sand. His head bowed forward, wracking sobs convulsing his body. Blood, snot and tears drooled from his face.

Olive let go of his arm and looked at the other boys. 'What's happened?' she almost shrieked. 'Won't someone please tell me what's happened?' She looked at Nigel, who came to a halt, clutching his stomach and staring at her as though she was something alien. The spotty blond-haired boy tried to speak, but 'Buh-buh-b-b-b-b' was as far as he got before he pressed the back of his hand to his mouth and turned deathly white.

It was the chubby boy who finally answered. His hair was thick with gore and red blobby stuff ran down the sleeve of his parka, but he seemed the least affected of the four. Hitching in breath he gasped, 'W-We f-found a . . . buh-body. I-in the cave . . . over there.' He pointed with a trembling finger.

Olive looked instinctively to where he had indicated, but of course she could see nothing. 'But why are you so . . . so bloody?' she said.

Toady swallowed and shuddered. 'I-it w-was all . . . ch-ch-ch-chopped up . . . into l-little p-pieces.' He clapped his left hand to his mouth. When he took it away it left a bleary, skeletal hand-print.

Olive felt ill herself. She said, 'I think you'd better all come back to my house. I'll call the police.'

Toady nodded. Richard got up shakily and spat into the sand. Olive took his arm again and helped him up the steps, grimacing at the sticky feel of blood on her fingers and its hot raw smell. Robin and Nige trailed after them like zombies, Robin swallowing continuously. Toady brought up the rear, wiping his face and hands and dabbing at his hair with a white handkerchief. When he got to the top of the steps, he tossed the now sodden handkerchief back on to the beach where it fluttered away over the sand like a fat red butterfly.

Inside her booth, Olive helped the boys take off their boots, then led the way upstairs. In the lounge she spread newspaper over the floor and furniture and the boys sat down. A heavy odour came off them, like a butcher's shop, only riper. There was also a sickly smell which Olive noticed came from Nige's left leg, spattered with vomit from his knee to his trouser cuff.

Strangely it was this, rather than the blood, which really caused her gorge to rise. She hurried into the kitchen, poured herself a glass of water and drank it down. As she crossed back into the lounge she remembered where she had seen the chubby boy before: in her dream

(pushing back the sheet and smiling at his twin)

last night. Though the dream had been horrifying in a way she couldn't define, recognizing the boy now caused her to feel nothing more than a weary inevitability. She was already in this up to her neck and the fact that the dream-boy was here in her flat only seemed to confirm what she already knew.

She went back into the lounge and the dream-boy looked at her. The handprint on his face was darkening to a crusty maroon. A name appeared in Olive's mind to go with the face: Toady. Of course, he was the boy Richard had been moaning about the other day, the Horror Club's newest member.

'How are we all?' she said, and was aware she sounded like a nurse determined to be cheerful in a terminal ward.

'*I'm* all right,' Toady answered as if it were a competition, and looked round at the others.

Robin shrugged. 'O-OK, I suppose.'

Richard didn't reply, but flapped a hand weakly. A blob of blood slid from his hair to his spectacle lens and from there into his lap.

Nige said nothing either, but stared up at Olive with wide panicky eyes. Olive moved forward to comfort him, then realized the boy simply needed to be sick.

'If you feel ill, go to the—' she said, but before she got a chance to finish, Nige was up and out. A moment later they heard the sound of vomiting and then the toilet flushed. Nige came back into the lounge, holding his stomach tenderly.

'Better?' Olive said.

He simply stared at her and sat down again.

She phoned the police and told them about the body. 'A body, madam? Are you sure?' asked the officer who took the call, sounding very young and rather awestruck.

In any other circumstances Olive would have been amused by his deference. Now, with a roomful of traumatized boys, she was anything but. 'Yes, constable,' she said acidly, 'a body. I haven't seen it myself, but I have four very shocked witnesses here who assure me they have.'

She listened to the voice at the other end, then closed her eyes briefly. Not bothering to cup the mouthpiece she said, 'The officer wants to know if it was definitely a human body you found.'

Richard shuddered. Toady said, 'Oh, yeah, it was a human body all right.'

Olive repeated this information into the mouthpiece. She listened then said, 'Thank you, that would be much appreciated. I'll expect someone shortly. Goodbye.'

2

Eileen Gardener snatched up the phone on the fourth ring. 'Hello?' she said, flapping her left hand to dry her newly applied nail varnish. She listened for a moment to the voice on the other end. Her left hand stopped flapping. The frown on her face gradually became a look of horror. 'What?' she shrieked in a voice so harsh it brought her husband running from the bathroom. He stood on the upstairs landing, looking over the banister, a towel held clumsily round his waist, water dripping off him.

'What is it?' he said, seeing his wife's stricken face. 'Is it Neil?'

Eileen looked wildly up at him, then jerkily shook her head. 'No, it . . . it's Richard. He—'

'He's not hurt, is he?'

'No. He and his friends have found a . . . a *body*.' This last word was spoken in a kind of bewildered wonderment.

'A body?' Derek said, staring at her. 'You mean a human body? A dead body??'

'Yes.'

'Well, where is he now? Who's that on the phone?'

'A policeman, Constable Heaney. Richard's at the police station with his friends. They want us to fetch him and take him to hospital to be treated for shock. The constable says he and his friends are covered in blood.'

Derek said nothing for a few moments. With Neil's stabbing last night, the strange episode with Richard that morning, and now this, he couldn't help feeling he was in the centre of a house of cards, the walls of which were gradually collapsing around him. 'Tell him we'll be there in twenty minutes,' he said at last. 'I have to dry myself first and get dressed.'

Eileen repeated this into the mouthpiece. She wouldn't realize until later that she had clenched her left fist during the exchange with the constable and the inside of her palm was now smeared with nail varnish.

Derek, leaving two soggy footprints on the stair carpet, squelched back into the bathroom. As he shut the door he was muttering, 'What a weekend! *What a bloody weekend!*'

3

Police Constable Trevor Heaney broke the connection with a jab of his finger. 'Your parents will be here in about twenty minutes, Richard,' he called across the room.

There was little response from the bespectacled boy huddled in the blanket and Heaney shrugged. 'Poor kid,' he thought, 'what a bloody awful thing to find.' The Constable was only grateful that he had been in the back office typing out a report when Inspector Lattersley had selected his 'cleaning up' squad to go out to the cave. Heaney could think of a thousand things he'd rather do with his Sunday afternoon than pick up bits of dismembered body and put them into plastic bags. Shuddering, he squinted at the next name on his list. Treadwell. Picking up the phone, he dialled the number he'd been given.

From his seat across the room Richard watched him. He and the others had been driven from Olive's house to the station, all four having refused point-blank to return to the cave. Even Toady, who seemed to have recovered quickly, had been adamant about that. Nige, in whose eyes shock still registered like a cloudy light, had gone hysterical when the suggestion had been made, had kicked and screamed at a constable who had tried to help him up. The constable, a young man with a worried face, had taken a surprised step backwards on to a colleague's toe, and it had been Olive who had finally calmed Nige, smothering his hysteria in her soothing embrace, clutching the boy until his outburst subsided.

He was quiet now, but he had a strange expression on his face, blank but somehow watchful. It was an expression that frightened Richard badly. His friend's body was rigid, the fingers that clutched the blanket around him hooked talons. Richard, who was not aware of the extent to which shock had rendered *him* uncommunicative and introspective, felt that if he so much as touched Nige the boy would explode into a whirling fiend, like the Tasmanian Devil in the Bugs Bunny cartoons.

His gaze shifted to Robin and Toady. Like himself and Nige, the two boys had washed their hands, faces and hair (though in Nige's case this had had to be done for him: when he had seen the blood running off him and swirling into the sink, he had curled his lip like a dog and begun to moan). All four of the boys now had blankets wrapped round them, primarily to keep them warm, but also to hide their blood-spattered clothes.

Richard looked to his right as the station door opened and someone came in. It was someone he recognized vaguely, but he couldn't think from where. His thoughts were fat and sluggish, languorous behind a sleepy curtain of shock. The man, who had curly red hair and was wearing a policeman's uniform, glanced at the boys, at first uninterested, then more closely. Richard felt alarmed. The man was staring at him so intently that it was obvious he knew him from somewhere. Richard continued to stare as the man approached and hunkered down in front of him.

'Hello, Richard,' the man said. 'Remember me?'

Richard swallowed. 'Yes I do,' he thought, 'but from where? From where?' He opened his mouth to formulate sounds from these thought-words when the man spoke again.

'Are you all right, Richard? Can you hear me?'

This new barrage broke his concentration and he closed his mouth. The man looked at him with what Richard knew was concern. Then he stood up, his dark uniform passing through Richard's fixed vision like a sheer cliff glimpsed whilst falling. He strode to the desk and began to speak to the policeman with the phone who had shouted something across the room. Richard saw the red-haired policeman point at him, saw horror, disbelief, filter slowly across his face. Then he was back, crouched in front of him again, speaking.

'Richard, it's me, Sergeant Glennon. Don't you remember?'

The words drove themselves like a wedge into Richard's shock. 'Glennon?' he said.

'That's right, son. You remember? At the hospital?'

Hospital. Flashing blue light, ambulance wail, hurrying figures in white coats, uncomfortable chairs, sludgy

291

coffee . . . *a line of glistening red footprints trailing up the corridor . . . leading back to the cave . . . the blood . . .*

'No!' Richard yelled. The substance of the police station seemed suddenly flat, two dimensional. He felt he could tear it aside with ease, and that beneath would be the real world – a buzzing mad world of dark disorder and torn bloody things that squelched and crawled and gibbered.

He whined like an animal and suddenly launched himself at Glennon. The policeman, startled, had time only to jerk back before Richard's arms encircled him in a clinging hug, the blanket fluttering to the floor. Richard buried his face in the policeman's neck, smelt Old Spice, the aftershave his father used. He felt the policeman's arms slide around him and the obscene images gradually began to recede. He tightened his grip, drawing a gasp from Glennon. The image melted like wax in fire. The chittering, buzzing madness that had filled Richard's head slowly dissolved into the slight hum of the overhead strip light.

'Hey, Richard,' the policeman murmured, 'you're safe here. There's nothing to worry about.' His words moved like grit against Richard's ear, calming, soothing.

Richard began to relax. He felt cocooned in safety. No, there was nothing to worry about. He released his grip on the policeman and leaned back with a sigh. Glennon's face was glowing with a mixture of emotions that Richard could not fathom. The policeman reached down, picked up the blanket, and draped it over Richard's shoulders.

'You all right now?' he asked.

Richard nodded. Suddenly things seemed much clearer, much more solid. The policeman behind the desk was standing with the telephone receiver forgotten in his hand, watching proceedings with concerned surprise. Robin's face held much the same expression, though in his eyes there was also understanding. On Toady's there was . . . what? A kind of shrewd and wary watchfulness.

Richard looked away. On his other side, Nige appeared not even to have registered his outburst. Nige's fists were curling like restless puppies within the blanket, but his gaze was fixed blankly on the floor. Richard reached out and touched his friend's back. Nige did not respond. He leaned forward, put his mouth close to Nige's ear, and whispered, 'Nige. Nige, can you hear me?'

This time he thought he detected a flicker in Nige's eyes, but apart from that nothing. He turned with desperation to Glennon. 'Why won't he answer me?' he said.

'He's in shock, Richard. He needs to go to hospital.' Glennon looked at his watch. 'His parents should be here fairly soon.'

Minutes later the station doors banged open and in strode Rosemary Figg. She was bulky in a cerise coat, colossal legs squeezed into fur-lined boots. Her face was very white with high spots of rouge on the slab-like cheeks. Behind her trailed Colin Figg, an unlit pipe in his hand.

'Where is he?' Mrs Figg cried, glaring around. 'Where's my baby?' She saw Nige huddled on the chair with the blanket wrapped around him, and with a cry of, 'Nigel!' advanced like a mother walrus preparing for battle.

Glennon rose to meet her. 'Mr and Mrs Figg, I assume?' Rosemary Figg ignored him. Glennon neatly side-stepped her, deciding it would be more profitable to speak to her husband. He explained the situation, stressing the urgent need to get Nige to the hospital.

Meanwhile Mrs Figg bent as low as her vast bulk would allow. She grasped her son's face in both hands and gave him a slobbering kiss on the forehead. Nige moaned and shied away, wiping at the smear of lipstick as though it were stigmata.

'Oh, Nigel, my baby, what have they done to you?' Rosemary Figg wailed. She glared at the other boys.

Richard and Robin looked away, cowed, but Toady stared back with defiance. 'We've done nothing,' he hissed. 'We found a body. That's why he's like he is.'

Mrs Figg looked as though she was about to explode;

she was not used to people answering back with such venom. 'You . . . you *delinquent*!' she blurted, and hugged Nige harder until all that could be seen of him was the crown of his head.

Toady gave an incredulous snort and looked away. Across the room Mr Figg, Glennon and Heaney exchanged glances. Mr Figg's expression was one of excruciating apology.

The station doors opened again, admitting a waft of cold air, and Derek and Eileen entered. Derek looked grim, his wife hollow-eyed, somewhat haggard. They peered around, getting their bearings, and saw Richard on the other side of the room. Both hurried over, Derek acknowledging the policemen and Mr Figg as they did so.

'Mum! Dad!' Richard said as his parents came over.

'Oh, so *you're* the boy's parents,' Mrs Figg said balefully, looking round at them.

Derek frowned, puzzled by her vehemence. 'Richard is our son, yes.'

'Your son! Well, just look what your precious son has done to my Nigel!' She moved back as though presenting a star guest, and they all looked at Nige. His wet hair was tousled by her affections; there was a fresh smear of lipstick on his cheek.

Derek's frown deepened. 'Done to your Nigel? I don't see quite what—'

'Look at him!' she shrieked. 'He doesn't even know his own mother! Look at the state he's in!'

'I hardly think that's Richard's fault,' Eileen said tartly.

Mrs Figg looked as though she was about to bite off someone's head. 'Not his fault? Not his fault? I have forbidden Nigel to play in those caves, and it is only because of your son's influence that he disobeys my orders. People like you shouldn't be allowed to have children!'

Richard felt his mother trembling beside him. 'Mum,' he warned miserably, but it was no use. Mr Figg was hovering on the edge of the group, trying to act as peacemaker. 'Now, dear, come on. Don't upset yourself.'

Derek's hand bunched into a fist and for one hideous moment Richard thought his father was going to take a swing at the fat woman. Instead, his voice low, he said, 'Look, this has nothing to do with Richard's influence. My boy—'

'Your boy is a hooligan!' Rosemary Figg shrieked.

'I've had just about enough of this!' Eileen shrieked back. As Mrs Figg turned to face her, Eileen poked her in the chest. 'Just who the hell do you think you are? People like you make me sick! You think your son is so bloody precious, don't you? You think nobody's good enough for him! If you had your way you'd lock him in his room all day and never let him have any friends, at all. God, you're . . . you're . . .' She sought for a word to express her rage. 'You're pathetic!' she screeched at last.

Richard listened to his mother, stunned. He had never, ever, heard her shout like this before. He felt a sense of horror, pride and unalloyed glee that she was standing up to the ogress. He saw Rosemary Figg's eyes bulge, her lips purse, her cheeks quiver. When she spoke her voice was hoarse and accusatory. 'Now I can see where your boy gets it from,' she said. She dragged Nige to his feet and smoothed down his hair. 'Come on, darling, we're leaving.'

Eileen stared at her, her teeth bared; Richard half-expected her to start grinding them together. At the door Mrs Figg turned back, her face twisting with hatred. 'I don't want your son ever to play with my Nigel again! You hear me? Ever!'

Then she was gone. The station walls seemed to tremble as she crashed the door behind her.

Glennon looked at Heaney and let out a long heartfelt sigh. Eileen, her rage now dissipated, sank on to the bench beside Richard. She covered her face with a trembling hand and after a moment began to weep.

Richard put an arm around his mother and kissed her; his father stood awkwardly by, offering a clean handkerchief to his wife's bowed head. Richard was exhausted. He felt as though his emotions had run a marathon over the last couple of days. He took the handkerchief from his father and pressed it into his mother's hand.

'That woman,' Eileen said, raising her head, dabbing at her eyes.

'A nutter,' Robin muttered and they all laughed shakily. Richard glanced at Toady and was once again disturbed by what he saw.

Toady had a strange, distracted half-smile on his face. It was the kind of smile an adult might wear when forced to endure the silliness of a juvenile party. Richard was used to Toady being sullen, bitter, self-centred, but this present mood he found even more disconcerting. For some reason Toady had been friendly this afternoon, unusual in itself, but since they'd found the body, since they'd been here in this police station, something else had been added to that friendliness. Not just shock, but . . . but a kind of . . . desperation. Yes, that was the closest to it. Toady looked like a person who had secrets too terrible to share.

At that moment Toady looked round and caught Richard staring at him and his smile widened. Richard returned the smile, though he made it a glancing one, turning away almost immediately. He didn't want to look into that haunted face too long for fear he would see something of the truth in Toady's eyes. Perhaps tomorrow, in the sane world of the school playground, he and Toady could talk. But just at the moment Richard wasn't ready, not while he still felt so vulnerable himself.

Trying to appear casual, he said, 'How are you feeling now, Mum?'

'All right, thank you, Richard,' Eileen said, and looked at the two policemen. 'I'm sorry about all that,' she said, 'but that woman got me so angry.'

Glennon smiled. 'That's all right, Mrs Gardener. We get a lot worse than that in here, believe me.' He winked at Richard. 'And how are you now?'

He shrugged. 'A bit better, thanks. Still cold and shaky though.'

'You'd better pop him down the hospital,' Glennon said to Derek. 'Get the doctor to check him over.'

'Yes, we will,' Derek said. 'Well, thanks again, sergeant.'

Glennon nodded and turned as the station door opened again. Mike and Sylvia Treadwell entered, Sylvia scowling, her hands stuffed determinedly into her coat pockets. From the tension between them it was obvious they had had some form of disagreement. Robin stood up as they came in.

'Right, well, that's three of you sorted out,' Glennon said when the Gardeners and Treadwells had left. He sat beside Toady on the bench. 'Now, what about you, eh?'

Toady looked at him and shrugged. From across the room Heaney said, 'The Tibbets are still not answering. Have you any idea where your parents are, Adrian?'

'My mum's taken my little brother to my grandma's. My dad should be in – but he's probably gone off to get drunk somewhere.'

Glennon looked at Heaney, raised his eyebrows. 'Do you want me to drive you home?' he said.

Toady stood up. 'Might as well. My dad hasn't got a car anyway. He'd only have to come in on the bus.'

'And you're sure you're OK to go straight home?'

'Yes, I'm fine.' Toady turned on a smile. 'No problems.'

'OK, well I'll take you then. You will be able to get in when we get there?'

Toady nodded and produced a door key from his pocket.

'Right,' Glennon said, 'off we go.'

4

Mo sneezed, hawked up spit and let loose at the opposite wall.

'You filthy sod,' Rusty said, watching the green blob of

phlegm slither down the damp plaster. The skinhead grinned.

'Yeah, well, the place needed redecorating.'

The boys were sitting against the wall facing the boarded windows, the door to their left, the fireplace to their right. It was the driest wall in the room, yet even so it felt damp to the touch. Mo was huddled in the blanket, his knees drawn up, his arms wrapped around himself. He had been sneezing all day and now he couldn't stop shivering. Rusty was sitting beside him, his blanket at his feet, eating peaches straight from the tin. In and around the fireplace was scattered the debris of the boys' brief habitation – beer bottles, baked bean, spaghetti and corned beef tins, a crumpled cellophane bread wrapper. In a little over twelve hours most of their provisions had been eaten, and there were some essentials they had since discovered they needed badly.

Rusty finished the peaches, drank the juice and burped. He flung the can at the fireplace, where it hit the wall above and bounced down into the grate. Then he stood up, licking his fingers and wiping them on his jeans.

'Right,' he said, 'what do we need?'

'Food,' Mo replied, 'bog rolls, fags, matches, somethin' to drink – not beer though, Rus, it just gets you thirstier. Er . . . newspaper, pack of cards, candles, torch batteries. And get me some Aspirin or somethin', otherwise this cold'll just get worse.'

'I can't remember all that,' Rusty said, patting his pockets. 'Haven't you got a pen or somethin' so I can write it down?'

'No, you'll just have to remember. If you forget anythin' you'll just have to go back for it, that's all.'

'Fuck you,' Rusty said. 'Right then, give me your money.'

Mo stretched out his legs so he could fit his hand into his jeans pocket and pulled out a number of coins. He counted them and gave them to Rusty. 'There you go.

There's just under five quid there. How much have you got?'

'About seven.'

'Good. Well, that should keep us going for a bit.'

Rusty pocketed the money that Mo had given him and went towards the door.

'Be careful, Rus,' Mo said. 'Don't let the coppers see you.'

Rusty winked. 'Don't worry; I'm only going to that Paki shop down the road. I'll be there and back before you know it.' He reached the door, dragged it open and passed through.

Mo called, 'Oh, and Rus?'

Rusty's head reappeared. 'Yeah?'

'Bring us back a nice bit o' tit as well, eh?'

Rusty sniggered. 'What do you want? Dog-tit or cat-tit?'

'Piss off. All right, just bring us *The Sunday Sport*. That'll do.'

'You sure you don't want a nice fat mummy-cat?' Rusty said.

Mo gave him the two-fingered salute. 'Fuck off, Perv,' he replied amiably.

Rusty grinned and disappeared again. Halfway down the corridor his voice came floating back. To the tune of *Tie Me Kangaroo Down, Sport* he was singing, 'Bestiality's best, boys, bestiality's best . . .'

Mo laughed and settled down to wait.

5

It was starting to snow again when the police car slowed to a halt in front of Toady's house. Glennon said, 'Here we are son. Do you want me to come in with you?'

He shook his head. 'No, thanks.'

'You sure? I don't mind waiting till your parents get back. I mean, the shock you've had it's probably not a good idea to be on your own.'

'No, honestly, I'm fine,' Toady said. 'I've got over the shock now.'

Glennon looked at him doubtfully and Toady forced a smile. 'Really, I'm fine,' he repeated.

The policeman looked at him a moment longer, then said, 'All right, son, you win. But remember, the slightest doubt and you ring the station.'

'I will,' said Toady, and got out of the car.

The wind instantly clutched at his damp hair, reducing it to a cap of ice. He turned and waved to Glennon, then trudged up the garden path. From the corner of his eyes he saw next door's lace curtains flicker and a wrinkled face gape at him, then at the police car by the kerb. Toady scowled at Mrs Prendergast and tried to think his teeth into fangs. However nothing happened – he couldn't have been concentrating hard enough – so he stuck out his tongue instead. The old woman's toothless mouth dropped open and the lace curtains fell back into place. As he pushed his key into the lock he smiled humourlessly.

He pushed open the door and went inside. Behind him he heard the police car drive away. 'Dad? Dad, are you in?' he called as he shut the door behind him. There was no reply.

He unzipped his blood-spattered parka and slung it over the banister rail, glancing up the stairs as he did so. His facsimile was sitting on the top step, watching him, elbows on knees, chin in hands. Strangely the creature's hair looked as damp as his own as though it too had been recently washed. Toady jumped slightly, then relaxed. His facsimile smiled.

'You gave me a shock, sitting there so quietly,' Toady said. The creature didn't reply and despite himself Toady felt nervous. 'What have you been up to?' he asked to break the silence.

'Oh, this and that,' the creature answered.

'I've been to the beach,' Toady said, struggling with his Wellingtons.

'Have you?' replied the creature as it descended the

stairs. It began to preen itself in the hall mirror. Toady's voice hardened.

'Yes. We went to our club cave. We found a body in there.'

The creature paused, half-turned. 'A body? What sort of body?'

'A dead body,' Toady said, 'a very badly mutilated dead body. It was all in pieces. Would you happen to know anything about it?'

The creature tapped its bottom lip with its index finger; its brow furrowed. All at once it said, 'Ah!' and looked up.

'Well?' Toady prompted.

'Ah. Yes. I'm afraid that was me. I'd forgotten about that. Yes, poor unfortunate man. It was just after you'd released me, you see. I was confused, I didn't know my own strength. I went down to the beach to recuperate, somewhere quiet where I could think. Unfortunately this man came along and tried to attack me – I don't know why. Naturally I panicked. I'm afraid I took him apart.'

It gave an apologetic smile and spread its hands. Toady shuddered; it might just as well have been talking about a beetle it had inadvertently crushed. 'You realize the police are involved now?' he said angrily.

'The police? What are they?'

'The police. Law and order. Don't you have laws where you come from?'

It was obvious from the creature's expression that it did not. 'Laws?' it enquired.

Toady searched for an explanation the creature would understand. It was so difficult to define what he had always taken for granted. 'Laws are to stop people from doing bad things,' he began, then remembered that just as the creature did not understand the concept of law, it also did not understand the concepts of good and bad. Slowly he said, 'It's a bad thing to harm someone – to steal from them or to kill them. This is because you are interfering with their . . . with their human rights, I suppose. People

301

have a right to live, just as people have a right to keep what is theirs, to keep what has been given to them or what they have bought.' He tailed off, beginning to realize what a mammoth task he was undertaking. Perhaps it would be easier just to present the creature with a text book and tell it to read it – but could the creature read? Doggedly Toady continued: 'A law is . . . well, it's a common opinion, I suppose, a common *written* opinion of what is right and what is wrong . . . that is, er, what is good and what is bad. Anyone who breaks these laws is dealt with by the police. And the police are special people who are employed to uphold the law.'

The creature took all of this in with an expression of polite interest. When Toady had finished it said, 'And what happens to people who oppose the law?'

'They're put into prison,' replied Toady, 'they're taken out of society and locked away where they can't do any more harm.'

'I see.' The creature thought for a moment, then said, 'So shall I tell the police what I did to the old man? I'm sorry I opposed the law, but I didn't know it was wrong. If I tell them, will they understand?'

Toady didn't know how to answer that. Finally he said, 'Do you want to tell them?'

The creature considered. 'I don't want to be locked up. That wouldn't teach me anything. Besides, physical constraints wouldn't hold me; I would escape. If someone escapes, does that mean he has beaten the law?'

'Only if he stays free. Really, by escaping you would only be breaking the law still further. You would be in more trouble.'

'Then I won't tell the police,' said the creature decisively. 'What happens now?'

'They'll make enquiries. They'll ask questions, try to find out who killed the old man. If they find out it was you, they'll try to catch you.'

'They won't find out. I don't exist for them. And even if they do, they won't catch me.' The creature raised its

302

hands in a flourish like a magician and dissolved in a wisp of smoke. A moment later it was back, still in its Toady guise, once again sitting at the top of the stairs. It chuckled like a baby and said, 'I can be whatever I like.' Then piece by piece it vanished, the last part to go being the head, the smile lingering like a memory.

Toady sighed and ascended the stairs. In his bedroom he pulled off his clothes, still damp and dark with blood. He stuffed the clothes into a plastic bag, grimacing at their coppery smell, and changed into fresh ones. As he carried the bagful of washing downstairs, he wondered why he wasn't happy. For years he had nurtured fantasies of getting revenge on his tormentors, of making them pay for all the humiliation they had caused him. Yet now that the opportunity to do so was at hand, Toady found himself confused, scared, repulsed by what was happening.

Violent death – real death, not the play-acting in his mind – was shocking and terrible. It stirred up the humanity and morality that, in Toady, had for years laid dormant beneath resentment and fear that resulted from being a scapegoat. At last Toady was beginning to draw the morality out of himself, was finally beginning to feel like a human being. It was only tragic that it had taken a man's death – for which he felt responsible – to act as the catalyst. If Toady could have sent the creature back he would have done, power or no power. But, he feared, it was now too late. The ball he had unwisely set rolling was rapidly gaining momentum; he doubted that he could make it stop.

6

Richard had been checked over by a young doctor called Howlett and declared fit and well. Now changed into fresh clothes, he was sitting with his parents at Neil's bedside, looking round the hospital ward.

It was a long bright high-ceilinged room containing

perhaps two dozen beds, all of which were occupied. A few of the patients were asleep, though most were awake, reading or talking to friends or listening to music via the personal radio sets above their heads. One man had his eyes closed in apparent ecstasy, his fingers twitching as he conducted an invisible orchestra. Further up the ward two men were gloomily playing chess, whilst another was peering at *The Sunday Times* crossword over half-moon spectacles.

The ward was warm, cosy even with the snow tapping the windows outside, but still it didn't alter Richard's view of hospitals. He felt uncomfortable here, as though the smell of sickness hung in the air like a predator's scent. Looking around he couldn't help but think that in every one of these beds someone had probably died at one time or another. He wondered what would be worse: dying alone in blood and terror in a dingy cave, or wasting away slowly here, in clean bright efficient public.

He shuddered. Over the past twenty-four hours death seemed to have loomed very close to him, to have come almost within touching distance. No longer was it confined to newstime statistics or stuntmen leaping away from explosions in *The A-Team*. Suddenly he felt horribly vulnerable, almost panicky with the knowledge that death could pluck him away any time it liked. He stared desperately at his brother as though the sight of him could quash his anxiety.

Neil was sitting half-propped up, his back supported by pillows, wearing blue and white striped pyjamas. On the other side of the bed his mother was fussing round, transferring some fruit she had brought from a plastic bag to a bowl on the bedside table. By her side his father was sitting quietly, hands locked together, slowly rotating his thumbs. Richard felt a deep fierce love for all of them, and a sudden aching grief at the knowledge of *their* mortality. Trying to swamp the feeling, he reached over the bed, took a grape and popped it into his mouth.

'Richard, I brought that fruit for Neil. Don't you go eating it all,' Eileen said.

In spite of himself, Richard smiled at her indignation. 'I've only had one grape Mum. If Neil eats that lot, he'll be on the toilet for a week.'

In the bed Neil sniggered, but immediately the sound altered to a gasp of pain. Though his back was well supported, the slightest movement still sent shooting stars along his spine and ribs.

Eileen winced in sympathy. 'Does it hurt much?' she asked.

'Only when I laugh,' said Neil. He shifted slightly, trying to make himself more comfortable. His face creased in agony once more. Eileen put a hand on his arm.

'Ooh, Neil, don't,' she said. 'Can't the nurses give you something?'

'Not just yet, Mum. I've only been out of the anaesthetic for a couple of hours.' He gritted his teeth and shifted again.

'Have you had anything to eat?' his mother asked.

'No, I don't feel like it at the moment. Maybe later, when the effects of the anaesthetic have worn off. At the moment I still feel a bit sick.'

'Oh, but Neil, I think you ought to eat something. Here, have one of these pears. They're ever so nice.'

'Oh, for goodness' sake, Eileen, leave the boy alone,' Derek grumbled. His voice must have been louder than he intended for a passing nurse glanced their way.

'I was only trying to help,' Eileen muttered, hurt. 'I want him to be properly looked after, that's all.'

Derek looked a little shamefaced, but said gruffly, 'I know, Eileen, but don't fuss. Neil will eat when he's ready. There's no point forcing food on him.'

Eileen reluctantly put the pear back into the bowl and scowled at her husband. A bad-tempered silence hung over the bed before Neil asked, 'Did the doctors say how long I'll be in here for?'

'The one last night said about a week,' his father replied.

'Oh, that's not so bad. Less time than I thought.' Neil

turned to his brother. 'Soon be back thrashing you at table-tennis, eh, Rich?'

A smile ghosted across Richard's features, then slipped away.

'You all right, Rich?' Neil said. 'You seem a bit down.'

Richard sighed. 'Yeah, I'm all right . . . you know . . .' He shrugged as though sloughing off a heavy coat.

Neil looked curiously at his brother, sensing something was wrong. He asked, 'What have you been doing today? Been out to the cave for a meeting?'

He was surprised to see Richard's eyes widen, to hear him stammer, 'N-no, I stayed in today. I was too tired to go to the beach.'

Neil tried to meet Richard's eyes, but couldn't; he had no way of knowing that his family had made a mutual decision not to tell him of the body in the cave. 'Something is the matter, isn't it?' he said, turning to his parents. 'There is something wrong?'

A glance ricocheted between his parents, then his father looked at him, mustering a smile. Heartily he said, 'No, of course not, Neil; there's nothing wrong whatsoever. Everything's fine.' He beamed fiercely to prove just how fine everything was.

'Don't try to pretend. I know when there's something wrong.' Neil looked at his mother. 'What is it, Mum? Please tell me. I want to know.'

Eileen reddened, glanced desperately at her husband. Before she could say anything, Neil asked, 'Is it my back? Are my injuries worse than I've been told?' He looked anxious, but Derek laughed off the suggestion.

'Good God, no. You'll be out of action for a week or two, but you'll probably be back playing rugby within a month. No, the thing is . . . well . . .' He faltered, looked at Richard then continued resolutely, 'Well, you see, Richard did go out to the cave this afternoon. And . . . well, he and his friends found a body in there.'

Neil jerked as though stung, then cried out, tears of pain springing to his eyes. When the throbbing in his back had subsided, he spluttered, 'A body? You . . . you mean a dead body?'

Derek nodded gravely.

'But . . . but whose was it? Was it someone who'd drowned and been washed up? Someone who'd died of a heart attack? What?'

'No,' Derek said quietly, 'it was none of those. No, I'm afraid the person had been murdered.'

'What?' Despite the shock, Neil this time managed to take the news without flinching. He stared at his father, then at Richard, his expression one of utter disbelief. For a few moments there was silence: even the patients in the other beds seemed to become momentarily still. Then at last he managed to babble, 'Who . . . who was it?'

'We don't know yet,' Derek said. 'The . . . er . . . remains were unrecognizable.' He flashed a glance at Neil not to ask any more questions, though he could see his son was brimming with them. Neil opened his mouth, then closed it again. Slowly, disbelievingly, he shook his head.

Derek continued, 'They think it was a man, possibly an old man, though even that has still to be confirmed. We were called out to collect Richard from the police station about an hour ago and then we came straight here.'

Neil looked stunned. He glanced at Richard, still shaking his head. 'God, I don't know what to say,' he murmured. 'Bloody hell, Rich, it must have been awful for you.'

Richard said nothing. His silence rubbed off on his parents, and within five minutes they were muttering awkward goodbyes to Neil. In the car on the way home Richard turned his thoughts to Olive, to the fact that the murder had happened just a few hundred yards from her flat which surely meant that she was in danger too. She was alone up there, vulnerable and isolated. The flats to either side of her were mostly occupied only during the summer months when the stallholders preceded the tourists into town.

The more Richard thought about it, the more afraid for

307

the old lady he became. His fear was not just because she was a friend, but also because she was the only adult involved in all this, the only one – Richard truly believed – who might be able to help them. 'Mum?' he said.

'Mm?' Eileen replied, glancing at him in the driver's mirror.

'Can we have Olive to stay for a bit?' He went on before she could refuse, 'I mean, they said on the news that it was going to get really cold and there was going to be a lot more snow, and I was just thinking, what if she gets snowed in and can't get to the shops to buy food? And what about the murderer? That cave is only a few hundred yards from her flat.'

He stopped breathlessly. In the driver's mirror he saw his father's brow beetle with doubt. 'Please,' Richard thought silently, 'please say yes.' Derek said, 'I don't know, Rich. Your mum will have a lot on when Neil comes out of hospital. She can't be expected to look after two infirm people, you know.'

'Olive isn't infirm!' Richard exclaimed. 'She's pretty sprightly for her age. She'll be able to help Mum around the house. Go on, Dad, please let her stay. I'm worried about her being on her own in that flat.'

For a moment his father said nothing; he was too busy negotiating the road ahead. The snow had thickened again to a blizzard; through the window a set of traffic lights were disembodied blurs of colour. The car crawled up to the lights, passing a bus stop at which people were huddled like sooty snowmen. At last Derek said, 'Look, Rich, this is a bit of a bad time at the moment. Things are tough enough without taking in lodgers as well.'

'Well, what if she stays with Gran and Grandad then?' Richard said desperately. 'I just don't like the thought of her being on her own.'

His mother leaned over the passenger seat and touched his cheek. 'You're such a kind boy, Dickie,' she said to him, 'so caring and thoughtful. I really am proud of you, you know.'

Richard felt embarrassed and absurdly touched. Clearing his throat he asked, '*Can* she stay? She won't be any trouble. I'll even make up the bed for her and give you a hand in the kitchen.'

He was relieved to see some of the tension in his mother's face dissolve as she smiled.

'Oh, I expect so. We're going to have a spare bed for a few days while Neil's in hospital, anyway, so we might as well make use of it.'

'Are you sure, love,' Derek asked. 'I don't want you taking on too much.'

Eileen glanced at her husband and Richard was heartened to see a renewed flash of spirit in her eyes. 'Of course I'm sure. It's not me who's the old lady, you know.'

'No, I know. But with all that's happened this weekend—'

'I can cope,' Eileen said firmly. 'What's happened has been a shock, but it's not as though one of the family's died or anything.'

'No, but . . . well, to be honest, I was thinking about the press attention. We're probably going to get reporters wanting to talk to the boys, and they might have one or two problems at school. Well, not so much problems, but their schoolmates will doubtless want to know all the grisly details. We could have a tough couple of weeks in front of us, you know, love.'

Richard saw the anxious look return to his mother's face and knew she had not considered that prospect. And neither, he had to admit, had he. He shuddered inwardly at the thought of being asked to relive the experience in the cave again and again; and also at the thought of Nige, who had seemed so frail in the police station, being asked to describe how the body had come tumbling down in pieces, what it had looked like, what they had thought at the time. He closed his eyes, drew a deep breath as though mentally bracing himself for the ordeal. When he opened them again he saw his mother's face reflect the same determination.

'Well then,' she said, 'the more hands there are to repel boarders, the better.' She saw her husband frown slightly and touched his arm. 'Don't worry, Derek, we'll just have to take things as they come.'

He was silent for a few moments, then he nodded. In the back seat Richard drew up his knees and looked out of the window. The landscape was obliterated by swirling white, completely unrecognizable. He found himself wishing their problems could be wiped so easily away.

7

The sight of the ruined head thumping to the cave floor and the avalanche of flesh which had followed had sent Nige spinning into a deep black place within himself. Only now was he beginning to emerge, though he still felt detached, as though a layer of fear was stretched like gauze between himself and reality. He knew enought to realize he had just come from the hospital, where soft calm words had at least partially prised him from his terror. Now he was home, his mother slobbering over him, repeating, 'My poor, poor baby,' over and over again when all he wanted was to be left alone.

As soon as he could escape from her clutches, Nige went upstairs and locked himself in the bathroom. He sat for a while on the toilet seat, staring at the towel hanging on the rail behind the door, feeling as though the mass of his thoughts were floating dreamily above his head. He felt tainted, stained, felt an awful sense of defilement at what he had seen. Acting mechanically, his body seeming to work independently of him, he stood, walked to the bathroom cabinet, and stared long and hard at his reflection in the mirror.

His face looked like a mask, something that could be plucked easily away. Nige thought of what lay beneath – things that were oozing and repellent – and he would have screamed if he could have drawn breath. He raised a hand, slammed one side of the cabinet over the other, and found himself gazing at three shelves packed with toiletries. His eyes alighted on a packet of razor blades cowering beneath the onslaught of his mother's seven types of deodorant. Without knowing why, Nige reached in, took the packet out, and extracted one of the razor blades from its little plastic box.

He held the razor blade between the thumb and index finger of his right hand and looked at it. The dull sliver of metal felt flimsy as paper, seemed to flicker almost slyly as it caught the light. Nige touched the blade to his wrist, held it there, and gazed at it for a long, long time.

At last, inadvertently, he nicked himself. Nige winced at the stab of pain, then his eyes widened as a tiny strip of blood filled the cut. Suddenly he began to shake, the razor blade slipping from his fingers, making a tiny metallic *tink* sound as it bounced on a tap and slithered into the sink. Nige leaned over the sink, vomited until he could vomit no more, then slumped to the floor and began to weep.

How long he lay there he couldn't say, but when he finally stopped crying he felt a little better. He climbed to his feet, blew his nose, and switched on the taps to swill the vomit away. The razor blade danced in the plughole and Nige fished it out, dropped it into the toilet and pulled the chain. When the vomit had been washed away, he rinsed his face, his skin flinching at the touch of cold water. He looked at his wrist, the cut now a tiny scab, though it itched like a mosquito bite. He clenched his fist, pressed it to his mouth, then unlocked the bathroom door and walked across the landing to his bedroom.

8

The smell of blood hung in the air long after the boys had gone. Ignoring the cold, Olive had opened the windows to get rid of it, had thrown out the sheets of newspaper on which the boys had sat, had scrubbed the carpet and settee

311

where trickles of blood had leaked on to the material. However, despite her endeavours the smell still remained, lingering beneath the disinfectant, as did a number of tell-tale pink stains on the floor and furniture. Olive's gaze kept returning to the stains, for like shadows on X-rays they were a mocking reminder that all was not well, that there was a creeping sickness infiltrating Starmouth, affecting all their lives. At last, unable to bear the tugging at her vision any longer, she dragged her armchair to the window, positioning it so it faced outside.

As she lowered herself into the chair, Olive felt her joints pop, could have sworn she heard her spine creak like a closing door. She leaned forward and pulled aside the lace curtain that covered the bottom half of the glass, squinting as she peered through the more active curtain of the snow to the sea beyond. In the dark it seemed to blend with the beach, though occasionally ripples, like darting silverfish, cut open the smooth blackness. Far away on what Olive assumed must be the horizon, a single light bobbed, probably a fishing vessel weathering the blizzard.

Her gaze shifted to the cliffs, which looked almost metallic in the moonlight. Had she been looking at them, she wondered, at the time the murder was taking place? Like Richard she had no doubt that the King Street Creature – as she now thought of it – was responsible for the deed. The thought of the crime being perpetrated so close by made her feel sick; she would never be able to look at the beach again without thinking of the slaughter that had happened there. In a way it was almost as though the killing had been committed to spite her, as though whatever was loose in the town was taking delight in squeezing the pleasure and security from her life.

Her thoughts were interrupted by the ringing of the telephone. Half-turning, she pushed herself up from the chair, her back and shoulders stiff from her vigorous attempt to cleanse her flat. By the time she reached the phone it had already rung seven or eight times. She snatched up the receiver before the caller could hang up.

'Hello,' she said into the mouthpiece.

'Olive, is that you?' The voice was youthful, but it sounded strained, weary.

'Richard, how are you?' she said.

'Fine, thanks. I went to the hospital and the doctor said I was OK. I'm at home now.'

'And your other friends?' asked Olive. 'How are they?'

'Oh, Toady and Rob are fine. They both went straight home from the police station. I'm not so sure about Nige, though; he was in a pretty bad way – he still wasn't speaking to anyone. His mum and dad took him to the hospital and I haven't seen him since.' Richard paused, then said in a more sombre tone, 'My mum and his mum had a bit of a row in the police station.'

'A row?' Olive said. 'Whatever about?'

Richard explained what had happened. 'She seemed to think it was our fault,' he said, 'as though it had been us that had put the body in the cave.'

'Well, she sounds to me like a very stupid woman,' said Olive. 'I expect you'll see Nigel at school though.'

'Oh, yeah, though I'd prefer it if we could all stick together as much as possible just now. I don't like the thought of Nige being in the same house as that blind man. There's something weird about him.'

'Blind man?' Olive snapped. 'What blind man?'

'Oh – of course, you don't know,' said Richard. 'He arrived yesterday, just walked up to the gate when we were in the garden. He called himself Donald somebody; I can't remember the exact name – something foreign . . . Pierrebore or something. Last night Nige had a dream where the blind man changed into some sort of monster.' Richard paused as he searched for words to express his unease. He said finally, 'I dunno; he just gave me the creeps, that's all.'

Listening to Richard, Olive realized there was probably much about this affair she still didn't know; things that had happened to the boys she hadn't heard about. She said, 'Richard, has anything else happened to you or your

313

friends over the last couple of days? Anything out of the ordinary?'

'Oh yeah, plenty,' said Richard. 'There's been the dreams. And then this morning I saw the wolf again. It was in my room; it . . . it nearly got me this time.' His voice faltered. He cleared his throat before continuing. 'Olive, what's going to happen? I'm really scared.'

She gripped the receiver tightly and tried to hide the fear in her own voice. 'Look,' she said as briskly as she was able, 'can we meet tomorrow? Together we might be able to make some sense out of all this.' It was a vain hope, but one to which they had to cling. At the other end of the line, she heard Richard clear his throat again.

'Actually,' he said, 'that's why I'm ringing. I think you should come and stay at our house for a bit. I mean, you're in that flat on your own, right by the seafront where the . . . the murder took place. We've all got our families around us, but you've got nobody, you're the most vulnerable one of all. And . . . and you might be the only one who can tell us what to do.'

The desperation in his voice was evident and Olive felt her spirits plummet once more. 'Oh, why depend on me?' she thought. 'I'm just as much in the dark as the rest of you. And I'm old, too old for this. All I want is to be with Harold again, to be happy and peaceful. I'm old, Richard. Old!'

'Will you come?' he asked.

Olive looked round the little sitting room, her gaze once more drawn to the pink stains. She was touched by Richard's offer, and by his concern, and she couldn't say she wasn't tempted: yet strangely she felt very reluctant to leave her flat. To her it would be like retreating, running away, being driven out of her home. Olive felt defiant – and also, though she refused to admit it even to herself, she harboured a secret fear that if she walked out of this place she might never return.

'Olive, please say you'll come,' Richard repeated, breaking into her thoughts.

She sighed again. 'I don't know, Richard. Your parents don't want an old woman like me around the house. It'll only mean extra work for your mother.'

'No, it won't,' said Richard. 'We've got a spare bed at the moment with Neil in hospital, and with this bad weather forecast Mum and Dad are only too happy to have you to stay. Please, Olive, go on? Please say you'll come?'

It was the sheer despair in Richard's voice that convinced Olive to say yes. 'All right,' she agreed, 'but only for a few days. I don't want to be a burden.'

'You won't be,' promised Richard. 'Look, can you be ready in half an hour? If we leave it any longer, my dad won't be able to get the car out of the drive.'

'Yes, half an hour will be fine. I'll just sort out a few things.'

'Great,' said Richard, relieved. 'I'll see you then. Bye.'

'Just hang on a minute, young man.'

Richard paused. 'Yeah?'

'You haven't told me why your brother is in hospital. Is it connected with all of this?'

'Oh no,' said Richard, 'he was stabbed last night at a party.'

'Stabbed?' repeated Olive, shocked. 'Is he all right?'

'Yes, he's fine,' said Richard. 'Look, Olive, I'd better go. The snow's getting deeper every minute. See you soon.'

'Yes . . . yes, goodbye, Richard.'

There was a click as he put the phone down. For a moment Olive listened to the empty buzz, then replaced the receiver, plastic chattering against plastic. Her hands were trembling and her stomach felt hollow, though exactly why she couldn't say. She glanced out of the window again where the snow seemed to form faces that snarled in at her, mocking her frailty. Screwing up her eyes, she peered beyond them to the sea. She could hear it rushing at the shore, but its substance, and that of the sky and the beach, had bled into a single mass of black. For a

315

full five minutes Olive peered towards the sound of the waves, hoping to catch a glimpse of movement – a blade of moonlight on the water or a cloud slipping across the sky. But she saw only darkness. Even the bobbing light on the horizon had gone.

9

'Is something the matter?'

Toady looked round from the window, where he was being hypnotized by the falling snow, and focussed his attention on the creature. It was sitting cross-legged on his bed, its features blank, unreadable. The only light in the room came from the angle-poise lamp on the desk, the fat bulb towards the wall where a concentrated pool of whiteness gradually tapered to shadow. Toady looked at the lamp, then turned back to the creature and shrugged.

'No, why?'

'You seem troubled by something, that's all.'

Toady sighed and turned back to the window. Snow tiptoed across the glass. 'It's the killing of the old man . . . I don't like it, that's all.'

There was a silence. Finally the creature said, 'I know that and I'm sorry.'

'Are you?' said Toady. He swung round, his face bitter. 'Are you really? Do you even know what sorry means?'

'Of course,' the creature said, 'to be sorry is to show regret for one's actions.' It smiled as though delighted with its ability to grasp the concept. Toady groaned.

'It's just words to you, though, isn't it? You don't really care.'

'Of course I care,' said the creature. It joined Toady at the window. 'Haven't you ever hit a fly with a newspaper? Squashed a spider with your foot?'

Toady frowned. 'I don't know; probably. But what's that got to do with anything?'

'A great deal. To me you are like insects. You're puny,

316

frail, short-lived. The death of the old man was of little importance.'

Toady stared at the creature, then shook his head in disgust. 'That's really sick. What gives you the right to take someone's life?'

'What gives *you* the right to kill a fly?'

Toady frowned, irritated by the line of reasoning. 'A fly is different. A fly can't think, it doesn't have feelings. I wouldn't talk to a fly. If you think I'm no better than a fly, why are you talking to me?'

'Because I want to learn,' said the creature earnestly. 'I want you to teach me just as I can teach you. You will never have my capabilities, but we can live in harmony. I want you to tell me when I make mistakes. I am sorry I killed the old man, I didn't realize what I was doing.' It held out a hand. 'Please don't be angry with me. I only want to be your friend.'

Toady looked at the proffered hand, hesitated for a moment, then shook it. 'OK,' he said, 'but you promise you won't kill anyone else?'

'I promise,' said the creature. It smiled and then abruptly asked, 'Do you know Peter Cushing?'

'Peter Cushing?' said Toady, puzzled. 'The actor? Well . . . yeah, why?'

The creature grinned and held up a finger. 'Watch this.'

Toady stared, fascinated, as the creature became taller and thinner. The flesh on its face melted away and its bone structure began to move beneath its skin. Its hair changed from greasy brown to a fine grey, and even its clothes re-made themselves – t-shirt, jeans and trainers becoming a neat grey suit complete with black cape, bow tie and gold watch-chain. Within thirty seconds the transformation was complete, and Toady found himself looking at a perfect representation of the actor, Peter Cushing.

'Wow,' was all he could say. Strangely he felt shy and tongue-tied as though this really was *the* Peter Cushing standing in front of him.

317

'Well? What do you think?' the creature said, still speaking incongruously in Toady's own voice.

'It's . . . it's brilliant,' Toady replied, 'perfect. Who else can you do?'

'Anyone you like.' The blue eyes twinkled and the Cushing-creature gave a charming smile. 'I have a vast and impressive repertoire.'

Toady was beginning to enjoy this game. He was about to ask whether the creature could change into Freddy Krueger when a sudden thought struck him. 'Hey,' he said, 'how come you know who Peter Cushing is?'

The Cushing-creature seemed amused by the question. It crossed to the bookcase, dark slabs of shadow beneath the familiar jutting cheekbones. It ran a slim finger down the list of titles, said, 'Ah!' and drew out a large hardback book. This it carried over to Toady, leafing through the pages, the watch-chain twinkling with light.

'Look here,' it said.

Toady looked, and saw a photograph of Peter Cushing as Doctor Van Helsing. 'I see.' He took the book and slotted it back into the bookcase. Thoughtfully he asked, 'Can you be . . . just a person? I mean . . . do you have to copy something or can you be just a straightforward person who doesn't look like anyone else?'

'I can be whoever or whatever I like.' A smile played around the lips of the Cushing-face the creature wore and it spread its hands. 'What type of person do you have in mind?'

'Just a boy. About my age. Fairly normal-looking.'

The creature gave an acquiescent shrug and began to change once again. It became shorter, its skin rosier, smoother. The veins that stood out on its hands melted back into the flesh. Toady's attention was focussed on the creature's face. He watched with utter absorption as its features altered. It was like watching Doctor Who regenerating on the telly, he thought, but here there was no blurring, no overlaying of images. Here he could actually *see* the face changing shape, the skin and hair

318

becoming a different colour, the wrinkles disappearing as though smoothed with an invisible iron. A smattering of freckles appeared on the creature's face with the suddenness of raindrops on glass; the eyes gradually faded from blue to grey to sludgy brown to hazel; the lips became a little more pert; the hollow cheeks filled out. A few moments later, Toady found himself looking at a boy of about his age with brown hair, hazel eyes and a face that was neither handsome nor ugly. The boy opened his mouth and a perfectly ordinary boy's voice came out.

'How's this?'

Toady nodded. 'OK.' He walked slowly round the creature, subjecting it to a few moments of critical scrutiny. At last he said, 'Maybe you're just a bit *too* average, though.'

'Too average? How do you mean?'

'Well, you don't have any . . .' Toady struggled for the right phrase '. . . distinguishing marks. You're a bit too unreal, too perfect.'

The creature touched its face, then opened the wardrobe and looked into the mirror on the inside of the door. 'Oh yes, I see what you mean.'

A mole suddenly appeared on its forehead and a small birthmark beneath its chin. Its teeth became a little crooked, its mouth a mite thinner. A few pimples sprang up on its cheeks and forehead, disrupting the blemish-free skin. Its hair curled at the edges, giving it a more tousled appearance.

'Better?' it said when these alterations had been made.

Toady nodded. 'Yes, much.'

The boy-creature grinned. It was a cheeky grin; infectious. Toady couldn't help but grin back.

'You'll have to have a name,' he said. 'At the moment I don't know what to call you.'

'Call me Toady,' the creature replied, though as it spoke it half-turned away, reducing its voice to little more than a mumble.

Toady stiffened. The smile abruptly slipped from his

face. 'What did you say?' he hissed, resisting the urge to grab the creature by the arm.

'I said call me Toby. What's the matter? Don't you like the name?'

Toady swallowed and relaxed slightly. 'Oh,' he said, 'yes. Yes, it's all right. Toby. OK, fine.'

The newly-christened Toby walked across the room and sat down in the big armchair. He was a little shorter than Toady and his feet only just touched the floor. 'Do you know,' he said, leaning back and causing the chair to creak gently, 'I think I quite like this shape.' It put its hands behind its head, closed its eyes and tilted its face up towards the ceiling as though sunbathing.

Toady looked at the slight figure, now dressed in a grey sweatshirt, black canvas jeans, football socks and white baseball boots with red laces. The creature had a slight smile on its face and he wondered what was going through its mind. He walked across to his bed and sat down. Casually he asked, 'Why don't you come to school with me tomorrow and meet my friends?'

Though it sounded natural enough, the word 'friends' felt strange in his mouth. Before this weekend, Toady would never have regarded Richard and the others as friends, even though they were the only kids in school who seemed even half-prepared to accept him. Thinking back, he felt a little ashamed of his behaviour towards them and also thought it peculiar how events since the seance had broadened his horizons, provided him with a more objective opinion of himself. Circumstances had forced him to open up, review his situation, and Toady was beginning to realize that in Richard and the others he could have real friends for the first time in his life if only he allowed them to be. If he could break down his own protective barriers he could have people he trusted around him, people he liked, people to share things with.

All this went through his head in the time it took for the Toby-creature to open its eyes. The creature looked at him for a few moments, then said, 'No, I don't think that's a good idea.'

'But why not?' said Toady, disappointed. 'You can teach them just as you're teaching me. Maybe you could even join our club. They were in on the seance too, you know. They helped to bring you here.'

'I'm teaching you because you're special,' the creature interrupted quietly. 'I thought you wanted to be different. I thought you wanted to get revenge on your enemies.'

'Yeah, well,' said Toady. He looked at the bleak world outside the window. 'Sometimes it's nice to share things.'

'Not chickening out now, are you?' the boy-creature said, and there was the hint of a sneer in its voice.

'No,' replied Toady. 'It's just that . . .' He shrugged, then turned suddenly, remembering a question he had been meaning to ask. 'Are these bad dreams my friends have been having anything to do with you?'

He looked hard at the creature, but its face gave nothing away, partly because the harsh light of the desk-lamp was shining across its features and scouring them of expression. The creature moved its head slightly and shadows sprang like splashes of tar across its eyes, nose and mouth. 'What dreams?' it said.

Quickly Toady recounted the dreams, emphasizing how real they had seemed to the boys. The creature listened with apparent interest, raising its eyebrows when Toady told of how Nige and Robin had had different views of the same dream, and of how the snowman had disappeared that morning when Nige had looked out of his window. When Toady had finished the creature shook its head. 'It's nothing to do with me.'

Toady was surprised. 'Are you sure?'

'Of course I'm sure. There aren't bits of me here, there and everywhere, you know.'

'No, I suppose not,' said Toady, though in truth he didn't know what to believe. He was sure the dreams had something to do with the creature, though whether it was

321

actually aware of the influence it was exerting he couldn't say. It suddenly struck him that perhaps there was more than one creature; perhaps the seance had awoken a whole colony of them and Toady was the only one who had managed to get his under some semblance of control. He felt chilled by the prospect, and with the ugly thought growing in his mind he blurted, 'Are there any others like you?'

'Like me?' The Toby-creature smiled and spread its hands. 'Not exactly, no. I'm proud to say that this is my own creation.'

'You know what I mean,' said Toady. 'Are you the only one of your race or are there more?'

The creature's smile grew and it ran a hand through its hair, preening itself once again. 'No,' it said proudly, 'as a matter of fact I am unique.'

'Well then, are you sure you've got full control over your powers? I mean, perhaps you caused the dreams without realizing it?'

'No way,' the creature replied, shaking its head. Abruptly it stood up, stuffed its hands into its pockets and strolled across to the window. 'I'm tired of all these questions.' It watched the snow for a moment, then turned to Toady with a sly smile. 'Come here,' it said. 'I want to show you something.'

'What?' asked Toady.

'Just something. Come on.' It held out a hand, inviting Toady to join it.

Toady got up from the bed and walked across to where the creature was standing. Ignoring its outstretched hand, he peered outside. 'I can't see anything,' he said. 'In fact, the snow's so bad I can't even see the other side of the street.'

The Toby-creature shook its head. 'No, it's not out there. It's *out there*.' It gestured grandly, sweeping its hand to emphasize distance.

Toady scowled. 'You mean go outside? In this weather? You must be joking!' He turned away, but before he could take a step back towards the bed the creature's hand shot out and grabbed his.

'Trust me,' it purred. 'You won't get wet, I promise you; you won't even feel the cold. But you must come with me. I've got something very important to show you.' It tightened its grip and Toady winced.

'Ow,' he said, 'let go. You're hurting me.'

'Sorry,' the Toby-creature replied, though it loosened its grip only slightly. Its boyish face regarded Toady with serene patience, obviously waiting for him to agree to its request.

Toady, who by now was beginning to feel a little scared, shrugged and nodded as though he had a choice in the matter. 'OK,' he said as casually as he could, 'what is it you want to show me?'

The Toby-creature grinned, showing its teeth, and Toady felt a shiver prickle his shoulder-blades. Despite the freckles and hazel eyes, the grin looked somehow bestial. 'Close your eyes,' the creature said, and Toady did so gratefully, not wanting to look at that grin for any longer than he had to. He stood for a minute, his body tense, the hand that was holding the creature's hot and sweaty. Once or twice he felt his fingers tingle as though a mild electrical charge was being run through them, but each time the tingle faded.

At last, his eyes still closed, he asked, 'What are you doing?'

'I'm trying to change us both,' the creature snapped, 'but you keep resisting. Can't you just relax a little?'

'Sorry,' said Toady and forced himself to relax. A moment later the tingling sensation increased, coursing up his arm and through his entire body. It was not an unpleasant sensation, but it was certainly strange. He felt suddenly cleansed, sparkling clean, as though his body had shed all its impurities. He was twinkling with radiance, floating on air. He had a sweet fizzy taste, like sherbet, on his lips. He opened his eyes and immediately it felt as though thin rods of brilliant light were springing from beneath his eyelids and leaping back in again like criss-crossing laser beams.

Despite the exhilaration, however, Toady was scared. He felt alien, uncontrolled, not sure how to cope with this new experience. The fear, though, lasted only a few minutes, and after a while he actually began to enjoy himself. His body, and that of the creature's, seemed composed of a billion points of glittering light, like complex microcosmic star systems. Their combined 'bulk' (a word which seemed far too clumsy to describe the state) was flexible, transcendent, retaining only a basic shape. It was forever bursting apart at the edges only to re-form again in an equally vague manner. Around them, Toady was half-aware of a rushing world of browns and greys and blacks, dowdy shapes that seemed thick and awkward in structure. He tried to speak and his words tinkled out in a beautiful stream of colour like music.

'Where are we?'

The creature beamed. *'You'll see,'* it said, and Toady marvelled at the reds and oranges and mauves that swirled from its 'body'. A moment later he felt himself passing between the dowdy shapes, passing right *through* some of them, and suddenly he was looking down on a scene where cumbersome ugly monsters crawled in filth, encased in a cacophony of harsh discordant noise.

'Now where are we?' he said. The distaste he felt at the scene showed in his words, a bruised array of blues and greens which pulsed sluggishly from his being.

'Look again,' the creature said. *'Can't you tell?'*

Toady looked, and indeed there did seem something familiar about the scene and about the monsters that slithered through the squalor. And the more he looked, the more he began to recognize. The monsters were white bi-peds, almost embarrassingly clumsy in their movements. Some were gathered around brown structures, some clinging together in a large open space in the centre. Almost all had small glittery objects which they kept attaching to the top part of their bodies. Along the length of one wall ran a kind of lighted barrier from which the glittery objects were distributed.

Toady peered harder, and it was as though veils were being torn aside in his mind, and as each was pulled away he gained an increasingly stronger realization of the significance of the scene before him.

The truth, when it came, hit him like a sledgehammer. He felt a wash of despair so acute it was like pain. *'These are people!'* he cried, the words spouting from him in a wave of blue-black. *'They're just people like me! We're . . . we're in some sort of club!'*

'Yes,' the Toby-creature said gravely, and, Toady thought, with perhaps a touch of sympathy, *'yes, you're right. The club, if it matters, is called The Glamour. It's in rather a disreputable part of Starmouth.'*

Toady made a movement which, in his physical body, would have been equivalent to a nod. The Glamour was notorious; stories appeared frequently in the *Gazette* about stabbings and glass-fights that had happened there. Toady looked now with dismay at the shabby interior, the human beings who resembled fat white grubs crawling in dirt. He wailed, *'Why have you brought me here? I don't want to see this. Take me back to my own house.'*

The creature, however, merely gestured towards the scene. *'Look again,'* it said, *'and you'll understand my reasons.'*

Unwillingly Toady looked. The discordant noise, which he now realized had been pop music, had ended, and a number of dirty yellow spotlights were highlighting a cramped stage at the end of the room. There were people clustered about the stage, some whistling, others stamping or shouting. A moment later a scratchy tune started up and a blond woman dressed in black leather appeared and began to cavort about the stage, encouraged by the largely male crowd.

'This is disgusting,' Toady said. In his present state he had no understanding of the sexual urge, no sense at all of physical longing.

'Look closer at the woman,' the Toby-creatured ordered, and there was a savage sense of triumph in its voice. *'Look at her face and tell me what you see.'*

325

With a sigh that spun about him like a spiral of yellow flowers, Toady once more turned his attention to the stage. The woman had now removed her leather bra and was teasing the audience by keeping her naked breasts tantalizingly just out of the reach of grasping hands. What was the point, Toady wondered, that the creature was so intent upon making here? Was it showing him its view of the human race? Was it justifying its earlier actions by presenting to him the filth of his own species? Toady peered at the woman, hoping to find some clue in her face.

At first, however, he could see nothing through the heavy make-up and coloured lights. The woman had now stripped down to a black leather G-string and was dancing seductively, teasing the men who were screaming at her to remove this last vital scrap of clothing. All at once she raised her head as though to blow a kiss to the ceiling, and seeing her face properly for the first time, Toady gasped. He felt suddenly sick and dizzy, was sure he was about to plunge from the sky and land with a crash on the hard wood of the stage below. He blocked off his senses, felt himself stabilize, then opened himself up again and turned to the Toby-creature.

'That's my mother!' he cried, the words emerging a deep dark purple. 'That's my mother down there, taking her clothes off!'

The creature said nothing. Toady turned back to the scene, feeling repulsed, sickened. 'Say this isn't real,' he pleaded. 'Say this is just something you've created. Why are you doing this to me? I thought you were my friend!'

'This IS real,' the creature replied, and there was something grim and final in its words. 'I AM your friend; that's why I'm showing you this. I'm afraid this is what your mother does for a living. This is what she is!'

'No,' sobbed Toady, 'no,' though in his heart of hearts he knew it to be true. For a long time now he had suspected something like this of his mother, but had never dared to admit it to himself. He could see her now, down below, degrading herself and therefore him. She had her back to the audience, the G-string around her thighs, and was wiggling her bare bottom from side to side. The image cut into Toady's mind like a steel blade and brought all the fury gushing out.

'*Whore!*' he screamed. '*Bitch! Cow! Slut!*' The words tumbled from him, gouts of red, livid as blood, clouding his vision. He continued to scream and shout until the words had formed a solid thriving wall of crimson in front of him, mercifully obliterating the scene below. Only then did he begin to weep, sparks of silver replacing the tears that would have come from his physical body. He felt sick, disoriented, no longer in control of the 'body' the creature had given him. '*Take me home,*' he wept, seeing nothing around him but sparkling lights, mingled with red, and the oily blackness of his despair, '*please, please take me home.*'

Then he felt a tug and a sense of movement and he curled up into a knot of darkness and allowed himself to be led.

10

Robin's father was a research chemist with the Starmouth Water Board and from him Robin had inherited an ordered, practical mind. Therefore, at the same moment that Toady was watching his mother strip naked before a clubful of leering men, Robin was lying back on his bed, trying to fit the events of the past few days into a mental category headed: Rational Explanations.

On the stereo Kate Bush was singing about *Them Heavy People*. Outside snow was swirling from a dark sky. Robin's mind kept going over the same ground again and again and again, and as it did so the knot in his stomach drew tighter and tighter.

Nothing had happened at the seance, he kept telling himself; the wolf Richard had seen had been due to his own imagination and the effects of the blizzard; the blurred image he himself had seen in the bathroom mirror was a trick of the light, a freak shadow on the wall; the bird in the warehouse had simply hopped to a lower level and flown away; there was nothing sinister about Nige's blind man; the dreams were brought on by the shock of the stabbing at the party, by Nige and Richard's silly spook stories; he and Nige hadn't shared the same dream at all – they had merely been similar, and that similarity had forced them to jump to conclusions; Robin hadn't really seen the mutilated head in the girl's hands the night before finding the body – that again was a conclusion he had jumped to due to his shock.

If he didn't think about them too much, these arguments sounded almost convincing. If he clung to them blindly, and if he carried through his decision to quit the Horror Club tomorrow, then maybe he would be all right. No, what was he talking about? That wasn't the reason he was resigning from the Club. It had nothing to do with the possibility that cutting himself off from his friends might encourage whatever they'd awakened at the seance to leave him alone.

No. That was ridiculous. There were two perfectly *logical* reasons why he was leaving the Club. The first was that since Toady had joined they never had any fun any more. The fat boy had put a dampener on things; all he did was bicker and moan and sulk. And the second reason, a more fundamental one, was that Robin was simply getting too old. He was sixteen now, might well be leaving school and getting a job in July. Bloody hell, he was even old enough to get married if he wanted to! So what the hell was he going round with a bunch of fourteen year olds for? He was more interested in girls and booze, discos, his future, than stupid horror movies. Maybe he would even get out of Starmouth completely, find a job in some other part of the country . . .

He sighed as Kate Bush came to an end and put on The Christians instead. It was cold in his room and he shivered: his father still hadn't fixed the radiator despite his promise to do it this weekend. Robin rubbed his stomach, which felt queasy, knelt on his bed and flipped a curtain aside. He looked out through a window that wore a beard of trickling ice.

The snow was relentless, draping everything in a fat white coat. The back lawn was a huge gleaming slab from which the bird table projected like a spindly scarecrow. The line of hedge which bisected the whiteness, separating the Treadwells' lawn from Mr Treeborn's opposite, looked like a strip of charcoal.

Robin's attention was suddenly snagged by a light which clicked on in Treeborn's house, and he looked up. It was a downstairs light, to the left of the back door, and through the bright rectangle of window Robin could see the edge of a fridge and some pine cupboards beneath which mugs hung on hooks. 'The kitchen,' he thought vaguely, 'Mr Treeborn has gone into his kitchen.' And then he jerked back, for a tall figure had stepped into the light, so close to the window that it was almost in silhouette.

At first, Robin felt embarrassed – he didn't want Treeborn to think he was being spied on – but this quickly turned to unease. The figure was so still, so motionless, it looked almost like a cardboard cut-out. It was thin too; no, more than thin – emaciated. Robin could see knobs of bone where the wrist and elbow and shoulder joints were, saw a suggestion of jutting ribs striped with shadow. This wasn't Treeborn. It looked more like an African from a documentary about starvation.

Robin shuddered. The figure was so incongruous here, so out of place, that it sent a chill through him. Perhaps it was a burglar he thought, but quickly discounted the theory. No, a burglar wouldn't switch on a light and stand in front of the window where anyone could see him, would he? Then who was it? A friend of Treeborn's? Perhaps even Treeborn himself, for Robin had never seen him without a suit on; maybe he really was as thin as that.

He stared again at the figure, at the black blob of the

head, hoping to distinguish the man's features. All of a sudden he had an overwhelming impression that the figure was staring straight at him; and, more than that, that it knew exactly what he was thinking. As though to confirm this, the figure slowly raised its stick-like arms, put its palms flat on the window, and began to scratch at the glass.

Robin gasped. Even from the distance, even above the howl of the wind, he could hear the squeaking of the man's fingernails. He pulled back from the window and yanked the curtain across, shutting out the figure and the night and the snow. He was trembling, his teeth chattering together, his stomach sore. The sound was still there, grinding on his nerves, like the ghostly chirruping of a trapped bird. Robin got up, lurched across the room, and fumbled his earphones from their place beneath the stereo. He plugged them in and put them on, then turned the volume up loud.

He sat hunched against the wall, eyes closed, concentrating on the music. When the record ended, ten minutes later, he cautiously took the phones off his head. His ears felt squashed, ringing from the music, an echo which slowly died away. Robin listened – then breathed a sigh of relief. Thankfully the squeaking sound had stopped.

11

Monday

Toady stiffened as he heard his mother's key in the lock. Once again he was sitting in the armchair in the darkened lounge, staring at the blank television screen and occasionally casting glances at the black china cat which was a new addition to the mantelpiece. It was well after one in the morning and his father and Simon were asleep upstairs, his father snoring like a pig. From outside came the sound of snow tapping on the windows like a burglar seeking entrance.

Toady felt empty, soulless, gutted by the burden of knowledge that had become his today. The front door opened and cold air blew in, causing him to draw up his knees. He heard his mother in the hall, swearing quietly to herself about the weather. A moment later the front door closed and the hall light came on, throwing a web of illumination through the open lounge door. Toady glanced at the china cat again, then he pushed himself up from the armchair and padded across the room.

He entered the hallway, where his mother was sitting on the stairs, peeling off black stockings that were drenched to the knees and spattered with mud. Pauline didn't see her son until he was standing right next to her. Then she glanced up, recoiled, realized who it was, and put a hand to her chest, giggling nervously.

'Adrian,' she gasped, 'don't ever do that to me again. You gave me a shock.'

Toady said nothing, merely continued to glare at his mother. He watched with loathing as she dropped one muddy stocking on to the mat and hitched up her skirt to unclip the other. Sensing she was being stared at, Pauline looked up, at the same time pulling her skirt back down over her thighs.

'Adrian, don't stare like that,' she rebuked gently, 'it's not nice.'

She expected him to apologize, or at least to look away, but he did neither. He continued to stare, not saying anything, and for the first time she noticed the expression on his face. Despite the fact that this was Adrian standing before her, she licked her lips nervously. Trying to keep her voice light, she said, 'Why aren't you in bed, love? It's past one and there's school in the morning.'

This time Toady did reply, though his voice was hoarse, accusing. 'I . . . saw . . . you . . .' he croaked, a hand coming shakily to his mouth as though to catch the words as they emerged.

The significance of her son's statement eluded Pauline and she waited for him to elaborate. When he didn't, her face adopted a concerned look and she stretched out a hand to his cheek. 'What's the matter, love?' she asked. 'Are you feeling poorly again? Have you got a temperature?'

Flinching back from her hand, Toady screeched, *'Don't touch me!!'* The force of his voice made his mother jump. He pointed a finger at her which was literally quivering with rage. *'Don't you dare touch me ever again!'*

Pauline half-rose, then thought better of it and sat down. She was stunned by the ferocity of her son's anger. She shook her head in bewilderment. 'Adrian, what's wrong with you?' she said. She glanced towards the open lounge door, searching for an explanation, and grasped at the only one that came to mind. 'Have you . . . have you been drinking?'

Toady ignored the question. He took a backward step towards the lounge door and pointed again at his mother. 'I saw you tonight. *I know what you are!'* He turned and stumbled into the darkened lounge so that his mother would not see the tears roll down his cheeks.

For a moment Pauline remained seated on the stairs, confused, one leg bare, the other still clad in a black stocking. She thought of what her son had said, and her mouth and eyes opened wide.

'Oh shit,' she breathed.

She got up shakily and went into the lounge. Adrian was a huddled mound in the armchair. He had his knees drawn up and his face in his hands. He was sobbing quietly. Pauline went over and sat on the arm of the chair by his side.

'Adrian,' she said, but Toady didn't respond. She stretched out a hand towards him, hesitated a moment, then tentatively touched his shoulder. 'Ade—' she began again, but didn't get time to finish.

Toady reacted to his mother's touch as though needles had been stuck into him. His head snapped up, his tear-stained face furious, and he twisted away from her grasp. *'I said, don't fucking touch me!'* he screamed, and swung out, catching his mother across the mouth with an open-handed slap. She jerked back with a cry and her hand flew to her lips. When she withdrew it a moment later there was a trickle of blood on her fingers.

'Oh Adrian,' she moaned unhappily. She reached out to him again, as though to hug him, but then thought better of it. Her hands dropped limply into her lap. In a bleak voice she asked, 'How did you find out?'

Toady glared at his mother. His face was red, his temples pounding; his hands were bunched into fists. In a clogged voice he snarled, 'I was there. I saw you. It . . . you . . . you were *disgusting!!*'

Pauline said nothing for a few minutes, though her mind reeled. She felt deep shame, not because of what she did, but because her son had seen her do it. Miserably she said, 'It's only a job, Adrian. I do it for the money, that's all. I . . . I don't let them touch me, you know . . . I'm not a prostitute.'

'*It's just as bad!*' Toady shrieked, and struck out again as his mother reached for him. '*Don't touch me!*' he repeated, his hand slapping against hers, banging it aside.

There was a long pause. Communication was hard, painful. For a moment the only sounds in the room were the softly ticking clock, the snow at the window, Toady's and Pauline's panting breaths. At last, in a dull voice, she said, 'Who let you into the club? Who told you I was there?' She slid off the chair arm and knelt on the floor to look him in the face. She drew her hands into fists and pulled them back against her chest as though praying.

Toady again glanced at the china cat. 'What does it matter?' he retorted. He felt furious, hateful towards his mother, felt he wanted to hurt her badly. All at once the urge was seized upon as though by an outside force and expanded within his mind like a balloon. So tangible was the sensation that Toady felt as though his own head were swelling to accommodate the thought. Alarmed, he glanced up at the china cat and saw its tail twitching in the shadows, its eyes glittering green. Immediately he heard a voice inside his mind.

'She's a whore, Adrian,' the voice said, 'nothing but a disgusting piece of gutter shit. You'd be better off without her. Hurt her, Adrian, burn her up. Use the power I gave you.'

The voice was breathless with a dark sadistic excitement, but to Toady it sounded persuasive and reasonable; it seemed to tap the very root of his undirected need for revenge. He nodded eagerly, eyes wild. He was shaking, fairly vibrating with anger. Sweat was pouring down his face, itching his scalp. He looked at his mother before him, head bowed as though seeking forgiveness. Her sobbing was grating and pathetic, serving only to make him despise her all the more.

Suddenly his hands shot out, half directed by him, half by the power that squirmed in his mind. They gripped his mother's hair, twisting into the bleached curls like barbed hooks, and wrenched her head back.

Pauline gasped, screwing up eyes that trickled mascara-tears. A moment later those eyes opened wide and a shocked sound came from her lips. But the sound quickly died when she saw the sheer hatred on her son's face.

Toady observed his mother as though from a long way away. He had a volcano raging inside him, a pit of fire that bellowed with heat. At the periphery of his vision he saw the china cat prowling the mantelpiece, its green eyes now glowing red. It was swiping ornaments casually as it went, so that they shattered on to the hearth in a series of mini-explosions.

All at once the voice was back, crackling yet sibilant, liquid fire.

'Use your anger,' it urged, 'use the power of your fury. Burn her, Adrian, burn the whore!' The last word became a long drawn-out howl and Toady felt his body heave as though he was about to throw up. There was a pounding in his ears, a sound so loud that his mother's panicked pleas were no more than the drone of a distant insect. He imagined the pit inside him bubbling and seething, fat blisters of lava popping on its surface. Suddenly with a whoosh of sound the pit erupted, and Toady felt as if heat and fire were pouring through his veins, as if he were a living volcano. He clung to his mother's head, digging in his fingers as his body shook. His mouth dropped open and it seemed that boiling water shot from it, scalding his exposed skin. His eyes were so hot they felt poached in their sockets.

He was terrified by the sensation, but he was also exhilarated. Never before in his life had he felt so alive, so powerful. The heat was rushing through and out of him, using him as a channel, scorching his insides – and yet in a strange way he knew he was unharmed. The heat continued to build and build, until at its height it seemed that he was standing in a tunnel of fire, a tiny speck impervious to all that was raging around him. He wallowed in the heat, bathed in it, gradually relaxed and simply let it flow through him. His vision was filled with red and yellow and searing white. He felt pure and clean and whole. He felt that the fire was flushing out all his impurities, taking his anger and directing it at its source. For the first time in a long while Toady began to feel truly happy.

And then, just when it seemed the sensation would last forever, he felt the power begin to ebb. The roaring died down, the colours faded, his body started to cool. Flecks of reality began to intrude, spreading and blending to form a whole. Toady blinked eyelids that seemed raw and heavy with heat, knuckled away tears that blurred his vision. He felt the armchair beneath him, saw the glow from the hall light. But there was another glow too, a strange moving glow that seemed somehow akin to what he had just experienced. The last of his – dream? vision? – slipped away and his eyes focussed on his surroundings. And now he saw what it was that was causing the strange moving glow in front of him.

It was his mother. She was on fire.

Toady's mouth opened in shock and he gripped the

arms of the chair as tightly as he had gripped his mother's head. Pauline was staggering about the room, her clothes burning, her hair a tapering crown of flame. The screams that were coming from her were high and piercing; it seemed inconceivable that such sounds could come from a human throat.

There was an appalling smell in the room of charred spoiled meat, and clouds of black smoke were creeping about the walls like shadows seeking form. The Toby-creature was dancing gleefully around the burning woman, laughing and prodding, like a mischievous boy taunting his sister with a stick. As Toady watched, his mother, now little more than a blackened burning shape, crashed into the wall and slumped to the floor. The Toby-creature whooped with triumph and stamped on her head as though it was a burning log that had rolled from the fireplace. There was a brittle crunch and a puff of ashes. Toady leaned over the ledge of the armchair and threw up.

Still grinning, the Toby-creature sauntered over to him. 'Come on,' it said breathlessly, 'take my hand.' Toady stared at the grimy hand it held out to him, too bemused and shocked to do anything. He felt woozy and light-headed, was finding it increasingly difficult to catch his breath. The fire was spreading from the black inert thing that had been his mother and was beginning to devour the carpet. The Toby-creature took Toady's hand and dragged him to his feet. 'Come on,' it repeated, 'we've got to get out.'

Toady felt himself being pulled towards the lounge door on legs like lumps of iron. His chest hurt with the effort of trying to breathe; he began to cough, tasting smoke, hearing only the fire's roar and his own thumping heart. He was only half-conscious as he was pulled through the hallway and out of the front door.

Once outside he began to revive quickly. He gulped in great lungfuls of air, shivered as the cold hit him, freezing the sweat on his skin. Supported by the Toby-creature he staggered towards the garden gate through snow that came above his ankles. So great was the change in temperature that by the time he had taken half a dozen steps he was trembling and sneezing violently.

He looked up and saw a number of dark figures clustered around the gate, neighbours who had been drawn to the fire like moths to a lightbulb. As he got nearer, a few of them cried and pointed at him, then someone opened the gate and rushed up the path. Toady felt exhausted, sleepy, as if he was viewing all this through a veil. The hands that gripped him were real enough though, as was the voice: gruff, urgent, coaxing.

'It's all right, son, take it easy. Is there anybody else in there?'

Toady tried to reply, but his throat was too parched to make any sound. He glanced to his left, hoping Toby would provide the answer, but the boy had disappeared. Toady tried again, suddenly desperate to confess what he had done, but all that emerged was a guttural croak. The large hands that were holding him gave a reassuring squeeze.

'All right, son, don't try to talk. We'll get you to hospital soon enough.'

He was borne to the gate where a number of women rushed forward like autograph hunters. Toady flinched back, thinking they might want to attack him for what he had done, thinking that they somehow *knew*. However, they simply draped blankets around his shoulders and offered words of comfort. The words became a meaningless babble in the roar from the house behind him.

He was taken to a car whose back door was open and gently coaxed inside. He sank on to the leather seat and someone sat beside him, a large woman who smelled of fresh laundry. As the car began to limp through the snow, Toady turned his head to look back at the house.

It was a mass of flames. The whole downstairs section flickered with light, and even as Toady watched a window blew outwards with a bang, causing would-be rescuers to dive for cover. The brickwork and the wood around the

337

windows were black, as was the smoke that belched into the air and blended with the night. Snow was still coming down fast, but it was melting before it landed, rapidly turning the front lawn into a watery mush. Toady kept expecting to see figures at the upstairs windows, blazing figures screaming for help, but he saw no-one. Simon and his father might well be dead by now, he thought, overcome by fumes as they slept. The inferno seemed almost gleeful as it devoured the house, sending it collapsing like a tumbling stack of soot.

The full realization of what he was and what he had done suddenly struck Toady. He was an orphan and a murderer. *He had killed his entire family!* He sat in the moving car, too shocked to move, too shocked even to breathe. Then, with the suddenness of a bursting dam, a new floodgate opened within him and he began to scream.

CHAPTER THREE

Replicas

1

As is the case with most domestic breakdowns, Robin could not pinpoint exactly when his parents' problems had begun. All he could recall was a vague series of niggling incidents which at first had resulted in either a quick flare-up or, worse, a sullen silence that had swamped the house like a grey blanket. Gradually these incidents had intensified until at this stage in his parents' relationship a blazing row over the breakfast table had become an almost ritual start to the day.

This particular morning was to prove no exception. The reason this time was that the quarterly telephone bill had just arrived, and Mike Treadwell, already in a foul mood because the newspaper was late, had taken one look at the amount due and had seen red. He didn't *like* arguing with his wife, and if the truth was told had given no thought to the possibility that their problems might lead to divorce, but it was a habit both he and Sylvia had got into and couldn't seem to shake off. For this reason his immediate thought had not been: 'Surely this is a mistake,' but: 'Who has that bloody woman been ringing now?' He had gone into the kitchen, still clutching the bill, and had made himself a strong cup of coffee. Having drunk it, he was now sitting, stony-faced with crossed arms, waiting for his wife to appear, the offending bill laid before him like exhibit A at a murder trial.

To his right, Robin was spooning muesli into his mouth as fast as he could. He knew that trouble was brewing and he didn't want to be around when it broke. But at the same time a small stubborn part of him, a part he had inherited from both his parents, insisted that he had a right to sit here and finish his meal, that he shouldn't feel obliged to make himself scarce just because his mum and dad were about to have another of their rows. He was not really hungry, and the muesli had the consistency of shredded cardboard, but that wasn't the point. All the same he hoped to be away before his mother did come downstairs, and halfway to school before the decibel level became too unbearable.

Unfortunately he was not in luck. Robin heard his mother coming downstairs when he was barely halfway through his muesli, and by the time she entered the kitchen, yawning and tying the cord on her powder blue bathrobe, he had given up all hope of escape. He braced himself, hunching over his bowl in preparation for the verbal missiles that he expected would soon come whistling around his head.

'Morning, troops,' his mother said pleasantly enough.

Robin opened his mouth to reply, hoping that a cheery start might defuse the situation, but his father had other ideas. Before Robin could say anything, Mike had scooped up the bill and thrust it under his wife's nose, holding it between thumb and forefinger as though it was something offensive.

'Can you explain this?' he said in a withering tone.

Sylvia scowled. Having sheets of paper thrust under her nose at the breakfast table was not her idea of a good start to the day. She plucked the sheet from her husband's hand and turned it round so that she could read it.

'It's a telephone bill,' she said, whereupon she opened her fingers and let it flutter back to the table, where it landed half in and half out of the sugar bowl.

Mike seethed. He snatched up the bill, scattering sugar over a wide area, and jabbed at the amount due.

'Two hundred and thirty-three quid,' he said, and duly repeated himself, this time allowing a note of incredulity to creep into his voice. *'Two hundred and thirty-three bloody quid!* Who have you been ringing? Bloody Australia?'

Sylvia was taking a mug from the cupboard. Robin saw her shoulders stiffen. 'Oh shit,' he thought miserably, 'here we go.' She turned, put the mug on the table and reached for the Nescafé jar.

'What do you mean, who have *I* been ringing?' she said, scooping coffee into the mug. She gestured round the table with the spoon. 'There's three of us in this family, you know, not just me.'

'Yes, but you're the one who spends hours on the bloody phone,' Mike retorted. 'Wittering on about nothing to those poncey hairdressing friends of yours.'

'Rubbish!' snapped Sylvia and banged down the Nescafé jar hard enough to send coffee granules dancing into the air. 'As I recall, you were on the phone for at least an hour yesterday, talking to that creepy golf friend of yours.'

Mike stiffened. 'What do you mean – "creepy" golf friend?'

'You know who I mean. That Ron Whatsisname.'

'Ron's not creepy!'

'Yes he is,' said Sylvia. 'He ogles the girls, he makes crude comments and his bloody hands are everywhere. Every time I see him he says, "How are you, Sylvia?" and proceeds to grab my arse. He's bloody pathetic.'

'Well, at least that shows he's normal,' Mike blustered, 'which is more than can be said about your friends!'

'Normal?' Sylvia laughed sharply. 'You call Ron normal? Give him another ten years and he'll be flashing to little girls in the park. If that's your idea of normal, Mike, you must be as warped as he is.'

Robin saw his father flush red and knew his mother had hit a raw nerve. From now on, he knew, the row would get nastier and more personal. He sat, sipping his tea, as the pointless argument raged on. 'I ought to be used to this by now,' he was thinking, 'it shouldn't bother me any more.' But he wasn't and it did. He finally drained the last of his tea, burning his throat, and put down his cup on the table.

He pushed his chair out with his feet and was making ready to slip away when the doorbell rang.

Immediately his mother and father stopped shouting and looked round, like two boxers curtailed by the three-minute bell. Sylvia got up and snatched at a cigarette packet that was sitting on the kitchen windowsill. She took out a cigarette, popped it into her mouth and lit it quickly with a lighter she took from her robe pocket. The front doorbell rang again. Sylvia gave her husband a black look and said, 'I suppose you expect me to go to the door dressed like this?' then without waiting for a reply went out into the hallway, pulling the two sides of her robe together to cover her cleavage.

Mike Treadwell grimaced and rolled his eyes. 'Women,' he said to his son.

Robin gave a stiff smile, but said nothing.

They both heard Sylvia open the front door. There was a brief exchange of conversation then Sylvia exclaimed, 'Oh, how lovely! Thank you!' A moment later the front door closed and she re-entered the kitchen. In her arms she carried a huge bouquet of flowers shrouded in transparent plastic.

'Look what I've had delivered!' she said, showing off the flowers as a proud mother might show off a new baby.

'Wow!' said Robin. 'Who're they from?'

Sylvia glanced at her husband (hopefully, Robin thought), but Mike Treadwell shook his head. 'Don't look at me,' he muttered. 'I didn't send them.'

'There's probably a card inside,' said Robin. 'There usually is.'

Sylvia peeled away the plastic, inhaling deeply as she did so. She crumpled up the plastic and dropped it on to the kitchen table, then looked among the flowers for a card. She found one clipped to the stem of a pink carnation.

'From an Admirer,' she read, flipped the card over to look at the back, then shrugged. 'That's all it says.' She put the card on the kitchen table and looked around. 'I'd better put these in water.'

As she rooted in the cupboard for a vase Mike picked up the card. 'An Admirer?' he said sarcastically. 'Since when have you had an admirer?'

'Oh, you'd be surprised,' Sylvia replied, 'I've got plenty.' She pouted her lips Marilyn Monroe-style to show she was joking and took out a cut-glass vase she'd had at the back of the cupboard for ages. She rinsed it out and filled it with water, then dunked the flowers in, arranging them so that they fanned out equally on all sides.

'Name one,' Mike challenged.

Sylvia opened her mouth to deliver a cheeky rejoiner, then paused. A thoughtful look came over her face. Her husband didn't notice for he was still staring at the small white card, but Robin did. He saw his mother glance towards the kitchen window and followed her gaze. There was nothing out there that he could see except a snowbound back lawn and a steel grey sky. Sylvia flushed slightly, and in an overcasual voice said, 'Oh, I expect it was just one of the lads at work having a joke.'

'Pretty expensive joke,' Mike muttered, tossing the card on to the table.

'Yes, well, perhaps they all chipped in. Perhaps they wanted to make you jealous.'

'Well, they haven't succeeded,' Mike said. He picked up the bill and brandished it in the air. 'Look, never mind the flowers, what are we going to do about this? I hope you don't think I'm going to fork out this amount of money all by myself.'

Sylvia sighed and held up her hands. It seemed that the delivery of the flowers had mellowed her somewhat. 'Not now, Mike, OK? I'm not in the mood for arguing any more. We'll talk about it later, when you get home from work – *after* you've rung British Telecom and queried the amount, that is.'

Mike looked dissatisfied, but to Robin's relief he

nodded. 'All right. But if this bill's right, there's no way I'm going to pay it all.'

'Later, Mike,' Sylvia repeated firmly. 'I'm sure we can sort something out.'

Mike looked at his wife a moment longer, then left the room without saying another word. Sylvia sighed and reached for the cereal. Her cheeks were still glowing a little. She looked at Robin, who was getting up from the table, and smiled.

'How are you this morning, Robbie?'

'All right, thanks.'

'Good,' said Sylvia. She looked at her flowers again and a smile that Robin didn't like – that seemed to contain secrets – flickered around her lips. 'Your spots look a bit better this morning,' she said.

'Do they?' Robin was surprised to find he felt little satisfaction at the news. He suddenly realized that this morning, probably for the first time in months, he had not woken up wondering whether, by some miracle, his spots had disappeared overnight. He would never have believed it possible, but there now seemed more important things to worry about.

'Yes,' said Sylvia, 'they do.'

Upstairs, while Robin was washing his face and applying his zit cream, he thought about the flowers. They had cheered up his mother and so defused a potentially explosive situation, but all the same Robin wished they hadn't been delivered. 'From an Admirer.' Who could that be? Robin didn't know, but he was sure of one thing. Despite what his mother had said, she had known who had sent those flowers, and it certainly wasn't anyone from work.

2

Richard followed the hot smell of mint downstairs to the kitchen. There he found Olive, sipping a cup of pepper-mint tea and sharing a slice of toast and honey with Sam.

She was wearing a white flannelette nightgown and her grey hair bristled with curlers. She fed the last of the toast to Sam and patted her hands together to rid them of crumbs then looked up at Richard and beamed.

'Good morning, Richard,' she said brightly.

'Morning, Olive,' he replied, stifling a yawn. He sat down and lifted his spectacles on to his forehead to rub his sleepy eyes. Despite her extra fifty-odd years, Olive looked a great deal sprightlier than he felt this morning. 'Did you sleep well?' he asked when his yawns had subsided. He stroked Sam, who was wagging his rump in an enthusiastic greeting.

'Like a top,' said Olive. She sipped her tea and watched Richard playing with Sam for a moment. From overhead came the brief judder of plumbing and the sound of running water. 'Richard?' she said at last, hesitantly.

Richard looked up. Olive's smile was gone and in its place was an expression which made him feel nervous. He released Sam, and ignoring the dog's pawing insistence to continue the game, said, 'What's the matter?'

Again she hesitated. She looked into her cup as though the words for which she was searching were written there. Abruptly she said, 'If we're going to do anything about this business, we're going to have to do it quickly. I've a feeling that the longer we leave it, the more powerful this . . . this thing will become. I think we have to go back to King Street, confront the creature at its source. I don't know how yet, but we've got to find a way, we've got to try.' She broke off, reaching for her cup. As she picked it up it rattled against the saucer.

Richard looked at her, but at first said nothing. He had been harbouring similar thoughts himself, yet still felt fear pushing into his body like cold numbing needles. Part of the fear was due to Olive's manner: he had never known her look so scared, so indecisive . . . so old as she did at that moment. He pushed aside the bowl he had just filled with two Shredded Wheat, and clasping his hands together said, 'When did you want to go to the house?'

345

Olive grimaced. 'I don't want to go, but I think we have to. This evening will probably be the best time. When you get home from school.'

Richard thought of the damp stinking room where the seance had taken place and a shudder passed through him. In a pale voice he said, 'Shall I ask the others to come too?'

Olive hesitated once again. She was loathe to put lives at risk, but the presence of the other boys might be vital. At last she said, 'Talk to your friends. Let them come to their own decisions. I can't make them come, Richard.'

In a desperate voice Richard asked, 'Isn't there any other way?'

'If there is,' Olive murmured, 'I can't think what it might be. The problem is, we have no focal point except King Street. Up to now the creature has attacked us through our thoughts and dreams and emotions. There's been nothing substantial, nothing physical to fight against.'

'What about the wolf? I'm sure it was the wolf that murdered the man in the cave and it's tried to get me twice as well. Maybe if we can find the wolf and kill it, all this will end.'

'Hmm,' said Olive, unconvinced. 'Tell me again about the times you saw the wolf. Tell me everything you can remember.'

When Richard had done so, Olive said, 'And you say this creature actually spoke to you?'

'Ye-es . . . that is, it didn't open its mouth, I just heard words inside my head. But it was the wolf that was speaking, I know that. I don't know how I know, I just do.'

'And what did the wolf say to you? Can you remember its actual words?'

'Not really. They didn't make sense and I was half-asleep at the time. All I remember was its last sentence: "I am the hungry wolf of your dreams."'

Olive raised her eyebrows. 'Very dramatic.' She looked thoughtful for a moment, index finger stroking her lips as though to coax them into speech. At last she said,

'Assuming then, that it was the wolf that killed the man in the cave, why didn't it do the same to you?'

Richard shrugged. 'I suppose it just didn't get the chance. On Thursday night I got home before it could attack, and then yesterday my dad must have come in before the wolf had time to do anything.'

'But you told me the wolf was sitting on your chest when you passed out. You said its paws were on your shoulders, pinning you down.'

'Yes, that's right. Its face was right above mine.'

'Then it failed to kill you through choice, not through circumstance,' Olive said firmly. 'In the time it would have taken your father to cross from the door to your bed, the creature could have snapped its jaws, escaped through the window and been halfway across the back lawn.' She paused and a smile flickered on her lips. 'Don't you find that reassuring?'

'Reassuring?' squeaked Richard. He had his hand on his throat and was appalled at how flimsy the skin suddenly felt there. 'What's so reassuring about it?'

'Well, don't you see? The creature must want you alive – your friends too. If it had wanted you dead, it would have killed you by now. It would have killed you as easily as it did that man in the cave.'

Richard shuddered. 'But why?' he asked. 'Why should it want us alive?'

'Why indeed?' replied Olive, and her green eyes narrowed. 'What possible use could you be? And why didn't it kill me when it had the chance?'

'You mean . . . you've seen the wolf too?'

'No, not the wolf exactly.' Briefly Olive told Richard about how the creature had tried to dupe her into taking her own life by throwing up enticing images of Harold. 'It was almost as though he was calling to me, as though he was pleading for me to join him.' She paused and blinked back what Richard suspected was a tear. 'It was all nonsense of course, all a trick played by that . . . that monster!' There was a brief rebellious flash of the old

Olive in the words, a glint of indignation in her emerald eyes. Then she lapsed into thoughtfulness again. 'But why so subtle? That's what I can't understand. If it wanted me dead, why didn't it just come along and kill me? I mean, it's obvious that the creature has enormous power, both physical and mental. It can change shape, it can infiltrate thoughts and dreams. What, then, is holding it back? What are its weaknesses?'

'Perhaps it can't kill us because we were the ones who brought it here,' Richard suggested. He looked suddenly eager. 'Maybe if we have another seance we can send it back.'

Gently Olive shook her head. 'No, I'm afraid that's not the answer. For one thing, I had nothing to do with bringing it here, remember. And for another, a seance is an invocation, not a banishment. I'm afraid sending the creature away will be a darn sight harder than letting it through was.'

Richard sighed glumly and Olive reached across the table and patted his arm. She had her own personal theory as to why the creature had made no real attempt to kill the boys, though for the moment she was keeping it to herself. Secretly she thought that the creature, in some perverse way, was trying to communicate with the boys, yet it seemed to attempt this communication only when they were at their most susceptible – alone or confused or even asleep. She believed that the creature's purpose was ultimately to dominate, not to kill, though why she couldn't say.

Yet that still didn't explain the caution it had shown in trying to end her life. The only explanation Olive could come up with for that was that for some reason it was frightened of her, perhaps apprehensive of her psychic power, limited and uncontrolled though that power was. Nevertheless, although confusing, the creature's apparent prudence did give her hope. It seemed to indicate that it was, as yet, still vulnerable if only they could find its weak spot. She said as much to Richard.

348

'But what could it —' he began, then stopped as Olive put a finger to her lips.

'Shh, I can hear someone coming. Your father, I'd say, judging by that rather tuneless whistling.'

Despite himself, Richard smiled. His mother always said his father's whistling drove her round the bend. He and Olive both listened to the clomp-clomp of descending footsteps accompanied by a rather flat and sombre rendition of the tune, *Born Free*. As the footsteps reached the bottom of the stairs the telephone started to ring and Richard heard his father curse. He pulled his bowl of Shredded Wheat towards him and poured milk on the cereal to keep up appearances. Olive smiled distractedly as though practising for his father and poured herself another cup of peppermint tea.

Richard ate his breakfast and listened to the one-sided telephone call. He wondered if it was the hospital ringing to say how Neil was. He couldn't hear all that was being said but enough to know that whoever was on the other end of the line was doing most of the talking. There were long silences, punctuated by an occasional 'Mm' or 'Ah' from his father. Finally he heard his father say, 'Well, thank you for ringing, sergeant . . . Yes, I will . . . Thanks again . . . Bye.' A moment later Derek entered the kitchen.

'Whoa, boy, get down,' he said as Sam gave him a gleeful reception. He fended off the delirious dog as best he could, attempting to hold Sam at arm's length to avoid getting hairs and slaver on his suit. He managed to reach the fridge unmolested, and opened the door to look for eggs. As he did so he said, 'Good morning all. I trust you slept well, Olive?'

'Oh yes, thank you,' said Olive with an effusiveness that Richard knew was false.

'Good, good,' Derek said abstractedly, and put his eggs on to boil. He took the folded *Guardian*, which he'd brought in with him, from under his arm and put it on the table. Then he sat down, grimacing at the white landscape outside the window.

349

'Was that the hospital on the phone, Dad?' Richard asked. He knew it wasn't by the word 'sergeant' that his father had used, but he didn't want to sound as though he'd been eavesdropping.

'No, it was the police; Sergeant Glennon to be precise. He rang to say that the body in the cave had been identified. Apparently it was—'

'*Alfie Bessle!*'

Derek looked at Olive, surprised. 'Yes, that's right. How did you know?'

For a few moments Olive didn't answer. She sat bolt upright, staring into space, her fists clenched so tight they looked like bunched-up chicken's feet. A stillness settled over the room, a tension that was almost tangible. Even Sam noticed it, for he cocked his head to one side and gave a small uneasy whine. The Shredded Wheat that was poised on Richard's spoon slithered off and landed back in the bowl with a 'plop'. The eggs that Derek had put in the pan jostled bad-temperedly as the water began to boil.

'Miss Pierce – Olive,' Derek said at last, 'are you all right?'

Olive blinked as though she'd been roused from a deep sleep and her mouth closed with a clack of teeth. She looked around blearily, then her eyes focussed on Derek and she smiled. 'I'm sorry about that,' she said. 'I must have had one of my little turns.'

Derek looked concerned. 'Is that serious? Do you want me to call a doctor?'

'Oh no, no,' Olive said, 'I'll be all right. Besides, it's nothing a doctor could deal with. It's mental, not physical.'

'Mental?' Derek said. It was obvious he was wondering what his family had taken on.

'Olive's psychic, Dad,' Richard hastened to explain. 'She gets these . . . these messages every now and again.' He had been in Olive's company a number of times before when she'd had one of her 'little turns', the most recent

350

instance of course being last Thursday when she had warned him against holding the seance. Once, he remembered, Olive had shuddered and burst into tears, stopping just as abruptly moments later. Richard had asked, 'Olive, are you all right?' to which she had responded, 'My little Darren has gone to the angels. Oh, my poor, poor baby.'

Derek moved to the cooker, where the egg pan was overflowing, and turned the heat down. 'I see,' he said, though it was obvious he didn't see at all. He turned and looked at Olive warily. 'How long have you been having these . . . these experiences?'

Olive shrugged. 'Oh, a long time now. Ever since I was a young girl, in fact. I remember my parents fretting over me when I was, oh, ten or eleven, I suppose. At first they thought I had a brain tumour; then it was decided I suffered from epilepsy. It was my Great Aunt, Felicity Anne, on my father's side who put them right. She'd been having turns like this for years, but hers were much more powerful than mine. She used to have visions, premonitions of great events. It was said she predicted Queen Victoria's death to the very day, and that was four years before the Queen died. She's also said to have predicted the start of the First World War, and one night in 1916 she went downstairs to where her sister was sitting sewing by the fire and said, "Bill" – that was her sister's husband – "Bill says you're not to grieve for him." Next day a telegram arrived to say that Bill had been killed in the Somme.' Olive paused a moment to sip her tea, then continued. 'I was twenty-seven when Aunt Felicity died. The last time I went to see her, she said to me, "Write this down, Olive. Twenty-two years from today, a man will walk on the surface of the moon." I wrote it down in a little diary I had and kept it through the years to see if she'd be right. When a man did walk on the moon, I fished out the diary again and turned to the entry I'd made. The date of the entry was the 20th of July 1947. She'd been just one day out.' Olive stopped here and looked up at Richard and his father. There was a strange faraway look in her eyes, but at the sight of their intent faces she seemed to come back to herself. 'But just listen to me, rambling on like a mad woman,' she said. 'I'm sure you don't want to hear about things that happened forty years ago.' She turned and looked out of the window, and Richard noticed a pained look on her face as though she was grieving for times gone by.

To cover up the awkwardness of the moment, Richard asked, 'Wasn't Alfie Bessle that old tramp who used to tell stories to the children on the seafront?'

Olive nodded sadly. 'Yes. He was a true gentleman was Alfie. I used to give him free palm readings in the summer when business was slack, and occasionally we'd go for walks along the seashore in the evenings. He might have been a bit smelly and dirty, but he was one of the most knowledgeable people it's ever been my privilege to meet. Do you know, he knew everything about Starmouth – its history, its geography, its flora and fauna, even its local gossip. Point out any fish or bird or crab or plant and Alfie would tell you all about it.' She broke off, shaking her head, and Richard saw tears in her eyes. Instinctively he knew they were tears not just of grief, but also of anger. He reached across and took her hand, stirred by a sudden sense of indignation. Olive's hand, although larger than his, felt small and bony, fragile as a baby chick. Richard gave it a gentle squeeze and was rewarded with a watery smile.

'What else did Sergeant Glennon say?' Richard asked his father.

'He said you weren't to tell your school friends about what happened yesterday. He said the police would get in touch with your headmaster and let him know; I suppose just in case any of you suffer any after-effects at school – delayed shock or whatever. Oh, and he also said that the story would be appearing in tonight's *Gazette*, but that the police would make sure your names were kept out of it.' Derek moved from the cooker, where he'd been ma-noeuvering hot eggs from saucepan to plate, and back to the breakfast table. Ruthlessly he sliced the top off his egg. 'You are sure you're all right to go to school today, Rich?' he said. 'You don't want a day off to recover?'

Richard looked at Olive, but she gave the tiniest shake of her head. 'No,' he said, 'I'll be all right.'

Derek smiled, shook out his *Guardian*, and looked at the headline on the front page. Tutting, he turned to the sport at the back.

'I'd better get going soon,' said Richard, pushing aside his half-eaten bowl of Shredded Wheat. 'It'll take a while to get to school with the snow so deep.'

'Hmm,' said Derek, and glanced out of the kitchen window where snow lay in a solid white mass about a foot below its rim, giving the impression that the window had been lowered overnight. 'I can see I'm going to have problems getting the car out this morning,' he muttered.

'Perhaps they'll send you home early,' Olive said to Richard. 'I should imagine a lot of people won't be able to make it in to school today.'

Derek licked egg from his moustache. 'Just think of your poor grandmother. She's supposed to be having her birthday party tomorrow night. I can see nobody turning up at this rate.'

Richard, who was halfway out of the room, turned back at his father's words. 'Damn!' he exclaimed, looking at Olive. 'I'd forgotten. We're supposed to be decorating the old folks' club tonight.'

'So?' said Derek. 'What's the problem?'

'Um . . . oh, nothing. It's just that I'd made other plans, that's all.'

'Well, you'll just have to unmake them then, won't you? If I'm getting roped into this, my boy, you certainly are.'

Richard looked at Olive with a 'So what do we do now?' expression. Olive gave the shadow of a wink.

'Never mind, Richard, I'm sure something can be arranged,' she said pointedly. 'I mean, you can't disappoint Constance, can you?'

'No,' Richard said. 'What time do we have to be there?'

T.—16

'Half-seven,' said Derek. He finished his egg, sighed, and reluctantly put down his paper. 'I suppose I'd better go and see if I can get the car out. Come on, Richard, hurry up and then you can give me a hand. There's a spare shovel in the garage.'

3

The smell, the damp, the cold, the boredom, Mo's relentless complaining: it was all combining to drive Rusty round the fuckin' bend. Being cooped up here, he thought, was even worse than being cooped up in Borstal, and that was what they were trying to avoid. At least in Borstal they'd get a proper bed, hot meals, clean clothes, decent toilet facilities.

'Pass us the bucket, Rus. I need another shit,' Mo said, breaking into his thoughts.

Rusty scowled. 'For fuck's sake, Mo, you only had one about an hour ago. Can't you wait?'

'No, I can't,' said Mo. 'It's not my fault, it's my bloody guts. I'm not well, you know.'

'Oh, fuckin' hell, don't start that again. You've only got a fuckin' cold.'

'No, its more than that, Rus. It's a bug or somethin'. I mean, I feel *really* bad.'

Rusty tutted unsympathetically, but slouched to the far corner of the room where a red plastic bucket was standing. The bucket was covered by a few sheets of newspaper, but it still stunk to high Heaven. It had been nicked from somebody's yard yesterday afternoon when it was realized they had nothing to shit into. They had previously been pissing into a corner in the kitchen, but neither of them fancied squatting in that rat infested place. Besides, Mo was now so ill that he probably wouldn't be able to make it into the kitchen and back without collapsing or throwing up.

Rusty picked up the bucket, almost gagging at the smell

and the weight of Mo's diarrhoea slopping from side to side. He carried it at arm's length over to the skinhead and set it down.

'Never mind about a bug, we'll both get fuckin' typhoid at this rate,' he said. He watched as Mo undid his belt and dropped his trousers and underpants, but turned away in disgust as his friend lowered himself gingerly on to the makeshift toilet. A moment later there was a grunt and a rapid sound like stones falling into soft mud: *thuck-thuck-thuck-thuck-thuck.* Rusty curled his lip contemptuously. 'That's fuckin' revoltin'.'

'It's not my fault, Rus, it's not my fault,' Mo groaned again.

'Who's fuckin' fault is it then?' Rusty hissed, spinning round.

Mo was crouched over the bucket, jeans and pants round his ankles, wiping his arse with the last of the toilet roll. Even in this dim light Rusty could see how pale and sweaty his friend looked, how he was clutched by continuous shuddering spasms. Yet despite this Rusty felt no sympathy; only resentment that the skinhead had chosen such an awkward time to get ill. Already most of their money had gone on cold remedies and reams of bog roll for Mo's hyperactive bowel.

'Give it a rest eh, Rus?' Mo said. 'I feel bad enough without you gettin' at me.'

With anyone else, Mo's plea might have met with compassion and understanding, but not with Rusty. Rusty saw Mo's sickness as a sign of weakness, an indication of the skinhead's true worth, or rather lack of it. Previously Rusty had respected Mo, had admired his toughness, his arrogance, his courage in dodgy situations; but the last twenty-four hours had swept all that aside, had shown Mo up for what he really was: spineless and weak, unable to endure even the slightest hardship. He was sitting back against the wall now, shivering, dragging the blankets around his gangly form. He made a pitiful and wretched figure, his tight denims and shaved head now giving him a skeletal look whereas before they had made him look mean. Rusty felt like walking over and kicking him, if only to goad some sort of reaction, some scrap of defiance. Instead he walked over, picked up the bucket and carried it back to the corner of the room, where he covered it once again with newspaper.

'It needs emptyin',' Mo said in a weak voice.

'Well, it'll have to fuckin' wait then, won't it?' Rusty retorted. He zipped up his jacket and made for the door.

'Where are you goin'?' Mo said.

'Out. I want to get away from this fuckin' place for a while. And besides, we need some more stuff.'

'How much money we got left?' Mo asked, drawing the blankets up to his chin.

Rusty put his hand into his pocket and took out a fistful of change. He counted it by the door that led into the hall, where there was more light. 'Fifty, sixty, sixty-five,' he muttered, then he started on the copper. 'Fuckin' hell, we've only got ninety-three pence left!'

'We need some more food,' Mo said (not that he had felt like eating today), 'and somethin' to drink and some more bog rolls—'

'I know what we need,' Rusty interrupted savagely. He dropped the money into his pocket. 'We need more fuckin' cash, that's what we need. We need at least another tenner if we're gonna stay here for the next few days.'

Mo ran a trembling hand slowly over his features as though to check they were still there. 'Maybe it'd be better if you went off on your own, Rus,' he said, 'got out of Starmouth altogether. You can give Ratzy a ring from wherever you end up, tell him where I am.' He sneezed violently three times, then groaned, wiping the snot from his face with the blanket. 'Honestly, mate, I can't fuckin' stay here. I need a fuckin' bed, somewhere warm. I don't care any more if the pigs arrest me. I just wanna get well; I've never felt as bad as this before.'

Rusty listened to Mo's speech, feeling a blend of

emotion that, for him, was surprisingly complex. On the one hand he still felt scorn and irritation at Mo's weakness, yet on the other he felt a warped sense of loyalty and pride, a sudden determination that he and Mo would see this through together. Strangely enough, he himself had been toying with the idea of leaving Mo to his whining and going to look for an alternative hiding place; but now that Mo had actually suggested the idea, Rusty found himself balking at it.

'Don't be daft, mate,' he said, walking over and squatting down by his friend. He put a hand on Mo's shoulder, smelling his sweat and musty sickness. 'I'll get you better, you'll see. We'll beat these fuckin' coppers yet.'

Mo gave a wan smile. 'But what we gonna do for money?'

Rusty straightened up. 'I'll go back and get some off me dad.'

'You can't do that, Rus. The coppers are probably waitin' for you at your house right now. They'll have you as soon as you step through the door.'

Rusty's eyes narrowed. His lank dirty hair hung over his forehead in almost girlish ringlets. All at once his face cleared. 'Got it!' he said.

'What?'

Rusty winked and tapped the side of his nose. 'I know where we can get some money. Just leave it to me.' He walked across the room, pausing in the hallway that led out into the hall. 'I'll be gone about an hour. You'll be all right here, won't you?'

Mo looked anything but all right, yet he nodded and patted the bottle of Night Nurse and the jar of Aspirin by his side. 'Yeah, I'll be OK. I'll dope meself up on this shit.'

'Right, I'll see you later.' Rusty turned up the collar of his jacket and stepped out into the hall, pulling the sitting room door shut behind him. It grated closed, blocking out much of the light from the hallway, highlighting the thin

357

gleaming strips that filtered through the gaps in the boarded windows.

Mo shivered and took a couple of Aspirin from the jar. He popped them into his mouth and washed them down with a swig of Night Nurse. Then he settled down to wait.

After a time, lulled by the dimness and the quiet and the somnolent effect of the drugs he had swallowed, he drifted into sleep.

4

'He's waking up,' the nurse said.

Constable Ledbetter put down his tea and looked at the boy lying in the hospital bed. The boy's eyelids were flickering slightly and his lips were peeling apart as though to form words. The nurse, a large woman with a blotchy complexion, hurried to the left side of the bed and bent over the waking patient.

'All right, Adrian, take your time. There's no need to worry. You're in hospital now,' she said.

Toady began to murmur. His body jerked, then his hand rose from the bedclothes and hovered above his chest. The nurse took it in her considerably larger one as though afraid it might lunge for his throat like a vampire bat. She smoothed his greasy fringe away from his eyes and touched his cheek to give him reassurance. 'All right, love,' she soothed, 'all right.'

Ledbetter pulled his chair around to face the bed, the rubber-tipped legs juddering over the smooth floor. The bed was curtained off from the rest of the ward by heavy green drapes and the sounds that filtered through were not unlike the sounds from the police canteen kitchen. Ledbetter asked the nurse, 'How long will it be before he wakes up?'

'A minute or two, that's all. He'll be a bit muzzy, but should be coherent enough.'

Ledbetter nodded, then they both looked at Toady as he

went through the processes of waking. The nurse held his hand and made comforting noises. Ledbetter adjusted his tie, feeling hot despite the chill of the day, and glanced out of the window. The ward was on the third floor and gave a good view of the snow-coated town, the harsh sky, a few gulls wheeling slowly. When he looked back, the boy was staring at him, eyes wide and startled.

'Who . . . where am I?' Toady gasped.

'Shh, love, you're in hospital,' the nurse said. 'You're all right, don't worry. You've been in a bit of an accident, that's all.'

'An accident?' Toady struggled to sit up, but his arms were weak and he slumped back again. He groaned, shaking his head, and closed his eyes – for a moment it seemed he might drift back into sleep. Then abruptly his eyes reopened as memory flooded back to him. 'There was a fire!' he gasped and stared at the green drapes as though last night's flames were being replayed across them. Once again he struggled to sit up and this time had to be restrained by Ledbetter and the nurse. He looked panic-stricken: his face crumbled and tears began to roll down his cheeks. 'I killed them all,' he wailed. 'I killed them . . . Oh no, oh God, my mum . . . I killed them all. *I killed them!*'

The nurse glanced worriedly at Ledbetter, but her voice remained soothing. 'Shh, love, shh. You didn't kill anybody. It was an accident, that's all. Just an accident.'

'*No!*' Toady screamed, and this time he thrashed at the arms that were holding him. Ledbetter panted with the exertion of trying to restrain the boy; the nurse, who had almost to climb on to the bed, was having even more difficulty.

Abruptly Toady's struggles ceased. He slumped back and began to weep, his whole body shuddering with the effort. 'Toby made me do it,' he blubbered. 'It was him, he showed me. He made me do it . . . I didn't want to . . . he made me . . . he made me . . . !'

Ledbetter still had a hand on Toady's shoulder, but now

he didn't have to apply even the slightest pressure to keep the boy in the bed. He looked at the nurse and mouthed, 'Who's Toby?' The nurse shrugged.

'Adrian,' Ledbetter said in a coaxing voice. 'Adrian, can you tell me who Toby is?'

Toady stiffened again. In a tremulous whisper he said, 'It's him. Toby is him. He did it . . . he . . . he made me do it . . . I don't want him here any more. He can do things . . . he can make *me* do things . . . I don't want to . . . Please, please don't let him. Please, no more.' He suddenly sat bolt upright, startling both Ledbetter and the nurse, and screamed, *'Don't let him in!* He's not my real friend. No more . . . send him back. *He can kill everyone!'* He hurled back his covers and tried to dive out of bed on the nurse's side, whimpering sounds issuing from his throat. Instinctively Ledbetter made a grab for him and managed to get a grip on the back of his pyjama jacket. Toady's forward momentum caused the material to rip slightly at the seam of the collar and his palms smacked on the cold floor. The nurse lunged forward and managed to curl one arm over his neck, the other under his armpit. She locked her hands over his chest and between them she and Ledbetter hauled Toady back into bed.

They got him settled again and the nurse pulled the covers up to his chest, tucking them in tightly at the sides. Toady lay, panting, sweat and tears glistening on his face. The nurse stroked his hair and made comforting sounds, but this time he seemed to have gone beyond consolation. His pupils had contracted to pin-pricks, his gaze was wild and vacant. Worriedly the nurse said, 'I'll have to give him another sedative. Can you hold him here while I go for some diazapam?'

Ledbetter nodded and the nurse hurried away. The policeman leaned over Toady, placing one hand on each shoulder to hold him down, though for the moment the boy's energy seemed spent. Ledbetter wondered if this Toby he had talked about was a real person or whether it was just some imaginary friend on to whom he had transferred his feelings of guilt. Whatever the answer, it was quite obvious that the boy was deeply disturbed, and Ledbetter suspected it would take many delicate hours of coaxing and cajoling before they got anywhere near the truth.

Suddenly he felt the boy slump beneath him and looked down, momentarily alarmed. He was relieved, however, to see Toady's eyelids fluttering, his chest rising and falling in a steady rhythm.

By the time the nurse returned with the diazapam, Toady was fast asleep.

5

When Rusty peered in at the sitting room window he saw Ratz lying back, chuckling at *Playbus*. The Polish boy was stolidly munching his way through a bag of prawn cocktail crisps, a bottle of what looked like homemade wine propped between his knees. Rusty waited until Ratz had raised the bottle to his lips and then banged hard on the glass.

He was delighted to see Ratz jerk, slopping wine down his chin and on to the front of his Motorhead t-shirt. When Ratz turned angrily to face him, Rusty stuck up two fingers and grinned inanely. Immediately Ratz's expression changed to one of astonishment: his mouth, still dribbling wine, dropped open. His eyelids stretched so wide that Rusty half-expected his eyes to leap out on springs.

'Well, come on,' Rusty shouted as Ratz continued to gape, 'aren't you going to let me in?'

Ratz stirred, and putting down the crisps and the wine hurried to the front door. He opened it and stood in the hall, looking warily at Rusty as if he half-suspected him to be an imposter. Rusty grinned and slapped Ratz's belly.

'All right, slobbo. How you doin'?'

'I'm OK, thanks, Rus,' Ratz said. 'I . . . er . . . yeah,

361

I'm OK.' He opened the door wider. 'Er, come in, come in.'

'Cheers,' Rusty said. He stepped through the door and strode unhesitatingly up the hall and into the sitting room on the left.

As Rusty passed him, Ratz noticed how dirty he was, noticed with his nose as well as his eyes. He wondered where Rusty had been hiding the last couple of days and whether he realized how keen the police were to get hold of him and Mo. Afraid that Rusty might have been followed, Ratz leaned out into the street and peered up and down it like a heavy in an old gangster film. The street was stodgy with snow and, as far as he could see, deserted. Satisfied that his friend had arrived undetected, Ratz closed the door and followed him down the hall.

When he entered the sitting room, Rusty was perched on the edge of the settee, eating the crisps and drinking the wine. Ratz winced inwardly at the thought of what his mother would say about the grubby mark that Rusty's jeans would undoubtedly leave on the upholstery. He considered asking Rusty to stand up, but in the end chickened out: he had never given Rusty an order and wasn't about to start now. Instead he sat on the rocking-chair by the big front window and waited for his friend to speak.

Rusty finished the crisps, staring at the man on the television who was pretending to be a tree in a thunderstorm. He screwed up the bag and flung it towards the metal bin in the corner, but it fell short by two or three feet. Ratz picked it up and put it in the bin. Nodding towards the television, Rusty remarked, 'This is a bit advanced for you, innit, Ratz?'

Ratz blushed red as though he had been caught masturbating. Secretly he loved all the children's programmes, especially the cartoons. Shrugging and trying to sound off-hand he said, 'I was just passing the time. There's nothing else on and I'm bored.'

'You should be in school learnin' somethin',' Rusty said, his voice heavy with irony.

'Snow's too deep. Besides, the coppers said I had to stay here until they'd sorted out this stabbing business.'

Ratz expected this to have some effect on Rusty, but the red-haired boy merely nodded. 'Yeah, I thought the pigs would have been here. They've been to our house too, but luckily me and Mo were out. What did they say to you?'

'They wanted to know who'd stabbed Gardener and who'd been in the gang.'

'You didn't tell them, did you?'

'Nah, course not,' Ratz lied. 'They already knew you and Mo were there, but I told them the only kid who had a knife was someone I didn't know.'

'Good lad,' said Rusty. He stood up, strolled to the window and looked out.

'The coppers are on the lookout for you and Mo, you know,' Ratz said, worried that someone might see his friend.

'Yeah,' said Rusty, but he didn't alter his position.

Desperately Ratz looked around for inspiration. His eyes alighted on the bottle of wine. Snatching it up he said, 'Do you want some more of this?'

To his relief Rusty turned from the window, came over and took the wine. He tilted his head back and drained the bottle, then sat down.

Ratz said, 'Where've you been these last couple of days anyway? I tried to phone you, but your dad said you'd gone away with Mo. I thought you'd be miles away by now.'

'Nah, we're still in the area – in fact we're a lot nearer than you think.' Rusty grinned, then just as suddenly the grin slipped. 'Only thing is, we've got a few problems.'

'Problems?'

'Yeah . . . you see Mo's not too well – he's got flu or somethin', and the shits like you wouldn't believe. I'll tell you, Ratz, it's costin' us a fuckin' fortune in medicine 'n stuff. As you can imagine, we're a bit short of the old readies.'

Ratz sighed; even his less than agile mind could see where this was leading. 'How much do you want?' he asked.

A slow smile seeped across Rusty's face. 'That's very kind of you, Ratz old pal. I reckon a tenner should do it.'

'A *tenner!* But I've only got a couple of quid.'

The look that Rusty gave him was not dissimilar to the one his father had given him on Saturday night after the police had left. It was a look that made Ratz feel as though he had let people down badly. Softly Rusty said, 'Come on, mate, you can do better than that. There must be some money knockin' around here somewhere. I mean, you're our last hope. If we don't get any cash, me 'n Mo are goin' to have to give ourselves up, and you wouldn't want that to happen, would you?'

'Nah, course not,' Ratz mumbled, 'but the thing is, Rus, I *have* only got a couple of quid. I mean, you can have that by all means, but I don't—'

'There must be some more somewhere.' This time Rusty's voice was silky, but it cut through Ratz's protestations with ease.

Ratz saw the look in Rusty's eyes, the cloudy, slightly manic look of absolute authority, and he sighed. Rusty was going to get his way; there was no question of it when he was in this mood. The Polish boy pushed himself up from the rocker and nodded at the staircase. 'All right, I'll have a quick look upstairs. There might be a few quid on my mum's dressing table.'

'Good man,' Rusty said. He watched as Ratz plodded upstairs, large buttocks swaying like footballs inside his patched jeans, then he stood up and casually strode over to the hissing gas fire. Above the fire was a wooden mantelpiece cluttered with ornaments. Rusty picked up a marble egg on a wooden stand, admired it for a moment, then slipped it into the inside pocket of his jacket. He did the same thing with a china figurine of a cherub-faced girl selling flowers. He re-arranged the ornaments so that there were no gaps, then mooched over to the dining area at the back of the room. Here was a mahogany dresser, the backboard of which contained three shelves which supported an arrangement of nine willow-pattern plates. More ornaments were crowded on the dresser itself. Rusty pocketed a small vase, an ivory horse and a miniature brass candlestick. His pilfering complete, he strolled back to the settee and sat down, gazing blankly at a cartoon entitled *Jimbo and the Jet Set* until Ratz came clumping down the stairs again.

'Here's all I could find,' Ratz said, opening his cupped palms to reveal a number of pound coins and some change. 'There's about eight pounds fifty here.'

'Cheers, Ratz,' Rusty said and held out his hands for Ratz to tip the money into. He transferred the coins to the pockets of his filthy jeans, then stood up to go. 'I don't suppose you could give us a bit of food as well, could you?' he asked as he reached the front door. Ratz looked pained, but nodded.

'I suppose so. What do you want?'

'Bread, cheese, stuff like that – stuff we can eat raw . . . Oh, and we couldn't have one of them bottles of wine as well, could we? And maybe a couple of bogrolls?'

The Polish boy sighed. 'Wait here, I'll see what we've got.' He clumped through to the kitchen and Rusty smiled, enjoying the power he wielded. After a few minutes Ratz returned with a plastic Asda bag. 'There you are,' he said. 'That should keep you going for a bit.'

Rusty took the bag wordlessly and peered into it. There was bread, cheese, wine, tomatoes, apples, a packet of biscuits and some Andrex toilet rolls. He hefted the bag in his right hand as though judging its worth by its weight. Then he grinned and slapped Ratz on the shoulder.

'Cheers, Ratzy,' he said, 'you're a pal.'

A window. That was all Mo wanted: to be able to look out of a window and see the daylight. The glowing chinks that dribbled through the cracks in the boards hardly constituted that, nor did the flat pale light that groped down the stairs through the hole in the roof. If Mo had not felt so ill, he would have gone out through the kitchen and into the yard, would have just stood there, breathing deeply, feeling the air moving against his skin. He had never realized before how much he took his freedom and his health for granted, would never have believed he could sink as low as this.

He snorted, spat, and groaned at the effort even that took. He had woken – how long ago? Twenty minutes? An hour? Two? The shadows and his illness gulped time, distorted his perceptions. All he knew was that he had been alone too long, alone with the stink and the filth and the darkness. He felt trapped in a cage of pain – his limbs like jelly teeming with needles, his stomach and bowels a pulsing machine that needed to rest. He moved constantly, ceaselessly, beneath his blanket, but couldn't get comfortable. He groaned aloud, swore, snarled with frustration. Nobody deserved this sort of misery – it wasn't fair, it wasn't fuckin' fair.

He reached for the Aspirin and the Night Nurse, then pushed them away, feeling sick. Without them the pain would grow, but Mo couldn't face taking any more medicine at the moment. His mouth felt furry as the inside of an old kettle, his nose and throat raw and itchy. Not a part of him was free of discomfort, not even his eye sockets which seemed to strain under the weight of his eyeballs.

A brief flare of joy sparked in him as he heard a thump coming from the kitchen: Rusty was back. Mo was about to call out, but an itch at the back of his nose transformed the words into sneezes which the walls of the room echoed back at him. Mo groaned, feeling drained, grimacing at the snot that had catapulted out of him and over his blanket.

He wished Rusty would hurry because he wanted to use the bucket again, wanted to shit more of his sickness away.

But Rusty was taking his time. Mo could hear him shuffling about the kitchen, dragging his feet as though purposely to disturb the dust. The skinhead felt irritable even at this slight delay, felt like screaming with rage at Rusty's lack of consideration. He hauled himself into a sitting position and took a deep breath.

'Ru-us,' he called, grimacing at the pain. There was no answer. He tried again: 'Ru-uus.' But this time the words had barbs which caught at his throat and he slumped back, exhausted.

However it seemed his plea had not gone unheard. The shuffling from the kitchen paused and then footsteps moved across the room and down the hall towards him. Mo lay back and closed his eyes, swallowing phlegm that burned his throat. Rus would be here in a second, he needn't be alone any more.

He opened his eyes again when he realized that the footsteps had stopped. For a moment exhaustion had almost plucked him back into sleep, but now he looked up, expecting to see Rusty unpacking a bag of groceries and grinning all over his face. But only the bucket, the manky old mattress, the squat settee, the fireplace with its mouthful of debris and the overturned bamboo table kept him company: Rusty was nowhere to be seen.

'Rus?' Mo said, turning his head towards the door, 'Rus, are you there?'

There was certainly *someone* there, for Mo could see a black shape hovering on the other side of the door, could see material framed by jagged shards of glass.

'Rus?' he said again. 'Rus, is that you?'

The shape lifted an arm and pushed at the doorframe. The door grated slowly inward and a figure entered the room.

'Rus, I knew it was you. Why didn't you answer me?' Mo said.

'I didn't hear you,' replied Rusty. He stood outlined in the pallid light from the hallway, his coiled hair an orange

367

corona, his earrings twinkling pinpoints of brightness. There was a strange, enigmatic smile on his face.

Mo asked, 'Did you get the money?'

'Money?' Rusty repeated the word as though it had no meaning for him. He seemed to withdraw into himself for a moment, his smile fading, then he re-surfaced and the smile returned as though switched on. 'No,' he said, 'I couldn't get any money. Sorry.'

'But what we gonna do?' said Mo, infuriated by his friend's fickle manner. 'What we gonna do without money?'

'Do? We don't need to do anything. Or at least . . . you don't.'

'What do you mean?' Mo groaned as Rusty strode into the middle of the room and turned to face him. The red-haired boy spread his arms wide like a conjuror encompassing the audience with his personality. Mo, who had been looking forward to Rusty's return, now wished he was alone again. 'Don't act weird, Rus,' he pleaded, 'I'm not in the mood for it just now.'

But Rusty's only reply was to widen his smile and his arms still further. Strangely Mo could still see a halo of light around his friend's hair as though blazing sunshine was pouring through it, but of course that was impossible for Rusty had now moved out of the light altogether. Mo closed his eyes tight, then opened them and looked again. The light was still there as though Rusty was generating his own, and now the graffiti on the walls around him appeared to be writhing and squirming like coloured snakes.

'Just fever,' Mo thought. 'Just fever giving me hallucinations.' He reached for the Night Nurse with a trembling hand, but, hallucination or not, he still screamed when Rusty's face began to bubble.

'Look at me, Mo,' Rusty was saying, a savage chuckling triumph in his voice, 'watch me change!'

Mo couldn't have taken his eyes away if he'd tried. Rusty's face was melting like a plastic mask thrown into fire. Fat blisters of flesh were welling up then bursting, spitting orangey pus on to the floor where it sizzled like hot fat. Mo saw Rusty's forehead slide down his face and engulf his eyes and nostrils. Soon only a glutinous oval with a mouth was left – a mouth that continued to gargle: 'Watch me, Mo. Look at me. Watch me, Mo.'

Mo whimpered and pressed himself against the wall, dragging his blanket up to his chin. Rusty's tongue began to swell from his mouth like an inflating balloon, purple veins standing out on its semi-transparent surface. The tongue continued to blossom until it was half as large as the melting head from which it had come. And then – BANG! It burst, spraying blood and glop over a wide area.

Mo cried out as his face was peppered with moist shrapnel. The stuff was burning him, for fucksake, was boring into his face like acid! Through his attempts to scrub the stuff from his skin, Mo saw Rusty undergo a further transformation.

His arms were still spread wide as though encouraging applause. Suddenly the skin began to shrivel from his hands, revealing a black glistening sap beneath. As the skin sloughed off, the thing that had been Rusty laughed. 'Are you watching, Mo?' it asked in a sludgy voice. 'Are you watching me change?'

'No,' murmured Mo, as though by denying this he could deny the creature itself.

'Liar,' chuckled the creature, and flexed hands which looked moulded from hot tar. 'Liar, liar, pants on fire.'

It spread its black fingers. Immediately they began to elongate and grope towards the walls like searching tendrils. Mo watched, his eyes holding no fear; the sheer impossibility of what was happening had pushed fear out of his mind. His body was a different matter but Mo knew nothing of his bowel contents erupting into his pants; of his fingernails, torn and bloody, clawing at the floor. Neither did he know that his feet were jerking spastically, his heels performing a rapid, manic drumbeat.

The creature's fingers, now three or four feet long,

reached the walls on either side and adhered to the damp plaster. The body between them was now no longer recognizable as human; it was a dribbling, melting blob of iridescent but rapidly darkening colours. It gave off a high rancid stench like chemical waste. It still had a mouth and a voice, but the mouth was now simply a feebly struggling gash and the voice a gurgling slurping incoherent mess of sound.

As Mo watched, the creature turned black and drew its legs and head into itself. Slowly, grotesquely, it began to swing, a rotten foetus in a black hammock. A sweet mad voice filled the room, echoing in Mo's head. 'Rock a bye baby on the tree top,' it sang, before dissolving into a peal of crazy laughter.

The hammock's rocking became steadily more violent, more manic. Mo stared at it in the way a hypnotist's victim might stare at a swinging watch. The rocking increased until it seemed the hammock would smash into the wall, but just before it could do so more tendrils sprouted from the main mass and clutched the ceiling, arresting it in mid-swing. There was a split-second pause – and then the tendrils began to move and spread, slithering over the plaster like a speeded-up film of ivy infiltrating a stone wall.

Mo watched, wide-eyed, as the tarry mass crept towards him. It was coming from all directions – around the walls, over the ceiling, along the floor. What tiny urge for self-preservation there was left in his mind coalesced into action, and slowly he began to drag himself towards the open sitting room door.

Surprisingly the creature made no move to stop him. It continued its leisurely advance, apparently unconcerned that its quarry was getting away.

Mo reached the door and rolled through it, coming to rest at the foot of the staircase. Away from the sitting room he seemed to revive a little, both from his ordeal and his sickness, and succeeded in dragging himself to his feet. He staggered down the hall, bouncing off the walls, hardly feeling the bruises he was collecting. He plunged through the open kitchen doorway at the end and promptly fell down. Picking himself up, he stumbled towards the back window. Through it he could see paradise: the rundown row of red-brick houses covered in snow, and the sky beyond, bright as a child's picture.

Suddenly he tottered back, letting out a wail of distress. Something hunched and dark had appeared at the window and was climbing through it. Mo backtracked into the cooker, jarring his coccyx. The humped shape slithered over the sill and planted its feet firmly on the floor.

It was Rusty. He had the rucksack on his back and was patting dust from his jacket. He looked up, eyes narrowing as he peered into the gloomy kitchen. 'Mo?' he said suspiciously.

'Rus!' Mo cried, his voice cracked and brittle. 'Rus, is it really you?'

'Course it's me,' Rusty said, 'who else would it be?' He approached Mo and his nose wrinkled. 'Fuckin' hell, you stink. Have you shit your pants or somethin'?'

Mo looked down and was astonished to find he had. 'Yeah,' he said, feeling shame despite the circumstances. 'Only it wasn't my fault, Rus. I had to, I—'

'You're worse than a fuckin' baby, y'know. Why couldn't you use the bucket?'

'There's somethin' in there, Rus,' Mo said, clutching his friend's arm. *'There's somethin' in there!'*

'In the bucket?' Rusty said, misunderstanding.

'In the room!' Mo wailed. *'There's somethin' in that room!'*

Rusty glanced in the direction of Mo's jabbing finger, as though he could see through the mouldering wall and into the room beyond. He frowned and turned back to his companion. 'You're really scared, aren't you?' he said. 'You've really got the fuckin' heebie-jeebies.'

'Yes, I fuckin' have! We've got to get out of here, Rus. We've got to get out *now!*' Mo grabbed Rusty's arm but his illness had weakened him and Rusty shook him off easily. The red-haired boy took a couple of steps towards the doorway that led into the hall.

'Where're you goin'?' Mo gasped.

'To see what's in that room, to see what's scared you so much.'

'No, don't,' Mo pleaded, 'don't go in there. There's some sort of monster in there, Rus. Somethin' . . . somethin' *evil*.'

'Evil?' Rusty snorted. 'Don't talk soft, Mo. It was probably just an old tramp or a dog, somethin' like that. You were probably half-asleep, didn't know what you were seein'.'

'No, no, you don't understand.' Mo sank on to the rubble-strewn floor, his back against the cooker. His illness was beginning to assert itself again, beating down the adrenalin that had temporarily provided him with energy. 'It was a monster, Rus, believe me. At first it looked like you, then it started to melt, and then it turned all sort of black and horrible.' He shuddered. 'If you go in there, it'll get you; you'll be dead for sure.'

For a moment Rusty looked uncertain, then he squatted down by his friend's side. 'There's no need to worry, Mo,' he said soothingly. 'I've got somethin' in here that'll beat off any monster.' He swung the rucksack off his back and set it on the floor. Swiftly he untied the straps that held it together. 'Have a look at that, Mo,' he said, holding the rucksack open.

All Mo wanted was to go away from this place, but nevertheless he leaned forward and peered into the rucksack. It was dark, but he thought he could detect movement in there, something shifting sluggishly. Too late he remembered that Rusty had gone out empty-handed, that the rucksack, the *real* rucksack, was back in the room with the monster. He had no time even to scream as a pair of black oily hands shot from the darkness and closed over his face.

'Hopes and dreams,' Sylvia thought sadly. 'Where the hell have all mine gone to?'

She plunged her hands into the washing up bowl, coffee cups clinking together beneath the soapy bubbles. Today was her half-day at Prime Cutz, the hairdressing salon where she worked, and she had just been given a lift home by a colleague, Nick Tracey, and his girlfriend, Janine, in their clapped-out Morris Minor which was painted in purple and orange stripes. Nick sported a pink mohican dyed yellow at the ends, and moved with the creak of leather, the jangle of ornamentation. Janine was vampiric in her long flowing dresses, her white make-up, panda eyes and her shock of blue-black hair. Over coffee they had both bombarded Sylvia with their future plans, and for a while she had become caught up in their enthusiasm. Now, however, they had gone, taking their energy with them, leaving her feeling even more trapped and depressed than normal.

The doorbell rang. Who could this be? Probably Nick, she thought, come back for something he'd forgotten. But when she pulled the door open, she saw Walter Treeborn standing on her doorstep, smiling widely.

'Walter!' she exclaimed. 'This *is* a pleasant surprise!'

'I hope I'm not interrupting anything?' Treeborn said. 'I'm off work this week, you see, and I saw you come home . . .'

'Of course you're not interrupting. It's lovely to see you. Please come in.'

She held the door wide and Treeborn stepped into the house. He was dressed casually in a yellow cardigan over a white, open-necked shirt, and grey slacks. It was the first time Sylvia had seen him out of his three-piece suit and she felt a small wriggle of pleasurable desire in her stomach. Immediately she admonished herself for the feeling: 'This is ridiculous. You can't be getting a crush on someone at your age!' But she was, and the proof was there in the hot flush that rose to her face and made her skin glow.

'I'm afraid I haven't brought any wine this time,' Treeborn said. 'I'm not much of a daytime drinker, you see.'

'That's all right, neither am I,' Sylvia replied a little too quickly, then added, laughing nervously, 'I can offer you coffee, though.'

'Ah,' said Treeborn, 'that would be lovely.' He gestured towards the lounge. 'May I go in?'

'Oh yes, please do.' Sylvia felt her flush deepen. 'What must you think of me, keeping you standing on the doormat?'

She ushered Treeborn into the lounge, her movements palpitant, skittish. An inner voice told her to calm down, calm down, but her body refused to respond. In the lounge Treeborn gestured at the flowers she had received that morning and said, 'I see you got my little gift, then?'

Sylvia's blush reached critical mass. Feigning surprise, she said, 'Oh, were they from you? I wondered who had sent them.'

'I hope you didn't mind? It's just that it's not often I get the chance to buy presents for a pretty lady. And after our chat the other night . . . well, I thought you needed cheering up.'

'Mind?' Sylvia exclaimed. 'Of course I didn't mind! It was a lovely thing to do, Walter, though you shouldn't have spent your money on me. You know, you're a very kind man . . . a *very* kind man.'

Treeborn smiled modestly. For a bristling moment the air seemed charged with unspoken thoughts. To cover her embarrassment, Sylvia said, 'Well, I'll get the coffee, then,' and hurried into the kitchen.

They drank coffee and sat on opposite sides of the room as they chatted. They talked of mundane things – work, the weather, family. Sylvia enjoyed the chat, felt lulled by the soft cadences in Treeborn's voice, but she felt frustrated as well. She felt that much was being left unsaid, that they were hovering outside a door beyond which was a room where significant matters waited to be discussed. More than once an awkward silence fell between them as they spoke and a mutual glance inched open the doorway. Then one or the other would panic, pick up a thread of trivia, and the door would slam shut again, leaving only echoes behind.

At 3.26 p.m., at precisely the same time that her son, Robin, was groaning inwardly that there was still half-an-hour of his physics lesson to endure, Sylvia got up from her chair, walked across the room and bent to pick up the coffee tray. As she did so, Walter Treeborn leaned forward and gently encircled her left wrist with his right hand. Sylvia looked up, heart thudding, face able to express nothing but alarm.

Treeborn said, 'Let's go upstairs.'

Sylvia froze. She had wanted this, wanted it badly, but Treeborn's bluntness had caught her off-guard. She was aware of his hand round her wrist like a bracelet of flesh, could feel its warmth, its pressure, with an almost heightened sensitivity. She looked into his eyes, into his cool blue glittering eyes, and then at his smooth skin, the jaw shadowed by stubble, and at his neat well-cut hair. For a moment she felt faint, unreal; he seemed dream-like, too perfect for her. Then she saw him swallow convulsively, and realized he was just as nervous as she.

'All right,' she breathed.

They went upstairs, hand in hand, not saying a word. They undressed soundlessly, climbed between the sheets that were deliciously cold. Though silent, their love-making was rapacious, hungry, flooding. When it was over, they lay in the drowsy afterglow, their sweat drying to leave goosebumps, Sylvia caressing her lover's penis tenderly. She stroked the sticky slickness of its tip, experiencing a glut of emotions: satisfaction, confusion, fulfilment, guilt, anger at the guilt. She looked up at Treeborn's face, seeing his jawbone from the underside, jutting from the neck like the flat of an iron. She tapped on his chest with one finger and he looked down at her,

375

opening dewy eyes, lips edging upwards into a smile.

'Mnnn?'

'You OK?'

He gave a single slow nod and closed his eyes again. 'Wonderful.'

Sylvia glowed inside and gradually relaxed. After a pause she said, 'I'm glad.' She twisted lazily to look at the clock on the bedside, and suddenly her back tensed and she sat upright, hair tumbling about her shoulders. 'Oh shit, it's nearly four o'clock! Robin'll be home in twenty minutes!'

She scrambled from the bed and hurriedly dressed. Treeborn followed her example, though in a more leisurely manner. As he was lacing up his shoes, he said, 'Actually, that reminds me. That's one of the reasons why I came round here.'

Sylvia was running a slide into her hair at the back, leaving wispy strands to curl down over her ears. 'Hmm, what's that?'

'Your son, Robin. I'm clearing some stuff out of my cellar this evening and I wondered whether he might give me a hand.'

'What made you think of Robin?' Sylvia said.

'Well, I don't really know many other people round here, and to tell you the truth, I'd feel a little awkward asking your husband.'

'Yes, I can see that.' She smiled. 'OK, I'll ask Robin when he gets in, and if he doesn't have too much homework, I'll send him round.'

'Thank you, that would be much appreciated.' Treeborn stood up and stretched, then went to the mirror and smoothed down his hair. As he was doing so, Sylvia chuckled.

'You know, Walter, you're a real dark horse,' she said. 'If someone had told me a week ago I would be doing this, I'd never have believed them.'

Walter straightened up and came across the room. He bent slightly and kissed Sylvia's forehead, then cupped her face in his hand. 'You don't regret it, do you?' he asked.

Sylvia smiled. 'No, of course not.'

'Until next time, then.' Walter kissed her again, this time on the lips, and they went downstairs. At the front door he said, 'You won't forget to ask Robin, will you?'

'No, I won't forget.'

'Thanks . . . Well, goodbye then.'

'Bye.' She closed the door.

This time when she was washing the coffee cups, Sylvia felt a warmth inside her that she had not known for a long time. She touched her own breast gently, trailed a hand down between her thighs . . . and smiled until it seemed her face would split.

8

Resisting temptation had never been Rusty's strongpoint. After flogging the stolen ornaments in a dingy junk-shop for fifteen quid, he had turned not towards Piling Hill, but towards the promenade and the bright lights of the Golden Penny Amusement Arcade. There, among the bleeps and buzzes and explosions simulated by microchip, he had fed eight of his twenty-three pounds to a greedy and tight-fisted fruit machine. Afterwards he had followed his nose to a Kentucky Fried Chicken, where he had ordered a Bargain Bucket and set to with a vengeance. Belching happily, sucking the grease from his fingers, he had then entered The Wharf, a pub frequented by Starmouth's fishermen. It was only after four pints of Guinness that he remembered he had some groceries to buy. However it was not until he was approaching the checkout in Asda, his trolley stuffed with food, that he counted the money in his pocket and discovered he'd only got seven quid of his original twenty-three left.

His first thought was that he'd been ripped off – probably by one of those fuckin' mackerel-hunters in the bar at The Wharf. However, when he totalled up the money he'd spent, he was astonished to discover he hadn't been robbed after all. Eight quid on the fruit machine, four or five on the Kentucky, three or four at the pub: that made a grand total of sixteen quid, give or take, which, deducted from twenty-three, left seven.

'Shit,' Rusty murmured, somewhat awed by the ease with which the cash had melted away. He wheeled his trolley to the freezer aisle and hung around for a few minutes, pretending to decide between a strawberry flan and a blackcurrant cheesecake. Then, when no-one was looking, he dumped a good half of the groceries into the freezer. Objective achieved, he sedately approached the line of checkouts.

It was around four-thirty by the time he arrived back at King Street. Twilit clouds were smudging the sky above him, painting the snow a hard minty blue. Rusty kicked open the gate into the yard, and with the bag of groceries clutched to his chest tramped up to the open kitchen window. He dumped the bag inside, then climbed in after it, musing happily on the afternoon he'd spent. He felt a sense of triumph in the fact that he had managed to elude the entire Starmouth police force yet again. 'What a bunch of fuckin' useless morons,' he thought, 'what a totally inept group of nipple-headed turds.' Having not seen a newspaper, he didn't know that the Starmouth police force now had more urgent matters than his and Mo's disappearance to worry about.

Once through the window, he wiped his grimy hands on his jeans, then stood, adjusting his eyes to the gloom. 'It's cold in here,' he thought, 'even colder than outside.' He picked up the bag of groceries at his feet, replacing a few of the items which had tumbled from the plastic lips. If he had been more observant, and if the sky had graced the kitchen with a little more light, he might have noticed the marks on the floor by the cooker, the scuffs and swirls that suggested a struggle had taken place. But Rusty was not observant, and the sky outside was deepening to prema-ture night, and so he passed the marks by, not realizing the significance they held.

Rusty yelled his friend's name as he shuffled down the dark hallway that led to the sitting room; and when the only reply was the echo of his own voice, he yelled it again. 'Mo! It's me! I'm back! Are you there?'

But again only echoes filled the silence.

'Probably zonked out on Night Nurse,' Rusty thought, and smiled evilly. 'I'll give the lazy fucker a fright.' He set the bag down in the hallway, propping it against the spongy wall, and crept to the sitting room door. The gaps in the door were like two square mouths lined with jagged teeth: through them Rusty could see the dim outline of the fireplace, rubbish clustered around it. He positioned himself beside the door, out of sight of anyone who might be inside, and listened. He could hear nothing, not even the soft breathing that would tell him Mo was asleep.

'Must be a really deep one,' Rusty thought, grinning. He braced himself, then leaped into action, kicking hard at the doorframe and springing sideways into the room. 'Arghh!' he screamed as he turned to face the wall where Mo had been slumped. He expected to see a shaved head struggling from beneath a blanket, flailing limbs pawing the air. Instead he was both bemused and disappointed to find the room empty.

He straightened up, muttering, 'What the fuck . . . ?' and looked around him. Everything seemed to be as it was when he'd left – the piss-stench mattress, the rotting settee, the upended table, the bucket with its chronic case of halitosis. Even Mo's blanket was still there, bundled against the wall, and the rucksack lying beside it in a deflated heap.

But where the fuck was Mo? Rusty crossed to the blanket and picked it up as though half-expecting his friend to be underneath. He shook the blanket out, grimaced at its smell of damp and stale sweat and dropped it again. Frustrated, he booted it into a corner.

'Mo?' he barked, irritated by the mystery, 'Mo, where are you?'

He heard something. Had it been a groan or just the

wind probing at the house? Whichever, it had come from the hallway.

He went out there, glad to leave the stench of the sitting room behind, though the raw sewage smell was now starting to encroach into all areas of the house. He listened for a moment, hoping for a repetition of the sound, but the silence had closed ranks again. He looked along the length of the hallway, up at the stained ceiling which was a jigsaw puzzle of cracks. A cord hung from the ceiling like an exposed vein, the web that clung to it vibrating feebly. Suddenly from upstairs came a sound like shifting rubble. Rusty jumped, then grimaced at his own nervousness. He stood at the foot of the stairs and looked up.

'Mo?' he called. 'Are you there?'

Lengths of timber were criss-crossed at the top like clumsy wattle. Chunks of masonry, some as large as television sets, lay among them. 'Surely he can't have gone up there?' Rusty thought. 'Not in his state!' He put his hand on the banister, whose layer of dust was grey and sticky, and cautiously placed one foot on the bottom step.

'Mo?' he shouted again. 'Mo, is that you?'

The reply startled him. The voice was low and groaning, but without doubt it belonged to Mo. 'Ruuuusss,' it wailed, 'heeeeelllp meeee!'

Rusty licked his lips. 'Mo?' he said, uncertain.

'Heeeeeellllp meeeeeee!!'

This time the voice was unbearable, encapsulating a lifetime's grief and pain. Rusty felt the hairs quill on his neck and arms, swallowed as a pulse began to tick at the base of his throat. For a crazy moment he was convinced the most sensible thing would be to flee that house just as fast as he could and never go back there again . . .

Then as quickly as it had come the feeling passed, and he felt shame at his fear, and on top of the shame the old familiar anger.

'Mo,' he snarled, stomping up two or three more stairs, 'just what the fuck are you doin' up there?'

This time the reply was simply a groan. From his vantage

point, Rusty could see a gaping doorway which led into what looked like a bathroom, and part of a wall beyond the debris. He could see blue and orange wallpaper which must once have been garish, but had now been bleached by the elements. He could see fingers of light groping among the debris as though searching for something of value. And in his mind's eye he could see Mo, lying beneath a dislodged beam or a hunk of masonry, his body broken and blood dribbling from his mouth or his ears.

He shook his head roughly, feeling anger spark through him again. He hated weakness, always had, in himself as well as others. He had always hidden his uncertainties behind aggression, preferring to attack even when the odds were stacked heavily against him. Perhaps that was the best that could be said of Rusty, the only thing that even vaguely approached a semblance of nobility: that he was no coward, that he was every bit as tough as he purported to be. Of course, this didn't mean that he was an advocate of The Fair Fight (as Toady and Neil Gardener would testify), but still . . . he had never run from anything, and he wasn't about to start now.

He shouted up the stairs, 'Hold on, Mo, I'm coming,' and began his ascent.

Like the rest of the house, the stairs were damp and rotten, the wood sagging and occasionally crumbling beneath his feet. Rusty took them slowly, keeping to the sides, holding on to the banister for support. One step snapped with a wet crunching sound and Rusty almost went tumbling back down again. Desperately he swung round, both hands closing around the banister rail, and managed to regain his balance. He expelled a sigh of relief and moments later reached the top of the stairs.

He peered through the criss-crossing beams, thankful for the light which poured in through the ceiling. The hole was about the size and length of three bathtubs laid end to end and ran almost the entire length of the landing, then widened out where the bathroom ceiling had collapsed. Through the landing ceiling, Rusty could see into the attic, and beyond that the underside of the house's sloping slate roof. It was from the attic that the timber had come; the roof's supporting framework looking like a chestful of smashed and splintered ribs. A second hole, huge and jagged, had been punched through the slates, which was where the light and the snow and the rain got in.

Rusty shook his head, turning his attention to the mangled bathroom. The tumbling debris had smashed the lintel of the door into a 'V' and ripped the door itself off its hinges. It was now lying among the rubble, a rectangle of white peeling wood, warped drastically by the elements. Through the gap it had left, Rusty could see a toilet, a sink and the edge of a bath, all full of snow. A carpet of snow also lay on the landing itself, which, with its lengths of timber and hunks of rock, gave the impression that some strange leafless forest had taken root.

Though the damage did not look irreparable, Rusty guessed that by now it probably was. The house had been open to the elements for so long that its floors and walls and ceilings must be crawling with rot. Even the three rooms leading off from the landing whose walls and ceilings were still intact were probably just as bad. Rusty could see large cracks meandering out from the hole in the landing ceiling and running down the walls and into the lintels of the three closed doors. He wondered what would happen if he tried to open any of them, wondered whether he would hear a warning rumble before being buried by hunks of saturated brick and plaster. He knew it was foolish to try, knew it was dangerous even standing here, but he also knew he couldn't give up now.

Sighing, he looked at the three doors, wondering which one Mo had taken refuge behind. He struggled between and under the wooden supports, taking care not to dislodge any of them, until he came up parallel with the first door. He stepped over a chunk of masonry whose layer of snow gave it the appearance of a melting wedding cake, and put his mouth to the damp wood.

'Mo?' he called softly. 'Mo, are you in there?'

Silence.

Rusty felt anger surge in him again, an anger that almost superseded his unease. 'I'm here to help you, you dim cunt! Why don't you answer me?' he thought. He gritted his teeth and tried again.

'Mo! Where the pissin' hell are you?'

Silence again, and this time Rusty had the strange idea that it was mocking him.

'Fuck you!' he yelled, raising his head and staring up at the hole in the roof. He flinched a little as the landing around him darkened, but it was only a grey cloud sidling across the edge of the hole like a transient bruise. Frustrated, he looked down at the landing again – and noticed shadows collecting in prints in the snow; well-defined boot-prints that led to the door at the end.

'So that's where you are, you fucker,' he murmured softly to himself. His triumph was mingled with irritation. 'Trust you to go into the room that's fuckin' furthest away.'

He clambered over the debris and squeezed between the wooden beams, following the footprints. Just before he reached the far door, he slipped on a patch of snow and barked his shin on a projecting lump of wood. 'Twat!' he yelled, meaning both the wood and Mo. He rubbed his shin with his right hand and clenched his left into a fist, eager to hit something. However he didn't trust anything he might hit not to give way. In the end he uncoiled his fist, vowing that he'd hit Mo when he found him, for leading him on such a wild fuckin' goosechase.

Breathing heavily, he reached out and gripped the door handle, which was so cold it felt sculpted from silvered ice. He twisted and the handle screeched, but when he pushed, the door opened easily enough. He went in, entering a room whose walls were so dingy that it was difficult to imagine what colour they might once have been. Opposite the door, in the outward facing wall, were two sash windows, the glass in them furred with dust and grime and letting in very little light. The place was stripped of furniture and the floor, like those in the rest of the house, was wooden boards. A few sheets of newspaper lay spreadeagled over the boards, but for what purpose Rusty couldn't imagine. Curiously he bent and squinted at the date on one of the sheets: November 24th 1979. Over nine years old.

He straightened and looked around him, at a loss. Despite the bootprints, Mo was not here. Rusty pivoted on his heels, looking up at the ceiling as though prepared to believe that his friend might be clinging upside-down in a corner somewhere. His eyes swept round the room a number of times before he realized that the dark rectangle set into the wall to the right of the doorway was a sliding wardrobe. He approached it and placed his fingers into the groove that served as a handle. Of course, this must be where Mo was hiding, there was no alternative. The room was silent now, which must have meant that Mo had passed out, probably drugged up to his eyeballs on Night Nurse.

He tugged and the door grated open a little, then stopped, its runners stiff with disuse. Grunting, he tugged again and the door opened a little further. He gritted his teeth and tugged a third time, and with a sound like a carriage rumbling over cobbles, the door abruptly came all the way open, almost causing Rusty to lose his balance.

'It's all right, Mo,' he said as he straightened up. 'I'm here now. Nothing to worry ab—'

His words trickled away as he saw what the wardrobe contained. For a moment he simply stared, frozen, unable to believe his eyes. Then messages encouraging physical reaction seeped outwards from his brain and he almost vomited on the beer he had drunk earlier. Clumsily his hands scrabbled at the handle and he heaved the wardrobe door shut. The muscles in his arms screamed as he himself wanted to.

He stumbled over to the wall and rested his palms and forehead against it, the horror clogging up his throat, his limbs shaking. He felt sweat bursting out all over him, blood sprinting through his veins, but deep inside he was cold. His mind raced, trying desperately to cope with the paradox just presented to it. 'How could Mo have been calling me?' he kept thinking. 'How could Mo have been calling me without a head?' His stomach finally gave up its tug of war, and Rusty spewed over the wall.

He wiped his mouth with his sleeve as from behind him he heard the soft click of footsteps. He swung to face the door, blinking his eyes to stop sweat from blinding them. In the dim light he saw a dark shape silhouetted in the doorway; a shape that stepped forward to reveal itself as a pale-faced man with slicked-back hair who was dressed in a black tuxedo.

'Hi there,' the man said.

The greeting hit him like a bullet and Rusty felt his legs collapse beneath him. He slid down the wall, stopping only when his backside reached the floorboards. That 'hi there' had been too much for him, coming as it did from the bloke who was most probably Mo's murderer, the bloke who had twisted Mo's head clean off. He felt defenceless, sickened, his stomach a barrel of queasy custard. Vomit rose in him again and he fought it down. At last he managed to squeak, 'Who are you?'

The man grinned, revealing teeth like piano keys. His eyes glittered making Rusty think muzzily of the fairground, of the blinking lights atop the carousel. When he spoke Rusty heard music behind his voice, gaudy candy-floss music, sinister and tinkling. 'I,' the man whispered, and leaned closer, bringing a smell like toffee apples, 'am your friend.'

'Friend?' Rusty murmured the word as though he had never heard it before. He looked up at the pale face and realized it was powdered, the cheeks rouged, the eyes rimmed in black eyeliner. A thousand silly thoughts burst in his head like popcorn: Dracula, queer, joker, devil . . . He gasped as the face swooped at him like a hatchet blade and pushed himself as far back as bricks and mortar would allow. Despite the cosmetics (or perhaps because of them),

385

the face wore the most evil, merciless expression he had ever seen.

'Yes,' said the man, 'friend.' A pink tongue blossomed from the mouth to lick bloodless lips: an innocent gesture – so why did Rusty feel a wave of fear so intense he almost blacked out?

If he had been able to think straight, Rusty might have appreciated the irony of the situation. Here he was – the local psycho, the nutter – lying pinned to the wall in fear of this made-up tart while not six feet from him lay the decapitated body of his partner in crime. Throughout his short life, Rusty had been labelled crazy, capable of anything, and it was a reputation he had revelled in. But those people who had given him the label had no inkling what true craziness really was. Those people had never met *this* man.

'Why did you kill Mo?' he whispered, feeling more puny and insignificant than he ever had before. He tried to rise, but his legs were not yet ready to support him.

Shoulders, like the sharp points of folded bat-wings, shrugged in the dimness. 'Why not?' came the reply.

It was an answer Rusty could have anticipated, but nontheless he felt the chill inside him shoot out tendrils. He opened his mouth and found himself bleating. 'Mo was – he was my friend!'

'Oh, really!' The man pouted. 'He was useless, a nobody; he would never have amounted to anything. I did him a favour by killing him.' He winked at Rusty and mimed twisting a chicken's neck with his hands. 'Believe me, his death was quick and clean. I assure you he didn't feel a thing.'

He took a sudden step forward, and the rush of panic the movement prompted in Rusty enabled him to scramble to his feet. He edged towards the window as a sudden thought occurred to him. 'What . . . what did you do with . . . with the head?'

The man's thin lips seemed to hiss back as he smiled.

386

Reaching into his tuxedo, he said, 'I have it here. Why? Do you want to see it?'

'No!' Rusty shouted. Reason dictated that something so large as a human head could not possibly fit inside the man's jacket, but reason was not a faculty that Rusty trusted any more. If the man said he had Mo's head, then he had it; there was no doubting him.

'Are you sure?' the man said, disappointment on his painted face. 'It won't take a minute to find it.' He withdrew his hand with the flourish of a magician, to reveal not a human head, nor even a bunch of flowers, but a metal blade – the self-same blade with which Mo had stabbed Neil Gardener just two days before. Light seemed to be drawn to the blade, to flash and twinkle in the darkness. Within the light Rusty saw his own scared face staring back at him and he shivered in fear. It was like looking at a reflection of his own mortality.

'You're not going to kill me, you know,' he said. He tried to make the words defiant but they sounded more like a plea. 'I won't let you kill me.'

'Kill you?' The man's chuckle, dry as the house was damp, rippled round the room. 'My dear boy, I assure you the thought never entered my head. Oh no, I didn't bring you here just to kill you.'

'Didn't *bring* me here? What do you mean by that? Nobody brought me here. I came of my own accord.'

The man threw back his head and laughed. 'Oh dear, you creatures are so easy to manipulate, aren't you? I planted the seeds for it all, don't you see? I created these circumstances for my amusement . . . The stabbing of Neil Gardener, your flight to this house, Mo's illness. Don't you understand, little boy – I'm responsible for *everything*.'

Rusty was still edging towards the window and now he began to shake his head slowly. 'You talk crazy, you know that?' he said. 'I don't know what the fuck you're on about.' His hand touched the edge of the window.

Cautiously he began to slide it towards the catch in the middle that locked the top and bottom frames together.

'No,' the man said, looking at him, 'no, I don't suppose you do.' He brought Mo's blade up to his mouth and licked its length slowly with the tip of his tongue. The action caused Rusty's stomach to squirm uneasily and his hand shook as it grappled with the catch.

'You won't get those windows open, you know,' the man said suddenly. 'I'm afraid they're fused to the frames . . . both of them.'

Frantically Rusty swung to the windows and tried to lever open first the right, then the left. 'Come on, come on,' he muttered as his muscles strained, but already he knew that what the man had said was true. He swung back again, and like a cornered rat suddenly found some of his old aggression. His hand dipped into the back pocket of his jeans and emerged with his own knife. He pressed a button and the blade sprang eagerly from its sheath.

'Right, queer-boy,' he said, trying to keep the tremor from his voice, 'let's see if you can really fight. You're not gonna take me as easy as you took Mo.'

The man seemed amused by Rusty's bravado. He was still holding Mo's knife vaguely parallel with his face as though it were a cigar, but now slowly, deliberately, he brought it round and placed the point in the cleft of his chin. With a sudden upward stroke he sliced his face neatly in half, then, even before Rusty had time to register there was no blood, dropped the knife and began to rip away the flapping skin as though it were a mask.

Rusty tried to scream at what was underneath, but found he hadn't the breath. The image of what now surged from the creature's collar burned into his mind like a brand, squeezed his bowels, his heart, his brain. Between the two flapping lumps of pink flesh was a glass orb like an upside-down goldfish bowl; and within the orb, like a kernel in a shell, was Mo's head.

Brown, shrunken, it looked as though all its juices had been extracted. Its eyes were dry empty sockets, its mouth yawning open. Slowly, horribly, the mouth started to move, to struggle tortuously into life. 'Ah! So *that*'s where I put the head!' rasped the voice that came out of it.

The shrivelled lips twisted into a ghastly smile. The creature raised its right hand and with its left began casually to twist off its fingers, crunching them at the second knuckle like celery sticks and dropping them to the floor.

Not surprisingly, Rusty had seen enough. In one motion he threw down his knife, turned, and hurled himself at the closed right-hand window. A moment later he was soaring outwards, trailing glass fragments like the brittle shards of some strange chrysalis.

He experienced one brief moment of exhilaration, one fleeting instant when he really believed he could fly. Then gravity seized him. He plummetted downwards, a drop of twenty-five feet, his body travelling faster than it ever had before. The ground he hit was well-cushioned with both snow and grass, but it still felt as though someone had set off a series of explosions inside him. His left leg, his abdomen, his spine, his rib-cage and his skull all became separate knots of crunching, excruciating pain. The pain spread, merged, encompassed his whole body, then mercifully dwindled into a swimming black numbness.

The last thing he saw before he was washed away was the startling redness of his blood seeping into the snow.

9

'Rob! Hey, Rob! Wait up!'

Richard saw Robin turn at the sound of his voice and hurried towards him. He took care not to slip on the slushy pavement as he struggled through hordes of his peers, nearly all of whom were wearing coats and hats and boots. Richard smiled as he approached the school gates where Robin was waiting, but when he saw his friend's expression his smile died on his lips. Robin looked less than pleased to see him – looked, in fact, positively pained. When he got close enough to be heard, Richard uncertainly asked, 'You OK, Rob?'

Robin shrugged. His skin was pasty, highlighting his acne, and his puffy eyes suggested he'd had very little sleep. 'Yeah, course I am,' he muttered. 'Why shouldn't I be?'

Richard let that pass. 'Mind if I walk with you?' he said.

It was obvious from Robin's expression that he did mind. His gaze shifted and for a few moments he stared at the bodies streaming past them, breathing out carbon dioxide in vaporous clouds. Eventually he sighed and from somewhere he mustered a smile. 'Nah, course not,' he said. 'C'mon.'

The two boys merged with the crowd, a little knot of silence amid the chatter. It was not that Richard didn't want to speak – he did, desperately – but Robin's expression didn't encourage it. After his initial hurt at Robin's reaction to him, Richard thought he now understood why his friend had responded in the way he had. Robin was trying to forget about King Street and the body and all the weird things that had been happening, and the only way he could do that was by avoiding everything associated with it. And that included himself and Nige and Toady.

Richard felt angry at this, not at Robin but at the creature. Without even trying it was disrupting their lives, destroying their friendships. If they were going to win through, they had to stick together, had to be able to spill out their fears and share the burden. Their problem was frightening, and talking about it would be painful, yet ignoring it would not make it go away.

However, despite his need to talk, Richard did not say a word until they reached the main road that branched into Beachside some ten minutes walk from the school.

'Nige and Toady didn't show up for school today, did they?' he said then.

He saw Robin stiffen slightly. 'I dunno. Didn't they?'

'No . . . I hope Nige is all right . . . you know, after yesterday and everything.'

Robin gave a discouraging, 'Hmm,' and the boys lapsed into silence once more. Richard had broken the ice, but had found the water beneath cold and unwelcoming. Nevertheless he knew that he had to plunge in, and soon, because they were coming to the end of the road where Robin turned left and he right.

'Come on,' he told himself, 'if you can talk to Olive you can talk to Rob,' though even as the thought formed he knew that this was different somehow. It was easy discussing problems with Olive; it seemed natural and normal. But revealing his feelings to his friends felt like breaking too many unspoken rules. As a result, the words jammed in his throat; he struggled desperately for the right phraseology as his and Robin's footsteps crunched on grit-peppered snow. He was half-aware of the end of the road getting closer and closer; one more minute and it would be too late to say anything.

All at once he blurted. 'How are you coping with all this?'

Robin stopped dead, breathing heavily. Richard saw him swallow and close his eyes. He seemed to stand like that for a long time as traffic and people went past and grey wisps of cloud crawled overhead. Then at last he opened his eyes and said, 'Coping with what?'

Richard was taken aback. He could understand Robin's reluctance to speak, but could see no point in his being deliberately obtuse. 'All this King Street stuff . . . and, you know, the body and everything. Are you dealing with it OK?'

Robin sighed again. He looked away from Richard, towards the end of the road, as though silently bemoaning the fact that another few yards would have seen him safe. When he turned back there was an expression on his face that seemed like a desperate but failing attempt to maintain his composure.

'Rich,' he said haltingly, 'last night I saw . . .' His voice cracked and he shook his head. 'Aw, no, bollocks! Never mind, it doesn't matter.'

'Rob, what did you see?' Richard urged. Fear was gnawing at him, but he had to know. 'Tell me, what did you see?'

'*I said it doesn't matter!*' Robin seemed torn by fury and indecision. 'I've got to get back,' he growled, and started walking. Richard ran and caught up with him.

'Rob, we've got to stick together on this. There's no point pretending nothing's happening, because it is . . . *it is* . . . C'mon, Rob, don't just walk away. I'm not your enemy, you know.'

Robin stopped again. He looked confused, wretched. He said, 'Look, Rich, I don't wanna be a member of the Horror Club any more. I don't like what's going on . . . with Toady and everything, I mean. I just don't wanna be involved any more, OK!'

He tried to move away. Richard grabbed his arm.

'But we are involved,' he said, 'all of us. It's not just a game, Rob. You can't just say I'm not playing any more and that's an end to it. This . . . creature, whatever it is, knows about us, and it's not going to let us go. We've got to fight it, Rob. We've got to do something!'

He stepped back as Robin shook his arm free. Looking at the fury on his face, Richard was certain the older boy was about to hit him. He saw Robin's hands curl into fists and he brought up his own to protect his face. But to his relief Robin's fists stayed where they were. Instead of hitting out, he merely started yelling.

'*How can we fucking do something?*' he shouted. 'We don't know *what* to do! It's not like taking on Rusty and his gang, you know, Rich. We can't fight it with our fists and hope it'll leave us alone! I mean, you can't fight fucking nightmares! You can't fight something that can rip a man apart just like he was a fucking doll!'

His voice choked into sobs. The few passers-by on the street stopped and peered across at the cause of the commotion. Richard tried to ignore them, and awkwardly consoled his friend, more distressed by his tears than he had been by his anger. He fished a crumpled but unused handkerchief from his pocket and held it out.

'C'mon, Rob . . . hey, c'mon mate . . . don't cry,' he said.

Robin took the handkerchief which he used to wipe his eyes. 'I'm not crying,' he mumbled. 'I'm just . . . aw, fucking hell, Rich, what we gonna do?'

Richard took the handkerchief and stuffed it into his pocket. 'Me and Olive are going back to King street,' he said. 'We're going to see if we can kill that thing . . . or at least send it back to where it came from.'

He looked at Robin to gauge his reaction. His friend's eyes, now more bloodshot and puffy than ever, widened. 'Rich, you can't!' he said. 'It'd be suicide to go back there. What are you gonna do anyway? How are you going to get rid of it?'

'I don't know,' Richard admitted, and grimaced.

'You're mad, Rich . . . you're bloody mad. You can't go back to that house,' Robin wailed.

'But what else can we do?' Richard protested. 'We can either sit and wait for that thing to come and get us, or we can attack it. Rob, the only thing we know about it is that it comes from King Street. We've got to go back there . . . there's no other alternative.'

He spread his hands desperately. He needed Robin's blessing on this, needed the assurance that going back to King Street was a good idea. All day he had been having doubts about the validity of Olive's plan, not to mention the absolute terror he felt at the prospect of returning to that hell-hole of a house; but if only Robin thought it was a positive step, then Richard thought maybe he could go through with it.

However Robin's expression offered neither support nor encouragement. His face was simply a reflection of Richard's own emotions: the panic lurking beneath the surface, the feelings of futility, the horrible certainty that any opposition they came up with would be no more than a spit in the ocean.

Seeing those emotions – emotions which he himself had

been striving to conceal – displayed so openly on Robin's face, caused the floodgates in Richard's mind to open at last. Despair rushed in, washing away the fragments of hope to which he had been clinging, drowning them, battering them, showing them up for the worthless props they really were. Olive, for instance, whom he had been pinning blind hopes on, he now saw was nothing but a scared old lady; her 'psychic' ability which he so revered was merely an uncontrollable oddity and not a potential weapon; her words, 'The creature must want you alive . . .' no longer seemed reassuring, but sinister, ominous. Or maybe she was even mistaken – maybe the creature was merely biding its time before killing them all.

Richard felt as though a black sea was rushing through his body, invading every pore, every fibre of his being. In that instant he knew he couldn't go back to King Street – not today, not ever – and he felt more wretched than he ever had in his life. He felt the backs of his eyes prickling, and like Robin before him, he began to cry.

Like a lost child he held out a hand, which Robin, after a moment's hesitation, took. And in a cracked voice, tears misting up the insides of his spectacles, he echoed his friend's words of a few minutes before.

'Oh, Rob,' he wailed, 'what are we gonna do?'

10

The thud of the newspaper hitting the doormat made Nige jump, a reminder that his nerves were still raw and delicate. On the television *The Transformers* were saving the planet from world domination, but as far as Nige was concerned they might as well have been dancing a jig. His mind was turned inward, concentrating not on the robotic heroes but on the bewildering array of messages that whirled and spun in his head.

He'd woken at noon, after fourteen hours of dreamless sleep, a sleep that his mind had imposed as a natural anaesthetic in order to botch up a few mental repairs. His first conscious thoughts on waking had been purely physical desires – hunger, thirst, the need to piss. Mentally he had felt peaceful, if a little sluggish, and it was only as the vestiges of sleep flaked away and the day progressed that unsettling images began to seep through the protective brickwork that had been built around his mind.

The first instance of this had been sparked by looking out of his bedroom window and seeing a round depression, like a pockmark, in the middle of the snow-covered lawn. That apparently innocuous sight had generated a wave of undirected horror that had burst in his mind like a firework, causing his heart to thud, his mouth to go dry, and a sudden picture, like a flash-frame, to blink into his mind, then out again, too swift to be properly examined. All Nige had managed to grasp from the experience had been an impression, a horrifyingly vague impression of being pursued by something vast and cumbersome and relentless. He had rushed to the bathroom, not sure whether he was going to throw up or crap his guts out. In the end he had done neither.

The second instance had been later in the afternoon, after being plied by his mother with a lunch of tomato soup and bread. Unable to stand her fussing any longer, Nige had retreated to his bedroom to play some music, choosing a U2 tape from the selection he kept on his shelf. He pressed the 'eject' button on his radio cassette only to find that the cassette compartment had a tape already inside. It was a normal enough tape – a Memorex C60 – but what puzzled Nige was the fact that he was sure he had never seen it before in his life. Curiously he rewound the tape to the beginning and pressed the 'play' button.

The voices on the tape, muffled and dull, meant little to him at first. He listened for a couple of minutes, and was about to switch off, when he realized that one of the voices was his own. With renewed interest he turned up the volume and listened more intently. The flash-frame images, a whole jumble of them, came with the first scream.

On the tape Nige was apparently pleading for mercy, screaming about teeth and claws and pain, but it was in his mind where the real turmoil was going on. The images pounded into his head like a series of hammer blows – burning candles, breaking glass, stench, darkness, terror. Nige jabbed at the 'stop' button, missed, jabbed again. The second time he hit it, and the silence caused the images to abate, but not before he felt his lunch rising to the back of his throat. He dashed to the bathroom and this time he *did* throw up, the tomato soup streaming from his mouth and into the sink like thin blood.

The third instance had happened just half an hour ago.

He had been lying on his bed, recovering, clutching his queasy stomach and trying to fight down the fear that kept breaking through the oily surface of his mind. In one respect he felt quite sane and lucid – he knew his name, his age, his address, which school he went to, details of his friends and family. But what he couldn't remember were *events*, particularly over the last few days. Just what had been happening to make him forget?

If he thought hard enough he could recall snippets. He remembered, for instance, sitting behind a school desk and wrestling with maths problems; getting drunk somewhere and seeing a fight; being slapped across the face so hard it brought tears to his eyes. And very vaguely he remembered walking on the beach, climbing over rocks . . . though before that memory became too clear he felt his mind shying from it like a nervous horse.

The recollection of these details, though, instead of satisfying him, only frustrated Nige all the more. He was sure that something else had happened, and was sure too that it was something important; important and . . . *bad*. Yes, whatever had happened had been so rotten and dirty and nasty that his mind was keeping it from him. Yet though this insinuated that trying to remember was perhaps not such a good idea after all, Nige simply could *not* leave the memory alone. For him it held the same attraction as a large and crusty scab. To pull it off would probably hurt like hell, but that still didn't prevent him from picking and probing.

It was while he was picking and probing that the knock came on his bedroom door. Nige looked up, surprised, wondering who this was. He had not heard his mother clomping upstairs, and his father was at work at Peevey's Insurance, where he was a broker. Nige stared at the door for a moment as though uncertain how to react, then tentatively called, 'Come in.' The figure that entered caused him to sit up sharply and his empty stomach to spasm again.

It was an old man with a white stick, whose black pebble-glasses matched his black suit. A harmless enough, even sympathetic figure, but one which caused the flash-flame images to erupt once more, sharp and unpleasant as migraine.

In his mind's eye, Nige saw the old man as . . . something else. But so vague and fleeting was the image that it was hard to tell exactly what. Again he had a sensation of darkness, of a bed containing something spitting and clawing, drawing blood. As though to swamp this image a name and a title suddenly rose like flotsam from the murky depths of Nige's memory.

'Mr Robespierre . . .' he murmured '. . . the lodger.'

'Nigel!' Robespierre returned affably. The thin un-shaven features wrinkled upwards into a smile. 'I heard about your unpleasant experience and just thought I'd drop in to see how you were feeling. Better, I hope?'

Nige said nothing for a moment. He was trying to grasp the images that the blind man's arrival had prompted, but already he could feel them slipping away, sand through the drainage grille of his mind. As before they left behind them a queasy stomach and a large dose of undirected fear, but this time, fortunately, neither in such great quantities.

Nige pressed a hand to his forehead as though to prevent the thoughts escaping through his skin, then, realising that the blind man was still patiently waiting for an answer, muttered, 'Oh . . . er . . . yes, thank you, Mr Robespierre. I'm feeling much better today.'

The old man grinned again, said, 'Splendid, splendid, I'll leave you to it then,' and departed, pulling the door closed behind him.

On the television screen an impressive and colourful array of animated explosions was now taking place, but Nige was unmoved. His nerves were still tingling from the thud of newspaper on to doormat. He got up from the settee, shuffled through into the hall and picked up the *Starmouth Gazette*. He unfolded it and looked at the headline on the front page.

GRISLY FIND IN BEACH CAVE it screamed, below which was a subheading: *IS A BEAST STALKING STARMOUTH?* Vying for importance with the text was a photograph of the cave in which the 'grisly find' had been made, and another of a grim-faced man with a grey moustache, beneath which was the caption: *Detective Inspector Warren Mace: 'I have never seen such mutilation.'*

Nige didn't have to read the text to know what the story was about. With a strangled cry he flung the paper away from him and pounded up the stairs, his heart racing, his stomach coming alive. In his head memories were unwrapping themselves like obscene Christmas presents. He reached the top of the landing and plunged for his bedroom, unaware of his mother standing at the bottom of the stairs, worriedly calling, 'Nigel, Nigel.' He opened his bedroom door and dived for the sanctuary of his bed. The sheets were cold but vaguely comforting, despite the fact that the nightmare crawled in with him.

He curled into the foetal position and lay still, shuddering, whimpering. Another part of his mind – an inner sanctum that hadn't yet been breached – heard the thumping on the stairs, the wheezing of worried breath. Words formed, and Nige began to whisper them to himself, repeating them over and over like a charm.

When Rosemary Figg entered the room moments later,

she heard: 'Mummy's coming, Mummy's coming, Mummy's coming . . .'

11

Richard's crying had acted as a purgative; it had served to loosen the knot that had been tightening and tightening inside him. The fear and the dread were still there, eating away, but by the time he arrived home he was thinking more clearly than he had all day.

He found Olive in the sitting room, *Starmouth Gazette* folded on her lap, face grim and lips pursed as though she'd been expecting him and knew what he was going to say. From the kitchen floated the strains of Radio 4, entertaining his mother while she prepared dinner. Sam, who was curled up on the rug by the fire, looked up when Richard entered, and wagged his stump of a tail, but was far too cosy to move.

Richard said hello to Olive and knelt on the rug, scratching Sam's ears. He and Olive exchanged comments about the weather, then she asked, 'How was school today?'

Richard shrugged. 'Fine . . . just normal, you know? There weren't many people there.'

'Did you get a chance to speak to your friends?'

'Only Rob . . . neither of the others showed up.'

'Ah.' There was a pause. 'Did you speak to him about returning to King Street?'

Richard nodded without looking at her.

'And?' said Olive. 'What did he say?'

'He thinks we're mad . . . he thinks it'd be suicide to go back to that house.'

'I see. Then it's just me and you, is it?'

Richard hung his head and sighed. He stared into the gas fire, which Olive was sitting well away from. After a moment he got up and went to sit beside her. In a halting voice he said, 'Olive, I can't go back to that house. I . . .

I've been sitting there at school today, thinking about it, thinking about everything that's been going on, and . . . I'm just *so scared*.' He broke off and gave a grim smile, cheeks flushing red at the admission. 'I mean, I feel such a wimp, you know, but I can't help it. In all the books and films and stuff, people just take these things in their stride, they just accept them and get on with fighting them . . . *they always seem to know what to do*! But I don't. I mean, all I know is, I don't – *I can't* – go back to that house . . . I'm sorry, but I just can't.'

He broke off, feeling the knot re-tightening inside him. He took off his glasses and began to wipe them, cleared his throat, determined not to cry again. Olive stirred from her position, stretched out her arms and hugged him to her. For a moment Richard was surprised, then he relaxed, feeling the old lady's warmth, smelling her smell. She smelt of lavender and of the dry, faintly musty smell that seemed to cling to old people. It was a smell that had comforted him as a small child when sleeping in his grandma's bed, and it comforted him now. He hugged Olive back for a moment, then broke off and looked into her face. He thought how deep her wrinkles were becoming, how clearly the strain was beginning to show. He repeated the question he had put to Robin just half an hour before, though this time without tears. 'Olive,' he said, 'what are we going to do?'

She fetched a sigh from deep within herself, though unlike Robin she had an answer of sorts. 'We're going to help Constance prepare for her party, and while we're doing it we're going to *think*. Then, later on, we're going to draw up a battle plan. We're going to write down everything we know, everything we can remember, and we're going to study it and see if it throws up any clue, any possible weakness that the creature might have.' She smiled apologetically. 'I'm sorry not to be more positive, but it's all I can think of for the time being.'

Richard nodded slowly. In his heart of hearts, he knew Olive's suggestion was merely a time-filler, a bauble of activity to give them the impression they were doing something useful. He thought it unlikely that anything would come of writing down their problems, though on the other hand it just might throw up something their confused minds had overlooked. He gave Olive a last squeeze and stood up.

'I'd better say hello to Mum and offer to help with the dinner. Do you want a cup of tea or anything?'

'Hold on just a minute,' Olive said. She unfolded the newspaper and began to flip through its pages. 'There's something in here I think you ought to see. I'm afraid it may come as a bit of a shock.'

'Not another one,' Richard's mind protested, but he thought he knew what Olive was going to show him. 'I saw it on the way home,' he told her, 'it was on all the billboards. Dad told me this morning it was going to be in the paper tonight.'

'No,' Olive said, and there was an apology in her voice, 'I don't mean that. I'm talking about this. Look.'

She held out the paper for him. Richard took it and looked at the headline she indicated. As he read the text he felt the knot inside him tightening, tightening, until it seemed to block the air in his throat.

THREE DIE IN FIRE TRAGEDY, the headline said, and beneath was a picture of a burning building, the skeleton black beneath a grainy confusion of smoke and flame. By the time Richard got to the end of the story he could feel the newly-repaired floodgates straining again. He sat down, shut his eyes and fought to keep them closed.

'Of course it may have been coincidence,' Olive suggested, though both of them knew that it was not.

Richard said nothing for a few moments; his voice was being strangled somewhere and wouldn't come. He sniffed, swallowed, wondering how much more he could take, how much longer his emotions could swing between hope and despair before something snapped. He wondered too about Toady, about what could have happened to make the house burn down. The fact that he was the only survivor seemed to bear some great and terrible significance. Richard knuckled his hands into his eyes, tried to breathe steadily and deeply. It didn't make him feel any better, but at least it enabled his voice to return.

'Poor . . . Adrian,' he said, amending the word Toady at the last minute; it seemed somehow inappropriate to use the hated nickname in these circumstances.

'Yes,' Olive agreed, 'poor Adrian. I rang the hospital this afternoon to ask how he was, told them I was a family friend. They said he was sleeping, under heavy sedation.'

'Lucky buggar,' thought Richard before he could stop himself, 'sleeping through it all,' then he immediately felt ashamed. Shit, his whole family was dead, he wasn't lucky at all. Not to mention the fact that in their situation sleep offered no guarantee of escape.

'We'll go and see him tomorrow if you like,' Olive said, 'if he's in a fit state to receive visitors.'

Richard nodded. 'Yes, OK. Maybe he'll be able to tell us something.'

'Mm, but we mustn't push him. We won't get anything out of him that way.'

'No, I know,' Richard said, and staring at Sam snoozing on the rug found himself wishing that *his* life could be that simple. It seemed astounding that just four days ago his main worry had been how he and his friends were going to avoid Rusty's mob at school. 'Is there anything in here about the stabbing?' he asked, reaching for the paper again.

'Yes, page ten. There, look in the bottom corner.'

The story, GATECRASHERS IN STABBING INCIDENT occupied perhaps an eighth of the page. It briefly related the events of Saturday night, gave a quick rundown of Neil's injuries and ended with the single line paragraph: 'The youths are still being sought by police.' Richard put the paper aside. 'Has Mum been to see Neil today?'

'Yes,' said Olive, 'she went at lunchtime. Apparently he's much better today and has been eating like a horse. It seems he's very bored, though, and wants you to hunt out some books for him. I think he gave your mother a list.'

Richard stood up. 'OK. I'd better go and see her now. She'll be wondering where I am.'

'Richard,' Olive said when he reached the door. He turned back. 'Try not to worry. I'm sure we'll think of something.'

Richard smiled, but knew she was only trying to make him feel better. He was almost out of the door when he heard her add, 'Oh, and in answer to your earlier question – yes please, I'd love a cup of tea.'

12

Robin's crying, too, had acted as a purgative, though in his case with different results. His confrontation with Richard had finally forced him to admit what he had been trying to deny all along, that there was something happening to him and his friends; something – for want of a better word – supernatural. The admission terrified him, but at the same time it caused him to feel great relief. Thinking back to how he had blubbered in the street, and of who might have seen him, both made his stomach crawl with shame and filled him with a fierce anger. He felt angry at the creature, the thing, that had reduced them to frightened children; angry at its sheer audacity, the way it had casually infiltrated their lives and set about picking them apart; angry mostly at its lack of respect for human life, the way it killed without apparent reason. Robin was more frightened than he had ever been in his life, yet as he trudged through the gritted, tree-lined streets of Beachside he suddenly longed for a confrontation, felt a seething urge to grab the creature by the throat and to strangle the life out of it.

His anger persisted all the way home, and was only slightly lessened by his playing Sigue Sigue Sputnik at full-blast and leaping round his bedroom, punching invisible monsters. When the record slammed to a halt he felt exhausted, his arms tingling, his heart pumping blood at breakneck speed. Despite the sub-zero temperature he was sweating, could feel it trickling down his chest inside his school clothes. He peeled off his jumper, yanked the knot out of his tie with one hand and rolled up his shirt sleeves. Then he greased his blond fringe over to one side and trooped downstairs.

His mother was in the sitting room, sipping a diluted whisky and reading the *Starmouth Gazette*. As Robin entered she peered at him guiltily over the half-moon lenses of her reading glasses and put the whisky on the floor by her chair. Smiling she said, 'Hello, darling, how are you?'

Robin slumped on to the settee. He meshed his fingers together over his stomach and puffed out his cheeks. 'All right, I suppose.'

'No problems at school?'

'No.'

Sylvia nodded, followed Robin's gaze to the blank television screen then looked at him again. 'Cold out, isn't it?'

'Mmm.'

She seemed about to say more, but instead picked up the whisky and began to sip at it again. Robin wanted to tell her not to, wanted to say she'd been drinking too much lately and that it disturbed him whenever he came home to find her red-cheeked and tipsy. He breathed hard, but the words wouldn't come; the thought of her indignation kept them at bay. Besides, she didn't really look drunk and depressed as she had on previous occasions. Her cheeks were glowing, certainly, but she seemed calm, even happy judging by the smile on her face. Robin slumped lower, stretching his legs out under the coffee table, and stared at the paper, urging his mother to finish it. Every so often when she turned a page, he caught a glimpse of the front-page headline: *GRISLY FIND*. He'd seen the full headline scrawled on news stands on the way home, but still wanted to read the story through. He knew it would probably disturb him by bringing into sharp relief memories he'd been trying to suppress; but at the same time he felt he *had* to read it – just as people passing road accidents have to turn their heads to ensure there are no mangled remains among the wreckage.

At last, unable to wait any longer, he blurted, 'Can I look at the paper, Mum?'

Distractedly Sylvia said, 'Yes, in a minute, Robin. I'm just looking at it first.'

He made a vague gesture with his hand. 'I only wanted to read about . . . about the body.'

There was a pause. Sylvia stared at her son, then closed the paper and murmured, 'Oh, I see.' She scanned the story on the front page, breathing slowly, her face revealing nothing. At last she said, 'Are you sure you want to see this, Robbie? . . . I mean, perhaps it would be better just to put the whole thing out of your mind.'

He shrugged, feeling uncomfortable. 'I can't just put it out of my mind, Mum. It's not as easy as that. I just want to see what they've written, that's all, want to know what they've found out since yesterday.' He held out a hand and added earnestly, 'I'm all right, Mum, honest. I'm not gonna freak out if that's what you think.'

Sylvia appeared to consider a moment longer, then silently handed over the paper. Robin read the story, aware of his mother's eyes on him, trying to keep his face expressionless. He was aware of his aggression towards the creature draining away, to be replaced by a nugget of icy fear as he was reminded of the mutilations it had inflicted. He suddenly wanted to put the paper aside, to turn its headline away from him, but because of his mother's attention on him he read through to the bitter end.

When he had done his mouth felt dry and his stomach was churning. He squeezed his tongue out between lips that felt like tacky cardboard, licked them, and cleared his throat. He flashed a smile at his mother to show how little the story had affected him, then turned back to the paper, idly turning the pages and hoping she wouldn't notice his trembling hands. He stared blankly at pictures of girls in bikinis (inappropriate for January) and fund-raising boy scouts smiling proudly into the camera. He gazed at the telly page for a full three minutes without registering a single detail of that evening's viewing. He felt he was beginning to get on top of his fear when he noticed the story on page seven.

He dropped the paper as though it had bitten him and wailed, 'Oh shit!'

Sylvia sat up like a startled cat. 'Robin!' she exclaimed, shocked.

Robin picked up the paper, found the story again and presented it to his mother's gaze. 'Sorry, Mum, but . . . oh, look at this.'

Sylvia frowned at the dismay in her son's voice, took the paper and began to read. The story was tragic, but common enough; three members of a family wiped out in a house-fire, the only survivor the eldest son. She looked at the picture of the burning house and felt nothing but puzzlement. In a bemused voice she said, 'I know. It's terrible, isn't it? That poor family.'

Robin leaned forward and shook his head. 'No, Mum, you don't understand. That kid, the one who survived, he's a friend of ours. It's Toady. He was with us yesterday when we found the body.'

Sylvia's mouth opened and a hand fluttered towards it in appalled realization. 'Oh no!' she gasped. 'Oh no, that poor boy! Oh, Robin, how awful!'

Robin said nothing. He felt too sick to speak. He wanted at that moment to tell his mother everything, to explain to her that it was even more awful than she realized. And what made him feel doubly bad was his inability to summon up even a fragment of grief for Toady and his family. All he experienced was a sense of shock at the event and a heightened sense of fear for himself.

He stood up, his legs wobbly, and stumped to the door. 'I'm going up to my room for a bit, Mum,' he said. 'I want to be on my own for a while.'

He lay on his bed for what seemed a long time, his mind whirling with thoughts too swift to grasp. 'Why don't you leave us alone,' he muttered, staring at the postered wall, bunching his fist and driving it into his pillow. 'Why don't you just fucking leave us alone?'

He closed his eyes, opened them again, twisted on his bed, trying to gulp back tears. At last he heard hesitant footsteps on the stairs and propped himself up on his elbows, waiting for his mother's knock. Sure enough a few moments later it came, together with a tentative enquiry. 'Robbie? Can I come in?'

He composed himself, breathed deeply, sighed, sniffed. 'Yeah,' he said.

The door opened and Sylvia's head poked round. 'Are you all right?' she asked.

For a second Robin had an overwhelming urge to laugh hysterically at the question, to leap about his room and whoop until he dropped. Instead he simply nodded. 'Yeah, I'm fine.'

'Well, you don't look it,' said Sylvia. She advanced fully into the room and pushed the door closed behind her. After a moment's hesitation she perched on the edge of the bed.

'You look tired,' she said. She stretched out a hand and traced a long-nailed finger through her son's fringe. 'It's been a rather shocking weekend for you, hasn't it?'

'That's putting it mildly,' Robin thought, but didn't say so. He lay back, his head sinking into the divot in the pillow that his fist had made. Sylvia placed a palm on his forehead and clucked sympathetically. 'Is there anything I can do for you?' she asked.

'No,' said Robin, 'I don't think so.'

'Are you sure?'

Robin sighed again. His mother's idea of sympathy always seemed to be to speak to him as though he was six rather than sixteen. He supposed it was the bane of being an only child, but all the same it irritated him. Ah well, at least he didn't have it as bad as Nige did from *his* mother.

He mustered a smile, feeling it stretch his lips. 'No, honestly, Mum, I'll be all right. I just need to relax a bit, that's all.'

'Of course you do,' said Sylvia, her smile sugar-coated. 'I think you're taking all this very well, Robbie.'

Robin grunted. He didn't think he was taking it well at all, but then his mother didn't know the full story. He watched as Sylvia lunged forward and closed a hand around the metal radiator at the foot of his bed.

'I thought it was cold in here,' she said. 'This radiator's still not working, is it? I thought your father was supposed to have fixed it this weekend?'

'Oh God,' Robin thought, 'here it comes, slagging-off time.' He shrugged to show the matter was unimportant and said, 'Yeah, well, I suppose he was probably too busy.'

Sylvia looked scornful. 'Busy my . . . foot!' She flapped a hand to emphasize the point she was about to make. 'When I got back from work on Saturday he was just sitting on his backside, watching the motor racing on television. Four solid hours he'd been there, watching silly little cars going round and round in circles. I mean, he could have done it then, but oh no! He's getting so bloody lazy, Robbie. He doesn't lift a finger around the house any more.'

She glared at Robin, inviting him to share her indignation, but he tried to appear indifferent. In his opinion both his parents were at fault, their main shortcoming being their lack of communication with each other. He hated being drawn into their arguments, especially when they were together and each tried to recruit him as an ally.

Firmly enough so that Sylvia was taken aback, he said, 'Mum, I really don't want to hear this just now . . . I mean, I'm not in the mood, you know, not after what's happened in the past couple of days.'

He saw a hurt look cross his mother's face, but this was quickly displaced by an expression of understanding. 'I'm sorry, Robbie,' she said. 'It was a bit selfish of me, wasn't it?' She smiled in sweet apology and touched his cheek. As though it was a logical progression of the conversation, and in a voice so casual it sounded unnatural, she said, 'Oh, by the way, I saw Mr Treeborn this afternoon.'

Robin's eyes widened and he stared at his mother. His immediate thought was that Treeborn had complained about being spied on last night. Then he noticed her flushed face and embarrassed eyes and the thought became: 'Flowers. That morning she'd received flowers. From an Admirer.' However before the thought could develop further, she was speaking again.

'On the back lawn . . . that's where I saw him. I was putting out bread for the birds, and he . . . he was out there. He asked me if I'd ask you something.'

Robin felt a coldness shudder through his body. 'It's about that figure at the window,' he thought, 'it's about that sound I heard.' Trying to keep his voice steady, he said, 'Oh, yeah? What was that?'

'He asked me to ask you if you'd help him clear out his cellar this evening.'

The request was so unexpected that it took a moment for it to register in Robin's brain. When it did he felt a sense of horror sweep over him.

'No, Mum, I can't,' he said, 'not tonight. I . . . I've got a lot of homework to do. He'll have to find someone else.'

Sylvia looked disappointed, as though it was her he was turning down. 'Oh, Robbie, are you sure? I got the impression he was relying on you.'

Robin felt uncomfortable, but there was no way he was going around to that house in the dark, not after what he had seen and heard yesterday. Shrugging, he said, 'I'm sorry, Mum, but I've just got too much homework, that's all. It's not my fault.'

'Well, you'll just have to go round there and tell Mr Treeborn you can't help him then,' said Sylvia.

Robin glanced out of the window. The sky was darkening rapidly, but for the moment it was still bright enough to be termed daylight. If he had to go to the house, then now was the best time, before the dark took control. Nevertheless he made one last attempt at avoiding the visit altogether.

'Couldn't I just phone him up? It'd be much easier.'

'No, you can't,' said Sylvia. 'You know what your father said about the phone bill this morning. For goodness' sake, Robbie, it's only over the back hedge. It'll take two minutes to walk round at the most.'

Robin sighed and swung his legs over the edge of the bed. He grabbed his trainers and a jacket and followed his mother downstairs. As he was lacing up his trainers in the sitting room he called, 'Did Mr Treeborn look all right?'

Sylvia was in the kitchen. At his question she poked her head round the door, a frown on her face. 'All right? How do you mean?'

'Well . . . did he look . . . strange? Different?'

Sylvia thought of Treeborn's new casual image and easy attitude. 'No,' she said. 'Why? Should he have?'

'Oh, er . . . no. I just wondered why he was off work, that's all.'

Sylvia relaxed. 'Oh, he's not ill if that's what you mean. I think he's just taking a few days off while the weather's bad.'

She went back into the kitchen, but popped out again at her son's next question. 'Does Mr Treeborn have anyone staying with him at the moment?'

'I don't think so,' Sylvia said; Robin's interest in Treeborn unsettled her a little. 'Why do you ask?'

'Oh, I thought I saw someone in his house yesterday . . . You know, through my bedroom window.'

'You haven't been spying on him, have you?'

'Oh no, nothing like that. I was just closing my curtains and I looked across and saw . . . someone who didn't look like him in the kitchen.'

Despite herself Sylvia felt a twinge of jealousy. 'Male or female?' she asked, trying to sound casual.

'Male, I think,' said Robin.

Sylvia smiled. 'Then it must just have been Walt – um, Mr Treeborn himself.'

'Yeah,' said Robin, 'I suppose so.'

He finished lacing up his shoes and pulled on his jacket. He had noticed his mother's slip. He approached the vase sitting on the mantelpiece and thoughtfully touched the head of a pink carnation. He turned and glanced out of the back window towards Mr Treeborn's house, then abruptly swung towards the door.

'I'm off, Mum,' he called as he stepped into the hall. 'I won't be long.'

Five minutes later he was back, teeth chattering, fingers numb, nose turning blue. 'It's freezing out there now,' he called as he unzipped his jacket and walked through to the kitchen.

Sylvia was washing leeks in a colander under the hot tap. As Robin entered, she looked up and smiled. 'Was Mr Treeborn in?'

'No.' Robin eased himself into a chair and rested his elbows on the kitchen table. A pie dish was laid out before him, pastry draped over it, and a plate piled high with grated cheese. Robin took a pinch of cheese and popped it into his mouth just as his mother turned from the sink.

'Hey!' she said. 'Hands off! That cheese is for tea.'

Robin grinned and stood up. 'I'd better go and make a start on my homework. I've got lots to do tonight.'

'You won't forget to go and see Mr Treeborn again later, will you, to tell him you can't come?'

'No,' said Robin, though as he trudged upstairs he hoped desperately that his mother would forget all about it.

However, after a meal that was taciturn but not unpleasant, Sylvia said, 'Right then, Robbie, you'd better pop round to Mr Treeborn's. He'll be expecting you.'

'Aw, Mum, do I have to?' Robin said. 'Can't I just phone him up?'

'No, you can't,' grunted his father from behind his paper, 'not unless you want to contribute to the phone bill, that is.'

411

Robin pulled a face. 'But I've got tons of work to do.'

'The quicker you go round there the better then,' said Sylvia briskly. She began to gather their plates together, scraping leftovers on to the top one. Looking at her husband she said, 'If you want any afters you'll have to get a piece of fruit. I haven't had time to make anything.'

Robin saw his father give Sylvia a black look and he hurried out of the room before the argument could start.

His heart was thumping as he walked down Treeborn's drive. It was only seven o' clock but it was already full night, darkness leaking between the glow of streetlamps, staining trees and lawns and houses with shadow. There was no-one about on the street, and the only sound came from the wind, which rustled leaves brittle with frost. Robin found himself wishing that Beachside was not quite so suburban, that the houses were not set so far back behind high hedges and lawns that were white with snow. Oh well, he thought, maybe Treeborn wouldn't be in again, in which case he could be back home within three or four minutes.

He had considered not coming round to Treeborn's at all, merely walking down the road until he was out of sight of the house, then going back and telling his parents that there was still no answer to his knock. However he knew if he did that, Treeborn would probably call to ask where he was and then his mother would be annoyed. He drew back his fist and knocked on the door, though not too loudly, noting with satisfaction that the window of the room to the right of the door, the sitting room he guessed, was dark behind thick curtains.

No-one came in response to his knock and Robin felt relieved. He was about to go when he noticed the piece of paper taped to the glass by the handle, the piece of paper headed with his name.

Nerves set in again as he ripped the paper free, though he hoped it was simply a note apologizing for Treeborn's absence and telling Robin to make it some other time. He turned and held the note towards the streetlamps, squinting at the black letters. The note read: 'ROBIN. GO AROUND TO BACK. DOOR OPEN. I'M IN CELLAR AND MAY NOT HEAR YOU KNOCK. WT.'

'Oh shit,' Robin muttered and debated what to do. Should he follow the note's instructions or simply go home and pretend he hadn't seen the note at all? He hovered, uncertain, then abruptly turned down the narrow path that led around the side of the house. No, better to get it over with now, while he was here. He wasn't forced to go into the cellar, after all. He could stand at the top of the steps and shout down.

He emerged on to a small patio at the back of the house which was as snowbound as the silent lawn. Only a slight difference in levels indicated where the patio finished and the lawn began. The house itself was as dark at the back as at the front. Robin moved stealthily to the back door, glad of the snow which swallowed his footsteps. To the left of the door was the sloping lid of a coal bunker, which he guessed must lead directly into the cellar, whilst to the right was the kitchen window, the window at which he'd seen the figure last night.

He moved to that window now and peered through it, pressing his nose and his gloved hands to the cold glass. The kitchen was in darkness, a room of shadows wrapped in grey-blue and black. After a few seconds the room disappeared behind a cloud of his own breath.

Robin pushed back from the window, turned and looked at his parents' house. The sitting room glowed like a fire behind red curtains, filling him with warmth and longing. If it wasn't for the waist-high hedge that divided the expanse of lawn into two he could have run across to it in thirty seconds and knocked on the glass, making his parents jump.

He turned back with a sigh. Even with his gloves on, his fingertips were freezing. At least Treeborn's house will be warm, he thought, and so thinking reached out to open the back door.

It whispered quietly as it swung inwards, releasing a

movement of air and a faint musty smell. Robin stepped in after it, still clutching the doorknob, stamping the snow off his trainers and on to the lino where it melted into small dirty puddles. He left the door open as he moved across the kitchen, skirting around a table made of shadows, noting a sink unit, fridge freezer, wall cupboards, other implements, all composed of the same substance.

He reached the closed door that led into the sitting room and put out his hand to the white square of plastic by its side. He pressed down the switch and electric light turned the shadows into gleaming technology. Or rather, not quite gleaming, for everything was coated in a fine layer of dust.

Robin looked around, a little disturbed, wondering where Treeborn had been eating and drinking these last few days. Certainly not here, for the dust lay on the kitchen table, the draining board, the mugs which hung on hooks beneath the pine cupboards. It wasn't a thick layer, perhaps three or four days' worth, but the kitchen was so spotless in all other respects that it was unsettlingly conspicuous.

He crossed the kitchen floor again, trying to brush aside his unease, inventing explanations as he pushed the back door shut. Treeborn must have been staying with friends over the weekend, or maybe he'd been eating out and hadn't needed to use the kitchen. He took solace in these explanations, though he couldn't help feeling that neither seemed to ring quite true.

As the door clicked, shutting out the cold, the musty smell closed in. The place must need a good airing, decided Robin, and was pleased that the house being shut up seemed to slot in with his theory that Treeborn had spent the weekend away. He edged round the kitchen table towards the cellar door, which was located in the kitchen's most unobtrusive corner. On the way he jogged a dangling mug with his elbow and jumped at the slight sound it made when it rocked. The mug reminded him that the house was silent even though Treeborn was supposed to be working in the cellar. And another thing: if Treeborn *was* down there, why hadn't he left the cellar door open and the kitchen light on?

Apprehension pressed in on Robin. His instincts told him that something was wrong here but he would not translate feelings into thoughts until he was out of this place and back in his own home. His hand was on the cellar door handle now, but he felt loath to turn it – or was it simply fear that stilled the movement?

'Oh, this is ridiculous,' he thought suddenly, twisted and pushed. The door swung open, bringing a consolidation of the musty smell, like old farts in a closed-up room. Robin peered down the cellar steps into the dimness below.

The light from the kitchen illuminated the first half-dozen stone steps and swam blotchily up the walls, but apart from that made little impression. It was almost as though the cellar's darkness was a swarming living thing that swallowed light, that closed in on itself with walls of black. Robin wanted to laugh at the thought, but he couldn't quite manage it. Apart from the kitchen light there was another light glowing below, a faint white circle, though it was so negligible as to be useless.

He held his breath, glaring until his eyes ached. He could see grey corners, black angles, but no identifiable shapes. He stood for a few moments, left hand on the cool wall beside him, right hand gripping the thin metal banister set into the stone.

All at once the apprehension swamped him again, the feeling – no, the *knowledge* – that something was terribly wrong. He shuddered violently, knowing he shouldn't have come here, thinking that there was still time, if he left now, to escape from whatever awaited him. He took a step back, and then another, until he was on the cellar's threshold. He reached out a hand to close the cellar door.

And froze when he heard a noise in the darkness below.

He stood, rigid, his breath a sheet of ice in his chest, his arm poised. From beneath him came a bump-thud-scrape of movement and the impression of something shifting in the black depths of the cellar. All at once Robin's heartbeat was too loud, his breath a series of pants which seemed to reverberate round the room. He swallowed, trying to still it, and succeeded only in making himself choke. As he doubled over, he saw the pinpoint of white light swing towards him, pinning him to the top of the cellar steps.

He clamped a hand over his mouth, but too late. A voice echoed off the walls around him.

'Robin? Is that you?'

He nodded, eyes streaming, not knowing whether to feel relieved or afraid. Without doubt the voice belonged to Treeborn, though Robin still remained convinced that something was not right here.

'Yes,' he managed to gasp, 'I've just come to tell you—'

'Splendid,' Treeborn interrupted. The torchlight bobbed, jerking ahead of Robin like an invitation. 'I'm so pleased you could come.'

Robin took a step forward, back over the cellar's threshold. 'Actually,' he said, silently cursing the whimper in his voice, 'I've come to tell you that I can't really help tonight. I've got too much homework, you see.'

There was a long pause. Behind the torchlight Robin thought he detected a hunched figure, black on black, though it was too dark to be sure. He waited, feeling uncomfortable, and at last Treeborn said, 'Oh, I see.'

The tone of Treeborn's voice suggested he was disappointed in Robin, and despite himself Robin felt guilty. Taking another step forward he stammered, 'I-I'm terribly sorry, but I really do have a lot of homework . . . I mean, any other night I would have been glad to help, but . . . I'm sorry.'

'Oh well,' said Treeborn, 'not to worry.' The torchlight plodded up the steps again and sidled around Robin's legs. Suddenly Treeborn said, 'I don't suppose you could help me for just a few minutes, could you? I've got rather a heavy trunk that I need to drag up the steps and I don't think I can manage it on my own.'

Robin felt trapped. He stood at the top of the steps, not knowing what to do. His instincts screamed at him to run, but reason, on the other hand, told him calmly that he was behaving like an idiot, that this was undoubtedly Treeborn talking to him, and that despite what he might have seen and heard in this house last night, there was nothing here now. Besides, whatever it had been couldn't be all that dangerous for it didn't seem to have done Treeborn any harm. He made motions with his mouth, and at last he said, 'Isn't there a light we can put on in here?'

'I'm afraid not,' replied Treeborn. 'Most of the fitting has rusted away and I've never got round to fixing it.' He joggled the torch beam, throwing shadows around the walls. 'Not to worry, though. This gives out plenty of light. I'll direct you down the steps so you don't fall.'

As Robin descended he felt he was leaving his stomach behind. He took the steps slowly, his feet tapping on stone that the torchlight turned to chalk. Outside the boundaries of the light, darkness pressed in on him, soft and moist as mouths. When he got to the bottom he stood on flat concrete, waiting while the light converged and the figure behind it stepped towards him. The musty smell was quite strong now, as though whatever was making it was very close.

'Here we are then,' said Treeborn and a hand closed around Robin's upper arm. Robin could make out Treeborn's spectacles flashing, his white collar standing out grey against his suit and tie. Treeborn swung the torch around, briefly illuminating sections of grey wall and a black metal ladder that led up to the coal bunker doors. The light came to rest on a large trunk just to the right of the ladder.

'There she is. That's what we've got to get upstairs.'

'Looks heavy,' commented Robin.

Treeborn snorted. 'You're telling me.'

Robin strolled over to the trunk. There were handles on its sides and he gave one an experimental tug. The trunk didn't shift. 'Christ,' he said and turned back to Treeborn. 'Is there anything inside?'

'There might be,' Treeborn replied. 'Why don't you have a look?'

Robin raised his eyebrows and hooked his gloved fingers under the rim of the lid. He tugged, but the lid refused to budge. 'It's locked,' he said.

Treeborn shone the torch on to the lock. 'There should be a key there somewhere.'

Robin looked down and sure enough saw a small key. He twisted it, hearing metal scrape on metal, feeling the lid rise a little as whatever was inside pushed against the release of pressure. He hooked his fingers under the rim once again and heaved upwards.

Immediately his eyes started to water and he turned away, feeling sick. The smell that hit him was swampy and farty, so tangible he could almost have bitten into it. He felt his gorge rise and fought it down, knuckled the tears out of his eyes that his stinging nose had produced. When the smell had abated a little, he turned back to see what had caused it.

He found himself staring into the cold, dead face of Walter Treeborn . . .

Time froze into a silent, screaming moment. Robin's eyes widened until they glared like the corpse's, though the terror in his was so much more alive. He scuttled crab-like away from the trunk, a shrill sound that tried to be a scream lurching into his throat. Behind him the thing that was impersonating Treeborn was chuckling, a dry sound like old leaves. Robin scrambled over the floor until he was at the foot of the metal ladder, then he turned to one side and retched.

Though he'd only seen the corpse for a moment, Robin knew the image would stay with him forever . . . the way the body had been snapped and broken in order to enable it to fit snugly inside the trunk.

He closed his gloved fist around the bottom rung of the ladder and heaved himself into a semi-upright position. His legs felt like wood, his stomach was convulsing painfully. He was facing the wall, his nose pressed against rough brick that smelt of coal dust. With an effort he swung himself round to face Treeborn's doppelganger.

The creature, the thing, still stood there, its arms out and its palms spread as though inviting Robin to embrace it. The torch was gone, though it was no longer needed for the creature was now generating its own light. A golden glow seemed to pulse from its skin, hair, clothes; a halo that was almost angelic. Robin watched, sick with fear and yet entranced, awed by the radiance.

The Treeborn-thing opened its mouth but no words came out; the mouth simply grew wider and wider. The black lipless hole that the mouth had become rapidly swallowed up the nose and then the eyes. Its features gone, what remained of the head abruptly collapsed in on itself, like the head of a china doll crumbling to dust.

Robin screamed and almost lost his grip on the ladder. The creature now stood before him, headless yet still sentient, dressed in black suit, white shirt, black tie. A chuckle echoed up from its empty collar and Robin felt a squirt of urine down the inside leg of his jeans. The creature raised its arms which reached into its shirt collar and emerged with an eyeball in each hand. The eyeballs were slick and gleaming, streaked with blood and trailing roots. The Treeborn-thing allowed the eyes to roll squishily on to its palm then squeezed its hands tightly shut. Robin's stomach lurched as he heard a *pop-pop* sound and saw colourless liquid, like half-set jelly, ooze out between the creature's fingers.

Slowly the creature opened its hands and Robin winced, anticipating the squishy mess inside. He gasped in disbelief when swarms of black butterflies flew out and coiled round the headless body.

Like a swarm of bees in a cartoon, they suddenly formed into an arrow shape and swooped at Robin. His

419

hands scrabbled at the ladder and he tried to drag himself out of reach, but it was no use. Within seconds they were all around him, shreds of fluttering darkness, filling his ears with the frenzied beating of their tiny wings.

Robin winced and gasped as he felt pinpricks on his exposed skin, squinted at his hands and saw his gloves being shredded, slivers of blood springing up like paper-cuts. The butterflies attacked his head, filling his senses. He whimpered, but dared not scream for fear they might swoop down his throat and choke him. He was being engulfed: drowned and eaten at the same time. He let go of the ladder with one hand and beat at his head, feeling fat writhing bodies bursting beneath his fingers. 'I'll be dead soon,' he thought, and the thought gave him comfort: at least it would mean an end to this fluttering hell. He felt his other hand, his left, loosening on the ladder rung, felt velvet unconsciousness staining the edges of his perception . . .

Then, just as he was about to submit forever, the attack ceased.

Robin opened his eyes to see the butterflies retreating, a swaying ribbon of black that writhed towards the cellar steps and disappeared into darkness. He ripped off his tattered gloves, ran a trembling hand over his face, felt tiny spots of blood, but nothing more serious. He swallowed, the spit clogging as chalk, and renewed his grip on the ladder. He screwed his head round, saw the creature still standing there like an incomplete shop-window dummy covered in luminous paint. It was so motionless that Robin could almost believe it *was* a dummy, that it was nothing more threatening. He began to climb the ladder, and was halfway up when he heard a rumble like a volcano about to erupt. He turned back and was horrified to see things moving, squirming, within the black emptiness of the creature's collar.

There was a noise – a whistling, screeching wail – and suddenly a tentacle, pale green and slimy, threshed from the collar, flopped on to the creature's shoulder and slithered down the front of its shirt. Robin heard material tear and realized that the underside of the tentacle was lined not with suckers but with serrated razor-sharp teeth. He began to moan and to scramble up the ladder as fast as he could, though suddenly his body didn't feel like his any more. Behind him he half-saw more tentacles erupt from the collar, accompanied by a green evil-smelling slime that sizzled and steamed where it hit the floor.

Robin was losing control. His breathing was a chaos of gasps; his right foot went for a rung, missed, and the metal bar cracked into his shin. He hung there for a long moment, his teeth gritted against the pain, sweat undermining his grip. What got him moving again was the sound of the thing shambling towards him, its tentacles slapping against flesh and slicing through air.

The coal bunker doors were above him now, and he reached up with one hand and pushed. The doors didn't budge and Robin thought suddenly of all the snow piled on top, of ice that had maybe frozen the hinges solid.

'No!' he screeched and reached up with both hands, leaning into the ladder to stop himself from falling. He strained and heaved, and was sure he felt the doors move just a little. He pushed some more, and then suddenly the strength went out of him. Horror filled his body as something wet and heavy plopped on to the back of his calf and began to caress its way round to his shin.

He looked back and the thing was right behind him, its tentacles swaying like seaweed fronds in a moving tide. The one that held his leg was tightening, and Robin felt sharp white pain, heard a ripping sound as his jeans – and maybe his flesh – were sliced open. He screamed and kicked and thrashed, felt bile bubbling into his throat and adrenalin surging through his body. He reached up and battered the right-hand door with both fists so hard that it crashed back with a splintering sound, admitting moonlight and cold fresh air and a sprinkling of snow.

Robin lunged for the opening, his hands closing around the door's wooden frame, dragging himself towards the sight of the moon. The tentacle, as though sensing its quarry was escaping, tightened its grip. Robin screeched, then began to kick out with even more urgency, imagining the teeth shredding through his flesh and muscle, grinding on the bone beneath. The only result of his attack, however, was more searing pain as the tentacle became even tighter. In desperation he kicked at the figure itself, trying to catch it in the throat, and succeeded in kung-fuing it squarely in its slime-smeared chest. As though taken by surprise the creature staggered back, its tentacles waving madly, the one coiled round Robin's leg whipping free and leaving fresh welts that made him scream into the night.

Weeping and gasping, he hauled himself through the coal cellar door. A loose nail ripped a shred of skin from his hand, making him wince, but it didn't slow his progress. He pulled himself up and out, swinging his legs over the side, the left one spilling blood freely into the snow. The air was so fresh, so sharp, so clean that it revived him a little, and he managed to fight down the dizziness that was swimming in his head and turn back to the task in hand.

From the cellar he heard a clatter and a scrape, and recognized it as the sound of teeth dragging over metal. Using all his strength he reached down, lifted the door he had thrown open and heaved it back into place. That done, he stumbled over the carpet of snow that was Treeborn's back lawn, stopping only when he reached the black line of hedge that separated Treeborn's property from his parents'.

He sank down, his back to the hedge, and looked fearfully at the coal cellar doors. Any moment he expected them to burst open, releasing a thrashing writhing nest of razored tentacles. Thankfully, however, they remained closed, enabling Robin to turn his attention to his mangled leg.

He almost fainted at the sight of his injury. His jeans had been torn open three-quarters of the way round his leg, calf to knee, as though by a chainsaw. Much of the flesh beneath had been torn open too and was bleeding profusely. His thigh and the wound itself was hot, burning, excruciatingly painful; but his shin and ankles were cold, and his foot so numb he couldn't feel his toes.

He blinked and exhaled, scooped up snow and pressed it to his sizzling forehead. 'A tourniquet, that's what I need,' he thought 'a tourniquet to stem the bleeding.'

He rooted in his pockets and came up with a grubby handkerchief which he folded into a wodge. Carefully parting the sliced denim, he pressed the handkerchief to his leg, hissing at the pain. Still watching the dark block of Treeborn's house, and particularly the doors, he stripped off his jacket, sweater, shirt and t-shirt.

It was freezing sitting there topless in the snow, but it was only a few seconds before he was buttoning up his shirt and pulling his sweater over his head again. When he had zipped up his jacket, he wrapped the t-shirt round his leg and tied it as tight as he dared. The handkerchief, now a sodden red lump, was tossed over the hedge.

Robin sat for perhaps thirty more seconds, breathing heavily, trying to regain some of his composure. Only now was the real truth sinking in, the massive horrible knowledge that Treeborn was dead, that that thing from King Street had killed him and taken his place, that the Horror Club was responsible for Treeborn's murder and for the murder of the old man on the beach.

Robin felt wretched, felt like screaming and crying, felt ludicrously like sinking into the snow and sleeping forever. He looked down at his left leg stuck straight out before him and saw pinpoints of red blossoming on the white material. 'I'll never complain about spots again,' he thought, and began to snigger uncontrollably, the tension and misery and shame and fear translated perversely into laughter.

When he had done he felt better, though not much. He was relieved to feel prickly life returning to his toes, and using the hedge for support he dragged himself to his feet.

Treeborn's house was still quiet, and whilst Robin was thankful for that he was also uneasy. Why hadn't the thing come after him? he thought. If it could change into what it liked it could surely have adopted a form capable of opening the cellar doors. He looked around – left, right, behind. All was snow and shadows, soaked in moonlight and a dirty orange glimmer that came from streetlamps he couldn't see. It was quiet here on the lawn – no, more than quiet: silent. Robin turned and looked over the hedge at his own house, at the red square of the sitting room window. He imagined his mother and father sitting there, watching telly. He was sure if he shouted loud enough they would hear him.

He leaned over the hedge. 'Mum!' he yelled. 'Dad!' He watched the curtains for movement, almost willing them to flicker open, but to no avail. Drawing breath, he tried again. 'Mum! Dad! Help me!'

Surely someone must have heard him that time; but no, still nothing moved. 'What are you, fucking deaf or something?' he muttered, and began to hobble off to his right, following the line of the hedge. He tried to climb over, but the effort only made his leg scream in pain. He tried to force his way through, but the tangle of branches prevented him. He was left with only one option: to go back the way he had come, around the side of the house, up the drive and out on to the main road. His main fear was that the creature would be waiting for him somewhere along the way, but that was a risk he would have to take.

He reached the point where the hedge came up to the high wooden fence that ran parallel with the side of Treeborn's house and marked the division of his and next door's property. The narrow path that ran between this fence and the house's side looked dark and forbidding, but to Robin's relief, empty. He began to sidle towards it, keeping the weight on his right leg, his senses alert for any sign of movement.

He was creeping into the house's black shadow when he heard the sound behind him. He spun, forgetting his

424

injury, and a white lance of pain shot into his thigh. Robin screamed and almost fell, but his hands snatched at the wooden fence and managed to keep him upright. For a few moments he felt nauseous, saw black blobs writhing in his vision, felt his breath become quick and uncontrolled. The thought of blacking out here terrified him and he fought hard against it. A voice inside his mind was screaming: 'Look behind you! See what that noise was!' but Robin knew he couldn't do that until he had suppressed the threat of unconsciousness. He gritted his teeth, clutched the wood of the fence hard and blinked until his vision returned to normal. Then, taking care not to make any sudden movements, he slowly turned his head.

There were things moving beneath the hedge. Dark things. Things he couldn't quite identify. They appeared to be burrowing up through the soil and the snow like moles, tossing earth out in long spumes to spatter black on white. Robin shook his head, murmured, 'No . . . no . . .' and began to hobble away. Behind him he heard the things climbing from their burrows, creaking and rattling like dry twigs. Robin knew he ought to keep going, knew he ought to concentrate on the path ahead, on reaching the road and finding somebody who could help him. He knew this, and yet the temptation was too great. He looked behind him.

And saw them.

There were perhaps eight or nine of them, and they were scuttling towards him on crooked limbs. They were small, less than a foot high, and they resembled something between twisted root formations and giant spiders. Robin could see they had faces of sorts – mouths at least, from which a soft, low chittering could be heard. And eyes like pinpricks of ochre which flashed when they caught the light.

Robin felt the terror mount in him again. Despite their diminutive size, these things looked utterly evil, in some ways even worse than that tentacled thing in the cellar. They also seemed vaguely familiar, and he suddenly realized why. As a child he had owned a Rupert Bear Annual and one particular story in that book had given him terrible nightmares. It concerned a creature called Ragetty, a tiny twisted root-like creature who lived under a tree and who burrowed his way out during a storm. Now it seemed as though Robin's childhood nightmare had come alive; Ragetty was after him, and there was not just one of him, but eight or nine.

He wrenched his gaze away and began to lurch towards the dark path at the side of the house. He heard himself blubbering between gasps, felt tears cold on his face. Behind him the chittering, the scuttling, was getting closer; it seemed almost on his heels. His left leg throbbed; his skin itched with the blood that trickled down it. He plunged into the darkness between the fence and the side of the house, his world a mass of chittering, scraping, scuttling, creaking.

Ahead lay the light, a chunk of driveway that curved into view at the end of the passage. It was covered in snow that glittered like orange crystals, and seemed as perfect and unattainable as the end of a rainbow. Robin guessed he would never reach it, knew that the only true reality was the flood of bristling black behind him, the harsh scrape of dendritic bodies on house-brick. He tried anyway, his feet pounding unevenly, his leg full of hurt. He felt sick at the thought of spiny claws on his skin, charcoal limbs raking his legs and back. More than once he felt himself stumbling, the ground coming to meet him; but always at the last moment it lurched away when he realized he was still running.

And then, incredibly, he was out.

Light filled the spaces around him, blinding him, making him skid on the snow that packed Treeborn's drive. The skid wrenched his injured leg and another scream tore its way out of his throat. Surely someone must have heard that scream, someone out walking a dog or driving home from work or in one of these quiet houses that sit behind high hedges and trees?

He looked up and down the sanded road and saw signs of life everywhere: cars parked in driveways, lights making windows into yellow squares, footprints pock-marking the snow. In the gutter across the roads a kiddies' trike lay on its side before a house which had a Vote Conservative poster displayed in an upstairs window.

All these clues to life, all these intimations of normalcy, and yet behind him the chasm still yawned.

Robin limped up Treeborn's drive, his leg a throbbing knot of cold pain from which he could feel his blood flowing like liquid body-heat. He was almost at the top before he realized the chittering sounds had faded behind him.

When he looked back, he saw that the creatures were still there, filling the gap between the fence and the side of the house, though they were no longer pursuing him. Their voices – if voices they could be termed – had quietened, adopted a reticent tone, and their ochre eyes were staring in what Robin fancied was fearful loathing. He wondered what was holding them back, what they were afraid of, and then suddenly it came to him: *the light*! Of course! These were creatures of darkness and shadow: they were as timid of the light as he was of the dark, probably even more so.

He laughed out loud, clapped his hands together and shouted, 'Got you, you bastards!' His outburst provoked a renewed chittering from the Ragettys, but Robin now felt safe as a kid who had made it home before the bullies could catch him. He laughed again rather hysterically, blew a loud and vulgar raspberry and gave them the V-sign.

And then one of them stepped boldly on to the drive.

And Robin froze, realizing that the nightmare was not yet over after all.

His breath was a ragged veil of steam, his leg a swollen chunk of pain from which his t-shirt hung like stripped skin. He began to back away slowly as the creature hissed at him, opening its mouth to reveal tiny razor-teeth identical to those that had lined the tentacles. It was still uncertain in its new environment, but it was gaining confidence all the time. Robin turned and began to hobble along the pavement, hoping to gain as much distance as possible before its companions discovered a similar courage.

He was just getting into his limping stride when the creature let out a high-pitched scream. Robin turned back, praying that this time the light had done its stuff, that this time he would see lots of little Ragettys dissolving to dust before his eyes.

But of course it was not to be.

The creature appeared to be looking at something on the ground, something it had found. 'Maybe there's a fiver down there,' Robin thought with crazy black humour. 'Maybe it'll take its ugly little friends to the pub and leave me alone.' He watched, knowing he should take this opportunity to make his getaway, yet unable to tear his eyes away, too fascinated by the creature's behaviour.

It was now swaying from side to side, its black body trembling with excitement, a high keening purr rolling from its mouth. It was staring at the ground, at its shadow Robin suddenly realized, with an expression of hypnotic, almost holy rapture. It seemed entranced by the way its shadow moved, by its crisp, dark outline on the snow.

And then it did something that caused fresh hackles of fear to rise on the back of Robin's neck.

It reached down and gathered up its shadow as though it was a piece of grey cloth.

Robin shook his head and began to back away again. He saw the Ragetty's thin slash of a mouth curve upwards, revealing more of its teeth. 'It's grinning at me!' he thought. 'The fucking thing's grinning at me!' His innards twisted into knots. He took a step backwards, and all at once his right foot skidded on ice and he fell, jarring his spine, cracking both elbows as his momentum took him on to his back.

He heard a triumphant chittering and looked up in time to see something floating towards him, something ragged that had tiny silver hooks embedded in its grey-black underside. He realized it was the creature's shadow and he scrambled away, ignoring the pain that flared throughout his body. The shadow landed just short of his right foot, settling to the ground and seeming to merge with it as shadows do. The creature, standing at the top of the drive, hauled it in like a fisherman hauling in a trawler-net. The shadow left thin furrows where its silver hooks ploughed through the snow.

Robin grabbed hold of a low wall with his left hand and dragged himself to his feet. His leg, his back, and both his elbows throbbed, giving him an image of himself standing there with his painful spots pulsing cartoon-red. He could see that the other Ragettys had emerged from the darkness now and were gathering up *their* shadows, and he turned and began to stumble away. Behind him the chittering, the scuttling, the scraping and the hissing started up afresh, informing him that the chase was on once more.

Despite his fall, Robin had a reasonable lead on the creatures, and he pushed his body to its limits, determined that the lead would not diminish. His own house lay a couple of minutes' walk away at the most, and if he could reach it before the creatures caught him he felt sure he would be safe. All he had to do was get to the end of this road, maybe fifty yards away, turn sharp right, go on for another ten yards, then sharp right again and another fifty yard dash to his home. One hundred and ten yards altogether, and already he had a five, maybe ten yard lead. Even with a body that felt like a punchbag, he was certain he could do it.

His technique was awkward – right leg lunging forward taking the weight, left swinging out sideways like a clumsy pendulum – but it was effective so long as he didn't slip. As far as he could tell through the pounding in his ears and the rasping in his chest he was sustaining his lead, and already the end of the road was looming; he was nearly half-way there.

He skidded round the corner, wincing as pain flared up again, but trying not to let it spoil his rhythm. He couldn't slow now, not even to shout for help, and besides he had an eerie certainty that even if he did shout no-one would come. This ten-yard stretch was the darkest, little more than a passageway that linked streets and led on to the main road and ultimately down to the seafront. What Robin saw waiting for him at the top of his street caused him to scream in panic and frustration, and to skid to a painful stop.

A Ragetty was squatting on a wall, having somehow got here before him. Its shadow-net was clutched in its spiny mis-shapen claws and it was grinning evilly. When it saw Robin it chittered, the noise sounding unnervingly like a mocking laugh, and scuttled down from its perch.

'Oh shit,' he muttered, the last word choking off into a sob. He looked back, saw the creatures behind him taking their time, creaking forward, their limbs working like twisted spiders' legs as they unfurled their shadow-nets.

In that moment the rage flooded through him again, the overwhelming sense of furious injustice. 'Leave me alone!' he shrieked, alarmed at how crazy he sounded. 'Leave me alone, you fucking little bastards!'

The Ragettys merely shuffled closer, spreading their limbs and preparing to cast their shadows. Robin believed if they had been human opponents he would have run at them, fought with them, no matter how many there were. But the thought of touching these things, of their charred spiky flesh on his skin, repulsed him and he turned away. Under the circumstances he did the only thing he could do: he took the left hand path that led towards the seafront, away from his home, away from hope.

Relentlessly the Ragettys pursued him. They remained a steady ten yards behind, forever threatening to catch him but never quite doing so. At first Robin failed to grasp the significance of this, but as time wore on their intentions became more and more obvious. They were herding him, he realized, forcing him towards something. But what? What?

Whatever it was must be near the sea, for whenever he tried to double back and head inland he always found one of the Ragettys, which had somehow got around in front of him, cutting off his retreat.

Over the next twenty minutes or so he tried outwitting them in other ways. At one point he stopped completely, refusing to go any further, but had to give that up when the creatures made it obvious they would wrap him in their shadow-nets and carry him if need be. He tried screaming and shouting, dodging up the driveways of houses and banging on doors, but no-one ever came. He saw no-one on the streets either despite the fact that lights were on behind windows and occasional faint sounds – music, televisions – floated to him on the night air.

'The Marie Celeste, that's what they ought to call this place,' Robin thought as he stumbled along. 'Roll up, roll up, folks, come and see the mysterious town of Star-mouth. Discovered one winter's morning completely deserted. Guaranteed to chill the very flesh on your bones.'

By the time he got close enough to hear the sea, he had slowed considerably and his breath felt like tattered cloth in his chest. The Ragettys had slowed too in order to remain their obligatory ten yards behind, and Robin was almost beginning to wish they would catch him, if only to bring an end to this whole terrible nightmare. He felt like a man in a dream, so exhausted he could barely lift his throbbing left leg from the ground. He felt battered, both physically and mentally, and the lurching streets had become a maze in which the houses were all exactly alike. At times he cried, as though being led to his execution, but most of the time he just stared at the ground, at his stumbling feet and the never ending snow.

The waves grew louder. They sounded excited, hungry. A wind sprang up, laced with a dry salty smell. Whatever was waiting for Robin was down on the beach, down in the

431

darkness where no-one would hear him. He looked up to see how close he was to the seafront, and then an old friend he thought had long deserted him, a friend by the name of Hope, threw him a final lifeline.

Ten yards away, at the end of the road, stood a fish and chip shop. Fluorescent lighting glared from its large front window and from its white plastic sign with blue letters that read The Happy Fisherman. Robin could not see anyone in the shop from this angle, but its glass-panelled door was propped open, and floating out on a cloud of steam was the unmistakable aroma of frying fish and chips.

Surreptitiously Robin glanced behind him. The Ragettys were ambling along about twelve yards back, obviously under the impression that their quarry had no fight left in him. He turned back, face set: the little bastards were about to find out just how wrong they were. He waited until he was just a few yards away from the chip shop's open door and then he lunged towards it, screaming, 'Help me! Help me! Please, please, help me!'

He flew through the door, his words becoming an incoherent yell of both pain and defiance. More pain flared as he twisted to slam the door behind him, but he felt only a savage glee as it crashed into its frame with a shuddering of glass. Fingers trembling, Robin secured the latch, and then for good measure rammed both top and bottom bolts into place. Then he turned, expecting to find himself facing one very astonished owner.

But the chip shop was empty.

Robin stood, his back against the door, staring at the metal counter as if he expected someone to pop up from behind it like a jack-in-the-box. Surely there was someone here; there was certainly every sign of occupancy. Glass tanks with hot plates for floors displayed steaming fish and chips under golden light; hot oil sizzled in the deep fat fryer in which hunks of bubbling cod occasionally broke the surface; white strips of glistening fish lolled beside a vat that contained porridgey batter. Robin walked to the counter as though the sound of footsteps might bring someone to serve him.

'Hello,' he called when no-one came, 'is anyone there?'

Apparently not, for there was no reply.

Robin glanced idly at the old-fashioned till, which stood on a table at the back of the room. Beside the till was a stack of newspapers, and his flesh crawled when he saw the familiar headline on the topmost sheet: *Grisly Find in Beach Cave.* Somehow seeing that headline seemed to prove that something here was badly wrong.

He jumped at the bursting sound behind him, the tinkle of falling glass. He turned to see the Raggettys clustered around the large front window which had become a spider's web of cracks. A fist-sized hole had been punched in the centre of the 'web', and even as Robin watched, one of the Raggettys hurled itself at the glass, causing the hole to widen, the window to sag inwards.

He looked round and noticed the door behind the counter. He lifted the counter's metal flap, slipped inside, and limped to the door, praying it wouldn't be locked. Fortunately it wasn't, and Robin stepped through just as the din of shattering glass filled the shop. He slammed the door on the chittering that swarmed towards him and twisted the key in the lock so savagely that he hurt his hand. Almost immediately the door began to shake under a barrage of blows, but Robin didn't think the Raggettys would be able to get through, not without some form of weapon.

He paused just long enough to let out a deep breath, then surveyed the room he had locked himself into. It seemed to be the place where the messier jobs, like gutting fish and peeling potatoes, were done, and it smelt of muddy brine. Along the left-hand wall was a formica counter streaked with water and blood, and beneath it an open fridge which contained filleted strips of fish packed in ice-trays. On the far wall was a sink full of dirty water in which potatoes bobbed; above that a window through which Robin could see dark walls and a snow-covered roof.

He crossed quickly to the door beside the sink, wincing as he heard wood splinter behind him. It seemed that the Ragettys were going to get through quicker than he'd anticipated. He unlocked the door, slid the heavy bolts across and pulled it open. He stepped out into the cold night, the excitement of escape mounting in him, the sound of the waves crashing away to his left. A mewling sound made his heart leap but it was only a cat prowling round a dustbin that contained rotting fish. Robin crossed the walled yard that the door had led into, pushed open the creaky gate, and turned right, away from the sea.

Five yards away, squatting in the alley like twisted mounds of darkness, were three Ragettys. Their shadow-nets were draped around their shoulders like shawls and their limbs creaked as they shuffled forward. Their ochre eyes glinted in the sparse light like the glass stares of old dolls. Mouths opened to hiss softly in the ravaged charcoal of their faces.

Robin screamed out one heart-rending word, 'Noooooo!', and then tears came, hot and bitter. He felt walls crumbling within himself, walls that let in defeat like the most agonizing poison. He turned and began to trudge towards the beach even before they could gesture him onwards. He didn't care now, didn't care about anything. All he wanted was for it to be over. Over and finished and done.

The waves reared up as he limped on to the promenade, drowning out the sound of the creatures behind him. The buildings were all in darkness, crouched behind street-lamps as though sheltering or trying to hide. Robin trudged across the wide road, through snow that had turned to slush, brown with exhaust fumes and sand. He came to a stop only when he arrived at the steps that led down to the beach.

He looked out at the dark hummocks of sand, at the black sea that gleamed sluggish as an oil slick. Shock and the cold were making him shiver, though Robin was hardly aware of it. He could see nothing on the beach and yet he knew there was something there, knew it as surely as he knew there were stars in the sky. 'This is it,' he kept thinking, but the true meaning of the phrase did not register; they were just words which had popped into his head and seemed vaguely appropriate.

He heard a warning hiss behind him and turned to see the trio of Ragettys standing no more than a yard away, one of them reaching out with its black limbs to prod him forward. He shuddered, still loath to feel the touch of those limbs on his body. Before the creature could make contact with his skin, he had started down the steps.

As he descended, he gripped the metal hand-rail to support his injured leg. It was throbbing again, a beacon of pain, as were his elbows and his back. Behind him the Ragettys closed in, though instinctively Robin knew they would not follow him down here. Their task was simply to wait at the top and cut off his only possible escape route. They were merely servants, sheepdogs: the shepherd waited somewhere below.

He wondered vaguely, as he limped downwards, why he was giving in so easily. After all, he had nothing left to lose, so why not resist and go down fighting? He thought of his tiredness, his aura of defeat, his intense revulsion from the creatures which had pursued him. All these things were part of the reason, though they were only a part. He wondered why Jews who'd known they were going to be shot had dug their own graves first; why soldiers in the Somme had gone over the top when there was every chance of being ripped apart by machine-gun fire; why members of the Light Brigade had followed their leader into a charge that had little hope of victory. He thought about all these things, and in each case all he could come up with was that it was the easiest thing to do. Even in conditions as extreme, as horrendous as these, compliance was easier than resistance.

He reached the bottom of the steps and stood silently, feeling the sand spongy and wet beneath his feet. Streaks of icy slush glimmered in the darkness like disembowelled jellyfish, though the incoming tide had eroded away most of the snow. Robin began walking towards the pier, the sea ushering him on, waves gossiping as he trudged past. 'Why not just stand and wait?' he thought. 'Why walk into danger willingly?'

The answer came easily enough: it felt better to be walking, altogether more purposeful. Though he stopped when he glimpsed dark movement amongst the towering legs of the looming pier.

Time slowed. Robin's leg throbbed, and the tourniquet, its knot unpicked by blood and flight, slid down his shin and around his ankle. He nudged it away and a breath of wind snatched at it, made it flap and ripple like a child playing at ghosts. A stronger gust whipped Robin's blond fringe across his eyes, made him gasp at its icy teeth. Whatever was moving amongst the pier's iron supports was man-shaped and cautious, and Robin shuddered as he thought again of the dismembered tramp in the cave.

He took another step forward. Despite his terror, despite the feeling that he was going either to shit his pants or spill his guts at any moment, he wanted something to happen. The tension was building inside him, buzzing like a wasps' nest in the pit of his stomach. Beneath the pier dark moved on dark; blackness bobbed among silhouettes of metal limbs matted with seaweed. Robin cleared his throat and took another step forward. In a voice half his age, he squeaked, 'Come out, please . . . whatever you are.'

The shadows responded. The darkness advanced, then slid into the semi-light of the beach. As the figure emerged, Robin staggered back, eyes widening, able to gasp only one single word: 'You!'

It was the girl from his dream. In the moonlight her hair shimmered; her face was radiant; a soft golden down on her arms and legs captured a halo that seemed to make her glow. She walked towards Robin on tiny naked feet, her shape immaculate beneath the scraps of clothing she wore. Her smile was soft as she held out her arms towards him.

'Robin, come to me,' she said.

'No!' he screamed, and backed away on spent limbs. He knew there was nowhere left to go, wondered what he had expected to happen that wouldn't have made him react like this. 'At least she's human,' he thought desperately to himself, 'at least she's beautiful.' Though the memory of what she had done seemed to defile that beauty, seemed to make her somehow even uglier than the Ragettys.

His stomach crawled with horror as she came striding towards him, though on a baser more primitive level he couldn't help feeling aroused. Her fingers were slim, made longer by fingernails that had been clogged with meat the last time he had seen her. They reached out and brushed his hand, nothing more than a touch, but enough to send warm ripples of electric pleasure through his body.

'Don't be afraid,' she said softly, 'I won't hurt you,' and all at once Robin wanted to believe her. He hesitated for a moment, but long enough for the girl's arms to enfold him, for her lips to press hard on to his.

For a few seconds he resisted, remembering her teeth tearing at raw meat, then he relaxed, responded. This was the moment he had been yearning for since the onset of puberty, the moment when he would hold a girl in his arms, feel her warmth and her softness, mingle his saliva with hers. He pawed at her, relishing her shape, her femaleness. He could smell her hair, fresh and clean, her skin, like and yet unlike milk, her perfume, dizzyingly fragrant. The whole experience was wonderful, magical; so wonderful in fact that already he had forgotten his fear. He wanted to ask the girl about the dream, wanted to know her name and why she was here, but this, his first taste of sensuality, had chased all else from his head. The kiss ended at last, and they broke away and looked at each other. Robin, his voice rough with emotion, said, 'I love you.' The words, too, were magical, though somehow not enough. He said them again: 'I love you.'

The girl smiled. Her smile was perfection. She said, 'I love you too, Robin. You do believe that, don't you?'

'Yes,' he whispered, for how could he not believe?

'I can help you,' said the girl.

She turned him round gently, pointed to the top of the steps where black and scraggy silhouettes could be seen. 'Those are part of what you awakened at King Street,' she told him. 'And I am part of it too, though they are dark, I am light. Sometimes our roles are interchangeable.' She took Robin's shoulders and turned him back towards her again. 'You do understand that, don't you?'

'Yes,' Robin whispered again, 'I think so.'

'And you do trust me, don't you?'

The nod was eager, ruled by flesh not thought. 'Yes, course.'

The girl relaxed. 'Then you'll do whatever I ask of you?' she said.

Again the nod. Robin blushed furiously. 'Yes, I'll do whatever you want.'

'Good,' breathed the girl. She closed her eyes for a moment as though she'd come through some long and difficult ordeal. When she opened them again, there was a red tinge to her pupils that was not unattractive.

'Succumb to me,' she said, holding out her arms.

Robin moved forward to be embraced, heard the girl's voice in his ear. 'Succumb to me, give yourself up to me completely. If you do that, we can be together for always.' She reared back, locked his eyes with her own. 'You will do that for me, won't you, Robin?'

'Yes,' he nodded. He buried his face in the girl's neck and began to kiss it. Between kisses he whispered, 'Yes . . . oh yes . . . oh yes . . .'

The girl smiled. Her eyes glowed red. And a love affair, of sorts, began.

PART THREE

Hybrid

'It's a hybrid of me – I'm a hybrid of he
You're a misfit of me – I'm a misfit of you
In limbo . . .'

Siouxsie and the Banshees: *Hybrid*

CHAPTER ONE

Party, Party

1

Edith Paites, fifty-nine years old, had moved to Starmouth from Liverpool in 1972 after the death of her husband, Bill. She arrived envisaging a nice little cottage by the sea, but seafront house prices had forced her back and back until at last she'd had to accept a narrow terrace in the more inauspicious surroundings of Piling Hill. However, despite this setback, Edith had, for a while at least, been happy. All right, so the area was not much better than Norris Green where she'd come from, but at least it was a change and at least the sea was only a ten-minute bus ride away. She had therefore set to with enthusiasm, determined to make her house into a home, and prepared – as she had been all her life – to make the best of a bad lot.

Time had passed. Years had slipped remorselessly away. In 1980 Edith's mother and father died within weeks of each other, and a year later her only son, David, and his pregnant wife, Sonya, emigrated to Perth in Australia. In the ensuing years Edith grew lonely, came to feel more and more trapped. She fell into a routine that seemed pointless and depressing, but that ticked on, week after week, like a time bomb.

Her pleasures, like her friends, were few. On Fridays she went to bingo, Saturdays were spent shopping in town, Sundays – when the weather was nice – she got on the bus and went to the beach. But apart from these things there was nothing else in her life, nothing that made her existence worthwhile.

Except, of course, for the soaps.

441

For as long as she could remember Edith had been a fan of soap operas. She enjoyed the depiction of 'ordinary' people living 'ordinary' lives. But in the last six or seven years, Edith's interest had slowly become an obsession, to the extent that soap operas were now the lynchpin of her life, the nuts and bolts that held her existence together. She watched them all, knew every character in every soap, could tell you more about them than she could about herself. Meals and outings were planned around *EastEnders* and *Emmerdale Farm;* housework was organized so it wouldn't clash with *Neighbours* and *Sons and Daughters.* During the devotional half-hours in which these programmes were on the screen, Edith would sit, entranced, phone off the hook, deaf to any callers that happened by and tried to distract her from her worship.

On this particular evening she was hurrying home through the streets of Piling Hill, her stomach tying itself into panic-stricken knots with the fear that she might be late for the beginning of *Coronation Street.* This was her favourite soap of all, and Edith could not remember the last time she had missed even a fraction of an episode. As she ran she cursed the oaf of a librarian whose fault this was, the moron who'd insisted she pay a 40p fine despite her protestations that the reason her books were overdue was because of the recent appalling weather and her subsequent inability to get out of the house. She thought of the smug expression on the librarian's face, the toothbrush moustache that twitched above his smirk. 'All right, here's your bloody money!' she had shouted at last after almost ten minutes of fruitless argument, and she had thrown the coins at him and laughed as he dived behind his desk.

But now it seemed the librarian would get the last laugh after all, for it was already seven twenty-seven, only three minutes to go before the start of her programme, and Edith was still a quarter of a mile from home. Despite the treacherous pavements, her feet flew across the ground, the crunching of snow competing with the rasping of breath in her throat. She glanced at her watch again and was dismayed to see that it had leaped on another minute. Seven twenty-eight, only *two* minutes to go now: but – and here was a chilling thought – what if her watch was slow? What if her programme had already started? Despite the cold, by the time she turned on to King Street she was sweating.

Edith lived at number eleven, six houses up on the left-hand side. As always she gave number one a sour look as she passed by, cursing its caved-in roof, the graffiti-strewn boards at its windows. It was a bane on the rest of the street, that house, a blot on what was already a depressing landscape. She was moving quickly, though not quickly enough that she didn't notice a dark hunched shape in the snow beneath the downstairs window. Must be a dog, she thought, a Christmas present whose novelty has worn off and which has been thrown out on to the streets. She clucked sympathetically, but had no intention of stopping. The waifs and strays of Piling Hill were not her responsibility, were they?

Then she saw the hand . . .

She stopped this time, breath whistling through her teeth, heart thudding like a piston. Her mind was a whirl of emotions: should she stop and help or should she hurry on and not get involved? Perhaps it was a tramp lying there, or a druggie, or a glue sniffer. Perhaps he would turn violent if she interfered. However, on the other hand, perhaps it was the victim of an accident; perhaps the person had been knocked down by a car, or stabbed, or mugged. She looked towards her dark house, as though that could show her the way, and then back at the motionless shape in the snow. For the first time she noticed the blood, the broken glass, looked up and saw the gaping shattered window. And suddenly her mind had decided for her, and she was hurrying up the path, wading through the snow to where the body lay.

It was on its face, one arm above its head, the other twisted grotesquely beneath it. Its left leg, too, was twisted,

443

and Edith suspected it was probably broken. At first, when she saw the head, she thought it had been smashed completely open, but as she bent closer she realized that what she had mistaken for blood was mostly curly red hair.

She reached out and placed a hand on the body's shoulder, then withdrew it hesitantly. Partly she was afraid of what she might see, but also she had remembered a warning from somewhere not to move accident victims. Her hand hovered like a priest's blessing until she happened to glance at her watch and saw it was seven thirty-two. With renewed urgency she took hold of the body, braced herself, and slowly pushed it over.

'Holy Jesus,' she gasped, and looked at the sky, afraid she was going to be sick. Snow clung to the man's face (or was it just a boy? It was difficult to tell), but it did little to mask his injuries. His nose, his mouth, one ear and what looked like his entire forehead leaked red, though much of the blood had congealed into crusty black scabs that resembled charred skin. The man/boy's teeth were a row of white splinters, many of which were embedded in the lips, and the nose had been crushed beyond recognition. The eyes were swollen shut, and the skin that Edith could see that was not bruised or lacerated, was white tinged with blue.

'Dead,' she whispered, shivering at the hollow finality of the word. 'Poor, poor mite.'

She reached out to take the man/boy's hand and then suddenly stopped, watching fascinated as a red shimmering bubble formed and then burst over a crusted nostril. A moment later the ruined mouth moved, spilling blood, and a sound like a gurgling cough hacked its way out of the throat.

'You're alive!' Edith cried and felt a mixture of both joy and pity. She unwound the scarf that swathed her neck and chin and bunched it into a makeshift pillow. Gently she lifted the man/boy's head and slipped the pillow beneath.

444

'That's to help you breath,' she babbled, and absent-mindedly wiped the blood from her fingers on to the snow. She rooted in her pocket and came up with a large crumpled handkerchief, which she spat on to and used gently to remove blood from around the man/boy's nose and mouth. 'Sh,' she whispered as he groaned, and a moment later she stood up, satisfied that she had done all she could.

Her joints popped as she got to her feet. Edith rubbed them and glanced at her watch. It was now seven thirty-eight, and she couldn't help feeling a moment of hollow resentment at the pathetic creature before her.

'You just lie there while I phone for an ambulance,' she muttered, and waded through the snow to the gate, then up the road to her own house.

By the time she had dialled 999, spoken to all the necessary people and given her name and address, *Coronation Street* was over halfway through. She settled down to watch the last ten minutes of it, feeling as though she'd deserted an old friend. She hoped desperately that the emergency services would not arrive and interrupt her before the programme had ended.

2

Coronation Street was just coming to an end when Sylvia said, 'Is Robin home yet?'

Mike was sitting in the armchair, his briefcase propped open on his lap as though he was about to dine from it. By his side was a copy of the *Starmouth Water Bulletin* from which he was jotting down notes into a ring-binder notepad. At his wife's question he looked up, raising his eyebrows above the tops of his reading glasses. 'Hmm, what's that?' he murmured absently.

'I said, is Robin home yet? Did you hear him come in? He went round to Walter Treeborn's, remember.'

Mike glanced towards the door that led into the hall.

445

After a moment he said, 'No, I haven't heard him. But then again, I haven't really been listening for him.'

'That's strange,' said Sylvia.

'What is?'

'Robin was only supposed to be going to tell Mr Treeborn that he couldn't make it tonight, yet he's been gone nearly an hour now.' She crossed to the back window, lifted the curtain and peered out. 'Also there are no lights on in Mr Treeborn's house. It doesn't look as if anyone's in.'

Mike sighed and slipped his pen into the pad's coiled spine. 'I shouldn't worry about it,' he said. 'Treeborn will have roped him into doing something. You know what a miserable old sod he is.'

Sylvia bridled, though a week ago she would have agreed with his evaluation. Trying to keep her voice casual, she replied, 'He was perfectly nice when I saw him in the garden this afternoon.'

Mike snorted. 'I expect he was. After all, he was asking you a favour, wasn't he? When I went round to borrow his torch last week he was very reluctant, tried to fob me off with all sorts of excuses.'

'Well, that's because you never return things! That torch is still sitting on the kitchen windowsill. I thought you only wanted it to change a lightbulb in the garage.'

'I did,' said Mike huffily. 'I just haven't got round to taking it back yet, that's all.'

'Hmph. Story of your life.'

'What's that supposed to mean?'

'Look,' said Sylvia, 'why don't you take it back now? Then you can check on Robin at the same time.'

Mike sighed again, deeper and more theatrical this time. 'Because,' he said, waving the notepad as he had waved the telephone bill that morning, 'I've got too much bloody work to do. I've got to address the whole department tomorrow, give them all the gen on these new filter systems we're having installed. I mean, I don't know why they consider me such a bloody expert! I'm just condensing the article from this magazine.'

'Well, why don't the rest of the department just read the article too?' Sylvia asked.

Mike shook his head wearily. 'You tell me.' He removed his glasses, rubbed his eyes with the back of his hand, and put his glasses on again. 'Besides,' he muttered, 'Robin ought to be able to look after himself. If he hasn't got time to help Treeborn then he just has to say no. Now, will you please let me get on with this?'

He turned back to his work, leaving Sylvia fuming at the way he had dismissed her. Inevitably their conversation appeared to be taking a turn down the road marked 'Argument' again. There was no wonder she was drinking and having affairs, was there? Anyone in her position would probably feel the same. Pushing herself to her feet she said, 'Well, if you won't take the torch back, I will! Unlike you, I happen to care about the welfare of my son, and I don't like people taking advantage of him!'

She stomped into the kitchen, satisfied to have vented some of her anger, and yet knowing that she had not been entirely fair on her husband. In essence what Mike had said was true – it *was* up to Robin to say no, and it *was* unreasonable to expect Mike to break off from his work just to see what his son was doing – yet it wasn't so much Mike's words as his attitude which had annoyed her. In truth, the possibility that Robin might be being exploited and kept from his schoolwork didn't concern her as much as she had made out. After all, it was only eight o'clock, plenty of time yet for homework, and after Robin's distressing experience yesterday, she was amazed that he could even think about school. No, the real reason she was concerned was because her whirlwind relationship with Walter had planted a seed of paranoia in her mind. She couldn't help wondering what would happen if Walter were to accidently let slip to Robin about their affair. How would her son react to such news? Would he and Walter have a fight or a heart-to-heart talk? Would Robin rush home to tell Mike or would he simply give her accusing looks? The worst she could imagine, the thing that really frightened her, was the image of Robin walking the snowbound streets, laying the blame for all the problems she and Mike had suffered solely at her door.

Her hands were trembling as she snatched up Treeborn's torch from the windowsill and went back through to the hall. As she struggled into her jacket, she poked her head round the sitting room door. 'Right, I'm going,' she said as if it were a final goodbye. Mike grunted, but didn't look up. Sylvia felt like throwing the torch at his head. Instead she left the house, slamming the front door behind her, and as she strode up the drive she wondered obscurely how it would have worked out if she had married Walter instead of Mike.

She was gone for a little over ten minutes. Mike, who had become engrossed in his work again, looked up when he heard her key in the lock, expecting to see her march in with Robin in tow. He was therefore surprised when she staggered in alone, panting heavily.

It took him a moment to register the wide-eyed shock on her face, but when he did he felt a tightness in his chest and throat, knew instinctively that something was wrong. He stood up, putting the briefcase on the floor beside the chair.

'Syl,' he said quietly, 'what's the matter?'

For a moment she stared at him as though he was a stranger. She had a smudge of dirt on her nose and her hair was tousled. The door key she was holding slipped from her fingers and bounced on the coffee table. Like a baby taking its first steps she stumbled towards her husband.

'Oh Mike,' she whispered in a voice as pale as her skin, 'Oh, Mike, he's dead.'

And with that she collapsed into his arms.

'Thank you all for coming. I really do appreciate it.'

Constance Gardener beamed round at her family and stooped to give Richard a kiss. She was a handsome straight-backed woman who looked strong and imperious despite her age. She had the same steel-grey hair, calm blue eyes and large hands as her son. After kissing Richard, she kissed Derek and Eileen, then turned and took the hand of her old friend, Olive Pierce.

'Oh, I'm *so* looking forward to tomorrow night,' she said effusively. 'You've made this place look so nice.'

'Yes, it does look lovely,' Olive agreed, admiring their handiwork. The church hall, normally a drab and rather austere room, had been transformed with curtains and tablecloths, balloons and streamers.

'Come on, it's time we were off,' Derek said, looking at his watch.

The six of them trooped out, switching off lights and locking doors as they went. Richard waved to Constance as his grandfather, Albert, eased his Datsun out on to the main road. All in all he had enjoyed the evening; the work and the constant conversation had kept the events of the last few days in the back of his mind. But as they approached Cedar Grove his fears began to re-surface. When they reached the house he made an excuse and went up to his bedroom, where he was joined minutes later by Olive.

'Right,' she said briskly when they were seated at Richard's desk with a large sheet of blank paper before them, 'here's what we have to do. We write down everything we know, starting with the seance on Thursday night. We make a note of the creature's movements, its actions, the forms it has taken, who it has appeared to. If any thoughts or ideas or questions pop into your head, jot them down too, no matter how ridiculous they seem.' She lowered the neck of the desk lamp so that it shone directly on to the paper, emphasizing its whiteness and creating an island of light. 'This is called brainstorming. Sometimes by throwing ideas around, people can come up with new angles, new outlooks. Who knows, we may have overlooked something vital, something that's been right under our noses all the time. Also, by writing everything down we may be able to detect some pattern to all this, perhaps even to the extent where we can predict the creature's next move and plan against it.' She saw the doubt on his face and touched his arm. 'It's worth a try, Richard. Even if we don't come up with any answers we'll at least have cleared the air and set everything out for future reference.'

'And much good will it do,' he thought, but nodded and tried on a smile. Picking up his pen, he wrote in block capitals at the head of the sheet:

THURSDAY   10.00p.m.   KING STREET   SEANCE

An hour and two sheets of paper later, Olive sat back and put down her pen. Massaging her writing hand she said, 'Well, I think that's about it. Is there anything we've missed?'

Richard looked at the sheets before him, reading them through slowly. Asterisks and arrows linked points, and questions had been scribbled wherever there was room. 'No, I don't think so,' he replied. 'Nothing I can think of anyway.'

'Let's see what we've got then,' she said.

What they did have, what seemed to glare out at both of them, were the *gaps* in their knowledge, the grey areas, the dozens of unanswered questions. Toady, for instance, was an enigma, and one they discussed at length. What had inspired him to suggest the seance in the first place? What had happened to him between then and now? Why had his family house burned down, leaving him the only survivor? Richard told Olive about Toady's strange behaviour yesterday; the friendliness that, after the body had been found, seemed to mask a kind of desperation. Olive in her turn mentioned her dream, the disturbing image of twins that had stayed with her. It seemed reasonable to assume that both these sets of circumstances must have had something to do with the events leading to the fire tragedy,

450

yet the whys and wherefores eluded them, and indeed only served to engender more riddles.

Robin was also discussed, for he also appeared to be harbouring secrets. True, he had told Richard about his dream – the girl, the bird and the snowman – but Richard suspected there was yet more he hadn't told. That afternoon Robin had said, 'Last night I saw . . .' and then had refused to finish the sentence. It seemed to both Richard and Olive that they had to talk to Toady and Robin in depth before they could begin to have a full knowledge of the situation.

Yet another riddle was that of the blind man in Nige's house – how did he fit into all this? Was he, like the wolf and Harold's ghost and all the dream-images, another product of the seance? Or was he simply what he appeared to be – a disabled pensioner enjoying a winter break? Richard broached the subject with Olive, who said there was nothing much they could do beyond speaking to Nige, warning him to be on his guard. 'After all,' she said, 'we can hardly ring up the Figgs and tell them to throw the man out, can we? I mean, firstly they wouldn't listen to us, secondly the old chap might be innocent – the creature might have used his image as it used Harold's – and thirdly, if he isn't innocent it might just goad him into some sort of action. No, I think the thing to do for the time being is to play it by ear, speak to Robin and Adrian and gather information. Perhaps they can tell us something which would *prove* the blind man is involved, and which we could then use against him.'

Richard sighed. It seemed their whole philosophy was based on coulds and maybes. He pointed at something on the list against which he had scrawled two large question marks.

'What about this? Even before the seance took place you touched my hand and knew something was going to happen. And then later, when I broke the glass against the wall, you said it was as though the whole room was shattering around you. What caused those things to

451

happen, do you think? Was that the creature's power or was that you being psychic again?'

Olive looked thoughtful. 'You know, when I touched your hand I found myself in another place, a place that was dark and full of . . . awful things. I saw a claw come at me out of the darkness, a huge swinging thing with great long nails.' She shuddered and clenched her fists. 'I think that must have been a premonition of sorts, though where that place was I've no idea – perhaps the creature's home?' She paused for a moment, stared into space. 'Maybe that's why the creature tried to make me kill myself; maybe by touching your hand I somehow opened a door into another . . . place . . . dimension. I don't know. Maybe the thing feels threatened in case I do it again.' She looked at Richard, shrugged. 'I'm not sure about any of this. I'm only guessing.'

'Yeah, and that's all we *are* doing,' Richard said, frustrated. 'We might as well face it – we don't really know anything, do we? We don't know what this creature is, where it comes from, how strong it is. All we know is that it kills; it seems to do whatever it likes, to whoever it likes. We've got no chance of defeating it. We don't even know where to start.' He threw his pen on to the desk, where it skidded across the smooth surface, hit the wall and bounced on to the floor. He caught Olive's eye, saw her glaring at him, and immediately felt ashamed.

'Richard Gardener,' Olive said sternly, 'I'm disappointed in you. I thought you were a fighter. I thought you believed in standing up for your rights. Maybe we're not coming up with any answers just at the moment, but at least we're having a go. If you give up now, then other people may be killed and you won't have lifted a finger to stop it. Do you want that on your conscience? Well, do you?'

Richard hung his head miserably. 'No,' he murmured, and picked his pen up off the floor. 'No, of course not. It's just that . . . oh, I don't know. I feel so . . . so helpless. Helpless and scared.'

Olive placed a hand on his neck and smiled sympathetically. 'I know,' she said. 'I don't blame you for feeling that way. But this monster has got to have *some* weaknesses. Nothing is invincible. Things may seem pretty hopeless at the moment, but we've just got to keep looking for the chinks in its armour.' She put her spectacles on the desk and stroked the back of Richard's hair. 'We'll call it a day, shall we? Tomorrow we'll go and see Robin and Adrian, and perhaps Nigel, and we'll talk to them. They say that two heads are better than one, so think how useful five heads might be.'

Richard returned her smile and nodded. He pushed his spectacles up on to his forehead and rubbed his eyes. Suddenly he sat up straight, his spectacles slipping down like a visor. 'I've just thought of something,' he said, and picking up his pen, he underlined the words WOLF, DREAMS, HAROLD and BLIND MAN. 'All this time,' he said, 'we've been assuming that the thing responsible for all these is one creature or one entity or whatever you want to call it. But what if it isn't? What if all these things are separate? I mean, I'm not saying it wasn't the seance that brought them here, but what if all the things have nothing to do with one another? What if the seance unlocked some sort of . . . gate or something, and they all came through separately?'

He looked wide-eyed at Olive. She swallowed and murmured, 'Pandora's Box.'

Richard frowned. 'What?'

'What you said puts me in mind of Pandora's Box. It was supposed to contain all the evils in the Universe. When it was opened, the evils escaped and engulfed the world.' She smiled unsteadily. 'It's just a story.'

Richard's eyes had become saucers behind the spectacles.

'It's just a story,' she repeated. 'Besides, it might be better if we *were* dealing with many separate forces – they'd probably be easier to handle than one large one. I'm still inclined to believe, though, that all these events come from the same source, the same creature.' She stood up, pushing back her chair and snapped on the main light. 'I don't know how you sleep with her in the room,' she said, indicating the *Carrie* poster on the wall. She smiled stiffly and picked up her spectacles. Richard could see that her hands were trembling.

'I'll see you in the morning, Richard. Good night,' she said and opened the door.

'Night,' he replied, and watched as Olive stepped on to the landing. When she had gone he picked up his pen and wrote two words on the bottom of sheet three: PANDORA'S BOX.

For the second time in two nights he slept with the light on.

4

'Ow! You little bugger!!' Maureen gasped as Gillian bit down hard on her nipple. She held the baby away from her to examine the teethmarks, stroking the area gingerly with the tips of her fingers.

Gillian gurgled and wriggled in her mother's arms, obviously anxious to continue her feeding. Maureen said, 'All right, but only if you promise not to bite me this time.'

Not surprisingly Gillian made no such vow, and it was with great reluctance that Maureen lowered her breast to the baby's face once more. As the little mouth clamped around her tender flesh, Maureen winced, but this time, fortunately, Gillian kept her fangs to herself.

As the baby fed, Maureen glanced at the clock. It had been over two hours now since the police had arrived and taken Ken to the hospital. There'd been an accident, they'd said: Steven was badly hurt, and, from what Maureen could gather, it seemed his friend Maurice was dead. She'd been changing Gillian's nappy at the time and had only half-heard the conversation. She had come pounding down the stairs to hear the rest just as a pale and frightened-looking Ken was shrugging himself into his anorak.

Her questions had provoked sympathy from the police, but also evasion. They wouldn't say what Maurice had died of, and all they would tell her about Steven was that he'd fallen from a window and was in a bad way.

Maureen had always felt that one day something like this would happen. Steven had caused the family a lot of grief and shame over the past few years, but despite this she still loved him. She loved him because she was his mother; because she had brought him into the world and had watched him grow up; because she had fed him and clothed him and cared for him all his life. Maureen knew it was not really Steven's fault that he had turned out how he was; it was society that was responsible. Just as it was society that was responsible for lots of other things: nuclear bombs, drug abuse, urban decay, cancer, pollution. Maureen knew that Steven was simply a victim of society. She knew because his social worker had told her so.

She looked up at the sound of a car drawing to a halt outside. Above the purring engine, she heard doors slam, the subdued mush of human voices. She heard footsteps crunching on grit and ice, but wasn't sure whether they were coming up the drive until Ken's key scraped in the lock and the front door opened then closed.

Almost primly Maureen removed her nipple from the baby's mouth and slipped her breast back into its bra. Gillian protested feebly, but there was no way Maureen was going to feed the child in front of Ken, not the way he stared hungrily at her as though she were committing some sexual act. Quickly she buttoned up her blouse, and was just putting a cloth over her shoulder to burp the child when her husband came into the room.

He looked terrible. Haggard, old, his skin puffy and grey. Maureen burped the baby almost mechanically, watching as he slumped into the old armchair which creaked like tired bones beneath his bulk. He closed his

455

eyes, brought stubby hands up to massage his sockets and forehead. His fingers pushed through his thinning hair, roamed distractedly over his dry scalp before coming to a halt. He sighed, long and deep, as though his body was crammed with troubles that needed to be expelled.

'Well?' Maureen's fear made her snap. 'How is he?'

Ken shook his head slowly as though trying to dislodge something. 'Not good, Mor,' he murmured, 'not good at all.' His eyes blinked open. They looked rheumy and bloodshot. The thought that he might have been crying made Maureen feel strangely antagonistic towards him.

'Not good? What's that supposed to mean?'

Ken began to label his son's injuries, counting them off on his fingers as though they were groceries he had to remember. 'He's got a fractured skull, two broken legs, broken arm, three broken ribs, broken pelvis, internal bleeding, hundreds of cuts and bruises.' His voice broke, appalled by the catalogue of pain it was reciting. 'Shit, Mor, he . . . he looks like he was hit by a train . . . His face . . . God, his face is terrible. At first I didn't recognize him. I walked straight past his bed at the hospital.' He stared at his wife as though imparting some great and terrible truth. His fingers inched forward for solace; Maureen, however, flinched back, and they encountered only empty air.

Ken slumped in his seat, shuddered like a dog. Quietly he said, 'He's unconscious at the moment. The doctors don't know when he'll wake up. They said . . . they said there may be a possibility of brain damage, but they won't know how severe or how permanent for a while yet.' He gulped, grimaced as though it was painful to swallow. 'He was hiding out . . . There's an old house on King Street . . . Him and Mo were hiding there, hiding from the police. They . . . they reckon that nutter found them . . . you know, the one who chopped up the old man on the beach. They reckon he got Mo, and our Steve escaped by jumping out of an upstairs window.' His face creased, he looked suddenly manic. 'Christ, Mor, if I

456

could get my hands on him . . .' He left the threat unspoken, but strangled air to clarify his intention.

Maureen was filled with a kind of numb horror. She was hardly aware that Gillian had fallen asleep in her arms. Her voice was hushed, awed, as she said, 'Then you mean Maurice was . . . was murdered?'

'Murdered, yeah. Christ, they found him in a cupboard . . . in a fucking cupboard! With . . . with . . .' He looked away.

Maureen stared at him. Ken gripped the arms of the chair and pushed himself upright. He threw back his head and let out a laugh that was harsh and staccato, containing no humour. 'You know what that bastard did to him, Mor? You know what he did to Mo? The coppers found his body; oh, yeah, they found that all right. But they didn't find his head! Can you believe that? *They didn't find his fucking head!*'

5

Tuesday

Fingers tapped softly, insistently, in a haphazard rhythm. Permeating the veil came breathing – deep and heavy; harsh and rattling; soft like the whistling of wind through thin trees. He imagined figures – dark, ragged, faceless – shuffling towards his bed, palsied limbs twitching as they searched for him. He longed to open his eyes, but was afraid that to do so might betray his hiding place. He lay still in the hope that the figures would pass him by, overlook him in their blindness.

A smell touched his nostrils, a sterile institutionalized smell. By his side something creaked, and he imagined a trapdoor opening, something rising from it. He felt his muscles tightening, hairs stiffening as though quilled by electricity. His flesh shrank from the thought of some vague appendage, phobia-formed, meeting his skin. He imagined ghost-touches, by turn wet, cold, hard, dry,

457

spiny, scuttling. Each seemed as real as himself, and each seemed to clutch not just his skin but his bones beneath.

He heard a sound, a sigh, felt warm breath like brimstone on his cheek. He was certain that something was leaning over him, craning its neck to peer into his face. He tried to stop his features from twitching, but his eyes rebelled, flickering to be allowed open. Despite the danger he had to see what this creature was; had to. *Had to.* His eyes felt gritty as he opened them, ancient stone doors spilling dust and rubble, blurring his sight. He blinked the debris away, peering through the veil at the brimstone-breather. A face – fish-pale, boggle-eyed – swooped at him . . .

. . . Toady flung himself backwards, causing the metal headboard to judder. His hand came up, forming a flimsy shield between himself and his assailant. For a second his racing heart jerked the room; confused messages whirled in his mind. He flinched as the face retreated, slowly relaxed as he realized its intentions were not hostile. He saw a jumble in the background, struts and bars, that gradually resolved into an ordered row of metal beds. Each bed contained a bulky occupant whose pale face seemed to blend with the pillow. The fingers, still tapping, were snowflakes on the window; the breathing was that of his fellow patients. At the end of the ward a nurse sat reading at a desk beneath a lamp that transformed her face into a tripe-coloured slab pocked with shadows. The lamp beside Toady's bed was for reading too, but the book it had been illuminating was lying on the floor like a broken bird, dropped in shock when he had startled its owner.

'Are you all right?' he was asked by the pale face that hovered above the dark blue police uniform. Toady recognized the man from a time when he had come awake beneath an avalanche of panic and depression that crushed his thoughts. He nodded, his head woolly, and croaked, 'Yes.'

He sat up, feeling heavy, parched. He touched his throat which seemed swollen as a plum. 'Thirsty,' he said and stuck out his tongue, which adhered to his lips like a drying slug to a rock.

The policeman nodded and reached for a jug of water on the bedside table. He poured some into a glass and gave it to Toady. Toady took it, drank, relishing its slightly chemical taste. He felt the water reviving him, easing the dry friction of body and mind. It ran to his stomach, made him feel a little queasy, but he held his glass out for more. The policeman only half-filled it this time, and as Toady raised the water to his lips, said, 'Whoa, take it easy. You'll make yourself sick.'

Toady nodded, sipped. By his side the policeman's chair creaked again. When the water was gone, Toady put his glass on the bedside table and leaned back. Looking at the policeman he asked, 'What time is it?'

The policeman consulted his watch. 'Just after two in the morning. You've been asleep almost sixteen hours.'

Toady rubbed his eyes and yawned. His mind was clearing bit by bit. He looked along the line of beds, peering suspiciously at each pale face. At last he turned and stared at the policeman, at his young narrow features topped with curly black hair. 'Why are you here?' he asked. 'Have you come to arrest me?'

The policeman smiled. 'No, I've not come to arrest you. I've come because of what happened yesterday. Because of the accident.'

'Because of the fire, you mean?'

'Yes,' the policeman said, 'because of the fire.'

Toady sighed and lay back, pushing his head into the pillow. He was silent for perhaps thirty seconds, then he sat up, plumping the pillow to use as a backrest. In a quiet voice he said, 'They're all dead, aren't they? All my family are dead?'

The policeman, Ledbetter, felt a tug of pity, felt the boy's grief as if it was beating off him in waves. 'Yes,' he said, trying to keep his voice neutral. 'Yes, I'm afraid they are.'

Toady breathed out slowly, a puncture that seemed to

go on forever. Finally, in a cracked voice, he said, 'It's all my fault. It's all my fault that they're dead.'

Ledbetter leaned forward and took Toady's hand. 'No, it isn't. Just because you survived you mustn't automatically think that.' He rubbed the hand as though to goad life into the boy. 'You mustn't blame yourself, you know. It was an accident, that's all. Just an accident.'

Toady seemed to consider this, but then shook his head. 'No,' he murmured, 'you don't understand. It wasn't an accident . . . it was Toby; he made me do it. But it was my fault for bringing him here in the first place. If I hadn't done that, none of this would ever have happened.'

Ledbetter frowned, puzzled. There was that name again –Toby – the same one the boy had mentioned that morning. He began to wonder if someone else *had* been involved in starting the fire after all, some friend of Adrian's perhaps, who'd scarpered when things had started getting out of hand.

'Adrian,' he said, 'who is this Toby? Can you tell me about him?'

Toady stared at Ledbetter. His reply, when it came, appeared to bear no relation to the question that had prompted it. 'It was Thursday night it happened,' he said, 'but it was Saturday morning before I was really sure it had worked. I just wanted some proof, you see; I just wanted to know that there was something there, that it wasn't a load of old rubbish like everyone seemed to think . . . But, honest to God, I didn't mean anything like this to happen . . . I didn't want anyone to get killed.'

His voice choked off; in his eyes was a plea for understanding. Ledbetter patted his hand, made shushing noises, determined to nip a repeat of that morning's hysteria in the bud. When Toady had calmed a little, he said, 'OK, let's just take this one stage at a time. Now tell me what was it that happened on Thursday night?'

'The seance,' said Toady.

Ledbetter looked blank, then repeated dully, 'The seance.'

Toady nodded. There was a long pause. Ledbetter stared at the boy, his face a mixture of concern, frustration and confusion. Toady stared back, willing to help but unaware that his mind was releasing details with such waywardness that the policeman could make no sense of them.

'Look,' said Ledbetter patiently, 'I think we'd better start again. Are you telling me that on Thursday night you held a seance?'

'Yes.'

'OK, well, we'll take it from there. Can you tell me where this "seance" was held, and who was involved?'

'There were four of us,' Toady said, 'me, Richard, Nige and Robin. We went to this house in King Street—'

'*King Street!*' Ledbetter's raised voice earned a disapproving stare from the nurse further down the ward, and he raised a hand in apology. Leaning forward he hissed, 'You mean King Street in Piling Hill?'

'Yes, that's right.'

Ledbetter leaned back, making his chair creak again. King Street was where those two boys had been found: he'd heard all the gory details earlier when he'd checked into the station on his way to relieve WPC Saunders from her stint at Adrian's bedside. The boy mentioning it in connection with the fire at his home seemed somehow eerie, yet perhaps it was only coincidence. King Street was, after all, only a couple of roads away from Latimer Street where Adrian had lived.

'Go on,' he urged. 'What happened then?'

Toady told him briefly about the seance, about how Richard had thrown the glass against the wall. 'But that wasn't the end,' he said. 'After that, weird things started happening – though most of them I didn't know about till later. Richard was followed home by a wolf, and then that old man was killed on the beach. I was still using the ouija board, trying to call the thing back. I wasn't having much luck, and then on Saturday I managed to break through. At first the thing couldn't communicate; it kept messing

461

up my mind, making me feel . . . funny. And then, eventually, it managed to get through and it told me all about itself. It's name's Toby – that's when it's being a boy, of course – and it was dead friendly at first. It killed the old man, but it told me that he was a mistake. It could change into what it liked, could get inside your head and make you do things. It made me kill my mum . . .' He paused here, picked up the jug with a trembling hand and poured himself another glass of water. He sipped, then continued: 'I didn't want to kill her, honestly. It took me to this place where she was . . . taking her clothes off . . . I was so ashamed, so angry, but I would never have killed her if it hadn't made me . . . I thought it was my friend, but it isn't. It's evil, it's got to be stopped. It's got to be caught and sent back before it kills anyone else.'

He was now trembling so much that the water was slopping out of his glass and on to the bedclothes. Gently Ledbetter took the glass, then urged him to lie back for a moment and close his eyes. Toady did so, and Ledbetter stared with pity at his chubby young/old face, wondering what was going on in that shattered mind. Little of what the boy had told him made sense, but there were a few points that worried Ledbetter greatly. One was Adrian's continued insistence that he had killed his mother (or at least that 'something' (Toby?) had made him kill her). Another, of course, was that reference to King Street (though Adrian could not possibly know about the horrors discovered there tonight), and a third was the reference to the old man killed on the beach (though Ledbetter knew that Adrian had been one of the boys who had found him).

The policeman mused on these thoughts, unsure whether Adrian's monologue had been intended as confession or accusation, or whether it was simply the ramblings of a disturbed mind. Without a doubt the oblique references were intriguing, perhaps even significant, but for the life of him Ledbetter couldn't see how they fitted into the overall picture.

King Street, he thought. King Street, Thursday night,

seance. Adrian is at King Street on Thursday night; he is in a beach cave finding a body on Sunday afternoon; on Sunday evening he is at home when it is gutted by a fire, killing everyone but him. King Street, beach cave, home; three places of unnatural death in four days. So what did that make the boy? Perpetrator, victim or Jonah?

He shook his head, sighed, and turned his attention back to the bed. Adrian had to be talked to at length, coaxed and cajoled to yield up the information in his scrambled mind. Ledbetter knew it would be a painful and harrowing process, but it was one that had to be undertaken. He hunched over and took the boy's hand again, which was cold and limp and clammy. There was no response from the figure on the bed. He put his mouth to the boy's ear and said softly, 'Adrian? Adrian, are you awake?'

Toady opened his eyes, a weary look on his face. Ledbetter said, 'Would you mind if I asked you some more questions? It's very important that we know what's going on.'

Toady looked very much as if he did mind, but he shook his head. 'No,' he said. 'What is it you want to know?'

'Can you tell me about King Street again? Can you tell me which house you were in? Whether you saw or heard anything unusual?'

Toady sighed. 'We were in the abandoned house at the end of the row. We didn't break in or anything – there was a window open round the back. And I've told you once, we had the seance. We almost called up the thing that was in the house, but Richard broke the glass and it seemed as though the thing had gone away again.' He shrugged. 'Of course it hadn't, but we didn't know that until later.' Suddenly tetchy he said, 'But I've told you all this. Didn't you listen the first time?'

'Yes, yes, of course I did,' Ledbetter replied quickly. 'I was just a little confused about some of the details, that's all . . . Tell me, Adrian, what were the names of the other boys involved?'

463

'I've told you that as well. Richard, Nige and Robin.'

'No, no, I mean their surnames.'

'Oh . . . Richard Gardener, Nigel Figg, Robin Tread-well.'

Ledbetter scribbled the information down in the note-book he had taken from his hip pocket. As he did so, he pondered over the name Gardener: where had he heard that name already tonight? He was just jotting down the last name – Treadwell – when it came to him. It had been in the station before coming to the hospital. The boys who had been found at the house in King Street had been wanted in connection with the stabbing of a Neil Gardener at a party two nights before.

Suddenly excited he asked, 'This Richard Gardener – does he have a brother called Neil?'

'That's right, yes.'

'And is that the Neil Gardener who was stabbed a couple of nights ago?'

'By Rusty's lot, yeah.'

'Rusty?'

'Steven Oates. He's a kid at our school. He's really crazy. He . . . he picks on me sometimes.'

This too was duly transferred into Ledbetter's note-book. It seemed that a pattern, a clique of events, was at last beginning to emerge. However there was still the riddle of who or what Toby was, and what part he had played in all of this. He appeared to be at the centre of each grisly event, yet Adrian had failed to name him among the crowd who had been at King Street on Thursday night.

'This Toby,' he said. 'I wonder, could you just tell me about him again? You say he was at the seance, and that he killed the old man and then made you kill your mother? I wonder, could you give me some more details about him? His surname, for instance?'

Toady sat up, a guarded look on his face. 'Well, Toby's not really a person . . . He's, well, I'm not sure exactly what he is. Sometimes he's a person, though he can be what he likes. When he's being Toby he's just a boy, but I've seen him as lots of other things as well. Once he was even Peter Cushing.'

Ledbetter looked baffled. 'Peter Cushing?' he repeated.

'Yes – you know, the actor.'

Ledbetter sighed. This was getting him nowhere. Changing tack again, he said, 'You said that Toby made you kill your mother? Can you tell me exactly what you meant by that? What he made you do to her?'

He watched Toady's face carefully, alert for any sign of distress or withdrawal. Toady, however, remained calm, though his voice was slightly strained. 'I'm not sure *exactly* what he did . . . I was really mad because of her being a stripper and everything, and . . . and somehow Toby got into my head, kind of directed my anger, I suppose . . . I don't know. All I really remember is standing in this kind of tunnel of fire, and when I came to, my mother was burning.' He turned away, a sickened look on his face. Ledbetter squeezed his hand, hoping he hadn't pushed too hard too soon, but feeling as though he'd got the information he'd wanted. As he had thought, Adrian's recollection of the fire was confused and hazy; maybe this was due to the fumes which would have made him light-headed, or maybe it was simply distress that averted the worst of the memories. Whatever the reason, the question of Toby's true identity seemed answered now too. The words Adrian had used – *somehow Toby got into my head* – had clinched it for him. Toby was not a real person at all: he was some form of scapegoat, a kind of hook on which Adrian was hanging his guilt. At any rate that explained why the references were so confusing, why the boy insisted on this idea that his 'seance' was somehow significant.

Ledbetter patted the boy's hand and said, 'All right, Adrian, you rest now. I'm sorry to have pushed you, but the sooner we find out what's going on, the sooner we can clear all this up. I'm going to phone through to the station, tell them what you've told me. I'm afraid we may have to ask you some more questions tomorrow. Do you think you'll be up to it by then?'

Toady nodded. 'Yes, I think so.'

'Good lad,' smiled Ledbetter. He stood up, the chair creaking in relief. 'I'd better go and tell the nurse you're awake. If you want anything, she'll give it to you.' He winked as though he and Toady were old pals sharing a secret. 'See you later, OK?'

'OK.'

The policeman walked the length of the ward, bent and had a word with the nurse sitting at her desk. She nodded and Ledbetter walked back, through a tunnel of breathing that was both restful and unsettling. He glanced at Adrian as he passed his bed, but the boy had closed his eyes again, a slight frown wrinkling the puffed skin of his face. Ledbetter pushed open one of the double doors at the end of the room and stepped from the gloomy ward into a quieter, less gloomier corridor.

He passed olive-green doors set in a white wall, some labelled, some not. His mind buzzed with what the boy had told him, though still his thoughts were blundering about, searching for a pattern. Whether the fire at Adrian's house had been accidental or not, it still seemed obvious that the boy and his friends were more deeply involved in the Starmouth murders than had first appeared. Adrian's story had contained so many coincidences, so many connections; though just how those connections were linked eluded Ledbetter for the time being. The only theory that came to mind was that all this was the result of some kind of gang warfare that had got out of control – and yet that didn't quite ring true either. There *were* gangs in Piling Hill, but generally their members ranged in age from sixteen to twenty-five and their forays into violence involved stabbings and street-brawls, not beheadings and dismemberment. Besides, the old man had been a threat to nobody: the only apparent motive for his murder was sadism. Added to which the fact that it had taken place on the seafront, some three or four miles from Piling Hill.

Ledbetter's thoughts were cut short by a groaning sound to his left. He turned and found himself parallel with a door marked 'Bathroom,' the line of light leaking from beneath it betraying its habitation. He stopped for a moment and listened, and was about to move on when the groaning came again. Perhaps it was caused only by the discomfort of constipation, but somehow Ledbetter thought not. It sounded too much like someone in distress, someone so feeble that they were unable to form words. He looked up and down the corridor in the vain hope that a nurse might materialize, then hesitantly he stepped forward and tapped on the door.

'Excuse me,' he called, 'is anyone in there?'

Another groan answered him, this time weaker than before.

'Are you all right?' he asked, realizing how pointless the question must sound.

On this occasion not even a groan met his words: simply silence, deep as a held breath.

'Look,' said Ledbetter, taking the doorknob firmly in his hand, 'I'm a police officer. If you can hear me, get away from the door. I'm coming in and may have to break the lock.' He listened for a moment, but there was no response. Perhaps whoever was in there had passed out. Experimentally he tried the knob, though he didn't expect it to be unlocked. He was surprised, therefore, when on twisting and pushing, the door came open immediately.

Bracing himself for what he might see, he stepped inside.

6

Had he rung the station, Ledbetter would have found that much of the exclusive information he had uncovered was not so exclusive after all. Sergeant Glennon, on desk duty, had a sheet of paper in front of him, one side of which

467

contained a column of names, the other a column of events. He had linked and interlinked these columns with arrows, creating a tangled mass that resembled the beginnings of a spider's web – a spider's web in whose sticky strands he felt he was rapidly becoming ensnared.

Gloomily he gazed at the results of his labours, chin resting on his hand, a mug of tea rapidly cooling by his elbow. He stared until his eyes began to smart, but nothing except theories and ideas presented themselves. After a while the overlapping arrows seemed not even to clarify matters, but to tie themselves into ever tighter knots, a warp and weft of baffling intricacy.

The sheet, which he pushed aside in annoyance, looked like this:

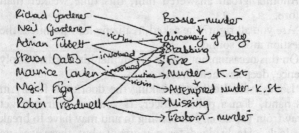

Like Ledbetter before him, Glennon had toyed with the idea of gang warfare and revenge killings, but also like Ledbetter he had quickly discarded this theory. If he had been dealing with big city villains then maybe the possibility would not have seemed so far-fetched, but he was dealing with schoolkids here – fourteen, fifteen, sixteen year olds – and not only that but schoolkids who (at least in the case of Gardener, Treadwell and co.) came from stable family backgrounds and had neither criminal records nor any history of mental disorder. No, Gardener and his friends were victims, not instigators. Glennon had seen for himself how shocked and upset they'd been after finding Bessle's body on Sunday afternoon. The most likely explanation, then, seemed to be that someone had it

468

in for the boys, someone who sent warning notes in the form of death and mutilation. Glennon could not conceive of anything the boys might have done provoking such revenge, but nevertheless following this line of thought did tend to give the murders a pattern, a kind of warped logic.

Take the first one, for instance: Alfie Bessle. Was it too unreasonable to assume that the body had been planted where the murderer knew the boys would find it? And the second: Maurice Landen. Did the murderer mistakenly believe that Landen was a friend of the boys and therefore involved in whatever it was they had done? The third death, Walter Treeborn, appeared the most logical of all: the man had presumably been killed in order to lure Robin Treadwell into a trap.

'But why?' Glennon muttered to himself. 'What the hell have they done to you?'

Never in his twenty-odd years with the force had he encountered murders of such brutal and callous ferocity. The injuries did not look as though they had been inflicted with axe or knife or shotgun: the flesh had been stretched, the bones sheared as though pulled apart by enormous hands. He picked up a pencil from the desk, broke it in two with a snap, and shuddered quietly to himself.

He thought of the call he had received that evening: Mike Treadwell ringing to say his neighbour was dead, his son missing. Though Glennon had always hated facing distraught relatives, he had gone along himself with Constable Bailey, and would never forget descending the steps into that dark cellar, shining his torch on to that white staring face in the open trunk. It had looked to him as though the man had been dead two or three days, though Mrs Treadwell claimed to have seen him just that afternoon. Still that was a matter for the pathology boys to decide. For now, all Glennon could do was wait.

He rested his elbows on the desk and rubbed his eyes, listening to the wet squishy sounds they made. As a rookie constable, violent senseless death had always upset him, sometimes for days, putting him off his meals, making him despair of the human race. Over the years he had become hardened to it, had learned to accept it as a sad but inevitable fact of life. But this case was bringing back all those old memories, was curdling his stomach like a bad meal, making him angry and depressed.

On returning to the station that evening, Glennon had called first the Gardeners, who had been out, and then the Figgs. He had told Mrs Figg what had happened and had warned her to keep her son close by. On learning of the murders and of Robin's disappearance, she had immediately become hysterical, claiming she knew something like this would happen if her son mixed with 'those hooligans.' She had gone on to demand a police guard on the house at all times, and when Glennon had tried to explain about resources and lack of manpower, she had accused him of being uncaring and of not doing his job properly.

In the end, cutting through her tirade and feeling like slapping her down the phone, Glennon had said, 'Look, madam, just keep the boy indoors where you can see him and I'm sure he'll be safe. Tomorrow I'll come and speak to him and we'll try to clear all this up. Goodbye.' He had replaced the receiver before she could reply.

Now he sat staring at the phone, at the sheet of paper, wishing there was something else he could do tonight. He wondered whether Adrian Tibbett had recovered consciousness at the hospital yet, whether he ought to get in touch with Ledbetter and warn him to be especially alert considering that evening's events. He put his hand on the phone, but then decided against it. No, Ledbetter couldn't do any more than sit by the boy's bedside, and ringing him would only draw him away from his vigil. Glennon sighed. He knew that colleagues of his were scouring the streets and following up leads even now, that pathology was working on the Landen and Treeborn corpses, that the house in King Street was being searched top to bottom. Beyond those walls was a hive of activity with himself at the hub but still that knowledge didn't

470

help his state of mind. He had never liked sitting around, which was why he'd been happy to progress no higher than sergeant at Starmouth. Though many of his colleagues had tried to convince him otherwise, Glennon had always regarded promotion as a shift towards increased paper and office work, had seen it as an unwelcome step beyond good honest coppering. He was looking forward to tomorrow when he could talk to the boys, try to wheedle information out of them that would hopefully throw the doors of this case wide open. He was looking ahead, twelve hours from now, when he hoped to have a suspect and an explanation; even twenty-four hours from now, when, with any luck, an arrest would have been made and charges pressed.

He sighed again. Twenty-four hours. It seemed such a long time. He continued to sit by the phone while the minutes ticked on and the snow came down, hoping against hope that something would happen to release him from his age of waiting.

7

The nurse had brought Toady two things: news and an apple. The apple he had been grateful for, the news not so. He was now sitting up in bed, his back propped by pillows, munching on the fruit and brooding on what she had told him.

In itself the news was not bad; it was the dilemma it created that troubled him. He had been informed that his Uncle Frank and Aunty Hilda would be coming to see him tomorrow, and that they would be taking him back with them to Leeds. Though he had never really liked his mother's sister and her gloomy husband, Toady's first reaction had been one of joy: the thought of convalescing in Yorkshire whilst the war either raged or petered out behind him held enormous appeal. He imagined himself snoozing till all hours, emerging only to eat, drink, watch

471

TV and be pampered to the point of indulgence.

But no; even as he thought this he knew he was only deluding himself. He could leave events behind, but he couldn't discard his conscience. If he left his friends in the lurch now he would be tormented by self-accusations of guilt, betrayal, cowardice, desertion. This newfound conscience was the creature's doing, a bitter-sweet legacy born from the need to reject its excesses.

He sighed and placed his half-eaten apple on the bedside table to rest his aching jaw. As well as his mind, his body too had been through an ordeal, a fact of which he was only now becoming fully aware. His flesh felt the worst: slightly baked, hot, as though a little of the inferno had seeped beneath his skin. His throat was rough, smokey. His chest hurt when he took too deep a breath. His limbs and his back ached from being in bed too long, and his head itched as though grit was trapped in the scalp.

He exhaled, sparking the pang in his chest, and wriggled down under the bedclothes. All around him the breathing of the sick pervaded the atmosphere, an orchestra whose music was respiration. He closed his eyes, and immediately he felt as though he were sinking into himself, the tension in his muscles and mind gradually easing. He did not realize how close he was to sleep until a voice in his ear said: 'Adrian.'

Though the word was softly spoken it cut through his slumber with ease. As before Toady's eyes drifted open to see a face looming over him, but this time he was not alarmed. 'Hello,' he said sleepily, and struggled to sit up, wiping at his eyes as though they were filmed with cobwebs. A yawn ballooned up his throat and out of his mouth, threatening to split his skull in two.

Ledbetter returned the greeting; he seemed agitated, excited. 'Listen,' he said, 'I've got something to tell you. I know how we can catch this Toby.'

At the mention of his adversary's name, Toady's drowsiness vanished. Sitting up, he reached over, took the apple and bit into it. Through a mouthful of pulp he said, 'Do you? How?'

'I'll tell you in a moment. But first you must promise to trust me. You must give yourself over to me completely, put your welfare into my hands. If you do that, then I believe we can win. If not . . .' Ledbetter shrugged '. . . well, who knows what might happen.'

For a long moment Toady was silent. The request was a strange one, and the look in the policeman's eyes somewhat disquieting. However the words that Ledbetter had spoken enthralled him, for they were pregnant with promise and hope. He stared hard into the policeman's face, hoping for some clue, but found only an eagerness that was almost lewd, glistening lips that opened to reveal just a hint of pink tongue. He was prepared to do anything to end this nightmare, anything at all, but he could not shake off his sudden reservations. Without quite knowing why, his mouth had gone arid, the apple in it like pulverized wood. He swallowed with an effort, then mumbled, 'I . . . I don't know. Can't you tell me what the plan is?'

'No.' Ledbetter shook his head. 'It's not for me to say.'

'Who then?'

'I'm afraid you'll have to wait till we get there.'

'Get where?'

'The King Street house, of course.'

There was a longer pause this time. The very name seemed to send arrows through Toady's heart. He poured himself some water, sluiced it round his mouth to quench the desert that was forming there. In a shaky voice he said, 'King Street? Why? Why do we have to go back there?'

'Because that's where the Toby creature is trapped,' Ledbetter said.

Toady's mouth dropped open. Could this be true? He couldn't imagine any physical barrier holding the beast, yet in his present state he was quite prepared to clutch at straws. 'Who . . . how did you do that?' he managed at last.

'The how isn't important,' replied the policeman. 'The fact is the creature is there and the place is surrounded. But they need *you* there. Now. Immediately.'

'But why?' Toady wailed.

'You brought the thing here. Only you can send it back.'

Toady's mind struggled to cope with this new revelation. 'Me? But . . . but I don't know how. I can't send it back by myself.'

Ledbetter smiled, put an arm around his shoulders. 'Don't worry. From what I can gather, you won't have to do much at all. Apparently they've got an expert there, some psychic or other. All you have to do is follow his instructions. I'm assured you won't be in any danger.'

His words did little to reassure Toady. The abruptness of events was confusing him. It was like sitting on a helter skelter which had just taken a swift and unpredictable new tilt. He felt scared to his stomach, felt dread flowing through his limbs like fever . . . and yet another part of him felt an enormous flood of relief, a need to believe that what this policeman was telling him was true; that all he had to do was follow a few orders to bring this whole dismal affair to an end.

'I . . .' he stammered, but Ledbetter cut in before the sentence had time to form.

'Well, what do you say? Will you do as I ask? Or do you want to see more people killed?'

'No!' said Toady; this was a concept he could grasp only too well. 'No, there mustn't be any more deaths.'

'Then you'll trust me?' returned the policeman.

The uncertainty was still there, sketched on Toady's face. Ledbetter leaned forward, his smile soothing, his voice like syrup. 'You *will* trust me, won't you, Adrian? You *will* do exactly as I say?'

There was another beat of silence, but the choice was nil.

474

'Yes,' Toady said.

'Good,' replied Ledbetter. He closed his eyes briefly, like a lover on the verge of climax. His hand tightened around Toady's shoulder.

'Then let's begin,' he said.

8

Daylight struggled through the closed curtains, giving the room colour and substance. In her sleep Sylvia whimpered and threw up her hands to fend off dreams that slumber had brought marching. She rolled over, but it was no use; the dreams would not go away.

She awoke with a scream to find she had the entire bed to fret in. The place beside her was empty, the covers thrown back, the pillow on Mike's side cool as a gravestone. 'Alone,' she thought in the panicky moment before her dream faded, 'I'm all alone.' But the sounds from downstairs disputed that, proclaiming the whereabouts of the bed's recent occupant.

She lay back, moaning, and spread her arms out to either side of her. At her core strands of nightmare still clung, but now they were delicate, ephemeral, and within moments had dissolved altogether. The sleep, all two fitful hours of it, had done nothing to ease her anxiety; indeed, it had worsened it, for it had unlocked the closet and allowed all her darkest fears to come tumbling out. Her stomach now felt gnawed, her head pulsed as though heart and brain had changed places. She glanced at the clock, saw the hands inching towards seven-thirty, and, groaning, tilted back her head.

She stared at the ceiling for a moment, then rolled on to her side, cramming her face into Mike's cold pillow. Oh, where was Robbie? Who had killed Walter? If there was a God, how could he allow such awful things to happen? Measured footsteps on the stairs snagged her attention, and she looked up as the door opened.

Mike entered, balancing a tray, his face dark with sleeplessness and stubble. 'I . . . I've brought you some breakfast,' he ventured, and held the tray out for her inspection. A bowl contained muesli drowned in milk; a plate held toast that was almost black and smeared with marge and jam; a mug of tea the colour of flesh exuded drifting fingers of steam.

It was a pitiful breakfast, but it was the first real thought Mike had shown her in months. So touched was she by the gesture, and so unstable were her emotions, that Sylvia began to cry.

'Don't,' Mike pleaded, and placing the tray on the floor, rushed to his wife's side. It had been months, too, since he had shown her any physical tenderness, but now he gathered her to him, crushing her against his chest.

'Don't,' he said again, 'please,' whispering into her hair.

Sylvia continued to bawl for what seemed like minutes, clutching at her husband's shirt-front, soaking it with tears, letting go only when the crying had become sobbing, then snuffling, then a hitching of breath. She felt Mike's arms releasing her gently, as though he was afraid any abrupt action might cause her to crack. She looked up into his face and saw an awkwardness there, an embarrassment, as though she was a stranger he had consoled instinctively in the street. She was hurt by the expression, but then he smiled and she saw it for what it *could* be: a small but crucial step on the road to reconciliation.

'Eat your breakfast,' he said gruffly, placing the tray on her lap. 'You're going to need something to keep your strength up.'

Her stomach protested, but Sylvia picked up a slice of toast and began to nibble at it to please him. She stirred the tea, sipped at it, and toyed with the muesli in her bowl. When she pushed the tray away minutes later, the food was virtually untouched, but Mike made no protest, simply took the tray and placed it on the floor.

'No news?' Sylvia said, clutching his hand. She knew

476

there wouldn't be – he would have told her if there had been – but she felt compelled to ask the question just the same.

He shook his head. 'No, not yet . . . but they'll find him, don't worry. I'm sure he'll be all right.'

His words were empty, desperate. They both knew it, but Sylvia nodded eagerly. 'Yes,' she said. 'Yes, they'll find him.' Then the sudden image of her lover's dead face gazing up from the trunk rose in her, and her hope crumbled. 'Oh, Mike, what if they don't . . . ? What if that bastard's done to Robbie what it did to Walter?' She gagged on the thought and began to sob afresh.

'Shh,' Mike said, 'shh.' He stroked his wife's back as she clung to him, rubbed her bare arms as though to massage reassurance into her. Already he was becoming used to their closeness again, hadn't realized until now how much he had missed it. He kissed her gently on the forehead and murmured words of encouragement.

'Just remember what the policeman told us,' he said. 'If the killer had meant to . . . to do to Robin what he did to Treeborn, then there was no reason he shouldn't have done it there and then . . . No, I'm sure Robin's alive somewhere. It's just a matter of finding him.' He rocked her like a baby and reflected on what else the policeman had said: that under the circumstances Robin could not be regarded as merely a victim, he had to be seen as a possible suspect too.

He blocked that thought from his mind. It was too ludicrous to think of his son as a murderer. No, Robin *was* a victim. He was out there somewhere – injured maybe, tired, hungry, alone . . . but not dead. Oh no, never dead.

Gently he untangled Sylvia's arms and looked into her stricken face. He leaned forward and kissed her, marvelling at the softness of her lips, wondering how he could ever have grown out of the habit in the first place. After lips, he kissed her forehead again, then her tear-blurred eyes, then the tip of her nose. 'Oh, Syl,' he whispered, pulling her to him once more. 'Oh, Syl, I'm sorry for being such a . . . such a stupid bastard these last few months.'

She said nothing. After a while, Mike mumbled, 'I'll make it up to you, I promise. You *and* Rob. Maybe, when all this has blown over, we can move away from here, find somewhere in the country, make a fresh start.'

He broke off, choked by tears. He wept openly, though not quite unashamedly. He was weeping not just for Robin, but also for his marriage and his life and the unfairness of it all. So wretched was his weeping that Sylvia could not help but weep too. More time passed as they huddled there in their sorrow and regret.

At last Mike stood, and swiping the tears away, crossed to the window. He pulled back the curtains, gazing at the drifting white landscape as he blew his nose. When he had regained his composure he turned, looking at his wife who seemed ghostly in the clean winter light. Her dark hair, slightly tangled, tumbled over slim shoulders; her skin and even her lips seemed bloodless. They stared at each other, man and wife, for a long, long moment until the spell was broken by a roaring from outside, the sound of a car engine idling to a stop. Mike turned again and glanced out of the window. 'It's the police,' he said.

Time halted. An almost tangible dread passed between them, a feeling that they were approaching the moment of truth. For a long moment neither moved nor spoke, then as the doorbell's din ratcheted through the house, Sylvia threw back the bedclothes and made for the door, dressed only in bra and pants.

'You get dressed,' Mike said. 'I'll go.'

She paused on the threshold, then nodded. As Mike pounded downstairs she dragged on jeans, shirt and sweater. Her hands fumbled with zips and buttons as though encased in boxing gloves, her ears strained, wanting and not wanting to make sense of the voices in the hall. She was just buckling her belt when she heard Mike ascending again, and she froze, staring at the doorway, suddenly terrified of the sight of him. He appeared and entered, his eyes wide, his face alight with a kind of fearful rapture. He crossed to her in three strides, gripped her by the arms and pulled her to him. She felt his heartbeat throbbing through her; his voice in her ear was between laugh and sob.

'They've found him,' he said.

9

The taxi driver eased the car to a stop in front of the hospital. Olive and Richard got out, and Olive paid the man with the money Derek had given her. That done, the two of them turned and trooped across the snowy pavement, through the gates, up the drive and in through the glass doors of the grey brick building.

Inside it was warm and suffused with the usual antiseptic smell. They were here for two reasons; to visit Neil and to meet sergeant Glennon. Because Derek had an urgent business meeting to attend in Manchester, and because Eileen had already committed herself to helping Constance prepare food for that evening's party, neither of Richard's parents would have the time to see Neil that day. Richard had therefore volunteered to go and visit his brother with Olive, and then to go on to school afterwards. The two of them had been getting ready to leave the house when Glennon had phoned.

The sergeant had told Richard he wanted to see him urgently, had said they had important matters to discuss. It was agreed, since they both had business at the hospital, that that would be their rendezvous.

Olive and Richard stood now in the main reception area, looking around. According to the clock on the wall it was only ten twenty, still ten minutes before they were due to meet Glennon; nevertheless Richard spotted the red-haired sergeant across the foyer, chatting to an old man with ragged clothes and a nicotine-stained beard.

479

He and Olive walked across, through a crowd of people who were milling around, many of them carrying appointment cards. The sergeant saw them and nodded a greeting, then patted the old man on the arm, obviously rounding off the conversation. The old man winked, touched a dirt-encrusted finger to the peaked balaclava he wore, and shuffled away, his mouth working beneath his whiskers as though he was chewing on something.

'Bodger,' Glennon said by way of explanation. 'He was a friend of Alfie Bessle's. His kind are keeping their heads low after what happened to Alfie.'

Richard and Olive watched the old man leave the hospital, then turned back to the sergeant. In response to his quizzical look, Olive thrust out a hand and smiled warmly.

'Olive Pierce,' she said. 'Richard's parents couldn't make it this morning so I'm acting as chaperone.'

'I see,' replied Glennon. He took the hand and shook it, but his words were not encouraging. 'Well, I'm afraid, Mrs Pierce—'

'Miss,' Olive corrected him.

'*Miss* Pierce. I'm afraid this is rather a private matter. Perhaps you would like to wait in Reception while I speak to Richard?'

Richard's spirits sank; he had been counting on Olive's moral support to see him through this. Before the old lady could reply he blurted, 'Oh, couldn't Olive come too? I mean she *is* virtually family. She's been staying with us the last few days and she knows everything that's been going on.'

'Is that so?' Glennon said. He rubbed his chin, looking thoughtful, then shrugged. 'OK, why not?' He led them down two corridors to a lift area in front of whose doors people were standing aimlessly, gazing at the floor-indicator lights. 'Sister Meecham has very kindly allowed us the use of her office for half an hour,' he explained. There was a 'ting' and the metal doors slid open. To Olive he said, 'After you, ma'am.'

They stepped into the lift and waited for it to begin climbing. As it did so, Richard watched the changing lights, enjoying the temporary silence. They got out on the third floor and Glennon led them down a corridor of doors and directions, stopping at a door marked: 'L. Meecham. Head Sister.' He took a key from his pocket, unlocked the door and pushed it open. Richard and Olive trooped inside.

'Now then,' Glennon said as he closed the door behind them, 'if you'd just like to make yourselves comfortable.'

The office was poky, lightless because no window faced on to the outside world. Sister Meecham had done her best to brighten up the place with prints and flowers, but it was obvious she was fighting a losing battle. Glennon switched on the light, making Olive blink as she lowered herself into a narrow leather-look armchair. The light dazzled the glass on the frames of the prints, hiding the pictures beneath. Richard sat on a wooden chair before a large desk, lowering himself gingerly as though afraid the seat might be booby-trapped. Glennon reached over and lifted Sister Meecham's chair from behind her desk, then set it on the floor with a thump. He sat down and leaned forward, elbows on knees. To Richard he said, 'Right then, son. Perhaps you'd like to tell me just what's been going on?'

Richard was startled by the abruptness of the question. For a moment he was at a loss for words, and looked a silent plea at Olive. The old lady shifted in her seat, cleared her throat to snag Glennon's attention, and when the policeman glanced at her, said, 'What exactly do you mean, Sergeant?'

Glennon sighed. His manner was relaxed, but the gaze he allowed to linger first on Olive, then on Richard, suggested he would settle for nothing less than straight answers.

'Well,' he said patiently, 'I know that *something's* going on . . . and I know that you, Richard, and perhaps even you, Miss Pierce, are in it up to your eyebrows.' He

481

brushed at an invisible speck of dust on his uniform, allowing his words to sink in. 'Now, I'm not saying you're criminals,' he continued. 'In fact, quite the opposite; I believe you to be in great danger. But if you continue to be evasive, then I'm afraid I may have to revise that opinion.'

His words did not quite constitute a threat, but they made Richard shudder nonetheless. The policeman went on in the same quiet, even voice.

'The evidence points to you, Richard, and to your friends, as central figures in this incident. Now we have here murders, attempted murders, people disappearing, a possible case of arson . . . all very, *very* serious crimes. If you're involved, Richard – and you are – I want to know in what capacity. If you're shielding somebody or being threatened by somebody, then it's better you let us know. Things are getting too out of hand for you to keep this to yourself any longer.'

His words hung in the room, their implication filling the tense silence that followed. Richard sat, head down, his cheeks blazing a confirmation of guilt, and even Olive struggled for a reply. She was wondering what the sergeant had meant by 'people disappearing,' wondering why he had added an 's' to murder and attempted murder, thus insinuating there'd been more than one of each. She had just decided to enquire about these points when Glennon said, 'Well?'

Richard squirmed as though the word was a hook and he a fish caught on it. He hunched lower, his face so red it looked about to explode. Glennon sighed, reached forward and gripped his arm, making him look up. When he spoke his voice was a rumble of both dissension and conciliation.

'Look, Richard, can't you see I'm trying to help you? All I want from you is the truth, and by keeping it from me you're effectively cutting your own throat.' He glanced at Olive, made it obvious his words included her too. 'I think perhaps it's time I told you what happened last night, made you see just how much danger you might be in.'

He went and stood by the door. His stance was casual, but his face was deadly serious. In a flat, almost cold voice he told them of Treeborn's murder and of Robin's disappearance, of the discovery of Mo's headless corpse in the room in the King Street house, and of Rusty jumping (or being pushed) through the closed window of that same room and almost killing himself.

He scrutinized their faces as he related all this, noting not just their shock, their disbelief, their distress, but also the way they both reacted (especially Richard) to the mention of the house in King Street – as though the place had a special significance for them both. When he had done, he paused a few moments to allow them to digest the information fully. Then he continued: 'This morning we found your friend, Robin Treadwell.' He held up a hand in anticipation of the obvious question. 'No, he isn't dead, but he's in a coma . . . and so is another of your friends, Adrian Tibbett.'

He heard Richard gasp. Quickly he went on: 'In neither case do the doctors know what has caused this state. Tests have been going on all morning and are still going on now. As far as we know, both boys are in reasonable physical condition. There are no signs of haemorrhaging, head injuries, heart trouble – in fact, nothing that is synonymous with a comatose state.'

He paused again. Olive asked, 'Wh-what happened to them then, Sergeant? Where was Robin found?'

'He was found in a seafront shelter early this morning. As to what happened – well, your guess is as good as mine. He had a few minor injuries, the worst being a rather nasty cut on his leg from which he'd lost some blood, and a touch of frostbite.' He unfolded his arms and held up a finger. 'But the Tibbett boy's case is even more unusual.'

He walked across the room and re-seated himself in his chair. 'It seems that Adrian regained consciousness around this time yesterday morning. Apparently he was hysterical, somewhat violent, and so the nurse administered a further sedative to help him sleep. He slept for a further sixteen hours, and woke round about two this morning.

'The officer on duty at that time was Constable Ledbetter, the same man who'd been present when Adrian had woken earlier in the day. Now, according to the nurse, the constable talked to the boy for a short while, then came to tell her he was going to make a phone call to the station and would return within a few minutes. The nurse spoke to Adrian, said he seemed perfectly fine, and even gave him an apple when he complained of being hungry. She returned to her desk, and a minute or so later Ledbetter returned and took his place by the boy's bedside.

'Now this is where things start to become a little strange. Apparently Ledbetter and the boy talked for a short while – the nurse was at the other end of the ward, but said she heard their voices as a kind of low buzz. After a few minutes the voices stopped and she assumed Adrian had simply gone back to sleep. It wasn't until a couple of minutes later, however, when she looked up that she realized Ledbetter was no longer at the boy's bedside. At first she thought nothing of it, thought he'd gone to the toilet or out to phone the station again; but when he still hadn't returned quarter of an hour later she began to get worried. She decided to check on Adrian, and it was then that she realized he wasn't just asleep but had slipped into a coma. Of course, not knowing what had caused it, there was something of a panic, and for the next ten or fifteen minutes things were pretty busy. When everything had calmed down, it was realized Ledbetter was still missing, and it was then that we were informed.'

Glennon shrugged and spread his hands; he looked a little flustered. 'Ledbetter never returned to the hospital and now nobody knows where he is. And another strange thing is that we never received the phone call he was supposed to have made to the station.'

His story ended there and was followed by a silence, thick as gas, which filled the room. Finally Olive asked, 'Where are the boys now?'

'In separate isolation units on the seventh floor,'

Glennon replied. 'Considering the unusual circumstances, the doctors weren't sure where else to put them . . . and also taking into account the connections between the boys, it was thought they might possibly have something contagious.'

'Can we see them?' Richard said in a small voice.

'Maybe, I'll have to ask. But first, Richard, I want to know the truth. Surely you can't hold back now after hearing about your friends?'

Richard turned away, an anguished look on his face. 'I . . . I can't tell you,' he said. 'I can't tell you why, but . . . I just can't. I'm sorry.'

'Do you know why your friends are in a coma?' Glennon asked softly.

Richard's discomfort increased. 'No . . . that is, I . . . no, not really.'

'But you know something, don't you? Why won't you tell me?'

'I can't, that's all! Don't you understand? I just can't!'

Glennon sighed as the boy burst into tears. He leaned forward, placed a consoling hand on Richard's heaving shoulder. To Olive he said, 'Richard said you knew of everything that's been going on. Can't you tell me, Miss Pierce?'

Olive looked as if she'd anticipated the question and had been considering it for some time. Reluctantly, she nodded. 'Yes . . . yes, I think it's time we told you the truth.'

Richard looked up, horrified. He had removed his spectacles and his face was drawn, his eyes red and puffy. He wiped away the tears on his cheeks with the back of his hand. 'Olive, you can't!' he wailed.

'We've got to, Richard,' Olive said firmly. 'The sergeant's right. We can't handle this on our own any longer.'

'But he won't believe us!' Richard said.

Olive turned to Glennon with a sad smile. 'He's right, you know. You won't believe us.'

485

'Try me,' answered Glennon.

So she did.

She told the story well, in a clear calm voice, neither adding nor forgetting a thing. Her tone disparaged sensationalism, but for all that the words were unbelievable. Richard listened in a state which bordered on near-panic, his hands jittering neurotically, his mouth so dry he could barely swallow. Now and then he winced, as though by revealing these events Olive was stripping away their defences, and frequently he stole glances at Glennon, but the policeman's expression never altered beyond a raising of the eyebrows and an occasional nod. To his credit, Glennon never once laughed nor butted in with a question, but in Richard's opinion this was not necessarily an encouraging sign. He couldn't help thinking that perhaps Glennon was storing up his ridicule and his contempt, that perhaps when the story was over he would unleash such a thunderbolt of scorn and anger that it would shake the building to its foundations.

But he didn't. Instead he expelled a long breath, stood up and wandered over to the wall, where for perhaps a minute or more he stared at one of David Hockney's swimming pool prints with glazed eyes and a slight frown wrinkling his forehead.

'You see?' Olive said at last. 'I told you you wouldn't believe us.'

Glennon turned slowly, shaking his head. 'I haven't said I don't believe you, have I?'

'You mean you do?' Olive exclaimed.

Glennon smiled an empty smile. 'Ah. Now I haven't said that either.'

He came and sat down again. Despite the infancy of the day he looked weary, haggard. Softly Olive asked, 'Then what do you believe?'

Glennon shook his head. 'I believe there's something very weird going on . . . *very* weird. But as for this story of seances and werewolves and snowmen that come to life . . .' He flapped a hand. 'Well, I mean!'

'But it's true!' Richard said fiercely.

Olive shushed him. She did not blame the sergeant for his scepticism; indeed, she sympathized strongly. The policeman's rational mind – forged by years of 'science', by a culture that fiercely defended its tunnel-vision reality – was no doubt informing him at this very moment that he was in the company of two seriously deranged and possibly psychotic lunatics. The old lady knew that ranting and raving was not a good manner in which to set about changing such a mind. The information she had unleashed was volatile as gelignite; it had to be handled lovingly, with sanity and prudence.

'I know it's rather a strange story, Sergeant—'

'Strange?' Glennon exclaimed. 'It's bloody incredible!' He stood up, paced the room, finally came to settle on the edge of the huge desk. 'Are you sure you haven't somehow been . . . mistaken?' he said hopefully. 'You know, maybe someone's playing a joke on you. Maybe this is all some elaborate hoax.'

They both shook their heads. Olive said apologetically, 'I'm sorry, Sergeant, I wish it could be that simple. But both Richard and I know what we've seen. We both know that what's happening is no trick.'

'But it's crazy,' Glennon said quietly. 'Don't you see? You're talking about monsters as if they really exist.'

'They do,' Richard said.

Glennon sighed and nervously stroked his chin. He looked from Richard to Olive, his face a jumble of expressions. There was a desperate kind of humour there, a sense of 'Hey, come on, stop pulling my leg'; there was a plea for sanity, for moderating the details of the story into a structure that the mind could accept; there was a wariness, both of being conned and of being in the presence of the unhinged . . . but underlying it all, deep at the root of all these attitudes, there was *fear* – a primitive fear; fear of the unknown; fear that what this old lady and this boy had told him might just be true. Olive recognized the fear and played on it.

'You said you believed there was something very peculiar going on?'

Glennon nodded warily.

'But why do you believe that?' she asked. 'What has happened that is so out of the ordinary it has led you to that conclusion?'

'Well . . .' Glennon looked reticent as a man negotiating a minefield '. . . well, there's the boys in the coma for one.'

'But you said it was thought they might have some disease, something contagious. That may be unusual, but it's not weird.'

'Well . . . it's a combination of things, isn't it?' he growled. 'It's everything put together. There's something strange about this whole business, something off-key. Take the pathology reports, for instance. This morning I received reports on the Treeborn and Landen corpses.' He paused, frowned, unsure whether to go on. However a raising of the eyebrows by Olive decided him; it was obvious he wanted to get things off his chest.

'I'd better start with the report on the Bessle corpse,' he said. 'As I'm sure you know, the body had been torn apart, divided into chunks, the biggest being the head. Now, at first it was assumed an axe or something similar had been used, but the reports show that no sharp edge of any kind was employed.' He paused, wiped a hand across his mouth, looked at Richard who was swallowing continuously. 'If this is worrying you, I'll stop,' he told the boy.

It obviously was worrying him, but Olive interjected with a shake of the head. 'No, I think we ought to know,' she said. She looked at Richard, smiling in sympathy. 'If you want to wait outside, you can.'

Richard made an effort to pull himself together. He tried a smile, but it was stillborn. Shaking his head he said, 'N-no, it's all right. I'll stay.'

Olive smiled again. Glennon went on: 'The boys in pathology were baffled as to how the body had been

488

dismembered. Apparently the skin was stretched to snapping point, the bones too. The pathology head, Doctor Arain, said it was as though the old man had been tied between two cars which had then driven off in different directions, and that this action had been repeated again and again and again.'

He grimaced. 'The Landen boy had been beheaded . . . but again it seems no weapon had been used. Rather it was as though the head had been *twisted* off. The spinal column was convoluted. It was a similar case with the Treeborn corpse. He was found in a tin trunk. His limbs had been broken, but not severed. He'd simply been made to fit into the trunk, snapped into a more convenient shape like a piece of wood.'

He licked his lips, grimaced an apology for reciting this list of atrocities. Olive looked ill but in control. After a moment she asked, 'And what do you make of these injuries, Sergeant?'

Glennon spread his hands. 'I honestly don't know. I was hoping that by talking to Richard and the others I could perhaps uncover some answers, shed some light on this whole affair.'

'But we've given you answers,' Olive said softly.

'They're not the ones I wanted,' Glennon muttered.

There was another short silence, almost a mutual one, as though they were boiling up a concoction so unstable it had to be allowed to cool every now and again. At last, still in the same soft voice, Olive said, 'Just what kind of answers *did* you want, Sergeant?'

Glennon ran a hand through his hair. 'I don't know. Something . . . something sane, something normal. I mean I can hardly go back and tell my men what you've told me, can I?'

'Hardly,' Olive muttered.

'So where does that leave me, hm? What *do* I tell them?'

Olive shrugged; she could suggest nothing. All she possessed was the truth and her own acceptance of it.

Shakily Glennon swung the chair he'd been sitting on back behind the desk and stomped to the door. Placing his hand on the handle he sighed, 'Come on, I'll ask if we can see your friends.'

It took a while to gain permission: they were told that the two boys were still undergoing extensive tests. It seemed that the doctors were now working on the theory that the boys had been exposed to some unknown virus or poison that was secretly paralysing the brain. To Olive this sounded a rather far-fetched and desperate idea, though infinitely more acceptable than the truth. Being an acquaintance of the boys, Richard was questioned for some time in an attempt to validate the poison theory but to the disappointment of the doctors he could not enlighten them. He declined a brain scan, but promised to come to the hospital immediately should he feel unwell over the next few days. In the end they were allowed in to see the boys.

There was not, however, much to see. Before entering each room, Glennon, Richard and Olive all donned disposable masks, gloves, caps and gowns. Robin and Toady were in separate but identical rooms, next door to one another on the seventh floor.

What surprised Richard about the rooms was their lack of medical gadgetry. He had expected his friends to be hooked up to all sorts of bleeping screens, on which he would see representations of heartbeats and brain activity and God knows what else; but the rooms were bare except for a bed, a chair, washbasin, a wardrobe and a couple of uninspiring watercolours on the walls.

The boys themselves looked to be sleeping peacefully. Their breathing, though shallow, was regular, and their faces, though pale, were still. Richard wondered what the creature had done to them to make them like this, wondered whether they dreamed, and if so what those dreams were about. He shuddered, his stomach revolving slowly: if he ever found out the answers to those questions, he hoped it was from Robin and Toady and not because he was in their position. In Robin's room he turned to the nurse and asked, 'How are they really?'

'Physically they're fine,' the nurse replied. She was a chubby West Indian girl called Rose. 'They're responding to stimuli, their blood pressure and heart rates are normal, their conscious level is constant.' She shrugged, as baffled as everyone by the phenomenon. 'If they don't wake soon they'll have to be catheterized and fed with drips but beyond that there's not a lot we can do.'

They watched Robin for a few more moments, but his empty face told them nothing. They left the room in silence, which thickened as they descended in the lift. At the hospital main doors, after they'd been to visit Neil, Glennon said awkwardly, 'This . . . er . . . this creature you told me about . . . Just assuming that I accept what you've said . . . can it be stopped? I mean, how do we catch the damn thing?'

Olive was putting on her gloves and scarf. She looked out over the hospital carpark, the new thin layer of snow already melting into the slush beneath. She turned back to Glennon as she buttoned up her coat. 'I'm afraid, Sergeant,' she said, 'I have absolutely no idea.'

10

It was either too much sleep or the aftermath of memory that made Nige's head pound. It roused him dry-mouthed and moaning, his hand flailing from beneath the sheets like a plant striving for growth.

He sat up, gasping, sweat sheening his body like sap. His clock read 11.32, and though daylight told him it was morning he had no idea of what day. He tried to think back, to recall a reference point from which he could work it out, but the hours and events became muddled in his mind, days and nights merging into a foggy grey.

He groaned, his stomach gnawing at itself. Losing time made him feel he'd been cast adrift. He sat for minutes, staring into space, while the sweat slowly cooled on his body. As well as his head, his bladder pounded too, screaming out its need to piss. He ignored it for a while, then at last he crawled into motion, unsettled by the stillness of the house.

His mother should be up and about by now, the rumblings of her housework competing with the television. Nige knew she never went out except when his father's car was available, and unless this was the weekend (which he was sure it wasn't) his father would be at work. He slid his legs from beneath the covers, feeling cold yet flushed at the same time. As usual the radiator was on tropical, but he shivered, thinking his hours in bed must have made him more susceptible to the cold. He buttoned up his pyjama top, grimacing at the feel of the collar on his neck, like a clammy length of wet rope, and stepped into his slippers. He took his dressing gown from the wardrobe and wrapped it around himself; bladder and head competing for his attention, he pulled open the door and stepped out on to the landing.

The house was so silent it seemed unreal. 'Mum,' he called, leaning over the banister. 'Mum, are you there?' There was no reply, no sign of life at all, and Nige frowned, puzzled. His bladder stabbed again, his head pulsed from the echo of his own voice. He shuffled along the landing to the bathroom, vowing to solve the mystery when he was physically capable.

The relief at emptying his bladder was so great he closed his eyes and sighed. The piss went on forever, bright yellow and steaming; he had to force the last drops out, he'd been holding it in so long. He rooted in the bathroom cabinet for headache pills, surrounded by the tidal wave sound of the flushing toilet. He found them, washed two down with a mouthful of tap water, then padded across the landing to the head of the stairs.

'Mum?' he called again, though by now he'd accepted she wasn't in. If she had been, she'd have come running to see if he was all right. He started down the stairs, the carpet hushed beneath his feet, the banister whispering as his fingers passed over it. The stillness made him think of Sleeping Beauty, the thorn bush growing around the Castle of Sleep. He reached the bottom of the stairs, the hall and the front door. An anorak, his father's, lay on the floor, beside which, on the Welcome mat, stood a pair of Wellingtons, scummed with brown ice and sitting in a pool of muddy water.

Nige picked up the anorak, tasting dry staleness on his breath. His mother never let them leave things lying around, always insisted everything was hung up and put away. The coat looked dropped in haste, the Wellingtons discarded in a similar manner. Just what had been going on? Why had his father taken off his coat and boots and then apparently left the house without putting them back on again?

Nige draped the anorak over the bottom of the stairs and turned towards the sitting room. He felt queasy and uncomfortable, certain that something was wrong. There was some fracture here, some dislocation in his reality. Because of yesterday's paper he now remembered it all. King Street, the dreams, the body . . . but strangely the memories didn't seem so intense to him now. Sleep, made deeper by the sedative the doctor had given him, had reduced the events merely to images. They were ugly, certainly, but distant, like someone else's memories that didn't quite gel in his mind. He entered the sitting room, saw pink and pink and pink. Everything was as it should be, and yet he couldn't shake off the impression of sleep, the sense of emptiness, abandonment.

He crossed the plush carpet, looked out of the window at the street outside. In front of the house his father's car was parked, an orange Vauxhall Viva, gaudy against the snow. Nige stared at it for a long time, wondered why it was there, where his parents had gone if not in the car. Were they at one of the next door neighbours? No; his mother thought the McNeils were common and the Poultons were snobs. Surely they hadn't gone for a walk?

The image of his mother waddling voluntarily through the snow was unbelievable. Then where were they? Perhaps he had been mistaken. Perhaps they were still in the house. Perhaps they were doing something quietly together, ridiculous though it seemed.

Sighing, he turned from the window, faced the voluptuous three-piece suite, the television, the ornaments, the bookcase full of encyclopedias. The lamps around the room were like giant pink buds with golden stems, the paintings were of tearful children with cherubic faces. A sudden rage overtook Nige, an urge to hit out at the unseen source of his confusion. He clenched his fists, but felt tears not aggression clogging the back of his throat. 'Wimp!' he thought angrily. 'Fucking wimp! That's it – go on, cry!'

He blinked back the tears before they could emerge, drew a deep breath and shouted so loud it hurt his throat, 'Mum! Dad! Where are you?' The silence mocked him, and he felt his anger crumbling. Robin and Rich wouldn't act like this, he thought; they'd know what to do. He shivered despite the warmth and drew his dressing gown tighter around him. He left the sitting room, padded along the hall to the kitchen, first checking the tiny downstairs toilet and the dining room that had been added to the back of the house.

Outside the kitchen door he paused, wary of entering. Despite himself, he still felt affected by his childhood conditioning, by his mother telling him this was *her* room and that he wasn't ever to enter without her supervision. Up to the age of eight he'd been terrified of this room, had seen it as some sort of secret chamber, bristling with an assault course of dangers: sharp knives that could cut deep; tripwires that would bring hot irons and kettles of boiling water crashing down; an enormous white monster called a freezer that trapped little boys in its cold stomach.

Even now Rosemary Figg regarded the kitchen solely as her domain. She absolutely forbade Nige to make himself a snack between meals (he thought this was because subsconsciously she didn't want him to end up like her) and even when he wanted a cup of tea or coffee she preferred to make it for him rather than let him loose in her precious kingdom.

He found himself knocking on the door before entering and shook his head in annoyance. If there was nobody in – which there wouldn't be – he would make himself something to eat and sod her stupid rules. He opened the door and peered around it to make sure it was empty before stepping inside. The kitchen backed on to a small laundry, another part of the extension which had eaten up most of the back yard. Nige could see through the half open door, though, that this was empty too, the washing machine silent, a basket of towels and sheets standing before it, waiting to be fed inside.

The kitchen itself was compact and, though cluttered, neat. His mother kept it spankingly clean, partly through pride and partly through fear of the health inspectors. The rows of tins and jars which contained condiments, beverages and herbs proliferated with flower designs. The walls were painted peach, the floor laid with tiles of a similar colour. Above the fridge sat a shelfful of cookery books, their spines displayed like status symbols.

Nige moved to the breadbin, took out the wheatgerm bread his mother thought would keep her healthy, and selected four slices. He put them on a plate, then looked around, still feeling odd, woozy, despite his sleep. There would be cheese in the fridge and pickle in the pantry, he thought. He took out the cheese, unwrapped it, then walked across the room and opened the pantry door.

There was no pickle to be seen; indeed, there was no food at all. The shelves and the tins had been removed, as had the pantry's floor and ceiling. Nige now found himself staring into a black brick shaft which stretched both upwards and downwards into impenetrable darkness . . . a shaft in which his parents' bodies swung from a single noose.

He stood and stared at the bodies for a long, long time –

at the rope which cut deep into their necks, at their bloated purple faces, their lolling tongues, their eyes which bulged like hard-boiled eggs. He noted the foamy slaver, now dried, which drooled from his mother's chin; noted also the way the bulk of her weight had stretched her neck, snapping the tendons inside, so that she resembled an enormous hog which some joker had dressed in blouse, skirt and fluffy pink slippers. He noted the way his father's upper lip had curled back like that of a rabid dog, the way his teeth had sliced bloody stripes from the tongue that had been forced from his mouth. He noted all these things . . . and yet he accepted none of them. His mind was collapsing in on itself, throwing up shutters, not allowing him to understand.

Softly, softly, he said: 'Mummy?' When there was no response he reached out a hand and tugged at the hem of her skirt. For a moment it seemed he'd roused her, then he realized she was just swinging, swinging, her slippered foot bumping the sooty brickwork with a soft and gentle sound.

He swallowed a boulder of saliva, looked beyond their bodies, up into the shaft where the rope thinned like the point of a spear before merging with the dark. There seemed to be something else up there besides the dark, something large with grey skin like an elephant's hide. Nige caught just a glimpse of it before it melted into the blackness, and immediately it was gone he put it from his mind. 'I'll see you later,' he whispered, and though that seemed somehow inappropriate, he softly closed the pantry door. That done he carefully wrapped up the cheese and put it in the fridge, then replaced the bread in the breadbin. He knew he hadn't eaten for a while, and knew he ought to, but somehow he just didn't feel hungry any more.

He left the room, feeling faint and sickly; he needed all his strength merely to turn the door handle. Inside his head his thoughts were tossing like an angry sea, hideous things threatening to break the surface. He walked into the hall, slippers kissing the carpet, and stopped when he reached his father's anorak. He ran his fingers over the cold material and a shudder passed through him. Then a scream lurched up his throat and threatened to choke him before breaking into fragments. Nige looked at the front door and a second scream followed the first, this time dissolving into a thin keening sound as it left his mouth. He had a sudden urge to get out of the house . . . out, *out, OUT!* He crossed to the door, twisted the Yale lock, turned the handle and pulled. Nothing happened. The door was locked with the key, and the key was nowhere to be found. Moaning, he walked round in small circles like a wind-up toy.

At last he stopped his circling and headed for the sitting toom. If he couldn't get out via the door, then he'd go through the window. He walked across the room, bumping into items of furniture that appeared to be trundling forward to obstruct him. At last he reached the window, his legs trembling, his vision a cloud. He reached up with hands that twitched like palsy and grasped the catch. Momentarily his balance tipped, the room spun, and he closed his eyes, something hot and fevered singing through his veins. When he had stabilized he opened his eyes, looked out of the window and let out an involuntary sob. Behind him the room had darkened considerably, this because the world outside the window had been replaced by perfect, absolute black.

He let go of the catch and put his fingers to the cold glass. He'd seen this limbo before, but finding his parents had buckled his memory and he couldn't recall where. Then a stray thought crystallized: 'Robespierre! The blind man had something to do with this!' He stared anew at the darkness as the thoughts rolled and spun in his head. The substance of the dark, or rather the substance*less* of it, seemed to work on his mind, made him feel that if he opened the window the dark would rush in and drown him. He closed his eyes, tried to assemble the tumbling thoughts, to reconstruct the blind man's role.

It was no use. He could remember nothing. He stared into the darkness again, looking for shadows, movement, definition, but he saw none of these things. After a while he began to feel sleepy as though the very deadness of the dark was sapping him, making him as much of a void as itself. He fought against the sleep, but it persisted, dragging down the eyelids, slowing his mind. In a way it was deliciously comforting, falling asleep here, wrapped in the drowsy honeycomb warmth. In another it was terribly wrong – he was allowing himself to be duped, rejecting the plan of action he knew instinctively he should follow.

But 'Sleep,' his mind told him, 'sleep, sleep, sleep.' And in the end sleep he did, still standing in the same position, breathing with the soft clarity of a young child.

He woke walking along a dark, featureless corridor in which his footsteps echoed hollowly as though he were underground.

He stopped, confused. Now where was he? His life was losing shape and pattern, a tapestry whose threads were quickly becoming unravelled. He looked around, felt claustrophobia seize him. The corridor was narrow enough for him to reach out and touch both sides, low enough for the top of his head to brush the ceiling. A vague blueish light was coming from somewhere ahead, and as his vision cleared he saw its source. A window at the end of the corridor; a window through which a night sky and a glowing arc of moon could clearly be seen.

He approached the window for there was no other way to go. It was waist-high, divided into four by the frame. The catch on the sill was large, painted with white gloss that had chipped and peeled at the edges. The catch was a metal bar punched with holes so that the window could be propped open. Nige took the bar and as though afraid of some trick, lifted it very slowly and carefully. However there was no trick. The window, relieved of the bar's pressure, swung open at the slightest push.

Nige stared at what lay beyond, breathed air that was clean and cold. The landscape that met the sky was rural, fields and patches of woodland divided by stone walls that from this distance looked like the bold black lines of a grid. It was a snow-clad landscape, though welcoming rather than harsh, quiet and still and perfect as a picture. He heard a sound behind him and turned slowly, saw shadows splashed across the walls and ceiling like tar. Within the shadows, just out of sight, something moved; something formless and cumbersome; something that may or may not have had dry cracked flesh like the hide of an elephant.

He turned back to the window, shuddered suddenly, heard his mother whisper: 'What's the matter, Nigel? If you're cold put a sweater on.' He looked at the ground beneath, the five foot drop on to a soft mattress of snow, and calmly he climbed on to the sill. For a moment he stared out across the panorama of field and woods, feeling like a bird about to take flight, and then all at once he was struck by a sense of déjà vu. 'I've done this before,' he thought, 'climbed up on to something to escape from something else, allowed myself to drop on to something that broke my fall.' Somehow that knowledge warmed him, it made him feel this was appropriate, that he was doing the right thing. He sat on the sill, letting his feet dangle over the side, then pushed himself away from the wall.

He closed his eyes a split-second before he hit, and the snow was hard and dry and wasn't snow at all. He was so surprised he fell forward, jarring his legs, the breath rushing out of him. He rolled over, using his hands to cushion the vulnerable parts of his body. He came to rest on his side, panting like a dog, his eyes still squeezed tightly shut.

When he opened them a moment later he was assailed by daylight so unexpected it was blinding. He squinted, a hand coming up to shield his face, until his eyes had adjusted to the light. When they had, he looked to see where he was, and let out a cry of astonishment. He was in his bedroom, back where he'd started, the clock on his table still reading 11.32.

He stood shakily, his legs hollow, stomach like a tinful of worms. Perversely he felt chilled by the ordinariness of the room, by the unexpected intrusion of the familiar into the grotesque. He tottered about like an old man, touching objects to make sure they were real, searching for cracks in the facade. He found none and sank on to his unmade bed, dragging his crumpled dressing gown around him. His body ached, his mind ached; he felt manipulated, pulled apart. He sat and shivered, an invalid trapped within his own confusion. At last he raised his head at the sound in the corridor outside.

He knew immediately it was a dark sound, a wrong sound, but it was fully ten seconds or more before he realized what it actually was. It was the sound of dragging, the sound of a vast bulk either hauling itself or being hauled towards his door. He felt blisters of fear burst inside him, fear made all the worse because the image that had caused it remained veiled at the back of his mind. He ran to his door, dropped the catch, stood panting with his palms and cheek against the wood. The dragging came closer, and now it was accompanied by something else; a tortured gurgling breath.

His throat closed up as the sound stopped outside his door. Whatever had made it was now less than a foot away, separated from him by a barrier of wood and plaster. He listened, hardly daring to breathe, his mind searching for that elusive association. He had gone downstairs . . . gone . . . gone to the sitting room . . . the kitchen . . . 'Oh, damn it! Come on, remember! Come on, come on, COME ON!'

His search was halted by the sound of fingernails on wood, so close they actually seemed to be inside his head. He jerked back from the door, looked at the place he thought the scratching was coming from, half-expecting the wood to crack and fall inwards. The noise was insidious, chilling, like the last feeble attempt to escape of a man buried beneath rubble. Nige backed away from the door as far as he could, stopping only when he bumped against the wall at the other side of the room. He let himself slide down the wall, and sat with his hands on his bent knees. His gaze never left the door, his eyes were rivetted there, attention held by the scratching and the slow, liquid breath. 'Who's there?' he tried to say, but the words that formed in his mouth were soundless.

At last the scratching stopped and only the breathing remained. Nige listened to it, feeling it would go on for ever, sensing an awful patience in the unseen form outside. His hands were gripping his knees so tightly it seemed they were trying to dig beneath the skin. His body was rigid, his teeth clenched, his eyes unblinking. However his bowels relaxed enough to release a little squirt of urine when the thing outside spoke.

'Niiigellll,' it said, the words low and gurgling as though forced through a mouthful of sick. 'Niigellll, open the dooorrr.'

Nige bit hard on his lip, tasted blood and shredded skin. After his terror the pain was almost welcome. 'No,' he breathed. 'No, go away.'

'I hear you, Nigelll,' the voice replied with sludgy glee. 'I hear you and I'm coming innn.'

The handle of the door rattled. Something began to thump against the wood.

'No!' Nige screamed, and felt wet heat flood his leg. 'No! Fuck off! Fuck off!'

The thing outside, whatever it was, paid no heed. It continued to thump, to shake the door handle, its quest for entry relentless. It spoke again, its words running into one another as though its vocal cords were liquefying. Nige could make no sense of the words, but the tone sparked a connection. It was a pleading tone, half enticement, half simpering petulance. It brought to mind an image of his mother swinging on the rope, her face purple and hideous. Image and voice merged, and he realized suddenly that this *was* his mother, this monstrosity outside. Somehow she had escaped the noose, dragged her dead and swollen body upstairs to his door.

She was speaking now, or rather pleading incoherently, her blue-black lips moving, trying to form words around a tongue that was a lolling bag of blood.

He drew himself into a tight ball and began to weep hysterically. He blocked his ears with his hands, but the sounds still permeated. In an attempt to stop them he started moaning, talking to himself, reciting his eight times table. 'Nine eights are seventy-two,' he chanted, and it was in the lull between this and ten eights that he realized the sounds had stopped.

He looked up, the room drowned through his tears. When he realized his bedroom door was wide open his heart almost screeched to a halt. It took a moment to focus on the figure standing in the doorway, the old man in the dark suit and spectacles holding a white stick. At the figure's feet was a huge bloated creature, its purple face fixed in a rictus grin. Nige caught just a glimpse of it before the blind man stepped into the room and slammed the door behind him.

'Mum,' Nige whispered as the thing outside began to moan and scrabble at the door once again. He turned his attention to the blind man, who was striding unerringly towards him. When the blind man was no more than two feet away, he stopped and bent down, nose twitching as though sniffing out his prey.

'Well, well,' he murmured, voice silky as cat's fur, 'we are in a pickle, aren't we?'

'Mr Robespierre,' Nige said. The name tripped off his tongue as though waiting for just such an opportunity. 'Mr Robespierre, what's happening?'

The blind man chuckled and thumped his stick on the ground. 'Nothing to worry about, my dear. Your time has come, that's all.'

'My . . . time?' Hunched against the wall, Nige resembled a savage or a creature at the end of a hunt. 'What do you mean, my time? Am I going to die?'

'Die?' Robespierre repeated and laughed uproariously. 'Oh no, no, no, my boy, you're not going to die. In point of fact you're going to do just the opposite. You're going to live!'

'Live? But . . . but . . .' Nige's brow furrowed with the anomaly. 'But I already live.' He flinched as the blind man crouched beside him, so close he could smell his papery breath.

'I'm a lonely old man, Nigel,' Robespierre said sadly, which to Nige didn't seem like any sort of answer. 'A very, very lonely old man.'

Nige said nothing. A renewed thumping came from outside, followed by a high distressed gurgle. Robespierre inclined his head towards the sound like a man listening to birdsong.

'Your mother,' he said, confirming Nige's fears. 'I think she wants to come in.'

'I know.' Nige nodded. 'She . . . she's dead, isn't she?'

Robespierre smiled sweetly, placed a hand over his heart in a theatrical gesture. 'Alas, yes. She perished some hours ago. However all credit to her for overcoming the disability. Your mother, Nigel, is a remarkable woman.'

Nige swallowed and looked past Robespierre to the door. 'What does she want?' he asked.

'Love,' Robespierre replied simply. 'In the end that is all any of us want.' He smiled and placed a hand on Nige's shoulder. His grip was like that of a bird of prey. 'Before she lays down her burden, she wants just one more kiss from her loving son. A simple and touching ambition, I'm sure you'll agree, though in these circumstances quite extraordinary.'

A kiss. The thought chilled Nige to the core. He pressed a hand to his mouth as though even now she was puckering blue lips around the disability of her erupting tongue.

'I don't want her here,' he whispered. 'Please . . . please make her go away.'

'Hmm,' Robespierre pondered the problem. 'I can't do that, I'm afraid, but I *can* get you out of here.'

'You can?'

503

'Oh, yes.' The blind man looked thoughtful, twirling his cane like a dandy. 'Actually, that's why I'm here. I've come to take you away from all this. In fact, if the truth be known, I am your Guardian Angel.'

'My . . .' The words remained unspoken. Even here, even now, they seemed ludicrous. However, the one concept Nige could grasp – and with both hands – was that of escape. Eagerly he asked, 'Can we go now?'

The Angel nodded. 'If you like.' And in one swift motion he reached up to his face and whisked away the dark spectacles.

Beyond which a world waited.

Nige saw lush green meadows plump with buttercups, a rolling landscape of hills and copses among whose trees rays of sunshine played like fairy children. He saw crystal lakes shimmering, ripe fruit heavy with juice and sweetness. He saw a fairground full of laughing happy people and a huge department store in which everything was free. He saw Christmas and Easter and birthdays all rolled into one, saw vast banquets laid out on never-ending tables. He saw fame and fortune and all its trappings, saw a liveried chauffeur standing beside a white Rolls-Royce, inviting him to luxuriate in its velvet interior. He saw all these things and more, saw his wildest dreams played out beyond the blind man's eyes. They were over in a flash, but Nige experienced them all fully, spent a lifetime of splendour and happiness within a single moment.

And so experiencing, wanted more.

'Is . . . is this for me?' he asked, wishing, yearning.

The blind man nodded. 'If you want it, yes.'

Nige looked again, then turned away for a moment to see what he was leaving behind. He saw fear and foulness and decay, and turned back to paradise, to the blind man, whose face, whose eyes, were the doorway.

'I want it,' he whispered. 'Oh yes, I want it.'

And somehow – floating, swimming – he entered his utopia.

Though he was dressed for one, Richard could not have felt less like a party. Outside his bedroom door the rush of running water and his father's electric shaver punctuated hurried conversations, most of whose sentences began with, 'Have you seen . . . ?' or 'Where's my . . . ?' Richard lay back on his bed, arm over his eyes like an old-time tragedian. All he could think of was that in a few hours time he and Olive would be back at King Street after all – where, he felt sure, this whole awful business would come to a terrible end.

King Street. Only yesterday he had sworn he would never go back. But circumstances change minds, and yesterday, it seemed, he'd still had a choice. Yesterday the Horror Club had numbered four; there'd seemed room to think and manoeuvre. But now . . . now the club had been decimated; he was the only one left, or at least the only one left standing. And as for manoeuvre, it seemed the walls had closed in so tightly he barely even had room to breathe.

He'd learned about the Figgs that afternoon, from Glennon who'd come visiting barely ninety minutes after their parting at the hospital. Richard had been planning to go to school after seeing his brother, but after Glennon's various bombshells he hadn't been able to face the prospect. The sergeant had entered the house awkwardly, his face pallid, like a naughty boy about to make some terrible confession. When he had said, 'I'm afraid I've got some rather shocking news for you both,' Richard's spirits had plummeted yet deeper into the well they had been occupying for the past few days. Hands cupping a mug of coffee, Glennon told them of Mrs Figg's death, her husband's disappearance, of Nige being found in a state of coma. With each new revelation, Richard slumped further and further forward, as though punctured, until eventually he began to release sobs that tore at his stomach like glass.

Glennon waited silently while Richard was comforted by Olive. In the kitchen Sam began to wuff, then to whine as though sensing and sharing their grief. When Richard's sobs had subsided, Glennon filled in the details, his voice flat, obviously affected by all he had seen.

'I arrived there not long after leaving the hospital. The first thing I noticed was the front door ajar, which I thought was strange considering the cold weather. I went in, shouted, looked around, but found nobody on the ground floor and no sign of disorder. I found Rosemary Figg's body upstairs, lying outside her son's bedroom door, and Nigel himself in the bedroom. There was no sign of Mr Figg, and so far we've been unable to locate him, though there is evidence he did arrive back at the house. Apparently he received a phone call this morning at work which threw him into some panic, and he left the office saying he had to go home immediately. His car's parked in the street, but he seems to have just disappeared – and so has that lodger, that blind man you were telling me about. We've searched all the guest rooms, but there's no sign of him or any luggage. In fact, as far as we could tell, it looked like none of those rooms had been occupied for weeks.'

He took a gulp of coffee. Olive asked, 'How did Mrs Figg die, Sergeant?'

'Asphyxiation,' Glennon said. 'The . . . um, marks on her neck would suggest she was hung.'

Richard made a gaggling sound. Olive exclaimed, 'Hung??'

Glennon nodded. 'Yes . . . but . . . well, it's not quite as simple as that . . . It appears she'd been dead a couple of hours before I found her. Where she was hung *from* we've no idea, and we don't know either how she came to be lying on the landing outside her son's bedroom. There are a number of theories, the most obvious being that the murderer himself stayed in the house, or returned to the house and took down the body.' He shook his head. 'Now, why he should do that we can only guess – perhaps to frighten or taunt the boy? – but the thing is, something happened *after* the woman's death which is more disturbing still.'

He paused again, drank more coffee. His voice was yet graver as he continued. 'When I arrived there, Nigel's bedroom door was locked from the inside – we had to break it down to get in. About three-quarters of the way down, the door was covered in rows of four long scratches, like fingernail scratches, but much too deep for any human being to have made.' He swallowed. 'Now, here comes the strangest part. One of Mrs Figg's hands was rigid like a claw, and there was . . . there was paint under the two fingernails she had left. The other nails had been torn off, and the fingers they'd been torn from were . . . were bleeding as though the wounds were fresh . . . None of the blood had congealed at all.'

He shuddered at the memory. Richard moaned and put a hand to his mouth. Olive looked shocked but composed, her trembling right hand lightly touching her chest. At length she said, 'But that would imply—'

'Exactly' interrupted Glennon as though he didn't want to hear her say it. 'It would mean Rosemary Figg made those marks sometime *after* she was dead . . . and we both know that's impossible, don't we?'

'Do we?' Olive murmured. She looked almost sad as she did so.

'Of course we do!' snapped Glennon. He looked momentarily furious, then shrugged wearily. 'Oh, I don't know. This whole thing is beyond me. I mean, corpses that scratch at doors.' He gave a sharp laugh that contained no humour. 'That story you told me at the hospital, I never thought I'd be saying this, but . . . I really think I'm beginning to believe it.'

He let his eyelids droop as though made of lead, expelled another massive sigh, then reached down and picked up his mug. 'Do you think I might have another coffee?' he asked. 'Or something stronger, if you've got it?'

'Certainly,' replied Olive. She made them all whisky-laced cups of coffee, and they sat round the fire, the old lady glancing at it nervously as she again related the events of the past few days.

Richard barely listened; he couldn't stop thinking about Nige and his vast mother who'd seemed immovable as a mountain. He drank only half his coffee, which left a bitter taste in his mouth, but the whisky combined with the warmth of the room made him feel pleasantly drowsy. He started to snooze, the snatches of conversation as Glennon and Olive discussed the situation like dreams within dreams. From somewhere far away he heard: '*So, Miss Pierce, what do you suggest we do now?*' and the reply: '*Well, as far as I'm concerned, Sergeant, there's only one thing to do. We have to return to King Street and re-enact the seance in the hope it will draw the creature back. We have to confront this thing at its source.*'

Sleep felt like layers of dark cloth through which Richard had to claw his way up. 'No!' he shouted. 'No, you can't go back! You can't! You can't!'

He opened his eyes and saw the two of them staring at him, their faces like swollen masks of light. His mouth felt stuffed with cotton wool as he said, 'It'll kill you if you go back. You know it will.'

Olive smiled sweetly and shook her head. Her lips seemed to move in slow motion, not quite in sync with the words. 'No, we don't know that, Richard. There may be a chance this creature doesn't know *what* it's doing, that it's simply trying to communicate. If so, we have to make it understand, make it realize all the chaos it's causing.'

Richard saw Glennon nodding, apparently content with this line of reasoning. 'No!' he said again. 'You know that's not true. This thing is evil. It tried to make you kill yourself, remember, and all those people it's murdered . . . It isn't mindless, Olive; it knows what it's doing. And *you* know too! You know if you go back you'll die.'

He saw the look on her face, saw that in truth she agreed

508

with everything he'd said. However, stubbornly she replied, 'No, we don't know that, not for sure. Besides, what else can we do? If we just sit back, it will almost certainly go on killing. Do you want to end up like your friends?'

At that, Richard fell silent. He was torn by indecision, felt conflicting emotions pulling him this way and that. In essence he knew that Olive's plan was the only way; that if they were to succeed they had to go hunting, had to confront the creature armed with whatever pitiful weapons they could muster. He felt suffocated by fear, paralysed by it, but if they were to succeed that emotion had to be overcome.

'All right,' he said at last, nodding his head and feeling like shaking it, 'all right, we'll go back to the house.'

Immediately he'd made the commitment a wave of nausea hit him, a blackness whose source turned in the pit of his stomach. He forced his lips to jerk into a tight smile as Olive gripped his hands and leaned forward.

'You don't have to come,' she said. 'I'll go back to King Street without you, if you like. After all, the sergeant and his men will be there, so it's not as though I'll really be alone.'

She squeezed his hands and Richard responded, grateful for her tenderness. However, tempting though her offer was, he could see she was urging him to refuse it. 'No,' he said quietly, 'no, I'll come. I've got to, really, haven't I?'

Olive looked at him a long time, but did not refute the statement. At length she said, 'All right, we'll go tonight. After Constance's party. The sergeant and I will arrange it while you get some rest.'

Tonight. The immediacy was terrifying. Nevertheless Richard nodded his agreement. However he said, 'I'll rest in a bit. I want to hear the plan first.'

Olive smiled and they fell to plotting again, unaware of the winter sky gradually darkening outside like mouldering cheese. Olive's suggestion that she and Richard be the only two present in the 'seance room' while Glennon and his men wait outside was met with opposition from the sergeant, whose policing sensibilities were offended by the notion of using civilians as live bait. Olive, however, employing all her persuasive charm, soon convinced him of the advisability of the scheme.

'It would mean telling your men the whole story if they had to be present as well,' she said, 'and what's more, getting them to believe you . . . Besides which, can you imagine trying to hold a seance with a dozen uniformed constables standing around the room? Not to mention the question of how those constables would react if the creature actually *did* put in an appearance . . . My guess is they would either attack it or run screaming up the corridor – neither of which would be conducive to good communication.'

She spread her hands and smiled rather condescendingly. Glennon still looked unhappy but nodded in reluctant agreement.

'OK, you win. But at the first sign of trouble, you yell and we'll come running. Whatever you think, Miss Pierce, you're both still my responsibility.'

'Very gallant, I'm sure,' Olive said, and leaned forward to pat Glennon on the knee.

'And of course Richard's parents will have to be told,' the policeman continued. 'I can't allow him into a situation such as this without their say so.'

There was a short silence. Then, very meaningfully, Olive said, 'Ah.'

'Problems?' Glennon asked.

The old lady exchanged a glance with Richard. 'Yes, Sergeant, I'm afraid so. You see, Richard's parents don't really know what's going on either. If we told them, not only would they not believe us, but they would almost certainly not allow Richard to return to King Street. And so, I do believe it's best to keep this just between ourselves.'

She looked hopeful, but Glennon shook his head. 'No,

510

Miss Pierce, absolutely not. I'm afraid I can't go behind the boy's parents' backs and OK his involvement in a situation like this. If I did, not only would I lose my job, but I would never be able to live with myself if anything happened . . . I'm sorry, but this is something I insist upon. Either Richard's parents give their permission or he doesn't go.'

Olive looked set to argue, then gave a short nod. 'All right, Sergeant, condition accepted . . . but at least let *me* speak to them. I know them better than you do, and I'm sure I'll be able to talk them into letting Richard come.'

The sergeant still looked unsure, so Olive gave him an appealing look which produced a hefty sigh. 'All right, you tell them,' he said. 'But I'll be checking that you've done so when I pick you up after this party.'

'Oh, absolutely!' Olive agreed, after which there was little else left to discuss.

Glennon took his leave. As soon as he had gone, Richard said, 'You know my mum and dad won't let me go back to King Street, Olive. When they find out the truth, they'll throw a fit.'

'They're not going to find out.'

'But . . . but you told Sergeant Glennon you'd tell them! You gave your word!'

'I had my fingers crossed,' Olive admitted, and held up her hand on which the index and second fingers overlapped like gnarled roots.

Richard was shocked. 'I . . . but . . . but what about when Glennon picks us up after the party?' he said. 'He'll know then that you haven't told my parents the truth.'

'Oh, I'll think of something,' Olive said, swatting the question away. She looked at Richard, noted his expression and thawed a little. 'I'm sorry, Richard, but this *is* the only way, believe me. If we don't go to King Street tonight, others will almost certainly die. I know I'm being deceitful, but it is in a good cause, isn't it?'

Richard shrugged.

511

'Well, look at it this way,' Olive said. 'Even if we told your parents the truth, they wouldn't believe us; or if they did believe us, they'd be absolutely worried sick in case something happened to you. They definitely wouldn't allow you to go to that house and they would probably be in as much danger as we are if they knew what we know.' She allowed this to sink in, then continued, 'Believe me, Richard, by keeping them in the dark we'll be doing them a kindness. We'll be saving them a lot of worry and anguish and pain.'

Richard was silent. Her argument made sense, but its method of execution left a nasty taste in his mouth. 'I just . . . I just don't like the thought of lying to them, that's all,' he said. 'Keeping the truth from them, OK, but actually lying.' He was silent a moment longer. 'And besides, what if something *does* happen to us tonight? That'll be even more of a shock for them. And what excuse can we give them for having to go to King Street after Gran's party?'

'Well, we can tell them about that boy, Mo's, murder – if they don't already know from the local newspaper – and say some new evidence has come to light which Sergeant Glennon wants us to see. I'll say the police think one of the summertime stallholders may be committing the murders, which is why they want me along as well. Don't worry, Richard, everything will be all right. It's not as though we're deceiving them in a bad way, is it?'

Richard was silent for a moment. 'I still don't know how we're going to stop Sergeant Glennon talking to them,' he murmured finally.

'Leave it to me,' Olive said confidently. 'Don't you worry about a thing. And now, young man, I think it's time you had something to eat and a good long rest. I don't want you fainting on me at the crucial moment.'

Richard ate some biscuits and lay on the settee. He thought about all the bad things that were happening – the deaths and the comas, having to go back to King Street, having to lie to his parents. He felt sick and depressed and afraid; wished – as he had after Neil's stabbing – that he could just go to sleep and wake up to find this all a dream. Though he had agreed to go back to King Street, he wondered where he would get the courage from when the time came, wondered whether he would be able to go through with it when the house came into view through the windows of the police car. At the moment he could not imagine finding the resolve to fight, pictured himself standing passive and unresisting as the creature did to him whatever it was going to do. He thought of himself lying in a hospital bed, lying in a row with his comatose friends. The Horror Club, club of zombies. *Night of the Living Dead*. In his mind's eye he saw those still white faces, the fourth and last of which was his own, and softly, so that Olive wouldn't hear, he again began to weep.

'What's the matter, Dickie? Are you ill?'

The voice was his mother's and it seemed to come from a long way away. Richard opened his eyes to find the curtains closed and the room illuminated by lamps. It took him a few seconds to remember why he was here, to realize that he must have fallen asleep. He yawned and rubbed the numb arm which had been trapped between his body and the back of the settee.

'No, Mum,' he said, 'just tired. Where's Olive?'

'Having a bath,' Eileen replied.

Richard yawned again and sat up. The small of his back was numb too, as though injected with anaesthetic. He said, 'How did it go today? How's Gran?'

'Oh, fine. We got all the food done, but she's a devil in the kitchen. How's Neil? And how did your meeting go with the policeman at the hospital?'

'Oh, Neil's fine, and the meeting was . . . was OK.'

Eileen dumped the bag she was carrying and sat on the settee. Richard drew up his knees to give her room.

'What's the matter, Dickie? You seem a bit fed up. What did the policeman say to you?'

Richard sighed and rubbed his back. The numbness was wearing off now to be replaced by a tingly throb. He wished Olive was here; they'd planned it so that she would tell the lies and he simply back them up. He said, 'I'll tell you in a minute. Do you think I could have a cup of tea first?'

Eileen stood up. 'Course you can. I was about to make one anyway. Just give me a minute to take off my coat and whatnot.'

She went out of the room just as the sound of water gurgling down a plughole reached Richard's ears. He lay back, relieved, hoping that Olive would make it downstairs before his mother returned with the tea. His face felt hot, his eyes smarting as though he'd been standing in front of a bonfire. He sat up and rotated his back, hearing the joints pop and crackle.

Three minutes later Olive was downstairs, her skin gleaming, grey hair tortured into place with curlers. Richard told her she looked like Hilda Ogden and she gave a louder laugh than the joke merited. Sam lolloped through the door, sniffing and wagging his tail, followed by Eileen with a tray of tea things.

'I heard you coming downstairs, Olive, and so I've made you a cup of your camomile. I hope that'll be all right?'

'Perfect,' Olive said, taking the cup. She made a fuss of Sam, whose tongue lapped at whatever skin it could find. In the time it took to drink the tea, Olive gave Eileen a carefully edited description of all that had been happening.

Eileen was horrified by what Olive told her. Though the old lady related the events as separate incidents, the links between them were plain to see and Eileen was soon asking awkward questions of her son. Who was doing this and why? What had Richard been up to that could merit such revenge? What on earth was causing his friends to lapse into these states of coma?

Richard muttered and squirmed, and shame-facedly claimed to be ignorant of the murderer's motives. He was grateful for Olive, who fielded and glibly answered the bulk of what was thrown at him with the skill of a courtroom lawyer. In the end Eileen, though still obviously shocked and worried, was prepared to accept that her son knew as little as he claimed.

Derek, however, when he came home, proved a tougher nut to crack.

'But you must know something?' he insisted for the fifth time. His reddening face betrayed his exasperation.

'No, Dad, I don't,' Richard said miserably.

'But you must do!' Derek replied. He ran a hand through his iron-grey hair. 'Look, you must have . . . done something, been somewhere. I mean, nobody gets persecuted like this unless there's a reason.'

'No reason can justify the murder of innocent people, Derek,' Olive said calmly.

'That's not what I meant!' Derek said, rounding on her. He looked at his son as if he wanted to shake the truth out of him. 'Just think, Richard, think. When you found the body on Sunday, was there anything else in the cave? Some small piece of evidence, perhaps, something you picked up that might incriminate the killer?'

Richard shook his head.

'I mean, it seems to me that the murderer believes you have some clue to his identity and is trying to shut you up. Either that or this is all some warped revenge because he didn't want the first body found.'

He looked thoughtful, musing over this theory. Before he could begin to pick holes in it and formulate more questions, Olive said, 'Yes, that's more or less what the police think too. Actually they want to collect us after the party and take us to the house where Maurice Landen was killed. It seems there's some evidence there they want Richard to see.'

Richard glanced at his father, saw him raise his eyebrows. 'Really? Well, it looks as though it's going to be a long night for us all, then.'

Olive looked uncomfortable. 'Um . . . well, as a matter of fact, I think they only want the two of us there. Er, Richard and me, that is.'

There was a pause. Derek looked from Olive to Richard then back again. 'You?' he said. 'Why you? We're his parents, we should go. It's up to us to support him.'

Olive spun him the bogus explanation about the police suspecting one of the summer stallholders. Listening to it, Richard cringed inwardly; it sounded so flimsy and ridiculous. He looked at his father, dreading his reaction, but Derek's face – which expressed confusion, annoyance and suspicion in equal measure – had not changed.

'I still don't see why we shouldn't come,' he said. 'He's our son, for God's sake!'

'I expect it's just a case of too many cooks,' Olive replied. She looked appropriately sympathetic. 'You know what the police are like. When they question a suspect, they don't have the whole family round offering advice.'

'But Richard's not a suspect!' Eileen exclaimed.

'No, no, you misunderstand me. That's not what I meant at all.' Olive reassured them that Richard would be in safe hands, that Glennon would drive them to King Street and back, and that she personally would make sure Richard was not upset in any way. He could see that his mother and father still did not like the situation, but were prepared to accept it if that was what Glennon had ordered. They were both, his mother in particular, strong believers in the wisdom of the law.

And now here he was, a couple of hours later, feeling utterly wretched. His parents had moved from the bathroom to the bedroom, and were getting changed, talking in low voices. Richard strained to hear the words, but it was no use; the walls reduced them to an insect-like buzz. He was certain they were discussing his and Olive's deception, was almost positive he heard his name mentioned more than once. Oh, why had he had to lie to them? If anything was going to happen to him tonight, he wanted to leave them with good memories of him, not with recollections of his dishonesty. He felt a lump rise to the back of his throat, felt his nose begin to run, the familiar pricking at the back of his eyes. Before this week he'd not cried since he was ten; now it seemed more natural than eating. He swung his legs round and sat up, whipping his handkerchief from his pocket. He blew his nose, lifted his spectacles and dabbed at his eyes. He wasn't going to cry again, he wasn't, *he wasn't!*

He didn't. He swallowed and had a choking fit instead which he did his best to stifle. The face trapped in the mirror was wan and thin. His mother called, 'Come on, Richard, we're ready.'

Minutes later they were in the cold car, his father revving the engine, which coughed like a geriatric before catching. Olive smiled at him, but Richard didn't see her. He was watching the house recede into the darkness as they pulled away and wishing he'd said goodbye to Sam.

'He's almost at the end of his tether,' Olive thought, looking at Richard. 'Do I have the right to do this? Is the problem large enough to justify deceiving the Gardeners and leading their son into danger?' She knew it was, but she still couldn't help feeling guilty. She'd never deliberately deceived anyone before, had always regarded cheats and liars as among the most despicable of all God's creatures. Even her fortune-telling and tarot readings were as scientific as she could make them.

'And yet look at me now,' she thought, 'telling lies as though there's no tomorrow.'

She bit her tongue on that phrase: if things went wrong tonight, then there very likely wouldn't be. She looked at Richard again. He was fidgeting, staring out the window with eyes that seemed glazed with sleeplessness. She felt she'd virtually bullied him into agreeing to accompany her to King Street, that she'd made him feel guilty and left him no choice. She wanted to reach out and touch him, stroke his hair and whisper that everything would be all right. However she didn't, because to have done so would simply have been to provide him with more empty words, more false assurances. She sighed and decided she had to give Richard more of a choice, had to make it clear that if

517

he didn't want to come then he didn't have to, whatever the consequences.

And yet if he chose not to come, Olive knew she might as well give up now. Somehow she felt that Richard was the key, was gambling on the fact that his presence at the house just might preserve their lives long enough for her to communicate with the creature. She knew, of course, that this was a horribly thin thread on which to hang their hopes, yet it was the only one they had and she was more than prepared to give it a try. She was scared of the prospect of finally confronting the creature, and yet in a strange way she was also excited. The creature's very nature, its capacity for casual evil, terrified her, yet there was an attraction there too, the fascination of delving into the workings of such a mind.

'We're here,' Derek said, jolting Olive from her reverie. She looked up, saw the church hall with light shining from its windows. They got out of the car, each clutching their gift to Constance, and made their way gingerly over the snow-packed pavement. Richard helped his mother, whose high heels were piercing the snow and making walking difficult.

The main doors of the hall formed a pointed arch, shaped like the head of a bullet. Derek pushed the left one open and they stepped into a foyer that was prickly with warmth. There were male and female toilets to the right and a small kitchen straight ahead at the end of a short corridor. The main room, where the party was being held, was to the left. As they stepped through the large square doors the first thing Olive noticed was a banner on the opposite wall whose red block letters spelled out the words: TONIGHT YOU DIE.

She gasped and thrust out a hand, catching hold of Richard's sleeve. 'What's wrong, Olive?' Richard hissed at her. 'What's the matter?'

She looked at him wide-eyed, then let go of his arm and pointed across the room. 'Look, Richard,' she said. 'Look there. The banner.'

'The banner?' Derek was by her shoulder, peering at her curiously. 'What about it?'

'Well . . . don't you see? Don't you see what it says?'

There was an uncomfortable silence, and immediately Olive realized the others must not be seeing what she saw. Richard looked at her, his eyes narrowed in an unspoken question. Derek glanced at the banner, then turned back, frowning.

'I don't see what's wrong with it?' he said. 'Dad and I put it up this afternoon. We thought it'd be a surprise for Mum.'

Olive struggled to find an excuse for her behaviour. She was saved from doing so by the appearance of Constance, who bustled over, glass in hand, trailed by a beaming Albert.

'Hello all!' she shrilled, hugging and kissing them each in turn, leaving smears of lipstick and the whiff of sweet sherry. They returned the greeting and handed over the presents, all of which were unwrapped and exclaimed over. As they made their way to a table which Constance had reserved for them all, Olive surreptitiously prodded Richard in the back. He turned and she indicated he should drop back a little, which he did.

'Richard,' she murmured, 'what does the banner say?'

He stared as if he wanted to be certain of its wording. 'It says "Happy Birthday, Constance". Why? What did you think it said?'

She told him and Richard paled, his jawbone clenching and unclenching rapidly. 'It knows,' he whispered in a strained voice. 'It knows what we're planning to do.'

Olive suspected he might be right, but she tried to look unconcerned. 'We don't know that,' she said. 'It's probably just trying to frighten us, throw us off-balance.'

'Do you think it's here?' Richard asked, looking around with panic in his eyes.

Olive shook her head, glancing quickly around the hall at the dozen or so arrivals, trying to detect something sinister, something different, in faces she had known for years. After a few moments she said, 'No, I doubt it. I think this is too public a place. The banner is probably just a warning – and a rather melodramatic one at that.'

She smiled stiffly and led Richard across to the table. She tried to appear calm and relaxed, but in truth she felt rather shaken by the incident. She wondered briefly whether it was worth even attempting to communicate with the creature (its rather stagey threat suggested an almost child-like cruelty that could not be reasoned with), then she cast that thought aside. Of course it was worth trying. If the ruthlessness was child-like, then it might be due to loneliness, a need for attention, any one of a hundred things. The sight of the banner had been disheartening, shocking even, but the motives of so complex a being could not be assessed in those three small words.

She looked at the banner again. Its words were running now, obviously meant to resemble blood. She grimaced at the tackiness of the image, like a poster for a cheaply made slasher movie. A few runnels of red paint (blood) reached the bottom of the white cloth and began to drip, unseen by all but her, on to the floor.

'Olive,' Derek repeated louder, making her look up, 'I said, did you want anything to drink?'

'Oh . . . er yes please. I'll have a dry white wine if you've got such a thing.'

'Dry white wine,' Derek repeated. 'And for you, Richard?'

'Er . . . a shandy please, Dad.'

Derek and Albert headed towards the kitchen just as a young, bearded man wearing a dog collar and holding a frothing pint appeared at their table.

'Everything all right, Mrs Gardener?' he asked, smiling round at everyone.

Constance looked up, her face flushed, and tugged at his sleeve. 'Yes, thank you, Roger, everything's wonderful. Come and sit down a minute and meet my family.'

The clergyman did so, and was introduced to Eileen and

Richard. Olive, who knew and liked Roger Baxter, watched him, thinking how self-assured he looked, how comfortable with his faith. She wondered if his gaze would be so serene, his voice so calm, if he knew what she and Richard knew.

They made smalltalk until Derek and Albert returned with the drinks and passed them round. Olive sipped at her wine, finding it just the thing to refresh her dry mouth. She noticed Richard staring into his shandy as though drinking it was an ordeal he had to endure, and tried to catch his eye. However he didn't look up, and a moment later her attention was diverted by Constance, who pointed out Major Bowers smiling shyly across at them.

The next half-hour saw many more people arrive, the majority of them between the ages of sixty and eighty, and all without fail peeling off overcoats, gloves, scarves, hats. Because of her proximity to Constance, Olive – as well as Richard, Derek, Eileen and Albert – was called upon to smile a great deal and to return the greetings that were showered upon them. She stared at what felt like hundreds of photographs of someone she didn't know's degree ceremony, which were shown her by a frail, wheelchair-bound nonagenarian called Dora; she was asked to hold a baby named Grant who dribbled constantly; she became embroiled in an interminable conversation about hip operations with Constance and Millie Small, the butcher's wife. When the tide of well-wishers began finally to abate, she was feeling positively skittish, almost high on her own false cheerfulness. Richard's fixed smile had become ghoulish as the parade of people increased, and at one point Olive had winked at him, and had been pleased to see a genuine smile blossom through the rictus.

Now Roger Baxter clapped his hands together and announced that people could help themselves to food. Constance and Eileen removed the cloth which had been covering the long table at the end of the room to reveal the buffet they'd been working on all day. People began to shuffle forward, picking up paper plates as they came, reminding Olive of a queue at a soup kitchen. Not for the first time she found it difficult to associate herself with her own generation; so many of them seemed tired, crippled, infirm. Derek and Albert moved over to the buffet table, arguing passionately about cricket. Now only she and Richard were left, he tracing aimless shapes in beer spillage with his finger. Olive sat on the seat next to him and said, 'Are you coming to get some food?'

Richard sighed and broke a solid piece of candlewax off the bottle in the centre of the table. Flicking it at the wall he said, 'I'm not hungry.'

'But you must eat something, Richard. You've hardly touched a thing these last three days. Come on, the food looks so nice.'

He shrugged, but followed Olive to the buffet table, picking up a plate from the pile. He hardly looked at the food he put on his plate, simply selected what was nearest to hand. When they were done they went back to the table where the others were already tucking in.

'Mmm, these little pastry things are lovely,' Albert said. 'What's in them?'

'Prawn and mushroom,' Constance replied. 'And they're called vol-au-vents.'

'Volley vents, eh? Hoy, Richard, you ought to try these. They're smashing.'

Richard grunted and sat down and began to nibble at a sandwich. As though to make up for him, Olive ate with gusto, surprised to find that she had quite an appetite. The dancing began in earnest soon after the food had been eaten. Throughout the evening music had been playing quietly in the background, but the ageing deejay, a friend of Albert's with the unlikely name of Seymour Weggle, gradually began to up the volume as more and more people took to the dance floor. In deference to the many generations gathered there, the music was a strange blend – Bosa Novas, Gay Gordons and waltzes rubbing shoulders with Bros, Rick Astley and the Pet Shop Boys.

Olive noticed that the banner, now to her eyes a running mess of red, was still dripping on to the floor, and she watched with distaste as it began to drip too on to people who passed beneath it. In particular she grimaced at one old man who continued to dance and laugh with his wife despite the fact that a crimson blob had spattered on to the side of his nose and was trickling into his mouth.

'Now's the time to speak to Richard again,' she thought as the waltz ended and a dose of old Motown – *Needle In A Haystack* by the Velvelettes – began. She leaned over, took his hand and gave it a tug. 'Come on, Richard, show me how to shimmy,' she said.

Richard looked less than enthusiastic, but Olive gave his hand a quick squeeze, hoping he would get the message. Apparently he did, for although he made a big show of groaning protests, he allowed himself to be hauled on to the dance floor.

'Over here,' she said under her breath, and they sashayed awkwardly to a spot that was relatively secluded. Moving her feet perfunctorily, Olive asked, 'How are you feeling?'

Richard shrugged, was silent for a long moment. 'Scared to death. I wish we didn't have to go back to that place.'

'You don't . . . if you don't want to.'

'What do you mean?'

She smiled at a couple who had moved too close to them, indicated to Richard that they should shuffle a little further away. When they had done so she said, 'I feel a bit guilty about all this . . . I feel as though I didn't leave you much of a choice this afternoon, that I more or less pushed you into agreeing to come to the house.'

'Oh no, Olive, that wasn't—'

'No, just hear me out. I decided earlier that I would ask you again this evening whether you were still prepared to come along. If you feel you can't face it, then I'll understand. You see . . . I don't want to force you into something you don't want to do; it has to be *entirely* your own choice. I don't have the right to make that choice for you, or even to influence it.'

There was a long silence following her statement, during which Richard scowled into the middle distance as he mused over her words. The Velvelettes were still bemoaning the difficulties of finding a good man, but now Olive barely heard them, simply moved her feet subconsciously in time with the rhythm. Light flashed and danced on Richard's spectacles like agonized thoughts; he hissed a sigh through clenched teeth. As the music came to an end he shook his head and raked the fingers of his left hand through his short fringe of mousey hair. In a low voice he muttered, 'I'll still come . . . I've got to really, haven't I?'

Olive felt a wave of relief so strong it made her shudder. However she said, 'No Richard, you don't *have* to. That's the whole point. If you don't want to come, you don't have to.'

She watched as he shook his head. 'I didn't mean that,' he said. 'I don't mean I have to come because you say I have to. I mean, well, it's just something I *have* to do. Do you understand what I'm saying?'

'Yes,' she replied with a smile and clasped his hand briefly. 'Yes, I understand.'

A smoochie began and Richard wrinkled his nose. 'Can we sit down again now?' he asked.

Olive laughed out loud, more a release of tension than anything. 'Yes . . . yes, sit down. I'll join you in a minute. I'm just going to the bathroom first.'

Richard turned and began to make his way through the swaying couples. Olive went the other way, towards the door. She did not feel ill, nor was she in need of the toilet: she simply wanted a few precious minutes to herself, minutes in which she could be silent, calm, thoughtful.

She stepped out of the door, closed it behind her, and shivered at the cold breeze that dried the perspiration on her arms and the back of her neck. The swell of chatter, distant now, was like the sea, she thought; bursts of laughter like waves breaking into foam on the rocks. She moved away from the door, across the foyer-cum-corridor on whose wall a noticeboard advertised a forthcoming jumble sale to raise money for the church restoration fund. She pushed open the door marked 'Ladies' and stepped inside, thankful to find the place quiet and empty.

She crossed to one of four washbasins along the wall, turned on the tap and dangled her fingers under the cool water. She brought her fingers to her lips, grimaced at the taste of metal, and then trailed her fingers across her forehead, allowing droplets of water to trickle down her face.

Her reflection in the large square mirror stared back at her, cheeks rosy. She leaned forward to confront herself more closely, but a fog of breath clouded the glass and forced her to draw back. Her knee began to hurt suddenly, a sharp *ping-ping* of pain that receded to a niggling ache. 'All right,' she said, rubbing the offending joint, 'I know you're not built for disco dancing.'

She crossed to the paper towel dispenser, extracted a rough sheet of pink paper, and dried her wet hands. The crumpled towel made a soft dull sound as she dropped it into the waist-high metal bin. Along the wall behind her, opposite the washbasins, were four cubicles, each with their doors shut, from behind which came the soft gurgle of plumbing. Above the sound Olive could still hear the party, though now only faintly.

'Silence is Golden,' she thought, and stood for a moment, enjoying the solitude and the calm. She was aware that if someone were to come through the door now, they would probably think her more than a little strange, simply standing there with her arms folded, but she didn't much care. Her knee began to throb again, and so she shifted her weight on to her other leg. She could have taken a couple of steps back and perched on the edge of a washbasin to relieve her discomfort, but she remained where she was; she had never been one to lean or slouch.

She was still standing there a few moments later when a

thump and a clank and a swirling rush of water from the far left-hand cubicle made her jump almost out of her skin. Her immediate thought was: 'The plumbing's gone haywire,' then she realized that whoever was in the end cubicle had simply flushed the toilet. The fact that someone was in there at all unnerved her a little; she could have sworn she'd been alone in the room.

She waited curiously as the lock clicked back and the cubicle door began to open. A second later a figure emerged, the sight of which turned Olive's legs to string, caused her to stumble backwards so that she smashed the base of her spine against the edge of a porcelain sink.

He was just as she'd always imagined; he'd stepped straight from her most appalling nightmare. A tree of pain cast its branches up her spine and across her shoulders, but that was as nothing compared to the pain that formed a tight searing column from her throat to her chest. She felt as though she were collapsing into the darkness of her body, heard her own blood roaring like a huge waterfall, her heart pounding manically. The darkness began to bleed from her eyes, obscuring her vision, dragging her into a deep and secret place. Her own fear flooded out, blocked her mouth, her nose, her lungs, froze her limbs into so much wood. She tried to speak, to scream, but could only gasp as the world slowed, as it became a stifling prison of ashes . . .

And then Harold touched her.

His skin was black and blistered, his features gone. The smell that came off him was like rank barbecued meat. His hair was a corona of orange flame, his clothes smouldering wads of ash that had fused to his melting skin. The hand that touched her had no fingers; it was a blackened lump, like a joint of meat shrivelled and forgotten in the oven. As he limped across the white tiled floor he left bits of himself in his wake, like a trail of bonfire remnants. His touch unlocked her voice, a strange key that opened her scream.

Olive, whose thoughts were becoming dreamy and disembodied, could not believe the sound had come from her. It was an animal sound, a primitive sound, that chilled the very core of her soul. Pain followed the sound – a horrible, biting, rending pain, like a hand reaching down and ripping her heart from its moorings. Unable to bear it, she let herself go, floated away, leaving the debris of what she had been behind. Her friend, the sea, began to soothe her, telling her everything would be fine. Slowly, imperceptibly, the gentle tide became a chorus of welcoming voices.

CHAPTER TWO

The Land of Nod

1

Wednesday, Thursday, Friday, Saturday

Alone.

That's what you are, Richard my boy. Completely and utterly alone.

Olive is dead; killed, they say, by a heart attack. But you know different, don't you? Your friends are dead too; or rather as good as: soulless puppets of flesh and blood, probably hooked up to tubes, drips, plastic bags by now, which piss-eat-shit for them.

What's that you say? You have other allies? Well, let's see, shall we? Let us determine just how useful those others really are.

Sergeant Glennon. A good man. Strong, brave, kind, loyal. In any 'normal' crisis he would be the ideal ally . . . but this particular crisis is anything but 'normal.' This is the kind of crisis which requires power, wisdom, imagination, knowledge – all qualities which, sadly, the good sergeant lacks.

So you see, Richard? Easy meat. Wheel on the next candidate.

Neil? Your parents? Ah yes, that great institution called *family*. But there, in that very word, lies the Achilles Heel, the soft underbelly which even the bluntest knife can split.

You see, my lad, there is no doubting that you could make them believe . . . but the crux is: dare you even tell them? You know as well as I do that your very proximity to them spells danger. But if you were to drag them in

528

further – and they, like Olive, died as a result of their involvement – well . . . need I go on? Matricide and patricide (even indirectly) are, they say, the most terrible of all crimes to bear.

So there you have it. Alone. Alonealonealone. It's a terrible word, isn't it? A terrible word and an even worse feeling. You have no-one to turn to, no-one at all. No solace, no hope, no light. You are scared Richard; you fear life, you fear death. But soon – very soon – you're going to have to choose one or the other.

So which is it to be? Fight or fall?

Fight? Did I hear you say fight? You hesitate, but yes, very faintly I heard you say it. I have to say I'm proud of you. You've chosen the hardest path – though in truth I believe you had little choice in the matter.

Your body is young, you see. Young and, despite everything, still strong. Your mind? Well, I have to admit . . . that has taken quite a bashing. Lots of scar tissue in evidence.

But scars heal.

Slowly.

If left alone.

And now – now that the decision has been made – it's time for you, Richard my lad, to rejoin the land of the living. No, don't struggle; it won't do you any good at all. I know this place is warm and dark, and yes, even safe, but I'm afraid you can't stay here indefinitely. You're an outpatient, you see, not a resident. You can come here to convalesce, but only now and again; only when you really need it. Yes, I appreciate your problems, I understand all that. But we all have problems, Richard. Existence itself is one enormous problem.

Look, if you're scared take my hand. There, that's better isn't it? Now, take a look over there. See those chinks of light? That's where you're headed; that's the dreamtime you laughingly call reality. I know this is all getting pretty heavy, but just trust me, son, OK? I've done this a million times before.

Now, let go of my hand. Take a step towards the light. That's it, keep going; don't worry, you won't fall.

There, you see? Easy as falling off a log. No, don't be alarmed; just a turn of phrase.

Please, Richard, don't start that again. Look, don't worry, you'll be fine. Yes, I mean it. No, I'm not just saying it to please you. All you have to do is keep moving forward like an arrow and you can't go far wrong.

That's it, you're getting the hang of it now. Do you think you're ready for the big one? You do? OK, brace yourself; here it comes.

On your marks.

Get set.

Go!

'Mum?'

The darkness split into shards, revealing such light that he felt the sun was falling. For long, long moments he was a speck in the heart of the nova; then, gradually, the glare subsided and his world dwindled back into microcosm.

A picture formed in front of his star-spangled eyes: his mother, sainted, her hair an aureole of light. He gazed on her divine smile, then realized the words he could hear as a rumble were her words, spilling from her gently moving lips.

'Mum,' he said again. 'Mum, I can't tell what you're saying.'

The light diminished further, became a window which threw bleached sunshine on to her back. Her face was in shadow, the features smudges of darkness, the skin grey. She shifted slightly and he screwed up his eyes against the harsh rays which stung his vision. Moments later his ears unblocked and he heard her words for the first time. They were nice words; words full of love; words meant only for him.

'Hello, Dickie,' the words went, 'it's lovely to have you back.'

He saw tears glisten in eyes that were dark with fatigue,

saw lips tremble in a face that was drawn with anxiety. She fluttered over him, smoothing his blankets with shaking hands, and made another attempt to speak. This time the words choked her, so she showed her emotions in a more direct way: she lunged forward and hugged him as hard as she could.

Richard held her as she sobbed into his neck, looked over her shoulder at the comforting familiarity of his room. In the time he'd been away it seemed summer had arrived; sunbeams lanced through the window, striping his floor and bed. On closer inspection, however, he could see the snow was still there, though melting now, patches of slate roof showing through the white like an outbreak of slick grey scales.

He said nothing until Eileen's tears had run their course and she'd broken the contact between them. Then, his mind clearing, he asked, 'What happened, Mum? What day is it?'

'It's Thursday, Dickie,' she said, sniffing, 'three o'clock in the afternoon. You've been in deep shock, unconscious for over forty hours. You passed out on Tuesday night when you found out Olive . . . when you found out she'd died. The doctor gave you a sedative to help you sleep. You were moaning and thrashing and crying out.' She broke off briefly, pressed a hand to her face in an effort to control her emotions. She managed, just, but there was a warbling quality to her voice as she continued. 'I've been so worried, Dickie. I thought you'd been . . . been taken. Like your friends.'

Taken? It seemed a strange word for her to use. Richard frowned, and Eileen, noting the expression, explained, 'Sergeant Glennon told us everything when he arrived at the church hall. He seemed very upset by Olive's death, and told us all about the seance and the killings and this awful . . . awful creature. Of course it was difficult to believe at first, but after a while he managed to convince us. Some of those things he told us were . . . were horrible. Just horrible.'

531

She shuddered and closed her eyes, pressing a clenched fist to her mouth. For a few moments Richard was silent. He felt a strange blend of relief and alarm that his parents had finally discovered the truth, and he also felt shame too because they would now know how he and Olive had deceived them.

He put out a hand and his mother took it, twining her fingers with his. Awkwardly he said, 'I'm sorry, Mum . . . I'm sorry you had to find out this way.'

She squeezed his hand, shushed him, leaned over and kissed his head. 'It's all right, Dickie,' she replied. 'It doesn't matter.'

'Yes it does,' he insisted, 'it does matter. We lied to you, Olive and I, and I feel really terrible about that. I'm sorry, Mum, honestly. I wish now we'd told you the truth.'

'Sh, Dickie, sh, I know you do. And it's all right, I understand. I know you were just trying to protect us and I think you've been very brave; your father and I both do. But there's no need to worry any more. We're here to help you now.'

She smiled, but Richard stiffened at her words. 'No, Mum,' he said, alarmed, 'I don't want you to help me. I don't want you and dad to get involved at all. If you try to do anything, the creature will kill you, simple as that. It killed Olive; it killed Nige's mum, and probably his dad too. I don't want the same thing to happen to you as well.'

'Shh,' Eileen soothed, 'that's not what I meant. The police are looking for the creature, and while they're doing that we'll be looking after you. Nothing's going to come into my house and take my son away while *I'm* here.'

She looked determined, but Richard said nothing; he was thinking of Rosemary Figg. As though to mask his thoughts from Eileen he said, 'Has anything happened these last couple of days? How're Nige and Toady and Rob?'

Eileen shrugged. 'No, nothing's happened; everywhere seems quiet. And there's no change in the condition of your friends. One bit of good news, though, is that Neil should be home this weekend. I went to see him yesterday. He can move about much more freely now. I told him about Olive dying, but nothing else. The sergeant thinks it was the strain that must have given her a heart attack.'

Richard nodded. His back felt cramped and he wriggled in his bed to ease it. He was surprised to hear a crackle beneath him like the sound of a plastic bag, and looked askance at Eileen.

'It's a rubber sheet, Dickie,' she explained. 'I had to put it on because you were wetting the bed. I'll take it off again now you've recovered consciousness.'

Richard nodded again, trying not to look embarrassed. He struggled to sit up and was surprised by how wobbly his arms felt.

'Here, let me help you,' Eileen said, and dragged him into a sitting position, plumping up his pillows.

Richard thanked her, grimaced as his empty stomach grumbled for food. He was surprised to find that he had rather a substantial appetite. 'I'm hungry,' he said, a complaint backed up by another burble from his abdomen.

'I'm not surprised,' replied Eileen. 'You haven't eaten since the party, and most of that you brought back up again. You sit tight and I'll go and fetch you something. What would you like? Soup? A sandwich?'

'Steak and chips,' said Richard, 'with peas and gravy. And onion rings.'

Eileen smiled. 'The doctor said you'd be hungry when you woke up – but he also said you'd have a delicate stomach. So you can have a snack now, and then maybe later we'll start thinking about the steak and chips.'

'OK,' Richard agreed reluctantly, then added, 'I'm thirsty too. Could I have something to drink?'

'Tea? Coffee?'

'Coke.'

'Oh no.' Eileen shook her head. 'Coke's too fizzy. You can make do with a cup of tea for now.'

Richard pulled a face, though in truth he didn't much

mind. As soon as Eileen had left the room, he began, cautiously, to think about Olive.

Her death, it seemed, had been the final straw for him, the event that had finally laid him low. She'd been a good friend and a valuable ally, and even when she'd been alive he'd felt pessimistic enough about their chances. Now that she was dead, however, and he was to all intents and purposes alone, he had a feeling he should have been wallowing in the deepest blackest pit of despair, should have been in the grip of the most mind-numbing fear imaginable.

The fact that he wasn't puzzled him greatly.

Of course he felt grief at her loss, felt it as keenly as if she were his own kin. He felt responsible too, to a certain extent; after all, he'd been the one who'd introduced her to this whole sordid affair in the first place. But his grief and his guilt manifested itself not as apathy and depression, but as determination, as a resolve to fight for Olive and all those others who'd died. He would even have gone so far as to say he felt a kind of vague optimism about the situation, felt that he could actually win this battle, if only he could work out how.

He wondered why he felt like this. Was it a false elation created by drugs or lack of food? Was his mind imposing some kind of temporary condition in order to keep him sane? Maybe his perverse sense of optimism was merely a flimsy veil masking the very blackest depression; perhaps anything at any time could tip him back over the edge.

There was, however, another possibility, and one which was altogether more uplifting. He wondered whether, while asleep, he'd somehow broken through some kind of barrier, shed the shackles of pain and despair which had become too much for him. Fight or fall: that had been his choice and Richard had elected to fight. As a reward he'd been given the gifts of purpose and courage, and his fear and his anguish had been banished from his mind.

Though this final alternative was the most spiritual, it was also the one that Richard was most inclined to believe.

534

He certainly felt more clear-headed at this moment than he'd done in days. He stretched his limbs which felt locked with disuse, and his spine which felt rigid as a pole. Minutes later his mother returned with a tray, which she set down on his lap.

'Eat up,' she said. 'You'll soon feel better when you've got this lot down you.'

Richard picked up his spoon and began to ladle the soup into his mouth. He felt an urge to gobble everything before him – soup, bread and biscuits – but he forced himself to take his time.

By the time his father arrived home at five-thirty he was dressed and walking about again. He hadn't been looking forward to his father's return, had expected anger and accusation, and was therefore astonished when his father showed him the same understanding and compassion that he'd been getting off his mother all day.

He relished his evening meal – steak, chips, peas and onion rings as he'd requested, with peppermint and chocolate ice cream to follow – and then afterwards, over coffee, told them everything, from the seance to Olive's death, and felt as though another weight was being lifted from his shoulders in their easy acceptance of all he said.

In the evening, on his own in his room, he spent half an hour inside his mind with Olive. He thought of her, just a week ago, telling him what it was like to grow old; he remembered her little flat which always smelt of herbal tea and seemed to embrace the sound of the waves; remembered too her giving Sam digestive biscuits and gently stroking his large head as he chomped them up.

They were small, private, tender, even banal memories, but somehow, now that she was gone, achingly poignant. He began to weep quietly, wondering as he did so whether the veil was at last coming down, whether the blackness would soon be rushing in again after all.

When he'd done crying, however, he found that the opposite was true. He felt calm, clean, purged by the catharsis of tears that his memories had brought. When he

535

dried his eyes he found it a simple task to relinquish his hold on his sadness, and to reinstate his previous feeling of vague optimism. He was both thrilled and awed with this new sense of control. He felt strong again, complete. Despite everything, he really began to believe he was on the way back.

He slept very well that night.

When he woke it was dark, but he felt so clear-headed, so unafraid, that he got out of bed immediately. Across the room the glowing numerals of his digital clock read 6.44 a.m., the sight reminding Richard of the last time he'd woken in the dead hour before dawn and seen the wolf's unblinking red eyes piercing the darkness.

'Six forty-four and all's well,' he muttered, and sniggered to himself, uncowed by the memory. He trooped across the carpet on bare feet, his legs still feeling a little hollow. When he reached the window he knelt down and ducked his head and shoulders beneath the curtain rather than pull it back. He rested on his elbows on the cold windowsill, propped his chin on his cupped hands, and stared out at the back lawn. Tufts of grass were beginning to sprout through snow that seemed lambent with moonshine.

The sight was soothing, almost mesmeric, and again the memory of the last time he'd done this – when he'd watched the wolf's paw-prints disappear beneath a fall of snow – failed to daunt him. Rather he felt peaceful, felt a sudden flood of well-being, as though for this precious moment all the elements within his own particular universe were in perfect alignment and creating something whole and meaningful within this apparently simple landscape.

So entranced was he by the sensation that he shuddered in awe, and felt a series of warm currents wriggle deliciously down his back. After this he was motionless, staring and staring until he became convinced that he'd managed to halt time itself by the sheer strength of his concentration. The pre-dawn sky, the black silhouettes of buildings and bushes, the white counterpane of grass-blotched snow soon seemed to be all that had ever existed or ever would. These elements filled his mind, *became* him, the snow like an empty canvas waiting for the bright paint of dreaming's pictures.

He slipped back into introspection, closing doors as he went. When he woke later, with daylight blazing through the window, he found himself back in bed. The strange early morning episode was only fractionally more substantial than a dream in his mind.

'It's Olive's funeral today. We didn't want to tell you yesterday in case you got upset.'

He looked at his mother, whose breakfast greeting this had been; she seemed uncomfortable as a child confessing the breaking of an ornament. He reached for the Shredded Wheat, momentarily the only movement in the room apart from the heavy rise and fall of Sam's ribs as he slept. He took out two Shredded Wheat and put them in his bowl. Sam snorted and growled in a dog-dream. Richard looked at him, then back at his mother.

'Oh,' he said neutrally. 'Are you both going?'

Eileen glanced at Derek, who nodded. 'Yes, of course. Are you going to come?'

Richard poured milk on his cereal. 'Yes . . . yes I am. What time does it start?'

The funeral was not pleasant, though only because so many people cried and pawed at him. Constance clung on to his arm like a cripple trying to walk, and Albert looked ten years older than he'd done three days before. It was things like this, the sight of all this misery, that upset Richard more than the flower-decked coffin, which he could not equate with Olive at all.

Roger Baxter spoke some nice words, something about the prospect of everlasting life superseding the earthbound sting of death, and they sang a hymn – *All Things Bright And Beautiful* – as the curtains swished across, hiding the coffin behind a screen of red velvet.

Afterwards it was time for tea and sandwiches,

reminiscences and more weeping, largely from old people whom Richard had never seen before. He took a breather in the bathroom, and there, while washing his hands, he looked into the mirror, smiled and said, 'Good-bye, Olive. Safe journey.' Somehow that simple farewell seemed much more appropriate than staring at a wooden box and singing.

The next day, Saturday, he returned to King Street.

He woke in the morning with the idea in his head and it persisted like a headache until lunchtime. Why he suddenly felt the urge to return he couldn't say; all he knew was that it was something he simply had to do. Maybe, he thought, it was another way of purifying himself, of flushing out the remaining dregs of his fear. Certainly he wasn't about to re-construct the seance alone or even to challenge the creature.

He set off at two, sneaking out of the house while his parents were watching TV. He'd left them a note: 'Gone for a walk. Won't be long. Love, Richard,' but he hoped to be back before they found it. The day was crisp and clear, the air so sharp it was like cold pins in his sinuses. He panted as he walked, his legs heavy, his eyes screwed into a squint against the harsh white sky.

Normally the walk would have taken him twenty minutes, but today it was more like twice that. In Piling Hill the snow was grey, churned by the feet of men and women whose tough, struggling lives were etched into the hard contours of their faces. Richard passed the usual gangs of kids, the usual shabby buildings and areas of wasteland. He saw graffiti, smashed windows, mouldering walls plastered with layers of torn posters like leprosy scabs. He saw a fight outside a pub in which bricks were thrown and blood was spilled, and heard an argument through an open window which was a screeching chorus of obscenities.

Last week, with Nige, he'd felt threatened here, unnerved by all he'd seen around him, but today, strangely, he barely gave it a thought. He looked on himself merely as an observer, as someone who could not be touched because he was not part of the surroundings. He didn't feel superior, merely . . . different. But different in a way that ensured his safety, not his persecution.

Around King Street it was quiet, as though out of respect for the terrible event that had happened at number one. Richard kept his head down, watching his feet, not allowing himself to look up until his hand was resting on the broken gate. Then he mentally braced himself and raised his head, breathing out slowly as he did so.

'Keep Out By Police Order': that was the first thing that registered, bold black letters on a white placard, mounted on a pole and hammered into the ground. Richard looked beyond the sign at the house, his eyes roving over the dirt-blackened brick, the boarded windows, the mess of struts and emptiness that had once been a roof. He tried to evoke some feeling at the sight, some measure of anticipation, anger, excitement, even fear, but to his astonishment he felt nothing at all. It was as though everything that the house had symbolized for him, all its associations with terror, corruption and death, had somehow been wiped completely from his mind.

He looked around, then pushed the gate open and walked up the garden path. The snow had been tamped down with many comings and goings over the past few days and twice he almost slipped. When he reached the front door, Richard tore off a long strip of grey paint, revealing the red beneath, which he absent-mindedly stuffed into his pocket. 'What a shit-pit,' he muttered, then kicked the door so that it boomed hollowly inside like an echo of pain. Smiling to himself, he tramped around to the back.

Here there were more police notices, and much of the rubbish had been cleared away. Richard saw that the window through which they'd entered nine days ago was now boarded up, as were all the others round this side of the house. Almost idly he reached out and tugged at a board, but the nails held it snug to the crumbling frame.

539

He considered finding something to lever the boards away, but then decided against it. The house was empty now, he was sure; he knew with absolute certainty that even if he broke in he would find nothing.

He shrugged and walked away, leaving the yard by the squealing back gate. As he picked his way gingerly over the icy cobbles, he began to wonder just what had impelled him to return. Whatever it was, it had certainly been the right decision, he thought; in coming here he felt he'd somehow exorcised another demon.

He got home a little under two hours after setting off, and closing the front door quietly behind him, sneaked upstairs. Quickly he stripped off his winter clothes, noting with satisfaction that the note he'd left was still on his pillow. He opened his bedroom door and listened, but heard only the murmur of the TV. He couldn't believe that they might not have realized he'd gone out at all. Crossing his fingers, he trudged downstairs, smiling innocently as he entered the sitting room. His father was snoring quietly in an armchair, his mother glancing through the evening paper. At Richard's greeting she looked up and returned his smile.

'Hello, Dickie,' she said. 'What have you been doing?'

'Reading,' Richard replied without a pause and sat down.

Later that evening he received the phone call.

2

No-Time

The boy trudged through the drifting landscape, searching for his name. He was certain it was around here somewhere. He'd had it not more than . . . well, not so very long ago anyway.

He reached up and wiped the dirt from his face. His hand was shaking with shock and fatigue. He stumbled to a stop, looked about him, then clenched his fists and his teeth. He closed his eyes, let out a long breath like a smoker exhaling poison. He stood for a moment longer; then, slowly opening his eyes, he wandered on his way.

'How long?' he thought. 'How long have I been doing this? Hours? Days? Months?' His memory and his concept of time had been devastated, scattered like the debris of a bomb blast so that now only twisted, broken fragments remained. He looked at the ground, at his relentlessly shuffling feet, his Puma trainers plastered with mud. He was in what seemed to be a ploughed field with no boundaries, from which leafless stunted trees sprouted like malformed hands.

He'd seen no houses on his travels, only ruins; and no people, only bones. He'd heard things – cries, screams, wails – but always distant, always muffled by the shifting yellow fog.

He was hungry, his stomach shrivelled to the size of an apple. Thirsty, too, his lips a red carapace of cracks, his tongue woolly as an old sock. He wondered how much longer he could go without food and water, how long before he joined the bones which dotted the ground like macabre milestones.

It would be so easy just to sink to his knees, he thought; then to lie full-length and drift to sleep in the mud. It wouldn't be so bad; a painless passing. Certainly much better than this endless wandering and confusion.

'Hup two-three-four, hup two-three-four, hup . . .'

The boy's head swung like a divining rod towards the sound, the booted feet crunching like gravel in his ears. He was about to call when it all slipped away, swallowed by the mud and the fog – another hallucination, like the sweetly singing girl and the football crowd chanting, 'There's Only One United!'

He swore, flapped a hand in a gesture of despair. 'It's not fair!' he thought. 'What have I done to deserve this? Why me? *Why me?*'

He raised his head and saw something gleaming dully ten yards away. More bones over which a straggly vine had grown, the skull grinning with sick indifference as creepers squirmed from sockets where eyes had once been.

He shook his head, muttered, 'No . . . no, I'm not going to end up like you.' And he walked on, leaving the remains as calcium for the soil, as home for the weeds.

The landscape was level, the horizon, when seen through the fog, constant. The boy trudged on, step after step after step, feeling like a hamster on a wheel, going nowhere.

Until: 'Robin! Ro-bin!'

The boy stopped dead, his eyes widening with realization. That was it! That was his name! He repeated it quietly, claiming it as his own; yes, it sounded right on his lips. And what's more, it unlocked other memories, snapped a few more jigsaw pieces back into place.

Memories such as . . .

At once his euphoria faded. Now that he'd found his name, he suddenly realized how unimportant it was, after all. It didn't help his situation. It wasn't food or water or a map. It was simply a word that could be carved on his tombstone – if there was anyone around to bury him when the time came, that was.

So locked was he in his thoughts, in the disappointing conclusion to his search, that it took a moment for him to realize just how the discovery had been made. His name had not flashed into his mind in a white explosion of memory, it had been shouted – which meant that there was someone close by who'd recognized him, someone who knew him well enough to use his name!

He swung this way and that, searching for the caller. 'Please God, don't let it be another hallucination,' he thought. His fingers, his spine, his scalp were tingling with apprehension. But there was nobody there, nobody, nobody . . .

. . . and then he saw that there was.

A figure was standing about fifteen yards away, squat and dark and plump, surrounded by fog. It was motionless and silent, though close enough to reach in a dozen steps, close enough to speak to.

Robin wanted to do both, but found he could do neither. He simply stood and stared, trying vainly to discern features on a face swathed in darkness and mist.

'Robin? It *is* you, isn't it?'

The voice was hesitant, strained and achingly familiar. It had a flat quality to it as though bouncing off fog. Robin nodded, then realized the speaker would probably not see the movement. Willing his vocal cords to work, he stammered, 'Y-yes . . . it's me, yes.'

The figure sighed and moved closer, tendrils of fog sweeping across its features and away like a delicate mask destroyed by wind. The mask gone, the features could now be seen: eyes red with tiredness, puffed cheeks and double chin, wide mouth stretched into a doubtful smile. The boy extended his hand awkwardly and said, 'Hello Rob, it's me.'

'*Toady!*' Robin cried, and clasped the proferred hand before it could disappear. He embraced the boy like a long-lost brother, conveniently forgetting that he and Toady had never been the best of friends. 'Toady, it's so good to see you!'

Toady returned Robin's embrace; it seemed that loneliness and fear had broken down the barriers of petty rivalry in him too. 'I'd prefer you to call me Adrian,' he said, though with none of the petulance that Robin was used to.

Robin laughed and slapped Toady on the shoulder, which made him laugh too. 'Sorry,' the older boy said, 'I forgot. Tell you what, whenever I call you Toady, you can call me Zit-face. That way both of us'll be careful.'

'OK,' Toady agreed, smiling.

For a while they simply stood there, looking at each other, each revelling in their newfound companionship. They might have stood there indefinitely if a sound had not shredded both the mist and their nerves. They turned as it cut through the fog, a great screaming-howling-bellow, like a herd of rampaging rogue elephants.

543

Toady went pale and seemed to totter on his feet; the last of the moisture in Robin's mouth dried in an instant. 'Maybe it's not real,' he croaked, but Toady shook his head. Huge pounding steps began to approach, like a thousand-strong army marching in unison.

'Come on,' Toady said, and rushing forward, grabbed Robin's hand. The boys began to flounder through the mud, their feet slapping like flippers, their breathing ragged. Behind them a huge snuffling breath could now be heard, then another bellow, this one full of rage or triumph. Robin risked a look behind him and saw something vast and dark blotting out the dim orangey-brown twilight.

'It's right behind us!' he yelled, and they doubled their pace, slipping and sliding as though in a nightmare. The hands which linked them were slick with sweat, but they kept the bond tight, and so prevented one another from tumbling headlong in the mud.

They ran for what seemed like hours, the sounds of pursuit fading beneath the smothering, pounding rush of their own bodies. At last Toady panted, 'Hang on . . . hang on . . . can't run . . . any more,' and they stopped, the younger boy bending double, clutching his stomach as though about to throw up. Robin listened, but the Howler seemed to have gone; silence had enfolded them once more. They stood, regaining their breath, until finally Toady straightened and murmured, 'Rob . . . where are we?'

A silence fell between them, for it was a question that evoked fear. Both had heard of limbo and purgatory, and both had secretly toyed with the notion that this was the place.

'What's the last thing you remember?' Robin asked, folding his arms tightly around him.

'I remember . . . being in a hospital bed . . . talking to a policeman called . . . Ledbetter.' Toady tailed off, shrugged. 'That's all.'

'And you woke up here?'

'Yes. I was in a bush. There was a branch sticking in my back. I remember thinking someone was poking me.'

Robin nodded. 'I remember being chased by some little black things . . . trolls or something, I don't know. Then I remember being on a beach – Starmouth I think it was – and there was a girl there . . . a beautiful girl . . .' His eyes glazed, then he blinked and shrugged. 'I dunno . . . Maybe that bit was all a dream. Anyway, I must've been asleep 'cos when I woke up I was here.'

'But where's here?' Toady wanted to know.

Robin shrugged, then stiffened as a thought occurred to him. 'Hang on a minute.'

'What's the matter?'

'Well, if you were in a hospital bed like you said you were, how come you're not wearing pyjamas?'

'I . . .' Toady looked down at himself and saw that it was true; he was now wearing his white Fair Isle sweater, faded jeans, and – strangest of all – his school shoes, which were in a dreadful state. 'I don't know,' he said lamely. 'I suppose I . . . I must have got dressed somewhere without realizing it.'

Robin scowled and sighed, frustrated by the mystery. Looking around, he noted that during their flight from the Howler, the colours of the landscape had subtly changed. The fog was now green, the twilight beyond a purplish-blue. The mud, however, was the same – black and clinging – as were the scrappy clumps of vegetation, and the bones which provided the only landmarks.

They began walking, heading towards the distant blurred horizon. They didn't discuss in which direction they should go, for there was only forward, nothing more. Their conversation as they walked was stilted, dealing only with practicalities, though both ached to put their scrambled emotions into words.

Gradually – very, very gradually – the landscape itself began to change. The vegetation, though still stunted and sickly, became more abundant. Rather than standing like lone scarecrows, bushes began to cluster together in groups, some even possessing a pitiful shawl of spiky leaves. Weeds and vines straggled in the mud, in places so thick that they formed a tatty carpet. And the mist began to thin out, breaking apart like cigarette smoke in the open air.

'Look!' Robin croaked suddenly and grabbed Toady by the arm. With his other hand he pointed. 'What's that?'

Toady sighed and dragged up his head with an effort. 'What?' he said with a hint of his old irritability.

'Over there, can't you see? It looks like . . . like trees or something.'

Toady rubbed his eyes and peered through the muggy haze. He saw that the horizon – so far a flat depressing plane of mud – now seemed different, bulkier, somehow higher. He glanced at Robin, saw the sparkle in his eyes, and the trace of a smile touched his lips.

'I think you're right,' he said cautiously. 'I think it is trees.'

Robin nodded eagerly. Both boys began to stumble forward. They were aware that trees indicated growth and fertility, which could only be achieved through nourishment – in other words, water. Apart from that the very sight of the trees was a psychological boost; it meant that the frightening monotony was not constant after all.

The horizon, however, was further away than it appeared – so far, in fact, that a crawling doubt began to surface in Robin's mind. 'It's a mirage,' he thought. 'We're going mad, seeing things that aren't really there.' Then, as though to prove him wrong, the horizon suddenly rushed forward and they *were* there.

And things were even better than they'd hoped. Instead of simply a line of trees, there was a whole forestful of them. True, they were not visually appealing – tall and black with fat gnarled trunks and branches that clutched dark handfuls of leaves – but at least they were real, at least they existed, and for the moment that was all that seemed to matter.

Robin moved forward, noting as he did so that the forest

was in fact man-made. The trees were regimented, though the rows were staggered so that nothing could be seen through the gaps but a seemingly impenetrable wall of thickly-grooved bark. He reached the first of the trees and placed his palms flat against it as though to push it over, and then suddenly he recoiled, a look of disgust crossing his face.

'*Urgh!*' he said, and held his hands out, palms spread. 'It's all cold and slimy. Like a fish.'

Toady was more cautious. He stepped forward and tested the wood with a single forefinger. 'Smells like a fish too,' he said, holding the finger to his nose. He took a handkerchief from his pocket, wiped the offending digit, then passed it to Robin. 'Here,' he said, 'use this, then chuck it away.'

Robin did so, and the two boys stood and looked at each other, Robin raising his eyebrows in silent appraisal.

'We'll have to go through,' he said. 'We can't afford to turn our backs just because the place stinks a bit.'

'Yeah,' Toady agreed. He flipped a thumb at the trees. 'You go first, I'll follow.'

'Oh, thanks, pal,' Robin said heavily, but set off, taking care not to brush the trees as he passed between them.

The forest was dark, the fishy odour almost overpowering. The boys felt dwarfed and insignificant as they moved among the silent black giants. After a while, however, the trees began to thin out, became healthier, smaller, younger, as though whoever had planted them had started at the outside and worked inwards. Robin wondered what they would find when they reached the centre of this dismal place – perhaps merely a ceremonial sapling, struggling for growth.

The vegetation became thicker. Bushes began to spring up in the gaps between the trees, tough and brown and sinewy, bristling with thorns that were hooked and serrated as shark's teeth. Robin negotiated one such bush, then turned back to give Toady a hand. 'Fucking things,' Toady muttered, sucking a finger from which blood was welling. Together the boys scanned the way ahead.

It consisted of a jumble of sorry-looking trees, more shark's teeth bushes, and increasingly uneven terrain and the ever-present mud. One advantage was that the fog had now all but dispersed, though wisps could still be seen here and there, hovering in branches like cobwebs.

'Look there,' Robin said. 'Those trees look different from the rest. Let's go and see.'

The trees in question were clustered together as though for safety. They were silvery, more upright than their neighbours, and they seemed to glisten in the dim light like giant solid slug-trails reaching into the sky. Their whip-thin branches formed graceful arcs in the air, bowed beneath buds as heavy and pendulous as a colony of plump yellow bats.

No. Not buds. More like . . . more like . . .

'It's fruit!' Toady exclaimed, and clapped his hands delightedly. He rushed forward and uncharacteristically launched himself at the nearest tree. However the branches were high – ten or twelve feet off the ground – and he was carrying too much weight. His hand flailed at empty air and he landed with a thump in the mud.

'Here, let me,' Robin said and stepped forward. He was taller than Toady, his frame considerably more athletic. He took a short run, then sprang high, fingers stretching for their prize. His hand closed around a piece of the fruit which his downward motion plucked from the tree.

He flinched from the branch's whiplash, then turned to Toady and grinned. 'Here, try this,' he said, before leaping again and snatching another piece of fruit for himself.

Clutching their manna, they stood facing each other, jubilant as bank robbers after a successful heist. They lifted their arms, brought the fruit to their lips and simultaneously took a large and ravenous bite.

'*Arghhh!*' yelled Robin and spat out his mouthful a split-second before Toady did the same. Beneath the fruit's tough skin was a creamy yellow pus which smelled of

548

vomit and tasted worse. Robin spat and spat until he could spit no more, and still the taste remained. 'It's like eating a boil,' he gagged, and felt his stomach contract, trying to expel food that wasn't there.

Toady's face was white tinged with green. He was staring fixedly at his piece of dropped fruit. 'There's maggots in mine,' he murmured, and clapped a hand over his mouth, his Adam's apple quivering like a trapped bird.

Robin looked – and his stomach gave the greatest lurch of all. There were indeed maggots in Toady's fruit, bright red maggots. Dozens of them were squirming and writhing with blind, senseless life, like animated viscera in pulped creamy innards.

'Oh shit,' he groaned, and drawing back his arms, threw his own piece of fruit at a tree. It hit dead-centre, spattering sap in all directions, and also releasing something like a fat brown worm, which twisted briefly in the air and then, astonishingly, straightened out like an arrow and flew away.

'Did you see that?' Robin gasped, turning to his friend. One look at Toady's face gave him his answer. Nauseated, he looked out over the diseased orchard, wondering what other delights lurked beneath golden skin. It reminded him of the Lucky Dip Machine on Starmouth's seafront – Each Plastic Egg Has A Prize Inside – only instead of toy whistles and spiders and bubblegum there was corruption and filth and decay.

'Come on,' said Toady, his voice faint, and began to walk away. Despite himself, Robin took one more look at the maggot-infested fruit and the stain on the tree; then shuddered and followed his friend.

The ground grew rockier, more hilly; the trees began to crowd in again. For a while the incident at the orchard muted the boys' appetites, but after half an hour of trudging, scrambling progress they began to feel hungry once more.

It occurred to Robin as they blundered through shrubbery and clambered over exposed roots that they

549

were now in a real forest, that the manufactured, regimented outskirts had been left far behind. Perhaps the final man-made contribution had been that vile orchard, he thought. He looked up, his reverie broken, as Toady yelled, '*Water!*'

The younger boy was pointing excitedly to a gouge in the hillside from which water flowed, swelling to a stream which cut a determined groove through the forest floor. Robin and Toady scrambled down to the stream, clutching at roots to stop themselves falling down the muddy bank. The water seemed clear enough, but neither risked taking a drink, though Toady squatted and dabbled his fingers and washed his face.

'Do you think it's fresh?' he asked, water dripping from his chin.

'Dunno,' Robin replied, 'I wouldn't bank on it.'

They stood, wistful as children at a sweet shop window, following the course of the stream with their eyes. It disappeared into a tangle of dense undergrowth and overhanging trees, the occasional dam forcing the water to spread and form marshland over which insects hovered.

'Come on,' Robin said, 'let's follow it. At least then we won't get lost.'

Toady rose, holding the small of his back, and they trudged on. The going was tough, the vegetation teeming, the ground boggy underfoot. Insects harangued them continually, and one species in particular – like tiny translucent crane-flies – had a bite like needles. At certain points the course of the stream seemed to stop altogether, seemed to span out into so much marshland that nothing was left to carry on. However a little exploration always unearthed the main artery again, normally a trickle that grew as it flowed, as though gaining confidence.

The minutes stretched on, became an hour, then two, then three. The boys' legs grew heavier, their appetites raged. They became snappish and irritable, Toady more like his old self with each minute that passed. Robin found himself wishing they were back on the mud-flats again: at least there the ground had been firmer and there hadn't been these fucking insects injecting them with God-know's-what.

At last they came to a hump-backed bridge beneath which the water gurgled into blackness. It was squat and primitive, constructed messily of uneven grey rock and crumbling cement, but it was neverthless an uplifting sight. It provided evidence that others had been here before them, that they weren't wandering through an uncharted wilderness. They climbed on to the bridge and sat down, their backs resting against the raised stone sides. What was better than the bridge itself was the road that branched off from it, left and right, for roads had to lead somewhere, didn't they? To the right, the road (in reality little more than a dirt-track) led upwards in a meandering fashion before it was swallowed by trees; to the left it dipped and was quickly obscured by undergrowth. Already Robin had mentally resolved that once they'd had a rest they would follow the right hand path. Perhaps this was due to some instinct that up was better than down, but whatever the reason, he felt sure the decision was the right one.

But, for the moment, rest.

He sank, yawning, on to the bridge beside Toady, and massaged his face with the heels of his hands. Mud and sweat plastered his clothes to him; his trainers felt like iron boots. Beside him Toady unlaced his Clark's school shoes and upended them to release bits of wood and gravel. Robin let his head fall back, filling his eyes with twilight, allowing his gaze to soar above the scraggy canopy of trees for the first time in hours. He felt giddy, as though he was looking down from the top of a skyscraper, and he clutched the rough ground beneath him. His eye was drawn to a plume of mist dissecting the sky like a scrawny wraith. He'd been watching the mist for a minute or more before the truth of what it really was hit him.

'Ade,' he said, and sensed the boy turn towards him, alerted by the urgency in his voice. 'Ade, look over there, in the sky. Just above that dip in the trees. There's smoke.'

Robin pointed and turned to Toady, who was scowling as he peered into the gloom. At last Toady saw the smoke and rolled his eyes, unimpressed. 'Oh yeah,' he said, 'so what?'

'So what?' exclaimed Robin. 'What do you mean, so what? If there's smoke there must be a fire. And if there's fire, there are very probably people.'

He waited for this to sink in. Toady looked at the smoke again, then back at Robin. At last, his voice tired but excited, he said, 'Oh yeah. I see what you mean.'

'Well, come on,' Robin said, 'let's go and have a look, shall we?' He struggled to his feet and waited, hands on hips, for Toady to comply.

Toady dragged on his muddy shoes and began to lace them up. 'Hang on, Rob,' he called as Robin impatiently set off along the right-hand path. A moment later he heaved himself to his feet and wheezed up the path after his friend. Robin grinned and clapped him on the shoulder, as though the smoke meant they were already saved.

For a while the path took them upwards, elevating them to the highest ridge of the valley, the occasional twinkle of water far below to their left. The path was relatively clear of undergrowth, though having to trudge uphill took its toll on them both. At one point Toady's ankle turned on a loose stone and he went down with a cry of pain. He would probably have stayed there too, had Robin not turned back and hauled him to his feet.

They took a short breather after this whilst they surveyed the damage. Toady's jeans were torn at the knee and there was some blood, but the cuts were only superficial. The sight of the ripped jeans prompted a memory in Robin and he looked down at his own left leg. For some reason (he couldn't recall why) he expected to see *his* jeans sliced cleanly open. However, they were intact, as was the limb beneath. Nevertheless an unsettling half-memory popped like a bubble in his head.

'Tentacle,' he muttered, not quite understanding why. Toady gave him a quizzical look, but was too tired to push for an explanation. After a while they dragged themselves to their feet and carried on.

They were both thankful when the path began to dip, even though the smoke was temporarily lost behind a jostling screen of black trees. As though emboldened by the dark, the vegetation on this part of the path was thicker, vines inching across like organic trip-wires. Robin prayed for the smoke to be something worthwhile and not simply some localized and inexplicable forest fire. He felt he'd pushed his body to its limits; it was a block of pain cased in fatigue.

After ten or fifteen minutes of trudging progress, the path suddenly widened, the trees appearing to draw back like respectful doormen. Instinctively the boys slowed, cautious of this new development, their eyes darting left and right. Robin peered through the gloom, saw what looked like a treeless plain ahead, a carpet of scrubby grass. He moved forward warily, Toady a few steps behind . . .

. . . and they emerged into a clearing like a Roman arena, in the centre of which was a cottage direct from the pages of a fairytale.

'Wow,' Robin whispered, feeling Toady's breath on his neck. The cottage was a squat cylinder shaped rather like a pork pie, the roof a dome of yellow thatch. The walls were bright orange, the windows black portholes, the door enclosed in a bower of pink roses. A knee-high picket fence, also painted orange, surrounded a neat vegetable garden through the centre of which a path led from a tiny gate. There was a well behind the cottage, every bit as quaint as the building itself, and from the cottage's stubby chimney smoke poured, the beacon that had drawn them here.

Neither boy knew what to say or do; they just stood and stared. Finally Toady muttered in a low voice, 'I wonder where they bought their paint from.' It was unlike Toady to make a quip like this, and even more unlike him to start giggling so hard a bubble of snot shot out of his nose.

'Woolworths,' Robin said, and became convulsed with giggles himself. They sniggered and shook like hyenas, more than a trace of hysteria in the sound. However their laughter died abruptly when the door of the cottage opened and a figure came out.

Or rather, *squeezed* out, for the door of the cottage was small – perhaps five feet high by two feet wide – and the figure enormously fat. It was a woman, they both saw, dressed in a floor-length dowdy blue dress, a white apron and a frilly bonnet tied beneath the chin (or rather, chins). In one podgy hand she clutched a wooden spoon, and from her mouth jutted a clay pipe. Though fat, she was tiny – perhaps four feet high – but it was not this, nor was it even her pipe, that constituted her most unusual feature. What would have made her stand out in a crowd – *really* stand out – was her beard: thick, straggly, a brilliant lime-green, it cascaded over her enormous bosom like a nest of some exotic bird.

Robin and Toady stood and gaped, not knowing whether to laugh or run. The bearded woman waddled beneath the bower, then turned to look at them, hands on vast hips. 'You boys,' she shouted suddenly, her voice high and piping as a midget's. 'You boys! Come here at once!'

Toady and Robin looked at one another, each waiting for the other to take the initiative. However both were reluctant, and the result was that they stayed where they were. In one sense they both felt a heady, almost euphoric sense of relief at finding even this degree of civilization, yet on the other they felt reluctance, trepidation, even fear at the thought of approaching this fearsome-looking woman and her gingerbread house.

'Well, come on!' she snapped, the pipe swivelling from one side of her mouth to the other, blue smoke puffing from it in little clouds. 'I haven't got all day, you know. Either you come of your own accord or I'll have to ask Ranulf to drag you!'

'Ranulf?' Toady whispered nervously into Robin's ear. 'Who's Ranulf, do you think?'

'*I* am Ranulf,' said a voice behind them.

The boys spun in the muddy grass, like weather-cocks whipped by a sudden wind. Toady gave a shriek of fear, and would have fallen to his knees in the mud had Robin not held him upright.

Ranulf was a dog, a huge black dog, his straggly coat decorated with multi-coloured twists of ribbon. He had the look of an Irish wolfhound, but was the size of a small horse, the top of Robin's head coming roughly to the level of his throat. Despite the cultured voice that had emanated from his vocal chords, he looked mean and fierce – small dark eyes, long yellow teeth, slaver collecting on his jowls. He stared at the boys implacably, steam rising from his nostrils as he breathed, paws the size of joints of meat planted in the ground.

Toady cowered behind Robin, gripping his upper arm so hard he felt sure it would bruise. 'What are we going to do,' the fat boy wailed. 'Rob, what are we going to do?'

'I suggest you go to the cottage,' Ranulf murmured reasonably. 'The Lady Liana has a most dreadful temper when roused.'

'The Lady . . .?' Robin said in a weak voice.

'Liana. An unlikely name, I know, but things weren't always so humble as this. Once upon a time the name rather suited her.'

'What happened?' Robin asked (part of his mind still rejected this scenario. Talking to a dog? What crap!).

'Oh, you know, the usual thing: revolution, forced abdication, annexation by the Zad. Liana and I came out of the Treaty of Idrias rather lightly as it happens . . .' he leant forward, lips curling back in a startling grin '. . . apart from that awful beard, of course.'

'Will you boys come here!'

Liana was now almost apoplectic with rage. The dough-like flesh above her green beard had deepened to a rich crimson. Ranulf looked at her, sighed, and said to the boys, 'You'd better do as she asks. I'll lead, you follow.'

'But why does she want us?' Robin asked nervously, stepping back as the dog's matted muscled flank passed six inches from his nose.

'She wants to feed you, that's all,' Ranulf said. 'It's her job, you see. Five Thousand Mouths Must Be Filled By The Results Of Your Toils As Penance For The Folly Of Arrogance. It's all in the Treaty.'

Bemused, the boys followed him towards the cottage, watching as he pawed open the orange gate and padded up the path. Flanking them were rows of all types of vegetables: carrots, turnips, cabbages, peas, cauliflower, squash, broccoli, even ears of corn. Some of the things had no right to be growing in such a climate and in soil that produced only blighted trees and lowly bushes, but growing they were, and not only growing but flourishing, all prime examples of their type.

'About time!' the bearded lady snapped in her peculiar sing-song voice. 'The way you dawdle, it's a wonder the Crowl hasn't got you.'

'The Crowl?' Robin repeated, but the woman had already turned and passed beneath the bower. A casual raising of the brows from Ranulf indicated that the boys should do the same.

The Lady Liana (Robin still could not get over the inappropriateness of the name) paused to bang the ash from her pipe on the wall of the house, then squeezed inside, assisted by a gentle head-butt from Ranulf. The dog stepped back as the boys followed, making no move to enter the cottage himself.

'Liana will take care of your needs,' he called. 'I'm off to dig for Wergles.' He turned and galloped up the path, leaping over the gate with the grace of a prize racehorse.

Robin, on the cottage's threshold, looked at Toady, whose face held a confused, slightly vacant expression. 'Come on, Ade,' he said, and squeezed his friend's arm reassuringly. Toady's eyes drifted back into focus and a fleeting smile appeared on his face. Robin leading, they entered the house.

They found themselves in a low-ceilinged kitchen dominated by a dark wood table. The walls were white, the floor tiled in reddish-brown. A cooking range of black metal took up most of one wall, in the heart of which a fire blazed, warming the room. There were shelves stacked with jars of herbs, a wooden tub full of muddy water and vegetable peelings. Hooks jutted from the wall from which kitchen implements hung, gleaming like weaponry.

'Well, come on, sit down,' Liana said, dragging two stools from beneath the table. The boys did so tentatively, watching as she placed two wooden bowls before them. 'I expect you're hungry,' she piped, bustling over to the cooking range, a comment which drew murmurs of assent from them both. Snatching a cloth from a hook, she heaved the vault-like oven door open, releasing a rolling wave of heat heavy with the smell of freshly-baked bread.

Robin had thought it was only in cartoons and among animals that mouths watered in anticipation of food, but now he felt his mouth filling with saliva and had to swallow quickly before it dribbled down his chin. His stomach danced a jig as Liana drew out a tray on which sat a mound of bread, golden brown, the size and shape of half a basket-ball. She placed the tray in front of the boys, then turned back to the cooking range again.

Toady and Robin leaned forward, breathing in the smell with rapt expressions. Liana folded the cloth she was holding into a wad and wrapped it round the handle of a pan that was bubbling on the range. She lifted the pan with both hands and carried it to the table. Carefully she tilted the pan over the bowls, pouring out its contents – brown and thick – and unleashing a new smell to swamp that of the bread.

'Well, go on,' she urged as she placed the barely empty pan back on the range. 'Don't just sit there slavering. Eat.'

The boys needed no more bidding. Robin lunged across, picked up the bread – still hot – and tore off a huge

557

chunk for himself. This he dipped into the steam-wreathed bowl, soaking it in the brown liquid that smelled of stew. He stuffed as much as he could into his mouth, and moaned with ecstasy as he chewed and swallowed. The broth was full of spicy meat and chunks of vegetable. Beside him Toady was gorging himself too, whilst at the head of the table Liana watched, hands on hips, black-button eyes creased beneath a frown that barely concealed her admiration.

The boys had a second helping, then a third, Robin reflecting as he polished off the last of the bread that they would probably pay for their gluttony later with a bout of indigestion. At last they pushed their bowls aside and leaned back on their stools, stomachs pregnant with food. Robin closed his eyes, still tasting the meal in his mouth, and sighed with pleasure. 'That was brilliant,' he said, 'the best meal I've ever had.'

Liana nodded curtly, muttered, 'Good,' and swept forward like an avalanche to snatch up their dirty pots. These she placed on the floor beside the tub of muddy water, and almost in the same movement took a wooden bucket from a hook on the wall.

'Now that you've eaten you can make yourselves useful,' she piped. 'I'm going to get some clean water from the well. You two, pour that sludge away. There's a pit on the other side of the clearing.'

She fixed them with a look which denied defiance, then, wooden bucket clenched in her fist, squeezed out of the house. They watched her pass the porthole-window to the left of the door, great bulk wobbling as she moved, wisps of green beard trailing over her shoulders. Robin groaned, spread a hand across his swollen stomach and heaved himself to his feet. 'Come on,' he said, 'we'd better do as she says.'

Toady looked up with drooping eyelids. 'But I'm so full,' he groaned. Nevertheless he too hauled himself upright, and together he and Robin picked up the slopping tub and manoeuvred their way out through the door.

The pit Liana had mentioned was at the far edge of the clearing beneath a half-circle of drooping twisted trees. It was a flat glistening bed of food remains and (Robin suspected) raw sewage, and was coated with a layer of steam so dank it was almost furry. A ripe sweaty smell saturated the area round the pit, tingeing (Toady fancied) the very air green. He and Robin held their breaths as they upended the tub and tipped in the peelings. Then they hurried back, gasping, carrying the tub between them like stretcher-bearers transporting a casualty.

They arrived back at the cottage to find Liana waiting for them. 'You took your time,' she said, then swilled out the tub with a little water from the bucket and slung it out the front door. 'There's ale waiting for you by the fire,' she told them before launching herself with gusto into the washing up.

Robin and Toady looked at the cooking range, noted their stools had been placed one either side of the fire and a frothing tankard of ale perched on the floor beside. They thanked Liana, then waddled over, still full from their meal, and sat down. They picked up their tankards, raised them to one another in silent salutation and buried their faces in the froth.

The ale was thick and sweet and left a tingling in the mouth, like a chocolate liquor laced with pepper. After one long draught, Robin felt his head begin to spin, and put his tankard back down to catch his breath. He blinked and looked about the room which jiggled slightly before settling. Toady, too, it seemed, was experiencing a similar sensation: his grin was now so wide that he looked more like a bullfrog than ever – a bullfrog wearing an ivory moustache of froth.

'This is wonderful, Lady Liana,' Robin said, using her name for the first time. Liana, her washing done, wiped her hands and turned to look at them.

'Hmph,' was her only reply, though Robin reckoned he saw her eyes crinkle and gleam at the compliment.

All at once the ceiling vibrated with a scraping thud,

and clomping sounds – certainly footsteps – thumped overhead. Robin almost choked on a mouthful of ale and looked up, alarmed, noticing out of the corner of his eye that Toady was doing the same. 'What's that?' he hissed, following the steps as they crossed the ceiling and began to descend unseen stairs.

Liana seemed less than perturbed. She had now lowered herself on to a stool – her vast behind almost swallowing it – and was sucking on her pipe vigorously. She hadn't looked up as the sounds had reverberated overhead, had simply focussed on the glowing fire as a child might focus on television. At Robin's question she scratched her strawberry nose and fixed him with a steady gaze. In a voice without inflection she replied, 'It's the idiot, that's all. He's been asleep. He sleeps a great deal.'

Toady stared at Liana, eyes wide and – yes – frog-like. 'Who's the idiot?' he asked, swallowing hard as though the question mark had stuck in his throat.

'The idiot,' Lady Liana said firmly, 'is the idiot,' and she looked at Toady as though he himself was a suitable candidate for the title.

The footsteps came to a halt directly behind a door which Robin had assumed to be a pantry or a broom cupboard. He was still trying to come to terms with the thought that the cottage had an upstairs at all (from the outside it had seemed too tiny), though now he came to think about it, he supposed Liana must sleep somewhere.

'Come in,' the Lady called wearily as someone or something began to rap on the pantry-that-was-not-a-pantry door. There was a short pause, then the door began to inch slowly open. Unconsciously, Robin and Toady drew back on their stools.

The yawning door revealed a figure – small, dishevelled, sleepy-eyed – who entered the kitchen. The figure's short black hair was stuck up from sleep, and his shirt hung wrongly buttoned outside his grey cords. At the sight of the boys his eyes widened in timid fear and he dived for the voluminous safety of Liana's skirt. Robin gasped and

Toady's mouth dropped open, froth clinging to his upper lip. Though the figure did not seem to recognize them, they recognized him all right.

The 'idiot' was Nigel Figg.

CHAPTER THREE

Through The Square Window

1

Saturday 7.40 p.m.

The phone rang. Eileen picked it up. 'Hello, Starmouth 704041,' she said. 'Eileen Gardener speaking.'

'Ah, hello, Mrs Gardener,' answered a voice. 'Could I talk to Richard, please?'

Eileen paused before replying; the voice was one she didn't recognize. 'Who's calling, please?' she asked at last.

'This is Constable Stevens, Mrs Gardener. Starmouth police station. It's about the death of Miss Olive Pierce. I'd just like to ask your son a few questions.'

Eileen relaxed slightly at the words 'Constable' and 'police', but tensed again at the mention of Olive. 'Oh, I see,' she said. 'Well . . . perhaps I could answer your questions for you, Constable? I knew Miss Pierce too, you know.'

'That's very kind of you, Mrs Gardener, but I don't think so. It's related to the . . . um . . . the other matter, you see. I assure you, I'm acting under Sergeant Glennon's direct orders. He has taken me completely into his confidence.'

The tone was smooth, diplomatic, reassuring, but since Olive's death Eileen had grown fiercely protective of her son. 'We-ell, I'm not sure,' she said. 'I don't want Richard disturbed just now. He's been through an awful lot, you see, and at the moment he's convalescing.'

'I quite understand the situation, Mrs Gardener,' the voice cut in, 'but I assure you I won't keep him for long.

And I promise not to distress him in any way.'

'Oh . . . all right,' Eileen conceded reluctantly. 'But you make sure it's only a few minutes. If you'll just hang on, I'll call him.'

She cupped the mouthpiece in one hand and shouted up the stairs, 'Richard! Richard!'

He peered over the banister. The drumming of water behind him indicated he was about to have a bath. 'What is it?'

'There's a phone call for you. A Constable Stevens from Starmouth police station. He says he wants to talk to you about Olive. Will you speak to him? You don't have to if you don't want to.'

'No, I'll speak to him,' said Richard. He crossed the landing and came down the stairs, barefoot. He'd taken his spectacles off, leaving deep red grooves at the side of his nose. He held out his hand for the receiver.

Eileen, however, didn't immediately hand it over. 'You're sure you don't mind?' she said first. 'I don't want him upsetting you.'

'Mum,' Richard said firmly. He flattened his palm and straightened his arm out, a gesture that said: Give. Eileen, unhappily, gave.

'Well, don't be too long,' she said. 'It's all right for these people. They don't know what you've been through.' Then she turned and headed back to the sitting room.

Richard watched her go, smiling a little; when she'd closed the sitting room door, he lifted the phone to his ear. 'Hello,' he said, 'Richard Gardener speaking.'

'She's a gullible bitch, your mum, isn't she?' the voice at the other end sneered.

Richard was stunned. For a few moments he could neither think nor speak. He put a hand to his face, which all at once felt sizzlingly hot, and waited for the words to form. At last, just as the silence threatened to become profound, he stammered, 'Who . . . who is this?'

'Oh, I think you know,' came the snappish reply almost before his own question was out. 'It's Me-me-me, your friendly neighbourhood Creature. Know what I mean, daddy-o?'

It sounded more like a manic game-show host, yet suddenly Richard felt fear – no, more than that; utter terror – slide through his chest as though a knife had materialized there. He swayed on his feet, fingers loosening around the receiver, a black cloud informing him that both he and it would soon meet the floor with a crash. He swallowed, saw swarms of red-black microbes clouding his vision . . .

. . . and then, like a just-in-the-nick-of-time superhero, the mood of the last few days swooped down to chase the blues away.

Richard felt it all wash over him in a soothing wave – the calm controlled anger, the determination, the feeling of self-confidence. His hand tightened around the receiver, squeezing the plastic until his knuckles glared white. In a voice so steely it chilled even him, he heard himself saying, 'Oh, it's you, is it? I've been looking for you. I wanted to tell you you're a fucking murdering bastard.'

There was a soft chuckle at the end of the line. The game-show host became a gently admonishing grandad. 'Tut, tut, tut, such language. Wash your mouth out, you naughty boy.' Another chuckle, then the game-show host was back. 'But enough chitty-chat. I'm just calling to say it's your turn, Dickie-Wickie. Be at the hospital in an hour and we'll have some fun. If you're not there, I'll be very, very angry. So angry, in fact, that I doubt your zombie friends and your dear bruvver will live to see the morning. Byee!'

Click. Brrrr . . .

Richard stood for a long time, listening to the monotonous hum of the dialling tone. The threats against his friends and his brother, though ugly and lowdown, had not really alarmed him, largely because the appointment the creature had fixed was one he had no intention of breaking. All week he had been expecting some form of contact, yet it had been the method, the conventional, even mundane use of the telephone system which had thrown him – he guessed intentionally. The creature, he thought, was doing all it could to catch him off-guard, to hurl him into as much confusion as possible before the final confrontation could begin. Well, Richard was just as determined that its crude attempts at gamesmanship would not work. From now on he would expect the unexpected; he would be ready for anything.

Breathing deeply he replaced the receiver, his eyes straying towards the hall window, beyond which darkness waited. From the sitting room came the senseless jangle of the television (*Come on and Blankety Blank, Blankety Blank, Blank, Blank*), from upstairs the thrumming splash of water. Richard checked his watch – 7.45. He'd better cancel (no, postpone; only postpone) his bath. His feet were cold, as were his fingers, but inside he felt OK: cool, calm, collected, as the saying goes. Feet padding softly on the carpet, he went upstairs.

2

No-time

It came to Toady suddenly in the darkness: the memory of what had preceded the hospital bed. It was so devastating that it knocked the wind from him, and he sucked in air, his fingers scrabbling at the bulky softness of the mattress. His gaze flickered to the ceiling, which was low and criss-crossed with dark wood beams.

'Rob,' he said, forcing the word out, 'Rob, are you there?'

He twisted his head to look at the mound in the bed across the room. It was just discernible, dark against dark, and at his words it humped up like a caterpillar. A groan issued from it.

'What is it, Ade? I'm trying to sleep.'

'Sorry, Rob, but . . . I just needed someone to talk to. I've remembered something. Something that happened to me before I came here.'

There was a short pause. Then Robin sat up and said, 'Oh, yeah? Hang on a minute.'

The sound of fumbling was followed by the rasping flare of a match. A disembodied hand directed it towards a fat white candle.

'What have you remembered?' Robin asked.

Toady sat up too: the candlelight seemed to have dispelled the suffocating weight of the memory, if not the distress it had caused him. For a long moment he was silent, all at once reluctant to put the memory into words. He looked at Robin, sighed, and then said in a dull voice, 'There was a fire. All my . . . all my family died in it. I caused it but . . . I was tricked somehow. There was someone else involved. A kid called . . . called Toby . . . Yeah, that's right. Toby.'

He faltered there, right hand flying to his face, index finger pressing the spot between his eyes as though a migraine had flared up. Silence again filled the room, but it was the silence of memory as Robin's own eyes opened wide. 'Shit, yeah,' he said, 'I remember now too. I read about it in the paper. You were taken to hospital, the only survivor . . . God, Ade, I'm . . . I'm so sorry. I don't know what to say. How could we forget something like that?'

Silence again, so deep that the candle-flame seemed to flap and flicker like a bird's wing. Toady shook his head. His voice, when he spoke, was flat, inflectionless.

'I think there's plenty more we've forgotten. I think some really bad things have been happening to us. I've been trying to think back, Rob, *really* trying to think, but the last thing I remember apart from the hospital and the fire is being picked on in the playground by Rusty's mob that day we had the Horror Club meeting, and then them chasing me after school and Rich's brother helping me out . . .' He frowned, his head-shaking growing more rapid. 'But that must have been . . .what? . . . two, three weeks ago?'

'Yeah,' said Robin slowly. 'Yeah, I remember that too.

That was the meeting where we decided to have the seance. And you got uppity 'cos Nige couldn't stay out late. Mind you, back then you were a bit . . . What's the matter, Ade?'

Robin had tailed off because of the way Toady was looking at him: wide-eyed, open-mouthed. 'What's up?' he said nervously. 'Have I just grown horns or something?'

'That's it!' Toady said. 'Rob, that's what caused all this. It was that seance – in King Street. Remember King Street? It was after that when all the bad things started happening.'

Now Robin's mouth, too, dropped open. 'God, yeah,' he said. 'The dreams . . . the girl on the beach, and that . . . thing she was holding.'

'And the body in the cave,' Toady added sombrely. 'Remember that, Rob? The body?'

'The body . . . yeah.' He shuddered. 'And the cellar . . . the thing in the cellar . . . all those tentacles . . . and the Ragettys.' He shuddered more violently and clapped a hand to his mouth. It was obvious from his expression that he was beginning to re-live his own personal nightmare of the previous couple of weeks, that memories were unwrapping in his mind like poisoned sweets.

And in his own too, Toady suddenly realized. The gaps in his memory were rapidly filling up, image upon image upon image punching – *drilling* – themselves into his head. *The seance continued . . . and concluded; seduction, shadow, Simon's screams. Himself in bed; learning to change; Peter Cushing; Toby; floating on air. His mother stripping; then destruction. Cleansing with fire and death as the cat prowled.*

Toady felt himself drowning, and clawed at the light which was his only salvation. 'Rob,' he gasped, and felt someone answering him, giving him strength. Bit by bit the memories ebbed. 'Rob, are you there?'

'I'm here, Ade,' came the confirmation in a voice that sounded as weak as he felt. 'It's all over now, that part of it. We're here, and that's all that matters.'

Toady came back to himself, saw Robin staring at him, white-faced. Shame and fear stuck in his throat, almost choking him as he tried to speak. 'Where are we, Rob? *What* are we? Dead? On another planet? Dreaming? What?'

He was aware of his own voice rising hysterically, and then Robin flapped a hand at him, twisting to glance at the door.

'Shh, we don't want to wake Liana up. I don't fancy facing her in a bad mood in the middle of the night, even if she is a midget.'

Toady nodded and settled back into bed again, his heart pounding. Robin continued, 'No, I don't know where we are. Or even what. But, well, at least we're alive. And at least three of us – you, me and Nige – are together.' He paused here and frowned, them murmured, 'I hope Rich is all right. I wonder where he is.'

'Do you think he's here somewhere . . . lost?' said Toady.

'I dunno. Maybe. Or maybe he's still in Starmouth.'

'Yeah. Yeah, I hope so.'

There was another pause as they contemplated the fate of their friend. Then Robin added, 'And at least we're well-fed, and we've got a bed to sleep in. Tomorrow we'll see if Liana, or even that dog, Ranulf, can tell us anything. But now I reckon we ought to get some sleep. We'll probably need it.'

He looked across at Toady. There was uncertainty in his face, but warmth too, and comradeship, and Toady was absurdly moved. 'This is what it's like to have a real friend', he thought, and had consciously to stop himself from rushing over and giving the older boy a hug. Instead he contented himself with a smile that he hoped conveyed all he felt. In a voice gruff with emotion he said, 'OK. We'll leave it till tomorrow. But I don't think I'll sleep tonight, Rob. Not after remembering about my family and everything.'

568

'You will,' Robin promised him.

And he did.

But not straight away.

The older boy made a move to blow out the candle. 'No, don't!' Toady snapped, then cringed as the echoes reverberated round the room. He met Robin's curious stare, blushing, a little shame-faced at his outburst. 'Could we leave the candle burning for a bit, Rob?' he asked. 'Please? If you don't mind?'

Robin looked at him, then shrugged and nodded. 'Yeah, course,' he said, 'if that's what you want.' He lay back with a sigh.

Toady lay back too, but he couldn't get comfortable. It was as though someone had filled his mattress with rocks. He glanced at the window, a porthole covered with a square of dark cloth like a magician's trick. There was no wind at all outside, and the house, despite its apparent age, didn't creak.

Over in the other bed, Robin's breathing began to level out, deepen. Toady suddenly realized he dreaded his friend going to sleep while he was still wide awake.

'Rob?' he said, and then, when his friend didn't reply, 'Oi, Rob?'

'Hmmm?' came the reply from across the room.

'Rob, how long do you think we've been here?'

'Been here? What, in this house you mean?'

'No. *Here*. In this . . . this place. This land.'

'Uhh . . . I dunno. Hard to say. Time just seems to kind of . . . melt here.'

Melt. Yes, that was a good word for it. Time just melted. It frightened Toady, the idea that time could be meaningless. Time was the yardstick by which they measured all things. Without time – without seconds, minutes, hours, days, months, years – there was nothing. There was only confusion.

Melt.

Meltdown.

He shuddered.

Silence endured for another indeterminate length. Toady wished there was a ticking clock on the bedside table. Finally, abruptly, he asked, 'But this *is* the first night we've had, isn't it? Since we've been here? The first time it's got dark?'

'Wha?' muttered Robin thickly, rising once more from muddy near-sleep.

'The first night we've had. This *is* the first night, isn't it?'

'Yes, and I intend to make the most of it. Just bloody go to sleep, Ade.'

'OK, Rob. Sorry.'

'Hnn.'

And again silence wrapped its arms about them.

Toady lay, thinking, ideas and memories bubbling in his mind, boiling up like water on a stove. He was naked in bed, and he subconsciously fingered his penis beneath the sheets, rolling the flaccid organ between thumb and index finger like a piece of plasticine. His clothes were downstairs; Liana had taken them away to wash as soon as they'd climbed into bed. Toady had felt vulnerable, uncomfortable, giving his clothes up, but it was done now, and besides Nige had been here apparently for a day or two (if such a time-scale actually meant anything here) and he'd been given his clothes back.

Nige. There again was a mystery. Even since he had made his entrance earlier as 'the idiot' he had behaved like a frightened deer. He had clung on to Liana's skirts, stared at the boys with large doe-eyes, and not uttered a word. Whenever either Toady or Robin had made a move towards him, he had whimpered and cringed behind Liana's flesh-padded frame. He had clung to Liana even though her attitude towards him seemed to be one of tolerance rather than affection, had even followed her up to bed, creating in Toady's mind a scenario both fascinating and repugnant.

But to get back to clothes. There was something . . . something about them that niggled him. The clothes he'd

570

been wearing – FairIsle sweater, jeans, shoes – what was it about them? It was an irritating feeling, like trying to remember someone's name, like having a hair stuck in the throat. Think hard, think hard . . .

And then sudden success as he realized.

The clothes he'd been wearing today were not the same clothes he'd been wearing when he'd been taken to the hospital after the fire. Robin had mentioned something about clothes and pyjamas earlier on, but it had taken this long for the realization fully to surface. The clothes that were at this moment drying downstairs (hopefully) had actually been in the house on Latimer Street when the fire had started.

And the house had burnt to the ground.

Ipso facto, the clothes he'd been wearing should now be ashes.

He lay for a long time, thinking about this. Maybe by some miracle his room had survived the conflagration, maybe the firemen had got there in time. Maybe they'd salvaged what they could, and some kind soul had brought all that was still intact to the hospital. Yes, that must be it. But still the thought bothered him. Things just didn't seem to fit. Nothing seemed to fit.

Melt.

He slept.

When he woke, the first thing he noticed was how low the candle had burned. Like a lop-sided dripping face with the hair on fire, he thought, and immediately an image of his mother – wheeling about the room, screaming, clawing at the fire-brand which her head had become – tore into his mind. He sat bolt upright, a spontaneous sheen of perspiration bursting from the pores of his skin. He swallowed, his throat so dry it clicked, and looked across at Robin.

The older boy was sleeping, his arm thrown up over his head, his face composed and oddly vulnerable. In the soft light his skin seemed unblemished, his acne hardly pronounced at all. Toady's gaze flitted back to the candle,

571

noting the candle-holder brimming with wax which quivered slightly like jelly. In one or two places the wax had spilled over and hardened, forming tiny grey-white stalactites.

The silence, velvet-still, was now so deep it seemed to muffle Robin's breathing.

Toady shivered and pulled his blankets up to his chin and watched the shadows playing on the walls. Absently he began to pick his nose with the little finger of his right hand, and contemplated whether to go downstairs for a piss. A moment later he almost pissed in his bed when the voice came drifting through the window.

'Adian!' it called. 'Adian!'

Only one person had ever called him Adian – without the 'r' – and that was his little brother, Simon. But Simon was dead, killed in the fire that Toady had induced, a fact that caused prickly dread to invade his body like a rash. But coupled with the dread was another emotion, and one that was perhaps strange considering that Toady had never had much time for the kid when he was alive. That emotion was love, and it manifested itself now in physical signs: in a throat that felt jammed by cotton wool, in eyes that were filled with tears.

'Simon,' he whispered, forcing the word past the obstruction in his Adam's apple. The child's voice had sounded lost, desperate, and Toady could not help but respond to it. He pushed back his covers and swung his stubby legs over the side of the bed. He stood up and padded naked to the window.

He peeled back the dark drape and looked out. The sky was starless and moonless, but nevertheless a dirty half-light seemed to come from somewhere, like hidden phosphorescence leaking from the earth. The room faced on to the front of the house – the vegetable garden, the clearing, the grim wall of trees – but it was high up, half-hidden by the overhang of the thatched roof. Toady's own sickly-yellow face stared back at him from its cage of glass. He leaned forward, almost resting his cheek against the cold cheek of his reflection, and peered into the darkness below.

The small blond figure was standing half-way up the garden path, flapping its arms. It was dressed in a BMX Bikers sweat shirt and football shorts. Its grey socks were puddled about its ankles and it wore sandals on its feet. Even from this distance Toady could see it was plastered in mud.

'Simon,' he whispered again, and his eyes blurred as tears ran down his cheeks. With his left hand he wiped them away and with his right he began waving frantically. He saw Simon's head cock towards him, lines of mud on his face like war-paint. A second later Simon began jumping up and down, flapping his arms even more vigorously. 'Adian! Adian!' he shouted in his excited high-pitched voice.

'Wait there, Si,' Toady mouthed, and pointed to consolidate the order. He wasn't sure whether Simon understood or not, but he doubted the boy would wander off anyway. Nevertheless he ran urgently across the room, stubbing his toe on the corner of Robin's bed. He slapped a hand to his mouth to stifle his cry of pain, not merely to avoid waking Robin but also because he had a strong yet obscure feeling that it was important he do this alone, that no-one else should find out about Simon's presence – not yet anyway.

He opened the wooden door, wincing at the creak it made, and ducked out on to the landing. To his left was the only other upstairs door, to Liana's bedroom, to his right a narrow wooden staircase. He began to descend barefoot, the wood rough against his soles, hoping a splinter was not about to complement his stubbed toe. He opened the door at the bottom and stepped into the kitchen, meagre light seeping through the windows, painting objects in gradations of shadow. He looked around and saw his and Robin's clothes draped over a rickety clothes-horse in front of the cooking range. They were damp but warm, and he pulled his own on quickly.

He spent a frantic few moments looking for his shoes, but finally found them, newly cleaned and polished, standing against the wall by the wooden tub.

His fingers were clumsy as he fumbled with the laces; clumsier still as he stood up and reached for the iron ring in the front door that served as a handle. The metal was cool beneath his palm; he felt a finger of sweat lightly trace the shape of his collarbone. He took a deep breath, bunched his muscles and twisted.

He was rewarded with a dry click and a shifting motion as the latch disengaged from its socket. He pulled the door towards him, admitting the night. The smell was a blend of bower-roses and something dank and sour which he suspected came from the cess-pit. He stepped beneath the bower and on to the thin grey thread of the path. Simon was there waiting for him, arms held out in a welcoming embrace.

'Adian,' he whimpered pitifully, 'I bin looking for you.'

Tears sprang down Toady's cheeks. He opened his arms and Simon ran into them. The top of the boy's blond head came barely to Toady's throat. Simon smelled a little grubby, but beneath was that milky clean smell that all little kids seem to have. Toady hugged his brother hard, realizing and regretting that this was the first time he had ever done so.

Simon's arms wrapped round his waist felt as thin as rope. 'I bin looking for you,' the boy said again. 'I bin scared. The trees are big.'

Toady hugged his brother harder, moved by his simple fear and his resourcefulness. They stayed that way for long silent minutes, until eventually they broke apart. Toady swiped a sleeve across his face to hide his tears.

'How did you get here, Si?' he said with a sniff. 'Where did you come from?'

The little boy looked at him, face creasing in puzzlement. 'Dunno, just came,' he said, shrugging. 'It's scary in the trees. I'm hungry.'

'Come on,' Toady smiled and took his brother's hand.

'I'll try and find you something to eat in the cottage.'

He was surprised when Simon resisted his tug and turned back, frowning. 'What's the matter?' he said. 'There's nothing to be frightened of.'

'Want Mummy n' Daddy to come too,' Simon said. 'They hungry like me. Can 'em come, Adian?'

Toady felt as though crushed ice-cubes had been dumped down his back. 'Mummy and . . . you mean they're *here*?' he spluttered.

Simon nodded. 'Mm. Over there. They said for me to come first.'

Toady looked where Simon was pointing and the ice-cubes were joined by needles. His little brother's dirty finger was stabbing in the direction of the cess-pit, where the trees huddled like witches. Nasty thoughts began to bloom in Toady's mind, but he tried to chase them away with a question.

'Er . . . what are they doing here?' he asked.

Simon shrugged, eyes wide and innocent.

Toady felt his throat filling up again, though this time not with love but fear. He had been toying with the idea that Simon had somehow survived the fire, and yet he couldn't help but remember Robin's earlier words: 'I read about it in the paper. You were . . . the only survivor.' Toady had been hoping, however, that he had somehow been mistaken, that some miraculous misunderstanding had occurred. After all, Simon was here, warm flesh, dirty hair, looking up at him now, solemnly waiting for a decision to be made.

'We're all dead,' Toady thought suddenly. 'This is Hell.' Yet he crushed the conjecture and replaced it with a further question. 'Why didn't Mum and Dad come to the cottage with you?'

Simon sighed, making it plain he found these questions tiresome. 'Dunno. We go fetch 'em. Come on.'

Toady knew there was something wrong about this, something very wrong indeed, yet he allowed himself to be tugged down the garden path and out of the gate into the clearing. He was still some distance from the cess-pit when the smell of it began to make him gag. The grass he was walking on was like shards of grey shadow streaked with black; the trees, though there was no discernible light-source, were probing and enveloping him with tar-black shadows of their own.

A sudden creaking to his left had Toady's head snapping round, his mouth dropping open in preparation for a scream. Shadows and trees seemed all one, a crawling of black, and from them Toady half-expected to see some charcoal nightmare that had once been his mother detaching itself.

However there was nothing – nothing but a spavined tree-branch twitching in the breeze.

'What breeze?' he thought. 'What breeze? There is no fucking breeze.'

'Si,' he said. His voice was tremulous, but steadier than he would have thought possible. 'Si, I don't think this is such a good idea. I think we should go back.'

His brother turned to face him, mouth set in a stubborn line. 'Mummy n' Daddy're hungry too,' he muttered, and only tightened his grip on Toady's hand.

'Yes, but . . . but if they want some food why can't they come to the cottage themselves? I mean . . . why can't they? *Why can't they, Si?*'

''cos they can't,' was all Simon said and resumed his tugging.

Toady shook his head. The stench of the pit was filling him now, making it difficult to think. It was putrefying, miasmic; it clutched at his throat and drew forth bile. It was almost solid, conjuring up images of decay like a host offering tempting titbits. Green spoiled meat teeming with flies; rotting flesh like soft cheese; fruit stuffed with pus and red maggots.

This last morsel was too much for Toady. He snatched his hand from Simon's grip, bent over double and puked.

He was staring at the pile of vomit spattered over his newly-polished shoes when a single word echoed round the clearing. It was a boom of authority, a retort like a shotgun blast. It made Toady raise his head a little, though his eyes were blurred from the effort of puking.

'Stop!'

Toady retched again and a thin stream of yellowish bile leaped from his mouth on to the oily ground.

'Stop I said,' the voice repeated, to which Toady thought: 'I can't help it. It's this bloody smell.'

He spat the last of the sickness from his mouth and finally felt his stomach begin to settle. He wiped fresh tears away from his sleeve and looked up. What he saw caused his bowels to contract painfully, gave him a brief exquisite moment of absolute terror.

Something huge and black was bearing down on him from across the clearing, something that seemed all slavering teeth and flashing claws.

It took Toady a moment to recognize this vision, though even when he did he was not sure whether to feel relieved or alarmed. This was Ranulf, Liana's dog, though it was a Ranulf transformed from the last time they had met. This was a Ranulf whose eyes were flaring lanterns; a Ranulf who would have put the Hound of the Baskervilles to shame.

'And he thinks I'm trying to escape,' Toady thought with horror.

'No, Ranulf!' he screamed. 'No, I'm not! I'm with my brother, Simon. We were just looking for my parents. We were going to go back to the house. Honest we were! Honest!'

It seemed that his words had had no effect: Ranulf continued to gallop. Toady imagined those giant paws trampling him into the ground, those teeth tearing at his flesh. His legs began to buckle and he half-hoped he would faint before the dog reached him.

However, when he was no more than eight feet away Ranulf padded to a halt. He stood regarding Toady, his lips curled back and froth collecting around his jowls. Steam puffed from his nostrils, an awesome symbol of his physical prowess. Even in the darkness Toady fancied he could see muscles rippling and gathering beneath the dog's matted black fur.

'Ranulf, I wasn't trying to escape, honest,' he babbled, 'I was just—'

'Walk towards me,' the dog cut in coldly. 'Don't look back and don't run. Just walk slowly towards me.'

Toady stared, his mouth half-open. Ranulf's attitude was all wrong. Toady had expected threats, bluster, anger. But the dog's body was rigid, his voice steady though shot through with tension. Cautiously Toady began, 'Ranulf, I don't think—' but the dog's icy voice cut in again.

'Just do as I say. No questions.'

Something uncurled in Toady's stomach, but he tried to retain a look of dignity. However, he decided that in this instance it was probably wiser to obey the dog's orders. He flapped a hand behind him, hoping his little brother would have the sense to stay put, then walked unsteadily towards the dog.

'Now,' Ranulf said when Toady was no more than a foot away, 'turn and look behind you. See what I've rescued you from.'

Puzzled and fearful, Toady turned. Then he shrieked and his bowels cramped painfully again.

Simon had disappeared.

And a nightmare had taken his place.

It hovered and swayed above the cess-pit, strangely blurred as though trapped within its own heat-haze. Its shape was constantly changing, though for the most part it was long and spindly, its limbs – if limbs they could be called – crooked as old twigs. It seemed composed of running green-black tallow, mucus linked by exposed bone, which gleamed startlingly white in places as though picked clean by birds. Its fingers were long and fleshless, its neck a glistening tangle of tubes and tendons. Its stomach, threads of stringy flesh like the cheese on a pizza, barely concealed an inner jumble of rancid chitterlings.

Without doubt it was the most repulsive creature Toady had ever seen.

And its face . . .

That was the worst of all.

Long and sallow, its cheekbones and the top of its skull were nothing but white bone and bits of floating matter. Its eyes were like soft-boiled eggs from which poisoned yolk leaked, and they roiled and slithered in their sockets as though in constant danger of sliding out. Its ears were lumps of chewed gristle, its mouth a slit sewn closed by thick black stitches. Its nose was a hole in the centre of its face within which things squirmed, like fish-roe on the point of hatching.

'You see?' Ranulf said casually as Toady huddled against him. 'You see how you've been tricked?'

'What is it?' Toady barely whispered.

Ranulf's voice was grim with distaste as he replied. 'The Crowl. A rather odious part of the Us.'

Toady's bowels spasmed for the third time, putting him in imminent danger of soiling his freshly-laundered jeans, as the creature ejaculated a sudden gurgling hiss. The hiss was followed by speech, which Toady thought strange considering that the creature's mouth was sewn up. Then he saw the source of the speech and he turned and buried his face in Ranulf's fur, wishing to see no more.

'Give me the boy,' the Crowl burbled, words which came from a tiny mouth which had opened in the milky vesicle of one of its eyes. Its next words were drowned in a sputter of yellow ichor, though Toady recognized 'mongrel' and something that sounded like 'fuck-stink', and assumed he and Ranulf were being abused.

To his credit, Ranulf's reply was calm, forthright and equally abusive. 'Screw you,' he said.

The Crowl hissed and sputtered, a noise like steak in hot fat. Toady risked a look between his fingers and saw fleshy lumps of the creature sliding off and dropping into the mire, where they glowed briefly like fungus, then went out. This was too much for him and he buried his face

again. Above his head the dispute over ownership continued.

'He's my little treat. I found him first. You look for
your own, slum-beast-mongrel-spit.'

'Like I said, screw you. The boy's coming with me to
the cottage. Bye-bye, Crowl.'

'Vermin-shit-turd. You bring him back here!'

'Sorry, no can do. Come *on*, boy!'

Toady realized he was being nudged in the direction of
Liana's cottage and he complied readily. Details of the
Crowl's hideous anatomy were branding themselves on his
memory. Behind them the creature continued to spit and
seethe, though it made no attempt at pursuit. Presumably
it was cowardly despite its appearance, given to trickery
and under-handedness rather than open conflict.

They reached the cottage. Now that the crisis was over,
Toady felt weak and trembly, though his mind was
whirring, wanting answers more than sleep. He hated this
feeling, the sense that comprehension was slipping away,
that reality was careering into the dark unknown recesses
of a side tunnel. What was 'the Us' that Ranulf had
mentioned? It sounded like something one of these weird
hippy sociologists would say: cosmic awareness, collective
unconscious, all that stuff; matters of which Toady had
only minimal knowledge and even less understanding.

He opened the cottage door, but before entering he
turned and asked Ranulf this question. The dog stared at
him as though deliberating, then he blinked and sighed
deeply.

'Time for questions in the morning, boy. Go and sleep
now,' he said.

Toady hovered on the threshold, half-resigned to
submitting to Ranulf's promptings. The dog had an air of
quiet authority about him that was hard to disobey. But
then he thought of the long dark hours before dawn, of the
way he would toss and turn in bed while his incomprehen-
sion burgeoned into near-panic. He knew that he would
never sleep without at least some explanation, and so as

Ranulf turned to leave he instinctively reached out and grabbed a handful of the dog's ribboned fur.

'No, Ranulf,' he said. 'No, I need to know now.'

The startled look on Ranulf's face was almost comical. Toady went on, 'I won't be able to sleep again tonight anyway, not after seeing that . . . that thing.'

The surprise on Ranulf's face changed to a curiously human expression of long-suffering. It was the look of a man who has been keeping bad news from somebody and knows he can delay its telling no longer. His tongue flicked out, a pink flatworm cleaning the froth from his jowls. He looked towards the trees, then turned back and inclined his head.

'Very well. But we'll go inside. It'll be warmer in the kitchen.'

Toady led the way, then held the door wide, wondering how Ranulf would fit through such a tiny opening. However the dog, though solid and powerful, was also lithe, and he slipped through the door much more easily than ever the Lady Liana could.

Once inside it was the same story. Ranulf looked huge in the kitchen, his head barely inches from the ceiling. Yet he negotiated furniture and brushed past the hanging array of kitchen implements without disturbing a thing. He padded to the cooking range and sat before it, luxuriating in the warmth retained by the black metal. Once there he turned to look at Toady, his eyes flashing hazel-yellow in the darkness.

'There are candles in the cupboard by the door,' he said softly.

Toady was a little irritated by the dog's air of command, but went over to the cupboard, opened it, and took out candles, candle-holders and matches. He lit four of these and carried two over to the cooking range, reminded as he did so of the first night in King Street, the night of the seance, a thousand years ago. He set the candles on the range, then said, 'Before we start, I have to go to the loo.'

Again Ranulf inclined his head, a gesture of consent that

Toady found somehow belittling. He crossed the kitchen to a small door, one of the three that was set into the wall. Behind the other two doors was the staircase and a pantry, but behind this was a short corridor which led to an alcove in which squatted a primitive commode. Toady completed the function begun by the first sight of Ranulf and exacerbated by the appearance of the Crowl, then he returned to the kitchen.

He found the dog in much the same position as before, candle-light playing over his haughty features, turning his eyes into nuggets of liquid gold. He didn't move even when Toady pulled up a stool and sat opposite him, simply stared at the light as though awaiting guidance. Toady wondered how difficult this was going to be; it already seemed obvious that Ranulf would volunteer nothing. He opened his mouth again to enquire what Ranulf had meant by 'the Us' when the dog stirred and said, 'Ah, Adrian. Welcome back.'

The greeting threw Toady more than it should have, and for a moment he couldn't understand why. Then it dawned on him: Ranulf had used his name. As far as Toady could recall, his name had never been mentioned in the dog's presence before.

'How did you know I was called Adrian?' became, then, his first question.

Ranulf looked at him implacably, though Toady thought he detected a sense of . . . what, quiet triumph? in the dog's eyes. Toady could not help thinking that Ranulf had subtly manipulated the conversation to his own ends before it had even begun, and he felt secretly enraged at this. However he tried not to show it, tried instead to concentrate on what the dog was saying.

'You have already encountered an element of the Us,' the dog informed him, 'an element which acquired this knowledge. The dispensation of such knowledge is entire throughout the Us. It is only the assimilation of it that is a more selective process.'

He stopped there, like a computer awaiting its next

instruction. Toady stared at him, wrestling with what he had been told. In the end, however, he had to give up. Hating both himself and the dog for his shortcomings, he said, 'I don't understand what you mean. What . . . what *is* the Us?'

Ranulf gave an exaggerated sigh, but secretly Toady thought he looked pleased. 'Oh dear,' he said, 'I can see I'm going to have to paraphrase to the point of idiocy. You will remember though, won't you Adrian, that what I'm about to tell you is vastly, crudely over-simplified?'

Toady nodded mutely: he was both too furious to speak and determined to keep the ball in Ranulf's court. The dog stared into the candle again as though it provided a focus of concentration. Then in a slow careful voice he continued: 'The Us is what we are – our eternal being. I believe the element of the Us which you have encountered you know as the "King Street Creature"?'

'You mean *you're* the Creature?' Toady gasped.

Ranulf shook his head. 'I'm not exactly *the* Creature, no, but we *are* both elements of the same whole. The Creature is, in fact, not really a creature at all. It is a . . . I suppose the best word you have to describe it – to describe *Us* – is a "state". We are what is, what has been, and what will be, and we exist in eternity. We have no beginning and no end; we reside in an eternal number of dimensions, an eternal number of forms, roles, moods. Everything you have seen since you've been here is part of the Us: me, Liana, the Crowl; the trees, the mud and the cottage; even the air you breathe, the food you eat. In a sense you are *inside* Us, within Us . . . Do you understand so far?'

Toady's mind was reeling. The very idea that Ranulf would have him believe felt as though it was making his brain swell like a balloon. However he nodded doubtfully, murmured, 'I think so,' and asked one of a queue of questions, hoping it would ease the pressure. 'But . . . how come we see you as things that we know in our world? I mean, you're a dog, Liana's a woman – even if she has got a green beard; this is a kitchen, a table, a fire; we've been sleeping in a bed; we even speak the same language. I mean . . . how can that be? How can everything be so close to what we know?'

Again that long pause. Ranulf looked at him as if encouraging him to say more. Eventually he replied, 'Because, as I've already explained, what you and your friends have seen are not *all* that we are. We exist in an endless number of forms, states, dimensions. Our elements – our atoms, to use a very crude term – are malleable, adaptable; they can be altered by the influence of ourselves and by our proximity to outside influences. In other words, you! Yes, it's true. You and Robin, even Nigel, are influencing and creating an environment out of the Us that you are able to cope with and believe in.'

'So you mean this is all in our minds? It's not real?'

'Oh no, no, not at all. This – Us – is as real as you are; in fact, even more so. But we have an extra dimension – we can be changed. Anything about Us – *anything* – can be changed in any way we like.'

Toady shook his head. Ranulf's explanations seemed only to be pulling knots tighter instead of loosening them. He said, 'OK, answer me this then. Here in . . . in this place, there's you and Liana, and you've been very kind to us – you've given us food and a bed and everything. But back in Starmouth, in our world, the . . . the Creature, the Us, whatever it is, is causing havoc, is murdering people, and all for no reason. Can you tell me why this is? Why it – why *you* are doing this? I mean, if you're so . . . so eternal, why are you operating on such a small scale? And why are you doing such awful things? I mean, you say you're boundless, that you can change into anything you like, so surely if you wanted you could squash not just Starmouth, but the whole world like a bug? So why is what you're doing so . . . so localized?'

He felt driven by anger, felt an urge to shake Ranulf by the scruff of the neck to get answers. However he resisted, waiting as the dog shifted position slightly. Finally Ranulf replied, 'Everything we do we see as important . . .

everything, Adrian. Importance, after all, is simply a question of degree. The Us is eternal, therefore everything which exists in eternity – which *is* everything – is important to Us, no matter how vast or trivial. You, for instance, are important to Us, yet by your scale you represent something that is infinitely smaller than the single atom which helps make up an amoeba in your world. To the Us, the life of your world is a click of the fingers, a blink of an eye. Yet, despite this, you *are* important . . . I'll bet you've never considered the importance of the atoms which make up amoebae, have you Adrian?'

Toady shook his head. Again, having to admit he had not gave him the impression that Ranulf was trying to make him feel inferior. In an effort to divert this, he said, 'But you still haven't answered my question about Star-mouth: why you're killing people? And why on such a small scale?'

Ranulf's eyes were lambent; his tone was that of a patient though condescending schoolteacher. 'Well, just remember what I've been telling you. We are boundless, eternal, we have the capacity to exist in every place, every time. Doubtless in another dimension your world *is* being squashed like a bug; in yet another it is reaping the rewards of our involvement. You see, Adrian, the key is always eternity; you must let loose your mind and embrace that concept. Now in *your* dimension, in *your* Starmouth, you have encountered an element of the Us which, though powerful, is petty, vindictive, destructive; a liar and a cheat. Though it is not a "creature", it does kill like one; it is driven by viciousness and spite.'

'But why? Why should it? And if you know this, why can't you stop it? Don't you have any control over yourself?'

Ranulf shrugged. 'It is not a question of control. You see, Adrian, what is done *needs* to be done. Our purpose, our overriding motive, is the acquisition of knowledge – *all* knowledge. To achieve this we need to explore all aspects of eternity, good *and* bad. And for this we need to adopt an eternal variety of stances and attitudes and approaches, we need to create situations and circumstances and to observe the consequences, to study the environmental reactions to the Us. Now, having said all that, I'd like to make it clear that I personally, whilst understanding and accepting the relevance of all approaches, am violently opposed to the approach instigated by the Zad – the approach employed in your particular dimension. And though this may seem contradictory and confusing, it's really not. You see, disagreement and dispute is also the basis for acquiring separate viewpoints of similar knowledge. Now do you understand?'

'Kind of. But what's a Zad?'

'*The* Zad. It's a title, like lord or duke or monarch. You see, in this dimension I was a prince and the Lady Liana was my mother, the queen.'

'Your mother!' Toady exclaimed. 'She . . . that . . . she's your mother??'

Ranulf nodded. 'Let me explain. The Zad was – is – an evil revolutionary. He stirred the populace into revolt, overthrew the monarchy and reduced us to this. My mother was forced by the Treaty of Idrias to adopt the form you see her in now (or rather, your perception of the form) and to accept an existence of drudgery, struggle and poverty. This heinous sentence was as a punishment for her supposed arrogance and uncaring attitude, though in truth she was a good queen, a just queen.

'I, by this Treaty, was turned into this, a dog, forced to scavenge in the woods for scraps. I am not permitted to eat any of the food which the Zad provides for my mother to prepare. To me, and me alone, it is poison.

'As for my father, well . . .' His voice dropped an octave; Toady could have sworn he saw tears swim in his eyes. 'He received the most vile sentence of all. He was put to death, dismembered slowly and publicly, piece by piece, a long and horrific process. The Zad declared this period a public festival; parties were thrown in the streets.

586

My father's slowly reducing body was placed in a cage for people to come and jeer at. They poked him with sticks, pissed on him, shat on him; he almost drowned in urine and excrement. In the end his head was given to the people, who kicked it into a pulp. Now any opposition to the Zad is dealt with in a similar way.'

Ranulf's voice had grown quieter and huskier throughout this telling, and now it tailed off altogether. For a few moments the two of them sat, dog and boy, one quiet with remembered grief, the other silent with horror. Then, gradually, the anomalies of Ranulf's story began to filter through to Toady's brain; confusion superseded his shock. Trying to adopt a tone both diplomatic and demanding, he said, 'But . . . but if you're eternal, how can any of this have happened? I mean, I'm not saying you're a liar, but you've been going on about having no boundaries, no beginning and no end, all that cosmic stuff, and yet now you're telling me you have a mother and father – which means that you were born – and that your father is now dead. I . . . I just don't understand, Ranulf. If what you've told me is true, then it seems to suggest that all this stuff about eternity is . . . well, is just a load of crap.'

He stopped, breathless, both triumphant at having sniffed out this anomaly and fearful of having called Ranulf's honesty into question. Ranulf tilted his head to look at him, and Toady thought he saw genuine pain in the canine features. In a weary voice, Ranulf said, '*All* that I have told you is true. In the Us – the eternal Us – there *are* no boundaries, yet we, I, am for now only an element of the Us residing within this one particular dimension. Therefore, in order to achieve structure, we create temporary boundaries within and for ourselves. Even in eternity, Adrian, there must still be discipline and order.'

Listening to this, it seemed to Toady that a sudden and blazing light, a light of truth and realization, had appeared at the end of a long dark tunnel. Barely able to suppress his excitement he said, 'But that means you're no different from us! You might be a part of this great, eternal, cosmic whatever, but that's no different to me being a part of the human race! You're born, you die, same as me, same as everyone! And just 'cos you can change dimensions and forms and stuff, and you share knowledge, that doesn't necessarily mean you're eternal. I mean, if you look at it like that, then that means *we're* eternal too – not personally, but as a race, a species. I mean, even if the earth blows up, we're still part of space, part of the universe, and that will go on forever. Maybe one day—' he paused here, eyes sparkling like a zealot's – 'maybe one day we'll be the same as you! Maybe we *are* you! Maybe we just haven't developed enough yet!'

He was sweating with the euphoria of this possibility. Ranulf, however, seemed implacable as ever. Toady thought he detected anger, doubt, even fear in the dog's soft brown eyes, but so fleeting was the impression he could not be sure.

'No,' Ranulf said, 'you do not understand. I doubted that you would. You aspire to greatness, that's all, but you can never scale the heights that we have achieved. You, your race, are puny, a scattered series of disparate elements locked into one dimension, one timescale. It is only we who can manipulate and expand that dimension, only we who can open up parallel histories for you. No amount of evolutionary development could make you like us.'

This last speech, Toady fancied, had been delivered in a sulky, guarded manner. Because of this, he decided to leave this particular line of argument alone for fear that Ranulf would become uncommunicative. There were still questions he wanted to ask the dog, questions relating to his and his friends' own personal plight, and about the state of affairs in far-off Starmouth. Therefore, reluctantly abandoning the existential tack, he said, 'OK, answer me this then. Why, if you're so powerful, couldn't you reach Starmouth without our help? I mean, how come we had to have a seance to let you in?'

He waited long moments for Ranulf's reply. Then the

dog said, 'There are . . . passageways between dimensions. Links. Places where structures blend, where powers converge. Disturbed places. The house at King Street is one such place. We – the Us – have access to all these links . . . yet, admittedly, we sometimes need help to cross them. But this is not a failing; in eternity, help always comes, sooner or later.'

'But why a seance?' Toady insisted. 'I mean, it seemed a good idea at the time. But now, after all this, is just seems a bit . . . I dunno . . . corny, I suppose.'

'It was not the "seance", not the ceremony itself, which allowed the Us to enter. It was the energy of your concentrated thoughts, your life-energies, which opened the link. The "seance" was merely an incidental.'

'I see,' said Toady, nodding. He had an image of a concentrated beam of thought, like a thread of light, flowing from the boys, cutting through the blackness of space to some nebulous area where the Zad waited. He imagined the Zad as a huge black spider crouching in the centre of an enormous web; imagined their thoughts striking the web, setting its delicate strands shimmering; imagined the Zad scuttling down that thread to its source.

He shuddered.

'Is it possible for me to get back to Starmouth and stop this Zad-thing from doing whatever it's doing?' he asked, and thought, 'He won't answer that,' as the silence following this question stretched and stretched like rubber.

Then, surprisingly, Ranulf said, 'Yes, it's a possibility. Though only if that is what's meant to be. Another way to acquire knowledge – to understand humility, for instance – is through defeat.'

'Then will you help me?' Toady asked. 'How do I get back?'

Another annoying pause, though shorter this time. 'I cannot help you directly – in this dimension the forces of Zad are in the ascendancy and the power of the Us prevents me – but, as much as I am able, I will point you

589

in the right direction. The knowledge you need to defeat the Zad is within you, and if events permit it will make itself known in due course. As for getting back, you must look for the link between this and your own dimension and pray that it is still open to you.'

'The link,' Toady repeated. 'What does it look like, this link?'

'For you it is a representation of the environment which houses your physical body. You and your friends must look for a hospital, then a room, then a bed . . . But because of your limited mental capabilities, the link which exists for you is only temporary. It does not have the power of the Us to reinforce it. There is no knowing how long it will be able to sustain itself.'

'But how do we find it? Which direction do we go in?'

Another silence. Then the dog said, 'You must search. That is all I can tell you.'

Toady was silent for a moment as he thought on this. Then another question occurred to him. 'Why did the Zad send us here? I mean, if we're some kind of threat to him because of what we know, why didn't he just kill us? Surely it would have been easier for him to have done that than trick us all in the way he did?'

Ranulf sighed, as though the answer to Toady's question was obvious. 'Because,' he said, 'you are the Zad's link. Your energies, your essences, your life forces, are what sustains the Zad in your dimension. Only by keeping you alive can he remain there. If he were to kill you, then the link would be broken and he would return automatically to this dimension.'

'But you just said we had limited mental capabilities! How can we provide a link for the Zad and yet at the same time create only a temporary one for ourselves?'

'Because the Us provides the extra power. The link can only remain if both elements, the strength of the Us and your own small but vital contribution, exist simultaneously.'

'So . . . so . . .' Toady put his hands to his head; his

brain was beginning to hurt as he tried to absorb and order all this information. 'So why can't *you* give us the extra power and get us back to Starmouth?'

'I can only influence the strength of the link if I am operating within it,' said Ranulf. 'If the Us allows, once you are *in* the link I can communicate with you, advise you, direct you, but I cannot influence its strength. You will be – as it were – the pilot, Adrian. You must hold the plane steady.'

Toady grimaced. The task appeared enormous. The metaphor which Ranulf had used seemed alarmingly appropriate: he was a little kid being placed in the cockpit of an aircraft and told to fly it. If he didn't, it could mean an end to his life and to the lives of untold others.

The thought horrified him and for the moment he decided to let the matter be. He asked a question he had already put to Robin, one he had been puzzling over ever since arriving in this fairytale-nightmare. 'Ranulf, what are we exactly? I mean, to myself I feel normal, flesh and blood, but if my physical body's in Starmouth, does that mean I'm a ghost? An illusion? A dream? A thought? What?'

He saw Ranulf's jowls crinkle into a smile, and couldn't help thinking it was at his uncertainty. The dog answered, 'Physically you exist in both dimensions, but your conscious mind is here in this one and has fabricated a form for itself. As I said, in Starmouth you and your friends are in hospital beds, in states which you know as coma. So in answer to your question, Adrian, you are neither ghost nor illusion nor dream nor thought . . . and yet you are all of these.'

'Oh, thanks,' Toady said heavily. 'That helps a lot.' He stared at one of the candles, dimming and brightening, rhythmic as breath. He asked, 'So does that mean we can't die here? I mean, if that Crowl thing had got me, it wouldn't have mattered because this isn't my real body; it's just something my mind made for itself?'

He was not surprised to see Ranulf shake his head. 'No,

just the opposite. If you were to die either here or in Starmouth, then the whole of you would die; both parts, if you like. If I had not rescued you from the Crowl, or if, for instance, the Zad destroyed the physical part of you in Starmouth, then the entirety of what you are would have no choice but to progress to whatever awaits you beyond your physical existence – or not, as the case may be.'

Toady shuddered at the implications of this. All that Zad-thing in Starmouth had to do was stick a knife into his recumbent form, or put a pillow over his sleeping face, and he would wink out of existence. He looked at Ranulf, noticed the expression of smug superiority on the canine features, and thought: 'You bastard.'

Though the dog had helped him, had saved his life and was willingly answering all his questions, Toady decided he did not like Ranulf very much. The dog possessed a great deal of what his mother had been accused of: arrogance. He used every opportunity to humble and belittle, to manipulate Toady into a position of inferiority – a tactic, the boy suddenly realized, that he himself had employed not so very long ago. Thinking back now, he found it hard to equate himself with the bitter, petulant, insecure boy who had goaded and tricked his friends into holding the seance. He felt ashamed of his actions, wondered what had used to make him think that everyone was his enemy. Was it due, as he had always believed, to a lifetime of being bullied? Or had he been bullied because of his attitude? Had his attitude, in fact, been somehow ingrained in his make-up from the beginning? Indeed, perhaps it had been this very attitude which had alienated him from his peers in the first place?

'What came first,' he thought, 'the chicken or the egg?' Then he looked up to see Ranulf staring at him as though reading his mind.

Without quite knowing why, Toady said, 'I got this book out of the library not so long ago. It was about this woman in America who'd been . . . y'know, physically abused as a child, and had developed all these personalities

592

in her mind to cope with it. There were, I think, about ninety-eight of these personalities, all with different names and everything.' He suddenly saw where this was leading, but couldn't stop himself. He continued, 'Anyway I was just thinking that you reminded me of this woman. Well, not you personally but, y'know, the Us. Except that in your case there aren't ninety-eight personalities, but about ninety-eight billion zillion recurring. That's what you are, Ranulf, the ultimate multiple-personality. Perhaps they ought to write a book about you.'

He laughed uncertainly, half-inviting the dog to join in. Ranulf, however, turned contemptuously away and stared into the candle. Toady's laughter tittered to a halt, leaving a silence to swallow them up. At last, penetrating the silence, came three words muttered and hard, the dog's black lips hardly moving as he spoke.

'You,' he said – and there was a sneer there too, not unlike the one Richard Gardener had heard over the phone-line in Starmouth – 'understand nothing.'

3

Saturday 8.33 p.m.

'There's a new series I'd like to watch at nine. It's about these two ex-SAS men who go off to fight in the Gaza Strip. I saw a clip of it yesterday. It looks very good.'

Derek had made this announcement at eight o'clock, but as usual by half past he was snoring quietly. This was their normal Saturday night ritual: switching to brain-dead mode in front of the telly, Derek sliding into sleep. At half-past eleven Eileen would begin to watch the horror film – tonight's was *Blood On Dracula's Lips* – whereupon Derek would lurch into wakefulness, stare uncomprehendingly at the screen for a moment, then blunder through to the kitchen to make the Horlicks and let Sam out.

Thinking of this, Eileen marvelled at how quickly their

593

minds had adapted to the situation, how the humdrum routines of life failed to be extinguished by the revelations of the past few days. In a way it was like a kind of schizophrenia. One half of their minds were full of awe, horror, wonder, whilst the other half plodded on, laying down the tracks of humble physical existence with a kind of blind, stupid stoicism.

She watched Derek's lips vibrating slightly as he snored, and thought that it was as though by weaving webs of mundanity they were creating an almost mystical barrier against the power of the 'creature'. Of course she knew this was nonsense – shopping in Asda, going down the chippy, watching TV, would no more repel an 'attack' than spit would stop an elephant – though she nevertheless felt comforted by the familiarity and the routine. She selected a coffee cream from the half-empty box of Milk Tray on her knee, which had been left over from Christmas, and popped it into her mouth. As the chocolate broke open and the coffee sweetness spread over her tongue, she switched her thoughts to her son.

Richard, of course, was the one in real danger. Yet this fact offered no comfort to Eileen; indeed it only served to make things worse. If she had the choice she would much rather bear her son's suffering than have him suffer himself, and she believed that ninety per cent of mums in the world would do the same. She was proud of the way Richard had coped; it choked her up to see the almost frightening sense of maturity he had adopted in the past two days. It was almost as though within his 'mini-coma' he had sloughed off the last awkward shackles of adolescence and emerged from the chrysalis a man.

Her thoughts were broken by Sam, who lifted his head and barked. Eileen, who'd become hyper-sensitive to noise around the house in the past couple of days, tensed like a cat. 'What is it, boy?' she hissed, and a moment later she had her answer. She flinched as white glowing eyes swept across the curtains like search-lamps, and relaxed only a little at the sound of a car engine dwindling to a stop outside.

Reluctantly Sam dragged himself up from his place by the fire and plodded to the door to do his guard-dog bit. 'Woof, woof,' he said to the hall through the door's glass panels, then as his acute hearing picked up the sound of footsteps approaching up the drive, 'WOOF-WOOF-WOOF'.

'Derek,' said Eileen. Three short hard raps on the front door made her jump and Sam bark all the louder. 'Derek, there's someone at the door.'

He surfaced slowly, opening one eye and then the other. He groaned and smoothed down his steely hair. 'What's that bloody dog barking at?' he muttered.

'There's someone at the door,' Eileen repeated. She was clutching the Milk Tray box as though preparing to use it as a shield. 'Go and see who it is, will you?'

Muttering, Derek pushed himself to his feet and trudged across the room. He nudged Sam out of the way with his knee as he opened the sitting room door. 'Shut up, Sam,' he grumbled, but the boxer ignored him, hackles rising.

Derek plodded down the hallway, trying to shake off the disorienting effects of being suddenly woken from a sleep that was somewhere other than in his bed. Around him was a sea of whispers – the shh of the central heating, the murmur of the wind. Sam's barking was muffled through the sitting room door, but the three knocks, repeated again, were sharp as stone on stone. 'Hang on, I'm coming,' he grumbled, twisting the latch and the handle and pulling the door open.

A blast of cold passed over and through him, chilling both his skin and the hallway behind. He shivered, a reaction intensified by the sight of the figure standing before him – bulky, black and shiny with a flat head. It was only a split-second, however, before he recognized Sergeant Glennon, wrapped up well against the cold.

'Ah . . . good evening, Sergeant. What can we do for you?' Derek asked.

Glennon looked at him, face as red as his hair. 'I wondered if I might speak to Richard?' he said. 'I didn't like to intrude before, but I was passing and I thought . . .'

He left the sentence unfinished. Derek held the door wide and stepped back. 'Certainly, come on in,' he invited.

Glennon thanked him and passed over the threshold, puffing out his cheeks. He wiped his feet, then stepped forward so that Derek could shut the door. 'It's cold out tonight,' he said as he peeled off his gloves and his coat. He draped them over the banister, then perched his cap on top. 'I hope there's not more snow on the way.'

'Hmm,' Derek said and led the way along the hall. He opened the sitting room door, pushing back Sam who looked to be spoiling for a fight. 'It's only Sergeant Glennon, love,' he said to his wife as he entered.

Eileen paled and glared at her husband. It had been the sergeant himself who had warned them to take nothing for granted, who had told them about the creature's ability to impersonate whomever it liked, quoting Olive's experience with 'Harold' as the example. 'Admit no-one, trust no-one, unless you're absolutely sure of their identity,' Glennon had said, yet here was Derek, letting in what *appeared* to be the sergeant without a second thought.

Her suspicion, however, quickly faded. Sam's initial reticence soon gave way to a puppyish wagging of his entire hind-quarters, as sure a sign as any that this Glennon was indeed the genuine article. The policeman's large hands petted Sam's body in the rough but friendly way that the dog seemed to like best, and were met with licks in return. 'Get down, Sam,' Eileen said at last, 'you're getting hairs on the sergeant's uniform.'

'Oh, I don't mind,' Glennon replied, 'I like dogs.' He looked up, raised his eyebrows and said, 'Is Richard about by any chance?'

For a moment Eileen was puzzled. She couldn't see any connection between liking dogs and Richard. She wondered whether the policeman was making some obscure and not-very-funny joke. Then Derek said, 'That's why the sergeant's come. He wanted a chat with Richard.'

'Oh,' said Eileen, surprised, 'I see. Well, I think he's having a bath just now . . . but didn't your Constable whatsisname get all the information you needed?'

There was a silence. Glennon looked at her blankly. At last he gave a tight smile and said, 'I'm sorry. I don't know what you mean.'

Eileen stared back at him. 'You know,' she said, 'your Constable . . . thingy. Stevens! That was his name. Constable Stevens. He rang up and asked to speak to Richard. He said he was acting under your orders.'

Glennon glanced at Derek, then shook his head. 'I'm sorry, Mrs Gardener, but I still don't know what you're talking about. I've never heard of a Constable Stevens. There certainly isn't one at Starmouth.'

'But there must be,' Eileen insisted; she looked at the two men as though trapped. 'He rang up this evening, said you'd taken him into your confidence, told him everything.'

'I'm sorry, Mrs Gardener,' repeated Glennon, 'but someone's been having you on.'

Eileen was bewildered. 'But who—' she began, then stopped as realization dawned. Her face filled with horror. 'It was that thing, wasn't it? That foul awful . . . *thing* rang me up.'

The room screamed out its silence. Eileen's hand rubbed at the ear the creature had spoken into as though it might have become infected. Then in a strained voice she said, 'Oh God, Richard!' and stood up, chocolates spilling everywhere.

She stumbled to the sitting room door and wrenched it open. Her foot burst a caramel on the carpet; the rest were devoured by Sam. For a moment she stood swaying in the doorway as though buffetted by a strong wind. Then she yelled louder, 'Richard!' and stumbled along the hall to the stairs.

The men sat watching in a tableau of stupefaction. It took her raucous shout to rouse them from their trance. As

Eileen plunged into the hallway, Derek turned and regarded the policeman almost quizzically. Then he muttered, 'Bloody hell,' and followed his wife from the room.

Eileen's shouts grew shriller, more panic-stricken, as her son failed to answer. 'Richard! Richard!' she screeched over and over until the word became meaningless. Derek was halfway up the stairs, Glennon close behind, when the cries abruptly stopped. The men halted, stood motionless, like pensive mannequins.

Eileen burst from Richard's room, waving a piece of paper, the signal for them to start moving again. Derek met his wife at the top of the stairs and caught her as she started to faint. He snatched the paper from her hand, read it, then passed it, pale-faced, to Glennon. The policeman scanned the tight block capitals written in red biro on the sheet of foolscap:

DEAR MUM AND DAD,
I'M SORRY I'VE HAD TO DECEIVE YOU AGAIN, BUT THAT PHONE CALL I GOT WAS FROM THE CREATURE. IT TOLD ME TO BE AT THE HOSPITAL AT 8.45 OTHERWISE IT WOULD KILL NEIL AND ALL MY FRIENDS. I HAD TO GO, BUT DON'T WORRY, I'LL DO ALL I CAN TO KILL IT. IN A FUNNY KIND OF WAY I THINK THIS IS JUST WHAT I'VE BEEN WAITING FOR. IF ALL GOES WELL, I MIGHT EVEN BE BACK BEFORE YOU FIND THIS NOTE, BUT IF NOT I'D BETTER SAY HOW SORRY I AM FOR ALL THIS, AND THAT I LOVE YOU VERY MUCH. YOU'RE THE BEST MUM AND DAD ANYONE COULD EVER WANT. PLEASE FORGIVE ME.

ALL MY LOVE, YOUR SON,
RICHARD

'Ah no,' Glennon sighed after reading it, then folded the note and put it in his pocket. All at once he felt tired, so tired that the skin seemed heavy on his face. He rubbed his chin, hearing the bristles scrape like sandpaper, then tapped Derek Gardener on the shoulder. He was comforting his sobbing wife, but turned at the sergeant's touch.

For a moment Glennon said nothing. He stared into

Derek's eyes and hoped his own weren't so haunted. He suddenly found himself wishing, as he'd never wished before, that he'd become an engineer like his dad.

'Come on,' he heard himself say, 'we'll use my car.'

4

Saturday 8.37 p.m.

Three buses packed with Saturday night revellers swept by Richard's outstretched hand before one finally stopped. He got on, panic burgeoning like nausea within him, aware that a good portion of his sixty-minute deadline had passed as he stood at the bus-stop contracting frost-bite. The bus smelt of perfume, after shave and hair gel; Richard felt like screaming at the laughing, chatting hordes around him, at the bus driver who seemed to think he was stuck in an invisible traffic jam. By the time Richard alighted from the bus it was 8.37, only eight minutes before his deadline. As soon as his feet touched the pavement, Richard started running.

He emerged from between two buildings and the hospital came into sight, lit up like an opera house in the darkness. Its grey stone shone like ice; its neon sign, 'Hospital. Quiet Please', burned red like an enticement to customers. Richard sprinted through the open gates and across the carpark. Three ambulances were parked either side of the steps like sinister ice-cream vans, one of them with its lights on. Richard ran between them, up the steps and in through the glass doors.

Immediately he was inside he began sweating. Before his spectacles steamed up he saw a clock on the wall poised at 8.40. Despite the time, he stopped for a moment to catch his breath and look around. There were a few people about, but nobody paid him any attention.

As he wiped his spectacles he thought it ironic how things had worked out. This terrible business had begun in a dark, dirty, evil-smelling place; now it looked

599

destined to end somewhere full of light and antiseptic-clean. His heart was thumping, his throat like sand; he was scared, but not for himself. Within him he still held that strange sense of peace, that cool determination and icy hatred for his enemy. He replaced his spectacles and glanced again at the clock. 8.41 it said, and he started to run once more.

'Excuse me,' the receptionist said as Richard passed by.

'I've got to see my brother,' he called over his shoulder without slowing.

He ran along two corridors – white, brown-carpeted, lined with pastelly pictures – and emerged into an open area, one wall of which was dominated by two lift doors. A button between the doors unnecessarily read 'Press', and Richard did so, then stood back to wait. 'Come on, come on,' he muttered as the lights above the lift descended leisurely from '8' to 'G'.

At 'G' there was an agonizing pause, as though the lift was debating whether to travel up to '8' again, then the doors slowly parted with a musical 'ting'. Richard hurled himself into the metal box and jabbed at the number '2'. The lift doors closed excruciatingly slowly. Just before they sealed him inside, he noticed the clock on the opposite wall lurch to 8.42. There seemed to be clocks wherever he looked here, mocking him with the shortness of their minutes.

At '2' the lift paused again, thought long and hard about opening its doors, then deigned to do so. Richard shot out, barging into someone whose white coat and stethoscope suggested he was a doctor. 'Hey, watch what you're doing,' said a voice, and a hand made a grab for his arm, though whether through instinct or aggression was difficult to tell.

'Sorry,' muttered Richard, and squirmed away from the hand before its fingers could close in a grip. Without looking at the doctor's face, he took to his heels down the corridor.

When he was sure that the man was not following, he slowed to a jog. Speed was all-important, but Richard knew that a flat-out sprint would only draw attention to himself and probably cause more accidents. Besides, he was only vaguely aware of the layout of the hospital and had to keep his eyes peeled for signs that would point him in the direction he wanted to go.

'Ward thirty-three,' he murmured as he came upon a junction with arrowed signs pointing in different directions. His eyes skimmed over -ology this and -opothy that until they alighted on a sign which read 'Wards 32–38'.

He grunted in satisfaction and increased speed again, turning right along a corridor which contained an un-manned desk on which a phone was bleeping. He passed olive-green doors, a poster about heart disease, a notice-board dripping with 'Thank You' cards. A nurse suddenly appeared round the corner, carrying something which Richard was too startled to register. He subconsciously slowed to a jog-trot and smiled nervously as they came parallel with one another. She smiled back but said nothing. They passed. He sighed with relief and increased speed again.

Round another corner; feeling as though the corridors were folding back on themselves like an Escher drawing. He saw a plaque above a pair of double doors that read 'Ward 32', glimpsed beds and people in them through the glass panels as he hurried on. A little further along, another pair of double doors, another plaque: 'Ward 33'. 'At last,' he whispered and, breathing hard, entered.

He spotted Neil almost immediately, halfway along the line of beds to his left, reading a magazine called *Rugby World*. He looked around for personnel, saw a bearded male nurse sharing a joke with a patient at the end of the ward. He began to sidle along the line of beds, aware of eyes watching him, hoping no-one would challenge him or call out. He was at the foot of Neil's bed before his brother looked up and saw him.

'Rich!' he said then, loud enough to make Richard

601

cringe. The younger boy placed a finger to his lips, an agonized expression on his face. A few heads turned their way; a man with half-moon spectacles peered long and hard like a schoolteacher rooting out miscreants. Richard smiled at him and felt a trickle of sweat run down his face. Half-moon didn't smile back, but, thankfully, returned to his book.

'Rich, what are you doing here?' Neil hissed. 'You look awful. Is something wrong?'

'Are you all right?' Richard said, countering his brother's questions with one of his own.

'Yeah . . . I'm fine,' answered Neil, bewildered. 'Why shouldn't I be? I'm coming home tomorrow.'

'You've had no strange visitors? There's been no-one, nothing . . . weird hanging about the ward?'

'Only you. Look, Rich, what is all this? What's going on? Are you in some kind of trouble?'

'No, no, nothing like that.' He shook his head distractedly, then glanced at the ward clock. It hovered on 8.43, then clicked on another minute. Richard began to back away from his brother's bed.

'Look, Neil, I've gotta go,' he said. 'I'll see you later, OK? Tomorrow, when you come home . . . or maybe later tonight.'

Neil rolled his eyes, exasperated. 'Rich! Will you please tell me what's going on?'

'There's no time now. I really have gotta go. Look, I'll explain later, I promise. I just came in to make sure you were all right.'

'Well, where are you going now?' the older boy exclaimed.

'Isolation ward. I've got to get there by quarter to or it'll kill them. See you, Neil.'

Out in the corridor again, Richard spun around and around, looking for a sign that would lead him to a lift or stairs. Seeing nothing, he began to run along the corridor past Wards 34, 35, 36, round a corner, past 37, 38. A door stood open to his left, from it the sound of voices. He ran past without turning his head, hoping the talkers hadn't seen him. The timbre of their voices remained unchanged and he sighed with relief once more. Seconds later his heart leaped as the familiar open area came into sight.

Richard ran to the lift doors, hit the button so hard it jarred his finger. On the wall was a photograph of black lungs, on the floor a rubber plant in a pot, the leaves yellow and sicky. 'You should see a doctor', he thought hysterically, then he noticed the clock on the wall.

'8.45', it screamed at him. 'You've missed your deadline, pal! Your mates are gonna die!'

'Aw, fuck, no,' Richard moaned. 'Sod it! Sod it!' He looked at the lights above the lift, saw them poised on '5', and snarled, 'Bastard!' He turned to the wall behind him, a reinforced glass door that led to a featureless stair-well.

He wrenched the door open, began to run up the stairs, feet slapping the concrete, palm squealing along the plastic-coated banister. His breath rasped, his clothes clung to him with sweat. He could smell himself, a sour hot smell of panic, and was furious that the creature's gamesmanship, if that was what it was, had got to him after all. He stumbled on the stairs, wrenching his arm. A sharp step lunged and bit at his shin. 'Fucking hell!' he screamed, dragging himself upright, pain singing in both limbs. His spectacles slid off and hit the floor. He scooped them up to find one lens cracked, one arm hanging loose. All the rage, all the frustration in the world boiled inside him, and with a yell that echoed and echoed and echoed he hurled his spectacles at the wall.

'Oy, what's going on?' said a voice, though whether from above him or below Richard couldn't tell.

'Piss off,' he muttered, still seething; then took a grip on the banister and continued his ascent.

Floor three, floor four: 8.47.

Floor five, floor six: 8.48.

By the time he reached floor seven – contagious diseases and supernatural comas only – it was 8.49.

Despite the time, Richard had to pause for a moment at

the top; he felt he was on the point of either throwing up or fainting. He gripped the banister rail and slumped over it, staring at the floor far, far below. It made his head spin and he squeezed his eyes tightly shut. His throat snatched at saliva, but couldn't find it. Centipedes of sweat danced over his skin, cooking him within the oven of his clothes. He unzipped his parka, the teeth rasping like a metallic tear.

He pushed himself back from the banister and opened his eyes. Red and green blobs shivered like half-seen jelly. His eyes focussed on the sign above the door to the right of the lifts. Without his specs it was fuzzy, but he could still read it well enough. 'Isolation Rooms 1–10' it said, 4, 5 and 6 of which were occupied by his three friends.

What he could see of the corridor through the door's glass panels was well-lit but empty. It did not surprise Richard that there seemed to be no nurses on duty. Of course they could have been inside the rooms, attending to their patients, but somehow he didn't think so. No, the creature would have got rid of them one way or another; Richard did not like to dwell on the possible methods employed.

He pushed the door inwards and stepped on to the brown carpet of the corridor. Immediately he felt the almost tangible sense of waiting, of expectation. The creature was here all right; he could all but see it, taste it, smell it. The door swung shut behind him, its heavy spring catching it and stopping it from banging. The profound, sealed-in silence made Richard feel completely isolated.

He was late, five minutes late, but somehow he felt that it didn't matter any more. The enraged, panicked scramble up the stairs had been pointless, for time was a nonsense here. As if to comfirm this, he noticed the clock on the wall was broken, the hands stuck on 6.22. But no, on closer inspection it seemed the clock was not broken after all. The hands were, in fact, still moving; he watched the second hand rotate on its never-ending journey. The clock was working perfectly, except for one small thing.

It was running backwards.

'Very clever,' Richard said, and let out a chuckle that sounded like a cough. He approached the first of the doors, room 4, the sweat cooling on his body. The silence had helped him regain his composure; the inner triad of peace, cold hatred and determination were re-establishing themselves. He reached the door and placed his hands on the handle, pausing just long enough to read the notice blu-tacked to the white wood.

CAUTION

SPEAK TO NURSE IN CHARGE BEFORE ENTERING

WEAR GOWN, MASK AND GLOVES

USE DISPOSABLE PLATES, CUPS AND CUTLERY

'Bollocks,' said Richard, and pushed the door open.

This was Robin's room. There was a smell of plastic sterility. Without letting go of the door handle, Richard took a good look round.

The room was as spartan as the last time he'd been here: apart from Robin and his bed it contained only a washbasin, wastebin, chair, and a painting on the wall of daisies in a field. The lighting was subdued; the floor-length orange curtains across the room gave the place a false sense of warmth. Richard let go of the handle and walked across to look at his friend.

Since his last visit, Robin had grown tubes out of his body from which sprouted a metal tree. The fruit on this tree were dangling bags of colourless fluid. Robin was on his back, his eyes closed, his breathing steady. Despite the orange curtains his skin was pale, almost translucent. Richard touched his friend's upper arm; the flesh felt clammy and cool. He was not sure whether this was a good thing or a bad one.

At least, he thought, Robin had not been tampered with. Though the lack of medical attention that his friend was receiving worried him. He touched him again, as though to ensure he was real, then walked back across the room, 'See you, Rob,' he said quietly, then went out, shutting the door behind him.

'OK,' he thought, 'one down, two to go.' Room 5, he knew, belonged to Toady. Without pausing to read the notice this time, he turned the handle and went in.

This might have been the room he'd just left, so similar was it in design and furnishings. Even the figure in the bed was similar in regard to position, skin colour and plastic tube decoration. In fact, there were only two significant differences between this room and Robin's, and only one of these concerned Richard. The first difference, the one that didn't concern him, was that the curtains were green and not orange, and that the left one was open, revealing half a large window which started at knee-level and stopped a foot from the ceiling. The second difference, the one that concerned Richard very much, was the presence of the creature that Toady knew as the Zad. It was sitting in the chair, its legs crossed, its head slumped forward, face buried in its hands.

When Richard stepped into the room, it raised its head very, very slowly.

5

No-Time

The breakthrough came over a breakfast of malty cereal garnished with dried fruit and what tasted like honeyed milk. Robin and Toady were sitting at one side of the table, Nige at the other. Robin was wolfing down his food, wiping a hand across his face each time the milk dribbled down his chin. Toady was merely picking at his breakfast, the after-effects of last night having destroyed his appetite. Nige watched the boys warily as he ate, crouched over, hand curled around the bowl like an animal protecting its young.

Suddenly Nige sat bolt upright and dropped his spoon with a clatter. Liana swung round from the shelves she'd been dusting and regarded him silently, eyes narrowed. Nige looked, thought Toady, exactly how Simon had looked when he'd sat on a wasp at the age of three – a brief, suspended moment of shocked astonishment before an abrupt landslide of screaming tears.

However in Nige's case there were no tears; merely a look of dawning, of revelation. The slim dark-haired boy slipped down from his stool and walked around the table to stand beside Robin. It was the first time he had willingly approached his friends, and now they too were wary. Robin swivelled on his stool to face Nige, wooden spoon clenched in his hand like an amulet.

'Er . . . hi,' he said nervously.

Nige stared into Robin's face, a look whose frankness was both winsome and unsettling. Robin licked his lips just as a hand shot out and a finger poked him in the chest. 'You,' Nige said – it was the first word they'd heard him say here, though others quickly followed. 'You. I know you. I know who you are.'

Robin did not know what to say. Before his mind could decide for him, Nige was pointing at Toady. 'I know you too,' he said, and walked round the back of Robin's stool to gaze into Toady's face. After a few moments more he confirmed his statement.

'Yes. I know you and I know you. I know both of you. Both of you I know. Both of you.'

Then, thoughtfully, he returned to his seat.

Toady, though surprised, was not as tongue-tied as Robin. As Nige picked up his spoon again, he asked, 'What do you know, Nige? Do you know our names?'

'Names,' Nige repeated, and frowned suspiciously. He looked at his spoon as if that might give him the answer. Then all at once his face cleared and Toady thought he'd got through. But Nige was simply rejecting the question, pushing it aside because he didn't understand its meaning.

The olive-skinned boy began to eat again. Toady looked at Robin, who shrugged indifferently. Toady, however, was not prepared to give up so easily and leaned forward to draw Nige's attention. Behind him he was aware of Liana watching the exchange with interest.

'Nige,' he said firmly. The boy's eyes flickered, but he did not look up. 'Nige, we're your friends. We want to help you. Do you understand that? We're your friends.'

'Friends,' repeated Nige, and this time did look up, a slow smile spreading across his face. 'Friends. Yes, friends.' He smiled some more, liking the taste of the word.

'Do you know our names?' Toady persisted, knowing from experience that the key to one memory could also be the key to many others. 'Nige, this is very important. You must remember our names.'

Nige's smile wavered, then his eyes hooded over and he began to eat stolidly once more. Toady made an exasperated sound.

'Give the boy time,' Liana said from behind him. 'He's confused at the moment. But he'll come round.'

Toady turned to face her. She looked back at him unflinchingly as if she hadn't spoken at all. There was no animation in her face; the only movement came from her hands, carefully filling her clay pipe. Toady wondered what she'd looked like before the Zad had forced her into this shape, wondered how much all this drudgery had changed her character. This, of course, was assuming that Ranulf had told him the truth last night. He wondered whether, as a queen, she'd smoked a pipe, and the image brought a smile to his lips.

Liana sniffed and looked down at her pipe as though disquieted by his smile. Sullenly she said, 'You were lucky last night. The Crowl is an evil element.'

'How did you—' Toady began, but knew the answer before he'd even finished the question. Of course: 'the Us', shared knowledge, all that stuff. It seemed, then, that

Ranulf had been at least partly telling the truth; there was no other way Liana could have found out about last night's events. Unable to sleep after his ordeal, Toady had heard her get up at first light and had followed her downstairs.

'You'll be wanting food for your journey,' Liana said, then put the pipe in her mouth and lit it. She looked at him shrewdly, eyes like obsidian in her doughy face.

The offer was like a put-down, a reminder to the boys of their dependence on her, and for a moment Toady felt an urge to refuse it. Then he remembered how they had almost starved on their way here, and so swallowing his pride he said, 'Er . . . yes please. That is, if you've got any to spare.'

Robin was scraping the last remnants of cereal from his bowl. 'What journey?' he said. 'And what the hell *is* a Crowl?'

Liana smirked. Toady sighed and ran a hand through his hair. He'd been putting off telling Robin about last night, largely because the thought of repeating all that Ranulf had told him was daunting. However, now that Liana had brought the subject up, he was going to have to offer an explanation. He pushed his bowl of half-eaten cereal aside, collected his thoughts and began.

The first part of the story was easy enough to tell, though having to describe the Crowl made him grimace with distaste. The second part, however, the talk with Ranulf, was altogether more difficult. Toady found himself halting and stuttering as he tried to remember all the complexities of 'the Us', frequently having to double-back on his account to explain points that he'd missed or glossed over. He was uncomfortably aware of his audience throughout: Robin, frowning and silent, obviously struggling for comprehension. Nige, giving the impression of enraptured attention, but his brown eyes empty, not taking anything in. Liana, who was, after all, part of the same stuff as Ranulf, who simply stood and watched his struggle with the same implacable intensity as her son/dog, and who made no attempts to help him out when he started to come unstuck.

609

He finished his monologue tight-lipped, feeling anger towards the bearded lady. 'And that was it,' he said, 'I went to bed then.' He swung towards her, shoulders stiff, face burning with resentment. 'Well?' he snapped accusingly. 'How did I do?'

'Fine,' said Liana calmly, her expression unchanging, the word little more than a twitch. She turned towards the pantry, manoeuvering round the table like a battleship round a buoy. 'I'll get that food for you,' she added with a finality that defied argument.

Toady gave up, and turned instead to Robin. 'Well,' he said, 'what did you think?'

Robin looked pensive; the mental cogs were almost visible, whirring in his head. Thoughtfully he asked some questions: why this, how that, what the other. Toady did his best to answer them, then both of them looked up as Nige began to speak.

'Nigel Figg! That's who I am!' he said, thumping his fist on the table. 'And you, you're Robin Treadwell, and you're Adrian Tibbett!'

Delightedly he began to laugh, the sound abandoned and infectious as a toddler's. Despite everything, Robin began to smile in response and a moment later Toady too joined in.

Their departure from Liana's cottage was low-key, without ceremony. Dressed in their newly-cleaned clothes and shoes (though Toady's shoes were still spattered with dried vomit), they stood out on the path, waiting. The trees around the clearing stood at a kind of twisted attention, snaring patches of bruised sky in their branches. The cess-pit lurked within its own foggy aura, its surface like glistening skin.

Liana oozed from the cottage and silently held out a sack. Robin took it and looked inside. He saw bread, cheese, fruit and a few chunky bottles containing some liquid or other. He thanked her and smiled, but she didn't smile back.

Nige said, 'Friends,' and moved forward without

610

inhibition to hug Liana round her vast waist. The bearded lady did not reject the hug, but neither did she acknowledge it.

'Well . . . goodbye. Thanks for all your help,' Toady said.

Liana replied, 'Hmm,' and went back into the cottage, closing the door behind her.

For a moment the boys stood looking at the closed door and each other, Toady again irritated by the woman's imperiousness, and again ashamed to see a parallel there with his own previous behaviour. Earlier on he had asked Liana, 'Which is the best way to go?' to which she had replied, 'One way is as good as another. Nothing is constant here.'

Toady now put this question to Robin. The blond-haired boy shrugged and looked around. 'I don't fancy going back that way again,' he said, nodding towards the natural tunnel in the trees through which they'd entered the clearing. 'I mean, according to Liana that link-thing could be anywhere. It doesn't have to be back that way, does it?'

'No,' Toady said, 'it doesn't. And I agree with you; I can't face that forest and all that mud again either – if it's still all there, that is. No, let's go this way. Though how we're expected to find the link at all is beyond me.'

The three boys walked up the path, Nige now seemingly happy simply to follow his friends. Once out the gate they turned right, cutting behind the cottage, giving them a view of the back of the house and the ancient well with its wooden bucket resting on the stone lip. As they entered the trees, passing once more into a land of twilight and shadow, Toady wondered where Ranulf was. After last night he would have thought Ranulf would have come to see them off, maybe even offer some last-minute advice, but this had not been the case. He shrugged, and tried to concentrate on the way ahead, as the cottage disappeared from view.

6

Saturday 8.52 p.m.

The creature was crying.

Richard stood just inside the door, frozen with . . . what? Fear? Surprise? Anticipation? He honestly couldn't say. He thought the tears on the creature's cheeks looked like cellophane, crocodile tears, and he stared at them, emotionless. The creature let out a sob, then raised its arm, hand reaching out entreatingly.

'Richard,' it whispered, 'help me, please.'

Richard closed the door behind him and took two more steps into the room. The hatred he felt was so cold, so intense, that it did not feel like hatred at all. He wished he had a gun with him now; if he had he believed – no, he *knew* – he would have used it. He would have pumped shot after shot into the creature's head until it was a pulp of bone and brains and blood. It did not matter that the creature had taken on the shape of a boy the same age as himself, did not matter that for some reason it seemed racked with remorse. Coldly, unemotionally, Richard would have killed the creature, and afterwards he would have washed the blood off himself, gone home and climbed into bed where he would have dreamt the dreams of the righteous.

However, Richard did not have a gun. And even if he had he doubted whether such a mundane thing as a bullet would have provided the answer to his problems. He had come here, in fact, without any conventional weapon at all; all he had was his own emotional equilibrium, the strange sense of inner calm that was like a manifestation of his own personal faith.

He took two more steps, then two more, until he was able to lean against the end of Toady's bed. He stood, arms folded, watching the creature weep. He wondered how he knew this *was* the creature, this boy who was both familiar and unfamiliar. He came to the conclusion that he simply knew, that was all; it was as though he had developed an extra sense, a creature-detector, that wheedled out the monster whatever guise it chose to adopt. 'Bloody good,' he thought with a kind of vague satisfaction, 'bloody useful'. He shifted his weight on to his other leg as the creature spoke again.

'Richard,' it said, its voice small, broken, 'I really am so, so sorry for everything that I've done.'

Richard opened his mouth. His lips peeled apart like flypaper, making him realize how dry they had become. He spoke his first words since entering the room, and was only mildly surprised to hear a voice that did not sound like his at all. 'I don't believe you' he said.

The creature seemed to deflate, its shoulders slumping, its limbs folding over one another as though it was trying to make itself as small a target as possible. The body it had adopted was a little on the portly side – plump hands, the suggestion of a double chin, a stomach which almost (but not quite) lapped over the belt of its jeans. It had swarthy skin, a wide mouth, a face and neck blemished with acne. Its hair was straight and black and a little greasy-looking, its fringe long, flicked to one side.

The conviction that he both knew and did not know this boy again gnawed at Richard, though it was nothing more than a minor distraction. It did not upset his sense of inner balance in any way; indeed, it only served to put him more on his guard than ever. He stared at the creature as the silence extended between them, regulated by Toady's deep breathing and the occasional muffled snarl of traffic far below. The large window gave a view of a starless night sky, heavy with smoggy cloud, and a few rooftops, black and angular, spiky with chimneys. The creature squirmed in its seat, a hand fluttering to its face, then looked up, meeting Richard's eye, squinting as though staring into the sun. At last, in a dull voice, it said, 'I don't blame you. I don't blame you for not believing me. But it's true, Richard, every word, I swear it. I . . . I've done some terrible things.'

Richard snorted. 'That's the understatement of the

century.' His arms folded and he jabbed an accusation at the creature's slumped form. 'OK, if you're sorry, how do you explain the phone call of . . . what? Just over an hour ago? How do you explain the threat to kill Neil and my friends if I didn't show up?'

The creature looked utterly miserable. 'I couldn't think of any other way to get you here,' it replied.

Richard snorted again, rolled his eyes disbelievingly, though in truth he was appalled to find himself wanting to believe that the creature's remorse was genuine. He had come here expecting some cataclysmic encounter, but instead he had found a subdued plea for aid and forgiveness, had found every indication that this whole ghastly affair could end in a simple and bloodless manner. This wasn't how it ended in the films and books, but then again this wasn't fiction. He thought of all the senseless deaths, thought of Olive, so still, mouth open, eyes wide. He looked at Toady, a living corpse, and almost welcomed the rush of cold hatred that filled his system like a drug.

'That's bullshit,' he said. 'You honestly expect me to believe that? Over the last nine days you've killed a dozen people, and now here you are blubbering about what a bad boy you've been and how sorry you are. What happened? Have you seen the light or something? And what do you expect me to say? Oh well, never mind, anyone can make mistakes? You're . . . you're . . . you're *unbelievable!* You're *sick* . . . *evil* . . . *vicious* . . . *cowardly* . . . *SCUM!* That's what you are. You're *vermin!* You don't deserve to live.'

He came to a halt, his voice strangled with rage, lifted a stiff hand to wipe the spittle from his chin. He expected the creature to respond to his tirade, to get angry, show its true self, but instead it seemed to dwindle, to wither, to push itself back into the chair as though it wished to merge with it and disappear. Tears began to run down its acned cheeks, and Richard grinned savagely, pleased to have caused them.

'I said I was sorry,' the creature wailed, 'and I am. I am,

Richard. I really am.' It hung its head, pushed a fist into its cheek in a slow-motion punch. 'I know I've been evil. I realize that now. But I brought you here because I wanted to explain why. And because I believe that together we can undo some of what I've done.'

Richard remained silent. The creature's tear-blurred eyes met his, then slid away again. They focussed on its chubby hands, wrestling together in its lap like naked, fat-limbed crabs.

'I did what I did,' it said bleakly, 'as a kind of test, as a way of assessing the human being from both a physical and psychological standpoint. I took people apart to see how they were made; I subjected them to stress, played with their minds to find out how they thought. I didn't realize this was an "evil" thing to do, honestly I didn't. At the time I didn't even know what evil was. I had – have – no conscience, you see, no sense of right and wrong. It was dark where I was. I was lonely, bored. It was you, Richard, you and your friends, who released me from that darkness.'

It paused there, wiped the tears from its face. Richard said, 'Go on.'

'I wanted . . . I wanted to become one of you, to live as you do, so that I wouldn't feel lonely any more. I had the ability to take on whatever shape I chose, but still felt alienated, an outsider. To *be* like you I had to *think* like you too, and so I decided to absorb the minds, the thought-processes and emotions, of you and your three friends. That way, I believed, I would be eliminating my only threat, the only people who knew the truth about me, and I would be able to live as a hybrid, as an amalgamation of the four of you, revelling in your thoughts and emotions.' It paused, sighed deeply, shrugged. 'The morality of this didn't occur to me. As I've said before, I have no conscience, and so my motives were selfish, concerned only with the improvement of my own situation. The effect on you all, the slipping into coma, this state of living death, didn't concern me in the slightest.

615

Unfortunately – or, as far as you're concerned, fortunately – in absorbing your friends' thoughts a sense of morality, your friends' morality, was forced upon me. I began to experience emotions I never knew existed before: guilt, regret, self-loathing. At first I tried to repress them, but they continued to re-surface, and not only that but they started to get stronger and stronger. Now it's as though they're pounding in my head, berating me for all the evil I've done. I hate myself now. I realize that I've perpetrated the most hideous, disgusting crimes . . . I agree with you Richard. I *am* vermin. I don't think I can live with myself, with what I've done, any more . . . I . . . I can't stand it . . . I just . . . can't . . . stand it.'

The creature dipped its head and began to claw at its scalp as though in an attempt to tear the thoughts from its brain. When it next looked up, Richard gasped at the expression on its face. It looked, he thought, like someone whose mind was ravaged by emotions too hideous to bear. It was the face of an Auschwitz survivor, of a Vietnam veteran, memories of atrocities swirling like ominous clouds behind haunted eyes. It was the face alone, the sheer intensity of it, which sapped all the anger and hatred from Richard's body. Instead he felt pity and horror filling him, felt a confused and sympathetic sense of tragedy and despair. He knew now that the creature was telling the truth, knew that such anguish could not be faked. He felt himself crossing the gap between bed and chair, laying a hand awkwardly on the creature's shoulder. 'It's all right,' he said roughly. 'Don't worry about it. Everything'll be all right.'

Empty words, he knew, for things were not all right. Already too much had happened to prevent things ever being completely right again. The shoulder beneath his hand heaved with the sobs of his enemy. An enemy who had been terrible but misguided, evil only through his own alienness. 'What do we do?' Richard said, and his voice was flat, dredged of all emotion. He was almost glad to hear his desperation as he repeated the question. 'What do we do now?'

616

The hybrid drove knuckles into its eyes and rubbed, pummelling the tears away. When it looked up its face was raw as sunburn. 'I have links with the dead,' it said. 'They're not gone for good, that's one thing. I can't make them live again, though I can bring your friends back. But I'll need your help.'

Richard removed his hand from the creature's shoulder, carefully as though afraid of setting off an alarm. 'What do you mean,' he said, 'by "links with the dead"? Do you mean you speak to them? Do you mean you speak to people's ghosts?'

He could not keep the scepticism from his voice, though in the past Richard had always been an enthusiastic believer in the paranormal. However the events of the past nine days had, ironically perhaps, made the idea of ghosts seem quaint and obsolete. He looked at the creature now, mulling over this latest revelation, slightly raising his mental guard once again. The hybrid stared back at him candidly, a curtain of fringe drooping over one eye.

'Yes,' it said, nodding, 'I speak to them. Does that idea seem so strange to you? After seeing me, after seeing what I can do, I would have thought you, Richard, of all people, would have found the notion acceptable. The flesh is not all that you are; I've shown you myself how it can be bent and shaped if only you have the will to do so. There are even examples of it among your own kind: people who walk on red hot coals without burning their feet, people who lift heavy objects such as cars off loved ones who've become trapped underneath. There are many states of being, Richard, of which the flesh is only one. The evidence for "ghosts", as you call them, is vast and unarguable yet you reject it simply because it can't be explained "scientifically". Your race, by and large, is a noble one, Richard, but it's also small-minded and timid. You're scared to admit what you know to be the truth.'

It was unsettling and incongruous, these words coming from a podgy, acned, awkward-looking boy. Richard's mind was racing; he was sure he had a million questions to

617

ask, but for the moment he could think of none of them. 'Ghosts', he thought, and still it seemed more unbelievable than the idea of the creature itself. When something impossible is shown to be possible, it tends to lose its aura of mystery. The creature was impossible, yet Richard had now accepted it, had slotted it into his way of thinking. Ghosts, however, were a different matter.

'I don't know,' was all he could think of to say.

To which a voice behind him replied, 'It's true, Richard. Every word.'

He whirled round so quickly that his neck clicked and sent a stab of pain into the base of his skull. A hand came up and slapped across his mouth; his other hand, his left, groped at the air as he tottered sideways, closing at last around the steel rail at the foot of Toady's bed. There was a progress chart hooked over the end of the rail and he dislodged it, causing it to glance off the side of his foot and skid away under the bed. The steel in his hand was reassuringly cold, but soon became warm as his own flesh as he squeezed it.

'There's no need to be frightened,' the voice said chirpily, 'it's only me.'

Olive Pierce was in a sitting position on the other side of the room, floating in mid-air. Her clothes, her limbs, were wispy, insubstantial, as though seen through a milky plastic bubble, but her face was vivid and radiant. Each feature, each wrinkle, was so sharply defined that it seemed almost *too* real, as though some unearthly graphic artist had taken the vitality of life and added to it. Also her voice, though recognizable, was clearer, more musical than Richard had ever heard it before. He stared and stared until his eyes began to smart through not blinking. Then, in a detached, farwaway voice he stammered, 'Olive . . . is . . . is it really you?'

The drifting figure laughed, a sound so familiar that Richard almost cried with elation. 'Of course it's me,' she said. 'I've come back to you, Richard. Thanks to our friend's mediumship, I'm finally able to speak to you again.'

An incorporeal limb gestured to Richard's right, and he turned to see the hybrid slumped in its chair in what appeared to be a light trance. The hybrid's eyes were open only slightly, revealing glistening crescents of white, and its cheeks were undulating as its tongue moved in its mouth like a slug.

'Our friend has the physical make-up to be the perfect medium,' Olive explained in her silvery voice. 'He – or rather, it – can move just as easily between this world and the spirit-world, you see. I've been looking for some such means of communication ever since the change, but oh, Richard, you've no idea how frustrating it's been not being able to get through to you. I have, however, been helping you in other ways. Tell me, how have you been feeling since waking up from your little sleep?'

'Er . . .' Richard's mind was in a turmoil and for a moment he was unable to respond. Finally he managed, 'Good. That is, y'know, calm . . . determined, sort of. It's as though it feels like things are suddenly going to turn out all right. I don't know why, but . . .' And then his eyes widened for suddenly he did know why. 'It was you, wasn't it? It was you making me feel like that?'

The apparition inclined its head modestly. 'Yes,' Olive said, 'that was me.' She smiled, her teeth white as a toothpaste commercial, her eyes flashing green as a cat's. Richard noticed that she was still wearing her spectacles and smiled at the thought of a ghost needing glasses. But then he thought, 'Well, why not?' If he was a ghost, he would probably come back wearing his glasses too. He would make sure he came back as people remembered him, so that he would be recognized.

'How . . . how's Harold?' he asked, unable to think of anything else. 'Is he there too?'

Olive's smile widened and softened. She nodded demurely and seemed actually to blush. For a moment

Richard saw her as she must have been five decades ago, the years melting from her face. She said, 'Oh, yes, Richard, he's here. And I can't tell you how wonderful it is to see him again. Things between us are just as they were all those years ago, only more so. He's been watching over me, you know, all this time, waiting for me to join him. We've got such a lot to catch up on, but before we do that I want to help you with your problems. I've learnt a great deal since crossing over; I've learnt that the "creature" is not really evil, but simply misguided, and that now it really does want to undo the wrongs it has done. You must listen to it, Richard, it's telling you the truth. Only by working together can you hope to bring your friends back.' The ghost paused here, shook its head. 'But listen to me, giving orders. I didn't come back to do that. I came back simply to advise, to tell you what I now know. The decision, the final decision, rests with you, Richard, you alone. Only you can form a judgement, only you can decide.'

The vision had been growing fainter over the last three sentences, and now on the word 'decide', it faded completely. Its features smudged, ran into one another, like a painting left in the rain; the voice grew steadily quieter as though a volume control was being turned down. Finally, with a sound like a fall of cobwebs, the clots of drifting grey that Olive had become rushed into themselves, disappearing in a silent dustless implosion. The last Richard saw of her was the glint of her spectacles, tumbling like a spark from a dying firefly.

For a moment he stood and stared at the spot where she had been, hoping that she would re-appear. However she did not, and he turned at the sounds of stirring behind him. The creature was waking, stretching its limbs, its face breaking into a yawn. It regarded Richard sleepily. 'Did she come? The old lady? Was she here just now?'

Richard nodded. 'Yes, she was.' He swallowed a lump that had risen in his throat, and half-turned to the window as laughter carried up from below. He frowned slightly, deep in thought, and then he asked, 'What do I do to get my friends back?'

The hybrid paused in mid-stretch. It looked at him, its only expression a slight wrinkling of its forehead. 'You would have to put your life in my hands, Richard. You would have to trust me completely. Do you think you're prepared to do that?'

A beat of silence. Then: 'But what would I have to *do*? I mean, exactly? What would it involve?'

The hybrid leaned back, steepling its fingers, the action of a man, not a fourteen-year-old boy. It regarded Richard through narrowed eyes as though gauging his suitability for a dangerous task. Finally it said, 'I would have to send you to where your friends are, and I warn you now it won't be a nice place. It'll be dark, soundless; you'll see or hear nothing except yourself. Your job would be to collect your friends together and begin walking in the direction from which you came, to find the point at which I'd be able to draw you back here. I'll do my best to guide you along the way, but most of it would be up to you. It'll depend on your instincts, and on your ability to remain calm and clear-headed. Do you think you could cope with all that?'

Again Richard nodded. 'Yes,' he said, 'I don't see why not. But . . . what did you mean by you would *send* me to where my friends are? I mean, exactly *how* would you send me? What would you do?'

'It'd be a little like hypnotism,' said the creature. 'You'd feel nothing except a gradual falling away, a gentle slide into a world going blacker and blacker. You may pass out, but try not to; if you remain conscious, it'll be easier for me to keep a hold on you from this side. You'll probably land with a thump, like jumping off a six-foot wall. The ground beneath you will be hard, though with a little give, and it'll look to you as though you've landed on nothingness. Don't let this disorientate you. As soon as you can, pick yourself up and begin shouting your friend's names. If possible try not to stray too far from your original spot; the further you wander the weaker the contact will become.' It smiled reassuringly. 'It's simple enough really,' it said. 'Any other questions?'

'Yes,' said Richard firmly. 'Why can't *you* bring my friends back? Why do I have to go? I mean, you sent them there in the first place, and you can bring *me* back. So why not them?'

The creature smiled again. 'Good point. The problem is, when I sent your friends I had little regard for their mental stability. I took what I wanted from their minds and then cast them away. Now, because of that, I find that I can't properly latch on to their thoughts. Their minds are too clogged with fear and confusion. Therefore I need an intermediary, someone who is actually prepared to go in there and physically bring them back. If you like, you're a deep-sea diver and I'm the person at the other end, back on the boat, pumping the oxygen and hauling you in once you've collected what you went down for. You see now how much responsibility you're giving me? You realize that I'll literally have the power of life and death over you? I want to make this clear to you before we start; I want you to know that if you don't want to go through with this after all the things I've done, then I'll understand.'

The creature's expression was one of concern and sincerity. Richard knew he would go through with it, yet still didn't commit himself; he had a couple more questions to ask first.

'Will my friends be . . . different in any way?' he wanted to know.

'Different?' The creature looked puzzled.

'You know? Will I be able to recognize them? Will we all look just as we do? And . . . and will I be able to communicate with them? You said they were "confused". Does that mean they're unbalanced?'

The hybrid raised its hands. 'Hold on, one at a time. Firstly, yes, you and your friends will all look exactly as you do now. Secondly, you personally will *feel* exactly as you do now. Your real body will be here, unconscious, but you'll still feel as though it's there with you, as though you're flesh and blood, as though you're whole. As for your friends' states of mind, well, I've said they will be confused and frightened. It'll be up to you, Richard, to calm them down, explain the situation. They certainly won't be "unbalanced" in any way; there won't be any permanent damage at any rate. Once we get them back here, it's likely that they'll recover very quickly. Everything will be fine, Richard. Both physically and mentally. I give you my word on that.'

Richard almost expected the hybrid to raise its fingers in a 'scout's honour', but instead it simply sat and waited for him to take the initiative. Was this rescue operation really going to be as straightforward as it had promised, or was this all a trick, another example of gamesmanship? He looked hard into the creature's face and saw the anguish still there, floating darkly behind its eyes. He realized it was a foolish assumption to make, but he was certain this time that the creature was telling him the truth. And then there was Olive too; had she been a fake? Somehow Richard didn't think so. He had one more question to ask; one more question and then he would be ready to commit himself. He asked it.

'Where exactly is this place you're sending me?'

The hybrid paused for just a moment, a slight frown creasing its face as it strove to explain. 'It's . . . it's a kind of limbo. It's within me, within my psyche if you like, though having said that it's not in here.' It tapped its head. 'You see, Richard, this isn't all that I am. There are other vast, invisible parts of me, mind-parts if you like, without dimension. I . . . this is difficult to explain, hard to put into words that you would understand, but . . . think of it as outer space, blackness that just goes on and on and on. It's a frightening place, I won't deny that; an empty, eternal place. But it's also *my* place, part of me, I have control over it. If you remember that, Richard, if you remember that and don't panic, then everything will be all right.'

Richard nodded slowly, his mouth dry, his stomach

turning over. He looked at Toady's recumbent form, unaware that in far different surroundings his friend had had a similar conversation. 'This is it', he thought, 'this is really it', and had time to reflect how unexpectedly things had worked out. He wondered what time it was: it seemed like hours since he'd walked through the door, but he suspected it was no more than fifteen or twenty minutes. He thought of his parents, wondered if they'd found his note yet, thought of Olive, no doubt off somewhere with Harold by now. He took a deep breath, gazed out of the window into the night. He felt Olive's magic still working within him, making him strong.

'I'm ready,' he said to the hybrid.

7

No-Time

He moaned in his sleep, squirmed this way and that, yet try as he might he could not avoid the thudding. It was part of him, part of his soul; it took his nightmares and it made them pulse. He glimpsed vague images, separate details that the thudding allowed him, but there was nothing solid, nothing he could hold on to. He had an impression of something bruised and fat, of skin like a fish's white underbelly, of something that dragged itself painfully along the ground towards him. He felt sick, disoriented; felt as though he were riding a carousel, the horses plunging and rearing, rearing and plunging, as though they would never stop. 'Next time,' he thought. 'Next time I'll see. I'll stop the light and I'll hold it and I'll see.' He waited, readying himself, as the pulse of darkness wound down, dwindled to its end. He held his breath. A silence. Then, like the workings of some huge and old machine, there came a slow, slow rising thud, the sound of a pulse. Growing. Growing.

As it swelled, the mist rushed away, layers of night-cloud shed by the sun. He waited expectantly; he flexed his hands to clutch at the light. Then, quicker than ever he remembered, it was upon him, a split-second of harsh stark reality, swift and blinding as a flash-bulb. He shot out his hands, plunged them into the whiteness, grabbed the detail, held it, looked. His eyes scrutinized, drank, digested, but his mind, making sense of the image, tried to rebel, tried to vomit it out again before it could poison his system. In harsh white detail he saw the rope-mark, the livid necklace of puffy flesh, red and oozing on the smooth (bloated), lily-white (corpse-white) throat. He saw his fingers in the flesh, pushing into white dough, saw breasts like basketballs in sacks, a stomach and arms and legs that were bloodless mountains of meat. He saw a face that was purple-black, a tongue all spoiled by decay, eyes shrivelled deep in their sockets. He looked into those sockets, saw a dead-stare, a dead-fish stare, a stare that was both tender and hungry, both loving and utterly mad. He tried to pull back his hands to let the light go, but other hands were encircling his wrists now, the fingers like plump white writhing worms. He screamed and kicked and punched but to no avail; the hands had him tight and they weren't about to let go. They dragged him, inch by inch, towards the mountain of dead flesh, towards black ruined lips that puckered grotesquely for a kiss. And, in his worst moment of his entire life, a great truth suddenly came to him. He realized, after all, that the light was not pure light, and that the darkness was not pure darkness. Within the light, he saw, there was a greater darkness, an awful unseen darkness, the most terrible darkness of all . . .

He woke with a cry on his lips.

He sat up, shivering, feeling the nausea flip within him, sensing the nightmare crawl back beneath the rock of his mind. His breath was sharp in the silent twilight-morning, his sweat sour, his muscles stiff where they had bunched and squirmed in sleep. He stood shakily, wondering where he was, wondering who his companions were. He felt he should have known them, but the nightmare had broken his mind again, had shattered the fragile framework of his returning memory like a delicate china vase. He stared at the boys – the blond one lying on his back like an effigy on a tomb; the chubby one sitting against a tree, head bowed as though examining something in his lap. 'Who are they?' he thought. 'And more to the point, who am I?' His head – in fact, his whole body – was still thudding, but as his senses returned he realized the sound came from outside him, an external force, and it called to him like a voice on the wind. He faced the forest, his head turning slowly as though trying to beam in on a signal. He felt an explosion of euphoria, for suddenly he realized what the pulsing was. It was his life-force, the beating of his own heart, and it was out there somewhere, calling to him. For the first time in days his thoughts sharpened, concentrated, converged. Then, as though drawn by invisible twine, he stumbled down the small hill and began to walk away from his companions, into the heart of the forest . . .

. . . Toady woke some time later and immediately felt guilty. He was supposed to have been keeping watch, but instead he'd fallen asleep, leaving them open to attack from God-only-knew what kinds of horrible things. He winced as he straightened a back which felt fused to the shape of the tree. He stood gingerly, his spine and neck clicking like a pocketful of pebbles. He stamped tingling feet on top of which legs and buttocks felt like dead slabs of heavy muscle. He looked blearily about him, a yawn dragging at his mouth, his gaze ranging over the dead forest and his nose filled with the dank mouldy smell that hung in the air. He looked to his left, to where his companions lay – and all at once his sleep sloughed away and he suddenly felt wide, wide awake.

'Rob!' he said, shaking his friend. 'Rob! Wake up! Nige has gone!'

Robin groaned, slapped at the hand which jabbed him, then grumpily opened his eyes. 'What? Whaddjamean? Gone?' He turned to look at the spot where Nige had been sleeping the night before, at the flattened earth, the dip where he had lain. Realizing that what Toady had said was true, he struggled into a sitting position, massaging the sleep from his face. 'Well, where's he gone?' he said, looking at Toady. 'You were on guard last night. Which direction did he go?'

Toady shook his head, shame-faced. 'I . . . I don't know. I fell asleep. He'd gone when I woke up.'

'You did what?' exclaimed Robin. 'You fell asleep?'

He scrambled to his feet so he could meet Toady eye-to-eye. Toady flinched and braced himself, in some ways still instinctively resigned to being kicked and punched by his peers. However Robin simply stood there, glaring, seething, trying to find words. At last he said, 'Can't you be trusted to do anything, you dick-head? If you felt sleepy, why didn't you wake me up? I mean, we don't know what's out there in that forest. Anything could've bloody come for us in the night. And now Nige is gone and . . . and . . . oh, sometimes, Ade, you're just a prat.'

Toady hung his head. He knew he was in the wrong, but he felt stung into a response by Robin's anger. 'It wasn't *my* fault!' he wailed. 'You shouldn't have asked me to keep watch in the first place. I was still dead tired from the night before. I tried to keep awake but I couldn't. Besides, I can't help it if Nige is stupid enough to go wandering off, can I? And anyway, I don't reckon there's anything in this forest except for insects and maybe a few birds and stuff.'

'What about the Crowl?' said Robin. 'How do you know there's not more of them?'

Toady stayed silent.

Robin saw how miserable he was and his anger evaporated a little. 'Aw, c'mon. There's no use standing here arguing. We'd better find him. He can't have been gone long.'

This was an assumption based on hope rather than conviction. They wore no watches here, there was no sun for them to speculate by, and the days and nights seemed to come and go almost on a whim, with no apparent set length. For all they knew, Nige could have been gone ten minutes or ten hours. Again Toady found himself wishing desperately for units of recognizable time by which they could structure and measure their lives. He said, 'Which way will he have gone, do you think?' and circled slowly, his gaze sweeping the forest.

'That way,' Robin said, pointing. A trail of muddy footprints led down the rise and cut a meandering trail through the undergrowth.

'We'd better get after him then,' said Toady. He picked up the sack of food, eager to be off. Robin stayed him with a hand on the arm.

'Hang on, we'll try shouting first. He might still be within earshot.'

They shouted for two, three, four minutes, but without success. At last Robin sighed. 'Nah, it's no good. Come on, we'd better go and look for him.'

They started down the hill, began to follow Nige's trail, Robin walking in the younger boy's footprints. The ground around them was mostly earth and scrubby brown grass, the trees tall and black and brooding. It had been this way all day yesterday, an interminable march through dingy humid forest, no way of knowing how many miles they had covered, or how many hours they had been walking, or even if they had been going in the right direction. Finally, as blackness had begun to seep in and weld the trees together, they found this spot, bedded down, and waited for the darkness to pass.

They'd tried to light a fire to keep any night-creatures away, but the only wood they could find was damp and crumbly and riddled with small white grubs, and so instead they had opted to keep watch in turns – Toady first until he felt tired, then Robin until *he* felt tired, and so on and so on for as long as the night decided to last. They'd left Nige out of this because, although seemingly happy in their company, he was still for the most part uncommunicative. Sometimes he mindlessly repeated what they said to him, sometimes he smiled and nodded as though he understood, and sometimes he simply stared straight through them as though they were not there at all. Robin had watched the dark-skinned boy closely but unobtrusively throughout the day, and had found himself wondering exactly what was going on in that mind. Nothing at all? Or far too much?

Now, however, Nige had gone, wandered away like a puppy who didn't know any better. The boys munched bread from the sack as they looked for him, and tried not to think of the fact that their supplies were dwindling. What would they do if the food finally ran out and this compost-heap of a forest just went on and on and on?

They walked for perhaps another mile before the first flash of colour struck their eyes. It was so unexpected in the landscape of black and grey and muddy brown that they were both, quite literally, startled.

'Look, what's that?' Robin said, pointing an excited finger.

'Looks like a plant or something. Flowers,' said Toady, and the two boys abandoned their quest for a moment and wandered over to examine their discovery more closely.

It was indeed a plant, the like of which neither had seen before. It most closely resembled a Yucca plant, with a thick pale stem and a spray of slender leaves at the top like an explosion of shredded paper snakes. However it also abounded with orange blossom, tight compact flowers like partly-peeled fruit, which gave off a pungent aroma suggestive of spicy Arabian markets, of peppers left out to dry under a South American sun. Robin poked the stem experimentally; the wood was tough and sinewy, though the outer layer was flaky as burnt skin. 'What is it, do you think?' he asked, and then looked around as though someone might pop up and tell him. 'And what's it doing here? It seems so . . . so out of place.'

Toady shrugged. The plant was an intriguing diversion, but they had more important things to do. 'Dunno. C'mon, Rob, we'd better carry on. We don't know how far Nige is ahead of us.'

They walked back to the trail, yet it was not long before

they were stopping once again. This time it was to examine an even more impressive plant, an enormous Venus fly-trap with purple-blue mandibles that bristled with spiny teeth, and pulsing yellow veins busily transporting nutrients.

'Wow, look at this,' breathed Robin, bending low. He jerked back as the plant hissed at him.

'Shit,' said Toady as it slowly unmeshed its 'teeth' to reveal a gullet that looked layered in moist pink rubber foam. The boys watched, entranced and awed, as it opened and closed, opened and closed its 'mouth'. It was almost as though it was inviting them inside for a closer look. Toady shivered at the thought.

They left the plant and moved on. It was obvious now to both of them that the flora of the forest was slowly but perceptibly changing. Over the next few miles they saw more greens and yellows emerge, saw things fatten up, become lush and healthy rather than grey-brown and lifeless. They saw flowers dotted here and there in clumps of colour, saw exotic straight-limbed trees bearing spade-shaped leaves and plump ganglions of fruit. It seemed incredible, it was in direct opposition to all the laws of nature, yet it was true: the drab dying forest was gradually transmogrifying itself into a thriving tropical jungle.

However, as with all things here, this was no conventional jungle. It was a hotch-potch of exotica, a riot of vegetation that seemed somehow ominous, disturbing to the eye. Tropical palms with slender trunks and flat polish-green leaves rubbed shoulders with reedy desert grasses, bamboo canes, obese spiny-bodied cacti. There were deformities here too, monsters of horticulture – purple two-headed roses that grew like warts on various plants; trees with delicate lilac trunks from whose top-knots thick yellow vines dangled to the ground like mummified octopuses; bloated green bulbs like baby pumpkins, which swelled and hissed angrily when you went near them, exposing an intricate tracery of blue veins like cracks in glass. This was a jungle's bastard child, an experiment gone wrong, a vast mutant of creation; fecund, sinister, grotesque.

And worse, it moved.

Its leaves rustled, its thorns rippled, its vines twitched and squirmed. Petals stirred like thirsty lips; the grass itself swayed as though a breeze was riffling through it. Both boys moved through this breathing, shifting landscape with nervous glances from side to side, acutely aware of their blood, their muscle, the tenderness of their young flesh. Toady dragged off his sweater, for with the tropical jungle had come tropical heat. Robin unbuttoned the shirt he was wearing, the armpits darkened by circles of sweat, the juts of his collarbone gleaming as though oiled. Their feet grew heavy, their breathing heavier; Toady reached into the sack and drew out a bottle of now-warm juice. He uncorked it and drank deeply, then passed the sloshing remains to Robin. The older boy tilted back his head, the neck of the bottle clinking against his teeth, and gulped down the rest of the liquid. When he was done he drew back his arm and flung the empty bottle away from him into the jungle. A few minutes later he said, 'I think I've lost the trail,' and stopped, his gaze ranging from side to side.

Toady stopped too, though reluctantly, for a few yards to his right a chest-high powder-blue orchid was slowly awakening. Its petals were unfurling like welcoming arms, its style quivering as though excited at the proximity of such a tasty morsel. 'Er, do you think we could . . . ?' Toady said, and pointed at the flower without finishing his sentence.

Robin looked, gave an alarmed grimace, then sniggered his unease. 'Yeah,' he said, and they moved to a spot which they hoped was out of the strike-range of all the nearby flora. They tried to find Nige's trail again, probing the jungle with their eyes, desperately searching for a bit of flattened undergrowth, a half-hidden footprint, a broken stem or leaf or branch. Toady looked back at the giant orchid nervously, half-wondering whether it was capable of eating an entire human being.

'I think it's best if we just keep moving forward,' he said. 'Maybe we'll pick up his trail a bit further on.'

They started walking again, their eyes darting to and fro, passing a coconut tree which dropped a sample of its hairy fruit as though trying to concuss them. Toady jumped back as the nut broke open on a rock, splashing oily milk on to the back of Robin's jeans. He was appalled to see the jeans start to smoulder where the milk had touched them, little curls of grey smoke petering out only when coin-sized holes had been burnt in the denim. Robin twisted to see where the smell was coming from, and paled when he saw what had happened. 'Shit,' he said, looking at Toady, and wiped sweat from his face as though that too could burn.

Further they walked, and further still, the heat beating down despite the lack of a sun. Their clothes hung, baggy with sweat; their lungs felt stifled by the sodden air. The jungle continued to rustle and creak, to whisper and mutter and hiss. Nige's trail was still lost to them, but all at once Robin halted, jerking up his head, then his hand.

'Sh,' he said. 'Listen.'

Toady stopped and listened, but all he heard was a noise like animals slinking through undergrowth, like litter dashing, dry-clawed, through wind-blown streets. He knew it was only the plants, and he shrugged, shaking his head. 'I don't hear anything,' he replied.

'I thought—'Robin began, then stopped and looked at his friend as though pre-judging his reaction. He swallowed, his Adam's apple glistening with sweat. 'I thought I heard music.'

'Music,' Toady repeated softly, and shivered without quite knowing why. He listened again, trying to cut beneath the jungle-sounds or maybe to rise above them. And then he sucked in air, for the jungle-sounds suddenly stopped, a momentary lapse as everything – *everything* – ceased its languid underwater dance.

And then they both heard it.

And it *was* music.

It came on a breeze that didn't exist, a distant hum of sound from which crystal notes and phrases occasionally jumped. It lasted only a few seconds before the jungle began to speak again, but in those few seconds they were able to recognize the song being sung. They looked at each other, Robin open-mouthed, Toady blinking rapidly as though trying to keep awake. The fat boy spoke first, his voice strange and awkward, a clumsy thing that spilled from his mouth and was unable to complete its sentence. All he said was, 'That wasn't . . . was it?'

Robin nodded, quickly, eagerly. 'Yeah,' he said, 'it was.' He gave a peculiar laugh. '*A Town Called Malice*. By The Jam. I've got that record.'

Toady laughed too, at this thing that was so mundane it was like a miracle, and the boys began to move forward, Paul Weller's voice like that of a holy man calling them to worship.

More of the pumpkin plants hissed and puffed up like bullfrogs; a line of delicate-stemmed tulips opened soft petals to reveal blobs of dilating jelly. The boys passed by, unheeding, as the music grew louder and louder.

They came across the record player sitting behind a bush. It was an old model, pre 1970s, a compact grey box, its casing scratched and battered. Its lid was open, revealing a stubby needle-arm ending in a thick metal fist. The record whirled beneath this fist, defying the jungle with music. The spindle that pushed up through the centre of the record was a blunt spike; the speed controls were chunky as the knobs on a cooker.

'It . . . what . . . how's it *going*?' Robin said, and wandered around to the back of the record player, picking up the grey cable that snaked from a hole in the casing. He reeled the cable in, until at last a white plastic plug dangled before his eyes. Both boys stared at this new impossibility, a record player without power that played on regardless.

The music ended, and Robin laughed harshly into the

silence that followed. With a whirr of automata the needle lifted and returned to its rest. A knob turned itself from 'play' to 'off' with a solid 'chunk' sound.

'What's it doing here? How does it play?' Robin said again.

'Don't worry about it,' Toady advised. 'Nothing here is how it should be.'

Robin shrugged and dropped the plug, which lay with its metal pins pointing at the sky, a dead insect on its back. The boys walked on, and didn't speak again until about twenty minutes later, when this time it was Toady's turn to stop.

'What's wrong?' asked Robin nervously, watching his friend's nose twitch as though he sensed danger on the air.

'I smell something,' Toady replied. 'Food. Meat. Bacon.'

Robin sniffed too, but at first all he could smell was the jungle. It was a green lush smell, chlorophyll and sap and swampy stillness. There was the heady scent of fruit in there too, and of scented blossom cloying as perfumed flesh. And then, just when he was on the point of saying, 'I don't smell anything,' it came to him, the sudden red fragrance of frying bacon.

'Aww,' he murmured, a sound almost of ecstasy. 'Yeah, I smell it now too. Where's it coming from, do you think?'

They followed their noses, breathing in so deeply that they began to feel dizzy. They moved in a half-crouch, hunters stalking prey, through grass like a sea of sword-blades jabbing at the air. They made their way towards a large tree that was chocolate-brown and covered in matted hair like an ape's limb. They rounded the tree, and gasped at what lay beyond. A brand new gas cooker, all gleaming white metal and sleek perspex. Both boys could see that its pipes were linked to nothing, yet it was merrily frying bacon, the rashers sizzling in hot fat, a blue corona of flame languidly licking the underside of a non-stick pan. Beyond the cooker was a table, a blue and white checked tablecloth draped over it, a chair tucked neatly underneath.

On the table was a plate, and on the plate a bacon sandwich steamed gently, mutilated by a bite, a semi-circle of teeth marks, revealing a cross-section – white, red, white – like a sliver of bone and marrow.

'Oh,' was all that Robin could say, and he half-stumbled to the cooker and turned off the gas. He reached gingerly into the pan to snag a piece of bacon, but snatched back his hand when Toady snapped, 'Don't!'

'Why not?' Robin said, frowning. 'What's the matter?'

'Remember the fruit,' replied Toady, which to Robin was warning enough. The older boy looked once more, longingly, into the pan, then sniffed the air, sighed, and went to lean against the table, arms folded.

After a moment he said, 'This is ridiculous. I mean, who's doing this? What's it all for?'

Toady looked thoughtful. He chewed his lip, wandered over to the cooker, toyed with the handle of the pan. At length he replied, 'I think, actually, maybe *we* might be doing it ourselves. I mean, remember what Ranulf said – that this world is kind of shaped by our own minds, that we subconsciously create a landscape we can believe in. I mean, maybe we're creating things from back home, things we want, things we miss, and putting them here. I know everything's weird, jumbled up, but they're still all basically things we recognize, aren't they? I mean, even the plants; we've never seen anything quite like them before, but we still know them as plants, don't we? We still know what they are.'

'Hmm,' Robin said, mulling this over. He wafted a hand at the jungle. 'But why do we make everything so bloody dangerous? Why is it all jungles and . . . and mud-flats? Why do we get lost and half-starve to death and get attacked by horrible monsters? I think I can do very nicely without Crowls and man-eating plants and coconuts that spit acid, thank you very much. Why don't we make a *nice* world for ourselves? Somewhere small with lots of signposts and friendly people and . . . and a McDonald's and an ice-cream parlour?'

He spoke this last sentence with relish. Toady grinned and shrugged. 'Maybe we're just masochists,' he said; then his grin slipped and he added, 'Or maybe Ranulf was talking shit. Maybe we're not creating this landscape at all.'

Robin stared at the table, his eyes glazed as though mesmerized by the sandwich on the plate. He murmured, 'Who do you think's taken a bite out of that sandwich? Do you think we magicked it there or do you think it was . . . ?'

'Nige,' Toady finished for him.

They looked at each other. A moment later they were shouting their friend's name again, something they'd been doing at intervals throughout the morning. However, as before there was no response. If it *had* been Nige, he was now either out of earshot or he would not – or could not – answer.

They moved on, finding their path again, hoping they were walking in a straight line. Not that it made much difference, Toady thought. The smell of the bacon had made them hungry, so they munched cheese from the sack as they walked, and kept a wary eye on the jungle's restless flora. They passed other enigmas, oohed and aahed and pointed, yet made a determined effort not to stop and examine everything they encountered. They saw a snooker table under a tree, upon which the balls had been set out neatly for a game; they came across a desk on which stood a manual Olivetti typewriter containing a piece of paper which bore the intriguing message, THE ZI; beside a bush a television, again unplugged, was switched on, showing an old black-and-white episode of *Doctor Who*; Patrick Troughton being chased through bleak corridors by a group of Cybermen. Robin found a book in the grass, a science-fiction novel called *The Planetarium* by a man named Bexley H. Thornton; Toady came across another record, a scratched old Tamla Motown single, *Reach Out, I'll Be There* by The Four Tops.

A little further along they came to the first of the signposts.

It was nothing more than a hacked tree branch being slowly strangled by vines, atop which was an uneven piece of splintered wood. However it was not the signpost itself but the message on it which was intriguing. Daubed in dribbling crimson, like the lettering on a pulp horror poster (or the banner that had greeted Olive Pierce at Constance's party), was the single word, RED, and an arrow jabbing straight out from the D, pointing off to the right.

'Well,' said Toady, and turned to look at Robin, 'there's your signpost. This must be one of your creations.'

'RED?' Robin muttered. 'What the hell is that supposed to mean?'

'I don't know. But . . . well . . . I don't much like the sound of it, do you?'

They stared at the signpost for a minute or more as though half-believing the cryptic message would suddenly change and enlighten them. However it didn't, and at last Robin turned with a shrug. 'Well?' he said. 'Shall we follow it or not?'

Toady felt both reluctant and eager; he found himself nodding and wishing that he wasn't. 'We've got to really, haven't we?' he said, both surprised at, and resigned to, his feeling that they had no choice.

Robin simply nodded back, and a moment later they were squeezing between trees and stepping over plants they had previously been careful to avoid. Toady felt his heart-beat quicken, had the impression that he was a tiny pulsing thing in a body full of pulses. However this did not make him feel safe; rather he felt he was a separate pulse, adrift and alien, something to be squashed and rejected when the opportunity arose.

What seemed like two or three hours later they had encountered six other signposts, all jabbing in the direction of RED. They followed each one grimly, Toady thinking really hard for the first time about what they were actually doing, thinking about the enormity – the almost impossibility – of the task they had undertaken. They were looking for a 'link', something apparently transient and temporary, which just *might* (though they had no idea how) get them home. Their chosen method was to wander aimlessly about a terrain of which they knew absolutely nothing. It was probably akin, thought Toady (too stunned by their stupidity and blind faith by this time to feel scared), to plonking a Martian down in the middle of Peru or Siberia and telling him to find Woolworths in Starmouth High Street without the aid of a map. He began to wonder how they could have been idiotic enough to set out on this journey in the first place, and then his attention was momentarily distracted as the jungle came to an end.

It was literally as abrupt as that. One moment they were ducking beneath leaves as big as tables, tiptoeing nervously past things that looked like rejects from *Little Shop Of Horrors*, and the next they had stepped out into the open, the sky above their heads, a vista of rolling hills before them, purple-green with heather and bracken and springy turf, and here and there a stunted tree. The boys looked at each other, then at the jungle, which was chopped back in a line as severe and regimented as that which had originally heralded the start of the forest. Robin put his hand out to a sinewy, green-stemmed trunk, touched the tree as though for reassurance, then plunged his hand beyond the tree, back into the jungle.

'My hand's really warm,' he said, 'much warmer than the rest of my body.' Then he curled the hand into a fist and snatched it back as though afraid it would become infected by something.

Toady said nothing. There was nothing much *to* say. Each puzzle, each miracle, each impossibility, both added to their wonder and yet in a way also detracted from it, made the astounding commonplace. Instead he shielded his eyes. The sky was still dull, shot through with reds and purples and greys, yet after the oppression of the jungle it was almost like sunlight. He gazed at something nestling in a far-off valley. He pointed towards this, to the two craggy hills like stooped old men supporting the sky on their backs. 'Rob, what's that thing over there? I can't quite see.'

Robin turned his back on the jungle uneasily and looked to where Toady was pointing. He realized for the first time that they were standing on a dirt-track which stretched towards the distant valley like a sandy thread. He squinted, trying to make out the thing that was like a giant blood-clot, a sanguine shadow on the horizon. The light shifted, and suddenly he saw towers and chimneys, walls and spires and roofs.

'It's a town,' he said, and turned to look at Toady who had realized at the same instant as he.

The chubby boy nodded his head slowly, a look almost of superstitious dread in his eyes. 'Yeah,' he murmured, 'it's a town all right.' He hummed a few bars of the song they had heard and made it sound funereal. 'A Town Called Red.'

8

Saturday 9.07 p.m.

'Come here, Richard,' the hybrid said softly.

Richard came.

Placing its hands on his shoulders, it murmured, 'You do trust me, don't you?'

Richard nodded.

'Then look into my eyes. Give yourself up to me. Succumb.'

Richard stared into the creature's eyes. And, as he did so, he suddenly saw those eyes begin to change. He saw the pigment recede from them, drain away, swirling brown like water down a plughole. It took only a moment for the creature to have new eyes. Eyes that were strange and fascinating. Eyes like clots of curdled milk in the smiling dark-skinned face . . .

9

No-Time

The road to RED was longer and hillier than either Robin or Toady had anticipated. When they struggled to the top of a rise, legs heavy as cement, it seemed they'd been walking for hours. True, the town now spread below them was appreciably closer than ever, yet it still looked dismayingly distant. It was like something constructed of fire and blood, an image so fervent that the mountains surrounding it appeared dull with shadow. 'Soon be there now,' Robin said, but Toady merely grimaced at his words. They started downhill again, their feet kicking up dust and scree which clattered ahead like excited children. RED ducked out of sight beyond the next hill, leaving only the horns of its mountains to scrape against the skyline.

'I'm knackered,' Toady panted, 'got to have a rest,' and upon reaching the bottom of the dip staggered to a large rock and sat down. A moment later Robin joined him, lying back briefly and closing his eyes, then sitting up and reaching for the sack of food which Toady had dropped in the dust.

'Not much left, is there,' he said, holding up a fist-sized hunk of bread and a third of a bottle of juice.

'No,' Toady agreed, 'that's the last of it.'

They ate and drank in silence.

When they had done, Robin stood up, stretched, and tossed the sack into the heather at the side of the road. 'Come on,' he said, 'we can't afford to get comfortable. We ought to try and reach RED before it decides to start getting dark again.'

Toady groaned and started to rise, then his face became alert. 'Listen, Rob,' he said, pointing to the apex of the next hill, 'something's coming.'

Both boys tensed at the approach of pounding hooves, the clatter of wooden wheels on stony ground. They huddled instinctively together, watching the brow of the hill.

Next moment it was as if a hole had been shot in the sky, bringing a spatter of blood. Then the red object began to descend towards them and Toady realized it was a cart drawn by a pair of flame-coloured horses. The cart appeared to be careering wildly out of control, the horses whinnying in panic, the wheels crashing and bouncing over loose rocks. The driver was a red blur, his whip-arm a slash of movement, and though he and his cargo seemed in dire peril of being hurled through the air like an explosion of acrobats, he was laughing uproariously.

'Here, Ade, behind the rock,' Robin urged, tugging at Toady's arm. The two of them crouched low, each moment expecting a splintering crash, flying wood, the tumbling of stricken horseflesh.

The cart thundered closer. Now it was almost upon them. They felt the earth and the boulder behind which they cowered vibrating with the din of its passage. Robin squeezed his eyes tight shut, clutched the rock so hard it began to crumble beneath his fingernails. Toady, though, couldn't stand not seeing how close the thing was getting, had to raise his head and look, if only to ensure that they wouldn't be hit. He resisted the urge for as long as possible, right up until the moment when the cacophony seemed to be all about them. Then, finally, his nerve broke and he popped up from behind the rock like a jack-in-the-box.

And found himself staring straight into the driver's eyes.

Their gazes locked for just a second, but to Toady it seemed like minutes. The eyes were slits of red in glistening black; they resembled plums sliced open, oozing a stripe of blood. They were hypnotic eyes, merciless eyes, glacial-cold as a snake's. They widened as they clamped on Toady, then narrowed, spitting a hatred that was almost tangible.

And then they were gone. Swept away in a flash of clamorous red, leaving only the languid heather, the silent rocks, the gently swirling sky. Toady put a hand on his chest where it felt he'd been injected with ice. He looked down at Robin, who was crouched at knee-level, mouthing at him. When he heard the cries of 'Whoa! Whoa!' from up ahead he turned back to look at the cart.

It had stopped in a cloud of dust, the sweating blaze-skinned horses stamping the ground. Through the dust the boys saw the 'cargo' move, then break apart into five squat figures. Their eyes widened as the dust cleared and the true nature of the figures became apparent.

They were naked, red and small as children. Yet they were also broad, their muscle-bound bodies tremendously powerful-looking. Their torsos and forearms were plated like an armadillo, but the colour reminded Toady of ridges of lobster shell, which rippled and creaked when they moved like a separate living thing. Their heads, jutting straight from the shoulders, were both ape-like and reptilian. Their black-red eyes, chilling and oily, were set beneath a bony overhang of brow. Their noses were flat and wide-nostrilled, their lips so protruberant they resembled beaks more than mouths. Their teeth were filed points, caging blood-red gullets and tongues like slabs of raw liver.

'Demons!' Robin thought, cold fear sluicing through him.

'Gargoyles!' Toady was thinking, 'like the ones on the roof of St Margaret's in Starmouth.'

The demon-gargoyles were shouting at them, calling in raucous voices. The boys homed in on what they were saying, confirming in their own minds that this was no welcoming committee.

'Fucking pinkers!' one creature was snarling.

'Get back to the shit where you belong!' sneered another.

The meanest-looking gargoyle, and, at a shade under five foot, the tallest, said derisively, 'Which fucking auction you escaped from then?'

The other gargoyles sniggered at his words as Robin said, 'Auction? I . . . I don't know what you mean.'

He was met by a barrage of insults.

The boys stepped back as one of the gargoyles leaped over the tailgate of the cart, picked up a rock and hurled it towards them. Toady ducked as the rock whizzed past his head. The rock-thrower licked his scaly lips and growled, 'Let's teach these fuckers a lesson.'

There was a rumble of agreement, but the driver of the cart, an old gargoyle with baggy skin and a few wiry strands of white hair sprouting from his wrinkled pate, shook his head. 'Nah, leave it, boys,' he advised. 'There'll be time enough for fun later.'

There were grumbles of disappointment, but the gargoyles concurred with their elder. The boys were relieved to see the creatures clamber back on to the cart which rumbled away, pebbles spurting from beneath its wheels. Not until it was a red speck in the distance did either of the boys move or speak. Then Robin looked at Toady, gasped, 'Fucking hell,' tottered to the rock and sat down.

After a few moments Toady joined him. He was shaking. 'You don't think they're all like that in RED, do you?' he asked.

'Only one way to find out isn't there?'

'You mean you still want to go there? Even after this?'

'Yeah, I think so. I mean, we don't have much choice, do we?'

Toady was silent for a long moment. He sighed deeply, torn by indecision. 'Rob, we can't go there,' he said at last. 'If the place is full of psychopathic gargoyles, we'll be dead within minutes.'

'We've got to, Ade,' Robin replied. 'We've lost Nige, we've got no more food, and the state we're in there's no way we'd be able to get back through that jungle again. We were maybe just unlucky with that lot. I mean, they can't all be as nasty as that, can they?'

'Can't they?' Toady said sullenly.

'No, they can't,' Robin said, wishing he could believe it

643

himself. He stood up, staring at the wheel-tracks in the road, at the blurred jumble of hoof-prints in the dust. 'We have to at least check it out, don't we? We should be able to see what the place is like once we get a bit closer. If it looks bad, then we'll walk round the outside and hope there's somewhere up ahead. But I warn you, Ade, I can't go on much further like this. I'm just about done in.'

Toady sighed but shrugged and nodded, and the two boys began to walk once again. Two hours later they were overlooking the town of RED.

The colour of the place, combined with its layout and its architecture, gave RED a quirky, surrealistic aura. It was perfectly square – probably three to four miles from one corner to the next – and its tall shabby buildings and narrow mean streets made the boys think of Victorian East End London. There was an open area in the middle in which 'people' (both gargoyles and 'pinkers' like themselves) milled about, and along whose sides market-stalls appeared to be erected. Despite the Victorian atmosphere, the boys saw neon signs flashing in the semi-gloom, red streetlamps glowing like dots of mould. They felt encouraged to see the 'pinkers', though it was not long before they realized that these people were doing the bulk of the heavy work, that groups of them were actually linked together like the chain-gangs of old.

'They're slaves,' Robin breathed. 'The pinkers are being treated the same as the blacks in America not so long ago.'

'I told you we shouldn't have come here,' said Toady. 'Let's get away before we're seen. I don't fancy spending my life as a gargoyle's slave.'

He touched Robin's arm, but the older boy, squinting, pointed at the town. 'Hang on, look. There're pinkers wandering about the market by themselves who're obviously not slaves. If they're free, then the gargoyles will probably think we are too.'

'Probably,' Toady emphasized, 'but not definitely. Rob, we can't take the risk.'

'We've got to. Turning back now would be the same as giving in. At least if we're moving forward, exploring new places, we'll have a fighting chance of finding this link.'

'Huh, fighting's the word. We'll probably get challenged to do a lot of that before we get out of there.'

Robin shrugged off his friend's protests and started down the hill. Toady followed, every instinct screaming at him to turn back even while his mind tried to convince him that what Robin had said was true. Maybe, if they behaved casually and confidently enough, they would be accepted as freemen. All they had to do was watch their step, keep a low profile and melt into the crowd at the first sign of trouble. Put like that it seemed that nothing could go wrong. Yet Toady's fear suggested otherwise as he forced his legs to pass into the welcoming embrace of the twin peaks.

There were no outskirts to the town. It began as abruptly as the jungle had ended. They headed roughly towards the centre, towards the market square, largely because there seemed nothing else to aim for. They tried to keep themselves to themselves as much as possible, yet they couldn't help but look around wherever they went, eyes agog.

RED was full of wonders and surprises. The dingy cobbled streets contained everything from massage parlours to kebab houses, the shops sold everything from strange antiques to electric guitars. On one corner the advertising hoarding of a cinema was a kaleidoscope of swirling lights; on another sat a quartet of red telephone boxes just like the ones the boys were used to at home. The 'people' (90 per cent gargoyle, 10 per cent pinker) were more cosmopolitan than the gang of thugs the boys had met back on the road. Those had been completely naked, but here most gargoyles were decked out in accessories. Wigs, belts, gloves, footwear and jewellery were the most popular; the boys did not see one gargoyle who actually condescended to wear clothes. The groups that came closest to doing this were the subcultures –

645

gargoyles with purple Mohican wigs and black leather jackets, studded belts and wristbands, padlocks on chains round their necks.

This, in fact, was one of the biggest surprises for the boys: that the gargoyles were not the clonal, sexless race they had assumed them to be. There were female gargoyles (slimmer and prettier than their male counterparts, with long tapering fingernails and large purple-nippled breasts) pushing prams which contained howling baby gargoyles; there were child gargoyles, cute as toys, playing in the streets, clutching lollipops or red balloons or their mother's hand. Old men gargoyles sat on steps, smoking pipes and growling together in low voices; smart young things in white boots and floppy white caps sat outside cafés, laughingly flamboyant with their pink cigarettes and glasses of red liquid.

It was a mish-mash of styles and cultures, of times and places, and running beneath it all was that ominous undercurrent of racial hatred. The boys were not actually physically attacked, but they were perpetually aware of the stares being directed at them, some merely curious but the majority openly hostile. They heard occasional muttered comments, 'dirty pinkers', 'filthy scum', but they studiously ignored them all. By the time they reached the market square, with its bustling throngs, its market traders promoting their wares, its bartering and haggling, a feeling of oppression was making them sweat.

They mingled with the crowd and began to browse among the stalls, relaxing a little now that they were out of the narrow streets and dim alleyways. There were more pinkers around here than anywhere else, most of them slaves but also plenty of freemen. Both boys had already seen that the pinkers were not really like themselves: they were dark-skinned, slim, lithe, their delicate, almost Far Eastern features uniformly blank. The freemen wore white robes and sandals; at best the slaves wore rags, at worst nothing at all. It was obvious that some masters treated their slaves with compassion and dignity, whilst others treated theirs as dirt. Robin shuddered when one procession of slaves jogged past, the heavy chain that linked their ankles jangling, the gargoyle behind them bulbous and mean-faced, lashing out with a whip. These particular slaves carried wicker baskets on their heads which contained live things that clawed and spat and thrashed about. However it was not this that made Robin shudder – it was their faces. Each slave had his left eye sewn closed and a deep diagonal red scar mutilating his right cheek. Robin knew that even if any of these men ever earned or bought their freedom, the taint of slavery would always be with them, livid on their faces.

The market-stalls sold a cornucopia of goods, some (like chattering plastic teeth and soap-on-a-rope) tackily recognizable, others of which had the boys gasping in wonder. There were animals that looked like circus deformities, crosses between snakes-and-squirrels, emus-and-chimpanzees; plants that were furniture or furniture that were plants – rose-beds, tulip-chairs, pianolas made from geraniums and vines and sunflowers; ornaments made from metal and sand and glass and string whose true shapes defied the eye (some moved sinuously, others squeaked and whistled and hummed in a parody of life); machines like cash dispensers with crawling things inside – red centipedal bug-eyed insects intended as gargoyle snacks.

Robin and Toady wandered among these incredible stalls, their mouths watering at the sight of all the food, their pockets agonizingly empty. They paused by a stall that sold miniature red mermaids in pink bulb-shaped jars, entranced by the tiny creatures' beautiful singing voices, by the way they lounged on thumb-sized rocks and flipped their fish-tails in a half-inch of water.

'Wow,' Robin breathed and bent low to examine one of the creatures further. He was sure she batted her eyes at him and he smiled bashfully, turning to Toady. 'I wonder what they'd say at school if we brought one of these back with us,' he said.

The proprietor of the stall, an old gargoyle wearing an array of silver rings and bangles and a purple cloth cap on his head, looked up from his newspaper. It was a pink paper whose red symbols looked like a cross between Arabic and geometry. He was sitting on a red and white striped deckchair, one of the familiar pink cigarettes jutting from his mouth. He stared at the boys without expression, his black-red eyes unblinking, and it was only when Robin picked up one of the mermaid jars that he spoke.

'What in Zad's name do you think you're doing?' he murmured then, softly.

'Er . . . um . . . nothing. Just looking,' answered Robin, taken aback.

The proprietor folded his newspaper and dropped it on the chair behind him as he stood up. He placed his large thick-veined hands on the counter-top and leaned towards Robin.

'Are you just stupid or are you taking the piss?' he said, a question to which Robin had no reply. The old gargoyle rolled his eyes, sighed heavily, and pointed at the store-front sign above his head.

Robin looked. The sign was written in the same gobbledeygook as the newspaper and beside it was a large pink cross. He began, 'What's the—' and then he halted, for suddenly he understood. He glanced up and down the row of stalls, noticed a similar cross on maybe one in four of them. He felt his cheeks burning, felt like hurling the jar in the gargoyle's ugly face, but he resisted. Instead he mumbled an apology, placed the jar back on the exact spot from which he'd picked it up, and turned to walk away.

'Hoy!' the old gargoyle snarled. 'Where the fuck do you think you're going?'

Robin turned to face him. 'Away. We're going away. We're obviously not welcome here so we're leaving.'

'Not without paying for that you're not,' the gargoyle replied, pointing at the mermaid jar. 'I can't sell it now you've had your filthy hands on it, can I? So just give me the money and then fuck off.'

'Money,' said Robin. 'Ah.' He made a big show of patting his pockets. 'I'm afraid I don't, er, have any money as such.'

The old gargoyle seemed to be expecting this. He banged his fist down hard on the wooden counter, making the jars rattle and the boys jump. 'Zchat!' was the word he seemed to shout, and a split-second later Robin and Toady found themselves surrounded by muscled red flesh, by snarling mouths full of pointed teeth, by four, five, six, seven, *eight* pairs of glistening black-red snake-eyes.

'Oh shit,' Robin muttered as four pairs of hands reached for him, another four pairs for Toady. He was picked up, flipped horizontal and carried through the air. He squealed at the tightness of the grips on his arms and legs, but they refused to slacken. Though he faced the sky he could smell the gargoyles – their hot meaty breath, the cold musk of their bodies that was both metallic and reptilian.

'Take these jokers round the back and slice them up,' he heard the old gargoyle say. Next moment the sky was lurching, and Robin's limbs were sending out sickening spasms of pain.

'What seems to be the problem?' another voice said then, and their journey was, momentarily at least, suspended. This new voice was harsh, guttural, obviously that of another gargoyle, yet there was a calm authority about it which gave an impression almost of kindliness.

'These wankers tried to cause trouble at my stall, ignored the exclusion rule,' the old gargoyle said. 'I gave them the chance to pay for what they'd soiled, but they refused. My boys were just going to pop them round the back, teach them a few lessons in etiquette. There's nothing here to concern you, Mister. I think it would be better if you just turned and walked the other way.'

'I see,' said the voice. This was followed by a pause so long that Robin thought the speaker had taken the old gargoyle's advice. However next moment the voice came again, this time the accent almost plummy, dripping with authority. 'Well, Mr . . . ?'

'Zniminee.' That was what it sounded like.

'Yes . . . well, sir, let me assure you that first I have no intention of walking away, and secondly the events occurring here do indeed concern me. I am not used to having my retainers assaulted in the streets, and especially not over such a trifling matter as this. We have travelled a long way, we are tired and we wish to proceed to our place of residence. I am sorry that my . . . ah . . . servants have transgressed your exclusion rule, but I'm afraid that we do not possess such a . . . such a *crude* social structure in Idrias. If it is an apology you want, then you have it, sir. Now, please, put down my servants and let us continue on our way.'

There was another pause, then the old gargoyle spoke again. He sounded impressed and a little fearful. 'You . . . er . . . you come from Idrias, you say?'

'Yes,' said the voice imperiously.

'Home of Our Eminence, the Zad?'

'Yes, that is correct.'

'Then . . . then it should be *me* who is apologizing to *you*, sir. I never realized, I'm terribly sorry. Boys, put these . . . er . . . gentlemen down. I'm afraid there's been a misunderstanding.'

Robin and Toady found themselves lowered to the ground, and stood swaying for a moment, white-faced. The eight gargoyles who had been about to 'teach them a lesson' slipped silently away, and for the first time the boys were able to see their would-be rescuer.

He was a paunchy, pompous-looking gargoyle. He wore a white-powdered wig on his bullet-sleek head and a monocle clamped in his eye. He also wore white kid-gloves, white shoes with spats, and twirled a white cane in his left hand. Across his chest, from right shoulder to left hip, lay a sash, purple with a zigzag golden stripe. He was so grotesquely comical that Toady almost laughed out loud, but managed to turn his mirth into a coughing fit at the last moment.

'Now, sir,' their saviour said, 'if you will allow me to pay for the damage caused we'll be on our way.'

'Damage?' the old gargoyle replied. 'Oh no, no, no, sir, there was no damage. But . . . but I'd be honoured if you'd accept the mermaid jar there – yes, that's right, the one at the far end – as a token of my . . . er . . . of my goodwill, as it were. Yes, and please call again, sir. And of course, feel free to bring these . . . er . . . your servants with you.'

The pompous-looking gargoyle picked up the mermaid jar the proprietor had indicated, said, 'Charming,' and passed the jar to Toady. 'Here, Adrian, you look after this for me. Now we really must get along. We're late enough as it is.'

He began to walk away, twirling his cane. The boys looked at each other in astonishment and then followed. Toady had been amazed to hear the creature use his name, even after Ranulf's explanations the other night about shared knowledge within the 'Us'. However this posed the question of why none of the other gargoyles in RED had known who the boys were, and it was a question to which Toady had no real answer. Maybe, he thought, you needed a certain amount of eminence, breeding, intelligence, whatever, to absorb the knowledge that was floating around and to use it. Maybe these other gargoyles *did* have the knowledge buried somewhere in their subconscious, but they were simply too thick to see it for what it was. He shrugged, looked at Robin, and clutched the mermaid jar to his chest. What did it matter what the explanation was so long as they'd been saved once again?

10

Saturday 9.08 p.m.

'Start, you sod!' Glennon shouted, and slammed his fist down hard on the steering wheel. He sat for a moment, fuming, then tried the ignition key again. The engine coughed and wheezed like an asthmatic, but stubbornly refused to catch. Muttering under his breath, Glennon threw the door open and stalked outside.

The bonnet seemed encased in ice as he wrenched it open and peered underneath. He knew this was pointless – he'd checked every nut and bolt at least five times already – yet he retained the faint hope that maybe this time the problem would leap up and smack him in the face. However the engine looked the same as before, an oily lump of metal and plastic with no apparent symptoms of debility. His hands roamed over it, prodding, poking, ensuring that things were tight, and again came away clueless.

'Still no luck?' said a voice by his shoulder. Glennon turned to see Derek Gardener there. His lugubrious face and casual stance masked his frustrated anxiety.

'No,' Glennon said, 'I'm afraid not,' and felt wretched at having to tell him so. They'd been here for half an hour already – a half-hour during which Eileen Gardener had progressed from anguished sobbing to screaming hysterics to a state of almost catatonic shock. She sat now in the back seat of the car, silhouetted by the street lamps, a cold, silent, unmoving presence. Though her eyes were blank, her hands rigid in her lap, Glennon could not help thinking that she accused him with each shallow breath she took.

He tore himself from his thoughts as he realized that Derek was speaking. 'Are you sure it's not the plugs?' he was saying. 'Maybe they want tightening or something.'

'It's not the plugs,' Glennon muttered. 'I've checked them twice already.' Yet he reached into the innards of the car and fiddled with them once again.

'The battery then. It must be that. Let's give it one more go with the jump leads.' Without waiting for a reply, Derek trudged round the back to fetch them.

Glennon raised his eyes heavenwards, saw a blackness that was almost soothing, vaporous clouds that seemed frozen to the sky. If the jump leads didn't work this time they'd have to . . . to go in the Gardeners' car!

He jerked upright with the force of this revelation, icy air snatching at his throat. Next moment he expelled a huge gout of ragged steam and tried to work out how they could have been so stupid. Here they were, in a life-and-death situation, trying to get *his* car started when Derek's had been available all the time! Hell, Derek had even backed his car out of his drive and parked it nose to nose with Glennon's so that they could use the charge from his battery!

Glennon stared at his car, and then at Derek's, his head shaking in utter bewilderment. Next moment the bewilderment gave way to suspicion and he slammed the bonnet down.

'Get in,' he said to Derek, who was holding out the jump leads as though offering a fistful of snakes.

'Pardon?' Derek said in surprise, but Glennon was already in the car and leaning over to shove the passenger door open. Derek got in, still perplexed, still with the jump leads trailing from his hand. 'I don't believe it!' he exclaimed as the engine roared into life with the first twist of the key.

'I do,' Glennon said grimly, slamming the car into reverse, spinning the wheel so they backed round in a half-circle. 'That creature's been doing something, messing with my car and our minds. It must have known that we were trying to get to the hospital.'

'How . . . how do you know?' Derek asked. He had to raise his voice above the caterwauling siren.

'It suddenly came to me. All this time we've been trying to get my car going, *when we could have used yours!*'

Derek looked as stunned as Glennon had felt just a matter of seconds ago. The sergeant glanced at the car-clock, saw it was ten-past nine, and gripped the steering wheel harder. If Richard had left the house soon after the bogus phone-call, he had already been gone for well over an hour. He would have reached the hospital long ago.

Glennon knew it wasn't his fault, yet if anything happened to the boy he didn't think he would ever forgive himself.

11

No-Time

'Excuse me,' Toady said, hurrying after their saviour, 'but could I ask you a question?'

The gargoyle had been leading the way through the bustle of the market square. Now he turned and regarded the boys thoughtfully. The black-red eye behind the lens of his monocle seemed to bloat and shift. He said, 'Yes, certainly, but only if you're quick. We haven't got much time.'

'Who are you?' Toady asked. 'And why did you rescue us? And where are you taking us now?'

'That's three questions,' the gargoyle pointed out, 'all of which will be answered in due course. Now come along, hurry. The auction is about to start.'

He rallied them with his cane, turned on his heels and set off again through the crowd. Robin and Toady looked at each other, then went after him. They didn't like the way the initiative was being taken from them, and yet their need for answers made them loath to end the acquaint-anceship here. Moments later they had reached the far side of the square where the crowds were not so dense.

Toady expected their rescuer to plunge into one of the many side-streets, but instead he stopped before a red stone building and gestured with his cane. 'Here we are,' he said, then turned and began to trot up the dozen or so steps that led to the huge front door. Feeling manipulated the boys went up after him.

This building was by far the grandest in the square. Elevated by the steps, it was guarded by a row of massive pillars and had intricate carvings of mythical, or maybe not so mythical, beasts clambering motionless about its elaborate stonework. At the top of the steps, the gargoyle turned, said, 'Come along,' and entered the building. The boys followed, and found themselves in a large high-ceilinged room which reminded them of a theatre. Rows of wooden chairs faced a stage which was bare but for a lectern. The lack of a carpet, stark furniture and sparse ornamentation should have made the place seem bare and echoing. However the almost exclusive use of the colour red created an illusion of close, hot oppression.

The place was about half-full with seated male gargoyles and pinker slaves standing against the walls. A smell hung in the air like the inside of a reptile-house. Toady, Robin and their gargoyle made their way down a side-aisle, the boys nervous of the stares they were attracting. Toady, however, was at least partly thankful that the dull rumble of chatter was drowning out the song of the mermaid in the jar.

'I'm afraid you'll have to stand,' their gargoyle muttered, pressing his face up close to Robin's. Robin had to make a conscious effort to stop himself recoiling. 'It's not a rule I agree with, but nevertheless we'll have to adhere to it. There's no point rocking the boat and getting thrown out before we've even begun.'

'Begun what?' Robin hissed back at him. 'What's it an auction *for*?'

But their gargoyle put a finger to his lips and said, 'Shh, it's about to begin.'

He spotted a seat at the end of a row towards the back of the hall and went to sit down. Resignedly Robin and Toady went to stand against the wall. Robin looked around him at the other pinkers and shuddered: their smooth blank expressions and vacant eyes made them in some ways even creepier than the gargoyles.

The chatter quietened as a figure came on to the stage. He was a grossly fat gargoyle with broken brown teeth and an armband embellished with a pink symbol. He wandered to the lectern, picked up a gavel and banged it down, killing the last few mutters of conversation.

'Gen'lemen,' he began, 'first of all I'd like to welcome

you to the auction an' just say that I 'ope you find what you're lookin' for 'ere. We've got a good selection of stock an' quite a large one, so I think it's best if we get started immediately. Now our first item, lot one, belonged to Pradle Geronimee. I'm told this boy is 'ard-working, loyal, good wiv electrics an' a good cook . . .'

The gargoyle babbled on as a pinker was prodded on to the stage. At first Robin thought the pinker would bring on some item, the aforementioned lot one, but then he realized it was the pinker himself who was for sale. He grimaced distastefully: so this was what the auction was – a slave mart. He should have guessed. He glanced at their gargoyle, who was following the proceedings with polite interest, and wondered what his purpose was in bringing them here.

Was he, he wondered, some kind of philanthropist, a well-to-do gentleman who used his wealth and his influence to relieve suffering? Was that why he had saved them back there in the street? Was he here now to buy slaves simply to set them free?

Robin tried hard to entertain this idea, but a much more sinister one kept bobbing above the surface of his optimism. Perhaps the gargoyle had rescued them simply in order to sell them here and make some money for himself. Robin feared that at the end of the auction he and Toady might suddenly find themselves put forward as last-minute additional items.

He brooded on this as the bids for lot one came thick and fast. The currency being used was apparently called lepri, and lot one's starting price of seventy-five soon rose to a hundred and sixty. As soon as the first pinker was sold the second was introduced and the process was repeated. As the auction wore on, Robin only half-listened to the gunfire of bids and counter-bids; he was much more concerned with keeping a watch on the dandy with the cane who had brought them here.

What Robin saw did not reassure him; indeed, it served

only to consolidate his suspicions. Their saviour sat quietly, his cane across his knees, apparently uninterested in making a purchase. At last Robin nudged Toady and whispered, 'I don't like this, Ade. What the hell's he brought us here for? We're on lot forty-six now and he hasn't even bid once. If he tries to put us up for sale, get ready to make a run for it.'

Toady looked at him worriedly, but after a moment he nodded. In a hopeful voice he said, 'Maybe he just doesn't feel there's anything worth buying.'

'Lot forty-seven,' the auctioneer announced. 'Now then, gents, 'ere's a strange specimen. This one was found wanderin' wild on the town's outskirts, an' he put up quite a fight, I can tell you. I won't pretend you wouldn't be takin' a risk wi' this one, but on the other 'and 'e could work out to be a sound investment. 'E's a bit on the small side, but 'as plenty of spirit an' should be all right for menials and then maybe later for studdin'. Now, who wants to take the plunge an' start the biddin'? Shall we say . . . twenty lepri?'

Robin barely heard these words, for his attention was taken by their gargoyle, whose attitude all at once had changed. Instead of leaning back in his chair in a relaxed pose, he had suddenly leaned forward and then risen to his feet; instead of the distracted smile and half-glazed eyes, he now seemed intensely interested in what was going on in front of him.

'Look at that!' Robin hissed, and nudged Toady in the ribs. He glanced at his friend and was startled to see the expression on *his* face. Toady was gaping, wide-eyed, wide-mouthed, at the stage. 'What's the matter?' Robin said, noting out of the corner of his eye that their gargoyle was now brandishing his cane like a sword.

'*It's Nige!*' Toady gasped, his voice loud enough to set gargoyle heads swivelling. Robin tried to ignore those glacial stares and turned his attention to the stage. It was indeed Nige; their friend was recognizable despite a black eye and a bruised swollen cheek. He looked barely conscious, his head lolling on his shoulders, his hands tied behind his back.

'I 'ave twenty,' the auctioneer was saying, 'from the gen'leman there with the stick. Now come on, sirs, who'll give me twenty-five? Twenty-five anybody? Surely the buck's worth that?'

There was a great deal of murmuring and shaking of heads. Meanwhile Robin's mind was racing in an attempt to come to terms with this latest of circumstances. It was obvious to him now that the gargoyle had known Nige was going to be one of the items for sale here and had simply been waiting for him to appear. But this being the case, what were the implications for the three of them? Had their movements been monitored all along, and if so, by whom? Or was this simply something to do with all that shared knowledge stuff that Ranulf had told Ade about, but which none of these other gargoyles seemed to possess?

Thoughts and fears chased themselves round and round in Robin's head. He was grateful for the gargoyle's intervention back in the market, but the creature's motives still worried him. Their progress in this place seemed an endless succession of jumping from frying pans into fires and back into frying pans again. Was their luck finally changing for the better or was this simply another inferno?

'Shit,' he heard Toady mutter, and surfaced from his reverie.

'What's up?' Robin said, looking first at their gargoyle and then at the stage.

'Someone in the front row's bid twenty-five.' But even as Toady said this their gargoyle was waving his cane in the air once again.

'Thirty,' said the auctioneer, sounding surprised and pleased. 'I 'ave thirty from the gen'leman with the stick. Do I 'ear thirty-five anywhere? Come on, surely someone will give me thirty-five? At this price we're virtually givin' 'im away.'

His glycerine eyes swept round the hall. It seemed, however, there were few bargain-hunters here today. 'Goin' once,' he announced, and looked round in the hope this would goad some reaction. 'Goin' twice.' He picked up his gavel and poised it above the lectern. He was just about to bring it down to complete the sale when a voice growled, 'Thirty-two.'

Toady and Robin expelled sighs of disappointment. Robin glanced at their gargoyle and saw the anger on his face. Suddenly he understood what was happening here: the gargoyle in the front row was a professional bidder, positioned to boost up the price of items in which the interest was low. If the professional won the bid, then the item was retained and sold next time around. Robin hoped fervently that their gargoyle had both the resources and the inclination to see this through.

He needn't have worried. Their gargoyle was now standing on the chair, his cane held rigid above his head. 'Fifty!' he declared, and glared at the hunched figure on the front row, defying him to bid against that. The auctioneer's mouth dropped open, then instantly snapped closed: Robin could see he was having trouble masking his glee.

'Fifty!' he exclaimed, waving the gavel. 'The gen'leman wi' the stick's offered me fifty! Does anyone wanna go higher? Fifty-one? Fifty-two? No? Right then, goin' once, goin' twice, *sold* to the gent wi' the stick!'

This was little more than a babble. Evidently he was anxious to make the sale official before the buyer had time to realize what he'd done and change his mind. The boys saw flat red heads twist to stare at the fool with money to burn. Other gargoyles nudged one another and grinned snidely and rolled their snake-cold eyes.

Their rescuer got down off his seat and made his way along the row and down the side aisle towards the boys. 'Meet me on the steps in two minutes,' he breathed as he reached them. 'I'm just going to fetch Nigel.'

'How did you—' Robin began, but their gargoyle repeated, 'Two minutes,' and passed by.

Robin and Toady looked at one another. The mermaid still sang in its pink jar. 'I don't know about all this,' Robin said.

Toady shrugged. 'Well, he saved our lives and found Nige for us, didn't he?'

Robin said, 'Yeah, but . . .' Then he shrugged and motioned for Toady to lead the way.

They made their way down the side-aisle, the million dollar question, Why?, flashing in bright red letters inside both their heads. They were parallel with the back row when a large red hand snaked out from nowhere and closed around Toady's forearm.

He bit back on a yelp of pain. The hand had the crushing power of a vice. For a moment he thought he was going to drop the mermaid jar, but managed to juggle it to safety with the arm that was still free. The owner of the crushing hand was a thickly-set gargoyle in an old straw hat, wearing a pink eyepatch.

'Like it up yer, do yer?' this gargoyle sneered, saliva spraying from his mouth.

Toady tried not to flinch at the ripe butcher's-shop smell that wafted over him. He stammered, 'I . . . I don't know what you mean.'

Eyepatch flashed a knowing look towards his cronies. There were three of them, and they were snickering and slapping each other like schoolboys.

'Prog here reckons you must have arseholes so wide you can shit sideways,' Eyepatch said. 'Or does he make you suck him, eh? Is that what he likes?'

'Leave us alone,' Robin said, more fear than bravado in his voice.

The cronies hooted; Eyepatch's single eye narrowed in savage amusement.

'You gonna make me, boy?' he gloated.

Robin didn't know what to say. In effect they were stuck here until Eyepatch deigned to let Toady go. Up on the stage the auctioneer announced, 'Lot forty-nine.' The gargoyle called Prog leaned over and hissed, 'This is ours, Grak.'

660

Eyepatch's hand opened and he pushed Toady away from him. 'Get going, fuck-face,' he snarled, 'go and lick your master's arse.' The boys hurried away just as he bawled out a bid: 'Eighty-five!' Toady rubbed his arm on which was an imprint in red of the creature's hand.

Their gargoyle was waiting for them on the steps, trying to support Nige's semi-conscious body as best he could. As the boys appeared the gargoyle snapped, 'Where have you two been?'

Briefly Robin explained what had happaned. A look of disgust crossed the gargoyle's face and he muttered, 'Barbarians.' He took the mermaid jar from Toady and indicated that the boys support their friend. They did so, and followed the gargoyle down the steps.

'Where now?' Robin said when they had reached the bottom.

'We'll go to my hotel. Once there I promise I'll answer all your questions.'

He led them out of the market-square via a narrow side-street. At the bottom he turned left, then right, then left again. Robin tried to memorize the route they were taking, but soon realized that the task was hopeless. The town of RED was a maze of alleyways, dank passages, back-yards.

It began to grow dark. An effect of this was the illusion that the streets were getting narrower, that the buildings were leaning over as though to squeeze out the sky. Robin had the strange idea that they were specks of matter flowing through some vast and intricate blood-stream. The mermaid jar in the gargoyle's hand was like an oil-lamp lighting their way.

In the darkness the gargoyles prowling the streets seemed more threatening than ever. Their red-slitted eyes appeared to catch the light like a cat's. The boys saw red-skinned drunks huddled in corners, prostitutes and drug-dealers plying for trade. They shivered as gangs of Mohican-wigged gargoyles passed them, brandishing clubs and chains.

661

'Are we nearly there?' Toady whispered in a voice tight with nerves.

Their gargoyle nodded. 'Not long now.'

'Heartbeat . . . Close . . .' Nige muttered, stirring in their arms.

'Sh, Nige,' said Robin, side-stepping a gargoyle who was hunched against a wall to his left.

They emerged finally into a street that was full of dilapidated warehouses. The street lamps here were so dim they seemed wrapped in layers of gauze. At the far end fire crackled in an ancient brazier; raucous laughter accompanied the cavorting of tall black shapes. There was a rustling in the street, litter stirred feebly by a gentle night-wind.

Robin shuddered at all the graffiti, huge pink crosses marching in rows on red brick like a giant's scrawled kisses to his sweetheart. Their gargoyle led them to a building they had both assumed to be abandoned. Red paint peeled from its walls, revealing more red paint beneath. The windows offered the boys no clue as to what waited inside; every last one was boarded up – just as, Toady thought uncomfortably, the windows in the King Street house had been.

'Hold on,' Robin said as their gargoyle stretched out a hand. 'Is *this* your hotel?'

The gargoyle nodded; pink light slid across its monocle like a wad of shifting skin. 'Yes. The place is shabby, I know, but I wanted somewhere unobtrusive. It's important that nobody finds us here; that we are not disturbed.'

Robin shivered at these words, they implied something threatening to him. However he and Toady had no choice now but to see this through. To try to find their way back through these streets in the dark, braving club-wielding gangs who were probably out looking for lone pinkers, would have been an act of suicide. They braced themselves as the gargoyle turned the handle and pushed the door open.

They stepped in after him, wrinkling their noses at the

ape-like smell. They found themselves in a filthy hotel lobby, the dust and grime only partly concealed by lighting so dingy it caused everything to seem made of rust. The wallpaper was stained and tatty, the carpet so threadbare that in places rough wooden boards peeped through like ribs.

To the left of the door was a desk. Between the desk and a huge board hung with keys sat a gargoyle eating what looked like a fistful of snot from which grease dripped. To the right of the door two pillars marked the border of a bar/restaurant area, a clutter of rickety tables draped with grimy tablecloths and surrounded by chairs. Opposite the door, beyond the desk, was a staircase, steep and narrow, leading up to a land of shadow.

Two female gargoyles sat smoking on the stairs, watching the boys through cold dead eyes. Their mean faces were plastered with yellow make-up and they wore black leather basques replete with buckles which creaked and jangled when they moved. They were leaning forward, their breasts swinging pendulously, hostility emanating from them like a wave. The cloud of cigarette smoke above their heads seemed to twist blackly within itself like a genie trying to form.

Their gargoyle walked to the desk. The hotel-owner, looking up from his snot-snack, saw the three boys and his eyes narrowed. 'What the fuck *they* doing here?' he snarled, dumping the green blob on a sheet of grease-proof paper beside him.

'They are my retainers,' the gargoyle said. 'I wish them to accompany me to my room.'

'Like hell,' the hotel owner replied, staring at his guest with undisguised loathing.

Even by gargoyle standards the hotel-owner was an ugly specimen. His arms were huge, an unwieldy collaboration of fat and muscle. A black snake tattoo curled from his wrist up his arm and finally ended in a fork-tongued head at his throat. He had a deep scar from his lip to just beneath his right eye, and a cluster of gold studs in each ear.

'I'm sure we can come to some . . . arrangement?' their gargoyle murmured, and from what appeared to be a pouch in his stomach withdrew a number of strips of purple and pink material. These he pushed across the counter with his fingertips, removing his hand only when they were directly beneath Scarface's nose.

Scarface looked at the strips for a moment, then placed a hand over them and nodded. 'All right, just this once. But I'll have to stick a bit more on your bill when you leave. That room'll need fumigating if these pinkers are gonna be sleeping in it.'

'Of course,' their gargoyle said, and Scarface gave him a key from the board. The gargoyle led the way upstairs, the two females squeezing into the side to let him pass. When Robin and Toady followed, still trying awkwardly to support Nige between them, the females were less accommodating. One of them deliberately blew smoke into Toady's face and the other reached up between Robin's legs and nipped him in the balls.

The gargoyle's room was on the fourth floor. By the time the three boys reached it, Robin and Toady were sweating and exhausted. Nige had begun to come round a little by this time, but had still needed carrying up the stairs. A dim lozenge of crimson light above each floor number was the only illumination the hotel provided.

The boys paused on the fourth floor landing as the gargoyle fumbled with the key to his room. The sweet song from the mermaid jar was not sufficient to smother the grunts and groans and shrieks, the sounds of violence and lust, which seemed to come from every other room and made their skin crawl. Their gargoyle pushed his key into the lock, twisted it and turned the handle. The door swung open and he led them into a limbo of solid blackness.

Or that was what it seemed at first. For almost immediately the pink light from the mermaid jar sprang in and gave the room a shadowy definition. There was a wardrobe, a chair, a bed and a bedside cabinet. There was

664

nothing else, not even a carpet on the floor or a bulb in the empty fitting.

Toady screwed up his face in disgust and Robin did likewise. The room's very walls seemed impregnated with a rank animal stench.

'Yes, I'm sorry about that,' the gargoyle muttered. 'It's nothing to do with me, I assure you.' He crossed to the bedside cabinet, placed the mermaid jar and his cane atop it and turned to face them.

'Close the door, Adrian,' he said then in a quiet, peculiar voice.

Toady didn't move. 'What?' he said nervously. 'Why?'

'Just do it, Adrian, please. Close the door.'

'And trap that smell in with us?' Robin said. 'No way.'

The gargoyle sighed and seemed to wilt a little. He placed a hand on his chest, then stepped forward to shut the door himself. Robin and Toady, still supporting Nige between them, shuffled into his path. There was a brief embarrassed stalemate, then Robin stammered, 'L-look, Mister, we're grateful for what you've done for us and everything, but . . . but we don't know why you've brought us here now. You said you'd give us some answers, and that's all we've come for, nothing else. If you try anything on, we'll fight you, I mean it; it's three against one. So look, why don't we just keep the door open, have a little chat, and then we'll go?'

For a moment only the mermaid's song and the muffled groans of unseen residents filled the stillness. Then the gargoyle gave an abrupt barking laugh and stepped back to sit on the bed. Waving a hand vaguely in the air he said, 'Is that why you think I brought you here? You think I . . . ?' He chuckled, both half-amused and half-astonished that the boys should think this way.

'Well, why *did* you bring us here then?' Robin said, embarrassment making him brusque.

'If you'll just close the door, I'll explain. I didn't want to be overheard, that's all.'

Robin and Toady looked at each other. Then Robin

gave a short nod and they manhandled Nige into the chair that stood between wardrobe and bed. That done, Toady walked to the door and closed it quietly.

'That's better,' the gargoyle said, and immediately slumped on the bed with a groan. He discarded his wig, monocle, gloves and sash, and just before he lay back Toady was sure he saw something gleaming wetly on his crown. The sight made him uneasy and he looked at Robin, wondering if he had seen it too. Robin, however, appeared more concerned with the smell, and hadn't noticed what had looked to Toady like a wound gone mushily gangrenous.

'Are you all right?' Robin asked as the gargoyle bent suddenly to pant and writhe. Defined in pink light and black shadow, the creature looked unsettlingly like a foetus in a womb. The mermaid's song seemed strangely to add to this image, as did the far wall, flowing with shadow like a black river. The boys saw the gargoyle's face contort, then its black-red eyes slide closed.

'I think he's ill,' Robin said, turning to Toady.

A voice came from the bed, a harsh gargling whisper. 'I'm all . . . right . . . It's just been . . . such a strain . . . that's all.'

All at once Nige let out a shriek, and almost simultaneously Robin and Toady stumbled back in horror. Robin crashed into the wardrobe, jarring his entire body, but barely even noticed the pain. *'Oh my God!'* he hissed, eyes fixed on the abomination on the bed.

With a wet ripping sound the gargoyle had burst open. A jagged fissure had simply split his body from chin to navel and black stuff like molten tar was now pouring out. The stuff trickled down its sides and began to pool on the grubby sheets beneath it. The gargoyle's arms and legs were jerking spastically and its mouth yawned in a silent scream.

'Let's get out,' Toady moaned and scrabbled for the door handle.

'*We can't leave Nige!*' Robin yelled, grabbing at his arm.

They turned back to see Nige rocking on the chair, muttering something so low that neither of them could hear it. Then their attention was dragged to the bed again as the gargoyle's mutilated body made a thick, wet, bubbling sound.

They both screamed as yellow-white froth suddenly erupted from the ruined body, fizzing and popping like sherbert, jetting from every orifice the gargoyle possessed. They saw the stuff streaming from its nose, its mouth, its ears and finally its eyes. Much more plentiful than the tarry gunge which had preceded it, it fanned out over the bed and began to plop on to the floor. Grotesquely, Toady was reminded of a washing machine gone haywire, vomiting out its suds in an ever-widening pool.

The gargoyle was quickly buried in the stuff. Robin and Toady stood rivetted, both wanting to leave and yet compelled in some way to see this through. The animal-smell, still rife in the room, was now joined by a high yeasty smell like mouldy bread. Nige was leaning forward in his chair, face intense, hands cupping his knees. Yellow-white muck streaked with black was pooling sluggishly around his feet.

Toady gasped as something dark, muscly-bony, gleaming with discharge, broke the surface of the foam. It wavered in the air for a moment like a hair-matted snake, then plunged back into the gunge again. Now Toady was reminded of calves and foals being born in that vet programme on the telly. But if this was a birth it was a hideous one – one for which the parent had given up his life.

The slick hairy limb reappeared, waving and jerking, trembling as though pushing against something. There was another sound, like a melon bursting beneath the wheel of a car, and next moment what was left of the gargoyle's body exploded. Toady and Robin ducked as hunks of red flesh began to fly about the room, Toady giggling hysterically as an entire hand smacked wetly against the boards over the window, then slithered down to the floor like a dead crab.

When the rain of flesh had stopped falling, he cautiously raised his head. What was now lying on the bed, amid the slimy debris of its birth, was indeed a foal. He could see its long limbs stirring, its flanks heaving as it drew breath. Then it opened its mouth, lifted its snout and he realized it was not a foal after all.

'It's a dog!' Robin gasped, his back still pressed against the wardrobe.

'It's Ranulf,' Toady said without thinking, and suddenly he knew that this was true.

Ranulf shook his head, specks of eggy gunk spattering in all directions. He struggled up on to his elbows and blinked his liquid-brown eyes. His fur stood up in sticky tufts; his mouth opened and his pink tongue emerged to lick himself clean. Slime sucking at his shoes as he stepped closer, Toady said, 'It is you, Ranulf, isn't it?'

The dog looked at him and a strange gurgling sound came from its throat. It curled its jowls and vomited a stream of yellow stuff on to the bed. 'Yes,' it rasped. 'Yes, of course it's me. Who did you think it was?'

Robin was at Toady's shoulder now, shaking his head. 'I don't get this,' he said. 'What is . . . I mean, I just don't get this.'

'There's nothing to get,' Ranulf said, rotating his head on his neck, stretching his limbs luxuriously. 'I was your rescuer. I've been following you since you left Liana's cottage. I simply changed my shape to . . . ah . . . blend in with the surroundings, as it were.'

'Changed your shape?' Toady said. 'I thought you couldn't do that any more. I thought the Zad locked you into the shape of a dog?'

'And so he did,' Ranulf replied, 'but his distance has weakened the restraints and I managed to override them. But still I had to use every last vestige of strength to maintain the shape. And it damned near killed me to do it.'

He gestured with a nod at the scummy results of his shape-shifting. The yellow-white froth was crystallizing now, becoming brittle and flaky, and shrinking as it did so like polythene held above a flame. As for the lumps of red flesh, they were liquefying like chunks of ice, dissolving each into its own little pool of redness. Toady looked with distaste at the hand beneath the window, saw nothing more than a shapeless blob. He said, 'I don't really understand this either.'

Ranulf sighed, closed his eyes briefly, then opened them again. 'What don't you understand?' he said wearily.

'Well, for a start, why you risked your life to save us. And also how you were able to. I mean, back at the cottage you said you couldn't help us.'

'I said I couldn't help you directly,' Ranulf said, 'but I am able to point you in the right direction. Within the Us the influence of the Zad – despite his absence – prevents me from actually helping you to find the link and defeat him. But at least I've been able to keep you alive, to bring you to this point. I suspect from now on the rest will be up to you.'

Robin shook his head. 'All this is a bit beyond me,' he said.

'Me too,' Toady replied, yet nevertheless he turned back to Ranulf. 'But why did you help us? Not that we aren't grateful, of course,' he added hastily.

'I helped you because, unlike the Zad, I am kind and generous. I believe in the preservation of good.' The dog's jowls crinkled into what the boys took for a smile. Next moment he rather spoiled it by adding, 'And because I want to see the Zad defeated even more than you do.'

'Ah' Toady thought, 'now that's the crux of the matter.' Ranulf saw the boys not as noble warriors, as fighters for good, but simply as weapons against the Zad. He obviously thought that if he could guide them through this landscape, lead them to a point where hopefully they would re-discover the link, then there was a possibility they might return to Starmouth and root out the creature's

Achilles Heel. Which would presumably mean that the Zad's power would go into decline and the monarchy – himself and Liana – would be in the ascendancy again.

The more Toady thought about this, the more he disliked Ranulf, despite the dog's endeavours on their behalf. He did not like the idea of being used as a political pawn, yet on the other hand the risks Ranulf had taken to bring them to this point seemed to imply that the creature was much more vulnerable on foreign soil than it was here among its own subjects.

Musing on this, Toady asked the question that had occurred to him before. 'Why don't those gargoyle-things know who we are? I mean, I thought everything here was all part of the Us? I thought it was all shared knowledge and that sort of stuff?'

Ranulf made a disgusted sound. 'Knowledge is available to all elements,' he said, 'but it is the absorption and assimilation of it which is important. What we have here are petty elements, elements motivated by hate, spite, greed, lust, all the baser emotions. Unfortunately with the Zad in power this now is the nature of things. When my family were on the throne, such elements were held in check.'

These words got Toady wondering whether the Zad's rise had in fact been a case not of evil replacing good, but rather of one evil replacing another, of anarchy superseding tyranny. However it was not the politics of this place which really concerned them. What did concern them was getting back to Starmouth and trying to deal with their own particular element of the Us.

'So?' he said. 'What happens now?'

'You must find the link,' replied Ranulf.

Robin groaned. 'Brilliant. I wish we'd thought of that.'

'*How* do we find it?' Toady asked, breaking in on his friend's sarcasm.

Ranulf considered. He scowled and clenched his teeth as though gripped by some inner turmoil. At last he said, 'As I said before, I'm not permitted to tell you.'

670

'But what exactly do you mean – not permitted?' said Toady. 'Why don't you just come right out and say it?'

'I can't . . . I physically can't.'

'Try,' said Toady.

Ranulf tried. He looked like a stroke victim trying to relearn speech – his lips struggling, his voice a jumble of inarticulate sounds.

Robin pulled a face. He was confused and exasperated; he couldn't help thinking that Ranulf was toying with them, for some reason playing a coy and stupid game. Flapping a hand he snarled, 'Well, if you can't tell us straight out, can't you give us some clue or something?'

His remark was meant sarcastically, yet Ranulf seemed to ponder it deeply. However when he replied his answer at first seemed unconnected to the question. Quietly – so quietly he could barely be heard above the mermaid's song – Ranulf murmured, 'This landscape means nothing to Nige. He is . . . detached from it in all but the physical. He is closer to the link than either of you . . . So close, and yet he doesn't understand.' And then he shivered as though a spear of ice had punctured him.

Toady and Robin turned their attention to Nige. He was rocking on his chair, staring into space, his lips moving in some personal incantation. Toady stepped forward, touched his shoulder, said, 'Nige? Nige, can you hear me?'

Nige stopped rocking. His bruised face was immobile, his wide, wide eyes dancing with pink light. He turned his head so slowly that Toady imagined the joints creaking like old iron hinges. Toady leaned closer to hear the words spilling from his friend's restless lips.

'Ba-dum. Ba-dum. Ba-dum. Ba-dum.'

'It's like a heartbeat,' he thought, surprised.

'Nige,' he said. 'Nige, where are you? What do you see?'

'Here.' A whisper, barely heard. 'I'm here.'

'What do you *see*?' Toady repeated.

'. . . Hospital . . . I see . . . heartbeat . . .'

Toady felt a surge of excitement. He straightened, his eyes shining.

'Well?' Robin demanded. 'What did he say? I couldn't hear him with that bloody mermaid ranting on.'

'He says he sees the hospital. He must have found the link.'

'But he can't have. He's been here with us. How *can* he see the hospital?'

'It must be in his mind,' Toady said, tapping his head. 'Don't you see? It must be in *all* our minds. We've been carrying it with us all this time.'

Robin sank on to the edge of the bed, the quickly-drying slime crunching into fragments beneath him. 'You mean we've come all this way for nothing?' he said blankly.

'Looks like it,' Toady said, and laughed. To Ranulf he said, 'That's right, isn't it? The link is in our minds?'

Ranulf never moved, yet his expression seemed to confirm Toady's words.

'So how do we get to it? How do we get inside our own heads?' asked Robin.

'Do what Nige is doing, I suppose. Concentrate. Block everything else out.'

Toady sat on the bed, cupped his hands around his eyes, and stared at a section of wall. It was a clear section, just above the bedside cabinet and the mermaid jar; a balloon of pink light from the jar blossomed over it like a glowing stain. He listened to the sounds in the room – the haunting sweetness of the mermaid's song, Ranulf's laboured breathing, the creak of Nige's chair as he rocked and his sibilant heartbeat chant – and slowly, bit by bit, these elements came together, provided a focal point of concentration whose centre was the pink-stained section of damp rough plaster.

Toady stared at it . . . stared . . . stared. And at last, for him, time stopped. The music of chair and breath and song and chant became a single coagulation of sound, and one that seemed to come from the wall itself. Everything else in the room melted away, became darkness, an irrelevance. Toady's subconscious imagined a chain reaction, an entropic devouring of everything – this hotel, RED, the jungle, the world, the universe – until all that was left was himself and the wall, the wall and himself.

And now dimensions were his to control.

The distance between himself and the wall closed, dispersed with a dreamlike suddenness. He and the wall *flowed* towards one another; they touched; the wall melted without effort over and into him.

He licked his lips and they were the wall's lips; he blinked his eyes and they were the wall's eyes. His fingers gently caressed the air, touched the cool flesh of the plaster, and immediately it dissolved, became air movements through his skin.

Now Toady was in the wall; he *was* the wall; he could feel his steadfastness, his symmetry. He felt the damp within him, chill and grinding as arthritis in his bones. And then he felt himself pushing away, moving on, leaving the wall behind.

He opened his eyes, not realizing they were closed. So aware was he of himself that he heard his eyes open clearly, a soft awesome sound like the magnified wing-beat of a passing bird. The darkness rose to reveal a grey desert, a rubescent sky across which dark clouds rolled like tanks. A jag of lightning some distance away tore the sky and corkscrewed into the ground.

Toady's heart leaped as he identified the building on the horizon. It was grey and square with many windows and large glass doors. A neon sign, 'Hospital. Quiet Please,' flickered sporadically like a stuttering cry for help.

'I've found it,' he breathed to the wilderness. 'I've found the link.'

He was disturbed to find he was alone. There was no sign of Robin, and surprisingly no sign of Nige. Toady began to jog-walk towards the hospital, the sand soft beneath his feet. He licked his lips and felt a spark *zizz* between them, as though the air was charged, ready to erupt.

He glanced at the swirling soup of red sky. It appeared to scowl. The hospital edged slowly towards him, and now Toady could see an ant lying on the building-brick steps: Nigel Figg, unconscious. He jumped at a sudden crack, and then a whip of lightning lashed the sky, roared into the sand not twenty feet away.

'Shit,' he muttered with feeling, staring at the after-image of the crooked bolt, the small storm of ashes. He began to jog faster, imagining something huge and flat floating above the clouds, tracking him. Next moment that image seemed confirmed as a third streak of lightning raped the desert not more than eight feet away. Toady felt sparks of pain in the soles of his feet, the tingling bite of electricity in his fingertips.

He began to run. His legs felt heavy, dragged down by the dense atmosphere. The hospital jerked closer, forlorn and grey as an image of loneliness. Toady was now close enough to see that many of its windows were smashed, and the sight moved him with foreboding. Suddenly he felt a pang in his chest, enough to make him mutter a startled, 'Ooh!' and touch the place with his fingertips.

This time Toady heard the lightning's screech of triumph. A split-second later his world was filled with blinding light and sizzling pain. His own scream rivalled the lightning's, and for a moment he was certain he was dead. Then he realized he was running, his legs eating the ground in an attempt to escape the crackling beast at his side.

He turned his head, his left eye blind; it felt as though a red hot coin had been pressed through it and into his skull. He saw white-yellow fire dancing on his arm and he yelled in pain and panic. He threw himself on the sand, rolled over and over, smelling singed hair, burned wool, porky-roasted flesh. His mind was full of the memory of his mother, a raging fireball, stumbling blindly as she burnt to death.

He clambered to his feet again, his legs pumping

blindly, making him run as though he could escape the pain. It was like nothing he'd ever known before, so intense he felt certain he'd go mad. It raked at his nerve-endings; he felt as though the left side of him was being drenched by a constant spray of acid. He cried as he ran, sobbed, 'Nige, help me,' as he came to the hospital steps.

The figure on the steps didn't move, and Toady collapsed on the cool, cool concrete. He pressed his roasting face to it, wishing as he'd never wished before that he could die right here and now. His was a world of agony; his head felt full of fire. He fell, spun into the fire, and slowly lost consciousness.

When he woke he forgot for a moment where he was. Then he moved and the holocaust woke too, and memory came flooding back. He flinched and groaned, at the same time aware that his heart was thudding strangely. It seemed almost to be telling him something, reminding him of something he should do. He lifted his head from the steps, and a second later was howling his pain at the sky.

He looked at the place on the steps where his face had been and felt a wave of dizziness wash over him. For a few seconds he was not sure whether he was going to faint or throw up. Eventually he did neither, and raised his head, though he thought if he looked down again he would probably do both. It seemed almost impossible to accept that the waxy red mask that had torn away from him and adhered to the concrete were strands of his own molten flesh.

He raised his hand in front of his face, hardly daring to look. As he did so he was aware that both eyes were working again, though the one he thought he'd lost was smarting and streaming with water. His arm was an horrendous sight, perhaps even worse than he'd thought. The sleeve of his sweater was a black ragged ruin, and in places was welded to the skin. The limb itself was red-raw, swollen and horribly blistered. It oozed greasy fluid like a sausage weeping fat beneath a grill.

Toady sobbed as he looked at his hand. It was lumpy, mis-shapen, the skin puckered and warped as though it had started to melt like wax and had then solidified again as it cooled. His fingers were gummed up, and as he moved them apart he let out another wail of agony. The fingers *tore* apart, little strands of semi-liquid skin linking one to the next.

'Oh God,' he rasped, 'Oh God, help me.' He swallowed and felt fire and a metallic meat-taste slide down his throat. He crawled on his hands and knees up the steps, to the body of Nige who was still unconscious above him. He shook Nige, croaked out his name, but his friend refused to stir.

His heart was thudding now, an insistent hand knocking painfully on the door of his chest. Toady muttered, 'All right, all right,' as if it were a parent nagging him to do something. He took hold of a step to help pull himself to his feet, and was surprised to feel the concrete crumbling away. He looked up at the hospital, noticed that its walls were crumbling too, that a crystal spider's web of cracks had spun itself into the glass of the large entrance doors.

The link was fading, he realized, rotting away even as he watched. A combination of this knowledge and the tugging of his heart saw him staggering unsteadily to his feet. He stumbled up the few remaining steps, the stone granulating like sugar in his wake. There was a powdery crack and a few more chunks of stone detached themselves from the building and pattered to the ground.

Toady placed his hand on the left-hand entrance door, and pushed. There was a screeching of rusty hinges followed by a crack, and then the door lolled drunkenly and collapsed with a crash into the hospital foyer. Through the cloud of white dust, Toady saw the jagged fractures in the floor, the sagging ceiling and gouged walls. There were heaps of rubble and plaster everywhere, and the main reception desk was splintered as though someone had attacked it with a pickaxe.

Toady sneezed three times, and each time it felt as if his face was ripping apart. Wiping his nose carefully on the sleeve that hadn't burned, he shuffled into the hospital. There were no sounds of human occupation, only the rumbling growl of structural decay. Powder sifted down from the ceiling and hunks of plaster slid off walls at an alarming rate.

Toady wondered where he should go and then realized that his heart was leading him. It was controlling his legs, dragging him along as if it was a huge hook attacked to a line in his chest. He felt as if he was being reeled in, drawn inevitably to some kind of epicentre. Though this lack of volition worried him it also seemed to mask the extent of his injuries, gave him a motivation he would not otherwise have possessed.

He went through a swing door and started walking along a corridor. There was strip lighting here, some of which still worked, some which was black and dead, and some which flickered and sparked like infant lightning bolts trying to hatch from eggs. Toady turned a corner, walked through another corridor lined with consulting rooms. He saw formerly pristine white linen stretched over doctors' couches now speckled with debris and mould. Everything metal was caked with rust; everything glass was either cracked or broken.

He came to an open area, saw a pot plant that had shrivelled to brown string standing before a lift that was stuck between this floor and the one below. The lift doors were half open: through them Toady could see the top half of the lift car, its lights flickering like a strobe, and above that an oil-black shaft, lift cables like exposed tendons.

The whole contraption was making an alarming creaking, grinding sound. Toady wondered how long it would be before the cables snapped and the lift went crashing to the basement. He backed away as a huge chunk of masonry hit the lift roof with a clang and bounced out of the half-open doors. His heart was telling him to go up, up, up, so Toady turned to the opposite wall behind him.

Here was a reinforced glass door. Inside the glass wire mesh seeped rust like clots of blood. Beyond this door a staircase looked in imminent danger of collapsing into its own stair-well. However Toady pushed open the door and without hesitation began to climb the stairs.

The stone of the steps was interlaced with cracks, and in places was the consistency of soggy cardboard. Toady was not sure whether it was his imagination which made him feel the whole structure was swaying and creaking around him. Plaster fell like heavy rain; huge cracks in the walls meandered between floors like negative images of light-ning bolts. In places the banister had given way, the plastic-coated handrail convoluted like a twist of liquorice.

Toady wondered where he was going: his heart was a bird, reaching for the sky. Part of him was filled with terror at the prospect of the building giving way around him. He couldn't help but think of demolition films he'd seen, buildings collapsing like felled giants into a house-sized cloud of their own dust.

When he reached floor seven he instinctively thought, 'This is it'. A sign above the glass-panelled door read: 'Isolation Rooms 1–10.' Toady pushed open the door, feeling his heart kicking against his ribs, surging into the back of his throat with a thumping juicy rhythm. He noticed a clock on the wall and wondered if there had been others in the hospital. Though the glass of the clock was smashed and coated with dust, he could still see the time: 6.22.

He crossed the brown carpet which with its covering of dust and rubble resembled a beach. Of the ten rooms, the doors of four had collapsed and were now lying half in and half out of the corridor. Beyond these doors Toady saw good-sized single rooms rapidly falling into decay. However his heart told him it was only one of the rooms, number 5, which concerned him.

He placed his hand on the handle. He twisted and pushed, not knowing what he would find inside. He was certain of one thing however; it would not be the unoccupied ruin he had seen through each of the other doorways. He was therefore surprised when it seemed at first as though this was exactly what it was. He saw plaster-stripped walls, a smashed window, a bulging ceiling trickling dust.

And then, turning slowly to his right, he saw the bed.

And, a second later, the figure upon it.

Toady's heart was now beating so fast it felt almost like a blur. The bed-frame was grimy with rust, the sheets stained and mouldy. Toady saw dirty tubes from a rusty metal stand feeding into a white arm. He focussed on the end of that arm; on the hand, milk-white with pale blue fingernails.

Though his mind told him not to, he felt himself walking towards the bed. He kept his eyes fixed on the immobile hand, almost superstitiously afraid of raising his gaze any higher. The hospital groaned around him, and now Toady felt he would welcome its collapse if it meant he did not have to confront whatever he'd been brought here for. He stopped beside the bed, still keeping his head bowed, like a grieving relative.

Part of the ceiling collapsed and Toady jumped, turning away for a moment. When he turned back the hand seemed to have acquired a greeny-yellow hue. He thought he was mistaken until he saw the skin pulling back from the fingernails. Next moment spots of mould appeared on it, turquoise and furry like poisoned rain.

Toady couldn't swallow; his disgust and his fear were too thick. He could smell the thing now, overripe, sickly-sweet, pungent as maggoty cheese. His heart hitched and he gasped, and then a thought surfaced in his mind. He suddenly knew that if he did not look into the figure's face he would stand like this forever.

Suffocated by the smell of putrefaction, his gaze crawled over the rot-stained pyjamas. Next moment he was staring into a face it took him an age to recognize. Shrunken discoloured skin, blotches of mould, lips peeled back over a clench-toothed smile . . . his legs almost gave way beneath him when he realized the figure was himself.

His mind went back an eternity, to a night when he'd seen a figure beneath the covers of his bed. The figure had sat up, pushed the covers off itself, and Toady had been looking into his own face. He was doing that now, but this time it was much, much worse. This time he was being shown his own death and he didn't know what it meant.

Was this thing on the bed himself or part of the creature? And why was he rotting away? Did that mean his Starmouth self had died? Were he and Robin and Nige stuck in this nightmare forever? Or would they wink out of existence, become nothing, once the process of decay here was complete?

Toady stared at the decomposing face, now more frightened for himself than he was of this empty dead thing. The skin was splitting, tearing like wet paper, the gums reducing to grey pulp and shedding teeth. Fungus was blossoming, furry-yellow, spreading like a crazy growth of beard. Toady felt tears slip down his face, sobs catch like food in his throat.

'Why?' he whispered. 'Why? I don't understand.'

And then the corpse's eyes opened and he understood it all.

12

Saturday 9.08 p.m.

'So gullible,' were the words Richard heard just before he felt himself falling. 'So, so gullible. Just like your mother.' But by then it was too late to turn back.

He did all he could: he clawed, he screamed, he kicked his legs like a swimmer, but nothing could prevent him spinning down the well that the creature had coaxed him into. He fell slowly, dreamily, like Alice down the rabbit hole, feeling wretched, scared, angry, and especially ashamed of the way he had been tricked. He felt he'd let everyone down – his friends, his family, himself – and he wept bitter tears of frustration. He thought he'd done with weeping, thought he'd wept enough to last him a lifetime, yet was unable now to stop the tears from flowing once again.

After a while, however, the tears did stop. And by this time Richard's struggling had stopped too and he was going with the flow, staring bleakly around him. He thought he glimpsed faces, scenes, at the edge of his vision, but when he twisted to see there was never anything there. 'The creature has won,' he thought. 'The creature has won.'

He had to bite his lips to stop himself from screaming.

At last the darkness was broken by an object drifting slowly towards him. It was an armchair, he could see, and there was a figure sitting in it, head bowed. As the chair came closer, he realized the figure was Olive Pierce, and that the reason her head was bowed was because she was knitting. Richard had never known her to knit before, yet in this distorted, semi-dream atmosphere the activity seemed oddly appropriate.

The chair drifted closer, then at about ten feet away it stopped. It hung in the blackness, aslant, near enough now for Richard to see the figure in detail. However, though it looked like Olive it was a desecration of her memory; drool spilled babyish from its lips. More distressing than this, however, were the words streaming from her mouth – a mumbling string of obscenities.

'Shit-fuck-bugger-cunt-bastard-shit-fuck-bugger-cunt-bastard.'

'Stop it!' Richard boomed to the darkness. 'Stop it! That's not Olive!'

The figure vanished, and a dry hideous chuckle echoed around him. 'So, so gullible,' whispered a voice by his ear, towards which Richard twisted as he fell.

A smell hit him, so foul it was like a fist, squeezing his gut, bringing tears to his eyes. He palmed the tears away to find Rosemary Figg hanging on a rope beside him. Her body was a sack of swaying blubber, her head a purple basketball from which eyes bulged, the colour of mushrooms. So tight was the noose, and so great her weight, that the rope cut a ravine through her neck.

'So, so gullible,' she whispered again, her black tongue causing an obstruction. Then she said, 'Excuse me while I—' but left the sentence unfinished as centipedes poured from her mouth.

Richard shrieked, twisted away, plastering his face with his hands. The movement caused his body to spin wildly. His stomach began to flip like an acrobat. He kept his hands over his face for a long time, long after the echoes of his shriek had died away and his careering body had stabilized. He listened for the sounds of the corpse beside him, but heard nothing except dark empty silence.

Slowly he opened his eyes. Removed the hands from his face. A grey screen hung in the darkness, the size of a screen in the cinema. As though waiting for him to look, a camera began to whirr and the screen came alive, a flickering of numbers from 10 to 1. The picture was jerky and not quite in focus, though was still far too clear for Richard.

He saw Nigel Figg in a butcher's shop lying on a slab. Nigel was in hacked pieces, a mess of blood, bone, skin and innards. He should have been dead, but he was piercing the silence with his screams. The butcher, raising his cleaver, smacking it down, had the head of a grunting pig.

No!

Robin Treadwell was in a grey stormy sea, splashing and crying for help. Behind him something black, furry, broke the surface of the waves. A moment later, with a bellow that it seemed would tear the world apart, a spider the size of a house rose streaming from the depths and engulfed him.

No! No!

Toady Tibbett was hanging upside down from a tree. He was pleading for mercy to an unseen shadowy thing in the foreground, holding an enormous knife. Next moment the thing shambled into picture, turned, and Richard saw himself, eyes glinting manically. He grinned, raised the knife and swept it across his friend's exposed belly. A stripe of blood followed the knife, then the wound gaped and Toady's intestines came spilling out like a nest of blind red eels.

No! No! No!

Each image was savage, callous, sickening, a miniature video nasty. The worst thing about them was their sense of glee, of celebration, as though the events being depicted were to be cheered and encouraged, as though morality should be found in degradation. Richard lowered his head into his hands and began to sob once again. His body felt light as a feather. And it was with a feather's grace that he felt his feet touch solid ground.

Hands fell to his sides, eyes opened once more. This time there was a semblance of reality. A muddy plain, the occasional black stunted tree, a murky purple-grey sky. And pervading it all, a thick yellow fog which blurred the landscape.

The place was so silent, so still, that Richard wanted to shout and jump . . . and it was for precisely the same reason that he was afraid even to move.

He stood for a long while, something in the monotony of the place insinuating itself into his mind, disrupting his sense of time to such an extent that he felt he was cat-napping then blinking awake again. At last, from the heart of a bank of fog, he heard slow measured footsteps approaching. He tensed, forgot to breathe. The footsteps trudged closer. By some acoustic quirk the fog both muffled and amplified them.

A man appeared through the fog: a dim mist-grey silhouette. By his side was a hulking lupine shape. Instinctively Richard feared this man, felt his heart begin to pound in terror. Mist stripped away to reveal details, the first of which were the black coins hiding the eyes of the gaunt unshaven face. But it was the lupine eyes to which Richard was drawn. They were slanted. Large. Glowing red.

683

I am the hungry wolf of your dreams.

Richard felt a shudder convulse him. He wanted to run, but sheer terror locked his legs. The wolf shrugged off the fog, slunk into view, and now Richard could see muscles rippling under the shaggy pelt. 'Mr Robespierre,' Richard said to the blind man, barely able to get the words round his fear.

Robespierre smiled and raised his white stick in greeting. 'Richard Gardener,' he said warmly, 'so pleased that you could join us.' 'Us', Richard saw, did not merely include Robespierre and the wolf. There was also something white, gull-like, hovering above Robespierre's left shoulder.

Try as he might, Richard could not focus on this third presence. It was like a faulty film-reel, fluttering, jerky, leaving echoes of its own movements to mask its true shape.

The trio came to a halt a few feet away. The wolf was panting, the steam that rose from its jowls more yellow than the fog. There was no sun and the mud was black as coal, yet Richard saw that Robespierre cast a shadow before him. And though the blind man was now motionless his shadow continued to move. Writhing, twisting, it seemed as though it was trying to escape the confines that linked it to the blind man's form.

'Where . . . where are we?' Richard said, feeling obliged by their silence to speak.

'We are here,' Robespierre replied, and waved his stick in an arc.

Next instant he had taken a step forward and brought his stick lashing down. It made contact with Richard's shoulder, forcing him to his knees with a yelp of pain. Before he could move, the wolf had leaped forward and closed its jaws over his face. Richard found himself staring into a glistening gullet edged with yellow fangs.

'And now we are here,' he heard Robespierre say.

Then the wolf closed its jaws with a snap.

Richard's eyes opened as he jerked from the dream. He

found himself in a chapel, weak light glowing through a stained-glass window. There were people in the chapel, some of them weeping, and standing behind a lectern was Roger Baxter dressed in religious vestments. Baxter was speaking softly, tenderly, relaying his belief in eternal life after death.

'Superstitious nonsense,' said a voice to Richard's right.

Richard turned to see Robespierre and the wolf, like angels of death, beside him. 'Why have you brought me here?' he asked, watching the gull-thing as it hovered above the congregation. He saw the creature alight on the flower-decked coffin within the red-curtained alcove, then flit away again, a blur of white.

'We have come to show you a great truth,' Robespierre said, and Richard shuddered at the smirk that played on his lips. 'Come with me,' the blind man ordered, then set off down the central aisle, the wolf prowling beside him.

Richard followed unwillingly. He realized they could not be seen here, that the congregation was not paying them even the slightest attention. The sight of himself, his parents and his grandparents standing in the second row disturbed him more than he would have thought possible. Constance was weeping softly, clinging on to his arm as though trying to pull it off. Somehow re-living Olive's funeral in this way was worse than the original ceremony had been.

Robespierre and the wolf entered the red-curtained alcove and stopped by the coffin. The gull-thing hovered above Roger Baxter's head like a trick of the light. Though he'd been expecting it, Richard felt his heart sink when Robespierre beckoned him over. As soon as Richard was in position, Robespierre reached down to lift the coffin lid.

'No,' Richard said feebly, 'you can't do this. It's not right.'

The blind man ignored him. Instead he took hold of each side of the coffin lid and wrenched. Richard gasped as the lid came away, nails jerking free with a tight ripping

685

sound. He looked round at the congregation, but they appeared not to have noticed a thing.

'Look,' Robespierre ordered.

Richard braced himself. His mother had told him that undertakers made corpses look like people asleep, but he was nonetheless apprehensive. He squinted at the coffin as though afraid something might fly at him. And then his mouth dropped open; he literally went weak at the knees.

There was no body in the coffin. There was not even a silk lining, nor even bare wood. Instead there was a vortex of darkness, a spinning whirlpool of black.

'What is it?' Richard breathed, mesmerized.

'It is the truth,' replied Robespierre in his actor's voice. He pointed at Roger Baxter, whose hands were clasped before him. 'As opposed to that,' he added derisively.

Richard, entranced by the maelstrom's languor, tried hard to shake the effect of it from his mind. 'No,' he murmured, 'I don't believe you.' And yet still he stared, drawn inexplicably to the whirlpool's lazy depths, to its vast coiling emptiness.

'Goodbye, Richard,' Robespierre said softly.

Even these words brought only a spark of dread to Richard's mind.

'Whaddyamean?' he drawled, and found himself climbing on to the coffin platform.

'Goodbye,' said the blind man again.

Richard placed his hands on the coffin's smooth edge. 'No,' he mumbled, 'I won't do it, you know. I won't—'

Then his words cut off as he pitched himself into the vortex.

13

The link

Though neither boy knew it, Richard's and Toady's experiences ran almost parallel. Only in Toady's case the journey was not one of corruption but of enlightenment.

The corpse had his eyes. Toady had always assumed eyes to be much the same, indistinguishable without the structure of the face to surround them, but he now knew that this was not the case. The eyes he saw in the rank mask of grey-green pulp were his and his alone, the ones he saw staring back at him whenever he looked in a mirror. He wondered how the eyes could have survived intact when the rest of the body was decaying, and then he looked into them, *really* looked into them, for the first time.

And he thought: 'Eyes are the windows of the soul.'

He saw a plea in the eyes, a desperate urgent intensity, so strong that it cut like a laser through the muddled emotions of his brain. Toady suddenly understood that the link, the true link, was not the hospital nor ever had been; it was *himself*, both the part of him that was here, the part that was in Starmouth, and this part, this miserable go-between, who was clinging on to its own temporary and gruesome pseudo-life with the desperation of a man clinging to a crumbling cliff-edge.

And if the cliff-edge should crumble away? If these anguished eyes in the ravaged face should close for ever?

Then the triplets – himself, himself, himself – all would die.

Toady understood all this in a second, and in the same second the link was made and he was on his way. He entered a strange slow stage of semi-dreaming, a softly echoing landscape in which he never lost consciousness. It was a state of calm, of beauty, of warmth. Toady almost began to wish he could remain in it forever.

And then, like and yet unlike Richard, he found himself drifting fully aware through darkness.

He was not falling but rising . . . or perhaps he only thought he was. Certainly he had the impression of progress, the feeling that he was going somewhere. The dark in which he drifted was not true dark, but then neither was it touched by light. He travelled as though wearing a pair of smudged grey goggles, and he felt calmer, more relaxed than he ever had before.

'Hello,' he said to the greyness, though more to test his sense of hearing than anything else. His other three senses – touch, smell, taste – were working fine. He licked his lips, tasted salt, and could still smell his own burnt flesh and singed hair commingled with his sweat. His spoken word, though deadened, came to him clearly as though he was speaking in a small room that had no echo.

He drifted . . . drifted . . . travelling towards himself. He thought: 'I wonder how long this journey will last.' And then a voice by his ear murmured, 'Before you arrive there are things I must show you.'

Toady spun slowly, alarm injecting him. A man hovered by his shoulder – swarthy, dark-bearded, twists of coloured ribbon in his matted shoulder-length hair. He had glittering eyes, wore clothes that had once been fine but were now grimy and sweat-stained.

'Who . . . who are you?' Toady muttered.

Thin lips curled within the growth of beard. 'Don't you know?' the man said.

Toady stared hard. The man was familiar. He was . . . he was . . .

'Ranulf!' Toady gasped.

The man-Ranulf gave a sardonic bow. 'At your service.'

'But . . . but I don't understand. What are *you* doing here?'

'I have come to advise you. Now that the link has been established, I am outside the Zad's influence.'

Toady remembered the conversation he and Ranulf had had in Liana's cottage. 'You'll tell me how to defeat the Zad?'

'I'll show you,' said Ranulf. 'Take my hand.'

Toady did so eagerly. Lights, stars, sparks, galaxies, suddenly blinded him, filling his senses. As he had once before, he was flying, swooping, rushing to some unknown destination. His surroundings were vague as a dream's backdrop. Then the vagueness became solid, real, and he saw . . .

A cave. A fire. Sand. Beyond the fire crouches an old man, overcoat shabby, hat battered and shapeless. His hands are held in front of him, feverishly kneading the exposed breasts of a young girl. The girl is beautiful, smiling faintly. Her hands rest lightly on the man's shoulders . . . The girl's hands suddenly change. Instead of fingers she now has metal spikes: long, gleaming, vicious. Lazily she places her hands on the old man's neck and pushes the spikes in. Blood comes out, spatters on the sand . . . The old man stops kneading her breasts and places his hands over hers. He begins to thrash and scream, gropes at the hands, punches the swaying breasts. He does it in slow motion, he is weak as a kitten, but the girl still winces at the blows and almost loses her grip . . .

Toady turned away, sickened. 'Why?' he gasped. 'Why show me this?'

'Because,' said Ranulf calmly, 'it shows that physically the girl in the cave is only a girl. If she had not taken the tramp by surprise, pushed the spikes in before he could retaliate, then he could have fought her and won. *If* he had not been so weak, *if* he had closed his hands around her neck and squeezed her air off with his thumbs, then he could have killed her.'

Toady looked at him, struggling to understand. 'And if he *had* killed her?' he asked. 'What? *What?*'

'Look again,' said Ranulf.

Snow. Deserted streets. Robin Treadwell, limping, half-sobbing, a wave of scuttling black behind him. They are creatures: small, spindly, charcoal-twisted. They carry nets over their shoulders and are herding Robin towards the dark rushing mass of the sea . . .

Toady shuddered, looked a question at Ranulf. Sighing, Ranulf said, 'The creatures, however fearsome, are only small, wood-brittle. *If* Robin had turned on them, *if* he had kicked out at them, scattered them, avoided their nets, then he could have won; he could have picked the creatures off one by one, could have broken them up like firewood.'

'And if he had done that?' said Toady excitedly. '*If he had . . .?*'

689

The scene shifted again.

Nigel Figg standing before an open pantry door, gazing with almost childlike wonder at the bodies of his mother and father hanging from a single noose. He tugs the hem of his mother's skirt and sets her swaying. In the sitting room he crosses to the window and suddenly the room becomes black. He walks down a dark narrow corridor, at the end of which a window shows a night sky and a rural landscape. He climbs out of the window and is in his bedroom. Something – the moving corpse of his mother – is outside the door. He crosses to the door, locks it, jerks away, backs to the opposite wall. He slumps down, hunches up, sobs with fear. A blind man enters and crosses the room, his manner enticing. As Nige gazes in awe, he removes his spectacles . . .

Even before the scenario had faded, even before Toady could ask his questions, Ranulf was speaking.

'Nigel is worn down by a barrage of fear, confusion, disorientation. *If* he had not been, *if* he had managed to resist the manipulation of his mind, he could have fought back. The blind man, for all his magic, is, in Starmouth, simply that: a man. Maybe not blind but certainly old, his bones dry, his muscles wasted. And the corpse on the stairs? Simply a corpse, despite its animation. Nigel *could* have pushed the old man over, *could* have side-stepped the corpse with ease, *could* have denied the warping of dimensions, the folding of the house upon itself. *Could* even have escaped.'

'If . . . ?' was the only word that Toady could think of. 'If . . . ?'

'Look again. *Look again.*'

Rusty slides down a dingy wall in a deserted house, his legs collapsing beneath him. A man in a black tuxedo, his hair slicked back, his make-up garish, smiles. Rusty has fear on his face; it makes him look surprisingly boyish. The man takes a step forward and Rusty scrambles to his feet. Cautiously he begins to edge towards a window dark with grime . . . The man puts his hands in his jacket, draws out a metal blade which twinkles in the gloom. Rusty reaches the window,

690

*fumbles with the catch, finally in desperation tries to lever the
window up. Unable to do so, he swings back, his knife in his
hand, meanness somehow ageing his face once more. Though
the man smiles, there is an instant of surprise, uncertainty, even
fear in his eyes. Then he presses the point of the blade into his
chin and deftly slits his face up the middle . . . He tears away
the rubbery skin, beneath which is a glass globe containing a
shrunken head. He begins to twist off his fingers and drop them
on the floor. Rusty, horrified, throws down his knife and dives
at the closed window. Glass shatters outwards as his body
bursts into the twilight . . .*

Toady saw Ranulf look at him, willing him to understand. He shrugged apologetically. Ranulf muttered,
'Don't you see? The boy, Rusty, is defeated by his own
terror. The Zad here is nothing but a man, despite his
psychosis. Only when Rusty resisted did the Zad counter-
act that resistance by changing in to something even more
fearsome . . . and this is the key: the Zad's capacity for
change. Once he has adopted a form, he has then to abide
by the rules of the physical dimensions and limitations of
that form. In other words, physically he becomes no more
and no less than the form he has adopted, and thus
becomes vulnerable *in* that form.'

At last light began to dawn in Toady's mind. However,
he saw difficulties. 'But if Nige *had* pushed the old man
over,' he said, 'if Robin *had* kicked out at the charcoal
creatures and scattered them, if Rusty *had* gone at the man
with his knife, what would have stopped the Zad from
changing into something even more horrible? Like a fire-
breathing dragon, for example?'

'Nothing,' said Ranulf. 'The Zad has to be defeated
while he is locked into a vulnerable form.'

'But how? How can he be stopped from changing?'

Ranulf smiled coldly. And suddenly . . .

*Toady found himself standing in his bedroom in Starmouth,
his eyes closed, holding Toby's, the Zad's hand. He felt tense,
but, strangely, not scared. His hand was hot and sweaty.
Every so often he felt his fingers tingle as though electricity was*

running through them. He heard himself asking: 'What are you doing?' and the reply he received was flustered. 'I'm trying to change us both, but you keep resisting. Can't you just relax a little?' 'Sorry,' Toady said . . . and then he found himself back with Ranulf again.

'You see?' Ranulf said to him. 'You see now?'

'Yes,' Toady gasped, eyes bright. 'Yesyesyesyesyes! *This* is how the creature can be stopped from changing, isn't it? Somehow . . . somehow . . . I . . .'

'Via the physiological/psychological chemistry of your body,' Ranulf explained, 'the Zad's power was stemmed and he was temporarily locked into the form of a small boy. Somehow, Adrian, you must do this again. The Zad's attempts at inducing fear, confusion, disorientation, have to be resisted, its lies have to be ignored, and it has to be restrained in a vulnerable form by both physical and mental bonds.'

Toady nodded slowly. 'But . . . but how do I get into that position?' he asked. 'And once *in* that position, how do I *keep* it there? Do I hold it down while someone chops off its head? Drives a stake through its heart? Injects it with poison?'

'You must think,' Ranulf told him simply. 'You must think . . . think . . . think . . .'

But all at once Toady had no time.

He suddenly came awake in a hospital bed to find he had a tube in his arm.

14

Saturday 9.12 p.m.

When Richard regained consciousness to find himself staring at a chair-leg, his mind was a complete blank. He could not, nor ever would, consciously remember what had happened to him in the whirlpool. For the moment he even failed to recall Robespierre and the wolf and the gull-creature. He felt like something empty waiting to be

692

filled, felt as though he were staring at a closed door beyond which memory pressed.

He looked again at the chair-leg. It was wood, squared-off, little flakes of varnish peeling away like sunburn. He looked at the floor, saw he was lying on a brown carpet, looked along the carpet to where a wardrobe crushed it. He turned his head a little, saw a wash-basin set in an alcove, white walls, a long window hung with green curtains, one of which was pulled back. Night stood dark outside the window; muffled traffic sounds and the occasional shout carried up from below.

'Where am I?' Richard thought. 'Where the bloody hell am I?' The answer, he was sure, was vital. He looked again at the window as though the darkness might clear his head, and was astonished to see a bed and two dancing figures reflected in the glass.

'Dancing?' he thought. 'Dancing? What the sodding hell *is* this place?' He tried to sit up, felt gluey waves of dizziness gumming his thoughts, and almost keeled over again. He blinked, regained his balance, rubbed his eyes. Looked hard at the figures and recognized . . .

. . . Toady and the creature.

For a few moments he simply sat, a spectator, as it all came back to him. He recalled succinctly now the small neat sounds of nails tearing free from wood, Robespierre lifting the coffin lid, and then . . . nothing. Or at least, nothing except a . . . feeling, a *flavour*, of something dark, mesmeric, worse than anything he'd ever known before. He shuddered, his mind veered away and turned again to the figures.

No, Richard now saw, not dancing. They were fighting, his friend who should have been in a coma but was not, and the creature. They were wrestling, struggling, blundering about the room. By the bed was a toppled metal stand, a ruptured plastic bag in a pool of fluid, a length of thin plastic tubing.

Richard stared for a moment at the tubing. His attention had been snagged by the redness on it. It made him think

693

of a smear of lipstick, but it was not lipstick, he knew. He swallowed and looked at Toady. And swallowed some more. Toady's face was very white and sickly, which contrasted sharply with his pyjamas, all dark red and shiny with blood.

15

Saturday 9.10 p.m.

Toady's immediate horrified thought on waking was: 'I've changed places with the corpse!' But then he realized he was not decaying. Relaxing a little, he thought about Ranulf, about the information he had been given in the link, about the way Ranulf's and the Zad's memories seemed interchangeable, fractions of a greater whole. He wondered about this – and suddenly it occurred to him that maybe this could cut both ways. Maybe the Zad, through Ranulf, knew what the boys had been up to. Maybe it knew that he had crossed the link. Maybe it was waiting for him now, standing at the end of the bed, a knife clenched tight in its hand.

Slowly, fearfully, he lifted his head to see. The Zad was indeed in the room, and the sight almost gave Toady a relapse. He wondered briefly how he could recognize the Zad even under its boyish exterior, wondered whether his time spent in its kingdom had heightened his perceptions, unlocked parts of his mind he hadn't even known existed. Whatever the answer, however, that particular line of enquiry was not really important just now. What *was* important was what the Zad was doing.

It was holding Richard by the shoulders and staring into his eyes. Toady noticed that the Zad's own eyes were pale as milk, that its frame was an unsettling blend of his own wide-mouthed plumpness, Nige's swarthiness and Robin's acned skin. Richard was limp in its grip. His eyes were open, his lips moving, but he seemed to be heavily drugged. The sight made Toady think of vampires, gave him the impression that the creature was sucking Richard's life away.

Stealthily he pushed the covers back, hoping the Zad would not notice the movement. As well as the tube in his arm he noticed there was also one snaking out of his pyjama trousers, and realized he'd been catheterized. The tube ended in a small round bag hooked up to a metal stand. Thankful that it was empty, Toady reached out, unhooked it, and tucked it into the elasticated waistband of his pyjamas.

Now he turned his attention to the IV in his arm. This was attached to a rather larger bag which was swollen with fluid, and Toady knew there was no way he could carry that across the room *and* grapple with the creature. It was only a thin tube; maybe he would be able just to pull it out. He closed his free hand around it, braced himself and tugged experimentally.

Instantly tears of pain sprang to his eyes. The feeling had been that of a huge needle piercing his nerves, and he could not help but cry out. Through his swimming vision he was horrified to see the Zad turning its head towards him. Its hands opened and Richard slipped through them, collapsing as though made of straw. Frantically, knowing that the element of surprise had already been lost, Toady kicked the covers from the bed. He swung himself into a standing position and lurched towards the creature. Behind him the metal stand toppled with a crash, the bags of fluid burst, as the IV – which he had removed only fractionally – wrenched itself from his arm. This time the pain was worse – white-hot, but in a way almost subliminal, like the deft slice of a razor. He halted momentarily as nausea swept through him, and again yelled out in agony.

He expected blood to spurt like a fountain from his arm, but instead it simply oozed and trickled. Nevertheless, by the time he reached the creature and embraced it, his hands were sticky and red. The creature, which had simply stood rooted to the spot as though in disbelief, now began to fight back. It writhed and kicked, punched at Toady's arms and back and the side of his head in an attempt to break free.

He hung on grimly, hung on literally for his life. His head rang with the blows it received; his penis felt stretched and uncomfortable, fitted with the catheter. Now and then he felt his body tingle and knew that the creature was trying to change. He desperately wished Richard would wake up, wished someone would come running, and shouted, 'Help! Help!' in the hope of attracting attention.

All at once Richard stirred and elation choked the words in Toady's throat. As though sensing defeat, the creature went limp in his arms, but Toady did not relax his grip. The creature began to stagger as though drunk, and Toady staggered with it in a clumsy, blundering dance. Then the creature's hand slipped into Toady's pyjama trousers, closed around the catheter and wrenched.

The pain was unbelievable. Toady screamed, his hands slipping from the creature's waist. The creature sprang free, like Batman escaping his bonds, as Toady dropped to his knees and was sick. The creature backed to the window, its head swivelling to take in both boys, its mouth stretched in a victory leer. It laughed, its eyes flared red, and fur began to sprout from its skin.

16

Saturday 9.12 p.m.

Toady's scream was so terrible that Richard almost screamed himself. He saw his friend release the creature, fall to his knees and throw up on the brown carpet. Toady's bloodied hands cupped his groin, an action which seemed to indicate he'd been kneed in the balls. He started rocking backwards and forwards on his haunches, eyes literally rolling with pain.

The creature backed up until it was standing in front of

the large window. A haze of sunlight seemed to play around its form; grey cloud, soaked with night, drifted behind its head. It was sneering, its mouth curled at the corners, and then it began to laugh. Its white eyes suddenly flared with red light and hair began to sprout from its skin.

Richard watched, fascinated, as the creature transformed before him. It was just like watching *American Werewolf In London*, a video which the Horror Club had hired only a few weeks ago. Fur grew from the creature with amazing speed, twined together, began to form a shaggy pelt. The jawbone elongated with an horrendous cracking sound as the mouth was replaced by a snout. The creature grinned and Richard saw its teeth growing longer, tapering to sharp points. Its body began to hunch, to grow muscly, its clothes to melt into the flesh.

'*No!*' screamed a voice, and Richard jumped, then turned to his right. Toady was staggering to his feet, horrified rage on his face. 'No!' he yelled again. 'No! I won't let you change!' He began to run towards the creature, then launched himself through the air.

The creature, half-man, half-wolf, raised its arms to defend itself. Richard saw talons spring from fingers that were reducing to stubby paws. Toady's full weight hit the creature, his momentum causing it to stagger backwards, its body slamming against the window. Just before the window shattered and the two bodies toppled out, Richard saw Toady take a grip on its fur.

'*No!*' Richard screamed, echoing his friend. '*No, Ade! Let go!*'

But he was suddenly alone in the room, shouting only at a man-sized asterisk of darkness punched into the glass. He heard a thump from below, a protracted pause, and then someone started to scream. He walked to the window like a zombie, poked his head through the jagged hole and looked down.

A small crowd was already starting to gather round the sprawled smashed bodies on the concrete. Richard could only wonder what they would think about the second one, the wolf thing, could only hope it had been splattered beyond recognition. The wind riffled his hair and he pulled his head in, taking care not to cut himself on the glass. He looked at the burst plastic bag, the pile of vomit, the IV tube with the blood on it . . . then he walked unsteadily from the room.

17

Saturday 9.16 p.m.

Glennon made it to the hospital in six minutes, swung in through the gates and pulled up in front of the steps just as the crowd started to disperse. Shocked faces turned towards the car's flashing light. Two stretchers, their occupants concealed by red blankets, were being wheeled slowly round to Casualty. At a glance, Glennon took in the sizeable spatters of blood on the slushy concrete, the shards of broken glass, and his stomach sank. He looked up, saw the shattered window, a green curtain – snagged by the wind – caught on a jagged edge. 'Isolation room', he thought inevitably, and threw the car door open. As he leaped out and started to run towards the stretchers, he heard Eileen scream out, *'Richard!'*

'Excuse me,' he said as he reached the first stretcher and twitched the edge of the blanket back. The brain had all but exploded on impact with the ground, but the face was still just discernible as Adrian Tibbett's. Sickened, Glennon moved on to the second stretcher, pulled the cover of that back too. Then he recoiled at the frozen snarl, the feral eyes glaring upwards in death.

'What . . . what is it?' he managed to gasp.

'You tell us, mate,' one of the stretcher-bearers replied blandly.

Glennon looked at the face again, then shuddered and concealed it with the blanket. He took great care as he did so not to touch the lupine snout. He cleared his throat, rubbed a hand over his mouth in an effort to regain his composure. 'What happened here?' he said. Then, 'Has anyone been up there yet?'

'No, mate,' the same stretcher-bearer replied, answering the second question. 'This only happened a few minutes ago. Just time to scrape them up off the concrete. As for what happened, well, as far as we know they just fell. The lad was clinging on to that . . . thing's fur so tight we had to prise his fingers away.'

Glennon nodded and turned as he heard running footsteps behind him. Eileen was approaching, Derek in tow; she had a manic look on her face. Glennon caught her as she tried to dodge past him, held her tight as she struggled. 'It's not Richard,' he said firmly, then as Derek ran up, his face a question he didn't want to ask, 'Don't worry, it's not Richard.'

'But they fell from one of the isolation rooms, didn't they?' Derek panted. 'It's where Richard's friends are in comas?'

'Yes. I'm going up there now. You and Eileen wait here.'

Derek shook his head. His mouth was a thin line beneath his moustache. 'No, we're coming with you. Richard might be hurt up there.'

Glennon hesitated for just a second; he was sure, however, that the drama was over, that the dead thing under the blanket was the 'murderer' they'd been searching for. He said, 'All right, come on. But you're to do as I tell you and let me lead the way.'

Derek nodded and they entered the hospital.

Three minutes later the lift doors opened on floor 7 and the three of them shot out. Glennon looked round, saw the sign for the isolation rooms, and shoved the door open so fiercely that it crashed back against the wall, gouging out some plaster. Derek and Eileen behind him, he then entered the first of three rooms with their doors standing open. He found his gaze drawn to the bed in which was a bemused but smiling figure.

'You're . . . ?' he said, grasping for the name.

'Robin Treadwell,' replied the boy. His smile widened as Derek and Eileen pushed into the room behind the sergeant. 'Hello, Mr and Mrs Gardener. We're back, aren't we? This is Starmouth? We're home?'

'Yes,' Derek said, nodding. 'Yes, Robin, you are.'

'Where's Richard?' Eileen demanded. 'Have you seen him, Robin? Is he all right?'

'Yes, I think he's with Nige. He's in a bad way—' Robin began, but before he could say more he was staring at an empty doorway.

Room 5 was a mess. Blood, vomit, broken glass, though thankfully no bodies. Glennon glanced quickly round, checked under the bed and in the wardrobe. He said, 'Don't touch anything,' then went back out into the corridor.

The door of Room 6 was only slightly ajar. Glennon pushed it open and entered. He saw the two figures almost immediately, one whimpering in bed like an animal, the other with his arms round his shoulders, comforting him.

'Richard,' Glennon said quietly, then winced as Eileen shouted, 'Richard! Oh, Richard, thank God!'

The boy in the bed – Nigel Figg was the name that surfaced in Glennon's mind – shrieked and scrabbled backwards, making the metal stand to which he was attached sway alarmingly. Richard said to him, 'Shh, Nige, it's all right,' then, turning to his mother, 'Keep your voice down, Mum. I don't think Nige knows where he is just yet.'

Eileen subsided, nonplussed. Derek said, 'What's been going on, Richard? What's been happening here?'

Richard looked at him and sighed. His eyes were wide but weary, full of pain. He said simply, 'It's over, Dad, that's all that matters. This time I think it's really over.'

700

EPILOGUE

Incy Wincy

In another part of the hospital was someone else who had fallen from a window, only his fall had been a quarter of the distance and he had been cushioned by snow and grass and had thus survived. For a while it was thought he might die, but only this morning he had been taken off the life-support machine, and now the doctors were no longer describing his condition as 'critical' but as 'dangerously ill but stable'.

He was virtually unrecognizable from the boy he had been before the accident. His face had swollen to twice its normal size and was all the colours of the rainbow; his red curls had been shaved off in order that his head could be opened up and a blood-clot removed from his brain; one arm and both legs were in plaster, the arm displaying a single scrawled message, 'Wake up you cunt, Ratzy'; he had an IV tube in his unplastered arm, another in his throat and yet another up his nose; he had been catheterized, and even now a faint trickle indicated that the bag was being filled.

When he had first been admitted, he had been given constant round-the-clock attention. Now, however, he had improved to the stage where his condition was checked only once every five to ten minutes. He had opened his eyes briefly that afternoon, muttered, 'Wha fuck?' and then lapsed back into sleep again. Now the faint trickle of urine subsided and it was silent in the room once more.

Suddenly the boy's lips parted as something flopped out and slithered down his cheek. It rested on the pillow for a moment by his right ear, quivering as though cold. It was a plum-sized blob of transparent jelly, cloudy in the centre, glistening wetly. It rolled along the pillow to the edge of the bed and plopped down on to the floor.

It made a slight slap as it landed, and was so still for a moment it seemed the fall had killed it. Then it began to quiver again and a hint of darkness appeared in its centre. Slowly the darkness spread, tentatively casting out tendrils as though the blob was being injected with ink.

Within minutes the blob was no longer transparent but completely black, and now it began, painstakingly, to change. It became smaller, drier, feelers began to sprout from its sides. When the process was complete, the blob had gone and a spider sat in its place. Quickly, as though alerted by the sounds of voices in the corridor outside, the spider scuttled across the room, found a crevice between wall and floor, and disappeared.

THE END

SHOCKER
by Randall Boyll

SHOCKER will give you nightmares!

A serial killer is plaguing Maryville, Ohio.

Jonathan is an all-American college student and football star. After an injury on the field, he lies unconscious – and has a terrible, realistic dream of the killer murdering his family. To his horror, Jonathan recognizes the killer. And the killer sees Jonathan.

Written with incredible power and pace, SHOCKER brings the reader into a terrifying world of murder and mayhem. A desperate young man must somehow find the strength of will to track down and destroy the evil force that inhabits a bloody assassin who will stop at nothing to survive.

SHOCKER is a novel of psychological and supernatural horror that follows in the tradition of Stephen King's *The Shining*.

0 552 13641 7

A SELECTED LIST OF HORROR TITLES
AVAILABLE FROM CORGI AND BANTAM BOOKS

☐ 09156 1	THE EXORCIST		*William Peter Blatty*	£3.99
☐ 13641 7	SHOCKER		*Randall Boyll*	£2.99
☐ 13034 6	COME DOWN INTO DARKNESS		*Clare McNally*	£2.99
☐ 12691 8	WHAT ABOUT THE BABY?		*Clare McNally*	£2.99
☐ 12400 1	GHOSTLIGHT		*Clare McNally*	£2.99
☐ 11652 1	GHOST HOUSE		*Clare McNally*	£2.99
☐ 11825 7	GHOST HOUSE REVENGE		*Clare McNally*	£2.99
☐ 13033 8	SOMEBODY COME AND PLAY		*Clare McNally*	£2.99
☐ 13323 X	BLOODLINE		*David St. Clair*	£3.99
☐ 12705 1	THE DEVIL ROCKED HER CRADLE		*David St. Clair*	£2.99
☐ 12587 3	MINE TO KILL		*David St. Clair*	£2.99
☐ 11132 5	CHILD POSSESSED		*David St. Clair*	£2.99
☐ 13532 1	SAY YOU LOVE SATAN		*David St. Clair*	£3.99
☐ 17255 7	HELLFIRE		*John Saul*	£2.95
☐ 17171 2	BRAINCHILD		*John Saul*	£2.50
☐ 17680 3	CREATURE		*John Saul*	£3.50
☐ 17466 5	NATHANIEL		*John Saul*	£3.50
☐ 17387 1	ALL FALL DOWN		*John Saul*	£3.50
☐ 17564 5	THE UNLOVED		*John Saul*	£3.50
☐ 17462 2	THE UNWANTED		*John Saul*	£3.99
☐ 10471 X	FULL CIRCLE		*Peter Straub*	£2.99
☐ 13466 X	STILL LIFE		*Sheri S. Tepper*	£2.99
☐ 13474 X	PRIME EVIL		*ed. Douglas Winter*	£3.99